He is a semi-disabled ex-soldier and retired police officer. He left the force in mid-'90s after a number of injuries and ill health. Highly commended on numerous occasions, he considers himself lucky to be alive. He's spent his last 18 months in Belfast, which included an undercover tour to thwart the IRA bombing campaign going on at the time.

His interests, apart from writing, include poetry, good music, art, history, fine dining and socialising with friends and family.

Widowed, he has four grown children and nearly a football team of grandchildren. He lives in Northern Ireland with his new partner and extended family.

He has two sequels completed in the DeJames trilogy and is working on another.

This novel is dedicated to all the members of the armed forces of all the democratic countries who are fighting and putting their lives on the line to protect their citizens and defeat the forces of the evil terrorist insurgency prevailing in the world at the moment. Lest we forget.

Davey C Bond

THE BIRTH OF THE SINGLE-HANDED VIKING

AUSTIN MACAULEY PUBLISHERS™

LONDON • CAMBRIDGE • NEW YORK • SHARJAH

A CIP catalogue record for this title is available from the British Library.

ISBN 9781528900522 (Paperback)
ISBN 9781528900539 (Hardback)
ISBN 9781528900546 (E-Book)

www.austinmacauley.com

First Published (2019)
Austin Macauley Publishers Ltd
25 Canada Square
Canary Wharf
London
E14 5LQ

This book would probably be lying on a shelf, gathering dust now but for the.help and encouragement of Liz Goodman, the late Jackie Johnston and the Fireside Crew in 'Fajoes'.

Martin and Janice of Virtual Secretarial Services, Wallingford, Oxfordshire. Big Jeff Morrow, landlord extraordinaire. Last but not least, my daughters and extended family who are waiting with bated breath and not a little degree of trepidation for the final product.

Thanks, guys.

A novel of action, romance and triumph over adversity
(The first in the DeJames family trilogy)

"You might be stupid enough to mess with the DeJames men but you certainly
don't mess with their women."

Table of Contents

Prologue

Bel-Aire, Hollywood, Los Angeles, California... Late March, 2011

Jamesey John DeJames came back from the balcony of his Beverley Hills penthouse apartment and gazed at his dying wife. His mind a conflict of emotions and thoughts. The sun was coming up over the dark Hollywood Hills, bringing light and colour to the scrubland, but there was no sunlight in his mind, only dark-grey clouds, bringing the storm of loss closer.

He threw his head back and gazed angrily up at the ceiling, hands raised in surrender, looking for mercy, an enemy to fight and devour to save the light of his life.

Nature's daily rebirth, he mused, wishing he could somehow infuse some of the awesome natural power into his beloved Collette and drive the cursed illness out of her. He couldn't grasp the concept that after they had loved so hard, played and worked so hard, she was being taken away from him so cruelly. It was pitiless and overwhelming. A travesty of life, something that should not be happening and was going seriously against the grain, call it what you will but it was very hard to handle and accept, and Jamesey didn't think he ever would.

"Leave the curtains open, I wanta see the sun. Now chill babe, I will always be wiv yah. Look after the kids, little blighters, the luv of my life so they are, so do yah best for them or I'll bleedin' come back to haunt yah," she whispered, her eyes glazed with the strong painkillers, her pupils black pinpricks. "Maybe we will take the kids to the beach later, little sods will love that," she giggled hoarsely, Jamesey not wanting to remind her 'the kids' were grown now and had flown the nest.

Jamesey had to grin, she was going to be a hard act to follow and he felt his love for her deep in his bones.

He left a gap of a few feet, and a shaft of sunlight made a corridor of light across the bed, illuminating her ravaged but still pretty features. A big man, topping six feet and strongly built, he crossed to the bed and lay down with her in his arms. She stared at his red/gold hair and then his ruggedly handsome face and into his artic blue eyes, which at one moment could be full of mischief, then the next with implacable, deadly intent, as sharp as flint.

At sixty-one Jamesey was still a very handsome man and incredibly attractive to women, but Collette never had to worry about him that way. He only ever had eyes for her, his little Collette. She would die content knowing that in thirty-four years of marriage, she had never stopped loving him. She worshipped the ground he walked on, and she knew, deep in her heart, he felt the same about her.

"Yer startin' to go a bit grey on top, mate! The ol' snow's comin' down on yer Barnet."[1] He smiled at her reverting back to her cockney accent after twenty years in the States.

Collette had done him proud in all ways. No man could have had a better woman to stand by his side through life. But for her he wouldn't be in the position he was in now. Top of the pack and master of all he surveyed. The 'alpha wolf' personified.

"Cor blimey! Who'd 'av thought a little Garston gal would've ended up in a bleedin' penthouse in Hollywood?"

"Fifty cents for swearing," he replied with a private joke from earlier in their marriage.

She was quite lucid now. He knew the end was not far off, the bastard enemy had prevailed and was rampaging, pillaging, raping and raising his realm and fiefdom, and he was going to steal away with the 'Holy Grail', his outstanding 'class act', his right hand, his irreplaceable Collette. He had seen it many times before in young wounded soldiers after battle. The battle was lost; the war was over.

"Ah wind in yer Gregory Peck[2], love. Yer know I'd give ya my shadow if I could get it off."

"You deserve everything you got, you earned it. I would run over broken glass barefoot for ya darlin', I would," he told her truthfully. "And give vindaloo curry up," he told her untruthfully, to which she gave a mocking snort of disbelief and a rueful smile.

The doctor put his head around the door, and Jamesey shooed him away with an impatient hand. He was sick of doctors and nurses hovering about. He wanted these last precious moments with Collette alone. He recalled as if yesterday her coming to his hospital bed in Belfast, forty years ago, taking charge, caring for him and mapping their future out.

In fact, it wasn't just a want. It was a need. To see her off safely on her long journey ahead. He knew wherever it was, it would be warm, safe and full of love, and she would be looking over him and their offspring.

"If yer go bald, you could get yerself a nice syrup of figs.[3] Get the gals chasing round after ya," she teased him. "Always loved your strong hair, lover."

He kissed her forehead. "There won't be another woman, kiddo," he breathed, admiring her sense of humour in adversity. She was a strong woman all right. "No one woman can replace you. No comparison out there. Anyway, thirty-five years with you has spoilt me."

"'Nothing Compares to You' – Sinead O'Connor – 1990. We used to dance to that in the ol' Peel," she said with a grin. "Hip to hip, mate, yah could have clamped a double decker bus when you were younger and kissed me with yah lips, fair took my breath away, so yah did."

"We will again, kiddo, for eternity and ever after," he promised.

"I'll wait for yer, Jamesey. It's been a privilege, mate," she whispered contentedly.

"The privilege has been all mine, baby," never having said a truer word in his life.

---

[1] Cockney slang. Barnet (town in North London) Hairnet to Hair
[2] Old film star – Neck.
[3] Wigs

Collette was fading now, smiling at God knows what. Memories and thoughts were in her mind. The light was circling around them, beckoning enticingly, promising her eternal succour from her pain. "Abba... Waterloo, EuroSong Contest 1974. We are getting our own Waterloo eventually, luv... Life is a stage ol' Willie Shakespeare said but the curtain has to close someday." She gasped for breath, "Oh how I lurved Abba... I don't feel myself, Jamesey... What the frig's happening?"

"Time for a tactical withdrawal, Collette, fall back, rest, lick your wounds and reassess." He chokingly fought back the tears. "You have to go now, darling. I'll follow on soon. God bless and keep a seat for me, dear heart," the temperature in the room dropped as the angels came down to escort her to the next stage of her incredible journey.

"No retreat, mate, you hear me," she whispered and died with a last gentle sigh, the light fading from her eyes and stealing away with her essence.

Jamesey looked into her once flashing gorgeous eyes for one last time before he closed them with a finality that nearly ripped his huge heart asunder. He'd lost his soulmate. He was bereft. He lay by her side and thought back to the first time he clamped eyes on her in a North London pub. He thought about her outrageous pink hair, smouldering hazel eyes flecked with green and gold, and the cheekiest, pert, denim-clad arse any soldier home on leave would ever want to gaze upon. Feck, and what a journey they had embarked on and travelled! Jamesey smiled fondly as he remembered, Collette cradled in his arms as if peacefully asleep.

* * *

Rabbie, Jamie and Petral DeJames peeked through a crack in the door. "Guess that's it then. Mum's gone," said Rabbie through wet eyes. Petral put her arm around him, "We'll be strong for Pop. He'll be devastated."

Jamie scowled, "She was robbed. At least Dick Turpin[4] wore a friggin' mask. I'm going for a drink. Let the old man get composed for an hour or two."

Despite the gravity of the situation, Petral laughed, "Mum would have loved that one... I'll drive you. You know how he hates a fuss... Smudger and Kim are on their way to keep an eyeball all on him."

Rabbie shrugged his jacket on, "Count me in. We'll go toast Mum. She certainly took no crap but surely covered us in a blanket of love and care. She was a legend in the face of adversity."

They stole quietly out, leaving Jamesey to his immediate grief as his mind wandered down over the years, seeking some type of last solace in his memory banks, then a big grin split his face as he thought of their first curry night, an army hospital in Belfast and the dragon of a Matron, and how whatever the seriousness of the situation or just the general annoyance of daily life, Collette was at his side to console and advise him.

His mind shot back to a grey, impersonal train station as he headed off to war, and the beautiful, vibrant young woman waving him off, blowing kisses, cheeks stained with tears.

---

[4] Seventeenth century highway man, a local hero likened to Robin Hood, hanged in York alongside his horse, 'Black Bess'.

The doctor hedged his way in, concerned. "Bloody diamond in a pile of coal she was," Jamesey informed him, "Now sod off for a few hours, I'll be reminiscing."

II

First Thursday in March, 2013, Midnight. Apartment 3B, 'The Poplar Trees' Apartments, North Village, New York City

Luca Valendenski tossed fitfully as she slept. Her dreams were of faraway shores and of a dead lover. She smiled in her sleep as she saw her lover's face and his arms opened wide to greet her. Suddenly, Galen's face disappeared and her dream became dark and menacing. Her exquisitely lovely face took on a frown as impending pitch-black clouds and shapes surrounded her and fearfulness gripped her subconscious. A large man in black strode towards her, hatred in his pace and eyes like steel traps.

She whimpered and rolled on to her back as beads of perspiration broke across her terrified countenance. The evil spectre was nearly upon her now, but as is the nature of nightmares, her legs were stuck fast as if cemented to the ground and she couldn't flee.

And flee she knew she had to, because, as sure as you could predict the oceans' tides, she realised this monster's only intent was to do her serious harm.

She watched him with fixated eyes. He stopped before her, laughed through a mouth laced with teeth like broken tombstones and reached out to grip the cringing young beauty in a deadly embrace, his odour rank and putrid.

Escape barred and swooning with fright, she knew the situation was hopeless.

A shaft of bright light broke from the side and a strong-looking man strode down its corridor, illuminating the scene. He wore a colourful tartan coat and exuded confidence as he faced the fiend.

"Go now, Luca. You're free. I'll handle this," and the rescuer confronted the evil entity.

Luca's legs were freed as if heavy shackles had been smitten off; she needed no second bidding and took off like an exotic bird released from a cage and rushed towards the shaft of light to freedom.

She woke with a start, heart thudding and sat up, disorientated, chest heaving. She had fallen asleep with her bedside lamp on. What a weird dream! Who was the stranger? He had a handsome face and a slight burr in his accent she couldn't place. Luca didn't need to think too hard as to who the man in black was. She shuddered at the thought and memory of him. "No more cheese and pickle sandwiches before bed again, my girl," she chided herself after putting the lamp out. She soon sank into a deep, dream-free slumber, happy her rescuer, whoever he was, was looking over her and monitoring her dreams and keeping her safe from devils, and she felt sheltered and secure.

In the alley, three floors below, a tall, beefy man in a black trench coat watched her light go out, "Soon, you bitch. Very soon I'll be calling," and he smirked evilly before heading off into the shadows, trailing evil.

Next morning Luca awoke and remembered nothing of her nightmare as she went through her morning routine, looking forward to her day.

Skipping down the outside steps, giving a finger wave to Mr Chin the caretaker, she almost slipped on the tiles but righted herself and laughed gaily with relief.

A clean-cut young executive, heading to work, offered a well-dressed arm "You 'kay, miss? Are yah hurt?"

She took his arm. "Vhy tank you so much, I am fine. Silly me."

He saw her across the busy road, and she gave him her dazzling smile in farewell, which broke several men's hearts everyday.

He eyed her departing slim back. *Silly? I thought she was absolutely enchanting.* You didn't bump into many angels first thing in the morning in the concrete jungle.

Across the street a large, bad-looking guy watched him from a car. "Move along, shitface," he growled, "That's my property and she ain't for rent."

Chapter 1
'A Real Deal in the Peel'
('When I First Saw the Light in Your Eyes'... The Fureys and Davy Arthur)

London, First Monday in February, 1976 – 11.00am

Jamesey John DeJames sat on the stool at the end of the bar in 'The Robert Peel' public house situated at the top of Watford's busy High Street in North London. By picking his spot he had a clear view of the doors, and if he glanced to his right, he could see the full length of the lounge bar through the partition and the entrance to that area as well. Entrances and exits were important considerations when tactical, on or off leave.

Jamesey never sat with his back to the door, he liked to see who came in so that he could react in defence if he had to and choose his exit if he had to withdraw quickly. He was a man who rarely backed down but liked to have the edge if he had to defend himself, the 'heads up' as they called it in the army. *Proper planning prevents piss-poor performance*, he mused. He doubted he would have to defend himself in The Peel, as the locals were friendly and convivial. They didn't give one iota about politics or the dire situation in the North of Ireland, where he had just come from a few days previously, returning to barracks in Aldershot after a gruelling six-month tour in the notorious 'Bandit Country' of South Armagh. Several of his comrades had returned in body bags and many others were lying up in hospital with horrendous injuries. *There but for the Grace of God go I*, he judged with a tinge of bitterness for his suffering comrades.

He shook his head in disbelief that in a part of the United Kingdom the only way to get around was by helicopter or on foot, treading warily to avoid booby traps, and never setting up a pattern. To drive the roads in their jeeps was courting death and tempting fate because of the huge landmines and roadside bombs the IRA[5] so cunningly concealed. Only the previous week Jamesey had watched the stream of red tracer from a heavy machine gun whizz past the chopper his patrol was aboard as the IRA had a last crack at the much hated paratroopers. A free, impromptu fireworks display by the so-called freedom fighters. The pilot had to take some stomach-churning, gut-wrenching evasive manoeuvres before landing in a field a few hundred yards from the firing point. The dazed paras, some covered in vomit from when their stomachs had objected to the pilot's antics, found that their attackers had fled across the invisible border. A brief gun battle had ensued across the disputed

---

[5] Irish Republican Army

19

line the frustrated troops were not allowed to cross before the bandits disappeared into the gloom.

Still, no casualties and no hits claimed. But long runs the fox, and Jamesey knew his path would cross the IRA's again in several weeks' time, when his battalion returned to Ulster for another six months, this time to war-torn Belfast, the paras being in great demand by the Army High Command in the troubled province. Not so much wanted by certain sections of the province's community after the debacle that had been Bloody Sunday, after the paras had shot down a number of protestors in Londonderry. The jury was out on that one and would be for many years to come, he guessed quite correctly.

This was his second leave in Watford. He had come last summer for two weeks to scout the area out and make plans, before heading off to Armagh. While here he got to know Ron and Eadie Mulligan, the proprietors of the pub and, liking them, he had decided to make it his watering hole. Jamesey was a guy that wherever he went, liked to have a base from which to forage out and return safely to.

The bar was filling up with the usual regulars: OAPs, shop workers on an early lunch, and a bunch of Irish navvies, who were working on the new ring road and shopping centre and trying to drink the bar dry of Guinness and Bushmills Whiskey.

He drank his Double Diamond ale contently. Ian Drury and the Blockheads were serenading him from the jukebox, something about 'On the Road to Mandalay' and 'Hit Me with Your Rhythm Stick', a catchy popular song. He chatted intermittently with Ron as he went to and fro, serving his clientele. It was good to feel safe and relax. It was a rare animal in his life of a paratrooper.

Jamesey was strong-willed and refused to dwell on the past, although the odd nightmare sometimes intruded on his sleep, but he had been warned about them in advance by the old Sweats when he was a young Penguin[6], it was all just part and parcel of the dangerous job he was in. 'Carpe diem' was Jamesey's view, 'Seize the day and live it to the full'.

He was a striking-looking man of twenty-six. Six feet two inches tall and wearing a size 13 boot, he was fit and muscular, with wide shoulders and a handsome ruggedness to his face and frame. Health and confidence oozed off him in waves. His head was topped with golden-red curly hair and with his clear ice-blue eyes and thick golden moustache, he had the look of a marauding Viking, looking for plunder. He knew he was attractive to a certain type of woman and had indeed had several, short-lived romances on various leaves and postings.

He was now footloose and fancy free. No piece of skirt was going to hold him back from achieving his goals. When he left the army in a year's time, he fully intended to establish the small security firm he had planned and was saving up for. He was his own man and beholden to no one. A new future was looming ahead and he was going to seize it with a strong grip and hold it aloft in both hands like Atlas the Greek god holding the world above his head.

Several pints later and he was chatting amiably with the Irish tarmaccers, who knew he was in the army but didn't give a damn and couldn't care one way or the other about the crazy war 'up north' in the troubled, occupied six counties. Jamesey was an easy man to get along with, he was a great listener and enjoyed all types of company, neither judging nor condemning the heady rich mix of drinkers he met and

---

[6] Trainee para

socialised with in the pub. Sometimes their cockney lingo and sense of humour flummoxed him, but he generally got the gist of the conversation at some point. People were generally the same the whole world over, and Jamesey had seen quite a lot of the world. "Treat people the way you would expect to be treated yourself and generally you won't get any anguish," his mother Beth had lectured him when he was young and he found it to be a good rule overall, although 'there is only so much crap a man should take' was his own motto. Still, his mother, who ran a sheep farm on the Scottish border, was a wise old bird, who took no crap and didn't suffer fools easily.

Jamesey also had a vast repartee of jokes and humorous stories he had picked up in the barracks and on tours, so when Ron had 'lock-ins', after hours when he felt 'Lily Law'[7] wasn't watching, Jamesey was in great demand. He sighed happily as he munched on a crispy liver pate roll Eadie had made him and gulped down more golden ale…bliss, pure bliss. He was a content man, happy in his own little world and looking forward massively to the next few years ahead, as the world was his oyster, his own devices and plans were his mistress and the road ahead beckoned enticingly before him.

The paras were worked hard, often to the point of endurance and beyond, but likewise, when they played, by crikey, they bloody well played hard too. He wondered how many of his guys he would have to bail out of the Glasshouse[8] on his return. There was always a price to pay for young men under military discipline who had been given a taste of freedom and misbehaved; apart from murder and other serious crimes, the army was understanding and had its own standards of practice.

This was the first leave he would spend in his new house, a three-bedroom semi he had taken a mortgage out on, situated a few miles outside town. His first big step towards total independence. He swigged more beer, one ear on the Irish tarmaccers who were as easygoing and humorous a group of guys as you could meet. "Salt of the earth" his mother would have said of them, having worked with and employed farm labourers her whole life.

"We reckon now, Jamesey, that if we cover all of yer country with the tarmac, in fifty years, then you're have to be buying the good Irish beef and wheat off us Paddies, so you will," said a big giant of a man from Cork called Brendan, his hands black from the said stuff and the same colour as his pint of Guinness.

Jamesey and Ron, who were chatting again, grinned. "You're only trying to get even for the famine,[9] yer bunch of Paddy Whackers," Ron laughed back.

"If you Brits had bought our corn, there would have been no famine, so there wouldn't!"

Jamesey laughed now, "Jesus, Brendan! That was over a hundred years ago. You Irish have memories like elephants."

"And this bunch smell like an elephant house," interposed Ron. "But their bleedin' memories ain't that good that they remember to go back to work after lunch."

---

[7] The police (pure as white lilies)
[8] Army Detention Centre
[9] 1845-1852 – When the potato crop failed in Ireland, over a million starved or emigrated, and they blamed the British Government for refusing to buy Irish wheat.

The navvies clapped and cheered, knowing their landlords and masters were good at winding them up.

"Another round of the Shamrock[10], landlord, and give the lad there a drink as well, to be sure."

Jamesey watched as a slim girl of about twenty came around from behind the bar to catcalls and whistles from the regulars. She smiled fondly at the old drinkers and began collecting glasses and emptying overflowing ashtrays. She was very graceful and fluid, but Jamesey noticed a nervous awareness in her actions, like he often saw in his young soldiers on active service. A lack of trust in her surroundings. Intriguing. Things were looking up. He liked the thought of the slip of the mysterious girl to chat up and unravel.

The young woman was quite diminutive in stature compared to Jamesey, about five feet two inches, he judged. One of the first things he noticed was her tight, pert arse, encased in a horrendous pair of skin-tight, fake crocodile skin trousers. Her legs seemed firm and shapely in the shabby slacks, her feet wobbling on high cork platform soles as she moved from table to table, leaving the glasses on the bar for Ron to put in the sink for her. Her fingernails, as indeed were the ones on her bare toes that peeked out from the dangerous shoes, were painted bright orange. She was wearing a scoop-necked vest, ivory coloured, which exposed the tops of her small creamy breasts when she bent over.

Small but definitely shapely, Jamesey noticed, and grinned when he thought of his best mate, and oppo, Steven 'Smudger' Smyth. He always said, with a nudge and a wink, when in female company, "Anything over a handful is a waste, mucker."

He wondered what colour her pubic hair was, because that's what soldiers on leave thought. It was impossible to guess as she had outrageous, dyed pink hair in a short feather cut. He studied her more covertly. She had a very pretty heart-shaped face and a dainty snubbed nose. The eyes were evenly spaced, a rich hazel with green and gold flecks when they caught the light, and framed by lustrous, long dark lashes. Her lips were full and pouty in a perfect cupid's bow. Whilst her manner seemed uncertain and insecure, her movements were done with a natural grace and deportment, pleasing to the eye, which complimented her quite sultry well-toned figure, almost feline in the fluid unconscious way she moved about. *She was a looker, all right*, Jamesey judged, and she either did not know it or was deliberately blanking it for her own, unknown to all but her, reasons.

As she went about her tasks, Jamesey decided she was a wee cracker. The locals treated her with affection, with the exception of one large, flabby dark-haired guy, who was sat alone at a table in the middle of the floor. Jamesey reckoned him to be in his early thirties. Everybody seemed to ignore him but it didn't seem to faze him at all as he studied the 'Racing Post', lord in his own castle. For some reason Jamesey thought of fascists in brown shirts and concentration camp guards.

"Cor lumey, fried eggs again today," he ribbed as she emptied his full ashtray. "Yer won't get lost in the fog with hair like that. Yer could get a job as a bleedin' Belisha Beacon."[11]

She ignored him as she lifted his empty glass and he quite blatantly stared down her cleavage. As she turned, he gave her a sharp nip on the arse with two fat fingers;

---

[10] Another round of Guinness

[11] First pedestrian crossing denoted by big lit orange globes

22

she jumped in pain and slapped him off. She mooched back over to the bar with the empties, looking slightly dejected but her pretty eyes flashing loathing and annoyance at the brute's action.

Jamesey, who was a good judge of character, decided she was hiding an inner sadness, and there was a definite air of melancholy about her which she just failed to hide. *Quite intriguing*, he thought. Something was slightly out of kilter about the lass, and he guessed she didn't worry too much about the way she looked or didn't care, it was as if she didn't want to be noticed too much, which was more the pity, because she was well worth looking at.

He decided that was very sad. Often his men in the platoon came to him with their problems, and he counselled them as best he could and kept an eagle eye out for signs of worry or distress in his young soldiers because a worried soldier was a distracted one, who could become a liability not only to himself but to his comrades as well.

Ron saw him watching and laughed. "That's our young Collette, one of Eadie's strays. Does the cleaning and other things about the place, and I bung her a few quid to pay for her lodgings. Bit of a broody mare at times. The missus will be opening a home for lost cats next," he chortled, running a cloth over the bar. "Keep the bloody rats down in the cellar anyhow, breed like bleedin' Vietnamese boat people the vermin," he laughed merrily.

Jamesey could sense a story coming but said 'broody mare' came mooching around behind the bar and Ron shut up. She cleared her way up to them and gave him a small, unsure, tentative smile and asked if he had finished with his glass. He noticed her neat, pearly white teeth and the tip of a small pink tongue as she concentrated on emptying his ashtray. At least she looked after them. He liked a clean mouth on a woman and laughed inwardly at the analogy because a very dirty thought had crossed his mind as he studied her sultry, provocative lips. He drained the last inch of ale and pushed the glass towards her. "I have now, my lovely. Any chance of another?"

"Thank you, sir," she said, taking the glass, "I'm not allowed to pull a pint yet. Ron ses I spill too much of the profits."

Jamesey smiled reassuringly at her. "Och lass, everybody has to learn. You'll soon pick it up," and he offered her his hand. A big, intimidating calloused hand, but it shot a warm sense of security up into her heart.

Ron grinned and went off to pour his drink. She hesitated before gingerly placing her small, dainty hand in his, his big mitt engulfing hers. "Jamesey John DeJames at your service, young lady," and he gave her a huge, happy, smiling, flashing, strong, white-tooth smile, wide open to invitation.

She shook his hand. "I'm Collette, Collette Stark. You in the army then? You must be bleedin' mad or very brave!" she said before easing her hand out of his, "Or both."

"Don't know about either of those," he grinned. "But for my sins, I took the Queen's Shilling[12]." Her hand felt very small and fragile in his. Like a bird's wing, small, delicate-boned. "Although I guess I have it long spent by now."

---

[12] Once enlisted in the military, you are given the Queen's or King's shilling to pledge allegiance

Ron deposited a perfectly poured pint in front of him before rushing off to serve the rapidly filling pub. Collette lingered on, interested in the big man across the bar with the soft burr to his accent. He was blatantly studying her hair, interest in what she considered was a pair of very clear, attractive eyes full of mischief. "Ya won't get much for a shilling these days, mate. Bleedin rip off when we went decimal."

"I think your hair is outstanding," he paused with a twinkle in his eye. "Did you do it for a bet or what?"

She blushed prettily and looked down shyly at her feet, tapping them about, distracted.

"Nah, was sloshed one night at a party and some mates did it when I was akip."

"Jesus! With friends like that, who needs enemies," he judged. "Hope you got your own back?"

She looked back up and mused on that before replying, her pretty fingers tapping on the bar top, "Nah, not these friends. They're a bleedin' rough pack, yer just let them get on with it and keep yer claptrap[13] shut."

"Nonsense. You have to stand up for yourself, lass, forget the Ten Commandments, we just have two commandments in the paras. It's our philosophy."

Collette didn't know what philosophy meant but was interested, "What're them then?"

"Number one, do it to them before they do it to you, and number two, if you can't, get bloody well even."

She pondered on this for a while, her lovely face lost in thought, then she said, "Yeah well, I guess that's okay for a six-foot squaddie, built like a bleedin' brick shit house, but it's not for a sack of bloody twigs like me."

His laugh rang out across the bar as he revised his opinion about her clean mouth. She liked his ringing laugh, liked it very much indeed. What she couldn't work out though was what induced him to take off in a perfectly decent aeroplane and then jump out of it thousands of feet above ground. She would have to ask him about that one day.

"There is more than one way to skin a cat, Collette. In fact, there are lots of ways," he informed her mysteriously. "The cat that bides its time catches more mice."

"Wot da frig would yah wanna skin a cat for anyway?" she questioned and added, "Though yah don't see too many moggies up near Mr Chin's Chinese take-out, nor mice, thinking about it."

He was off again, laughing uproariously. She certainly had a sense of humour. She smiled, strangely pleased she had amused him. He took a big swig of his pint, still chortling.

"And don't put yourself down, Collette, if you're a sack of twigs, then you're a very pretty one, very pretty indeed."

She blushed furiously and hastened down to the sink, at Ron's bidding, to wash glasses. He noticed she gave him the odd glance over her shoulder, not exactly smouldering looks but lingering, inquisitive ones. He dismissed her mentally as just a nice young girl flattered by the attention of an older man of the world. Master of his own destiny, if some lucky terrorist didn't soot or blow him up, and supreme emperor of the universe he vowed to build and expand on in the years ahead.

---

[13] Cockney slang for mouth

24

"Ach no, mate," they shouted back with their rich brogues, "We're off with the Irish flu."[22]

The Paddies eventually did go off back to work, and the clock ticked down to three and closing time.

Collette was picking up the loose change off the bar to put in her tips jar when Jamesey pushed across the accumulation of small change he had gathered over the afternoon, "Here, Collette, add that to the collection. Would you like to go with me for a bite to eat when you're ready? I have to get a few shirts after and could do with some female advice as to colour and style. I have as much fashion sense as Ken Dodd has in shirts, which is zero," he laughed and gave her an elbow nudge, "I need you on this one, mate."

Her eyes lit up and he was gratified. She seemed tidier today, wearing a figure-hugging pair of jeans that showed her pert bottom off to perfection and a nice light blue, cable-knit jumper. Red and blue were definitely her colours. Her lovely eyes shined and sparkled in anticipation of helping him with his shopping.

They went to the Skandia in town, she had a mixed grill and felt very posh. Then they went to Burtons, where he bought a couple of shirts that she picked. It made her feel very close to him. To be asked for her guidance by such a handsome, self-assured beast of the male species in her small enclosed zoo was a novel feeling. She hadn't talked about any personal things over lunch, and he didn't push for anymore of her background, feeling she would tell him in her own time. That night he dropped her home after the pub... Collette was falling in love, her heart was fit to bursting in her breast. She was missing him already and couldn't wait to get to work tomorrow.

II

Next Day

Collette was behind the bar when he arrived the next day, and she gave him a lovely smiling greeting as he took his customary stool. Her heart skipped a beat as she studied his handsome profile, and she chided herself for acting like a schoolgirl with her first crush; she was a mature twenty and not a moon-struck teenager.

He gazed around the bar, assessing. It was very quiet, just a few of the retired regulars were playing a subdued game of dominoes, the tiles clinking as they slipped them to and fro and Slimy Barry at his usual table, flicking through the 'Racing Post' his greasy brow furrowed in concentration. *He couldn't pick a winner if it kicked him in the arse*, Jamesey assessed bitchily.

Jamesey lit his first cigarette of the day and watched as Collette carefully poured him a pint of Double D. She looked very young and fresh in neatly pressed jeans, a pink blouse and a heavy woollen dark-blue cardigan, which reached below the knee. He liked the way she chewed her lips in concentration as she strove to pull the perfect pint.

"Mornin', Jamesey," she welcomed him and deposited the perfectly pulled pint before him, "did yah get a good kip then? I dreamt that bleedin' shark was in me bath an' was chompin' me legs aft'."

---

[22] Too drunk to go to work

He laughed and pushed a ten bob note over. "You must have a huge bath, lass. Thought you weren't allowed to pull pints?"

"I came in early, didn't I, and practised, and Ron ses I can serve when it's quiet like," she told him proudly. "I gets in a bit of a tizzy when it's busy, dun I."

"Well, good for you, kiddo. You'll soon be running the place single-handed. You're looking very fresh and pretty today." And she was. Her hair was shining and her eyes sparkled with pleasure at his compliments.

"This one's on me, mate. I've already paid for it owt me tips," and she pushed the note back at him, her fingers brushing his, lingering.

Ron came limping in from the back, "Morning, Jamesey. Just restocked with draught Guinness. Christ, those navvies can fairly guzzle it down. The Irish muvvers must have had it in their milk and the young 'uns got a tolerance for it."

"Good for business though, Ron. Where's the good lady then?"

"Up the shops, ain't she? Buying new clothes wiv me profits, ain't she?" Ron eyed Jamesey as he sank some of his ale, then inspected the slops tray. Satisfied, he patted Collette on the back fondly. "Nice one, I'll make a barmaid of yer yet, young un."

"Can I have your phone, Ron? I want to ring one of my guys and it's business."

Ron understood. He had done his national service. "Sure, come round to the office," and he lifted the flap at the end of the bar.

Jamesey rang his Sergeant and best mate in Tavistock in Cornwall, and they chatted about the upcoming tour and the hundred and one things of an admin nature they had to put in place when their leave ended. In the army you got paid twenty-four hours a day, three hundred and sixty-five days a year, leap years included. You were never, ever really off duty, physically or mentally. Steven 'Smudger' Smyth was an efficient no-nonsense soldier but well-liked and respected. He had gone through the arduous para training with Jamesey, and they were more than mates, they were brothers in arms.

It was Smudger who had suggested Jamesey look at Watford as a start-up spot for his security company, and Jamesey was trying to talk him into joining him as a partner in the venture. "Be like bloody Batman and Robin," he told him with his big self-effacing smile.

When he finished his call with a promise to keep in touch if anything he had forgotten occurred to him, Ron came in with two double Johnnie Walkers for them.

He sipped the sharp whiskey, liking the burn as it slipped down his strong throat. "Cheers, Ron...better not let Eadie catch you on the hard stuff," he advised with a grin.

Ron smiled smugly. "She won't be back for a while yet, not when she's on a free spree." He waggled a tube of polo mints in Jamesey's face, "Just in case, though."

"You're a dark, devious man, but I admire your style."

Ron sat and grimaced as he rubbed his right knee. Tall, stout and greying, he was the epitome of the ruddy-faced landlord and played the part to perfection.

Forced to retire from the Metropolitan Police when a blagger[23] he was chasing had took his right patella out with a pair of nostrils[24], he had made a resounding

---

[23] Armed robber
[24] Sawn off shotgun

success of The Robert Peel, the pub named after the founder of the London Police Force in the eighteenth century.

"I dunno, Jamesey... Wots this bleeding hold wimmen 'ave over us men? Yer spend nine months of yer life trying to get outta the bleedin' hole and the rest of yer adult life tryin' to get back into the bloody thing... Cor blimey mate, I dunno, I really don't."

Jamesey grinned at Ron's pained expression. Obviously, Eadie wasn't giving him his proper ration. "You know, Ron...you are so bloody right. Weird isn't it, but I guess it's what makes the world go round."

Ron sloshed another dose of Scotch into their glasses, "Get yer gums around that me ol' son...wimmen...different species, mate. You can't live with them, but you can't live without them."

"You're right I guess, Ron. Never had the privilege yet... You see ladies are from the planet Venus and men from the planet Penis."

Ron's turn to laugh. "Yer can say that again, me ol' cocker...the ol' one-eyed spitting python is a hard taskmaster... Still, I wouldn't swat Eadie for all the tea in China but doncha be telling her that, her head's swollen enuf as it is."

"Naw baw, mate. She's a good one, is Eadie." Jamesey promised. "So...what's the story with young Collette then?" he asked tentatively. "I didn't want to push too hard yesterday."

Ron looked at him knowingly. "Interested in her, are yer? She had it rough mate, I can tell yer...why doncha ask her yourself? Take her out for a curry. She might open up to yah. Be good for her."

"Might just do that," and leaving money for the phone call, returned to the bar, thoughtful.

Trade was picking up and the tarmaccers were in, and Collette was getting flustered. Jamesey gave her a reassuring wink.

"Thought you bloody women could multitask?" sneered Barry, tapping his empty pint pointedly on his table as Collette pulled Guinness and shots of Bushmills. She breathed out through pretty pink pursed lips, exasperated. "I've only got one pair of hands, Barry, dun I? I'll get to your soon."

"Give the lass a chance, man. She's doing her best," Jamesey told him pleasantly but firmly.

"Why don't yer mind yer own, soldier boy? I'm a fucking regular here. Why doncha bugger off and find some niggers to fight?"

Jamesey, who had a couple of coloured guys in his platoon, felt his hackle rise. "Whilst I am spending my own money on drink, I'll drink where I want, what I want and when I want, so put a sock in it and watch your foul mouth in future," he said with such deadly menace that the whole bar went quiet. You could have heard the cockroaches mating in the kitchen.

Barry just gazed open-mouthed, not being used to being stood up to. He might be overweight but he was big and mean and handy with his fist. No squaddie wanker took the piss at him in his bloody local.

Ron came quickly round from behind the bar "Okay, gents...that's enough, give us your glass, Barry, and I'll sort it."

Jamesey pointedly turned his back to Barry but he was ready for him if he wanted to rough and tumble. Collette looked worried and Jamesey winked at her. "Manners maketh the man, my father always said," he proclaimed loudly to no one in particular.

Big Brendan from Cork picked up on that and went into a lengthy disposition about a bad-mannered leprechaun, a goat and a prostitute and gradually, the atmosphere eased and guffaws had literally began as Brendan reached the climax of the story.

Barry just sat and stared malevolently at Jamesey's impervious back. *Fucking squaddie import.*

Eadie arrived back laden with designer shopping bags. Ron groaned and shook his head in mock disbelief and everyone laughed.

"Last orders, please," he roared. "And make 'em bleedin' big uns, so I can keep Queen Sheba here in the style she's accustomed to."

Eadie smiled sweetly at him and whispered in his earhole, "Maybe we'll go upstairs for an hour, Ron. Have a little lay down for a bit."

A crooked, lascivious grin crossed his face. "Right yah pack of heathens, hurry up and drink up."

Collette went and stood down by Jamesey, still a bit anxious about the altercation with Barry. He appeared totally unconcerned by it all.

"Fancy going out for a curry, Collette? Don't fancy eating on my own."

"Dunno, never had a Ruby Murray before."

He looked at her flabbergasted. "You've never had a curry before? Good God, lass, you haven't lived and who the heck is Ruby?"

She shrugged prettily, her small breasts joggled, "Ain't ever been asked before, 'ave I. But that would be lovely, Jamesey, tanx ever so… Ruby Murray, country and western singer in the fifties. Apparently, she was hot stuff."

He rubbed his hands gleefully, pleased that she looked pleased, "You just wait, lass. I'll soon show you what hot means."

She smiled back uncertainly, not sure what he meant by that, "I'll bleedin' try anything once," she answered with mock bravado. "Yer only bleeding live once, mate."

He knocked the rest of his pint back in two huge gulps. "I'll go ring Clive the taxi. See you outside."

He strolled past Barry, who was last to finish as usual. Barry scowled menacingly at Jamesey's back. As if sensing this, Jamesey stopped and smartly about-turned, walked back and placed both hands on the table either side of him.

He leant over and spoke quietly into Barry's face, "You touch her again, Barry, and soldier boy here will be practising some very painful unarmed combat moves on you."

Barry swallowed the last of his mild and bitter, his eyes locked implacably with Jamesey's. "I'm bleeding looking forward to that, soldier girl. My pub. My rules."

Collette could feel the temperatures drop as the two antagonists stared each other out. She knew that if not today, soon it would boil over into something very nasty and dangerous. She shivered as if someone had walked over her grave. Men were so frigging territorial.

Ron hadn't missed the confrontation. "Right, me ol' Chinas, enuf the chit-chat. I have tah lock up."

Jamesey straightened and gave a huge exaggerated yawn. "After you, Barry. You're boring me witless."

Barry shrugged into his padded anorak. "I be seeing yer, soldier girl," and he put his face into Jamesey's, "Watch yer back, cunt. Gets dark early." And he swaggered out, sniggering.

"Probably tah flash at the school girls up the park in a coat like that," laughed Ron to ease the tension. Collette just looked uneasily at Jamesey.

"More likely school boys would be my guess," grinned Jamesey. "Right, curry-time people, my stomach thinks my throats been cut, I'm that hungry."

Collette rushed out back to get her coat. 'Slimy Barry' forgotten, looking forward to a new life's experience and looking forward to getting the most out of a few hours with the most intriguing man who had ever taken an interest in her in her life, a dynamo of a male whom fate has crossed her path with.

Eadie watched her rush out and shook her head, "Young ones, Goodness Gracious, Great Balls of Fire."

Chapter 6

New York, New York... One Hell of a Town

('New York Empire State of Mind'...Leone Lewis)

First Sunday in March, 2013

Late evening – The Russian Club

She sipped on the expensive champagne with half an ear cocked to Constantine and his friend's conversation. She thought about the handsome man she had shared breakfast with on Friday morning and wondered if he was home from his climbing trip. A small rueful grin crossed her lush red lips as she wondered what it would be like to share breakfast in bed with him. Probably very pleasant, she surmised, never having had that experience with any man yet. The thought was exhilarating, and she did not dare let herself dwell on the thrilling idea of what might happen in the bed before breakfast, that was much too deep to contemplate. A shiver of sexual anticipation ran up her back and caused the fine silky hairs at the base of her spine to rise.

Constantine asked if she was okay, and she nodded her assent as he gazed at her admiringly with his black soulful Russian eyes. In his late twenties and darkly handsome, he was the epitome of the Russian male. He worked at something in property sales. His father owned the club, and he spent most of his spare time there, with his small circle of hangers-on, buying endless bottles of vodka and champagne. She speculated there were a few lines of cocaine too as they disappeared into the back restrooms at frequent intervals and came back giggling and animated. She knew Constantine would very much like to share breakfast in bed with her, among other things, but she suspected he'd probably shared breakfast with a number of the young women who frequented the club and she didn't want to join the queue. Not to be just a page in his history of sexual conquests or a notch on his strained bedpost.

Still, he was convivial company and it was great to be able to chat away in her mother tongue with other young Russians who were far from home and talk about the motherland. The latest movies and fashions. What Putin would be up to next. Would he invade the Ukraine, Belarus? Why had he not wiped out the Chechens? Which made Luca cringe.

She wondered what Reena and Dmitri were doing, and she missed them deeply. She thought of the old Director and of a grave on a windy hilltop. Dark, lonely thoughts in a crowded, lively place. You were never alone in New York, except in your own mind.

New York people, if you allowed them, were always so much in your face, bustling and hustling everywhere. In her first weeks she though if she heard "Have a nice day" ever again, her head would explode and it was a lot for a country girl from Drasnov Valley to get around, but now it was the norm and she was a real "Have a nice day" gal now and had fallen deeply in love with the giant.

The day she found the lost child a steely resolve formed and helped fuse her shattered heart together. She cooked her mother a nice supper and placed her ballerina ensemble away in her trunk. Time passed and she returned to university, where mixing with other young people helped restore her interest in things in general. The attention given to her by potential suitors raised her confidence and reminded her she was an attractive young woman. She became vibrant again and her former caring, unselfish nature rose to the fore once more.

She was hugely popular, finding other young students who had faced adversity in life and helping them through their tragic circumstances, bolstering her own inner strength and resolve at the same time.

She found she was able to look back on her relationship with Galen without breaking down in tears. She could remember all the good, happy things they had done together without that deep wrenching pain that had previously always been present. Luca was well on the mend, but she still declined all invites to 'take coffee' with single men. She was saving herself for someone special. She sighed prettily, which Constantine noticed and he patted her knee consolingly. Luca was a deep one.

Luca removed his wayward hand with a smile to defuse things. No sirree…despite many offers from eligible single men, and indeed many married guys chancing their arms, Luca's gallant knight had not come galloping down Fifth Avenue on his charger to make her swoon and her heart flutter.

At twenty-one she passed her degree in Art and Design with outstanding honours, getting the highest merit in the university's records.

Her mother was delighted and when Reena, Dmitri and Mikhail, the old Director, came to the awards ceremony, they talked about her future. The Director pulled some strings and she was offered an eighteen months' post as a paid lecturer's assistant. She had lodgings and free access to an English language course. The 'men of influence' also agreed to continue her stipend for that period, so she was financially much better off and was able to rent a small house for several weeks on the Baltic coast during the humid month of August.

She took her mother, Dmitri and the Director there for a holiday and they had a fine, relaxing time, doing little else only swimming or fishing in the frigid waters and eating well. At night they made fires and grilled some of the many varieties of local sausage or cooked wild trout or pollack in tinfoil with herbs and butter.

Gazing into the dying embers one night, the Director beside her happily sipping the local moonshine laced with honey that he claimed helped his old bones and aided his sleep, she realised he was the grandfather she never had. Her father, an only child, had been raised by a distant aunt when his own parents, who were 'intellectuals', had disappeared in mysterious circumstances when he was a baby and her mother's parents had both died young. There was talk of Nazi camps but Reena always clammed up and refused to talk about it. Her lips were sealed.

She stared at the old man and saw, in the lines and crevices of his craggy face lit by the mellow glow from the red embers, a wealth of life's varied experiences and the trial and tribulations he had so bravely fought through over the many rich years of his life. She reached over and took his gnarled, calloused hand in her own soft gentle one, and he felt the comfort and welcomed it. The love they had for each other was reflected in their eyes by the firelight, and he was glad he had the privilege to be able to help this talented young woman as he knew his time in this life was short.

"I have a lot to thank you for, Mikhail, for your kindness to me and my family."

He gazed, mesmerised, into the fire, thinking back to and speaking about his time with the Resistance when the older men had made him do his lessons around the camp fire. They also made sure he got his fair share of the meagre food ration. "True comrades, all dead now from the Nazi headhunters or the sadist Stalin's purges," he paused and gazed fondly at her, "As for your thanks, nonsense child! What goes around comes around. As I have helped you, so too will you help others in the future. You have a strong aura of compassion and kindness about you, Luca, that encourages and inspires others. It is a wonderful gift, but beware that people do not take advantage of it and hurt you."

His words would prove to be prophetic.

She looked into the depths of the fire and saw strange shapes and forms she could not put names to. A pine marten killed a nesting bird somewhere in the black forest behind them and Luca shivered. Life could be cruel but nature knew no boundaries, eat to survive or be eaten yourself, but at least nature's cruelty wasn't malicious. A kitten playing with a mouse was only honing its apprenticeship in survival. It wasn't wanton cruelty, it was survival. "You would have made a wonderful father but your unselfish nature denied you that. Now I hope you look upon Mama, Dmitri and I as your family."

He smiled happily. "Lithuania has been my mother and father. Lithuania has raised me, been kind to me and indeed punished me, but yes, I am honoured to be accepted into your fold. Spasibo my labyyanka."

She loved his sharp intellectual mind, fostered by years of study and teaching but also the product of a huge natural intelligence. He was one of a rare breed. A giant of a man. A prophet in her eyes, of hope and tolerance for humanity.

"And look at the thousands of students who have passed through your classroom, Mikhail, they are your offspring in a sense as well, your children. You must be so proud of what you have achieved."

Misty-eyed, he remembered, "Yes, I have a lot to be thankful for. The human mind has a great capacity for forgetting the bad things and remembering only the good times. It's a great mental self-defence mechanism. Mankind would become extinct and perish without it."

Luca squeezed the phenomenal old man's hand tenderly. "Tell me about your nephew Simon. He sounds so interesting."

Simon was four years old when he was liberated from the Auschwitz concentration camp in Poland on the 15th of January, 1945. The son of Theo, Mikhail's brother, and his wife Meta, neither of whom survived the brutal, sadistic regime, he was just skin and bone and had to be treated for TB when he was found. He was later repatriated to England, by a Jewish relief organisation, as it was feared if he was sent back, alone, to anti-sematic Russia, he would 'disappear'. He spent his first year in England in an orphanage.

Captain Justin Webb[25], of the Royal Horse Artillery, was an impressionable twenty-three-year-old when he was one of the first liberators into the foul hell of a

---

[25] The Russians liberated Auschwitz in January 1945, but it is a little known historical fact that they had forward advance commonwealth liaison officers attached to them. The

68

death camp, where God only knows how many millions the mad man Hitler and his insane cohorts had massacred, and it was an experience he would carry his whole life. He called it his "dark side of the moon on his sunny earth", his unwanted awakening of man's inhumanity to man, and he claimed because of its effect he was never the same since.

Justin found Simon under a pile of lifeless children; he was barely alive and looked like a sack of twigs with huge staring eyes. He looked after the boy, feeding and clothing him, until he could hand him over to the Red Cross, who were severely out of their depth dealing with the massive influx of concentration camp survivors and were overwhelmed by the numbers. The world was to witness the most displaced refugee persons' crisis ever known in written history.

Justin took a note of Simon's refugee number and had his photograph taken with the child, which he always carried with him afterwards. A memento of that atrocious hell.

Most of the records before they fled were hastily destroyed but Justin got lucky. The inmates were all tattooed with a number on the inside of their arm when they arrived in the camp, and Justin managed to trace Simon and his parents using that number. The family had been deported from Vilnius, Lithuania, just days before the advancing Russian army re-took the city the previous September, and sent to the camp. They had already had a terrible war but now they entered hell.

Simon's father had worked for a while in the property sheds, where the belongings of the inmates were sorted into different categories and sent to the now crumbling Third Reich. The records showed he had been assigned to sort dentures and gold fillings before he fell ill and was sent 'up the chimney', in other words, he was gassed with Zyklon B and then burnt in the ovens in the crematorium. Originally a pesticide, the Nazis put a whole new spin on the term 'vermin control'.

His mother, Justin saw from her photo on record, was a pretty dark-haired woman in her early twenties. She was dressed in a thin striped prison uniform and looked terrified in the snap. The old Jew in charge of the records remembered her and what had happened to her.

"Ja, she was very attractive," he told Justin, "And the big SS Officer, Sergeant Major Muller, who was in charge of the Guard Squad, took her as his own. He was a vicious thug, a demon from hell and in cohorts with the devil. Auschwitz was his playground and he played hard."

Justin quizzed the old Jew about this and found out that as each train of 'sub-humans' arrived, the officers and NCOs took their pick of the women and used them as they saw fit. When they grew bored with the current one, they discarded them, most were sent to the gas chamber, the lucky ones were shot first, and the guard just picked a new one from the next train. "Human livestock. That's all they were, except cattle were treated better," he sighed. "No, cows had more value than the Untermensch and were prized."

"Muller was a brute, his discards were not amongst the lucky ones, he liked to beat the women to death. It was rumoured he even put a few in the ovens while they were still alive," the old Jew told him, tears heavy in his rheumatic traumatised eyes.

---

atrocities found at the time were initially suppressed by the authorities, afraid of shocking the general public. Captain Justin Webb was one of those officers.

"A pack of bastards to the man they were. Like a pack of hyenas, they fed on the weak and laughed after, may they rot in hell for eternity. God's curse on them."

He thanked the Jew and much to his delight, gave him a packet of John Player Navy Cut cigarettes. He walked away in disgust, his young mind able to fully comprehend the daily regime of total sadism that had made up this abhorrent camp.

Justin played with Simon in the Red Cross transit camp that night, spending his last free time there with the boy he had saved. The British were pulling out the next day, leaving the area to the Russians, much to the horror of the local community.

* * *

It took Justin six weeks to track down Sergeant Major Gerhard Muller to a small internment camp five miles outside the heavily bombed German city of Dresden, which was famous for pottery production.

Muller was a rough, coarse thirty-year-old from the port of Hamburg. He stood over six feet and was very well-built. Being a psychopath and a natural sadist, he had enjoyed the war and believed that after he served a few years in jail, he would be welcomed back with open arms by the criminal underworld of Hamburg, where he had flourished before the war began. Pimping young girls, stealing off the ships, strong-arming and arson, Muller was into everything.

Muller had reckoned without Captain Justin Webb. Justice has many shapes and forms. Justin was determined that in Simon's family's case, justice would be served.

Arriving late one night at the small camp, Justin found it was guarded by a platoon of tough paratroopers, and he introduced himself to the platoon commander, Lieutenant Mike DeJames, from the Scottish borders. Over a bottle of Johnny Walker, he told him the story of Simon and his parents. DeJames listened intently, sickened when Webb told him about the camp and the inhuman conditions. When Webb finished, DeJames called his Sergeant.

"Go get that bastard Muller, now, handcuffed! He's goin' for a drive."

Muller duly arrived, grinning at the change in the tedious routine and asked for a cigarette. Muller and his pack of torturers had fled south before the Russian advance, knowing if the Red Army got their hands on them, it would be a prolonged beating and a bullet in the back of the neck from a Makarov pistol. The British, on the other hand, were a soft bunch of wimps and they treated their charges well.

"Will I sign him out in the book, sir, as per force orders?"

"I don't think so, Sergeant," DeJames replied laconically. "I believe you're in the middle of an all-night poker game, please go and carry on. Take that crate of Pale Ale in the cold store and enjoy yourselves and no fighting." The Sergeant grinned, happy. DeJames could be a hard bastard, but he was scrupulously fair and never asked the men to do something he wouldn't do himself. He had proved himself in battle and the men would follow when he led, "Roger on that, sir. You won't hear a word off us until morning."

DeJames looked at him knowingly, "Kay, Sarge, see you at muster parade. I'll be here all night."

The Sergeant slammed to attention and marched out, steel-shod boots crashing across the linoleum.

"Zigarette bitte?" asked the hopeful Sergeant Major.

"Get him in the jeep, Justin. Let's get this turd sorted out."

70

They drove the bemused and more and more alarmed Hamburger deep into the deciduous forest surrounding the area. It was dark and dank, ancient trees watching eerily.

"Was ist los? Weir commen?" asked a concerned mass-murderer.

Justin looked at him. "What's wrong, comrade? Meta Siminion…ring a bell in that thick head of yours? Wife and mother you killed, you piece of scheisser."

"Nichts Meta. Nein. Nein," he protested.

They found a clearing and threw Muller out of the jeep. By the light from the headlamps, they beat him to within an inch of his life as he screamed and cried for mercy. "The shoe's on the other foot now, you murdering bastard," Justin snarled as he slammed his ammo boot into his ribs.

"Hilfe, hilfe. Meta nichts mein." He implored. "I vos sheir gut da Meta."

The British officers had both had a long and bloody war and had seen things no young man should ever have to witness. Man's inhumanity to man on such a vast scale that no one's mind could fully contemplate the enormity of it. All DeJames wanted to do was get back to the Cheviots and help his mother on the sheep farm, his father Killian had died at Arnhem during the failed 'Operation Market Garden' the previous year, and Justin wanted to get back to his Art department in the grammar school outside Sutton Coalfield.

They kicked him about some more and Muller cried like a baby. He looked up at the two officers, he knew his torturers, often handpicking his own, and his gut instinct told him that these two were not sadists by nature. They wouldn't have the stomach to inflict prolonged suffering on another human being.

"Bitte, bitte, sirs. Das var is over ja? Nichts spiel. Mein Herrs for Gott in Himmel."

Justin was wavering and DeJames saw it, but he had heard the sketchy reports of his father's death and that strengthened his resolve. It was believed that when the brave para had surrendered after running out of ammo, the SS had shot him dead, totally ignoring the rules of the much abused Geneva Convention. He looked down at the pathetic former SS man and pulled his Webley .45 revolver from his holster and pointed it at Muller's head.

"Too right you won't be telling, old chap," he said, and shot him stone dead. "For my dad at Arnhem and the innocents you stole, you piece of shite," and wiped the brain matter off his toe cap on the brute's hated uniform that had instilled such terror into so many for the last two decades.

The disturbed birds took off and made quite a din before silence settled again in the trees. A breeze in the trees rustled their leaves as if applauding their actions.

"Thanks, Mike, even though I hated what he did, I don't think I could have pulled the trigger."

"Just vermin control, Justin. Let's get this thing back to camp. He quite disgusts me."

* * *

The official story was that Captain Webb wanted to talk to Muller about his activities at Auschwitz, and when he was brought to the guard room, he went for a gun and DeJames shot him dead. No one seemed that much concerned and the two officers shook hands and parted company. Bonded for life.

71

* * *

A year and a half later Justin was back in Sutton Coalfield, running his Art department and mighty happy to be home. It was by sheer chance he found out that Simon was in a small home for displaced Jewish children near Coventry and went to visit. The staff were amazed when he showed them the photograph and told his story. When they brought the six-year-old Simon out, the instant bond formed again, a bond of love brought on by extreme adversity. Justin later said that fate had carved a path for Simon and him, with a shocked God's blessing.

The young Jewess who ran the home, Shiva Toye, had also lost her family in the camps. She herself had escaped their fate because they had sent her to live with relatives in England before the war started. Shiva had trained as a doctor and, as a fully qualified GP, used her training to care for the children who came to the home as many arrived undernourished and with a variety of illnesses, traumatised and terrified.

Originally from Cologne, she was very striking with her even features and, unusual for the race, lustrous, naturally blonde hair. Most weekends when Justin came to take Simon out, she joined them, and it didn't take long for them to fall in love. They married a short time later and adopted Simon.

When Justin broached the prospect of them having children of their own, Shiva gently but firmly rejected the idea. Between what she had seen while working in the camps after the war and dealing with the children back in the home in England, she had seen too much pain and suffering.

"What? For the next madman like Hitler or Stalin to come along and throw them into camps and kill them?" she shuddered, "No thanks, not after what I have seen."

"But they said it can never happen again," he argued gently.

"They said that after the Great War. It was meant to be the war to end wars, but it happened again, and they probably say that after every war. Let's just stay focused and do what little good we can in this depraved world."

Because he loved her and didn't want to cause her distress, he reluctantly agreed.

"Anyway," she laughed, "I'm a GP...never ending supply of rubber johnnies. Just because we won't be baking a cake, doesn't mean we can't have lots of fun mixing the dough."

He liked the thought of that a lot, she knew just how to cheer him up.

As Simon Webb the young boy grew to be a confident and talented man, he studied hard and became an accomplished artist and architect very much in demand for his expertise. As a young man, the only real blight on his life was the fact that he had trouble maintaining a lasting relationship with women, but he put that down to the trauma he had gone through as a child.

When his beloved adopted father died, he reverted to his birth parent's surname, and it was as Simon Siminion he travelled to New York in 1968.

He was still grieving the death of his beloved 'dad', Justin, when he met the American interior designer Peter Schuster and they hit it off straightaway. Much to the surprise of them both, they fell in love and before long they were in a totally committed relationship. They found a place together and established Schuster, Siminion & Co, Interior Designers. They worked well together and the company was a great success, attracting not only the nouveau riche but also some of the old moneyed families to their client lists. Shiva, now a successful GP in Coventry, was delighted for them and very proud of the part she had played in making Simon the man he was.

Simon had done some research on his family tree and discovered he was related to Mikhail Gideon through his birth mother, Meta Gideon, who was the Director's sister. When he found out he had a blood relative, he traced him, and they corresponded for many years building a strong friendship. When the Director told him about Luca's plight, he asked to see her portfolio and when he received the email, he was so impressed he decided, there and then, to offer her a trial contract with the firm.

Luca jumped at the chance of twelve months with such an important company and arrived in New York in the fall of 2009, just three months before her twenty-third birthday.

She had expected New York to be large, but she was amazed at the sheer diversity of the population, from the variety of goods and foods on sale to the hundreds of accents and local enunciations of the language.

She felt overwhelmed and awed by it all. The place was massive. Her English was good but all the local dialects left her confused.

She would stand for hours people watching; she never tired of listening to their incessant chatter. One day a young policeman noticed her, standing all agog, and asked her if she was okay. She told him she was fine and that she was newly arrived from Russia. As it was getting late, he insisted on walking her home to 'Poplar Trees', where the lovely Mr Siminion had helped her get an apartment, in the village area. Very chic and cosmopolitan.

"You are a very kind man, Officer," she told him, "I am going to put you very high on my 'Nicest Person List'."

The cop was thrilled by this and, after seeing her to her door, went about his duties glowing with pleasure. Luca had that effect on people and made many friends among the people she met; most of these people thought of it as the 'Luca effect', and no one was immune, except Luca.

She loved her job and threw herself into her work and very soon she began to reap the rewards of all the hard work. Her talents became recognised and as word spread, Simon discovered a lot of clients asked for her.

They would call and say, "Hey, have you got that Russian chick, Luca? She did some work for Meta and Marty, and I would like her to look at my place."

The partners were very pleased as they watched her client list grow, and Simon felt justified in keeping her on after the temporary contract ran out. She was a sublime talent. The consummate bohemian artiste with a quirky, creative eye for colour and tone and a knack for detail her dead lover Galen had installed in her.

She soon became accustomed to the hustle and bustle of life that made up her daily routine in the big city. Every day was a new adventure waiting to happen.

She loved going to her office and she soon made friends with her work colleagues. She made friends with a married couple, Wendy and Bob Havilland, who lived in the apartment near her, and they became number one on her 'Bestest Friends List'; they also were her mentors on city life and the social scene.

Luca sent money home on a regular basis, and she also opened a saving account that she added to every month, with the intention of saving enough to eventually bring her mother and brother to the USA. No matter how much she loved being in New York and how many friends she made, she still missed them every day.

She occasionally visited The Russian Club in the village when she felt homesick. While reading the local 'Russian Émigré' paper one night, she noticed they were advertising for a part-time singer. She made a tentative approach and wowed them with her audition. They loved the beautiful, graceful girl with the voice like a nightingale and hired her to sing on Wednesday and Sunday nights.

So it was that first Sunday night in March after singing her 6–9pm slot, drinking with Constantine for an hour and dodging his well-meant advances, that she was ready to leave. Constantine saw her out and flagged a yellow cab and paid her fare in advance.

"It is only a ten-minute walk, Connie, I don't mind."

"You're not walking at this time of night, baby," he argued, "It's dangerous."

She scoffed, "Who would hurt a woman in these crowds?"

The taxi driver leant out his window, "He's right, miss. It's no trouble at all, better safe than sorry."

"Okay, tanks, guys. You're very kind to Luca."

She kissed Constantine on the cheek and climbed into the back of the taxi, flashing her gorgeous, mini-skirted legs, much to the delight of both men. The taxi driver carried the small bag of groceries she had purchased earlier up the steps to the door.

"There you are, miss."

"Oh you are such a darling. Tank you. See you again."

The driver left, a big cheesy grin on his face as the Luca effect hit again.

She strode in, keen to get into her comfortable apartment and get her work started. She saw the elevator was out of order, but she couldn't have cared less and she skipped lightly up the stairs. The way her mind judged it, the taxi had saved her a walk. 'Quid pro quo'. What goes around comes around.

Across the road three men watched from a car. "We'll give the bitch an hour to get started while we go have a beer. Fucking turn me down!" fumed Harry Hanlon.

"You sure about this, boss dude?" asked Arturo Calves, his driver.

"As sure as li'l ol' green apples, Bubba. Now get into gear."

Hell was an hour away for Luca, and she was about to embark on an adventure so unexpected, she would not have thought it possible.

* * *

Dark clouds hid the moon as the sinister trio drove off in search of alcohol and illegal substance abuse.

As they passed a lone woman heading home from her late shift, Hanlon gazed at her fleetingly and she shuddered from the pit of her stomach, afraid, and hastened her stride, her feminine intuition telling her the three men in the car were no friends to the gentler sex and were bad news, very bad news indeed, and God help any girl who crossed their paths tonight.

Chapter 7
The Fine Art of Eating a Ruby Murray
('Ring of Fire'...Johnny Cash)

He waited outside for her, having a quick drag, as became his regular custom in the days ahead. He had purchased her a packet of Embassy Red with his loose change from the vending machine in the vestibule.

"Ta very much, Jamesey," she said when he gave them to her "I'm gagging for a drag. Eadie don't let me smoke around the punters. Ses it looks bad."

"And so it does, lass," he agreed as they walked off arm in arm towards the car park around the corner, where Clive was waiting, probably toking on a big joint.

She took his arm. He was smiling in anticipation of his meal. He was a huge curry fan, having decided years ago that it was one of life's underrated secret delights. He had tried them all around the world and was looking forward to introducing this slip of a lass, who had been deprived of them for so long, to the addictive pleasure they had to offer. Culinary heaven beckoned and he lengthened his stride, making Collette skip and jump to keep up, hanging on furiously to his arm. "Christ, mate...slow up... It's like you're heading off to the last supper to meet Jesus and his gang before they scoff up all the grub."

"Never had a curry, indeed," he snorted, "Well, my mission today is to put that right, lass."

She smiled nervously, "'Ope it don't burn the gob off me, mate, and for Gawd's sake slow down."

"You'll love them, young missy. They are highly addictive," adjusting his pace for her.

"So's bloodin' chocolate but you don't have to put a bog roll in the fridge before yah eat a Mars bar."

He guffawed at that, liking her witticism, Clive was waiting in the car park for them, smoking a suspiciously long roll-up that smelt pungent and herby. "Bet yah didn't get a fag coup[26] wiv dat one, Clive?" Collette remarked. "Gis a drag on that, Reggie man?"

Clive gave her a peace sign with two fingers. "Peace and love, sister. If it's good enough for Bob Marley, it's good enough for me. Free Ethiopia for God's children, brothers and sisters."

* * *

---

[26] 'Fag coupons' – In the '70s you got a coupon in the brand you smoked, which you saved up for goods.

They drove to Abbots Langley, a few miles out of town, where Clive knew of a good all-day Indian. They were shown to a table for two and seated. Collette liked the spicy smell in the room and marvelled at the sitar music, which sounded strange and exotic to her untrained ear. "Certainly ain't the Beatles. Never heard Paki music before," she remarked, her mouth already watering.

"It's Indian, actually," he informed her, "In some parts of India when they dance, the men dress up as women, make-up and all, and the women as men."

That stunned her for a moment, then, "So how do they bloody well know who wears the trousers in the house, then?"

The waiter gave them menus and Jamesey ordered two large bottles of Cobra beer for them. "It's Indian beer, especially brewed to accompany curry."

"Cor blimey, this is gonna be a real experience, ain't it? Tanx ever so much for bringing me with yah, Jamesey."

"No problem...pleasure's all mine. I like a bit of company, especially attractive company, when I go for a meal." She squirmed subconsciously in her seat, pleased she was his centre of attention and revelling in it.

She blushed at the compliment. Had she heard right? He thought she was attractive; things were definitely looking up. She wondered if she told him how handsome she thought he was, whether he would scoff and tell her to get her eyes tested. It was the way he was, she intuitively knew, realising she was getting to know him better and secretly thrilled. He exuded such a powerful charisma, and she believed he was totally unaware of what a huge magnetic personality he had. She watched him carefully. In her eyes, he was the 'cream of the crop' and owned to top bulldog's gonads.

He was watching her eyeing the menu with a bemused look. It was all mumbo jumbo to her. How the frig did the Paki wallahs think this was the Queen's lingo? It was all double Dutch to her.

"Do you want me to pick what I think you'll like and do the ordering? Are you very hungry?"

A look of relief washed across her concerned face. "Yes please, Jamesey. I could eat a scabby donkey 'tween two mattresses." She paused, blushing at her manners, "Sorry, well yes, I am a tad peckish, so I am."

He chuckled and summoned the waiter. They had vegetable samosa, onion bhajis and roshni kumbi for starters.

He told her what was in each dish. She loved the samosa, little deep-fried pancakes folded over, said the bhajis tasted of cinnamon and the deep-fried garlic mushrooms, "Outta this friggin' world, mate." Collette was in a whole new world of culinary discovery and loving every bite, taste and swallow. *Funny ol' world*, she mused, *How one day could be so wonderfully different from another.*

He mused over the main menu before deciding on a fiery king prawn vindaloo for himself and tandoori lamb morposond for Collette, garlic naan bread, poppadoms and a selection of side dips to accompany the course.

As they waited, he told her there was actually no such food as curry, "No, they reckon Curry was a supply officer in the British Army in India in the eighteenth century. He noticed the locals adding chillies to their meat to preserve it and did the same with the army rations to make them last longer, stop it going off in the heat. The soldiers developed a taste for it, liking the hot flavour."

He raised his hands and looked knowledgeably at her, "So there you go, a local food now cherished and adored worldwide," wondering himself just how true the veracity of his statement was, amused himself.

But she seemed to take it all in with interest, so what the heck, no harm done.

It amazed him how gullible people were. He met many a chancer in the army, who would lie about the colour of their own shite to get out of some unwanted duty or tell tall stories until grass grew out their arse, but their listeners took it all in, hook, line and sinker.

It was a dangerous trait. Look at Hitler with his lies about the Jews that the German people took onboard, resulting in attempted genocide of a whole race, and Lenin and Stalin ranting about Communism and equality for all. *Yeah right*, he scoffed mentally and resolved when he started OLC, he would never act on face value alone until he had sussed out the full facts. People lied for hundreds of different reasons. Look at politicians, he scoffed again. The cockneys called the Houses of Parliament the 'Houses of Porky Pies', Lies.

Collette had been watching the look of concentration on his face and was intrigued, "Ground control to Major Tom. You coming back to earth, luv? Wot yah thinking abaht then?"

So he gave her the exact discourse of his thoughts, and she listened, rapt, thrilled he was sharing his thoughts. Cor blimey, you were never stuck for conversation with Jamesey.

He ended his recounting and tore back into his food like a starving wolf.

"Yeah well, everyone tells off Porkies now and then for whatever reason known only to them, but I reckon you should be Prime Minister, you've got what Ron calls moral fibre, mate."

He swallowed and chuckled, "Naw, no politics for me. I'm gonna go my own way instead of getting tarnished by hobnobbing with that corrupt bunch of tossers."

She liked that word – tarnished – and stored it away in her mind for future use. He was certainly educating her, and he didn't even know it.

"That guy Curry was a diamond geezer. Let's drink to him," and they clinked glasses and toasted the legendary officer Curry.

"The officers used to stand watch over their men and make sure they ate all their ration of chilli meat up. It made them perspire, so they drank lots of water and thus, they didn't get dehydrated under the hot Indian sun."

"Christ, they must 'ave had cast iron stomachs in them days. Gives a whole new meaning to that Johnny Cash song."

He eyed her. "Okay, I'll bite. What Johnny Cash song?"

Her eyes sparkled with mischief. "You know the one… I've got me a burning ring of fire."

He exploded into laughter. She was a sketch and a half. Other diners looked over at the good-looking couple and smiled, their bonhomie infectious.

"Probably stopped the soldiers chasin' the dark girls about, the ones wiv the jewels stuck to their foreheads."

"How yah work that one out then, Collette?"

"Well, if yer gonna be running to the bog all night wiv yer ring on fire, yer ain't gonna be in the mood for any 'hows yer father'[27], are yer, mate?"

---

[27] Very old Cockney for sex

He was off again. Where the heck did she come up with them? She was a wee jewel herself.

He gulped some beer down, half spluttering and signalled for two more. He had to tell Smudger about Collette. He would adore her.

A beaming waiter brought the aromatic food over with a flourish. He had overheard some of their conversation, "Your STEW, sir. It what curry mean in Hindu, sahib."

Jamesey guffawed. "Stew, Captain Curry, as long as it's hot and does the job, my friend."

Collette at her food nervously, then found a steely resolve, "Well, in for a bleeding penny, in for a pound," and got stuck in bravely.

She liked her dish very much, the glow of the chillies numbing her mouth but the exotic taste seeping through. "Like being at the dentist," she mumbled between mouthfuls, watching Jamesey munching happily away, lost in his own little heaven. There weren't any good Indians in South Armagh. Just bandits.

Her meal of spiced lamb cooked in a clay oven with chilli, cumin, coriander and yogurt was delicious. "Not too hot for you?" he asked her solicitously as he tore her a chunk of garlic naan off.

"It's fantastic. Bit 'ot but I'll manage."

He let her try his curry. She pierced a prawn with her fork. "I don't normally eat anything with more than four legs, but I'll try it today," she popped it in her mouth and chewed.

She nearly choked on the red-hot morsel and spluttering gulped down some beer. He grinned. Her gestures and mannerisms were highly entertaining.

"'Ow the Christ on a crutch can yer eat that, Jamesey? I'd need a fire hose by the table and asbestos knickers."

"You have to work up to it, Collette. Takes years of practice, and don't blaspheme. Keep your options open." He drifted off again, "Life is a game of swings and roundabouts, when you're on the swing, you go up high, then down low; on the roundabout, you're going around in a continuous circle, and you can't get off until it stops. Well, I'm going to make my own rides and go my own path," he filled his fork and gulped more curry, "And hot curry, or Indian stew", and he laughed, "will always be high on my swings."

She waved her hand theatrically in front of her open mouth. "Sorry, Jamesey, thought me ticker was gonna stop tocking there for a while. Me bloody tonsils are melting."

He reached over and wiped a smear of curry off her chin. Composed now, she smiled. She liked the kindness of him. She wasn't used to being looked after or the centre of attention, unless it was some drunk looking into her knickers and then she sidled away off to a safe distance. Like she used to do with that sod of a dad of hers, she thought sadly.

"Penny for them?" he asked intuitively.

"Was just wondering what all those dips were?" she hedged.

He knew she wasn't and was thinking of darker things. He was getting to know her too but he indulged her.

He pointed out the apricot sauce, the mint yogurt and various others and explained if the meal was too hot, you put some on the side of your plate to make it cooler.

"Cor, bleedin' clever, the Indians."

"Except these, chilli onions," and he spooned some onto his curry, "makes it hotter."

She marvelled, "Yer really, really must 'ave a cast iron gob, Jamesey."

They finished their meal, mopping up the last of the juices with the remains of the bread.

"That was absolutely bloody brilliant. Tanx so, so much, Jamesey," she told him truthfully.

"My absolute pleasure, Collette. Your convivial company."

She didn't know what that meant but took it as a compliment. "Wish I could use long words and know what they meant. You must think I'm a real dunderhead?"

He squeezed her hand, "One, I don't think that, and two, it's never too late to learn."

She belched demurely behind a small hand and giggled, "Pardon moi, si vous plait… Manners maketh the woman."

"See, you speak French, there's hope yet."

"Heard that on Bergerac[28], didn't I?"

"Besides, in some countries it's considered bad manners not to have a good old burp after a meal," he informed her, chewing on a toothpick. "It shows you appreciated the food."

"Like where?" she wanted to know, interested.

Her mouth had a lovely pleasant glow after her meal. Her first foray into the intricacies of Indian cuisine.

"Well, some Arab countries. The Sahara Bedouin Arabs would take it as a great insult if you didn't burp and might cut your tongue out."

She gawked at him, "No way, mate."

"Yep, every way. The Japanese like a good burping, as do the cannibals on Java."

She was goggle eyed, "Cannibals, bloody 'ell."

"Yep, and high in the Andes mountains in Peru, you're expected to burp and then sleep with the host's wife."

"No friggin' way," she gasped, shocked. "That is way beyond gross. No bugger's sleepin' with me after hamster and chips." She looked whimsical. "I would love to see a foreign country. See how the people live and speak and what they ate." She sighed, "Don't suppose I ever will, though."

She looked very sad fleetingly. He moved his chair around a bit closer to hers. She forced a grin. "Doncha listen tah me, Jamesey. I can be a right moody bitch at times."

He took her hand. "Where would you like to go if you ever got the chance?"

"Hollywood, Jamesey, Hollywood," animated now. "I wanna see the studios, walk on Marilyn Monroe's footsteps, drink cocktails on Sunset Strip. The whole caboodle."

He squeezed her hand, revelling in her enthusiasm. "Tell yer what, lass, if I ever make it rich, I'll take you. My treat."

A sense of déjà vu hit her but she hastily cast it away. Insecurity gripped her. She couldn't let herself hope something so wonderful or exotic could happen to her.

---

[28] Detective series in '70s, set in Jersey.

She looked up at his handsome face and deep into his clear blue eyes. Searching for his soul. Looking for his inner being, for the very core of him, for that elusive thing that made this great man what he was and wanting some of it herself. God, how she wanted it!

"You know, Jamesey," she said slowly, "If ever a man's going to make it to the top, I'll put my last shilling on you any day."

At that moment in time Collette just had no inkling of how prolific her words would be. Jamesey patted her hand and sat up straight. He had admired her appetite, not knowing she lived off the spare rolls in the bar that weren't sold at lunchtime and hamburgers from the chippy. Eadie made sure she got a decent sit-down roast dinner every Sunday in between opening times. Collette helped Eadie cook it, learning from the older woman, which was more than her bitch of a mum ever did for her, but during the week ,she refused to sit down to meals with them, trying to be as independent as she could and affording Ron and Eadie some much needed privacy.

Jamesey watched her intently. He could see the inner turmoil and regret that sometimes crossed her face. She was a fascinating blend of hard on the outside and soft in the middle.

"You from Watford originally, Collette? Where's your family then?"

She visibly flinched. The waiter placed a tall sundae glass of iced lemon sherbet before her. She took a couple of mouthfuls with the long-handled spoon before sighing and putting it down and looking him in the face. "You really, really don't wanna know about me, Jamesey." She said through ice-cold red lips. "You really don't."

He put both hands on hers, his turn to look into her face. "Oh but I do, Collette Stark. I really, really do."

"It ain't good, mate. Not good at all."

"Then prepare to shock the unshockable."

She looked deep into his honest, charismatic eyes. She didn't want to lose him now, not after only finding him. Make or break? Was honesty the proper policy here? She decided to take the bit between the teeth and tell the truth. She began talking quietly, looking him full in the eyes. "I was prostituted as a child." He never flinched, never moved a muscle or blinked. It seemed as if the room was deadly still and they were two actors on a stage. He just squeezed her hands. "Me muvver was a whore."

A tear like a newly born pearl welled and trickled down her soft cheek. He brushed it gently away with a big thumb, his demeanour one of tenderness and concern.

"I think you need to get it all out, Collette. Before it does more irreversible damage to you, lass. Damage no one can repair, and I'm right here for you. Everyone has their cross to bear."

She looked at this handsome, brilliant, gorgeous fucking fantastic man before her and such an aura of utter trust radiated off him that she knew he was right, and it was time she began talking again as an inner glow started slowly building and building inside her and the more she talked, the more the glow took shape like a giant bubble for good. A bubble that finally needed to be burst and let fly.

* * *

80

Collette Janet Stack was born on the 11th of April, 1956, the first child of Trevor and Beatrice Stark, in a rundown semi-detached council house in Garston, a suburb of North Watford. Her father was a hospital porter in Watford's busy Shrodell's Hospital. She never saw much of her daddy in her early formative years. Like many working-class men in that era, he went straight to his local pub after work, stayed until closing time, then staggered home blind-drunk to crawl into bed, ready to do the same routine the next day.

Money was tight and regular meals and adequate heat were in short supply. To supplement the meagre income, her mother took a job at 'The Queen Boudicca' pub, just outside Garston. Boudicca had been the warrior queen who rebelled and led the ancient Britons in revolt against the Romans in the second century AD and sacked and razed Lundinium (London) to the ground.

Beatrice was no warrior queen. She was a common prostitute. Queen Boudicca had two daughters who were defiled by Roman soldiers, which led to the revolt, but there the similarity between the two women ended. Because unlike the queen, Beatrice never cared one way or the other whether her daughter was defiled or not. In fact, the child's welfare and general well-being was of little interest to Mrs Stark at all. Her so-called mother basically didn't give a monkey's toss about the fruits from her womb. Any maternal instincts were only a nuisance, and she didn't feel an iota for the squalling brat who always wanted feeding and made such a fuss.

It was a case of do the minimum to keep the brat alive as long as I am okay Jack and fuck the rest of the world.

Beatrice would take regulars around the back of the pub and 'do it' for a few bob and a drink. She took to leaving a growing Collette alone for long periods in the house, often resorting to tying her to her cot.

Her father was of no use. He would just come home drunk and fall into bed to sleep it off. Concerned neighbours did what they could for the tragic little mite, often taking her under their roofs and feeding her and bathing and changing her spoiled clothes, but what she really needed was a mother's love and attention.

A number of times she went into the temporary care of the council but was always returned when Beatrice managed to get her act together for a few weeks. "Fir me first few years, I didn't bleedin' know who me mum was or where I lived. I was like little orphan Annie," she told Jamesey wryly, trying to make light of it, but he saw deep in her eyes the young, haunted, traumatised child she had been. He patted her hand soothingly, the picture of concern, but inside he felt only a terrible sadness for her and a seething anger at her parents, who in his book should have been drowned in a bucket of water at birth.

The waiter brought them coffee, brandies and After Eight Mints, and offered them coloured aromatic cigarettes from a wooden cedar box. Collette had never been treated so well in her life. She was agog! The Pakis, Indians, or what you called them, had gone up mega style in her esteem and she vowed never to look upon the as second-class citizens again, "'Ere, Jamesey, why is there no beef on the menu?"

He wiped his mouth with linen, "The cow is sacred. They think they are reincarnated gods."

She gawked, having no retort to that.

"Cor blimey guvnor, if this is how the other half live, I'm goin' on the transfer list." It saddened him that a simple meal in a nice restaurant meant such a big deal to her.

She continued her account. When she was seven, her mother fell pregnant, "Dunno how me mum and dad found the time. They were like ships in the night, passing and both alkies. Anyhow, they probably weren't his anyway, she had more bleedin' men than Dyno-Rod cleaned drains." She was very bitter, the strain of those early traumatic times plain to see on her face.

For the next four years she practically raised the twins, Michael and Frankie, on her own, badgering her parents for money for milk and food for them, often stealing it off them when they were drunk and getting a belting for it when caught.

Her father's drinking got worse and he got violent, slapping Collette around and sometimes using his belt on her.

"Had you no immediate family, Collette? Aunts and uncles, grandparents?"

She explained her mother, an only child, had lost her parents in 'The Blitz' when Goring's Luftwaffe had razed large parts of London to the ground. Her father's family wanted nothing to do with him, sick of his drinking and violence. "Now, the stray dogs in the street got more loving than me and the bruvvers."

Collette missed out on a lot of schooling, and when she went to the local secondary at eleven, she could barely read or write. She looked down, upset, crossing her face and her eyes moist, "I came home one afternoon and Mike and Frankie were gone. Clothes and toys away. Me sow of a muvver was laying on the sofa pissed. When I asked her where me bruvvers were, she laughed and said she'd handed them over to the social, 'cause the little sods were getting too bleedin' cheeky."

She was crying now, and Jamesey moved to sit beside her and put his arm around her and offered her his hanky. She blew her nose and wiped her eyes. "Sorry, Jamesey, you must think I'm a right moody cow."

"Frig no, I think you're a bloody hero," he said to her surprise. "It's good to get things off your chest. You must have been bottling it up for a long time."

"I loved me bruvvers to bits and I've never seen them since. The cunts in social say they are not allowed to say where they are."

He got two big brandies for them and lit her a fag as she continued, her fingers digging into his strong forearm.

The next year or two were bad. Her father started to come to her room at night and would touch her up. Her mother belted her across the face when she told her. She took to locking her door and barricading herself in at night.

One night her father came home with a couple of mates, and they beat her door down and tried to rape her. They paid her father money. He had prostituted her. She let them strip her, played with their half erections and kissed their foul drunken mouths, pretending to go along with it. Her father was pleased, reckoning he was onto a nice little earner. She begged to go to the toilet and promised to come back. She fled naked to a neighbour's and spent the next three years in a children's home.

"Nobody wanted me. I was too old. People wanted younger kids to foster. Can't say I blamed them, who the fuck would want a muppet like me?"

"What about your parents? Do you ever see them?"

"Nah, me dad's dead, I laughed when I heard he got stabbed. He was seeing some bloke's wife and he knifed him, now that guy's doing big bird.[29] There's an uvver family torn apart, thanks to good ol' Trevor."

---

[29] Long prison sentence.

He wiped her tears and squeezed her hand, "Me mum's still about. Still boozing away, so I hear. I see her walking about town now and then, but I don't go near her. She don't give a monkey's toss."

"So there yer go. The sad life of Collette Stark. Left school at fifteen, barely able to read and write. Hit the drugs scene, dossed around from floor to floor. Always on the scrounge and probably going to end up on skid row."

She flicked her fingers as if something had just come to her. "Shit no... Am already on skid row... Thanks very much, Mum and Dad."

He looked at the pretty young woman, tenderness and concern foremost in his mind for her. He talked to her for an hour. He told her she was young, attractive and intelligent. How she was only twenty and it was never too late to better herself. He drew her out and she told him about the drugs scene and how Eadie had befriended her when she met the lost young woman in The Peel. She took her on and Ron had found the room she was in now and paid the rent out of her pay.

Jamesey showed her the other side. How lucky she'd been to escape from her terrible past without anything worse happening. How when her brothers became adults, she would have access to them again. He talked about drink and drugs and advised her what qualifications to get so she could get better employment. And of some of the terrible things he had seen on his tours around the world. The starving children in Africa, the child prostitutes in Malaya, the terrible conditions of the slums in Belfast and the sad plight of the Greek refugees in the camps on Cyprus after the Turks invaded.

He bolstered her confidence. Complimented her and bummed and blew her up to a level where she started to feel good about herself. He threw a wad of notes down on the table for the impatient waiter. "Sod it, Collette...when you've been as low as that, there is only one way to go and that's up. Don't let the miserable fuckers get you down. You get your act together and spit in their eye on your way up past them."

They left in search of a taxi, she was surprised to see it was fully dark. They had talked for hours.

He let her hold his hand. It felt warm and safe in his. "What did yer reckon on the Ruby Murray then?"

"It was awesome, Jamesey, thank you... I feel like a new world's been opened up to me." She looked up at his strong profile, meaning the words in more than one sense, realising at that moment she was in love with him and wondering at the wonder of it and what the frig to do about it.

* * *

Back in The Peel Jamesey settled in for the night. Ronnie got his pint. "Young Collette seems happy, mate, whatcha do to her? She can be a right moody cow."

"It's the endorphins in the curry, Ron. They make yer happy. Bloody addictive."

Ron laughed, "Endorphins, my arse. That randy wee bitch 'as the hots for yer mate."

"Leave it out, Ron, she's just a child."

Ron leered knowingly. "She's a female, mate. Remember our chat? Different species. Different planet."

"Once it's covered in thatch, mate, it's ready for visitor."

Jamesey shrugged, "What will be, will be, pal, now get your finger out your arse and get me a pint of Double D and a snort for yourself, you miserable sod."

The bar was quiet that night. Jamesey played a bit of pool with a few of the regulars he had got to know, then sat chatting to Ron and Eadie.

Collette shuffled about collecting and washing glasses, covertly watching him and glowing inside.

'Slimy Barry' watched, keeping quiet. He would bide his time and spoil their happiness when the opportunity arose. He had his own plans for Collette. She was vulnerable and when soldier boy left to hopefully get blown up somewhere abroad, he would strike and have the vulnerable girl under his wing.

He was a fantasist, his perverted mind addled by years of alcohol, and he dreamt about Collette every night.

He noticed she kept her distance but that would change once the squaddie bastard was gone.

"'ere, Jamesey," said Eadie, "They been eating curry in London town since 1715 for frig's sake, I saw a recipe some toff wrote in an old book."

"Yeah, so Captain Curry is a load of bollocks, mate. He never existed," chirped Ronnie.

Jamesey took a long swig, "Well, army legend says he made his guys eat curry but hey, if it opened her mind and she enjoyed the story, more power to him, I say."

They both agreed and called last orders.

* * *

He dropped her home again, and declined her offer of coffee.

Clive the taxi thought he was a strange one indeed.

* * *

Collette tossed and turned. She couldn't get Jamesey out of her head. Cursing, she threw the bed covers off and got dressed.

Fuck it, if the big man wouldn't come to her bed, she would go to his.

She got her coat on, added the hat, scarf and mitts he had got and looked in the mirror, still half pissed from earlier, "Well, as Mary bleeding Poppins would say…practically perfect in every way," and left determinedly.

Half a mile up the road by the football ground, she passed three drunken yobs. Young guys in jeans and Doc Martens. Late teens, early twenties.

They bounced after her, laughing and jeering. "'Ere, darling, nice arse."

"Fancy a quickie? Give you a fag."

They surrounded her, one stopping in front and grabbed her by the shoulders, "'Ere, luv, gis a blowjob… I ain't had one for ages."

She looked into his tepid, alcohol-ridden eyes, "I reckon, mate, the first one you ever get will be your last." And slapped him full force across the face.

He staggered back and his mates laughed derisively. "You wanker, a girl," they jeered.

He faced her and raised his fist to her, "Let's get the slag and bang her."

Suddenly, a big Ford Granada painted in red, yellow and black stripes of the Ethiopian flag pulled up, and Clive the taxi bounced out, dreadlocks swinging and the half-smoked joint in his mouth sparking.

Collette breathed out, very relieved to see him.

"What's going on here, brothers? That's my sister of the skin."

Two faced him, the other sensible one standing back.

"Fuck off you black bastard and mind your own," snarled the one who had stopped her.

Clive wasn't a small man. He had faced racism ever since he had arrived in London ten years ago.

He eyed the thug, approached and gave him the 'Rastafarian Kiss', a head butt straight to his nose, which sent him straight down, squealing, blood spewing out in fountains.

His mate went for him and Clive raised his right knee level to his midriff and kicked him in the groin, "And that's the Bob Marley 'Ballistic Throat Equaliser', you honkey tonk wank."

The third youth just gawked at his two sprawled comrades, "Nothing to do with me, I'm only here for the beer, I'm a student."

Clive laughed, "Get the children home. Collette get in the car NOW, before the rozzers[30] come."

* * *

He drove her back to her lodgings, rolled another joint, "Okay, little adopted sister of Ethiopia... What the diddly squat was that about?"

She told him about the curry meal and how much Jamesey had helped and been so good to her and that she just wanted to be with him.

Clive rolled the joint for her and sighed.

"Collette, Collette, little bird. You going about it all way wrong. A mon like the Jamesey geezer, they carve their way through life, they ain't da nine to fivers, happy to sit da drift out, babe. He sees...he goes...he gets or dies in the doing. He's a one-man hurricane looking for a shore to devastate, then land on and seize all he sees for himself, babe, and his own."

Collette took a big drag, reflective, the Moroccan Gold calming her. She wouldn't admit it but she had been very afraid before Clive pulled up.

"Know what he is, Clive... He's a bleeding modern day Viking. Firm and fair but looking to build and rule his own empire."

Clive sucked deep, "Yah sister, he is that. And he will, yah know. He is the man. Him and the prophet Marley are two of a kind."

Collette ruminated, "So what dah frig do I do, Clive? Is there room for me in his wake?"

Clive grinned, "Jamesey's a big fish, oh big, big little sister, you gotta hook him craftily, nice and easy, go with the flow and reel him easy, because..." and he snapped his fingers, making her jump, "if the line snaps, you'll never see the dude again."

---

[30] Police officers

85

She climbed out, "Sorry for all the grief, Clive. You're right…" She kissed him on his cheek, "Bloody brill what yah done tonight, Holmes. You're a hero in your own taxi."

He guffawed, "Get in with you, sister. I gotta get some shut eye before I earn more bananas tomorrow."

She lent in the window, "Yah wanna come up for a coffee, mate? I got Bob's latest tape. It's brill."

He eyed her and laughing started the engine, "Yeah, right, and if Big Jamesey hears I was in da room with his bitch at dis time in da morning, he'll rip my dreadlocks off and make me eat them," and he drove off.

Collette watched him go, grateful. Thank fuck above he had come along. Whatever was going to happen in this new journey she was on, she would make sure Clive the taxi would benefit.

She looked up at the full clear moon above. *Oh, what stories and tales of things you have seen, but you won't, you benign God. Let us make our own paths and roads, and they will lead us to whatever will be, will be, will be*, she thought, her mind everywhere in the cannabis trip, not knowing where the fuck in the depths of her mind that had come from but sensing big Jamesey's influence there.

Well stoned, she went back to bed, the presence of a huge, blond-haired warrior standing guard over her.

She slept well with that concept soothing her frayed nerves.

Chapter 8
Wined, Dined and Ketamined
('Lucy in the Sky with Diamonds'...The Beatles)

Early Fall 2012 to 23rd of December, 2012

December 23rd, 2012

'Handsome Harry Herbert Hanlon' was anything but. His associates had nicknamed him 'Handsome Hanlon' but they were careful never to say the derogatory title to his face. At forty-two years old, he stood just over six foot high and was well filled out. Despite a large beer gut gained by his own overindulgence in substantial quantities of Guinness stout and steak dinners with fries daily, he was strong-looking and beefily menacing. But it was his face that let him down. Bald, except for a fringe of lank ginger hair, he had a wide, sloping forehead and a long face that tilted down and tapered into a weak double chin. His mouth was extra large and filled with enormous yellow teeth like gravestones. Coupled with a slight overbite, it was unattractive in itself. 'Equestrian featured' someone had once unkindly described him as they hurried to get out of his company.

But it was his eyes that gave his true character away. Massive and close-set and slightly protuberant, with big hooded eyelids, they were the colour of very pale amber. Cold and callous, people who first met him shivered to the core when he turned his gaze on them. They were soulless. His dead father described them as the shade of a sick cat's piss. Even his own mother found it hard to look into them for any amount of time.

They say not to judge a book by its cover and it takes all sorts to make a world, but the sad fact of the matter was that Harry was bad. Rotten through and through. One sad, sick, sadistic guy and unfortunately, he had set his sights on Luca Valendenski. She had rejected him and by jeepers would she pay. She would pay hard! She would rue the day she turned him away. Then again, he might just snuff the bitch out and be done with it. His regard for human life, particularly the female species, was as high on his agenda as swatting a stinging mosquito on his foul neck. He was going to give her a taste of hell, and it was going to be very painful, if not deadly.

The Hanlons immigrated to New York when Harry was ten. His father, Harold senior, had owned a chip shop on Belfast's ultra-loyalist Shankhill Road. Heavily mixed up with the vicious protestant paramilitaries, Harry senior had his finger in many pies. Drugs, racketeering, counterfeiting, extortion and illegal gambling. He was into it all. He taught his son from an early age the twin arts of crime and how to cook fast food. He reckoned if you couldn't survive on one, you could survive on the other.

When a huge drug deal went wrong and a vast amount of cash went missing, his violent paramilitary Godfathers looked at him suspiciously, and he decided it was time to flee. He had seen what they done to innocent Catholics they picked up off the streets in the corrupt, nasty little sectarian war that was going on at the time and Harry Snr determined he liked being attached to his manhood and kneecaps. So he gathered up the stolen money and his family and fled to America.

Settling in New York, he opened a small steakhouse in Queens and put a special on at night: 'As much as you can eat in an hour for five bucks'. It was a roaring success and ten years later, he had six houses across New York and taught his son everything he knew. It never ceased to amaze Harry senior how much certain New Yorkers could eat in an hour. New Yorkers were either mega gluttons, Mister Blobbies or anorexic twig insects, he decided in his tight-minded bigoted loyalist mind as he threw a free mega salad onto his plate as well.

Raised in a two-up, two-down, single-course red brick slum in Crimea Street off Belfast's ultra-loyalist Shankill Road in the sixties, Harry Snr had been brought up on a diet of boiled spuds and cabbage, with a bit of bacon through it on a Sunday if he was lucky. So it was no wonder with his new property he ate like a sumo wrestler and drank like Richard Burton. The times of poverty were gone, American prosperity was in force and bugger the cholesterol level.

Harry Jnr grew up a surly, argumentative young man. He had a natural animal cunning and a foul mouth. Unappealing to females and unable to sustain any type of friendship with man or woman, he frequented prostitutes and lowlifes and paid for his company. His father was making a good living, and he got a salary helping run the restaurants, which kept him flush[31] with money.

He was always in trouble as a young man for minor crimes of violence and sexual harassment of the staff, and Harry senior was forever bailing him out and paying witnesses off. As Junior got older and wiser, he became cuter and picked his targets and his associates more carefully, young thugs he could get to watch his back and go alibi for him if and when required, for a price of course. Not surprisingly, this was a common occurrence.

The police in Queens suspected him of a string of rapes and even of making a snuff movie involving a young Albanian illegal immigrant but they had no grounds for arrest and frustratingly waited for him to slip up and leave DNA. People were afraid of him, and he revelled in the feeling of power it gave him. His victims were afraid to give evidence against him, still bearing the bruises, the other lowlifes he just paid off. The dollar was God in New York.

Handsome Harry Hanlon was a dangerous psychopath, and he was used to getting what he wanted and he wanted Luca Valendenski. Wanted her so bad it hurt.

When Harry turned thirty, his father dropped dead during 'Happy Hour' in their steakhouse in Queens from a massive coronary. Fast food may have made his fortune for him, but it also killed him at the young age of forty-eight. *Ah well, quid pro quo*, thought Harry Jnr, who now owned eight 'Happy Harry's' steak restaurants, each run by an independent manager. The money was just rolling in. He even set up a nice little illegal drug-selling cartel amongst his less salubrious, underpaid staff in his steak houses. It was a nice little earner.

---

[31] Got money on the hip.

His mother, long suffering, not wanting to be there when her son eventually met his sticky end she was sure he was coming to, packed her suitcase, emptied the secret bank account she'd been filling for years with skimmed money and fled back to Belfast, not leaving a forwarding address. Harry shrugged his shoulders, not caring less. Let the old bitch go. He was on his own now and could do what he wanted without being nagged at. Women should be seen and not heard, unless given permission to speak.

Harry liked the prestige of being a successful businessman. He wasn't stupid by any means, and when he saw a large bistro for sale on the edge of Manhattan, he purchased it and decided to go upmarket to attract the stockbroker belt in, the yuppies and Park Lane set. He would open the most exclusive meat restaurant in 'The Big Apple'.

He approached Schuster & Siminion after a contact in the trade told him they had a fine reputation as regards designing interiors for the more trendy, upper-class restaurants. It was a Monday morning; the leaves dropping and twirling in Central Park that Simon called Luca into his office and introduced her to 'Handsome Harry'.

Dressed immaculately as usual in an olive-green short-waisted trouser suit, six inch stilettos and a butter-coloured silk blouse, he was instantly smitten and went onto his best behaviour mode and judged he would launch a charm offensive. Every bitch had a price.

"How do you do, Mr Hanlon? It is getting colder by da day."

"Please call me Harry, Miss Valendenski, if we're going to be working together."

"Den you must call me Luca. Now, vat can we do for you?" she asked the strange-looking man, it not being her nature to think of anybody as ugly. It was a bad mistake. Give Handsome an inch and he would take the whole ruler. He sensed the goodness of her makeup and he got excited at the thought of breaking her into his deviant ways.

He took her down to the premises. It was basically a long room, about seventy feet by forty, with kitchens at the back. It had been a bistro, dark and intimate, flock wallpaper and worsted carpets. They discussed various themes. He was enjoying her attractive company.

"I want it upmarket but historical. Atmospheric, you dig?"

"Vell how much you wanna spend, Harry? I'm tinking like seventeenth century aristocratic Boston meat house. Lots of bricks and wood and fires, da?"

He liked it, "No expense spared, babe. Pull it apart!"

Luca beamed, always thrilled at the start of a new project. Mr Hanlon was always so positive.

"I'll do you some drawings, Harry. I won't let you down."

And she didn't. She put her whole heart into it. They met several times in his steak houses, and she showed him her ideas and drawings, enjoying the free dinner he insisted she ate and having his driver, Arturo, drive her back afterwards. *Softly, softly, catchee monkey*, Handsome decided, determined by her character that she wasn't like the loose women he normally consorted with but high-class and worth the wait.

In no time her contractors had gutted the place out. Luca found a salvage yard in Newark, New Jersey, that supplied her with several thousand red bricks reclaimed from a seventeenth century mansion demolished in Boston. From an old boatyard in

Maine, she discovered a pile of oak planks a hundred years old, still wrapped in ship's canvas. She bought two Queen Anne fireplaces with large mantles from an antique yard in Charleston over the internet. On her day off, she trawled the markets and bric-a-brac shops and acquired mirrors, candlestick holders, hunting and sporting prints and a host of other things. When she saw a lot of a hundred pewter tankards on the internet, she snapped them up. It was looking good.

Handsome called in every Monday to see what she had gathered up over the weekend, and once a week Arturo collected her after work. Luca took her plans with her to one or other of Handsome's steak houses and they had dinner and debated the project. Luca was having fun and thoroughly enjoyed the challenge. Harry was supportive and such a gentleman. Such a shame he had no one close in his life. She bet he would make a great family man.

Simon Siminion noticed Handsome was becoming quite a regular in the office. Often popping in to see Luca with a sudden inspired idea or some trinket he had picked up which he considered might go well with the theme. He stroked his chin thoughtfully one Wednesday afternoon in mid-November when Harry bustled in carrying flowers and chocolates for Luca. He occasionally brought little gifts. It made Simon uneasy.

Most of his female staff were older than Luca and had families or partners, they were also more streetwise. If they were apprehensive with a client, they either refused point-blank to do work for him or took someone along with them to meetings. The beautiful, blonde estate agent Suzy Lamplugh was uppermost in his mind. She had vanished in London, showing the mysterious 'Mr Kipper' a property, never to be seen again.

Simon sat behind his desk and mused. Over the years a few of his girls had been 'touched up' or assaulted. He had normally dealt with it himself but he was in his twilight years and his long term partner was dying of cancer. Maybe he should invest a few hundred bucks on a private investigator and have Hanlon checked out. Invasion of privacy and data protection prevented him from accessing civil records, but a good PI had ways around that, and it may be worth spending a few bucks to keep whom he looked upon as his adopted daughter out of harm's way.

Hanlon came out of Luca's office beaming and saw Simon watching him. There was just something about him that made Simon very, very ill at ease. He tried to find a word for it. *Unsavoury? Unsuitable? Tacky? Yeah, possibly all three, but dangerous?* Then he thought back to his youth and the death camps and chided himself for being a bigot. *Sure, was it not on the back of bigotry that Hitler and his Nazis rose to power and look what that brought about? So Hanlon was an ugly sod and had a strange way about him but hey... Live and let live. Hatred breeds intolerance and divides society.*

Harry stuck his head in the door, "That is one talented girl, Mr Siminion. She's priceless. She reckons she'll be done before Christmas."

"Come in, Mr Hanlon, please. Yes, she was a great find. We are all extremely proud of her."

Hanlon sat. "Quite an experience this whole project. It's so interesting. It kinda grips yah. Hope I've not been making a nuisance of myself popping in and out all the time?"

Simon observed him closely. He was no fool. Was Hanlon genuine? Putting up smokescreens perchance?

"Not at all, Harry. We pride ourselves in keeping our clients happy and informed at all times," he paused. "Luca's a distant relative of mine. She's like the daughter I never had."

"Yeah, she's great. Listen, here's another cheque. Luca needs to get some big crossbeam in between the bar and the dining room. I'm gonna go pick my fiancée up and take her down to see the work in progress."

After he left, Simon sat reassured. He had a fiancée. Well, well!!! Harry just had a genuine interest. He surely knew Luca would never have any romantic notion in him. He called her in and they had coffee and chatted. She seemed her normal, happy, confident self. No, the venture would be over in a month or so. No need for a private detective. Clients come and clients go. It turned out to be one of the worst decisions of his life.

Hanlon rode down in the elevator gloating. He hated Jews. He sure had put one over on the old kike. Shame Adolf topped himself before he could have gassed every single one of the scum... Hopefully, the Islamic State dudes take a million or two out with a smart bomb.

II

The opening of 'Ye Olde Black Bull Pub and Steak House', licensed to sell the finest wines, beers, ales and intoxicating spirits on the 22nd of December was a resounding success. Luca had done Schuster & Siminion and her client proud. The outside was heavy teak vertical planks painted black and the gable was painted green, with the name emblazoned across in old style writing. The windows were bevelled and comprised of diamond-shaped panes of bottle glass in lead frames. A hand painted sign on a swinging pole showing a large horned black bull hung above the stout wooden door, guarding the entrance.

Luca had converted the first thirty feet into a bar and waiting area. The floor was heavy oak planking and weighty woollen rugs. The walls red brick with small alcoves and ornaments. Old prints of hunting and country scenes adorned the walls with horse brasses and old period bottles and vases. Ancient milk churns and jugs held dried flowers and an antique plough dangled from the ceiling. The bar was heavy timber and well stocked. The furniture was chunky, the seats old beer barrels padded with Spanish leather and the tables made from similar planking to the bar. One of the fireplaces was opposite the bar, packed with logs and imitation flames. Candlesticks with electric lights illuminated the room, merrily. The prospective customer felt immediately welcomed in from the cold, the dark street outside immediately forgotten.

Going through to the dining room, again the floor was oak planks. Luca had designed curved red brick vaulted walls and ceiling. Three booths on both sides and a genuine seventeenth century oak table and chairs that seated twelve down the middle. The fireplace was at the end, again with the electric-effect fire.

A pair of hunting muskets hung crossed over the mantle. Two crystal chandeliers hung from the ceiling, emitting dim orange lighting. Various artefacts lined a variety of nooks and crannies, a collection of clay pipes, leather saddles and bridles, buckles and riding crops and decrepit swords and bayonets added to the old-world atmosphere.

Above the door was a huge mounted bull's head, with horns nearly three-foot long. She had got it from a Spanish bullfighting website. Harry loved it. At the touch of a button, smoke came out of its nostrils and it snorted loudly. He called it 'El Diablo Toro', the devil bull. She had also cleverly put long mirrors at the end of each kiosk, and with soft candlelight, the use of crystal tableware and full silver service, the effect was stunning.

Harry had spared no expense on the menu either. Best Aberdeen Angus and Porterhouse steak from the UK, veined, two inches thick Kansas marbled steak, foot wide Texan rib eye, Irish spring lamb, Welsh lamb rack and cutlets, the venison was from Canada. Finest Polish gammon from Silesia and a huge selection of sausages from Germany and salamis from Italy. For the adventurous, there was horse meat from France, water buffalo from Thailand and just to please and impress Luca, wild boar from Russia. He even got reindeer steaks in for the festive season and the staff wore Rudolf red noses.

Harry bragged to his patrons, "If we ain't got it, give us a week and we'll get it for yah."

Of course, the prices were astronomical but that was the name of the game. He also hadn't stinted on advertising and opening night involved several famous food critics. Some minor VIPs, people from the Tourist Board, the Chief of Police and his wife, a famous TV anchor woman and a guy big in a famous soap re-run on television. To top it off, a small three-piece cello, violin and lute in one corner. The staff were dressed in period costume. Two Cordon Bleu chefs had been hired and tested by Harry for par excellence and several crates of Dom Pérignon were doing the rounds and loosening tongues in the bar.

"Vow, Harry! You have certainly splashed out… I am sooo impressed."

He looked at her. She was outstanding in an off-the-shoulder black cocktail dress, pearl choker and hair in a French plait adorned with a white ribbon. Her eyes sparkled like smoky quartz crystals in the subdued light, flashing enticingly when the candlelight and mirrors caught them.

"Couldn't have done it without yah, babe."

Luca laughed and kissed him on the cheek. "Dat's so kind, Harry, but it's your night. My job is done. I am pleased da, vith the result."

He signalled a waiter and had her glass refilled with champagne. He could feel on his cheeks where she had kissed him. He could not think of a time when a woman had last kissed him without payment.

Probably his mother when he was a small infant, and he had his doubts about that if he was honest with himself.

The night went, as they say in the upper toff echelons, swimmingly.

The drink flowed, the crystal glasses gleaming in the mirrors. The food was cooked to perfection, Harry watching the food critics anxiously. Luca had wild boar medallions in red berry sauce for starters, then Aberdeen Angus sirloin with asparagus in butter and salad. It was fantastic!

Harry sat at the head of the long table and she to his right. He kept topping her glass up with different wines, looking her approval. She liked that he valued her opinion, not that she was a great wine connoisseur. She thought of her mother and Dmitri in Lithuania and wished they were here with her. They would be so proud. She was getting quite tiddly now, but she reckoned she deserved it. Her easygoing nature made it hard for her to refuse Harry's frequent topping up of her glass.

A lady from 'Architects Review' interviewed her, and Harry showed her photographs of before and after. She was impressed and Luca later got an award for Best Young Innovative Interior Designer in New York, 2012. It was an award that later held bittersweet memories for her.

After the speeches, during which Harry praised his young designer up and down, they sat in the bar and drank yet more champagne. Luca looked at the thinning crowd.

"Vell, Harry…this was outstanding night." She burped discreetly into the back of her hand. "Sorreee…me bit sloshed," and giggled demurely, delighting him.

Harry laughed. He refilled her glass, "And well you deserve to be, kiddo. One for the road and I'll get Arturo to take you home."

She didn't see him slip the powdered ketamine in. She took a hefty swig and burped and giggled again…" Xcusey me again…no, tis 'kay, Harry, my neighbour coming at twelve for me."

He was aghast. He hadn't foreseen this. He wanted her in his car helpless on the ketamine and into his apartment. He had a whole night planned for her, which involved a camcorder, ropes and vibrators. Luca peered at him half unfocused and patted his hand. She wasn't that stupid. She knew he liked her, and she had noticed that no one else from Schuster & Siminion had been invited. She knew also he had no fiancée after Simon mentioned it. She still put it down to just his fragile male ego, not any badness in him that he had lied, but a girl had to be careful. She took another wallop of champagne. Shitski, it was strong.

"Dis my last drink, Harry… I have go liddle girls room. Don't go away." He smiled indulgently, a proprietorial gleam in his way. 'Dirty Harry' wasn't going nowhere.

In the ladies she felt very, very nauseous and light-headed. Her arms and legs tingled unpleasantly. She had felt tipsy and half-drunk thirty minutes ago but now it was like she was paralytic. Every movement and step required great concentration. Time seemed to slow down. Luca managed to turn a tap on and watched the water flowing, mesmerised at the silver torrent. "Is so kool, da, sooo, sooo kool. Like da molten liquid silver, vowski."

A large lady came in. "Hey, you okay, honey? Are you ill? You're as white as a sheet."

Luca gaped at her, bleary-eyed. "I not da great. Help da? Spasibo."

"I think you need a hand. Hold on. Keep holding that sink, child."

Her whole mood had changed. She felt depressed. Paranoid. The tingling in her arms and legs was worse. The walls kept swimming in and out. Suddenly, she couldn't care less. She felt euphoric and free. Two waitresses got her out and into her warm, fake brown fur coat. They got her outside into the still, crisp December night. Harry came out. She could barely move her arms or legs now. Harry's face spiralled in and out of focus. He looked to be grinning, leering with his big choppers. Instead of one horsey face, he had a whole herd.

"Thanks, girls. Arturo's away to get the car. Away back in and attend to the guests. Time is money."

The girls fidgeted and hesitated. The boss-man mightily spooked them out.

"I said away to fuck!" he snapped, "Or you won't be getting paid."

They left reluctantly. He steered Luca to the narrow alley at the side of the building. Got her down a few feet into the dark.

"I love you, Luca. I'm gonna have you tonight. You're gonna love it, what I've planned so long for."

He began kissing her. She wanted to vomit. He leant against the wall and fondled her breasts. Where the fuck was Arturo with the car? He wanted this fresh meat home for his own special recipes from his own sad, perverted cookbook. A car pulled up. About time. He left her propped up. She was paralysed.

"Where the fuck have you been, Arturo?" he shouted stepping out of the alley, waving his hands.

He stopped short when a huge man with a crew cut got out of a Crown Vic.

"What you saying, buddy? You gotta wire loose or something, dude?"

"Sorry, man, thought you were my driver. Can't get the fricking help these days."

Big Bobby De Havilland looked at the grotesque man in the dinner jacket suspiciously, an instant dislike.

"Whatcha doin' up that alley anyhow? They no restrooms inside or you perving?"

At that moment Luca slid helplessly down the wall and moaned softly.

"What the frig?" and Bobby strode past him and up the alley to help Luca up. When he got her into the light, he recognised her. "Jesus Christ, Luca! What you doin' down there? Yah tights are all laddered."

He looked around angry but the guy with the face like a horse had gone. Bobby got her into the front of the Crown Vic and buckled her in tight. He had borrowed the car off Mr Chin, the caretaker, and was fifteen minutes early. He was extremely glad he was now.

"Should have brought the van, and I could have strapped her on the roof-rack," he mumbled annoyed at the state of her. "Fresh air would have sobered the minx up."

Tears were now rolling down Luca's face and she was drooling. He wiped her face with his hanky, concerned now. "You 'kay, Luca? Yer gonna be sick?"

She didn't move or answer. Another car pulled up behind. A flash-red BMW. He pulled off and rang Wendy on his mobile and told her the score.

"Never known Luca to get pissed that bad. Get her back here and I'll sort her out."

"'Kay, babe. See ya in twenty."

Wendy would know what to do. She was a friggin' lighthouse in a storm, was his Wendy.

* * *

94

Hanlon observed the big guy drive off. Cursing under his breath, he rushed out to Arturo and slapped him hard around the face as he climbed out of the Beamer, knocking him back in.

"Where the fuck were you, man?"

Arturo clambered out, rubbing his cheek, annoyed. "Some galoot smashed a bottle in front of the car and gave me a flat. I had to change it," he snarled back and showed Harry his dirty hands.

"For fuck's sake. 'Kay get in and grab Liam and get the ketamine and the coke from under the bar and take it to my office. Just in case."

The Chief of Police strolled out, puffing on a big cigar. "Great night, Hanlon. You done us proud." For a senior cop, he hadn't done his background checks and was totally unaware of Hanlon's reputation and nefarious activities.

Hanlon recovered himself. "My pleasure, Chief. Hope you'll be a regular."

"Sure. That Water Buffalo was outstanding," he paused. "Listen, my wife says there was a young woman in the toilet very drunk. Not good for business, you know."

Harry thought furiously as Arturo and Liam came out with several thousand dollars' worth of drugs on their person and walked nonchalantly past the big policeman to the car.

"She's okay, Chief. I just sent her home with a friend. Diabetic and forgot her insulin."

"Great. Good man, Hanlon. Wish all our citizens were as conscientious as you."

Hanlon tried to look suitably pleased at the Chief. Inside, he was raging. He wanted to make Luca a home movie star and all his plans had been thwarted. But he wasn't beat yet. Not by a long way.

He would make that two-timing devious cunt pay, and she would rue the day she slighted Harry Herbert Hanlon. He would give her a good horse-whipping with the crop.

All women were bastards, including the slut of his mother, The Queen of the Ice Cold Heart.

* * *

Hanlon was on a mission and he wasn't to be deflected. Women needed to be put in their place and do what they are told and if they strayed across the road that his rules dictated, they would be punished and suffer, suffer hard! Pack of sneaky, devious bitches looking for equality. No bitch jaywalks on Harry Hanlon's highway.

Only thing they were good for was shagging, breeding and waiting hand and foot on the dominant gender.

Harry gave a crooked, malevolent grin, "There's a new male equality commission in town and he was 'Head Enforcer', so watch your back, you Russian whore... HARRY'S COMING FOR YOU!!!"

Chapter 9
The Demise of 'Slimy' Barry
('A Boy Named Sue'...Johnny Cash)

"You Should Never Start Something You Can't Finish, You Tosser..." Jamesey John DeJames

To promote the British egg industry in the mid-seventies, before the high cholesterol scares and the damage MP Edwina Currie did with her salmonella allegations which nearly wiped the industry out, there was a much played advert on television. It showed a businessman with bowler hat and umbrella riding to work on a giant egg, the purple lion stamp of the Brit egg industry emblazoned on the side. The music, a catchy jingle, extorted everyone to 'Go to work on an egg!' It was an addictive tune and would be heard whistled in the streets by kids hustling to school and all over as workers headed off to the café for the full British fry up. Billboards promoted the message to the masses and it could be seen on the sides of buses conveying the populace to and fro and on the windy platforms of the underground tube stations.

Collette was very happy that cold, February Wednesday morning, her cheeks flushed by the chill. She'd known Jamesey for over a week now and they had gone out every afternoon, then he dropped her home at night, but despite her exhortations, he never came up for tea and biscuits, or anything else for that matter, she thought wistfully. For once it was dry and a wintry sun made an apprehensive appearance, giving a semblance of mock warmth but brightening the grey streets pleasantly and cheering the pedestrians up. Pigeons cooed and played on high ledges.

She reflected back to the afternoon he had taken her for a curry meal. She had enjoyed her time with Jamesey and had surprised herself by opening up to him so much. He was an easy guy to talk to and she liked he didn't give her as much as pity but good sound advice. She liked it when he covered her hand reassuringly with his big mitt as she confided in him about her brief flirtation with the mad drugs scene.

Collette had expected condemnation or at least a good tocking off. Jamesey just shrugged and told her that at least she had the wits to pull herself out of the dirty morass that had sucked many young people in, ruined lives and wrecked youth's potential. She had been vulnerable and prey to older people with no scruples, and he likened them to the shark in Jaws, stalking the weak, making her laugh. Then she was gobsmacked when he divulged about a mad weekend he had in Newcastle before he joined the army and got out of his tree on wacky baccy and purple bombers. His mother had beaten the crap out of him with a birch stick and locked him in the shearing shed overnight.

"She's only five foot two," he said, "and she still scares the crap out of me! But unlike yours, Collette, she was always there for us one hundred per cent. She is the Annie Oakley[32] of the Cheviots."

She liked the sound of his mum and wondered wistfully if she would ever meet her. Probably not, she surmised. Berwick on Tweed was hundreds of miles away, although it sounded beautiful. The furthest Collette had ever ventured was Southend-on-Sea in Essex, the nearest seaside resort, where all the cockneys fled to for the day at the first hint of a heatwave, gorging themselves sick on jellied eels and cockles, heading home at the end of the day tanked up on booze and stippled with sunburn.

She entered the bar, humming the catchy jingle. Four or five of the old hands were in, guzzling down mild and bitter. Men who used the bar as a second home. Lonely people with problems who liked to get a bit of company and chat about all manner of things, and the more they drank, the more they talked. She chuckled to herself. God, she had heard some crap talked over the last while and then, she mused. She had heard sad stories too, often heartbreaking, and some of the old hands had told her their tales and warned and advised her of the darker sides of life. Collette now concluded they were looking out for her, not badgering her, and she also realised she had been moping about like a wet dish rag in a world of self-pity. After unburdening herself to Jamesey, she felt positive again and could see tomorrow ahead and put all those sad yesterdays behind her. Her bubble had well and truly burst for the good.

"Hindsight's a dangerous creature at times. It can make a person bitter," he told her. "Look at you; you're a young, attractive woman. Healthy and intelligent. Get yourself some objectives to better yourself, plan them out and go for them like a hungry tigress. That's what we do in the paras. Advance forward, never retreat. It's our credo and reinforced by the spilt blood of patriots through history."

"So the paras never retreat then, Jamesey? Do they fight to the last man?" she questioned him fearfully and looking at him. The thought of him standing blasting away with his machine gun at overwhelming hoards of turban-clad natives scared her deeply. She didn't want to lose him now.

He had guffawed, "Nope, we do a tactical withdrawal. Lick our wounds, assess the situation and move forward again. And that's what you have to do in life. Move forward, stop, rest and assess and move forward again. Works every time."

Fuck! He was so bloody positive, it oozed off him in droves, and she could feel it rubbing off on her, and indeed, had lain last night after he dropped her home and reckoned she would go for some qualifications. He had rendered to her the value of reading. How it opens the mind, fastens new ideas and gets the imagination tuned in and gives you something to think and talk about aside from daily matters. Right, she thought, she would see about doing English literature and language and ask Jamesey later if he wanted to browse WH Smith's, the bookshop, and maybe recommend some authors for her.

Collette was still humming as she passed Barry, who looked like he had had a rough night, and she noticed there was no one behind the bar. Ron must be down in the cellar, changing the kegs or sneaking a wee dram in the office.

---

[32] Famous cowgirl in 1890s, renowned for her sharpshooting.

"'Ere, Pinky. Why you so bleedin' perky[33]? Somebody go da work on yer fried eggs last night then?" Barry inquired, a malicious gleam in his alky eyes, menace and foulness in his demeanour.

She stopped, hands on hips, and regarded him coldly, her look as frosty as the morning. Normally, she would ignore the prat but she believed now was the time to stand up for herself. She wasn't a piece of dirt for the slob to wipe his boot on every day.

"Wotcha mean by that, Barry? Even if I had, it's none of yer bleedin' business what I do outa hours. So keep yer big conk out!"

Barry sighed contently. At last he had a reaction. He'd break the little bitch now. Snotty little cow. Women should know their place in life, and it was time to teach her that.

"Keep yer bloody pink hair on. Why yah getting yer knickers in a twist or have you left 'em in yer soldier boy's bed?"

The bar went deadly quiet and all attention was directed on the two antagonists. Although rooting for Colette, they wanted to see how she handled herself. Usually, she acted like a second-hand rug and let Barry walk all over her. It was showtime and best of all, it was free.

"You keep him out of this. He's ten times the man you are. Now, drink yer pint and keep yer Khyber[34] shut!"

Barry scowled, "Bleedin' cradle snatcher, that's all that geezer is! You should be spreading them for someone yer own age!"

Collette felt an all-consuming anger and clenched her fists at her sides. "You've a dirty mind. I don't spread 'em for no one."

Barry laughed uproariously. "Bollocks, you soppy tart! Does he not take yer home every night? How's he find the eggs then? Does he use a magnifying glass? Seen bleeding bigger Cadbury mini eggs than what you got, you dopey mare."

She felt the tears welling. "'Ave yer looked at yerself, Barry? You've bigger titties than those page three girls in 'The Sun'. Yer put Sam Fox[35] to shame. Why don't yer feck off up to the bogs in the park and find yerself a toy boy to rent, you nonce?"

That got a clap and a cheer from the old hands. "You tell the waste of space, young un'."

"Yer can't bleedin' speak to me like that, you loose cunt! I'm a regular. Now clear me glass and ashtray and tell Ron I need annuver pint if he values me custom at all. Jump to it you tart, Gawd lumey."

"Clear yer own crap and less of the claptrap. Yer call me a cunt again, I'll get you barred and the next time you touch me arse, I'll fucking clock yer[36]!"

An incredulous look crossed his features. "Bar me! Clock me! Did yer bleedin' 'ear that lads? I've never been so insulted in me whole life."

"Well, yer bloody well have been now, you fat tosser. Why don't you fuck off home for a wank, you loser?"

---

[33] Pinky and Perky – cartoon pigs on television.
[34] 'Shut your Khyber' – Big valley in Pakistan/Afghanistan, cockney for your mouth.
[35] 'Samantha Fox' – First page three topless model in the Sun newspaper.
[36] To hit/thump a person.

"I'd rather have a wank than waste it on a poxy whore like yer," he retorted vulgarly.

Barry had hurt her on Monday night. He had pinched her hard on the left buttock, nearly breaking skin and leaving a purple welt. His touch disgusted her. She had scrutinised it in the toilet and had cried with humiliation. Well, enough was enough! She wasn't taking any more crap off the likes of him. She would stand her corner from now on and get some self-respect back. She was glad Jamesey wasn't in yet. She knew he would batter Barry good and did not wish to spoil his leave.

"I'm gonna make a complaint to Ron about yer, yer smelly prick. I don't 'ave to take yer bigotry against women any longer. It's the seventies for Gawd's sake. Get with the times, yer nasty sod!"

Barry seethed. "Bigotry. Yer couldn't even spell it, you thick twat. Do what cha want. Ron won't bar me... I know all about his lock-ins[37], and he won't want that gettin' out, will 'e?" he snorted viciously.

"We'll see about that dickhead," and she flounced past him, very aware of the nasty, tense situation in the bar and saddened for the old regulars who didn't need this palaver and probably felt uncomfortable, not knowing whether to get involved or not.

As Collette passed Barry, he rose fast and reached out like a striking cobra with his right hand and gripped her left buttock in a hard grinding pinch. He was strong and pain shot through her, ambushed, protesting posterior like white-hot flame. She gasped in anguish and Barry twisted gleefully.

"I'll grab yer skanky arse when and where I want, young missy. So get fuckin' used to it!"

The old hands were shouting at him to leave her be and several rose up hastily to come to her aid. She was in agony and knew he had broken skin. She spun around, breaking his grip, and slapped him full handed with her right palm across his left cheek. The sound reverberated around the bar like a low velocity gunshot. Barry stood his ground and managed to grab her right wrist and dragged her into him, his flabby cheek stinging and starting to redden. How fucking dare she raise her stinking hand to him!

"Yer wicked bitch! I'll teach yer a lesson," and drew back his fist to punch her, radiating violence, his pale alcoholic eyes gleaming in anticipation of the hiding he was going to give the uppity slag.

II

Jamesey DeJames had come early to the bar, and Ron had let him in the side door. They had decided that because Barry always started on Collette when Ron was absent from behind the bar on a chore, they would lay an ambush. They had also agreed to let her handle it herself until or if it got out of hand, not wanting to embarrass her by insinuating she couldn't look after herself. Everybody needed a hand in life at times, but Jamesey believed it was time Collette started to stand up for herself at this time at the start of her adult life if she wanted to move onto better things.

---

[37] To drink after hours

"She's got what I call TUF syndrome, Ron," said Jamesey. "It's a rare phenomenon in a young girl."

"What's that then?" he asked, mystified, as they sat in the office just off the bar, smoking and having a sneaky 'White Horse' whiskey. Ron hoping Eadie wouldn't catch him and start grousing about his blood pressure again. A few whiskies of a morning never hurt no man.

"It's the 'Totally Unknown Factor'. Some girls have it and some don't. It's a female mystery that nobody can describe yet alone put into words, but it's totally alluring and compelling and Collette has it in bucketloads. Oodles and oodles of it."

Ron sipped his drink, pensive. "Yeah, it's that hidden attraction some women 'ave. Eadie oozed it when I courted her. Like the moth to the flame or the rabbit to the lamp, I was bleedin' trapped, waneye. Yer keen on her, then?"

Jamesey grunted. "Well, yeah. Who wouldn't be? But one, she's too young for me, and two, you know this Ron, you done your active service against those EOKA B[38] mob in Cyprus, I'm for Belfast, mate. The friggin' Rah[39] is topping a few hundred a year. I don't want to hurt her or let her become a fatal distraction."

Ron felt for the younger man. He knew Jamesey was not being selfish but acting out of common decency. He remembered the heartbroken widows and orphaned kids at the funerals of his murdered comrades and could see the sense of his argument but still…when it was offered on a plate as Collette seemed to be doing.

"Well, yeah, I guess so. But what's a seven-year difference, mate? Frig all! You should grab a bit of happiness when yer can, Jamesey. It don't come around often and in this crazy day and age, it's often in short supply. Make hay whilst the sun shines, mate, before it pisses down." He slapped Jamesey on the knee, "Mah ol da used to say never look a gift horse in the mouth."

This time Jamesey reflected. "Give us a bit more that Scotch, you tight sod." He drank the fiery brew down. "Yeah, guess yer right. I bow to your experience of life's wealth gathered over the years. I'll just take it slow and see what develops. I really do enjoy it as it is now. It's flattering to the male ego."

"What? Pretty young woman hanging off yer arm and swooning all over yer? Takin' in every word yer say? Worship in her starstruck eyes. All a-tremblin' and adorin'. Give us a break, mate. Wise up."

Jamesey grinned. "Partly. But I do like her. She can be bleedin' hilarious and she just ain't stupid. She's good company. She is endearing herself to me, and okay she can be an airhead when she wants to be, but it's all an act. I like taking her out and buying her things. I like it when she's pleased and surprised. It's different. I've never been in a situation like this before, Ron, and it's kind of nice. I'm enjoying my leave and I put it down to meeting Collette."

They sipped at their whiskey again. Ron gauged Jamesey had it bad and just refused to acknowledge it. Bleedin' paratroopers were stubborn sods. They had to be to survive.

---

[38] Greek terrorist movement led by Archbishop Makarios to drive the British out of Cyprus. They got their independence in 1964.
[39] 'RAH' – Republican Action Heroes – A local name for the IRA in Republican areas in the Provence.

"Yeah, well. Watch Eadie. She's in full match-makin' mode. Reckons you'll make and I quote 'Oh such a 'andsome-looking couple'," he said in high falsetto. "A match made in heaven."

He laughed at Ron's comic impression of his wife. "Jesus, she'll have us married off next! Don't let her catch you taking the Michael[40], Ron. Eadie will knock your block off."

Ron grimaced, "Don't I friggin' know it. But she's at work. She's had her booked in at the hairdresser's tomorrer and takin' her up herself. Oh, yer can't walk out with Jamesey looking like a stuck traffic light, she ses, Gawd bless her kind heart."

They roared again, appreciating the male bonding. Ron was a great guy, Jamesey concluded, forced to take early retirement from the Met's Flying Squad and now walking with a permanent limp. He had turned The Robert Peel into a resounding success. A real man of the world, Jamesey surmised he could get some useful contacts off him when he started On la Guardia.

They had been talking quietly with the office door ajar and could hear the going on in the bar. They heard Collette come in and the row start. Jamesey stood and listened. He screwed up his face. That Barry was a nasty piece of work, but Collette was holding her own.

"I'll have to speak to her about her language. Christ, she can curse with the best of them!"

"She'd put a boatload of Bombay Dockers to shame," agreed Ron.

They deemed it was over when Collette said that she was telling Ron, and then he heard her cry out, a cry for help. His damsel was in distress.

"Time to do a Zorro," he told Ron and flew out the office and saw Barry had her arse in a vice-like grip and Collette swivelled around and clocked the yob hard across the face with full force.

About bleeding time, grinned Jamesey.

Jamesey vaulted over the bar easily, his feet not touching Formica and landed with a thud, and as Barry drew his fist back, he covered the gap in three mighty strides. He caught Barry's fist with his left hand, spun him hard round and smacked him full force in the centre of his fat face with his right fist. The table crashed over and glass broke and the fat thug fell back, howling in a combination of pain, rage and frustration, clots of blood erupting from his shattered septum.

"Oh, Jamesey," Collette cried and rushed into his comforting bulk. Relief flooding across her anguished face.

Barry wasn't finished yet. He heaved himself up and grabbing a pint bottle of brown ale, he smashed it across a table edge and advanced at Jamesey and Collette, the jagged broken bottle thrust wickedly before him.

"C'mon, yer squaddie bastard. I'll give yer an extra arsehole in yer throat with this!"

"Don't yer fuckin' dare glass anyone in my bar!" shouted Ron from behind it.

"Shut yer clap, yer crippled rozzer[41]," sneered Barry. "Action man here is gonna be shitting glass for a week."

---

[40] Michael Fish – Television weatherman famous for wrong predictions.
[41] Police officer.

Jamesey eyed him as he came forward and got a shaking Collette behind him and pushed her gently over to Ron, who had come from behind the bar and gathered her to him, keeping a safe distance.

Jamesey half crouched in a defensive stance, right hand open and arm out, left arm lower and half locked. Right foot forward, left back, legs half bent and leaning half forward, watching his enemy intently, eyes like chips of flint. Barry was swishing the lethal edges from side to side aggressively, in wide semi-circles, an evil grin slotted across his foul mouth.

"Come on then, Barry. Let's see how good you are at fighting a man then. You've had your fun and games with Collette, you bullying bastard."

Barry grinned, "I am so, so looking forward to makin' yer bleed, soldier girl."

Collette stared at Jamesey. She had never seen a more dangerous sight in her life. His normally laughing blue eyes were like Artic ice and fury blazed in them. The calm, pleasant countenance she was used to was replaced by one of intense concentration, and violence radiated in heatwaves off him. He looked supremely confident and by his professional deportment, she knew what she was looking at – a born warrior. He was in full fighting modus operandi, implacable in his resolve, and she knew here was a man who would never back off and that he would fight to the last drop of blood in his body. Despite the awfulness of the serious situation he was in, her heart swelled with pride for she knew with total clarity that here was a man she would follow to the ends of the earth and back and would stick by him through thick and thin, proud to be by his side.

"Eadie, get me baseball bat!" yelled Ron alarmed. "Quick like, gal."

"Yer fuckin' cut him, Barry, I'll swing for yer," screeched Collette, struggling now to get free from Ron's strong arms.

Jamesey gave a nasty, evil little laugh. "Time to end this, Barry. Time to pay the piper. You should never start what you can't finish, you tosser."

Then to everyone's astonishment, he proceeded into the arc of wicked swinging glass, his arms flashing. He seized Barry's wrist with his right hand so fast it was a blur, twisted his arm out to the side like a gooseneck, moved in and head butted him full in the face. What Ron later described as the famous 'Glasgow Kiss'. Barry went over to his right as Jamesey pulled down on his locked wrist. A siren screamed nearby as Barry went sideways, Jamesey straightened and with his left foot fast kicked Barry's legs out from under him, spun so his back was to the thug and twisted harder on his wrist holding the deadly broken bottle. He brought the other hand to join the first and as Barry hit the floor sideways, his wrist bone snapped in two. The bottle dropped and Barry howled in animalistic agony. Collette had never heard anything like it. The sound of his wrist breaking was like an axe chopping through thick ice.

Tyres screeched to a halt outside. More sirens shrilled. Jamesey let Barry drop fully and then gave him an almighty kick in the stomach and another to the head, his noggin bouncing hard, slapping off the lino, blood and snot spraying out in a dramatic arc, in green and red technicolour.

Bloodied teeth spilled and clattered like thrown dice from the slob's mouth, across the hard floor, leaving jagged stumps.

Three coppers burst in, batons drawn and raised. Jamesey gave them a look of such malevolence, their blood chilled. They stopped in their tracks and these were men not easily frightened.

"Jamesey, Jamesey. Enough, babe. Please darling," implored Collette, struggling madly to break free.

Jamesey smirked evilly; years of training to be violent had taken hold now. He was on a different planet. He eyeballed the cops hungrily. Just young kids, he judged. Easy meat to a seasoned paratrooper. He knelt and grabbed a whimpering Barry by the hair, viciously wrapping his hands in the greasy mess with force, twisted Barry's head around so their eyes were only inches apart and whispered into his bleeding, shattered face. Nobody knew what he said, but the look of pure terror that crossed Barry's face was a sight to behold, and he wet himself then in a big steaming puddle.

Collette would never forget this day for the rest of her life. Neither would Barry.

Ron had put his arms around Collette when the fight started, and she turned to him now and said softly, "Let me go, Ron. I'll talk him down."

Jamesey was staring hard at the cops as they gingerly edged forward, trying to encircle him.

"Let the man go now, sir! Move away from the broken bottle!" instructed the nearest officer.

The peelers might have been young but they had all been to bar fights, Watford on a busy Saturday night was like a mini Beirut, and they understood from just the look of the big man before them he had the potential to be a very dangerous adversary. A berserker. More cops inched in. Jamesey beamed widely.

"Well, well. Watford's finest! No fucking retreat guys."

He then stood and gazed at them stoutly and raised his fists in a classic boxer's stance. He stood there like the Rock of Gibraltar. Collette had never witnessed such a magnificent sight in her whole life.

"Christ, Collette," whispered Ron, "go get him offside, quick!" and released her.

She rushed up and wrapped her slender arms around his big strong waist from behind and reached up on tiptoe. "Tactical withdrawal, baby. Lick the wounds and reassess," she whispered pleadingly in his big lug hole.

An ambulance arrived and the moaning casualty was carted off to claps and cheers!

Ron moved and began to explain to the police what had happened. The regulars backed him up, and Ron asked them to lower their batons. Collette felt Jamesey's muscles relax, and she pulled him back to his stool, made him sit and stood in front of him protectively. No frigging plod[42] was gonna hurt her man. Eadie pulled him a pint and chatted away inanely to calm him down. Two of the regulars had got a mop and broom and were cleaning the mess up.

"Make sure yer put plenty of bleach down where that dirt bag Jimmy riddled[43] himself!" she ordered them. "I'll buy yah all a drink."

Collette and Eadie still stood defensively around Jamesey. "Ron'll sort it," she said confidently. Collette hoped so.

The Duty Inspector had arrived and came over; Eadie poured him a double Irish. He was a pleasant enough man but capable. He assessed the situation easily enough.

---

[42] Police officers.
[43] To urinate – wet oneself.

"Was in The Green Jackets[44] myself, Ron tells me you're just back from the X[45], that's always a rough tour."

Jamesey grinned. "Was a piece of piss, except for the crap beer over there."

The Inspector chuckled. "You paras are all mad bastards. Glad to see you're keeping the tradition going. Ta, for not beating me boys. I would have had to get The Sweeney[46] in to top yah!"

Jamesey smiled widely back. "Another Irish Inspector? Probably the best thing to come out of that place. The Mighty Bush. [47]"

They chatted amiably for a while. A police photographer took a few snaps and disappeared. A CID man came over and arranged for Collette to come down with Jamesey the next day to make a statement.

"Have to be in the morning. She's getting her hair done in the afternoon," said Jamesey happily.

The Inspector surveyed her pink bonce with interest. "I think that would be a wise decision, miss. I've seen people arrested for less and it's a distraction to drivers." He grinned and she scowled at him.

"How the 'ell did cha know 'bout that?" she inquired, annoyed that the surprise was now an open secret.

"Just do. We have our ways," chortled Ron. "Male intuition, ain't it?"

Soon the bar was back to normal and the Micks arrived in, miffed to have missed the action, always keen to have a go at The Filth.[48] Collette went to the ladies with Eadie and showed her the nasty bruise and cut Barry had inflicted on her. Eadie bathed it with TCP, making her wince. She was then violently sick down the toilet, and Eadie brought her into the office and got her a drink of brandy and port to ease her stomach. Jamesey had seen her white face and came in and knelt in front of her and stroked her pink mane.

"Good girl. You sure showed that prick," was all he said before leaving, keen to get back to his pint as the adrenaline left his body and put a thirst on him.

Collette radiated and glowed with pride. She felt she could walk on water if he so commanded her to. Eadie noticed and sighed. "Oh the follies of youth."

Back in the bar, Ron said to Jamesey. "Subtle? I'd hate to see you angry, mate."

"That was only a little ripple in the mighty DeJames ocean. Sorry about your table."

Ron smiles, "Well, at least Barry the wanker's gone."

"Yeah, he'll be sucking hospital food through a straw for a week or two, anyhow."

"Reckon the tooth puller be making a few bob as well... Nuvver Double D?"

The Irish called for a joke. He joined them. Collette and Eadie came out to listen. He noticed a bit of colour back in her face and was pleased. Eadie seemed to be

---

[44] Famous former Rifle Regiment based in Winchester, Hampshire. The Sharpe Series with Sean Bean were based on them.

[45] Town of Crossmaglen in South Armagh. Very dangerous posting during 'The Troubles'.

[46] Armed, plain clothes police anti-robbery squad made famous in the series with John Thaw and Dennis Waterman.

[47] Bushmills Whiskey from Northern Ireland.

[48] Police officers.

keeping her well supplied with brandy. He wondered what she would be like pissed and sighed. Probably a hilarious handful. He had a feeling he was going to find out later.

"There's this guy with a hunchback drinking in the pub. Comes closing time, he heads home. It's a cold night, so he takes a shortcut through the churchyard. A big goblin jumps out and grabs him."

He was interrupted. "Goblins ain't big, yer know! They're little green tings, so they are," said Mike, the big, bald guy from Limerick.

"This one is. It's an American goblin from Texas and everything's big over there."

They laughed but Mike's not done. "Ach, sure. It's not cold in Texas and they're only two tings come from Texas and that's steers and Queens."[49]

Jamesey chuckled, "You've been watching too many movies, Mike... Okay! This is a Texan goblin on holiday in an Irish graveyard in winter. How's that?"

Mike grinned, "Sure, and ye have the way of the words with ye, so ye do."

"Right. So the goblin says, 'Give me that hump' and snatches it off the guy's back and puts it on his own back and runs off laughing madly."

Pauses for a swallow, the Micks enjoying the craic. They were good men. Hard but fair. He thanked his lucky stars they weren't here when the cops were or there would have been a riot. Rioting seemed to be a national sport across the Irish Sea. The kids were taught it from when they were knee-high to a grasshopper.

"Anyhow, next night he's in the pub, all cured, standing straight and proud telling his story, when his mate, who has a badly deformed leg, asks, 'If I wandered into the graveyard, would the goblin cure me?' 'You can but try,' says his pal. So after the pub closes, he enters the graveyard and the goblin jumps out. The man says to him, 'Would you like a deformed leg, Mr Goblin?' And the goblin answers, 'No, thanks' and pulls the hump off and puts it on the man's back. 'But you can have this hump. I'm fucking sick of it.'"

They erupt in stitches and Jamesey happily drunk with them for a while, throwing out one-liners. "What's the difference between a police car and a hedgehog?"

"What?" they asked, guzzling the Shamrock contentedly.

"The pricks are on the inside in a police car!"

Collette put some change in the jukebox. Stevie Wonder comes on 'You Are the Sunshine of My Life'. She passes him and says, "That's for you from me, babe, My Apollo."

He liked that. He was her moon...!!! Later, he put on Marie Osmond 'Paper Roses' because Eadie said that Collette loved it. At closing time, he waited in the small foyer in the entrance way when she came out and saw she was flushed-looking and giggling.

"Ron's annoyed at Eadie cos she kept giving me brandy. Said I was in shock, so she did, medicinal it was, wasn't it?"

Before he could reply, she had one arm around his neck and one up his back inside his coat. She pulled him down into a smouldering, open-mouthed kiss, her tongue seeking his urgently. He gave up all resolve and wrapped his arms around her and returned her ardour with a passion. She was something else. The kiss went

---

[49] Famous line from the cult Vietnam movie 'Apocalypse Now'.

on for an extremely long time as he lost himself in her heat and felt the comfort of her, the air crackling above their engrossed heads as their lips crushed into each other, both lost in the moment that possibly spelt the start of a new road ahead, with both their feet on it.

Eadie watched through the crack in the door, thoroughly approving.

Such a handsome couple! About bleeding time!

Chapter 10
Watch Out There's a Stalker About

"Oh Lawdy, Lawdy... She Can Walk Again... It's a Miracle. Praise the Lord," Bobby Havilland

December 23rd, 2012

Big Bobby Havilland parked outside the apartments, looked over at Luca and sighed heavily. Goddammit, she was in some state, slumped into the seatbelt, staring straight ahead. "Wendy's gonna be none too happy with you, little missey," he told her, wiping some drool off her chin with his hanky. "Not happy at all. No siree."

He got her out with some effort, holding her arm over his shoulder and putting an arm around her waist. "Can you lift yah tootsies, Luc?"

She never answered, her head slumped and eyes riveted on the frosty pavement. She was a dead weight. "Ah, guess not." He half dragged her, half carried her up the wide marble stairs, her feet trailing along behind her. "Yah gonna ruin them nice shoes," he scolded her. "They would sell a kidney for a pair like those in Iraq."

Mr Chin was hovering in the foyer and he let them in, face anxious. "What the damn wrong with Miss Luca?" and darted around and got her other arms and they proceeded down the hall. "She's as drunk as a skunk man. Too much soup and I don't mean the Heinz 57 variety."

Mr Chin tut tutted. "I've never seen her like this. It not like her."

"Well, you better believe it and my missus is gonna kill her."

Mrs Chin came out with her little Pekinese, Confucius, and jabbered at her husband in a torrent of indecipherable mandarin, the little dog running around their feet in an excited circle, yapping happily. His tail wagging rhythmically like a metronome.

"She say get her in a cold shower clothes off then into bed and roll her on her side so she don't choke."

Bobby thought about that, "I reckon Mrs Havilland would have something to say about that," he grinned. "Nice thought, though."

They made an incongruous sight as they proceeded down the hall, Mr Chin in sharp contrast to the huge bulk of Bobby, Luca slumped in the middle.

Bobby exhaled in exasperation when he saw the 'Out of order' sign looming out vindictively on the elevator doors. "For lawd's sake, Mr C, does them dam things never work?"

Mr Chin shrugged. "I tell owners."

"Only one thing for it I guess, hombre," and he slung Luca over his right shoulder, arm firmly across the back of her shapely legs and proceeded to trudge up the first flight of stairs, the Chins following like devout acolytes, the little dog gambolling up and down the steps excitedly. Bobby thinking if the Chins weren't there, he would kick the little fur ball into touch. He wasn't a great dog lover, especially after Bagdad, where packs of starved, rabid dogs used to follow them dangerously about.

All was going well until the last flight, when Luca gave an almighty belch, then vomited copiously down his back and trousers, splattering; Confucius and making the Chins dive for cover. "I get mop, I get mop." And Mr C rushed off and Mrs C gobbed off in more mandarin, stepping daintily around the steaming mess.

Bobby groaned and shook his head. "You are really, really going to pay for this, Luca. If you were mine, I'd give you a dam good spanking." Then dismissed that thought and locked it away for good. Luca was too attractive for ideas like that; besides, she was his buddy and he felt protective of her. He guessed life was hard enough for a single woman in New York, especially for one thousands of miles away from home and family, trying to adjust to life in this vast, unfeeling metropolis.

"If my daughter in China, I give her damn good flogging." Mrs C admonished in broken English.

He moved aside to let her pass, "Go knock my door, Mrs C, and get Wendy before she pukes again."

Wendy met him at the top of the last flight. "Honey, I'm home and bearing gifts," he panted as he put on a final spurt, sweat beading his big brow.

Wendy stood, hands on hips, Mrs Chin by her, and her arms crossed. "Look at the state of yah, Luca. For Chrissake girl, watcha thinking of?"

"Does not speak or respond. Outta her skull so she is," Bob explained. "More life in a zombie movie."

"That's not good babe," Wendy said concerned, "Dump her on the sofa."

He did as told, glad to be home. He put her in the recovery position, worried she was going to be sick again, which she promptly was, all over Wendy's pride and joy. "Yah missed me, Luca. Too quick for yah."

"Ah well, at least its leather." Wendy observed, increasingly concerned. "Go put your duds in bin bags and I'll get Luca sorted. She can't go home like that, and get a shower, you stink."

"Why's it always carrots, Wendy? When you barf after too much drink."

"It's the enzymes in the pancreas. Turn the food orange, now skedaddle."

He thought about that. So why was sweetcorn still yellow on rearrival?

"Okey-dokey," and he hastened off, glad he had his Wendy on hand to handle things. She was one smart cookie.

Wendy got a bucket of water and soapy cloths and cleaned Luca and the mess up, she knelt before the distraught female and sighed, "How the darnation did you get into this state, kiddo? Thought you Ruskies could hold your liquor?"

A flicker of recognition flitted across Luca's eyeballs.

"Help me, Vends, please, help me, Da?" before she sunk back into her stupor. Wendy frowned. This was not the Luca she knew. This was an animal in distress. Definitely something was out off-kilter here.

She changed Luca into one of Bob's sweat tops, which hung down to her knees, and wrapped her in one of his huge dressing gowns, she put a cold flannel over her brow and got her a pillow and settled her down for the night. "Tank you, Vends. I love you," she mumbled before dropping off to sleep. After being sick, she had felt a bit better and her limbs felt a bit lighter, the numbness was easing and she was semi-aware of what was going on around her. She knew she was in Wendy and Bobby's apartment and that she was safe but had no recollection at all of leaving 'Ye Olde Bull' restaurant or the time in between. In her sleep she dreamt she was with Galen walking in Lithuanian forests, and he was warning her to be aware of danger coming and to be very, very careful.

Wendy watched her friend sleeping as Bobby dandered back in dressed in his 'Army Engineers Rock n Roll' sweats. He saw the pensive look on her face, "What's the score, honey? She okay?"

"She'll have to stay here tonight. We'll have to keep an eye on her."

He flopped down on the chair, "You go to bed, babe, you're on earlies tomorrow. Old Bobby a watch the drunkski Ruski huski."

Wendy yawned, "We'll watch her together, she's my best mate but I'll tell ya, if I get my hands on the punk who got her pissed, I'll swing for him."

She went and sat on his knee. She was starting at 6a.m. on the children's ward and didn't need this crap but what could she do? She knew Luca would watch over her if the roles were reversed, but still. It was uncharacteristic of her pal. "You did brilliant tonight, honey," she told him, "Luca owes my big strong man big style."

He beamed at that. He liked being owed by young beautiful ladies. "Guess so. Ain't never seen her like that. She is gonna be one sorry gal tomorrow when Mr Hangover comes a calling."

Wendy nodded in agreement, watching Luca's chest rise and fall. They fell into an uneasy sleep, Wendy's bullshit antennae on full alert and doing overtime.

* * *

Wendy did her rounds and stopped at young Johnny Bristow's bay. The eleven-year-old was jumping up and down energetically on the bed, full of restless, pent-up energy. His dark hair was just staring to sprout back after his last round of chemo. "Right you, stop bouncing and into bed, you're making me dizzy."

He flopped down, spread like a starfish. "Frig's sake, you can do nothing in this place."

His dad woke up. He had slept in the chair all night. "Staff Havilland. Good morning. Johnny, apologise now. Right now. I mean it, son."

Wendy scrutinised the man's tired and exhausted face. "He's okay, Mr Bristow. Just bored is all. Aren't you, Johnny? And I can't blame him."

"I just wanna get outta this dump and go play with my pals."

Wendy sat down and put her arm around him "Yeah well, eat your breakfast up, brush your teeth and be nice to the doctors, and I reckon there's a good chance you're going home today."

They both looked at her hopefully. Johnny had a very rare form of leukaemia, but they had caught it quick and zapped the bastard out of him and the likelihood of it returning was extremely remote. They were awaiting his test results but Wendy's friend in the lab had told her he was all clear. There were two types of news on the kiddies ward – good and bad. When good, Wendy felt great pride and achievement to see her little charges leave. When bad, she put her comforting hat on and consoled them. Happily, she would not have to don the sad hat today.

"The doc's be around about nine and will speak to you, but I suggest you gather up his stuff, Mr Bristow, and sort yourself transport home."

Six weeks was a long time for a child to be cooped up in a ward, and one or other parent had been at his bedside the whole time. They were a credit to themselves, not like some they got in, always complaining and pointing fingers accusingly.

She left the beaming guys and hastened to the staffroom and got a small Tupperware container out of her bag and headed off down to the lab.

Her friend Sally was chief technician that morning, and she gave her the sample and headed back up to the busy ward.

After doctor's rounds, Mr Bristow asked to speak to her. Johnny was getting dressed. He was going home to see his pals, a big cheesy grin across his face.

She took him into a spare room, and he broke down in huge wracking sobs of relief and she hugged him to her ample bosom. "I thought we were going to lose him. I'll never be able to thank…"

She shushed him and gave him a tissue. "We don't need thanks. You take him home, Mr Bristow, and enjoy him. He'll soon be bringing girls home and breaking his curfew."

He laughed and dried his eyes, the past six weeks already just a bad memory, "You girls are incredible."

She shooed him out, "Yes, I know we are. Good luck now."

A happy, relieved father left with a bounce in his step. He would never forget Staff Nurse Wendy Havilland though.

At the nurses' station she phoned Sally in the lab. She listened intently, her face as white as a Japanese geisha girl's white, thick make-up, before slamming the phone down shocked.

"Fuck's sake. Unbefuckinglieveable. By crikey the shit's gonna fly high when I get home."

* * *

Luca woke at nine and peered at Bobby through slitted, bleary eyes. Her head felt like a horde of lunatics were running around in her head, bashing empty dustbins with golf clubs, accompanied by a discordant full brass band. Her mouth felt like something very furry and rotten had crawled into it and died, her arms and legs were sore and tender, and her stomach was going around like a cement mixer full of noxious substances.

The big guy was reading The New York Post in his armchair. She licked dry and cracked lips. "Bobby, please go get da gun and put me outta da misery."

He looked over the paper at her, "I don't have a gun, Luca. Gotta Black and Decker drill? Bit slower, but it'll do the job."

She groaned pitifully "Niet, too noisy. What da hell happen to me?"

"Well, legless, pissed, rat-arsed, drunk as a newt are a few things that come to mind," he tapped the paper. "I see the financial share index for alcohol consumption went off the board last night."

She curled up under his big robe, sweat doting her forehead. "What you need, my gal, is a good army breakfast," he said maliciously, "fried eggs, greasy bacon, big, fat sausages…"

He never finished because she jack-knifed straight and hung over the edge of the sofa and dry wretched into the bucket.

"Black pudding, diced onions and mushrooms in butter, fried bread and heaps of beans for roughage."

She gave him an evil look and wrapping the robe around her, staggered down to the bathroom.

Bobby threw his hands in the air like an evangelical preacher. "Oh lawdy, lawdy. She can walk again. It's a miracle. Praise the lord."

When she came back and collapsed in a forlorn heap on the couch again, he took pity on her and got her a pint of pure orange juice and two dissolvable solpadol in water. "Wendy ses lots of vitamin C and pain relief so drink up."

She did, gratefully. She was parched. The hissing of the dissolving tablets seemed to fill the room. She gulped them down, then promptly fell back to sleep.

Big Bobby grinned and slunk off to make his breakfast. He hadn't been joking and made himself the full works. He was a big man with a big appetite. His philosophy was…never mind poverty…throw another sausage in the frying pan.

Luca woke at lunchtime. "Da fizzys, please Bobby, more da fizzys. I beseech you. Fizzys."

He got her them, complaining. "Bad enough I was her human elevator and spew post last night, now I'm her Goddamn drug dealer."

She gulped them down eagerly. "Ah da vunders of over-the-counter prescription drugs."

"Saved yah some eggs and bacon if you're ready to eat."

She physically snarled at him and went back into a deep, dreamless sleep.

"Only trying to help," he grumbled and flicked through the sports channels for a match, leaving it on mute.

* * *

Wendy got home at three. He knew by her face there was trouble ahead. She was livid, seething with rage. It came off her in huge waves and he sensed the underlying unease off her.

She tossed her bag on the coffee table and knelt down by Luca and checked her pulse. "How's she been? Is she walking and talking?" she asked through thin lips and got a thermometer out of her bag and took her temperature.

"Well, yeah. She went to the bathroom, drunk her juice up. She's slept most of the day…like having a pet cat. Now you wanna tell me what's up before you burst a blood vessel?"

"She's one lucky girl, believe me. Kitchen, now."

He followed her meekly down. When Wendy was like this, she was Miss who must be obeyed and no arguments.

"So what's the story, morning glory?" trying to lighten the mood.

"What's the story?" she hissed, "Some dirty smelly cunt of a perverted bastard tried to date rape our best buddy, that's the fucking story."

He gripped her by the shoulders to face him, "Whoa, whoa. I'm lost here. Tell me slowly from the beginning. Take a breath."

She gulped air, composing herself. "Okay, some pervo gave her ketamine, so he could have his evil way with her, our pal. I do not fucking believe it but it is true." And she broke free and kicked a cupboard door hard.

111

He sat her down at the table and poured her a slug of tequila. She drunk it down with shaking hands and he topped her up and sat opposite her. He was getting annoyed now himself. "Right, whadda hell's ketamine and how'd ya know all this?"

"I took a sample of her vomit into the lab and got it tested. That's not a booze hangover, she was drugged and she's lucky to be alive. Special 'K' the pervs call it."

Bobby was known for his easygoing nature but he was not a man you wanted to cross. A ruddy glow of anger infused his big cheeks. "So what's da ketamine do then? You saying Luca was spiked?"

"Ketamine Hydrochloride. It's PCP. An analogue. It shuts the nervous system down," she explained, "vets use it to knock horses out. It's dangerous for humans. Way too strong. Can stop the heart."

He gripped the table. "We better get her to hospital, pronto."

She put her hand on his. "No, she's okay here. I asked the ward doctor for advice. They'll only do what we're doing. Fluids and rest. Painkillers. We'll hang onto her for a few days, keep a close watch on her."

Bobby blew out his nostrils. "Frigging perverts. He isn't getting away with drugging Luca. No frigging way Jose."

"Whatcha gonna do, hon?"

"I've a suspicion who did this. This is a job for the cops," and he marched over to the wall phone and punched in 911, grim determination on his face. Wendy often forgot he had done ten years in the military and could be very demanding when he put his mind to it, sometimes in the bedroom, much to her pleasure. He had the reins now, and she realised she had been dithering, in two minds what to do.

He gave his name and address and demanded the police, "Whatcha mean can we come down the precinct? Our buddy was ketamined last night, and I want the detectives out rightaway."

"Whatdya mean why did I not report it last night? We didn't know until today. I am not psychic, ma'am."

"Whatcha mean all resources are tied up? I know it's near Christmas. I don't give a fart in a spacesuit. I want the tecs up now or I'm gonna ring the Mayor's Office and ask him why the do diddly squat I pay rates if I get squat service for them. I done Eye Rack."

"Whatcha mean? I am not bringing the poor girl to the station house to sit for hours amongst the whackos. We need to catch the beast and now before he strikes again. The ladies ain't safe with this perv spiking their beverages."

"Yes, a fart in a spacesuit. Yes, it's a good one you've never heard before. The detectives will be out in an hour. Thank you, ma'am, and happy Christmas to you too." And he hung up, proudly.

Wendy rushed over and hugged him. "Wow, that sure told them, honey. You were outstanding."

He preened, feeling he was absolute ruler in his own little realm. "Yeah, well, can't let the authorities walk all over yah or there be anarchy. A man's gotta stand up for his ladies."

"I tink I owe you both da big apology for being da drunken bitch and making da mess."

They looked down and saw Luca standing in the entrance. She was softly weeping. Wendy ran down and pulled her into a tight embrace, "You're not a bitch. We're just glad you're okay, honey."

112

Bobby marched down and wrapped his massive arms around them both. "Doncha worry, Lucs. Nobody messes with Robert Eisenhower Havilland's women folk and gets away with it."

Luca snivelled happily, revelling in the tight embrace. She thought she would be up da shitski creekski without a paddle and suddenly she was flavour of the month… Americans were so bloody well unreadable at times.

* * *

Wendy ran her a bath, gave her more fizzys and washed her hair for her. Bobby got her clean nightwear and when the detectives arrived, she was sitting on the couch in pink flannel pyjamas and a blue robe, looking young and innocent, hair gleaming but still very pale.

She had drunk more orange juice and felt a bit better but her limbs were still very weak and sore and she was lightheaded.

Wendy had carefully explained what she had found out, and Luca was speechless with shock and very, very frightened.

She finally managed to speak. "Tank you Wendy. I knew I wasn't da pissed dat bad. But da kettlemined now dat ver' spooky."

"Yeah, sure is, honey, there are some creepy weirdos out there, but you're safe now."

"You're so clover, Vends. You should be on da cop show, Blue Blood, with Tom Sellick."

Wendy giggled. "I used to fancy him when he was Magnum, but not now. Some leap from Magnum to police commissioner."

"Tom Sellick was a chocolate ice lolly?" she asked. That confused Wendy, who gave up on it. Obviously, a Russian thing. "And the great news is the big guy's in full protective mode and insists you stay with us over Christmas, so no buts or you will hurt his feelings."

Luca clapped her hands in delight. "Dat's so cool. It is how you say, a done deal."

Bobby was sitting guzzling Coors. Wendy had hid a box in her closet and gave him them as a reward.

Luca jumped up in his lap, gave him a big hug and a smacking kiss around his cheek. "Tank you, Bobby. I think you saved me last night from da ver bad experience at da hand of da pervos. You now number one on my hero list."

He blushed and squirmed, "Ah shucks, Luca girl, was lucky I was early. The army taught me punctuality. It's always stood me in good stead."

She climbed off, "Yes, vell, I tink you're amazing. I owe you way, way da big style."

Wendy was watching, amused, "Enough Lucs or he be getting an even bigger headski than he's already got."

The buzzer went.

"That'll be five oh," guessed Bobby.

"Who five oh?" asked Luca.

"Hawaii five oh. Old cop show," and he hastened down to let them in.

"Steve McGarrett was the lead guy. Head of detectives," explained Wendy, over her shoulder.

113

"Was he as gorge as Tom Sellick, Wendy?"

She thought about that, "About evenly matched, I reckon. Carved from the same block of studly man stone."

* * *

The detectives were two ladies from the Serious Crimes Against Women's Unit, accompanied by a police doctor. They introduced themselves as Detective Annette Hurst and Janet Gillespie. Hurst was a strapping blonde in her late thirties, and Gillespie a stocky haired brunette of comparable age. They had worked together for many years and were seasoned, unshockable veterans, both married with kids, and they juggled career and home life expertly.

They gently quizzed a nervous Luca, and the doctor took her down to the bedroom for an examination and to take a blood test. They were concerned that she might have been sexually assaulted before Bobby found her up the alley.

"That was quick thinking on your part, Mrs Havilland. We'll make it official and get a report off the hospital lab and it should show up in the blood test. Ketamine's a dodgy PCP that hangs about in the system for days," Annette told them.

"Yeah, lucky you got there early, big guy. You need to keep an eye on her for a day or three. You definitely saved her from a seriously bad experience at the least," chipped in Janet, who had been tapping furiously away at her laptop.

"Coffee and cookies, ladies?" beamed Wendy, feeling pretty good at their praise and Bobby guzzled more Coors, basking in being the hero of the moment.

"Christ, yes," the tecs agreed, "We've been run off our feet dealing with complaints from the office parties."

"Yeah, the hospitals are flat out with drunks," said Wendy, getting up. "Guys who only drink once a year and think they're superdick and any female at hand is fair game."

"Not all dudes, babe," Bobby argues, insecurely.

"No, not you, lover. You want more Coors? I've got a six pack hid under the sink," she assured him.

When Luca came back down, embarrassed at the intimate examination and red-faced, the surgeon talked quietly with the trackers. "Definitely no sexual assault. In fact, I would say the young lady would be quite unfamiliar with that aspect of things, if you get my drift."

They did and the doctor let himself out and they resumed their seats. "Now, Hanlon. Would that be one Harold Herbert Henry by any chance, originally from Belfast?"

Booby had noticed the tecs glance at each other when his name came up. He slurped more beer as Luca told them about meeting him and eating at his steakhouses and designing Ye Olde Bull for him. Bobby was getting annoyed again, the strong beer swirling through his system.

"So you had a number of meals alone with him? Did he come onto you at all?"

"Vell, he asked me out on dates a few times, but I turn him down and he used da bring little presents to da office. Flowers and candy but he always was so sweet and pleased da see me."

Bobby guffawed. "I bet he was. Goddamn it, Luca, what were yah thinking, girl? Eating alone with him, stringing him along?"

Luca was getting upset, flustered, "I not how you da say, encourage him. It vas just da work."

"Yeah, right. Wendy and me have friggin warned you before about safe protocol with men. It's dangerous out there and you were stupid."

Luca still felt very unwell and fragile, "Am sorry, Bobby. I never thought, you know."

He exploded. He cared deeply for Luca and it was really hitting him now how close she had come to disaster. "Goddamit, Lucs, that whacko was gonna rape you and there was frig all you could do about it and what have I fricking told yah about watching your drink and leaving it unattended. That ketamine crap didn't get in there on its own. Oh here's Luca's drink sitting all lonesome, so I'll hop in and comatose the silly bitch."

"That's enough, Bobby. Can't you see Luca's hurting?" snapped Wendy.

And she was. Bobby had never talked to her like that before. She could see by his strained face he was livid with rage. Her lower lip quivered, and she sat up straight, fists clenched. "I never left da drink unattended, Bobs..." she managed before the dam broke, and she rushed off and locked herself in the bathroom, Wendy trotting down after her, glancing back and giving him the evil eye.

"I think you've made your point, Mr Havilland," said Janet wryly.

"Yeah well, it had to be said. She's so fucking naïve, and I hope I got through to her. Men follow her about, tongues lapping the pavement and she's totally unaware of it."

"Well, she's certainly aware now," snapped Annette, "And hopefully, it'll be a hard lesson learnt for the poor girl."

"It's only because we care about her," he groaned, "she's no one in New York and she's a fricking stalker's wet dream."

"Well yeah, she's beautiful. We'll get our personal security guy to chat to her and get her all the pamphlets and bumf."

"Good she's a couple like you looking out for her. You might have just saved her life last night."

He was mollified now and a bit ashamed. "Guess I was a bit hard on her, poor kid, but I had to get it outta me."

Wendy had coaxed Luca back down, and Bobby bounded over to her and pressed her to him, his big arms going around her shaking, slender frame. "Sorry, Lucs. I was just so Goddamn angry and afraid for yah."

He led her to the couch and sat holding her hand, Wendy on the other side, holding the other.

"No, you're right," she said in a small voice, "I am da silly person. Idiot. I be more da careful now."

"Good girl. You know Wendy and me luv yah. We just wantcha to be safe and happy."

Wendy looked at her big hubby. She sometimes forgot he'd been a trained soldier and had been to war. He had scared the crap outta Luca with his tirade, but she had to come to the decision he was right and her respect went up a notch for him. Luca was a stalking magnet that would attract all sorts of weirdos and she couldn't see it.

"I'll get you another Coors, dear, and juice for you, Luca. Lots of fluids."

That surprised him but he had seen the dawn of realisation on his wife's face, and he knew he was back in the good books. He grinned happily, hero of the hour again.

After Luca, shuddering, identified Hanlon from a montage of twelve photos on Janet's laptop. "Dat him, dat Harry."

"Ugly critter, ain't he?" sneered Bob, "Tell me, why have you his photo on your files?"

The tecs looked uneasy, "We're bound by data protection acts and invasion of policy crap but listen carefully, Miss Valendenski, that is one sad, dangerous dude, so beware," explained Janet.

Annette knelt down before her, hands on knees, "You be very, very careful, Luca. Let your friends know where you are at all times, and if he comes anywhere near you or even you see him in the street, you run, and get home. If you can't, get in a crowd and ask for assistance." She looked straight in Luca's scared eyes. She was very frightened now and trembling. Wendy put her arm around her. "I am not messing about here, Miss Valendenski. He's very, very dangerous and until we get the situation under control, you take no chances. Do you understand me?"

She nodded vigorously, terrified.

"I'm gonna go down 'Ye Olde Fricking Bull' with my trusty slugger and sort that dirt bag out for good," growled Bobby. "And what's that gonna do? You'll end up in the slammer and that douchebag will get a big lump of compo and he laughing at yah as he picks his next victim," warned Janet.

"Yeah, leave it to Cagney and Lacy here," said Wendy, referring to the old cop show, "So what's the plan, ladies?"

"We'll get a warrant off the Circuit Judge to search his premises and home and pull him in and grill him."

"And we'll need full statements off you both but we'll get them in the morning. You look exhausted, Miss Valendenski."

"Please da call me Luca. I am sooo, so sorry for being such a pain in da butt."

The tecs smiled kindly. She was a pleasant young woman, very beautiful. Pure stalker bait. "We'll go drag his sorry butt out of his 'Olde World' steak house. He won't be chasing after any fresh meat tonight," Janet assured her.

What they hadn't told her was Hanlon was prime suspect in a number of rapes in the borough of Queens but even worse, they had intelligence to say he was making violent pornographic films and was suspected of actually having made a 'snuff' movie of an Albanian immigrant. Many of the rape victims had said Hanlon had stalked them beforehand, but he hadn't left DNA yet at the scene, which was always at night and the perp being hooded. A psychological profile done by the FBI's Behavioural Science Unit at Quantico said the attacker hated women, was a serial predator and a danger to all lone single women who he preferred, was a social outcast but well-organised and patient. He probably had his own rape kit and had good resources and cash flow. He enjoyed the game and was a natural-born sadist. It concluded he didn't think he would ever get caught and was smarter than law enforcements. He would carry on his crimes until he was taken down. He was the most dangerous type of sexual pervert and would be a danger to women his whole adult life.

* * *

The lady tecs got in their car. "Let's get back up and go get this animal out of circulation."

"Yeah, and hopefully the muvver will resist arrest, and we can put the bastard down," agreed Janet.

"Be cool, wouldn't it, but I reckon he's too cute for that."

"Be nice though, wouldn't it?" Fingering her Glock 45auto, "Save a lot of paperwork."

Annette pulled out into the traffic. "Only way that guy's going down is in a box six feet under."

"Let's go get those warrants and rock and roll, partner."

"You got it, gal," and Annette laughed, "Cagney and Lacy, indeed. They were like old gals in the seventies."

Janet looked at her, "True but there were Hanlons then and Hanlons now and always will be."

"It's a sick world, full of human trash. It will always need Cagney and Laceys, sister."

"And we're the garbage collectors, kid, keeping the pavements clean of the whackos. Let's go do it, deputy."

* * *

Luca's stomach rumbled and Wendy laughed. "Are you hungry, kiddo?"

She realised she was ravenous, "I could eat da Great Bear of the Modena[50], I think!"

Wendy was pleased, "That's great. It's the body beating the drugs." She glanced at her man, "What about you stomping on down to Mickey d's and getting us gals vittles?"

Bobby had been thinking about Hanlon and what he would like to do with him. This included the use of a pair of secateurs, a Black and Decker drill and a blow torch.

He came out of his fantasy. A trip to junk food land was one of his favourite excursions. He really was high up on the brownie point chart if Wendy was sending him. "Sure will, hon. Fresh air does me good, and the first stray dog I see I'll boot up and down the street and pretend its Hanlon."

Luca was aghast. "Please don't kick da poor little dogs, Bobs, it not their fault."

He laughed. She really was so Goddamn naïve.

"He's only joking, dear," explained Wendy patting her hand. "It's just his weird sense of humour."

"Oh 'kay. You could buy da stray dogs da burger, Bobby."

He tied his laces and left chortling. She was something else, buy a stray hound a burger he could eat himself. He didn't think so, remembering the dogs in Iraq. Vicious brutes, like Hanlon.

Wendy and Luca sat discussing Christmas. Bobby had gone overboard with the decorations as usual. A large fibre tree gleamed with red, white and blue lights, fake Santas sang when you passed them, and he'd hung enough streamers and tinsel to run the length of Third Avenue.

---

[50] Old name for the Russian 'Motherland'.

Wendy thought it was gaudy and tacky but Luca loved it, a little girl look of wonder on her face when she first saw it.

"And I help you cook da dinner, Vends. You teach me how da makes the mince wincey pies and chest nutty stuffing?"

"The mince pies come out of a packet, Luca, and the butcher stuffs the big bird for us. It's New York, kiddo. Convenience city."

"Oh 'kay. I guess it gives people da pay packet to make dem for us."

Wendy hadn't thought of it like that. "Anyhow, I'm doing a half shift in the morning. Eight to twelve on the kids ward. Bobby comes up at lunchtime dressed as Santa with little prezzies for the little ones. They love him. Think he's a giant climbing frame and swing all over him."

Luca looked at her beseechingly, "Can I come with you, Wends, to play with the liddle ones? I buy dem da candy fluff and stuff."

Wendy smiled fondly at her. She was so easily pleased and kind-hearted "Course ya can. They'll love yah, Luca," and Wendy meant it. They would. Kids and animals gravitated towards her like matter in space to a black hole.

Afterwards, they sat up full and replete. Luca had gobbled down two quarter pounders, a mega chip, coleslaw, beans and a giant coke and finished Wendy's fries as well.

"It's the drugs. Makes yah crave food."

Luca burped daintily and giggled. "I am da pig, but da happy pig with my bestest friends. Tank you so much."

Bobby grinned, feet stretched out, "Did I tell yah about when I got home from Eye Rack the first time?"

"Oh Gawd. Not the poor ol Rusty Saga," laughed Wendy. "It's his Goddamn party piece."

"Yep, Wendy was staying with the old dragon up in New Jersey, weren't yah hon?"

"My mother's, Luca. He arrived there pissed as a skunk. Mum and Bobby don't always see eye to eye."

"Well, apart she's a self-righteous, two-faced, teetotal witch we get on okay." He grinned.

"They love each other really, in a strange lost in space kinda way," Wendy explained, "Go on, love."

"Yeah well, I arrived home on leave to see my little lady, para-let-ic, I can tell yah. No booze in Basra, babe."

"And he staggered in and crashed on the couch, so Mom very kindly drove out and got him a huge McDonalds," Wendy explained.

"Yep, and I wolfed it down, chomp, chomp, chomp," and he gnashed his big choppers at Luca making her flinch and giggle, "But it didn't sit well with Captain Morgan and Jim Beam and back up it came like Mount Washington erupting. Whoosh. The full pyrotechnic fountain, more colour than Joseph's magic dream coat."

Luca laughed. Delighting in the close intimacy with her best buddies.

"Yep, as it burst forth, I aimed fir the old crone, but she ducked and it went all over old Rusty, her Golden Retriever. It a been hovering for scraps."

"And it got more than it could chew, I tell yah," guffawed Wendy. "Poor thing was near drowned."

Luca was in stitches, "Poor Rusty. Gosh imagine that, death by da Bobby's vomit."

They laughed heartily. "Yep, she made me sleep in the garage and never got me a McDs again."

"Vot happened to poor Rusty den?" Luca asked.

"Ah hosed him down and now when I visit, he hides behind the TV and won't come out."

Luca yawned and lay out, her head in Wendy's lap. "Poor old Rusty. He never eats da cheeseburger again. So sad," and fell asleep.

"That's good. She'll sleep easier tonight. Safe with her pals."

"Yep, am ready for the cot myself," agreed Bobby. Wendy winked at him, "And you just might get tonight what you didn't get that night at Mom's."

He grinned lasciviously. "Yehaa, time for lift off."

He marched off, whistling the theme to 'Juliet Bravo', a UK cop show from the '80s that was being re-rerun on cable.

It was all law and order tonight in 3B, The Poplar Trees Apartments.

II

Two detectives came up first thing in the morning. A grizzled old war horse with thirty years' service and his younger companion, a clean-faced guy of thirty just graduated to Detective and who seemed dazzled by the beautiful white-faced Russian girl. He likened her to a snow princess from a Hans Christian Anderson fairy tale. It was why he'd joined the boys in blue, to serve and protect beauties like these.

Bobby watched ruefully. If he asked Luca for her cell number, he would punch his lights out, she was fragile and hurting and the last thing she needed was a strange man's attention. But the young dude was the picture of courtesy as they took detailed statements off them.

The good news was they had picked up Hanlon easily enough, and the lady tecs had been putting the screws on him all night. Bad news was no ketamine had turned up at his house or 'Ye Olde Bull' but they were tearing the steak house apart. "Not good for business this time of year, but life's a bitch." The old vet grinned. "Swings and roundabouts."

"He'll need plenty of steaks for his black eyes when I get my hands on him," growled Bobby.

"Never heard that, did we, Maurice?"

"Sure didn't Gareth," agreed the young one.

Afterwards, Luca had a long soak and put a nice dress and hosiery on, made Bobby a huge Spanish omelette and hash browns for lunch and put her long winter coat on.

"I go to da office party; I have da speak to Philli."

He donned his Dodgers baseball jacket, "I'll walk yah. I get bored when Wendy's on earlies and there's no fricking work at this time of year."

As they left the phone trilled, "Hold on, Lucs."

She waited by the elevator, which was working for a change. He came down scowling. "'Kay, big guy?"

"Oh yeah, just some telesales dude. Florida time shares for heaven's sake."

She accepted that. It had in fact been Annette Hurst. They had to let Hanlon go. Lack of evidence. He was admitting to nothing and no ketamine had turned up. "Probably dumped down a drain and knocking the rats out in the sewers, but we'll keep at it. You tell that girl to be careful."

So much for going to the cops, he thought, he'd tell Luca later after she'd enjoyed the party.

They walked along side by side. Luca watching passing men, afraid one would be Hanlon, despite thinking he was in the cop shop. Bobby hoping he did bump into him so he could rip his fucking head off, knowing he wasn't. He knew Luca meant well but an omelette for lunch? No, an eighteen-inch torpedo with all the trimmings and a pint of coffee was real working men's food, not that there was any work for self-employed electricians in this Goddamn recession.

The office party was in full swing. Everybody running around with silly hats and squealers, clutching paper cups of wine or punch, the village people blasting out YMCA over the speakers.

She saw Philomena Rourke across the room and headed between the dancers to speak to her when suddenly, she was grabbed from behind and spun around, startled.

"Gotcha now, Miss V," a male leered. She pushed him away hard, both hands to his chest. He went sprawling, dropping his mistletoe and cup of punch, shock across his face.

Everybody stopped and looked accusingly at her. She saw it was Derek, the office junior boy. She rushed and helped him up. "Sooo da sorry, Derek. You startled me."

"That's okay, my fault, Miss V," he said forlornly, then something primal came over her. She cupped his face with both hands and proceeded to snog him hard. He stood transfixed, so she wrapped her arms around him and gripped his hair and really went to town on him, pressing her beautiful body into his spindly youthful one.

She forced her tongue into his mouth, tasting his sweet punchy breath, and he hugged her back into it now. He thought he had died and gone to heaven.

The room fell silent. She released him, leaving the heat of his arousal behind. "Happy Christmas, Derek," she said and she spun and grabbed Philli and dragged her into her office. Derek stood panting, not believing his luck, and the room erupted into claps and cheers. A dazed Derek got more punch. That was one beautiful older chick, and he went to find a younger version.

"What the hell was that about, girl? Derek will be jerking off to that for months."

Luca knew what it was about. She was asserting the power she had over men, not the other way round, "Don't be da crude, Philli. He's a sweet young man."

Philli laughed, "And sweet young guys don't jerk off, yeah ride on, sister. Here, thought yah sick with the flu? You're very pale."

"It not da flu, Philli. I got da drugged by Harry Hanlon. Da cops have him in the clinky."

Philli couldn't believe her ears. "I frigging knew that dude was a flake. I told Mr Siminion I didn't trust him. Sit down, girl, I'll get yah a drink and you can tell me everything."

Luca did and Philli was speechless. "That Goddamn perv. I'll fucking swing for him."

Luca's cell went. "Dat be Bobby. He acting like da big sheep dog around me."

"And thank fuck for him. I owe him a mega drink."

Luca answered then gasped in shock. "Harry, vot you doing? You drugged me bad."

"You forgive me for getting you arrested," amazed.

"You love me and wanna start again," flummoxed.

"Harry, dar never was a start. I hate you," she shouted, then listened in disbelief. "You vant me to come and spend da Christmas at your home? I don't tink so, Harry. I am hanging up now. Do not ring me again."

He rang back five times before she turned her cell off. "I guess I have da change da sim. New number." Then the desk phone went. She looked at it nervously.

Philli snapped it up. "That you, Hanlon? Luca's not here, now frig off and rot in hell, man."

"You fricking what? You saw her come in? You stalking her, you sad bastard."

"You love her? You date drugged her, you pervert. You stay away from her or I'll fricking swing for yah."

"You'll stick what? Up my what? You sad muvver. One, that's physically impossible, and two, I'm ringing the cops on you, you whacko," and slammed the receiver down.

"Who's handling the case, Lucs? We have to nip this in the bud, kid, to stop it growing into something very, very nasty and creepy."

They rang Annette and Janet. Luca was too upset to speak. Simon Siminion had been appraised of the situation and was horrified. He gave Luca a brandy and rang his attorney at home.

"Yes, I'll tell the Judge what he said to me, Detective Hurst, Goddamn right, I will," raged Philli.

Four hours later they were in the night court. A very sympathetic Judge listened to them and Luca's attorney. There was no sign of Hanlon. The tecs had scanned the borough to serve the writ on him, to no avail.

"Miss Valendenski. I am issuing a personal protection order against Harold Henry Herbert Hanlon. If he comes anywhere near you, he can be arrested and incarcerated straightaway."

"Also a Restraining Order. If he sees you on the street or accidently bumps into you, he must back off straightaway. He cannot telephone you, e-mail you, write to you or communicate with you in any way. If he does, he will be incarcerated for a minimum of six weeks, okay, young lady?"

Luca looked at her feet, "Thank you, Judge, you're ver' kind and I'm keeping you away from your family."

The Judge eyed her, he could see how a man could become infatuated with a beauty like her. "Nonsense, we can't have this kind of behaviour going on, not on my watch. In the old days a man who uses vile language like that to ladies would be horse-whipped. Merry Christmas, folks. Court dismissed."

They trooped out. "We'll serve the papers on him, Luca, and keep an eye out. You be careful."

"Tank you, Annette, Merry Christmas," Luca whispered.

"Come on Lucs, I ain't leaving your side until this things sorted," Bobby announced. "Let's go get a pizza."

* * *

121

February 26th 2013

But things did calm down and Hanlon was neither seen nor heard from. Luca resorted back to her cheerful happy self, and Bobby let the leash out a bit. But she was careful. The few times she dated men, she never let herself be alone with them. Made sure she knew them and never left her drink unattended.

That night she attended the 'Fashion Institute of Technology' in Manhattan for a gala dinner and she was awarded 'The Best Young Innovator' award for interior design 2012 for her work on Ye Olde Bull restaurant.

It was a bittersweet moment, pride in her work but bad memories of Hanlon. She took Constantine from the club and they went in his dad's limo, Bobby and Wendy as guests, much to their delight.

"I could get used to this," exclaimed Bobby, guzzling down the free champers.

After, she let Constantine kiss her on the apartment steps and paw her breasts for a bit before shooing him off home with a carefree laugh.

She knew he wasn't Mr Right and wondered wistfully if Mr Right was ever going to come along.

Across the street Handsome Harry Hanlon watched from a shop door. "Soon, Luca kid. Soon. I'm all juiced up for you, so I am. You'll pay bitch... You'll pay hard."

Luca shivered and fled back in tired, rushing through the empty hallways to the safety of her apartment.

Things were very soon going to get down and dirty, and Luca was going to need all the help she could get.

Chapter 11
The Green, Green Grass of Home
('Tiger Feet'...Mud...1976)

They clattered up the high street, laughing and joking nosily like school kids, her shoulder bag swinging in step to their stride. Jamesey had bought it yesterday in Next for her when shirt hunting. Real leather. She soon had it filled with essential bots and bobs a chic girl about town needed when walking out with her boyfriend.

After battering Barry, the drink had flowed, and Collette had drunk more than her usual amount but couldn't have cared less. She was euphoric at standing up to the vile slug, even if it had turned nasty, and a strange creature that had lurked in the shadows of her mind had reared and come to the fore and she realised what it was – self-respect and dignity all rolled into one, and now she had regained some she wasn't going to lose it again.

She pulled a bottle in a brown paper bag out, took a healthy swallow and passed it to Jamesey. "Vodka, I welched half a bottle off Ron. He's pissed at me because Eadie kept topping me up wiv brandy."

He took a nip, grinning. He reckoned Collette drunk would have been a hilarious handful. He guessed he was going to find out later. He was more than half sloshed himself. Passersby looked at them. Some disapproving, some amused.

"Whatcha lookin' at, yah stuck up old cow?" she snapped after a particularly disgusting look from a well-dressed madam with a Pekinese.

"Steady, tigress," scolded Jamesey.

"Snobby old bitch," she laughed, carefree, as he took another swig and passed the drink back to her. "Strange you can drink in public, but it's gotta be outta brown bag."

She put the bottle away and then said cheekily but nicely, "Yer must have bloody hollow legs, luv," she quipped at him. She had somehow got his arm round her shoulder and a slim arm in his coat and around his waist. Her arm resting boldly across the curve of his arse. He was very aware of it. *She was playing the minx today,* he guessed, *Miss Sophistication, look at me, bless her.*

"Guess the bag thing's to stop the 'old soaks'[51] drinking in front of the mums and kids. Makes sense in a way and brown[52] so the cops know whose drinking and can keep an eye on them."

She hopped up and gave him a big kiss on the check, her eyes flashing at him in admiration. They were bright and sparkling with the sun and alcohol. He wanted to

---

[51] Alcoholics.

[52] Watford Council By-laws said you could drink alcohol out of a 'brown' paper bag in public.

dive deep into them. Collette was falling into his every nuance and look now, captivated by his presence; she'd never met any bloke like him before. "He's a one off; they broke the bleeding mould when they made him!" she used to tell her friends later, proudly.

"I never thought of that, Jamesey. You're so fuckin' clever. It's a good thing then, at least the rappers will not be influenced by the alkies."

All the free drinks he had drunk after his joke-telling were sloshing around in his belly like a big wave. "Yeah, well, enough of the fucking and bleeding. From now on I am going to deduct 5p from your tips every time I hear you curse."

She stuck her tongue out saucily, "Bollox! Nothing wrong wiv a bit of bleedin' and fuckin'."

They were looking in each other's eyes. He had diverted them up Church Lane[53] to the public toilets, his bladder felt fit to burst. She blushed a deep red to match her hat and scarf. She looked into his sexy pale blue eyes and thought of remote Scottish lochs for some reason. Distant drums and advancing redcoats entered her mind and she shook her head, Christ, that strong brandy was catching up fast.

"I meant bleedin' well saying' it, not doing it," she recovered quickly.

He smirked, enjoying her squirming against him. "I know what you meant and that's 25. Already," and he went into the gents, leaving her none the wiser of his cryptic remark. She groaned, 25p would get her a packet of king-size fags.

When he came out he saw a group of seven or so young people, dressed in the latest gear, large pointed collared pattern shirts, bomber jackets or parkas, turn-up jeans and Doc Martin 12 lace boots for the lads, long knee-length thick woollen cardigans, pastel blouses and maxi or miniskirts that buttoned up the front and knee-high boots with three inch soles and square ends for the girls.

They were clustered around Collette, joshing her. Several were overtly smoking long joints, the sickly sweet smell of cannabis hanging in the air around them. An attractive girl of twentyish with long, blonde, curly hair was drinking Collette's vodka and twirling her red hat around a finger with her other hand.

"Where yer been. Coll? That pink's bleedin' fading out. We can do yer annuver one – what colour yer like? A nice day glo green a be a class act."

"Ah, fuck up, Susie; you ain't half caused me such bleedin' grief already."

Jamesey got into the middle, waving the smoke away with his hand and grabbing the hat off the twirling finger and putting it back on Collette's head.

"Who you then?" Susie asked with interest. "You wanna drag on a joint? Tune in, turn on and drop out."

"That's 35p now, Collette," he admonished her. She was standing with head hanging down. "And no thanks, miss, don't do that shit, it scrambles the brain," and he shook Susie's hand. "Jamesey John DeJames, now give us that vodka back."

She eyeballed him unashamedly, up and down as he took a swig and passed it to Collette.

"Nice, very, very, nice, 'ere, you wanna hang out with us? We're going up to the park to drop some. Mike's got some blotters[54]."

---

[53] Al Murray, the comedian known as 'The Landlord' was born in the 'Three Bells' pub at the junction of Church Lane and Main Street. Allegedly on the 'pool table'.

[54] Acid drugs soaked onto blotting paper.

Jamesey laughed derisively, "You'll fuck your head up with that stuff. No ta me and Collette's going shopping, isn't that right, darling?"

"You ain't bleedin' going with her are yer? Look at the state of her, she's a muppet."

Jamesey turned to face a tall, pimply yob, "What? You a pooftah, son? Do you not know a good-looking lass when you see one or are you a turd shoveller?"

"Who are you calling a pooftah, squire?" and the lad squared up to him, the others crowding about with menace.

Susie, who was obviously leader of the pack, pushed into the middle, "Leave it out, Dennis, he'll wipe the ground wiv yer." She spun around to him and placed both arms around his sheep-skinned arms, tugging. "Come on, Big Man. Come wiv us, yah can get a drink later and yer never know yer luck."

Collette flew at her screaming, hands raised like talons, "You ain't fuckin' dropping them for Jamesey, you poxy slut," and grabbed the blonde's hair in two hands, pulling and tearing violently. Jamesey caught her round the waist and lifted her off the ground, her back into his chest, causing her to release her grip. Susie fell back on her arse, her legs flailing apart, revealing black tights and knickers.

Jamesey barged backwards through the stunned group so his back was to the toilet wall, keeping his head back to avoid Collette's wildly bobbing one. She was thrashing her legs and flailing her arms demonically, mad as hell, her only intention to get at the blonde bimbo and claw her eyes out. Scared people scuttled and past quickly, faces averted. Bloody yobs. What was Watford coming to?

"For heaven's sake, calm down, Collette. She was only joking. Tactical withdrawal, kiddo."

The group was gathered in a semi-circle aggressively around them and Jamesey reckoned a few flick knives and cutthroats might be produced. Susie burst in, rubbing her tender arse and faced a murderous Collette.

"Friggin' hell, gal...ah was only joking. Gis a break. Sorry about doing the hair, I thought you and me's 'pearly gates'[55], gal?"

"I don't bloody Adam and Eve[56] you at times, Susie. Tryin' to get my man up the 'apples and pears'[57]. You'd give him the 'Pony Trap'[58]. You're a real old 'brown crapper'[59] at times."

Jamesey was lost now on the cockney twaddle but eased his grip a bit on Collette, who had ceased struggling. Letting her stand against him, trembling with rage still. He was very aware of her small breasts squashed against his forearms and her taut arse pressed into his groin.

"Yeah, well, I didn't know he was your guy. Tell you, wot – I'll get you a drink tonight in The Peel. Big Ronnie has music in the lounge on a Thursdays, don't he?"

Collette relented and leaned back into him, swaying. He swore blind she was rubbing her gorgeous behind against his groin on purpose and if she didn't stop, he would find himself in an awkward position.

---

[55] Mates – friends.

[56] To believe, or not.

[57] Stairs.

[58] Clap...Gonorrhoea

[59] A slapper – A slut.

"Yeah, well, okay and sorry for pulling yer noggin. Yer won't get in if yer stoned up, though. Big Ron and Eadie will put yer out. We don't tolerate drugs in The Peel."

"Thank God for that," and Jamesey marched her away by the hand, 'tout suite'.

Susie and the gang watched them go, "See yah tonight, Collette." She turned to her mate, Sharon, "Ow dah frig, Coll pull top notch like that? He has me 'dream topping'[60]." She had noticed his semi-aroused state and envied Collette. He was a big man in every way. She wouldn't mind 'climbing his steeple'[61], one bit.

Sharon giggled. Her eyes glassy. "Don't think I'll get in The Peel tonight, Susie. Let's go Littlewoods and half inch[62] something nice for you to wear later."

* * *

"How much do you owe me now then?"

They had found a bench on the frosty grass by the church.

"20p, cos every time you cursed, it's 5p off and you swore three times. Quid pro quo."

He was impressed, "How'd you know Latin, then?"

She tittered, "Heard it on Rumpole of the Bailey[63]."

She was calm now and had insisted on sitting on his knee. She watched him warily, not knowing if he was annoyed with her or not. He smiled and stared back at her. She was as light as a feather, but when she had flown at Susie, it had taken a considerable part of his strength to restrain her.

"Fair do. You know, Collette, if I duffed every guy in the bar who chatted you up, I would be doing time in the Scrubs[64]."

She liked that, "Would yah go to the pokey for me then?"

He said nothing, just wrapped his arms tighter around her.

"I'm sorry, Jamesey. That Susie just gets me bleedin' goat[65]. Anyhow, I don't reckon she'll wanna 'rough and tumble'[66] wiv me after that, do yah?"

God, she was a class act! "Guess not. Not if she's any wit. You scared the crap out of her. And me," he added.

"5p – crap."

"Negated. You said 'bleeding'."

She stamped her foot, annoyed. Her toes peeking out from the awful platform shoes were white and cold, and she was shivering as the afternoon light faded. She cupped his face with her gloved hands and gave him a lingering kiss, her tongue probing his. He was lost in her lips, in just her pure essence. The TUF factor working on him, confusedly, its hold becoming harder and harder to break. She pulled him up.

---

[60] Sexually turned on. (Sopping)

[61] 'Climbing his steeple' – To have sex.

[62] To steal. To 'pinch'.

[63] Courtroom drama on television.

[64] 'Wormwood Scrubs'. Maximum security prison in London.

[65] Gets in my throat…to annoy.

[66] 'Rough and tumble' – To fight.

"Come on, babe, you'll be getting 'Chrissie Lloyds'[67] sitting on a cold park bench too long."

He followed her meekly, her dragging on his hand. He hadn't a clue what 'Chrissie Lloyds' were, would have to ask Ron. He took her into Top Girl on the High Street and choose her a lovely thigh-length dark thick woollen jacket with a square collar. All the rage at that time.

"Jesus, Jamesey, you don't have to do that." But he could see she adored it and he put it with the counter girl and turned and studied her before searching madly through the racks. He hated clothes shopping and wanted to get out as quick as possible.

Plus he was hungry and he wanted a good plateful of high cholesterol food, so he could get through the next part of the drinking day.

He glanced at a happy, tipsy barmaid and another desire gripped him. A desire to please and spoil her and make her happy in every way. Every way.

At the start of the sixties, end of the mid-seventies, the miniskirt came into fashion in a storm of condemnation from the church, politicians, the Women's Institute and anxious fathers but much to the delight of the young men and Casanovas of the day. Singers like Sandie Shaw and Lulu showed their lovely legs on 'Top of the Pops' and when Abba came on the scene, the men were bewitched by the blonde Agnetha and the auburn Anni-Frid.

In to the mid-seventies, the maxi skirt came in. A full-length skirt that brushed the ankles, some even covering the feet, much to the relief of many, including some sections of the young ladies, who were sick of freezing their asses off. Also the midi came in at this time, a cross of the two, normally worn with a suit. The skirt coming down to the knee.

Jamesey picked her a nice beige linen midi suit. A pair of stonewashed Levi's with frayed bottoms and a thick tan belt and a red frilled blouse to go with the suit and a couple of warm jumpers. He thrust them in her hands.

"Here, go try them for size."

Collette's eyes were agog. She was visibly excited but wanted to keep her self-respect. "I can't, Jamesey, I really can't. It ain't right."

"'Course you can. I've to pick up a big Yankee win from the bookies," he lied and spun her round, slapped her bum and pushed her towards the changing rooms.

"I'll pay yer back out me tips," she shouted back as she skipped happily away.

The counter girl, a sultry redhead called Karen was amused, "You treating your little sister then?" No way was this big well-dressed hunk of a man going out with that girl. She believed she was a good judge of men, but couldn't know that when it came to women, Jamesey did not conform to normal expectations. He was a unique man and didn't comply unless it suited him. There were enough rules and regs in the army to obey and he tried to bend them all the time.

"Something like that, love. Time she got some new gear."

"Gosh, wish I'd a bruv like you. Mine's as tight as a duck's arse and that's watertight."

Jamesey laughed, liking the girl, "Yeah, well, Collette's like a duck too. Calm and serene on the surface but paddling like crazy underneath. So if you could go and give her a hand to change, I'd really appreciate that."

---

[67] Lady champion tennis player.

"Yeah, sure, be my pleasure." She bustled off, wondering if she could get his phone number.

After a lot of swapping and changing, she was a petite size eight and Jamesey had picked a twelve, Collette shyly modelled for him, and he thought she looked stunning, especially in the suit. He thought there was a resemblance there to a young Audrey Hepburn.

"Right, get them jeans and a jumper on, and we'll ask the nice lady to put the crocodile suit out to pasture."

Collette went off coyly and Karen laughed, "She's such a sweet little thing."

Jamesey grimaced, "You really, really don't know her. Do us another favour. Would you get a few packs of undies and stuff? He blushed. "You know, tights, socks, boulder holders."

Karen went to do his bidding and he went to the shoes and got her a knee-high pair of black fashion boots, a pair of brown Doc Martin's and a pair of four inch stilettos. He judged her as a size four and he was correct. Infantry soldiers were good at judging foot size; feet being crucial to the job.

When Collette came out, he sat her down on a chair, took her platforms off gingerly and tossed them to Karen, "For the scrap heap, pet?" He knelt and eased a knee high pair of white socks up her dainty calves and put on the Doc Martin's and laced them army style for her. She watched, content, liking his competent touch on her leg and the spoiling.

At the counter she put her new coat on, dazed, and he grabbed a handful of cheap fashion jewellery off the spindle rack on the counter. Necklaces, tawdry finger rings and earrings and added them to the mix as Karen bagged and totalled.

Collette put her hat and scarf on and said, bemused, "I feel like Eliza bleedin' Dolittle"[68] and they all chuckled.

"5p," he winked.

Jamesey paid with his American Express card, mentally crossing his fingers that he had enough on his account, and relieved when Karen, after phoning, gave him the slip to sign. They gathered their purchases up, and he left Karen a fiver tip, which was a day's pay, much to her delight. She watched the couple wistfully as they left. Lucky cow!

They went to Littlewoods cafeteria for plaice, chips and peas, washed down with strong tea that Jamesey surreptitiously topped up with vodka to end the bottle. They giggled and chatted quietly, thick as thieves; Collette kept stroking his hand and played footsie under the table with him. At one stage she stroked up his thigh and when she got too high, he stopped her.

"Easy, tigress, you might pick off more than you can chew."

She winked sexily, "Mmmm – chew… I like chewing. It turns me on. Can I have a hot dog later? A big, long, hot juicy one?" She gazed at him with pouted lips and innocent eyes provocatively.

He felt himself stiffen. She was still half pissed, he excused her, but loving her wicked sense of humour. "Have to see if hot dogs are on the menu later," he replied, still tipsy, then guffawed at his own bravado.

---

[68] Film in the fifties with Rex Harrison, who turns a prostitute into a lady.

128

They stopped at the photobooth by the door and got a sheet of six photos done in the automatic machine, pulling faces, kissing and putting their noses into the lens, like teenagers. She made him sit still and be serious for the last two.

"Yer can take one back to barracks and show the boys the super young catwalk model you pulled."

He laughed and slapped her rump. She liked it and felt a stab of warmth down below her, pants moist. She had heard the married women in the lounge sniggering about their husbands liking a bit of 'slap and tickle' and guessed it meant a spanking and wondered what it would be like in a loving relationship.

Her dad used to whoop her across the bare arse with a belt, leaving welts and her bruised and crying in agony. She gazed at Jamesey as they waited for the pictures to drop into the slot. She knew with total certainty and female clarity that the 'Big Man' by her side would never lift a hand to her, unless she asked him. She pondered things she had never thought about before, intrigued by the images in her head.

It was after seven and Collette rushed through to the back of the pub with her bags to confab with Eadie, her lovely eyes aglow with excitement. Jamesey claimed his stool and drank down the pint Ron gave him, gratefully.

"What's Chrissie Lloyds, Ronnie?"

"Oh, yah mean Nobby Stiles[69], Jamesey. Bunches of grapes."

"Do I?" perplexed he drank more beer, "All you cockneys are mad in the head."

"We're a unique breed," agreed Ron.

II

Later Ron was saying to Jamesey, "Gawd's sake, man. Now Eadie's seen all Collette's new clobber, she expects me to take her out tomorrer to buy her a new outfit," he paused, "A landlady in my position has to look good for he punters or standards will slip," he mimicked in a high voice.

Jamesey smiled, "Sure, she's worth it. She's a cracker, is Eadie. Damn beautiful when she dresses up." He had heard her sneaking in from the lounge to listen to Ron and reckoned he could score a few brownie points, even a free pint.

"Aye. She's a good ol' gal. A man couldn't get a better 'trouble and strife'[70]. She's a treasure." Ron grinned. He had heard her as well, Jamesey guessed.

Eadie clattered in and stood by Ron as if she had just come in as normal.

"Go pull Jamesey a pint on the house, love, and get yourself a double Bell's on me. We'll enjoy the music tonight and have a few and relax."

A beaming Ron went to do her bidding. She chuckled, "Yeah, I heard all his ol' guff. He's not a bad 'un."

"He's a true gent, Eadie. 'True Blue'[71] so he is," he agreed.

Eadie mused; maybe if Ron behaves, he might be on a promise later tonight. Having a young woman in love around the bar dropping hormones all day was starting to affect her libido. She said, "You know young Collette's over the moon, doncha? She's up on me bed having a cry."

---

[69] Manchester United and England footballer.

[70] 'Trouble and Strife' – The wife.

[71] Top class

Jamesey squirmed, "Yeah, well, she deserves a bit of spoiling and when I'm 'flush'[72], I like to spread it about."

Eadie held his hand thoughtfully. "You know, don't string her along. Young women her age fall in love for what they think is life and most end up getting brokenhearted."

He wasn't used to this type of talk. He was more used to the rough barracks humour and the tough women who frequented the bars in Aldershot, where the paras were based. Gang bangers and Sanger bangers who hung around the guard posts. Hard girls but demanding, who took a strange pride amongst themselves in shagging as many soldiers as possible.

"Dunno about her loving me, Eadie, but I'd never hurt her. I've made it clear I'm only back for a few weeks leave. Don't need complications, do I?"

Eadie patted his hand affectionately as Big Ron came back in with their drinks, "I know you won't, Jamesey. Thank you. You're a gent."

Collette came in and gave them a smile, clear-eyed now, and bustled around clearing the glasses and accepting the locals' wolf whistles as if it was a normal occurrence and they liked what they saw. Eadie looked at him, eyebrows raised.

"Scrubs up well, don't she?"

Jamesey's eyes nearly popped out of his head. She was wearing the red blouse that he saw was very thin and transparent, with a black bra underneath, the jeans and the killer stilettoes.

Her hair was washed and gleamed under the light, and she had blue eye shadow, mascara and shiny lip gloss. She looked ravishing but what pleased him most was she looked happy and confident. A woman in her own right, free to come and go as she pleased without fear or favour.

She flounced past the table where Slimy Barry had sat and put a quizzical look on her face and a finger quizzically up, "Something's wrong; something's amiss. That fat wanker Barry's not out on the piss."

The punters chortled uproariously, "Oh, I forgot. He'll be sucking food through a straw and pissing into a glass bottle for weeks," and she flounced off again to wolf whistles and shouts of mirth. She was mugging it for all its worth and loving it and so did they.

Jamesey agreed. He thought she was the most beautiful thing he'd ever seen. What the fuck was he to do about it?

"She looks like dynamite," Ron commented, quoting a line from a 'Mud' song.

"Yeah, well, watch it don't all blow up in your face, Jamesey," said Eadie, face inscrutable. "You either give her your all, mate, or break it off tonight before it's too late."

* * *

A three-piece band played in the lounge bar that night. A guy on electric guitar, one on a keyboard and a smooth operator of a singer with a fake tan dressed as Tom Jones. Ruffled shirt, pomaded hair, gold medallion, the whole shebang.

Eadie and Loiuse, the night girl, looked after the lounge bar and Ron did the public bar. Collette flitted between the two, collecting glasses and tidying up with a

---

[72] Got money on the hip.

happy, carefree grace. Life was good in her own little world; in fact, it was fucking incredible when Jamesey was there.

The lounge filled up, mainly married couples and rowdy women who had left the hubby at home to watch the kids. But also a smattering of single men leaning on the bar on the prowl for a bit of 'strange'. Then band started off with a Tom Jones number 'Delilah', then he sang Elvis 'Guitar Man' and 'Hound Dog'. They were good and the crowd cheered and sang along and a few couples danced; the atmosphere was convivial.

Jamesey drank steadily, catching Collette's smiles at him as she moved to and fro. She blew him a kiss, which he plucked out of the air. He observed the single guys watching her but wasn't worried. Those beautiful eyes were for him only.

Collette's friends came in and took a table, Susie waving at him and he waved back. Eadie went over and spoke to them, and they placed their order and Collette took it over on a tray. She knew Eadie was checking they weren't stoned. Jamesey saw the look of surprise and envy when they saw the new Collette and was pleased for her. Slap it up them. She was her own woman. She would not be going to the Park again and dropping bombers with pervs and dregs again. Not on his watch.

The band struck up Fleetwood Mac's 'Albatross' and she came and took him by the hand, and they danced very, very close, her hands up his back and in the hair at the back of his head. He was very aware of her body pressed against him and the heat of it. She smelled of perfume, he wondered where she got that. The scent was sharp in his nostrils. Very arousing. Her hair smelt of Vosene shampoo. She must have taken a bath.

He lingered over that thought for a while as she pressed her breasts into him, her nipples hard and sharp. He, again, thought what they would feel like, the nubs like bullet heads pressing against his chest. A high-velocity charge of lust gripped, which he tried to shake off. Collette's flirting and trust were really getting to him.

She kissed him when the music stopped, hard on the lips, and went back to her work, giving Susie a bitchy look of triumph as she passed. He sent Susie's gang a drink over, a kind of 'no hard feelings' gesture and chatted to a few of the guys at the bar. They got the message that Collette had eyes only for him, and they quit ogling her. The Big Para was way too hard to get into Barney Rubble[73] with.

They danced again to T-Rex's 'Metal Guru', and she was light and nimble on her feet. They got close again to 'Little Green Apples' and after that bounced about to 'Tiger Feet'. Susie and the gang joining in like a riot, twirling around and stomping their feet.

Jamesey got her a drink after, she wanted a Snowball, and he got Eadie to slip a brandy in and took a whiskey himself, liking the bite of it. The last dance was of course, Tom Jones 'The Green Green Grass of Home'. She wrapped herself around him like a second skin and snogged him, her tongue deep in his mouth, what she later called 'a tonsil tickler'. When the song ended, she let go reluctantly and said wistfully, "I could 'ave bleedin' well stood all night snoggin' yah."

He grinned, "5p, but the feeling is mutual."

She punched him playfully and whisked off to gather the last glasses as Ron roared, "Time, gentlemen. Pllleeeaase. Have you no bleeding beds to go to?" and chortled his famous landlord's chortle, much to the regulars' delight.

---

[73] From Flintstones cartoon – 'Trouble'.

He waited outside for her, having got a bottle of Advocaat on the book for her. He sat with his legs half out the front seat of the taxi, chatting half drunkenly to Clive the driver. He'd had a great night's craic but could see a dilemma ahead. He hoped Collette was sloshed and would just want to go home but somehow, he doubted it. He could plead Brewer's Droop[74], but that would insult the para psyche.

She came out with her bags and got in the back, a little unsteady, he thought. Eadie's words rang in his head and hope rose. Clive drove off.

"Home, my lady, to get yer beauty sleep?"

"His house, Clive. What 'bout that Bob Marley and 'Buffalo Soldiers'? Class song or what?"

Clive agreed mightily. Jamesey turned to Collette, "We'll drop you off, babe. Sure, I've only a sleeping bag. Where you gonna kip?"

She looked at him as if he was mad, had just grown another head and both were bleeding, as did Clive, a look of utter disbelief on the big Rastafarian's face.

"It ain't a problem, luv. Eadie lent me her airbed," and tapped a bag, "It's got a foot pump an' all."

Then he just had to laugh. She was certainly resourceful.

"Hey, that Eadie's one kinky lady," said Clive, and he and Collette laughed loudly together. Jamesey sighed drunkenly. *He will follow where I lead.*

He gave in to the inevitable "Home, McDuff, and don't spare the horses."

She looked delighted and wriggled about the seat to the radio's music before suddenly going still and gazing lovingly at him. He observed her sit in the darkness and met her eyes in the mirror. She was as immutable now as some sacred beautiful Indian goddess. Streetlights flashed intermittently across her face like a kaleidoscope, like an old black and white film showing her face frame by frame. He had never seen a more mysterious pair of female eyes as he steadily kept her gaze on his. Absolutely no need for any words between them.

Clive, normally a gregarious type of guy who liked to chat to his fares, could sense the sudden charged tension between them and knew something was about to start. Honkies needed to chill out more and become sexually liberated. Up the Ethiopian birthrate. No muff too tough in Africa.

Collette watched him intently. She could comprehend, under his easy going exterior, that he was uneasy and she knew why and was intent on putting him at ease. She knew she was in control now. He was snagged in her snare, wrapped up tight in her strong gossamer web of desire. She loved him and she wanted him and she was going to have him, and she was just totally focused on the next few hours ahead. She would make sure she gave him a night he would never forget and sod the morrow, it would look after itself. Carpe diem.

She smelt old fag smoke in the car, the harsh alco fumes dying on their breath, Clive's aftershave, something tangy and exotic, even a whiff of cannabis. Clive must park up between jobs and have a joint or two she guessed. She could smell the engine oil, its hot odour coming up through the transmission, and the scent of the pine air freshener shaped like a Christmas tree and hanging off the interior mirror. But most of all she smelt sex. Impending sex to come. No, she decided, two people falling in love who were about to embark on and cement their relationship by making love with each other.

---

[74] Too drunk to get an erection.

In the body heat of musk wafting from Jamesey and in the wetness between her thighs. In the deepest parts of her, the parts she guarded and protected instinctively, over time, and only ever given out on a few occasions, at times of her choosing and when she played with herself, in the lonely hours, falling asleep unsatisfied and lonely. Tonight she was going to give them to this beautiful, big, strong, decent, thoughtful man and give him something he would always remember, and if that was all it was going to be, just a few precious hours, then so be it. Collette would accept that and cherish this time forever just for the sheer Goddamn privilege of going with him for at least one fantastic time. She had never felt so tuned into another human soul. It'was surreal. It was surely God-given from the beautiful head angel she couldn't name, but she was sure it was meant to be. This was going to be a landmark event in her young life.

Clive pulled up at Jamesey's and their eyes unlocked. She saw a pleasant new semi, three bedrooms, he had told her. Their upper half clad in white sparkling horizontal wood and a small open porch with the outside light on bracketing the frosted glass front door.

"Home, folks. You left your light on, Jamesey."

"Security, mate, keep the bentsgers away."

Something stirred in her breast, warm and comforting. 'Home'. Her eyes moistened, she actually did feel as if she was coming home, that she was approaching the end of a long, dark, lonely road and bright, welcoming hearth light was waiting to envelope her in its loving embrace. An emotion she never had before, had been deprived of. The safety and security that should have been hers as a right as a child cruelly stolen off her by self-serving, callous parents…

Chapter 12
Violent Intruders
('I Need a Hero'...Bonny Tyler...1977)

New York, First Sunday in March, 2013 – 10.54pm

She had changed into a light pair of rose-coloured pyjamas and looked as pretty as the drawing of the pirouetting ballerina she was working on at her drawing board in her living room. Her brow was furrowed in concentration as she drew adroitly with pastels, gradually shaping and defining the imaginary figure of the graceful lead dancer.

The buzzer on her front door beeped three times. She walked down the hall, opened the door wide and found her friend and neighbour Wendy Havilland standing there dressed in a white terry robe, her curly hair backlit by the dim hall lights.

"Got ya pizza, Podnah, Bobby took a mad fit and drove to Grimaldi's under Brooklyn Bridge for deep pan."

"Ah tank you, Vends, pizza my favourite snack da, you so ver' kind."

Wendy brushed past her and plonked herself on the sofa. When she opened the box, a rich aroma of food filled the room, and Luca's mouth watered as she poured Wendy a glass of Chardonnay before grabbing a slice and munching into it happily. God, pizza was so USA and free of restraints. It was the edible musical feast of Elvis Presley, Buddy Holly and Frank Sinatra rolled into one food symphony, totally U.S. of A.

"Big gahoot always buys too Goddamn much, he's afraid they'll run out and he won't get his fair share."

Luca laughed through a mouthful of pizza, Wendy was a riot, she was always complaining about Bobby but they adored each other despite being an unlikely couple. Luca wondered what it would be like to be one half of a full on loving scene like that but thought it unlikely in the foreseeable future. Until she was fully established in her career and had saved enough to bring her family over and get them settled, romance was not high on her to-do list. Galen briefly crossed her mind and she sighed, things might have been so different if not for an Italian anti-personnel mine half the size of a cola can.

She was brought out of her daydream by Wendy prattling on about her husband, "Wotcha think, Luca? The big gahoot got seven different toppings and Grimaldi's ain't cheap, ya know. With his work all but dried up, we have to tighten our belts or we'll be down the Swanee, but he reckons not when it comes to pizza."

Luca digested this along with her food, she was still trying to get the meaning of many things Americans said to her but she got Wendy's gist. "You ver' lucky to 'ave da big strong man to drive all that way to buy his chick pizza, it romantic, I think. He da bestest guy." And she meant that. She adored 'Big Bobby'.

Wendy eyed her thoughtfully then laughed, she knew Luca was lonely but wouldn't admit it. She worked too hard and shunned any hint of a relationship starting. She had teased the truth about Galen's tragic death from her over a bottle of tequila, and she felt for her buddy who was still hurting even if she didn't realise it. Wendy reckoned a nice man who could rock her world both in and out of bed would be the making of her friend but Luca was an idealist and was waiting for Mr Right; God only knew when he would come along, if ever. Although she loved Bobby, she was a pragmatist and didn't believe in the 'perfect man'. She could see the faults in people and so long as they weren't harmful or dangerous, she accepted them for what they were.

"Yep, I guess yer right, Luca, he's a big guy in every way and I wouldn't change him for The Empire State Building," she laughed, "Well...maybe Trump Towers, hon."

Chewing, Luca mused, why would Wendy swop her pal Bobby for a building?

She swallowed and wiped her full, sensuous lips with a tissue. "Da, Bobby da coolest dude, anyway, Vends, I met a man on Friday and we had breakfast together. Vas very pleasant. He vey handsome, da?"

Wendy was standing scrutinizing Luca's drawing; the girl was such a talent, "Whatcha mean breakfast? Who is he, babe? What's he do? Goddamn it, you're a dark horse," she feigned shock but was really thrilled for her pal. "Holy crap! This was worth the visit or what?"

Luca laughed and clapped her hands with delight, "I only met him, Vends, he lives on da fifth floor. We ate at Mama Jocelyn's and he walk me to work." Wendy demanded details and Luca told all.

Yep, the girl seemed keen, maybe there was a glimmer of light in Luca's dark tunnel of love. She grinned to herself at the simile and a crude thought crossed her mind.

"'Kay, kiddo. Leave it to me. We'll arrange a foursome and I'll vet the mother for ya."

"But he might not even like me, I don't vant ta scare him off and vey you need da vet?"

It was too much for Wendy. She looked at the beautiful young woman in amazement, "For Chris' sake Luca you're a dude magnet. Does he walk with the aid of a guide dog and use a white stick? Is he like mentally deficient when it comes to scoring with Russian women?"

"No, Vendy," a confused Luca retorted, "I think he has all the facilities. He is so, so good-looking."

Wendy rose to leave, "Then it's settled, hon, he has sight, he's a man...he'll be looking into your drawers. They are all the same, one track minds. You keep them closed and locked tight like Fort Knox until 'Big Bobby' and little ol' me suss the dude out...'Kay...? Night honey."

"Vy he vant to look in my drawers, Vends?" asked Luca innocently.

Wendy headed down the hall, "Yah knickers, Luca, he'll be looking ya to drop 'em," and she laughed uproariously. Luca was so naïve at times; it was endearing but so un-New York. "Have to go, kid, early start." She closed the door after her, shutting off her laughter.

135

Luca went down the hall and put the chain on the door, smiling, she liked making her best female friend in the whole world happy. *Look in my drawers...drop my knickers. Why not just say he would like to get me into bed and be done with it?* she wondered and went back to her drawing, pleasantly replete and getting nicely tired, ready for her lonely bed.

She would go to bed soon, alone. An image of her and Robbie waking up together one day in the future invaded her thoughts and made her tremble as long fingers of excitement probed her nether regions. She shivered deliciously, the time was 11.25pm.

* * *

11.28pm

Hanlon peered around the corner of the landing from the top stair, he grinned down at his two partners in crime and gave the thumbs up. Breaching the apartments had been easy as security was a farce. Mr Chin locked the big glass doors at 11.30pm and the residents used a simple intercom system for any visitors who called after then. They had sneaked in through the back service door that the slit eye never locked until twelve with the bins.

He smiled evilly at his cohorts, excitement coursed through him like a rich tonic...at last he would have the Russian bitch that had thwarted him for so long. He had played this scene over and over in his head and was panting in anticipation as he had watched the blonde woman leave a few minutes earlier and head to her own apartment further up on the right, facing the front.

Billy Crichton gave him the thumbs up. A small but powerful man, in his mid-thirties and prematurely bald, he had worked for Hanlon for several years as a general dogsbody. Socially inept, and a failure with the fairer sex, he hung onto his master's coat-tails and was happy to receive his unsavoury cast-offs. All the same he felt uneasy tonight, Hanlon wasn't normally so overt in his criminal activities but the boss was fixated on that Luca bitch. He looked down at Arturo Calvos who shrugged. 'C'est la vie.'

Calvos was a lean man in his thirties with beady eyes set in a ferret-like face. He wore his grey hair long and pulled back in a ponytail. A psychopath, like his boss, he had done several stints in prison for rape and sexual assault and was on parole after his last escapade with a French tourist. He knew if he was caught again, it would mean a life sentence, but he wasn't really that clever and was easily manipulated by Hanlon, who tended to use him as a whipping boy when things went wrong. Anyway, Harry was so annoyed at the sneaky cunt that he didn't intend to leave her alive to tell any sneaky tales.

He hefted the light tripod with the camcorder over his shoulder and followed Hanlon, as he headed off to Luca's door, halfway up the hall on the left. Hanlon liked to film his sexual conquests, it made him feel powerful and as if he had achieved something of merit. Watching his movies sure beat the reruns of Friends or Frazier, although he wondered what the TV psychiatrist Dr Crane would make of his strange hobby.

Luca was working on the ballerina's tutu, biting the tip of her tongue in concentration, when the buzzer sounded again. She sighed and stood, what did Wendy want now? Had she forgotten something or had a row with Bobby? They could be like squabbling children over a sweet at times.

She traipsed down the hall, not noticing the buzzer hadn't sounded three short rings, her and Wendy's security code. She never even noticed the intercom hadn't gone, her mind was so full of the intricate folds of the dancer's costume. She hated being interrupted when in full artistic flow.

She pulled open the door to the full length of the security chain and peered distractedly into the hall. The blood seemed to drain out of her when she recognised her stalker grinning at her. "Harry...vot you doing here?" she gasped, as she gathered her senses and tried to slam the door. A heavy fist crashed through the gap and caught her high on the left cheek, crunching bone. Her vision exploded in a phalanx of stars and she fell backwards, stunned, shocked and in disbelief.

Her years or rigorous training paid off, and she was still fit and quick; she changed the fall into a backward roll, leapt up and raced for the living room as Hanlon put a heavy shoulder to the door, snapping the light chain. The three men rushed in like evil carnivores chasing a wounded deer, Arturo pushed the door closed after them, not waiting for the lock to click. He was keen for his share of ripe female flesh.

Luca slammed the living room door and grabbed the phone off the small table beside it. Wendy had told her to buy a cordless that she could carry around and take to bed with her but she had seen, and fell in love with, a dial phone from the seventies. She cursed in Russian and had barely dialled the nine when Hanlon came charging through the door, nearly knocking her over again. He reached for her as she stumbled backwards but she nimbly avoided his grasp and regained her balance. She turned right and ran down the short hall to her bedroom, slamming that door too. Fuckski, was she dreaming?

She leant with her back to the door and wondered where she had put her cell phone; she was so careless at times. Hanlon was hot on her heels and hit the door, it opened nine or ten inches before she exerted her weight and it snapped shut with a thud. She knew she couldn't hold him for long, so she screamed. Her face smarted where he had punched her and her eyes watered. Please, somebody help her.

Through blurred vision she spotted the elusive cell on the windowsill beside the bed, she screamed again but knew it was useless because the apartments were thick-walled, well-insulated and double-glazed. Her bedroom window looked out over a passageway that backed onto a shopping complex and, being a side apartment, she had no immediate neighbours. She was a deer trapped in a cul-de-sac and savage hunters wanted to impale her gentle flesh as they snapped at her heels.

"Open up, Luca, or I'll take the door off its frikkin hinges. No escape from Harry, you bitch."

Luca's mind raced, "Vot you vant, Harry?" All she needed was half a minute to get to her phone, dial 911 and, if she could smash the window with the bedside locker, yell for help.

"Ya know what I want, babe. I wanna make ya a movie star. You'd be famous, honey pie," and he sniggered with that heehawing horsey bray. "The new Marilyn Monroe, but not for long."

She shuddered. The detectives had told her about his perversions, and she was terrified but she gathered up a deep inner resolve and, saying a silent prayer and with one eye on her phone, she tried a last desperate gambit. "'Kay, Harry. Sounds like fun, da. Give me a minute to put something nice on, da."

Hanlon chuckled nastily, "Holy cow…see guys she can't resist me. One minute, honey, then we'll huff and we'll puff and we'll blow the door down," and he laughed like a braying horse again.

Luca's blood ran cold as she ran across the room, crept quietly over her queen-sized bed and grabbed her cell. Her thoughts were troubled; he wasn't alone; what kind of sick pervert was he? Why hadn't she got a lock fixed to her bedroom door? This was New York and not the relatively crime-free Drasnov Valley. She had sat and watched American crime movies with her girlfriends, The Boston Strangler, Son of Sam, Silence of the Lambs and others like them and they had laughed through their terror, never imagining it could happen to them. Reality could be a kick in the teeth and it was here now. And reality was kicking hard and with extreme viciousness.

She pressed the on button… Nothing happened… No light came on; she had forgotten to put it on charge. Her heart raced and she felt icy fingers of terror claw down her scalp and spread horribly through her body as the door was kicked wide, and Harry stood there, wearing a long black and white herringbone trench coat and a dark suit, in all his horrifying glory, a salacious leer plastered across his foul face. "Showtime, Miss Bo-Peep."

"You are one lying, sneaky cunt," he yelled and bounded over the bed grabbing her lovely hair and yanking viciously. As she landed in the gap between the bed and wall and his heavy, steel-shod leather brogue caught her below the left knee and ran down the length of her shin, peeling skin, before stopping at her ankle. "Fricking try and call the cops on me, bitch!" he screamed in her face as she flailed at him with her fists but he was too strong, and he hurled her onto the bed, smacking her heavily around the head.

She tried to crawl away from him but Arturo joined in and held her right arm above her head as he pawed at her breasts and ripped her pyjama top open. He had quickly set the camera up at the end of the bed to be turned on and adjusted when Harry said. He liked them restrained, helpless and cowed before he started shooting, he was a true artist. The top came off with a rip like frying bacon. Billy stepped on her to get to her other side where he grabbed her left hand and pulled it, painfully, up to join the right one.

Luca bucked and kicked out frantically. Hanlon was trying to grab her legs but she was strong and caught him with several kicks to his upper body and thighs. He roared in frustration and caught her right foot in his left hand, "Keep fucking still," he snarled and raising his knee up he stomped down on the bottom left of her belly with his hard shoe. Luca screamed, the pain was excruciating but she rolled to her right with her hips, freeing her left leg. Harry was really annoyed now, he kicked her hard in the lower back and grabbed for her legs again but despite the agony, she carried on kicking. Luca wasn't going to succumb easy for these sad sickies to fulfil their evil game.

138

Arturo had got her thin vest up and put a hand over her mouth. She bit hard into his palm. He roared and punched her in the head before pummelling her breasts with his fists in anger. Billy was egging him on, "Hit the sad bitch. Look at those babies go," before he pushed Arturo away and tried to sink his teeth into her left breast. He missed but got a hard grip on the soft underside of her left breast and sunk his diseased canines in deep, snarling and growling like a rabid dog, which basically was what he was…an animal.

Billy was a biter; he loved nothing more than sinking his teeth into soft, yielding flesh. She screeched in agony before he released her, blood running down his chin, leaving a perfect impression of his teeth below her tortured breast.

Hanlon, meanwhile, had had enough of her flailing legs, "Chrissake, I haven't all night, ya know."

He grabbed her left leg hard, spread her wide and proceeded to kick and stomp her into submission with his left foot on the thighs and belly. Luca was seriously winded, her breath left her with a whump and she struggled to get it back. A glancing blow off her right thigh caught her between the legs and she thought her lungs and heart had quit working as the pain, heavy and brutal, ripped through her lovely young body.

She was almost spent now, her breath coming in small pants and moans. Old prayers came to her mind, and she saw her mother and Dmitri crying over her grave, Galen was standing at the end of an avenue lined with flowering cherry trees in full blossom, his arms open to welcome her to his safe domain. "Come, my true darling… Come down the avenue of sprouting blossom… Grace us with your beauty… Come to Galen… Come to succour and peace."

Tears ran unchecked down her cheeks as she mourned for her lost innocence and for all the poor women who had trod this path before her. Darkness, filled with evil black, long-winged mocking birds, hovered before her eyes as she felt herself slipping and sliding remorselessly down into a pit of foul-smelling, stinking black mud.

11.37pm

Suddenly, the bedroom door swung open with a crashing bang. "So what the fuck is going on here then?"

Luca blinked and gazed through misty eyes at a very angry-looking Rabbie Hamish DeJames standing braced in the doorway. He was absolutely fuming, his fists clenched and obviously ready for war. He looked magnificent in the full force of his battle fury.

Hope blossomed in her heart and careered through her bruised and battered body, and with a last Amazonian effort she broke her arms free and screamed, "Help me, Rabbie…pleesse…in the name of Virgin Mother…please help me."

139

II

Rabbie DeJames entered the apartments and sighed when he saw the 'Out of Order' sign on the elevator. Resigned, he hoisted his rucksack more securely on his shoulder and trudged gamely up the first flight of stairs, his thick rubber-soled boots making little sound on the thick pile carpet on the steps.

It was late and the apartments were quiet, the lighting in the hallways dimmed on the evening setting. It had been a long weekend but very satisfying, he reflected as he trudged up the stairs. All the kids had been tested on the various outdoor activities and passed with flying colours. The weekend had cumulated in a big 'cook out' at his dad's cabin in the Catskills, by way of a celebration. It had been great fun but hard work, but Rabbie revelled in the challenge of helping the youngsters. They were a class act and worth the effort. He had got a great sense of satisfaction seeing the look of achievement on their faces when they got their certificates, and he was proud of them.

He laughed to himself, the young ones had had a complete ball, full of mischief and pleased with their accomplishments, they had run riot and it had taken all of the staff's remaining energy to get them fed and watered and herded onto the bus for the journey back to the 'Big Apple' and home.

After seeing them off and having a quick 'Bud' with Mal, it was now after eleven thirty and he was glad to be almost at his own front door. He had reached the third flight and as he turned right into the corridor that led to the next, and thank God, near the final flight of stairs, his mind was on a shower, supper and bed, maybe a movie on Sky before sleep. Maybe a can of Mex chilli and micro fries. Way to go.

As he passed apartment 3B, he smiled to himself as he remembered that was where the lovely young Russian girl, Luca, lived. He wondered if she was still sitting working on some clever design for a rich client or perhaps in bed resting. The thought of her in bed, horizontal, in some skimpy nightwear, intrigued him and he chuckled, "Down, Rabbie boy," he chided himself. After his last foray into romance, he was still stinging and what would a beautiful young artisan see in a rough, old warhorse like him anyway? Still, it was nice to be able to dream and it didn't cost anything.

He paused as he took the first step up the next flight of stairs, the rucksack strap cutting into his shoulder. He took another step, something didn't feel quite right! He paused and thought, something seemed wrong, but what was it? Still, bed beckoned. He was weary and a full day ahead tomorrow…but sod it…something was amiss, but what the hell was it?

During his times in the Royal Marines, it had been hammered into him time and time again 'always look for the unexpected', even the smallest indication that something was out of the ordinary could be the difference between life and death. Trust your senses, and Rabbie was a guy highly tuned in and switched on. He had seen bloodshed and indeed had shed his own, for Queen and country, just like his father, and his father before and all down the lineage of the DeJames family through the aeons of time.

He shook his head ruefully, this was New York for Christ's sake, he wasn't on active service now but the doubt still niggled in his head. He had seen something out of the ordinary but what was it?

He sighed and turned back, retracing his steps along the corridor, his highly tuned instincts now alive. He reached Luca's door and stopped, God forbid she

140

should open it and find him lurking there, scaring the crap out of her and making him look like some type of pervert.

The door was dark brown, solid mahogany with a small peep hole. New Yorkers liked thick doors and this one looked okay. He glanced down to where the door met the ground and like a light going on in his mind, he realised what had been bugging him. Small twigs burnt made big bonfires.

He went cold as he removed his rucksack and knelt down to examine the slithers of wood that lay on the carpet. They were fresh, the splintered wood gleaming starkly in the dimmed light. Still kneeling, he put his ear to the door but all was quiet, no sound from the television or radio, and there didn't seem to be any movement but he couldn't rid himself of the feeling something was very, very wrong.

He gave the door a tentative push with his fingertips and it swung open without a sound. His senses sharpened and a feeling of menace came over him, and his mind gave him a healthy shot of adrenaline, making his hair stand on end. He put his marine tactical head on…trouble ahead.

He examined the door and it became obvious where the wood splinters had come from when he saw the security chain had been forced and was dangling loosely. Was it a burglary? Where was she? Should he wait and do the sensible thing and retreat and phone the boys in blue…? Naw, feck it, that's what civilians did… He would advance to contact and assess the situation as it developed.

He eased his way down the dark hallway, past the closet and storage space, to the living room door, which was closed tight. Fuck it, Rabbie… Go for it, you wuss.

When he opened the door, he found himself in a brightly lit room that had been beautifully decorated by a feminine hand in bright colours. A large drawing board, with drawings attached, stood on an easel and pens and pencils lay on a table beside it. There was no sign of Luca. Strange. Where was she?

He noticed her apartment had a different layout to his own; another corridor led off from the far right corner and another closed door was at the end of a short hallway in the middle of the wall on his right. The hallway probably housed another closet.

He was trying to decide whether he should call out when he noticed the telephone had been ripped out of the wall and thrown onto the floor. The hair stood on the back of his neck, and he shed all of his civilian persona and went into full tactical mode. Advance to contact and locate the enemy.

He cursed himself for leaving his cell phone in his rucksack. Too many complacent years as a civvy.

He crossed the room to the blue panel door on his right; all his senses were on high alert as he entered the small arched foyer with the closet, as he thought, to his left, and braced himself.

A small slither of light came from under the bedroom door; at least he wouldn't be entering the unknown in darkness, where anybody would have the element of surprise on him. He knew in all probability he had a fight looming ahead of him, but he'd be able to see his foe and assess how best to deal with them. How lethal the measure of the situation would dictate he had no idea.

The sound of a violent struggle and excited male voices, gloating, vicious, crude and crass came from the other side of the door. There was a loud crack of a slap on flesh and a muffled female scream.

Should he go back, get his cell out of his rucksack, dial 911 and leave it to the professionals?

141

Fight or flight?

He adopted a fighting stance…fuck it…he WAS a professional and flight was not in the DeJames vocabulary. If that was Luca in there being attacked, she needed him and needed him right now.

He gripped the ball-shaped brass door knob, turned it and flung the door open wide with a crash. What he saw inside caused the hackles to rise, chilled his blood and turned his fight mode up to the highest notch as more adrenalin flooded his system, and he became once again a lean, mean Green Marine fighting machine.

* * *

He scanned the room and his gaze fell on the queen-sized bed that took up the left-hand side of the bedroom and at this moment contained a semi naked Luca who was being held down by three men. He saw she was bleeding high on the left cheek, bruises were rising and she was in extreme distress.

One guy, in his mid-thirties and slightly built, was kneeling on the bed to her right, holding her arms above her head with one hand and covering her mouth with the other. Another man about the same age was standing in the space between the bed and the window, which overlooked the alley. He was leaning over her, one hand groping her breasts, which were exposed since her white vest was pushed up and bunched under her chin, and the other trying to pull her rose pink satin pyjama top off her left arm.

Rabbie noticed several buttons that had been ripped off it on the bed, glinting opaquely in the light like discarded gems thrown away, carelessly. The air in the room was one of menace and depravity.

The third man, and the one Rabbie judged the most dangerous, also stood in the narrow space between the bed and the wall. Rabbie reckoned he was in his late thirties, six feet or so, well-built and nearly bald, except for a fringe of red hair around his skull. His face was long and vicious, with large yellow tombstones for teeth. Evil radiated from him as his large head swivelled and he locked eyes with Rabbie. His gaze was penetrating, offering a world of pain with no remorse for anybody who stood in the way of him getting what he wanted.

He wore a black and white herringbone coat that came to his knees over a dark suit. He had his right foot on the floor and the other was pressed into Luca's left leg just above the knee, causing her legs to spread wide. In his left hand he held her ripped pyjama bottoms and his right hand was raised in a fist over the desperate struggling girl's flat stomach, ready to punch.

Rabbie assessed and assimilated all this information in less than a second, rage pumping through, tensing up his muscles and winging through his nerve ends as it prepared his body for instant violent action.

"So what the fuck is going on here then?" he growled. "Get your dirty maws off that woman now, you pack of stinking bastards, or by fuck you will rue the day you crossed paths with Rabbie Hamish DeJames, you tossers."

The men paused in their sordid activities and looked at him in surprise. "Butt your arse out of this, buddy, this is a private party. She's my lady, 'kay," the big ugly guy said through his teeth, "Luca likes it rough doncha, honey?"

Rabbie caught her eye and realised he had never ever before seen such a terrified look on a woman's face.

Luca saw her chance and wrestled her arms free from the restraining hand, as soon as her mouth was no longer covered, she pleaded, "Rabbie... Rabbie help me," before breaking out into a desperate scream.

It was time for immediate action and an enraged Rabbie didn't hang about. He ran forward, bounded onto the bed and took off landing full force with a double footed kick to the bald guy's chest, causing the brute to scream out in agony before crashing into the wall and sliding down to the floor.

As Rabbie rose up like a striking cobra, half on the bed and half on the floor, he caught the guy in the corner an almighty whack in the face and was pleased to feel bone break under the impact with his elbow. From his position astride Luca and with one foot on the floor, he delivered a number of blows to the head and face of the last of the villains, causing him to holler and roll off the far side of the bed. With a rush of adrenaline and anger, Rabbie grabbed the man he had elbowed by the hair and the back of his trousers and tossed him across the bed to land on his friend, who was just regaining his feet, and they went down in a tangle of arms and legs, roaring in pain and anger.

"Right, let's be havin' yer, ya pack of scurvy bastards," yelled Rabbie as he bounded back over the bed after them and proceeded to give them the hiding of their lives; enjoying the crack of hard knuckles on flesh.

Luca took the chance to scramble up the bed as far out of harm's way as possible, eyes not leaving Rabbie. He was hard, very fast, supremely coordinated and quite magnificent in his violent disdain for the thugs.

The older man was now up and had ripped the lamp off her bedside table. He climbed on the bed astride Luca and raised the ceramic base to smash into the 'spoilsport's' head.

"Rabbie, look out," she screamed. "He's behind you."

Rabbie pushed the two beaten thugs away and turned sharply. The lamp caught him on the lower left side of his head and neck just as he ducked and it smashed into a hundred pieces, a fine spray of blood misted the air, and Rabbie reeled, stunned, and shook his head like he was drunk. Seeing this Luca raised her left knee up hard between the legs of the slime ball who was conveniently close, and he howled in agony and dropping the lamp retreated back to the floor, one hand clutching his groin and the other fumbling in his overcoat pocket.

He pulled a small automatic out and pointed it, shakily, at Luca's face. "You fucking bitch," he spat as he prepared to shoot.

Rabbie leapt across the bed and grabbed his wrist with both hands and twisted the pistol away and up just as the thug pulled the trigger. Several loud cracks filled the air and the smell of discharged cordite further enraged Rabbie. He wrestled the firearm away from the man and beat him over the top of the head with it in the way cowboys called 'pistol whipping', only stopping when the dark red blood ran in rivulets down the ugly face and he collapsed to the floor, groaning in agony.

Rabbie turned with a growl to the other two intruders who took one look at the angry big man, now holding a gun, and fled from the room, tripping over each other in their haste to escape.

Silence descended and trickles of plaster dust from the bullet holes in the ceiling drifted down to the floor. Rabbie took several deep breaths, trying to get his temper back under control. He made the gun safe and zipped it into a pocket of his fleece jacket before turning back to the bed.

He faced the dazed girl sitting there and could now see she had several injuries, "Luca... Luca, are you okay?" He approached her slowly, not wanting to scare her more than she had been already. She raised her slim, bare arms to him imploringly, "Get me out of here please, Rabbie," she begged.

He lifted her in his strong, comforting arms from the much abused mattress and carried her into the sitting room, where he gently laid her on the couch and piled some cushions behind her to make her comfortable.

"We really must stop meeting like this, Luca," he quipped, "And you never even asked me to the party."

She just gazed adoringly at her saviour in her own twilight world of shock and pain.

III

There was no sign of the other two thugs in the room, it seemed they had fled the building, and the way the couch was placed meant Rabbie could tend to Luca and keep an eye on the bedroom door at the same time.

Rabbie had slammed it shut behind them but he really hoped the thug still in the room would try and make a break for it, because he would seriously like a chance to rip the bastard apart, limb for limb, for what he had done to this beautiful, trusting young woman, who was now watching him closely out of silver-grey eyes that were dulled with pain.

He concentrated his attention on Luca; she was in shock, her breathing was fast and her eyes glassy. He checked the pulse in her long slim neck and found it racing madly. She had a nasty cut on her right cheek bone and her eye was already going black.

As he pulled her vest down he noticed her breasts were bruised and scraped and welts were rising on her upper body; he also couldn't help noticing her breasts were well shaped and above average size. He was sad for her, knowing how young women cherished and looked after their vital assets. Goddamit, what was wrong with these sickies, who wanted to scar and blemish such exquisiteness?

He examined her stomach, which was also abraded and swelling up with the bruising, he was worried now, and although he was a fully qualified medic and kept up to date with all the modern trends as part of his job with OLG, he realised he needed an ambulance. Internal bleeding could kill as quickly as external and was harder to detect.

He decided to end his examination as quickly as possible.

Her left forearm was red and swollen so he gently placed it across her chest, he guessed it was probably broken, "Can you hold your arm there, Luca, and keep it still?"

"Yes, Rabbie," she said and held it with her right hand, still watching him intently, the shock set deep in her eyes.

Would she ever trust a man again? he wondered. Anyway, her reactions told him she was responding, it was good to get the injured person involved as it kept their mind alert and off what had happened to them.

He continued his visual check and saw the nasty looking gash down her right shin that had been caused when the thug had stomped on her leg.

144

"Can you bend your right leg?" she did and he was relieved. He pulled a bright patchwork throw off an armchair and wrapped it around her legs and midriff.

Remembering from his training that you need to comfort and reassure the patient he told her, "I don't think it's too bad, Luca. You'll be okay. I'm gonna get an ambulance...are you in pain anywhere else?"

Tears were now running freely down her cheeks, and she went very, very pale as she answered, "He kicked me...you know...down there. Very, very hard, da?"

Rabbie blanched. What the hell was the world coming to? As soon as he could leave her, he was going in to sort that big bastard out properly. Who the hell did he think he was? Hurting and terrorising this lovely, pleasant young woman. Rabbie was absolutely livid. He wanted to rip the ugly bastard's head off and beat him with it.

As if reading his mind, Luca stroked his arm with her good hand, "He not worth it. You good guy, don't lower yourself, Rabbie." The effort to reassure him seemed to exhaust her and, she slumped back onto the cushions.

Rabbie heard sounds and movement in the hall and, presuming the neighbours were gathering, was about to shout for assistance when a curly haired blonde woman in a fluffy white dressing gown came bustling in carrying a green plastic first aid kit. She stopped dead and raised the kit in front of her, "Oh mah Gawd...Luca...get away from her, mister...right now. Bobby, Bobby...get your Gawd damn butt in here, there's one still here." The accent was pure Brooklyn.

A man mountain rushed in brandishing a baseball bat. Easily six feet seven, twenty stone and rugged. He was dressed in a string vest, shorts and trainers (at least a size sixteen) and made an imposing figure with limbs like girders that rippled with muscle.

"It's okay... Wendy! Bobby! He saved me. Hanlon's still in da bedroom. Dis is Rabbie, da?"

Wendy rushed over, "Outta the way, man, I'm a nurse."

Rabbie let her in and retreated to the chair, his head throbbed, and he could feel the wet blood on his neck, although he didn't think he was badly hurt. The big guy eyed him suspiciously, the bat still raised in a two handed grip ready to swing.

"The cops are coming," he growled, "I told them to bring the medics. I locked the other two dickwads in the janitor's closet...now, time for a chat with horse face...the fucker."

Wendy gave Rabbie a lint pad, "Hold that to your neck dude, you're bleeding."

Rabbie did as he was told. "Whoa...what two, big man?" he asked.

"The two I caught coming outta Luca's apartment, I guessed they were up to no good, so I restrained them," Bobby said smugly, smacking his bat in his hand, "I locked them in a closet for safekeeping."

"Right, mate...great stuff. Guard that bedroom door, and don't let the fucker out until the cops come."

A bat-wielding Bobby marched over to the bedroom door. "Don't you worry, Luca kid, Uncle Bobby's on the grid now," he said as he entered the bedroom and closed the door.

Wendy had one arm round Luca and was looking under the blanket and feeling gently with the other hand. She probed the flesh at the top of Luca's legs and she winced. Luca had been watching Rabbie, and he smiled reassuringly and winked at her, she managed a weak smile back.

He saw the look of distaste that crossed Wendy's face as she carried out her examination and felt sorrow for the young Russian. At that moment he also felt strangely ashamed of his fellow man and his own masculinity.

Once again it seemed Luca read his mind and she reached her right hand out to him, he held it tentatively, strangely reassured. She squeezed his fingers tightly.

"Thank you so much, Rabbie." The 'thank' came out sounding like 'tank' and the 'much' like 'mulch', he had never heard such a sexy accent. She was like a beautiful, fragile princess from a fairy tale.

"Sorry, I never got on the case quicker, Luca, really I am."

She looked him steadily in the eye and he wondered at the loveliness of hers, "I tink maybe you saved me just in the nick of time and for that you are now number one on Luca's 'Gallant Knights List'."

He grinned, quite thrilled at that. This was the second of many times he would hear of her lists. "You really do keep lists about people, Luca? I thought you were only kidding."

She smiled the smile he would come to adore, "Of course, does not everyone? I am from Russia, you know."

Big Bobby came out of the bedroom, closed the door and stood on guard, a smile of satisfaction on his face and still slapping the bat into his palm. "Donkey head ain't going nowhere except in handcuffs and on a stretcher," and he grinned, "Nice bit of pistol whipping for a 'Brit dude'."

IV

Before the police arrived, Luca had introduced Rabbie to Wendy and Bobby Havilland from 3A and told him how they were number one on her 'Best Friends List'. Bobby almost crushed his hand when he shook it. The guy was a veritable 'Giant Haystacks'[75] and Rab blew on his bruised fingers.

Bobby had heard the shots and rushed out, grabbing his trusty 'slugger' in passing. He had bumped into the two bleeding thugs rushing out of Luca's flat and a fight had ensued, which he had ended quickly with a few well aimed whacks with the bat. While he was locking them in the janitor's closet, Wendy had called the police and grabbed her first aid kit before the two of them rushed into Luca's apartment.

Wendy was a senior nurse on the children's ward at Manhattan General Hospital, and Bobby was now a self-employed electrician after serving a ten-year stint in the American Army Engineers Corp, where he had learnt his trade. He had done two tours in Iraq and, when he was liquored up, he liked to say, "Hell, Iraq…sure did Big Bobby help turn the lights back on for those folks." Both in their mid-thirties they had been married for ten years, and he never said anything about the misery and depravation he saw to his Wendy.

"You better lose the bat before the cops arrive, Big Guy, they can be funny about things like that," Rabbie advised as he heard them pounding up the stairs. Bobby quickly hid it in a closet.

---

[75] Famous British wrestler in the seventies/eighties, built like a barn and fair-haired.

The cops arrived in a flurry of blue uniforms and chattering radios and mayhem ensued until two steely-eyed detectives arrived and gently pressed the basic facts of the matter out of Luca and Rabbie.

When the medics arrived, they fussed over Luca and put her on a drip of fluids and gave her a shot of OxyContin before putting her left arm in a plastic splint and a padded sling.

Wendy cleaned Rabbie's head and neck with antiseptic fluid on a cloth. It stung like crazy.

"You're gonna need a few staples in that, man. You were lucky."

"Yeah, Luca warned me just in time. Do you think she'll be all right?"

Wendy lowered her voice as Luca was being eased onto a wheeled stretcher, "That piece of shit stomped her bad. He gave her a kick downstairs, if you get my drift. Thank Gawd you came along in time."

Rabbie hissed through clenched teeth as Wendy applied more of the fluid, "Evil bastard, I should've shot him." Wendy tittered, she liked this cool Brit.

When he had handed the gun over to the cops, gingerly, the two detectives seemed happy enough with his account of events but told him not to leave New York in the immediate future, and he was to hand his passport over whilst they checked on the sequence of events.

The medics looked at his wounds, all on the left side of his head and the top of his neck. "X-rays and staples, dude. Probably a few lumps of china still in there."

It took quite a while and quite a number of cops and medics to get Luca and her stretcher down the three flights of stairs and into the ambulance. The residents watched in distress, patting her hand or stroking her hair as she was carried past them. The always cheerful, pretty young émigré was a popular and valued member of the apartment community. God damn! What was New York coming to? Bring Giuliani back.

Rabbie took time to dump his rucksack in his apartment and grab his passport for the tecs, he remembered to bring his cell with him as well.

* * *

Luca was on the left of the ambulance and Rabbie sat on the bed on the right as a paramedic slapped a temporary dressing on his wound. She held his hand the whole way as they flashed through the light traffic, lights and sirens blazing.

"How you feeling now?"

She yawned and faced him, "Safe and fuzzy."

"That's good then."

The ambulance turned sharply into the hospital grounds and howled to a stop at the entrance to the emergency room…

"Yes, safe 'cause you're with me and fuzzy cause they gave me funny pills," she elaborated.

He squeezed her hand, "I won't let anyone hurt you tonight, Luca."

"Tank you, kind sir," and she closed her eyes.

She had beautiful long, dark lashes, he noticed. In fact, he decided that beautiful was too inadequate a word to describe her at all. Sublimely heavenly, angelic, top totty vied to mind. He imagined her on his arm, all dressed up, going into some swanky restaurant, envious male heads turning, then dancing intimately somewhere discreet.

He smiled at his thoughts. Be nice but the last thing Luca needed was some old has been 'Brit' marine coming onto her, still…you never knew in life what was around the corner.

As the ambulance shuddered to a halt and the attendant killed the engine, silence descended. Luca pulled his hand to her mouth and kissed the back of it with her engorged, swollen lips that made him think of freshly opened rose petals.

"Tank you again so, so much, Rabbie. I tink you saved my life tonight."

He stroked her hair, she looked frightened again, "You're gonna be fine, Luca, it's all over now."

"They will be here as well, Rabbie…getting treatment." She looked hesitant, "What if they escape and come after me?"

Rabbie didn't believe in political correctness. It was all a load of political crap. He just believed you treated people as you expected to be treated yourself, whatever their race, gender, colour or creed.

All this crap from the politicians, social workers, church people and shrinks who made excuses for the criminal fraternity was a load of bullshit.

If you stole a dollar off your pal, you were a thief, simple as that.

As for paedophiles, rapists, child killers and other criminals of that ilk, he had no pity for them. Shoot or drown them all and save the decent taxpayers a shed load of money.

Well, that's how he felt as he sat along beside Luca. He really, really wished he had killed Hanlon and been done with it, and then this charming young woman could get on with her life and sleep easy at night.

The medics opened the doors. "I won't leave you, Luca…but those guys are going nowhere. I'll get a couple of my blokes from OLG to guard you as well."

She looked reassured as they wheeled her out and down on the ambulance lift and pushed her towards the ER entrance, where attendant nurses waited at the door for her.

He walked at her side and she looked up into his face. Her eyes were the colour of a light summer rain cloud, flecked with shades of silver and blue; they were incredible.

"You know, Rabbie, the Enrique Iglesias song 'Hero'? It must have been wrote just for you, because you will always be mine."

Rabbie grinned, "I think the 'happy pills' are kicking in again."

"I don't tink so," she smiled demurely back despite her anguish, "Some tings are soooo so meant to be, my 'Gallant Knight'," and she squeezed his hand and held on tight.

She wasn't going to let go of the powerful comfort of it; anyway, it seemed to fit hers just right. Very compatible.

He walked along beside her, and such an overpowering surge of protectiveness hit him for this young beauty, it made him dizzy and he shook his damaged head to clear it.

He knew with a steadfast resolve that a herd of wild mustangs could not drag him away from her side that night.

Chapter 13

Love at First Stroke... Beanz Meanz Heinz

('I'm Caught in a Trap... And I Can't Walk Out...')
Elvis Presley from His Song 'Suspicious Minds')

Collette got out with a clatter of heels, bags scraping against the car door. Christ, she was near pissed. She tottered down the short paved open-plan drive as Jamesey counted out the fare from a handful of change, tipping Clive a quid.

"Thanks, mon, yer a gent."

Jamesey beamed, "We'll see about that," and went to climb out. Clive paused him with a hand.

"And one very lucky, lucky bastard. Give her one for Ethiopia, my boy. Make Bobby M proud, you honky tonk[76]."

He got out laughing uproariously, "Get away on you, ya silly sod. Away and find somewhere to spark up[77]."

Jamesey staggered up the drive, searching for his keys so he could let Collette into his home. He managed to get the key in the door and opened it up and reached in and flicked the hall light on, then spun around and lifting a squealing Collette, bags and all, into his arms, carried her over the threshold and bounded up the bare stairs with her. If she was determined to let him ravage her and then break her heart, he might as well enjoy it. He was not anything at all but a realist. Carpe diem! If she wanted to seize the day...so be it, but he would certainly give her something to seize. He had the reputation of the paras to keep up and he took that very seriously indeed.

* * *

She came massively with a huge thrust into his groin, and he felt her velvet sheath clutch and tremor around the whole length of his shaft. She rose and bit into his shoulder and clawed his back with her nails, shouted "Bleedin' fuck, fuck, fuck," and lay back exhausted, her eyes rolled up into her head, supine on the pillow, panting through her mouth in small gasps. She couldn't talk or look at him after for fifteen minutes or so and he got worried. She just lay with her legs clasped tight around his waist, eyes closed, watching the dance of light behind her eyelids.

Collette knew it was going to be good but Jamesey had just blown her mind to pieces. She knew she would never be the same again. She was in sexual after shock and it had been seismic. In all her infrequent adult sexually active years, she had

---

[76] What coloured people nicknamed a white man.
[77] To roll and light a joint of cannabis.

absolutely no idea or conception that sex could be so overwhelming. She was in apres-sexual coma, stunned the whole length of her gorgeous, young, active body.

She eventually pulled his worried face down into a slow lingering kiss, when they finished, she took his face in both hands and gazed up at him, in awe and adoration.

"Jesus fucking wept, Jamesey. If that's what they teach you in da army, where the fuck do I sign up?"

He pinched her nose gently, "Don't blaspheme, hon. It was okay then?" male insecurity creeping in.

Collette nodded, "You blew my mind, and everywhere else, you big gahoot."

"Great. Do you want a glass of Advocaat?" and climbed off her, making her fanny burble gently for a few seconds as air escaped. She mourned the loss of his penis in her. Jamesey heard it but being a gent, pretended not to. He thought it was endearing. Made her more human, one of the boys.

Fuck the drink, she thought. She wanted more of his fingers, tongue, lips and big cock!

"How about some slap and tickle? You know? Hanky, panky?"

He was so big, strong and massive, and he loomed over her like a cliff face. "Are you sure? Don't want to hurt you." This was new territory for him and he was unsure of the protocol.

She nodded her assent and looked in his eyes. He saw it was important to her for some odd reason.

He lifted her closed legs up with his right forearm behind her knees and gave her a sharp tap with his left palm across the buttocks.

"What have I told you about blaspheming? Take that."

Collette liked that; she liked it intensely. She wanted more but he stopped and went back to his drink.

"Didn't think you would be into this kinky stuff, Coll."

She pushed him back, "Oh shut yer trap." She knew he was eyeing her ass again. "I'm bad and need a good spank across the buttocks."

He sat on the edge of the airbed. She went and lay across his knee, draped across him, her beautiful arse raised in full view of his hot stare. She heard him audibly gulp.

"Wot 'bout a bit more hanky panky, Jamesey? Real stuff."

He looked again at her gorgeous derriere, quivering now with anticipation. He never guessed the loving sex they had an hour ago would come to this. It was extremely exciting. He stroked the pinch mark and bruise Barry had left. He wanted to be certain. To him she was a lovely fragile bird to be nourished and cherished when it was let out of its cage. Allowed to fly in certain areas but to be contained in others.

"What you got in mind, Collette?" he asked, hesitant, an alien trait to his nature.

She turned her head up to him from his lap with demon eyes, "It's a done deal job, mate. You give me a bit of hanky panky and you get a bit back of wanky."

He placed his right arm across the top of her shoulders and gave her a fairly hard slap across the buttocks, the sound a dull crack.

She gasped and moaned, "More, babe. Harder, more."

He gave her six across the left cheek and six across the right. They bounced. Her arse cheeks flamed a pretty red. In an odd way it was strangely satisfying, but he wondered just who was dominating who?

He decided to regulate his level of pain spanking on a scale of one to ten and would not go over a five, whatever she demanded. He would not hurt her, although he was into it now. Why not? If it pleasured her, it pleasured him. He gave her what he considered a low four, the clap of the smack sharp in the still room. She gasped.

"Oh yeah – mmmm ouch. You get it now, luv. Fuck that makes me horny."

Somehow she'd opened her legs, her left leg nearly draped on the floor. Back arched, she had brought her left hand up under her belly and was fingering herself furiously. As she came, he gave her a few more slaps and she cried out in raw unadulterated passion as her orgasmic juices spurted down her stiff, probing fingers.

His erection was huge and needing attention as it dug into her belly. "You are the dog's bollocks[78], babe. Fair dos."

She climbed off him panting and knelt between his legs and gave him such a blowjob that he would never forget it.

If anything Collette believed in equal rights, in giving back. As he came and filled her mouth with his hot spunk, he reached down in passion and pinched and nipped her bum with his hands as she swallowed his hot seed; she came again, quivering and sucking in air frantically.

"Bend me, shape me, anyway you want me, as long as you love me, it's all right." She sang softly to him after. Content and sated. "Flower power. Make love not war," she quoted.

He laughed, still wondering about this strange sexual interlude.

"Wild thing... Rolling Stones... That's you, Collette."

She squeezed his balls, rolled off and took a big gulp of her creamy drink, "You better believe it, honey."

They lay atop his sleeping bag afterwards. She was incredibly loving to him. Lots of hugs and kisses. She got him a glass of whiskey. She praised his male prowess, how no man had ever made her feel so good and on and on in between sips of creamy Advocaat. She thanked him and he placed a huge digit over her swollen lips, shushing her.

"You don't have to thank me for nothing. There's no debt 'tween you and me. What's mine is yours from now on; whether it's my love or my last fag, it's yours."

She hugged him and silent tears trickled down her cheeks, she felt safe and wanted. He looked into her eyes, the colour of fine whiskey in the subdued light. He saw a new dawn in there as her inner sun arose and broke cover, and he saw she had reached full womanhood and it was an intimate, sweet and cherishing moment.

"And what's mine's yours, Jamesey. I'd give yer my bleedin' heart if yer needed a transplant."

He guffawed quietly, "Don't ever lose that sense of humour, Collette. It's a fine asset and will help you get through this troubled world we live in. Every day is a blessing and something to work on and move forward through as best we can...or so my dear old mum says."

---

[78] The best.

151

She eyed him adoringly, "Yer 'ave always something positive to say, babe," and kissed him for the hundredth time. "And yer mum is a bleeding prophet, so she is." They had a toast to his mum, then their friends and others.

He looked at her carefully, "Err…can you tell me what that last thing was about? The hanky spank," one big eyebrow raised.

She mused for a while, "I dunno…s'pose it's a trust thing. Ain't had much cause to trust anyone yet in me short, sad life. Wanted to see what it was like."

Jamesey understood and his heart went out to her, "So you trust me now, then? I'd never hurt you, darling, or let anybody else. But be careful love. Curiosity killed the cat."

She hugged him again. He licked a drop of Advocaat off her chin with his tongue, relishing the taste of her and the intimacy. He was very, very relaxed now.

"Yeah, well. I wanted to see what it was like, didn't I?" she quipped. "Yer gonna find I'm game for anything, mate. Life's too bleedin' short. I'll try anything once."

He smiled happily down at her, not believing his luck. He'd found his dream woman.

II

('I Thought Love Was Only True in Fairy Tales… The Monkees – 1969)

He left her dozing at seven, tracksuit and Bergin on, and went for his ten-mile tramp[79]. It was the way he was and it sweated the drink out of him.

He ran across Croxley Moor and followed the canal until it reached the River Lee.

He pushed himself hard, vaulting fences and crushing the winter grass as he completed his circuit, passing the Croxley Green paper mill that made the famous 'Basildon Bond' writing paper and sprinted up the steep hill into Rickmansworth.

He realised, through torrents of dripping sweat, that he couldn't wait to get back to his little Collette.

Collette was standing in his kitchen, wearing his red para T-shirt and nothing else.

He admired her slim, supple pale legs admiringly. She had searched and ransacked his fridge and cupboards, and she found one of these new-fangled 'toastie' machines and made a batch of cheese and tomato toasted sandwiches and had a pan of baked beans simmering on his two-ring butane gas cooker.

She was washing up the glasses from the night before, singing an advert from the television, "For hands that wash dishes can be soft and gentle as your face with mild green Fairy Liquid."

She was in a daze. Living a dream and had to keep busy, before she swooned and kept pinching herself to make sure it was real and not a dream.

Collette was deeply in love with 'Big Jamesey' and life was fucking fantastic.

He burst in, dumped his Bergin and crushed her to him, and they went into a sizzling, ear-cracking kiss.

---

[79] What the 'Airborne' call a run and speed march, weighted down, over a distance.

She broke for air, mentally engulfed in his huge persona, "Where were yah, love? You're all sweaty. I made yah toasties and beans."

He laughed, "A million housewives everyday pick up a can of beans and say… Beans mean Heinz," and he lifted her onto the workbench, dropped his trackies and made love to her again.

She was amazed, very turned on. Doing it in the kitchen!!! Standing up. Fuck, why not? This was definitely a class act!

She sang another advert jingle in his ear after he had sated himself and her very pleasurably, "Any time… Anywhere… Any place… That's Martini."

He grinned, "So you're my Martini girl, then?"

"Of course, babe… Ah told yah… I'm game for anything… Now get off me, the foods getting cold."

* * *

He ran a bath afterwards and she jumped in when he got out, had a good scrub and let him dry her hair with his green army towel.

They dressed and he used his newly connected phone to ring 'Whacky' Clive as he called him, to take them to The Peel.

All Collette wanted to do was lay upstairs with him, make love, sip Advocaat and listen to music.

"Hey come on, Collette, routine's important, it's what separates us from the monkeys," and he paused, "Anyhow, tonight's a new night and all the better for the wait."

She ran her fingers up his strong chest, tentative, musingly, "So I can come back tonight, love? I don't want to impose!"

He kissed her on top of the head, "Hey, I told you, my home is your home."

Tears trickled down her cheeks. She would remember this past week her whole life. It would be engrained on her memory like letters carved in granite by a master stone mason.

Whatever the future held, it would be her epitaph of love, hope and a new future.

* * *

Clive tooted his horn and they left.

"Wot yah want for tea tonight, Jamesey? I'll go up the shops and get something nice outta me tips."

He said, half singing another popular advert on the television for the dairy industry, "Cheese please, Louise… No, sod it, we'll go to the Skandia and get a full steak dinner, the whole thing, onions, mushrooms, petit pois and Diane sauce."

She climbed in the back, and he closed the door for her and jumped in the front.

Collette had never had a steak dinner, the nearest she had got to that was a Fray Bentos steak and kidney pie. Her life was opening up big style.

Clive looked at the radiant pair and shook his head, making his dreadlocks rattle. He was pleased for them. They made a nice couple, for 'honkies', and he classified them as blood friends.

Tom Jones was singing 'The Green, Green Grass of Home' on his eight track car stereo system, and Collette was bouncing around on the back seat, dragging on a No. 6[80].

"You okay, sister, you in the grove?"

"Chilled out, Clive, thanks man, me arse a bit sore but it's cool."

Clive stared at Jamesey, who reddened, "She fell on it, Clive. Too much brandy."

Collette laughed, "Yeah, brandy makes yah randy, whiskey makes yah frisky and gin makes yah sin."

The men laughed, "What about the mighty Jamaican rum and vodka, sister?" asked Clive.

Collette laughed, "Too much rum makes yah deaf and dumb, and vodka is a drink for sluts and commies."

Clive laughed and Jamesey was impressed. She was quick and smart, and it was an attribute he was determined to bring out in her; he would plan it like a military mission. She was a natural talent that had not had the space or circumstances to flourish, and it would be a crime to waste it and by crikey he would make sure it blossomed; besides, he fancied the socks off her. He reckoned he had found his soulmate and looked forward to the ride ahead.

Clive pulled up at The Peel, grinning. Their mood was infectious. Power to the people, dudes.

Jamesey paid him handsomely.

"'Ere, Clive, Ronnie's got a three piece on Thursday night. Take a break and bring that Roxy girl up. I get then do some 'Reggie' for yah and a bit of Barry White."

Clive thought that a good idea. No racism in The Peel. "Argh, the heathens Meister Barry White, consider that a date, honkies," and he drove off.

They entered the bar, arm in arm. Eadie took one look and just knew. She just bloody knew… Bleeding Norah. She couldn't wait to get Collette alone and quiz her. The girl was blooming like a new rose that had found a shaft of summer sun. Well fertilised, in every place and sense.

Jamesey took his customary stool, "Right, go you and wash lots of glasses while I demolish lots of pints of Double D."

She took his face in her soft hands and gave him a smacking tonsil tickler, the regulars watching agog. She pulled off with a satisfying squelch, "Yes, master, your wish is my command," and skipped off behind the bar.

"'Ere girl, I want all the horse's mouth[81], you hear me?"

"Later, Eadie, I'm in bleeding shock, ain't I?" then called to Jamesey, "'Ere, love, would yah put a few tunes on the box. Bit of ELO, Sweet and Tom Jones?"

He jumped up, fumbling for change, "Of course, my precious flower."

Eadie's hands were up to her face in surprise, "Gawd luv a duck, Collette, you've got Jamesey tamed."

Collette was filling the sink, "Naw, Eadie, you never tame a guy like that. He's a bleeding tiger," and she nudged her with an elbow, "In every sense of the bleeding word, leader of the pack so he is, but I'm hanging onto his tail and I ain't letting go and I'm enjoying the ride… Well, after last night," and she laughed salaciously, "The

---

[80] Players made No. 6 and No. 10 small cigarettes for the masses. Ten No. 6 cost 12p in 1976.

[81] All the gossip.

rides, the all-night riders." She shouted over to Jamesey, "'Ere, lover, out the Shadows on 'Ghost Riders in the Sky', in memory of Slimy Barry," and the whole bar laughed and cheered. What a dynamic duo!

Eadie gasped and poured herself a port and lemon.

Ronnie came up from the office, "Wot you girls laughing about? And bloody Norah, Eadie, you're drinking port at lunchtime." They grinned knowingly. This wasn't talk for men. They would sort it later over a pot of Rosie Lee[82] and cream cakes.

"Get yourself a Bells, love," Eadie told him. "Every day is a blessing."

So he did. Bloody women. Different planet, different species.

Collette nudged Eadie and said quietly, "'Ere, missus, I might need the airbed for quite a while."

Eadie whispered back, "That's okay, but if it gets a puncture, you can bleeding repair it."

Collette grinned, "I'll buy you a new one, mate. You might not want it back if you knew the things we've done on it."

A shocked Eadie reached for more port.

---

[82] Cup of tea.

Chapter 14
Emergency Room
('When You're Tired and Lonely'... James Taylor)

I

Luca lay on the bed in a cubicle, a young trainee nurse fussing over her, "The doctor will be here soon. She's great," tucking the blanket in tighter under her slim hips.

She was very afraid. She had seen lots of police standing further down the corridor and guessed they were guarding Hanlon and his vicious underlings. She shuddered as she recalled their vile hands pawing and groping at her body and the utter terror that had rose in her as she realised there was no escape. Trapped like a rabbit in a snare, a blood-lusted pack of wild, rabid dogs eyeing her greedily.

She then recalled the moment Rabbie had entered her bedroom and their eyes had met; she had never felt so much intense relief in her life. She knew she owed him a massive debt of gratitude. She was very sore despite the drugs and wished her mother was here. She wept softly.

"It's quite quiet for a Sunday night. Well, until you arrived. Doctor Buchanon will soon get you sorted," the young dark-haired girl told her, re-tucking the blanket around her for the tenth time. Concerned. Miss Valendenski was one lucky lady.

Luca thought back to the beating Rabbie had given her attackers. She had never seen a man move so fast in her life. It was something from an action scene, like from an old Jean-Claude Van Dam film. Or a Bruce Lee kung-fu movie. Fast, furious and vicious. She shivered again as she recalled Hanlon pointing the gun in her face. She had seen right up the evil eye of the barrel. No, it hadn't been a film. In reality, it had been an evil, vicious affair. She wondered what she had done to deserve such violent attention. She tried to be nice to everyone and hated to cause offence or hurt people. She prided herself on her humanity and was confused.

She heard shouting down the hall and was afraid again.

"Do you know where Rabbie DeJames is?" she asked the nurse, nervous.

Before she could answer, the selfsame came around the curtain, flanked by two huge men in dark clothing. "Hey, Luca, how you doing now?" He was bruised and battered but calm and confident. A collectiveness about him. An unflappable safety curtain.

Intense relief flooded her again, and she put her good hand out, which he took and held reassuringly. It felt good, instant Dutch courage.

She saw his left eye was black and dried blood crusted under his nostrils. The knuckles on both his hands were covered in dressings. "Are you hurt vet bad, Rabbie?"

He laughed, "I've had worse hangovers. This is Big Mal and Dan, known as little. They are from On La Guardia and are going to guard you tonight."

"Doncha worry about a thing, lil' lady, we'll keep ya safe an'all," Dan replied in a broad Texan accent. He was also called Desperate Dan, after the cartoon character, because he ate nothing but steaks and meat pies. He stood at 6'8" and had crew cut blond hair. She looked at him in awe. He was a living, moving mountain of a man.

Big Mal laughed. He was Rabbie's chief of operatives and reached a mere 6'4". He was dark and swarthy-looking and totally bald. "As long as we keep him fed, Luca, that is."

She smiled, comforted by their sheer bulk and huge presence. "You'll need a bulldozer to shift this pair if they don't want to move." Rabbie reiterated, seeing the relief in those exquisite grey eyes.

A doctor in green scrubs, accompanied by several nurses, entered. They shooed the men out curtly and closed the curtain briskly.

"Hi, Luca, I'm Grace Buchanon. I'm the physician in charge of ER tonight." She was in her forties, with fine fair hair held back in a bun, freckles and gold-rimmed glasses. "Now let's have a look at you dear and see what we can do to help." She radiated competence.

She also radiated kindness and warmth, and Luca relaxed a bit, glad she had a lady doctor.

They pulled the blanket off and eased the backless gown across to expose her injuries.

Dr Buchanon examined her from head to toe, tut tutting, paying lots of attention to her stomach and thighs, which were stippled and mottled with bruising and swollen. Like ripe fruit left out too long in a hot sun.

She examined her pelvic and pubic area gently but thoroughly and shook her head at the swelling around her vagina. "And you say this animal kicked you down there, Luca?"

"Da, he kick me very hard indeed, Doctor, I was vinded bad."

"Okay, this is what we're going to do and then take it from there, 'kay," and the doctor reeled off a list of orders to her staff and patted her hand. "Don't be worrying, young lady. We'll soon have you right as rain and fit as a fiddle."

But Luca was worried. She didn't know how fit fiddles were or why the rain was right. She was a young fertile woman and wanted to have children one day with a man she loved. "Do you think there is any permanent damage done, Doctor?"

She looked at the young lovely Russian woman. She was stunningly attractive. She was used to women's concerns. In twenty years at Manhattan General ER, she had seen things that defied belief and sometimes shook her faith in mankind. She wouldn't know until the X-rays and tests were complete but she knew Luca had internal bleeding and was concerned. "Call me Grace, dear. The human body is stronger than people think. Lots of defence systems. Now you can relax and my staff will get the ball rolling."

Luca thanked her, deciding that this incredible woman was going to go high up on her 'Most Competent Persons' List'. "Please call me Luca, Dr Grace."

Rabbie was at present No.1 on her heroes list and she reckoned he would be hard to shift, if ever. Her very own Rambo and Sir Galahad rolled into one.

They wheeled her down for the X-ray at the end of the corridor, flanked by her two man mountains of bodyguards. Wendy came hustling down, dressed in her favourite work-out tracksuit.

She took her good hand. "Hey, kiddo. How yah doing? Bobby's just parking up. We had to give a statement to the cops or we'd have been down sooner." Wendy chattered on, trying to keep Luca distracted as they passed the cops guarding the prisoners. There was method in her madness. Being a highly experienced nurse, she chatted away for hours to the sick children on her ward and made it into an art form and often chattered away incessantly to Bobby, sometimes driving him to distraction. Sometimes doing it on purpose to annoy him if he was on her crap side. She liked when Luca visited because she could chatter away with the best of them and livened up her day.

The grim-faced cops nodded and greeted them as they passed.

"How are you, Miss Valendenski?" asked a young cop, who had been one of the first on the scene.

"I tink I be okay, tank you soo so much, Officer." That made his night as she gave him one of her most dazzling, bewitching smiles.

Suddenly, a voice shouted out from behind a curtained cubicle "Luca, Luca… I love you, baby. Tell the cops the truth honey, and I'll forgive yah. You know you've never had it like I've given it yah."

Wendy saw Luca freeze and tense up and stormed swiftly past the cops and nearly ripped the curtain off in her rage as she burst into the cubicle.

"You Goddamn mother-fucker!" she screamed at Hanlon, who was sitting on the bed, legs dangling, "Hurt my pal, you're dead, buster." And she flew at him, swinging and punching, taking him by surprise, cracking him a hard slap across his already bruised face.

Luca sat up on her elbow. "Please fetch, Danny. She my bestest most friend."

Big Danny waded past the stunned cops, followed by Mal, caught Wendy in a double crossed armlock around the middle from behind and heaved her up and out of the cubicle, Wendy kicking furiously and shouting obscenities at the surprised villain.

Big Mal's eyes met Hanlon. "That's one fucking crazy bitch."

Mal clocked him a blow to the face, which knocked him back, his head thudding hard into the wall as the cops surged in. "You should mind your manners around ladies, dog breath." He left, passing the grinning cops and closing the curtain. "All yours guys. He fell off the bed, poor perve."

Big Danny was still clutching a fuming Wendy, her feet dangling above the ground.

"Now you all calm down, little missy. That piece of coyote dung ain't worth the trouble."

"I'm gonna sue your fat arse, you mad bitch!" roared Hanlon.

There were several loud thwacks on flesh and it went quiet.

"Never saw or heard a thing, did we, fellas?" stated a grizzled old vet of a Sergeant, who had a daughter about Luca's age.

His men nodded and agreed as Bobby came storming down the corridor. "Hey pal…what the hell yah doing manhandling my wife? Put her down before I knock yer lamps out."

"Jest doin' mah job, sir." He gave a slow, lazy grin, "Ain't safe to release them crazy possums."

"Oh, put her down, Danny. You behave, Vendy. I don't vant you getting in trouble," said Luca.

Danny placed her gently down. "There you all go, ma'am."

"I smacked the shitbag a good un', Luca," gloated Wendy in triumph.

Luca smiled. "Tank you so much, Wendy. Can I go to X-ray now?"

The two big bodyguards eyed the equally big arrival with interest. They sensed a kindred spirit. They followed the bed down to X-ray.

"No offence intended, hombre. That sure is one hell of a wild cat you got there. She sure got spunk."

Bobby grinned. "She sure can be that, but she is normally quite nice unless you try to steal her Cheerios."

They laughed. Big Mal introduced himself and they shook hands. "You ex-army, man? Did yah do Iraq?"

"Sure am, dude. I helped rebuild Baghdad and put the lights back on." An unspoken bond of comradeship was instantly formed between the three as only can be between veterans of war. Those who had donned the uniform of war for their country.

At X-ray Rabbie was just coming out. "I heard the commotion, I guess you lot were at your work? You lot are not safe to be let out in public."

They snickered. The attendants wheeled Luca in. She looked very pale and tired, he thought, worried.

"Hanlon fell off the bed and banged his poor head," said Mal. "Made a silly claim this little flower hit him, as if."

"I was getting that sucker good," gave off Wendy. "Until that big galoot stopped me."

"That's sure one feisty gal you got there, Bobby," said the huge Danny in open admiration.

"I have to get back to see the quack," said Rabbie "See what's happening. Sure has turned out to be some night."

"Mighty interesting, hombre," drawled little Dan, "Now where's that doggone all-night canteen?"

* * *

Grace Buchanon had expertly assessed the X-rays and her suspicions were correct. Luca was bleeding internally from the left kidney.

Apart from that, she had a fracture in her left forearm, a hairline fracture in her left cheekbone, severe bruising on her stomach, bite marks on her breasts and thighs, a nasty abrasion several inches long on her right shin and various lesser cuts and abrasions. She watched the young woman, who lay in shock, her friend holding her hand. She hadn't complained once as they had poked and prodded at her and had indeed thanked them. She was a lovely natured young lady, and Grace was determined she get through this as easily as possible. She was worried about the kidney, which was swollen and bleeding quite heavily, and had paged the duty renal specialist to come and give his opinion. Luca turned her head and smiled tentatively

159

at her. Luca knew her recovery was in Grace's hand. She smiled back and strolled over to the bed.

She had upped the pain relief, had her on plasma and had a catheter inserted so she could pass urine pain free, which had embarrassed Luca immensely but her friend, an off-duty nurse, had assisted and reassured her constantly.

"Okay, young lady. We're doing great. We will get that arm in a cast. Bathe and dress that abrasion on your shin, which should heal up fine without scarring, and take things from there, okey-dokey?"

"Tank you, Grace. Vhat about down there, is much damage? Is numb."

Grace patted her leg. "Well, you're bleeding from the uterus, which is good, believe it or not. I don't see any evidence of any permanent damage. It's just old mother nature kicking in, flushing out the system after getting attacked."

Luca looked reassured. "So will it stop by itself then?"

"Yeah, should do, when the swelling goes down a bit. Apart from that, I'm more worried about your kidney. It's bleeding very badly, and we have to get it to stop before it causes permanent damage."

Luca looked sad. "I guess I won't be going nowhere for a while then. I couldn't go back to my home anyway. It's too scary."

Wendy hugged her gently. "Now don't you be worrying, Luca. We'll sort all that out as it comes up."

A dark-haired man with glasses came up, "Good evening. I'm Mr Shilburn. Kidney expert extraordinaire. Now let's have a look at these X-rays."

He studied them for a long time on the screen, hhrumping and hhrumming. He then examined Luca's stomach gently before conferring with Dr Buchanon outside.

Wendy noticed the urine in the catheter was very dark and knew from experience that it was blood. She hoped her pal didn't lose it. She would give her buddy one of her own, if the need arose.

Dr Buchanon summoned one of her nurses out and gave her instructions quietly.

Grace came in. "We're going to take you to theatre, Luca, and shoot that mother with adrenaline. Mr Shilburn is going to do it himself. He's the best, I can assure you. It's essential we stop it."

"What's adrenaline do?"

She was nervous now. Wendy squeezed her hand.

"It coats it and kinda seals it. Nature's super glue. You won't feel a thing. We'll knock you out with a local anaesthetic and we'll do everything at once. Clean and dress those bumps and cuts, put that arm in plaster and when you wake up, you'll be much more comfortable."

Luca nodded. "Okay, tanks. Lucky I have such a great hospital to come to, is it not, Wendy?"

Grace smiled. She was so adorable.

"Would you go see how Rabbie is, Wends? I am worried about him."

And caring, Grace added on.

"Theatre six at two-twenty, Doc," the returning nurse told Grace.

II

Rabbie was running the event of the night over in his mind, trying to get the sequence of events right and working out what else had to be done. Like his father, he was a practical man and dis what had to be done as and when needed. He who waits is beat, his maxim.

He hadn't the huge bulk and presence of his father, topping in at just over six feet and fourteen stone of lean, well-muscled body mass, and he had his mother's colouring, the dark hair and blue eyes and her quick mind and tenacity. He was confident, dependable and friendly by nature, and like his father, he didn't judge a book by its cover but treated people equally until they proved themselves otherwise. Still, he was no pushover and believed in getting the job done, but with his easygoing manner he was approachable and fair, so his employees happily did their best for him and benefited from his support and backup.

He knew his father would not have promoted him to head of office unless he merited the job, and he knew the guys considered him capable. He thought himself very lucky to be in a job he enjoyed and got satisfaction from. His father didn't suffer fools gladly and could be merciless in his business dealings but Rabbie was more laid-back. It was hammered into him from an early age that nobody was any better than anybody else and that life was a lottery but you took the openings and made the best of them, that everyone had their own unique talents and you used them accordingly.

A junior doctor was taping his hands up. She was a pretty little thing from Brazil with black wiry hair, wicked eyes and flashing pearly teeth, and she was flirting with him outrageously. Another time he might have been interested but the Russian girl was on his mind big style. He had seen some pretty grim things in this huge sprawl of a city and around the world with the marines but tonight had thrown him. He had walked in upon pure evil manifested. That any man could attack a young woman like that was inconceivable to his good nature. He knew it went on. To walk in on an attack and to be able to stop it was very satisfying but the mere fact it had happened at all was distressing to him in the extreme. Plus the fact that the deviants were filming the attack was mind-boggling.

"You know you're a bit of a celeb, Mr DeJames? It was very lucky you came along and saved that poor woman from those bastardos."

"Should have killed the bastards and done us all a favour," he growled.

She laughed, secretly thrilled to be treating this human superhero. "They'll get what's coming to them, amigo. Guess what makes us different from them? We are human and they are just animals with no feelings, comprendí?"

"Wish words from one so young, Doc, but don't insult animals. Those guys are just bad to the core and need locked up and the key threw away."

She started on his other hand, pleased he was treating her as an equal. A lot of the patients whom she treated in ER either looked through her because of the colour of her skin or tried it on with her and she had to warn them off. Nights were worse, when they had to have armed guards on to protect them from the drunks and druggies. The cops were never away from the doors, dealing with complaints and assaults. She would be glad when her rotation was over, and she would get on a ward and deal with the sick and needy, not the whackos and space cadets. Still, Rio de Janeiro was as bad, if not worse.

She finished with his hand. "There, all done. No fractures. Just bruised and cut. You must have fists of iron," and she stroked his hand admiringly, grinning.

He smiled and she thought it took ten years off him. He was a clean-cut, good-looking man. "Thanks, Doc, you're very kind. I appreciate it. Bet you'll be glad to see the back of me?"

"Not at all. You're a refreshing change. We don't get much thanks in here."

"I can believe it," he commiserated. "Still, least you can go home and sleep with a clear conscience. It's a noble trade you're in."

She thought about that, "Yeah, it true. Never looked at it that way, now lay back and relax until they find a bed on the ward for you."

He did as bid. Because of his head injury, he had to stay in for observation overnight. A medical insurance thing. There was no fracture or concussion but rules were rules and it meant he could keep an eye on Luca. He'd good tight security on her. You never knew who the lowlifes like Hanlon knew, and it would be in his interests to silence her good. He wasn't too worried about himself. Mal had slipped him a 9mm Glock with a 14-round mag and it was within easy reach in his coat. He was ultra-aware and professional and any contract killer the likes of Hanlon could hire would be bottom of the tree, lowlife scum, and Rabbie and the boys would see them coming a mile. Some of the gangs in the boroughs would take a hit for a few grand or a pro for fifteen thousand but because of the nature of the crime, a pro wouldn't touch it for love or money. There was a certain honour amongst thieves and crimes against women and children were frowned upon. He knew Hanlon and his crew would be segregated when on remand on the maximum security facility on Rikers Island, amongst the serial rapists, paedophiles and other pond life, but hopefully, when convicted and put out in the general prison populace the bastards would get their just deserts. Sex offenders were looked upon as the lowest of the low by your banged up thief and robber, many of them having families of their own, and Hanlon would pay heavily for his heinous crimes against the fairer sex. Through his work Rabbie had many contacts in the cops, the prison service and the criminal fraternity in general, and he would make sure he did. What goes around comes around, and Rab would call a few favours in. Quid pro quo.

He scowled at the ceiling. He wasn't a vindictive man by nature but he believed in justice. If you can't do the time, don't do the crime. If the American legal system, slow and cumbersome and often handing out trivial sentences or making wrong decisions and at times seeming to care more about the welfare of the perpetrator then the victim, couldn't give Luca the justice, and with it the peace of mind and safety any woman living in New York deserved, then by all that was good and decent, Rabbie Hamish DeJames would make sure she got it by fair means or foul. He would use every tool at his disposable to ensure it happened, with lethal intent, with extreme prejudice.

He got up and strolled down to see her. He was light-headed with the OxyContin. The medics didn't like to give morphine with a heavy head injury but once the X-ray had ascertained his head wasn't broken and they had stapled him up, they had given him a good dose and everything was light and fuzzy. He could see why so much of it was stolen and sold on. OLG had done quite a few ops in the hospitals around the boroughs to stop the thieving in the very lucrative trade.

Mal and Danny were at each end of the corridor and Billy-Jo was outside the cubicle. He went in. Luca was crying, so he put his arm around her and got her some tissues. She was annoyed because she thought she was a nuisance and fussed over his torn hands and black eye, blaming herself.

It was strange to have this feminine fuss made over him as he was independent by nature and Juliette had not been the fussing type, unless it involved her own welfare or comfort. He regarded her carefully, searching for the right words to put her at ease. She was pale and nervous as a newborn colt but still undeniably beautiful. He talked gently to her and soon coaxed a smile out of her. She was afraid of going down to the theatre but he soon allayed her fears.

She chatted away shyly, then with more confidence. She thanked him profusely but he didn't want her thanks, what he had done he would have done for anybody, and it just happened to be a God-given bonus that the person he had been allotted to save was the most striking, gorgeous heaven-sent creature to ever have graced his company and who had tugged heavily at his heartstrings from the first time he met her that fateful Friday morning. When he looked at her injuries slow, steady rage seethed within that Hanlon had sullied her by sticking his dirty, filthy hands on her, but he kept himself calm and collected because he knew if he showed his anger, it would just upset this gentle soul all the more.

When they came to fetch her for theatre, her eyes darted around like a trapped animal stuck in a speeding truck's headlamps, so he gave her his hand and she clung tightly. He accompanied her to the elevator and cracked away with the nurses, and she made jokes about the mess he had made of her bedroom, and he marvelled at her inner strength and resolve. She was a plucky one all right. Young girl, and let's face it she was very young, he thought, to be all alone in a big, bad New York, thousands of miles from home and family. He felt strangely proud of her and gratified to be in her company.

He left her laughing and Dr Grace grabbed him and chased him up to the ward. Mal went up with him. They put him in a small room at the end of a corridor on the sixth floor of men's medical. "At least yah on your own, dude," observed Mal, "Least yah won't have to listen to old guys snoring and pissing in a bottle all night."

"Guess that's one way of looking at it, although I don't intend being in too long."

A nurse came in with forms and took his vitals. Temp, pulse, blood pressure. She made him get into bed. Mal covertly slipped his Glock under the pillow and slipped off to find coffee with the grace and stealth of a jaguar hunting prey in the jungle at night. Mal had killed many times over in Iraq, and God help the fool who thought he could take him down.

He felt strange sitting in bed. He guessed he kept getting small jets of adrenaline when he thought about the events earlier in Luca's bedroom. Probably delayed shock, he assessed. Everything had happened so fast that afterwards he hadn't had time to let his mind get to grips with it. God knows how poor Luca felt. Invaded and violated like that out of the blue. It was a hard place to get to know, the wastelands in the sick country that existed in the heads of beasts like Hanlon, who spewed out their sick fantasies into real life and left their broken victims trailing in their wake like garbage thrown over the prow of a ship for the sharks.

Mal came back with a much needed caffeine boost and they sat for a while discussing tactics before he slunk off again, silent and deadly as the night itself.

Rabbie lowered the bed and gazed at the poor paintwork on the ceiling. He considered himself very lucky in life. His early years were spent between Watford and Northumbria. His mother spent as much time in Petral Hill Farm as possible.

She was a loving parent, who showered them with the love and affection she had been so cruelly denied and that most kids took for granted. His father was a giant of a man, firm and fair. He was away a lot of the time on business but when he was home, he always had time for them. As a boy Rabbie idolised him and came to listen and learn from him. He told great stories and anecdotes and Rabbie learnt to get hidden wisdom from them.

As he got older, he deduced his mother had a very deprived, stifling childhood. She had two brothers, Uncles Frankie and Mike, who visited regularly and who did the OLG accounts, but any talk about her parents became out of bounds.

She became a great outdoors woman. His gran taught her to ride and shoot, and they spent many a happy holiday picnicking on the moors or tramping along Hadrian's Wall, searching for Roman pottery and artefacts the rabbits dug up.

They also spent many days along the rugged Northumberland Coast, watching the puffins and petrels swoop and dive for fish. He loved the ocean. It had no favourites and demanded respect.

From a young age Rabbie could read a map and compass. His father and Uncle Smudger taught him rock-climbing, how to stalk a deer and trap rabbits, how to build a fire and cook and pitch a tent, navigate by the stars, and how to build a shelter in the bracken and survive when the weather came down, and a thousand and one other secrets of the great outdoors.

At twelve he was fit, well-nourished, with boyish good looks and was starting to look at girls in a different, exciting way. He had passed the eleven plus and his father sent him to grammar school in Hexham, and he spent his teens living with his granny and helping on the farm. He learnt all there was to know about sheep and could shear with the best of them. He would tramp the Cheviots with old Mac and learnt to work the dogs and listened in awe to ghost stories of Roman Legionnaires appearing out of the mist and savage Viking battles around the crackling, smoky campfire.

He did well at school but at seventeen, his whole world was turned upside down. His father moved them all, lock, stock and barrel to New York, the mighty Big Apple. It was a serious culture shock to them all. He hated it at first. The term concrete jungle took on a whole new meaning. It was vast, packed and totally overwhelming. It never stopped and the inhabitants hustled and bustled about 24/7, like thousands of ants looking for prey to take back to their skyscraper anthills.

He knew his father was an important man. On school holidays he used to go home to Watford, and he would call up to OLG HQ to see his dad and generally get under everybody's feet. There was a steady stream of people in and out his dad's office. Smart businessmen in suits, fit-looking guys in jeans and bomber jackets, military types and seedy, strange-looking little men in anoraks with caps and furtive glances. He knew his father had his fingers in many pies. He was often quoted in the press or appearing on TV, giving his views as a security consultant.

But he settled down eventually. He was in the gap year between school and university when his father put him to work in the outer office, filing and learning the ropes.

He'd lost his virginity at fifteen after his birthday party to a farmer's daughter in his granny's barn, when he and his mates had spiked the punchbowl with Bacardi. He suspected his granny knew but she seemed more amused than annoyed, but the girls his age in New York were a different breed. They were spoilt, pampered and predatory. They prowled in packs, devouring susceptible young guys up, then getting

164

rid of them and putting another notch on the head-board, before running back to the pack boasting about their latest conquest.

After having his heart broke twice in six months by coquettish socialite beauties, and having his first marijuana hangover, he tightened his belt, vowing never to let another Yankee temptress undo it and decided to do something positive. He was pining for the wide open moors, the smell of a peat fire and the gentler vowels of a pretty, unassuming border lass.

His father had said he would get him a good American campus. Yale or Harvard. He could major in business studies or security consultancy, then come into the family business but Rabbie had other ideas. He wanted to be his own man first and see a bit of the world.

He applied to the Royal Marines for a deferred commission. He corresponded in secret and was accepted. He would do a year at university, then as a boot neck[83] in the marines, and then two years as an officer, a final year at university, and then another three years owed to the forces. He liked the independence it gave him.

Using the excuse he missed his granny, he flew over to England and did the week's selection in Lympstone and passed with flying colours. The instructors were impressed with him. He was already a fit, young outdoors man and he was well-suited to the rugged life ahead. He had his parents' blood and sense of purpose in bucket-loads.

Arriving back in New York, he went to see his father as a matter of urgency. He expected fireworks to fly as he faced the big man behind his huge desk and in a firm voice told him what he had done. Shaking inwardly, he was expecting a severe bollocking.

Jamesey listened, amazed, fingers steepled. He sat unmoving for several minutes, "But why the marines? What's wrong with the paras?"

Rabbie laughed, "I could never understand, Dad, why you would want to take off in a perfectly good aircraft, then jump out of it. At least if a boat sinks, you can swim off."

Jamesey smiled, reminiscing. "Never heard it put that way before. What are you going to major in?"

"Security consultancy and ancient history at Edinburgh Uni. Gran says I can stay with her," he answered warily.

"Oh does she? So she's on the act, the wily old vixen. Your mum's going to miss you, as I am, of course."

Rabbie wasn't expecting this, "So we're cool with this then, Dad?"

The big man leant back in his big swivel chair, "I didn't expect anything less of you, lad. I'll give you an allowance to ease the way, like father, like son."

He stood and got his coat, "You know your granny wasn't too pleased when I ran off and joined the army," he put his coat on, "There's a maverick streak in the family line that surfaces now and then...come on."

Rabbie followed him out, pleased and relieved, "Where we going, Pops?"

"Down to fifth. There's a wee bar run by a pal does the finest single malts, you need to learn good Scotch from bad if you're going to survive Edinburgh, and don't

---

[83] In the eighteenth century the marines, in hot climates used to put a square of leather across the back of their neck to prevent sunburn, which was a flogging offence.

call me Pops, that's something corn does when heated. Always remember your roots, laddie, and be true to them."

* * *

Rabbie looked at his watch. It was the early hours. He wondered how his men were getting on guarding Luca. He should go down and see them, boost morale. That was his excuse anyway to check on her. Interesting, this new protective side to him. Very modern man. He hadn't really felt it for Juliette.

He dandered down the corridor, smiling at the memory of the day he had got drunk with his Dad at McKendry's on Fifth.

They had staggered home inebriated to the apartment to a shocked Collette, and she had scolded them, then laughed at their antics and fed them bowls of rich beef stew and dumplings. His younger siblings had enjoyed the break in routine, and Jamesey had later took them to the pictures to see 'The Lion King' and then McDonalds. The man had the stamina of an elephant. Happy days.

He lingered at the nurses' station. The bored young nurse manning' the fort perked up at his arrival. Word had spread of the events earlier and despite the deadly nature of it all, the nurses agreed it was so Goddamn romantic that a film should be made about it starring Daniel Craig and Angelina Jolie.

* * *

"Why, Mistah DeJames. What can I do yah all for? You'll shoulda pressed the buzzer," she asked in a deep southern accent. She was another looker with blonde hair and blue eyes and skin the texture of peach skin. "Ah, a lady from the Deep South. Where are you from?"

"Ah am from Myrtle, Alabama. Just a tiny dot on the map."

"Then it should be noted in tourist guides for the beauty of its women folk."

She gave a tinkling laugh, "Why, Mr DeJames. Ah do declare. How gallant, you are a charmer, sir. What can I do for ya all?"

He asked where Luca's room was. God there were some cracking nurses in this hospital or was it just the OxyContin?

The nurse grinned and clicked on her computer. "She's on the ninth floor. Ward 3. First bed on the right in Bay B."

"Thanks, nurse. Back later."

"It's Amanda to you, sugar, and you take all night if you want to."

"It will take as long as it takes," he replied.

"And that's the way ah like it, honey," she replied wickedly.

He hastened off, hand over his mouth, laughing joyously. Those girls were something else, but one thing was sure, they were angels to the very core of each of them.

* * *

He found her looking forlorn and tired. He had intercepted a pleasant Irish nurse taking tea and toast. She was surprised to see him again. He administered to her needs and when she was replete, he sat on the bed with an arm around her and they

166

chatted. She seemed to welcome the company. Before he knew it, he was sitting on the bed with his legs up alongside hers, and suddenly she was asleep, nestled into him and he hadn't the heart to wake her. He felt his eyelids drooping. Another big Irish nurse came in and told him off but he talked her into letting him stay and drifted off to sleep and dreamt of deep blue seas, battle-grey destroyers and his old shipmates when he'd been a young, carefree marine.

III

As Rabbie nursed his sore head, he dozed for a while, the drugs coursing through his system, making him light-headed and relaxed. The New Yorkers would have called it a 'power nap', but his old comrades in the forces called it 'getting a bit of shut eye', and the rule of foot in the marines was to get it when and where you could because you never knew when you might get the chance again.

He had begun training at the Royal Marine depot in Lympstone in South Devon four months short of his nineteenth birthday. Already a skilled outdoorsman, fit and familiar with firearms, he had cruised through the training, revelling in the challenge, the tenacity that ran in his genes refusing to let him give up on the gruelling, blister-forming route marches, the bruising assault courses and long exercises on windswept Dartmoor, where sleep was frowned upon and they were pushed to and beyond the limits of endurance. "Sleep is for wimps and woosies," the instructors would scream before goading and pushing them onto yet another task that seemed near impossible but somehow, by sheer guts and determination, they achieved. Those who fell by the wayside failed and were never seen again. Many started, most dropped out, and the small bonded unit that survived passed out on the square and received the much coveted green beret with its brass globe surrounded by laurel-leafed cap badge. Jamesey and Collette had flown over to see their son pass out, and as they watched the new marines do a beach assault from landing craft and blast to bits targets in the sand dunes with an impressive display of firepower, Jamesey had to admit there was a lump in his throat. He was proud of his firstborn. The lad had turned out well. *Prefer a good airplane myself but I guess it's one way of getting about*, he thought.

Jamesey laughed. "Wouldn't fancy that bunch of hairy-arsed squaddies storming our beach house in Los Angeles." OLG was going from strength to strength and Jamesey was spending his money wisely. "I just can't see them on Malibu Beach, can you?"

"Oh. I don't know, Jamesey," Collette mused. "Los Angeles seems to attract all sorts; the lads might fit in all right."

"Yeah, it certainly attracts all the whackos, weirdos and misfits, so I guess a load of fit, horny Brit marines would go down a storm."

Rabbie came panting up to join them and his father shook his hand. "Well done, lad. Pretty damn impressive."

Collette kissed him fondly. She missed him at home but hadn't stood in the path of him leaving. She knew once a DeJames made his mind up, there was no deterring them.

"Your dad reckons you should bring your mates over and stay at the beach house."

"Are you mad, Mum?" he said aghast. "The Angelinos would gobble them up and spit them out. Christ, they would never see fair England again."

Jamesey laughed. He knew what Rab meant. Most of the recruits were from working-class backgrounds and if you unleashed them in a 'where anything goes place' like LA, they would go crazy and God knows what would happen. In all likelihood, many of the recruits had joined the marines to see a bit of the world but until they got settled down and served a year or two with more seasoned men to guide them, they were loose cannons. "You're probably right. Malibu is just not ready for your rufti tufti mob," he agreed.

Rabbie took the whole platoon and their relatives out to dinner that night, courtesy of OLG. His father was already quite a famous man in his own right now. He was strong and charismatic and the media loved him. With his powerful physique, golden locks and artificial hand, they had dubbed him 'The Single-Handed Viking', and he watched his father fondly as he networked the room, chatting easily with the young soldiers and their kin. *Probably looking for promising candidates to join OLG after their service ended,* he guessed. His father never missed a trick and never forgot a face.

After three weeks on the farm, it was off to 45 commands in Arbroath in Scotland, where he joined mountain troop, where he was to do six months as a 'bootneck' before he started university.

For six months he tramped the majestic Highlands, climbed sheer granite rock faces and practised exercises in the waters of the frigid lochs. He learned off the old sweats and honed his skills and learnt new ones.

In an elite unit like the marines, the training never stopped, and they spent more time out of camp than in and slept rough and he became ultra-fit and aware. He did a four-week survival course run by the elite Special Boat Service, the British equivalent of the American Navy Seals, and he judged it to be the hardest four weeks of his life, but he persevered and passed and vowed one day to be a SBS man and wear the winged dagger.

That September he left his new comrades reluctantly and headed off to Edinburgh to start his degree in Business Studies and Ancient British History. Being on a full scholarship and pay from the army, they owned him now and he owed them at least three years' full service. He found the students immature and juvenile after his harsh introduction into adulthood through portals of Special Forces training but he was easygoing and laid-back and taking his father's advice, he picked a few friends carefully and watched the antics of his peers with amusement. Young people, let off the leash, in the time away from home, tended to run amok and overindulge in most things.

He steered clear of the inevitable drugs scene and the heavy-drinking party culture that seemed to go on every night, spending his weekends and half terms helping his granny on the farm or climbing with the university club.

He did well at his studies, which he found mundane, but he found the secondary course in Ancient History fascinating, particularly the Roman era and the building of Hadrian's Wall. They were hardy folk in those days, he decided, and only the strongest and most adept survived. Good, strong gene pool around Northumbria.

During the long summer breaks, he went to the summer camp with the Territorial Army and keep his skills up to scratch. The camps were often abroad and they trained with other armies from friendly countries, ending in long exercises that culminated in mock battles and he thoroughly enjoyed it.

But he was no prude and when he wanted to, he went out and could drink with the best of them. He was a fit, attractive man, highly eligible, and young ladies sought him out and he had a few carefree flings, breaking them off when things got too intense and fleeing back to the sanctuary of his granny's house. He had a career lined up and he wanted to get established before settling down.

Easters he sojourned back to the States, enjoying family life and spoiling his young siblings Jamie and Petral, who it seemed were getting bigger and developing fast at an astounding rate in-between his visits.

During his second year, he met a beautiful first year student called Samantha McKay Sinclair, Sammy to her friends. Blonde-haired, brown-eyed and legs up to her armpits, she latched onto Rabbie during a boisterous do in the student's union for 'Aids Relief in Africa', and she soon coaxed him into her bed. She was so beguiling and good company and mischievous that Rabbie was smitten for a while. His feelings deepened.

Her father was 'something in the city' and mother an honourable something or other of a debutante, who spent most of her time shopping, lunching and planning dinner parties.

Sammy was studying Forensic Medicine and wanted to solve murders "like the lady in the Tess Gerritsen books," she told him, Rabbie could see nothing wrong with that. Rabbie's only ambition at that time was getting her kit off and getting his hands on her fine body, and Sammy was as keen as he, and they shagged for Scotland for several months, unable to keep their hands off each other.

He spent several weekends at the family townhouse in Edinburgh. He found her father highly pretentious and the mother a pain in the butt, and he wondered where his lovely easygoing Sammy had got her genes from. Likewise, he took her to 'Petral Hill Farm', to meet his gran, and Beth enthused over her and thought she was just lovely.

Rabbie realised he was falling in love and debated with his conscience about what to do. Not too many guys met a prime catch like Sammy so early in their lives, and it would be a shame to let her slip out of his fingers. They were dating heavily now, she was certainly getting under his skin, and she understood his commitment to the army, indeed she said she admired his steely resolve in doing his bit for Queen and country.

He flew her over to meet his parents on a long half term. He was subconsciously seeking his parents' approval, although he didn't realise it at the time. The visit went very well. His dad liked her very much and she got along like a house on fire with Collette, going shopping and swopping recipes.

It was all the approval he needed and instead of slinking off like a fox in the night who has fed from a chicken coop, he stood his ground and let the relationship bloom around him. He could see marriage and eventually kids, and he knew they could sort things out and juggle their careers accordingly. They were two young, adaptable people of the nineties and the world was their oyster.

That second summer of university passed in a romantic whirl for the infatuated couple. During the break he had to go on a six-week exercise to Cyprus with the TA, and Sammy gave him a night to remember before he left and waved him off, vowing her profuse love and asking him to come back home safely to her.

It was 1998 and the world seemed a fine and wonderful place to Rabbie as he yomped across the plains and mountains under the sweltering blanket of heat of a Cypriot summer.

The last week they were high up the Troodos Mountains, trying to track down an elusive mock enemy, when he was surprised to be called back to Battalion Headquarters and even more surprised to see his Uncle Davey sitting in the mess tent waiting for him.

His uncle greeted him uneasily and sat him down. He too was in the desert fatigues, and Rabbie eyed the Winged Dagger emblem on his arm with the 'Who dares wins' logo of the Special Air Service emblazoned underneath.

His Uncle Davey was a bit of a mystery to the young DeJames. He had joined the army at sixteen and rarely came home. He was tall and rugged and deeply tanned and to be a Captain at twenty-eight in what was considered the hardest fighting, most professional army unit worldwide was a mega achievement.

Rabbie wiped the sweat off his brow with a face veil and gulped down a pint of concentrated orange juice. "Uncle Dee, never knew you guys were here, what's up? I guess you SAS guys were the enemy because you're like ghosts and we still haven't found your camp."

Davey sat down, knee to knee. He wasn't good at this type of thing. He didn't do the emotion thing well normally, leaving the breaking of bad news in the troop to his senior NCOs. "I've come to take you back to Scotland, lad. You've to pack your kit and we are flying out of Akrotiri in two hours."

Rabbie rose quickly, knocking the chair over. "What is it, Uncle? Is it Granny? She was fine when I left."

"No lad, it's Sammy," he righted the chair and made Rabbie sit. "Car crash. So sorry, son. Ran into a lorry by all accounts."

Rabbie looked bemused. "A lorry. But she's a great wee driver. Is she going to be okay? Is she in hospital?"

Davey shifted uneasily. "She never stood a chance, Rabbie. The road was wet and it was dark. She was taking your gran her birthday present, and well, let's say she ran out of road."

Rabbie recalled his uncle helping him pack his kit. Ten hours later they were back in Scotland and first thing in the morning at Sammy's home in Edinburgh. Grief has no boundaries and Rabbie sobbed broken-heartedly with the devastated parents, whom he hadn't particularly liked but who were now reunited with him in grief.

His uncle booked them into a small hotel and was there for him one hundred percent. He stood by his side at the funeral, holding him up both mentally and physically as his lovely Sammy was lowered into the rich brown Scottish earth with a finality that nearly broke his heart.

"'Tis strange, Gran," he told his sad gran in a whisper, "She wanted to bring murderers to justice by studying dead bodies and now she is one," and his shoulders heaved and his granny and uncle led him away and fed him whiskey from a hip flask and made him smoke a cigarette.

But worse was to come to compound his deep and so unexpected grief. Death tended to bring those left behind together, for however long that may be.

After the wake in the church hall, Davey took him back to the hotel and in the bar ordered double Glenlivets, no water.

"Listen, Rab. Sammy's mum took me aside and asked me to pass something on."

Rabbie looked into his uncle's uneasy eyes before going back to his whiskey.

"Yes, it seems at the post mortem they found Sammy was pregnant. About six weeks, they reckon." Rabbie cringed at the thought of that lovely, vibrant young body being cut open. A body he adored and worshipped, that he had fine-tuned his skills as an eager lover on, before his uncle's words sunk in and the full import of his words sunk home. "She was having a baby. Our kid. Oh sweet suffering Jesus. What a sad, fucking bastard of a life we live in."

Davey gripped his shoulder hard. "I'm not a great man for the religion, Rab, but I do believe that we all face some judgement after we leave this fucked up place. Shit happens but if it's any consolation, she was young and innocent and she's got company to see her through the journey, so to speak."

That night Rabbie got blind drunk. His uncle never left his side and when he finally passed out, got him to bed, cleaned his vomit up and stood watching over him all night.

Next day they travelled back to the farm and his granny's tender mercies. Davey loitered for another few days before slinking back to his unit, a much unwanted job done to the best of his abilities.

Rabbie shifted uneasily around the bed, awake now, wondering what Luca was dreaming about.

His uncle had extorted him to throw himself into his army career before leaving. "I've never been great with the ladies, Rab, I chase them, shag 'em, and leave them but you put this behind you and let the army be your family for a while and you'll soon heal."

Rabbie shook his hand gratefully. He would never forget what the hard SAS man had done for him.

His dreams went deeper, closing in and demanding attention. He pulled the hurt girl closer into his side, and she murmured something in Russian in her drugged stupor and moved in closer, her arm hugging him tight and it was a comfort to him as his dream state whisked him away to a hot, scorching desert and he prepared himself to take on an evil, merciless foe.

Tactical Map of Attack on
Shahib - Mahayeh Prison   11/6/04.

A.B.C.D. - Watchtowers
1. CELL BLOCK
2. OFFICES + ADMIN
3. QUARTERS
4. GATES
5. MESS HUT
6. G/POST + BARRIER
✳ SEMTEX LANDMINE
⊙ MILAN A/TANK
✳— 30 Cal M/GUN

Scrubland
(dense)

D
80 M
2.
C
3.
1.
A
100 M
4.
5.
6.
B

(Desert - Hard Sand)

PUR COAST
8.3 KM

200 M

X16
(SCREE)
RV WADI
POINT 1

Tripoli
83 k
FP
ROCKS

(Hard Stoney
Ground)
Z 11
Z 11A
Z 11B
Z 12

(SCREE)
ROCKS
X16
X 12A
Take Out
Enemy:
Cover
withdrawal

X 12A
ROCKS
Mission
Z c/s - Take Fort -
Rescue Hostage:
Time Frame: 20 Mins
from detonation

(Not to exact Scale:
Elevation: 120 ft Asl)

Withdrawl
Time Frame:
2 hours 15 Mins.

As drawn by Lt. B. Cooper.
Z Troop. SBS

172

IV

The Rise of Red Viking Alpha

June, 2004, Northern Sahara Desert, Libya

They lay in the scorching rocks watching the approach road to Al-Shahib-Mahayeh prison. A wary eye out for scorpions and the ever-present camel spiders, which gave a nasty bite if disturbed; fortunately, non-poisonous but painful. The female of the species was the most dangerous. Bigger than the male, a body the size of a small football covered in dun-coloured hair and long, extending legs. They hunted as a pair at night, the male going up the camel's leg and under the belly, bit into it with razor-sharp fangs, numbing the area with a natural freezing agent like novocaine. The female then stood under the camel on her long legs, ate a hole through the stomach and feasted. Sometimes she entered and laid her eggs inside and the offspring would spawn, eat and exit their warm nest when ready to face the world. They weren't even real spiders as they only had seven legs but they were vile things. Rabbie shuddered despite the extreme heat. Of course, easier pickings were welcome and one of his men, off-watch, had woken in the early hours with a female spider squatting over his face, eating into his cheek. He had despatched the loathsome thing with his commando knife and the medic had stitched him up. How the fuck he had not screamed in terror, Rabbie did not know. But it goes to show the high training to become a member of the elite Special Boat Squadron paid off. He didn't envy his man's future nightmares.

No, there were not just human enemies in the Sahara Desert. Between the heat, lethal creepy crawlies and venomous snakes, it was a vast merciless cauldron of hell. It was the stuff horrors were made of. Blistering heat at dawn and paradoxically often freezing at night. The devil's stomping ground, where the unwary perished and the heat drove men into crazed gibbering wrecks.

A small, very pale scorpion was lodged in a crack near his left elbow, and he knew the lighter coloured, the more deadly the venom. The big, black ones could give you a nasty sting like a bee but the pale ones could send you into paralytic shock, writhing on the ground in agony. They came out in the coolness of the night to hunt, and Rabbie was going to crush the bugger as soon as it showed its deadly head.

He sighed as he lowered his binoculars and wiped the stinging sweat out of his eyes and wished he was back tramping the Cheviots, where the air was clean and friendly. The only thing that might sting you was a cloud of midges or the wild bees in the woods that his mother would search for. On finding the nest, she put them to sleep with smoking rags and stole their honey. Manna from God spread on warm crusty bread with butter.

He had completed his degree and passed with honours before doing his officer training, which he cruised through but despising the bullshit in the barracks. He revelled in the outdoor training, honing his skills as a professional soldier, which was a unique art in itself.

Rabbie emerged as Second Lieutenant DeJames, a handsome, intelligent, extremely fit young man, eligible and in his prime. He took female company when he got it but never sought it out. The intense pain he felt after losing Sammy was

173

slowly dripping away like muddy water through a muslin cloth. There would always be a residue of her memory in the back of his mind, first love being the hardest to forget, and he decided on no more permanent attachments until later in life. None of this, 'Oh look, we're a couple, joined at the hip for ever and ever' malarkey. Tell that to the ones left behind after road crashes, sudden fires, terrorist ambushes, indiscriminate murders and muggings that went wrong and the other plethora of myriad events that could snatch your heart's love away. Leaving the 'Grim Reaper' gloating and sated in his heinous lair, lapping up your grief.

No, Rabbie decided. If true love ever came his way again, he wouldn't shy away from it, he would go with the flow. He certainly wouldn't be making the effort to find that elusive thread that could lead him to eternal love. Was there life after Sammy? he pondered. His name would be on no dating agency list.

He had served two years in Mountain Troop, serving tours of Bosnia and Kosovo, then six months on the training team in Lympstone, before attempting the arduous, vicious Special Boat Squadron course.

The Squadron ran along the lines of its bigger sister, the Special Air Service. Only numbering a hundred or so men, it was considered the toughest fighting unit in the world and very few completed the highly secretive course. Rabbie was one of those few. It was a prerogative for him, and he came out the other side as a man with a clear mind of high initiative and able to survive on the bare minimum in the harshest places on earth and spit in the eye of the devil with contempt. They said that if heaven was on the verge of being overrun by the 'Devils of Hell', the last two angels left guarding the 'Pearly Gates' would be two SBS warriors.

Rabbie had his own squad, which was Red Squad, but because they operated on and under the sea, they became known as Red Vikings, and Rabbie's call sign became Red Viking Alpha. They were fearsome warriors.

Rab was a full Lieutenant when the Twin Towers fell. He knew the face of modern warfare was changed forever. He already had several covert ops under his belt. Black ops that were guarded under the fifty-year rule of the Official Secrets Act and the government would deny ever happened if made public. When 'Desert Storm 2' commenced in 2003, Rabbie's troop was in the front. Going ahead with their SAS brothers, feeding intelligence back to the ground troops, bringing the jets in to take out hot positions, snatching prisoners and generally causing mayhem. Hitting complacent Iraqi strongholds hundreds of miles behind enemy lines before disappearing back into the hills like ghosts. The Iraqis were terrified of them and well should they be…they never knew where they would hit next.

Afghanistan came immediately after, and they cleared areas deep in Taliban territory so the troops could safely put 'Forward Fire' bases in. Time off was in short supply but when they were pulled back from the front, exhausted, bedraggled, lean and mean, their spirits and indomitable will unbroken, they partied and boy, did they party hard. They were a big hit with the nurses and female signal staff, who took their own stresses and frustration of war out in the comfort of the hard, muscular bodies of the outstanding fighters.

Rabbie was a Captain now. The SBS worked in four-man patrols, and he often led four or five of these on jobs to thwart the Taliban in their own terrain. He bumped into his Uncle Davey several times; indeed, they were on several joint missions. They would chew the cud and swap stories. Rabbie was at the pinnacle of what a fighting soldier could achieve. He was still in awe of his uncle, who in the echelons of the Special Forces was a legend in his own time and a man whom his men would follow to hell and back without question.

Rabbie had left the service the year before Major DeJames won the Victoria Cross and lost the love of his life. The beautiful Swedish combat nurse, Sonja Erikkson, at the Battle of the Fort of the Dark Raven's Wing. It brought them even closer together, an unbreakable bond between two men who had endured the burden of their true loves being extinguished before their allotted time on earth. Where they never saw the benefits and bonuses of slowly growing into and flourishing over the years in a special, loving relationship that in all probability would have resulted in marriage, a secure home and wanted children. Instead, their young lives were stolen in an instant, snuffed out like a damp finger snubbing out a candle. Leaving darkness in the hearts of the men they left behind, who would always cherish the memories of the beautiful, young, carefree girls they had loved. That picture would never age, locked in the recesses at the back of the mind to be taken out and played over and over again like a forgotten silent movie.

Brien Cooper, Rab's Lieutenant, crawled up beside him and raised a hand – five minutes before the guard change. He nodded, focusing on the job.

Al-Shahib was a small fort, dating back to the time of the Crusaders. Its walls were thick and crumbling, its dungeons deep and ominous. A platoon of Gaddafi's defence forces patrolled the fort twenty-four hours a day. They were relieved every forty-eight hours, and Rabbie was to hit them at change-over time. Taking out the relief force in one foul swoop and the defenders, when they were complacent after a long shift and seeing their relief arriving.

He noticed the plume of dust approaching a mile or so down the single track road. Tripoli was 80 kilometres to the southeast and the nearest settlement, a mud brick village of goat herders, twenty klicks[84] away posed no threat. They would be in and out in minutes and heading back to the coast, eight clicks away, for pick up by submarine and back to Malta; mission accomplished or so he hoped.

Rab had twelve heavily armed, hairy-arsed, seasoned vets with him. More than enough to take on the lightly armed militia platoon awaiting relief.

The reason they were there was because the mandarins in the foreign office had seen the unrest in the Middle East spreading. Hoping to topple the likes of Colonel Gadaffi'and other tyrants and replace them with democratic regimes, they had been spending the taxpayers' money and inserting agents to foster discontent, raise bands of guerrilla fighters, train and arm them ready for the impending coup that was coming.

Unfortunately, an agent had been caught and incarcerated in Al-Shahib, a notorious torture centre reserved for special prisoners. He had been nabbed coming ashore in a dhow two nights previously. When the boat had been searched, a cache of arms and explosives were discovered.

Although the agent had an impeccable cover as living in Wazi as a mechanic, spoke fluent Arabic and looked the part, he was, in fact, Sergeant Fred Salter from Norwich and there wasn't a drop of Arab blood in his body. He was also a member of the SBS and the boys were going to get him back dead or alive. Another deep cover operator had told his contact he had been roughed up and flung in the cells in solitary; denied light, food and water. Standard softening up techniques before the

---

[84] One kilometre.

interrogators arrived from Tripoli. Rab knew Fred Salter would be a hard nut to crack but every man had his limit and lives depended they get him out in one piece ASAP! Already the 'Mad Mullah', Gadaffi, was screaming an international conspiracy but no one took notice of his insane chants any more. This was a man who authorised the blowing up of an American jumbo jet over Lockerbie in Scotland, killing hundreds aboard. He supplied the IRA for years with arms and explosives. The British Government had a serious score to settle with the mad man, and in a strange way it was up front and personal for Rabbie too. The grenade that took off his father's hand in Glenmacadoon Square[85] in 1976 had come in on a boat from these very shores.

His men were laid up either side of him now, sinister-looking in the fading light, the desert sky a rainbow of deep purple, mauve and indigo as it lost the savage sun that had been its tormentor all day. The truck, engine growling, was a hundred yards off now, two hundred yards to his front. Rabbie concentrated on the small scrub they had painted with the luminous marker the night before as they dug the forty pounds of Semtex explosives under the road, enough to take a small block of flats out. Overkill? Certainly. Rabbie and the guys liked blowing things up and the bigger the bang, the better.

The truck reached the marker and he pressed the button on the handheld detonator, which sent a radio signal to its sister embedded in the pliable blocks of instant death, and all hell ensued. An eye-searing blue flash and then an ear-splitting crump, followed by a fiendish blast, blew the truck and its occupants fifty feet into the air. It ripped metal and flesh into fragments; soft organs like hearts, eyes and lungs vaporising. The huge wooden gates, fifty yards away, were blown off their hinges with a hideous shriek and several guards were crushed to jam beneath them. The guards in the two watchtowers were blown off their perches and flew screaming through the air, dead before they struck the ground.

As one they charged through the swirling dust and debris for the fort. Rab swore a turbaned head landed in front of him, sightless eyes accusing. They stormed in, and Lt Cooper led half the troop to deal with the guardroom and quarters and Rab sprinted for the spiral staircase that led down to the dungeons. He blasted the lock off a barrel gate, kicked it open and sprayed a full mag of thirty rounds from his H&K33 down the dimly lit stairs. Another trooper lobbed two grenades down and they bounced musically down the stairs before detonating with an ear-cracking roar and orange flash.

Magazine changed, Rabbie hurled down the stairs. Two dead guards lay at the bottom, peppered with shrapnel, blood pooling. A corridor stretched before him. He snatched the keys off a bloody belt and proceeded down. Four heavy, metal studded doors either side. Gunfire above him subsided and they reported the fort secure. The first four cells were empty. In another a group of several women and wailing children filled his torchlight with desperation etched across their features. Hostages. He ushered them out and pointed them to the stairs. He continued his search, his men behind him.

Another empty cell. Next one, a dead man hanged by chains from a wall, flies gorging on him, and the stench was ripe but he hadn't been dead long. He was horribly mutilated. Another empty cell, the floor caked in blood and faeces.

---

[85] The Battle of Glenmacadoon Square, Belfast 18th July, 1976.

"Can't see this place getting into the Michelin guide," one of the guys remarked. Rabbie had to concur.

The last cell yielded two young male Arabs. Relief flooded across their faces when they told them they were British Army. They asked for their brother in the next cell. Rab shook his hand sadly and directed them to the stairs; they needed no second bidding. Where the hell was Fred Salter?

At the end of the corridor another narrow spiral set of steps led into pitch blackness. "You down there, Fred?"

"That you, Captain DeJames? I thought I heard you knocking."

Rabbie laughed and hastened down and entered a small cell. "I got the executive suite, comes with its own bucket," said Fred from his chains on the far wall.

He chuckled and found keys and unfettered him, "You okay, buddy? Can you walk?"

"Bit of a hiding but boy am I glad to see you," he said rubbing his chaffed wrists. "Got a fag?"

Rab lit him a Du Maurier, his Uncle Davey's brand. "You know these things will kill you. Gotta go, mate, the natives are hostile."

Fred followed him up the stairs. "At least you get to choose, and you gotta agree a good shag's all the better for a smoke after."

Rabbie laughed. Fred was your typical SBS trooper, and he knew his dad wanted him for OLG when his time was done.

* * *

They left quickly and melted into the desert, taking the hostages with them and leaving eighty dead militia men to make their way to paradise behind them. Inah' Allah dudes. The jihadists called it 'the honeyed death of martyrdom', and the 'Red Vikings' had just given them a whole jar of it.

Two klicks into their journey they stopped and fed and watered the grateful ex-prisoners. The charges they had laid went up with an impressive thud and lit the desert sky for miles around. Al-Shahib-Mahayeh was no more. A smoking mound of rubble and the spirits of its tormented and dead were released and soared into the sky and became one with the trillions of desert stars. The purity of the desert night air washing across the marauders' faces, leading them towards the coast and safety.

Brien Cooper and his brick were bringing up the rear. He noticed Brien was limping. "You okay, mucker? You want me to get you a taxi and take you to casualty?"

Brien sniggered derisively, "I think I'll wait, thanks very much. Just a blister."

"You're getting old. Think you'll keep up?"

"I'll race you to the beach, young 'un," snorted Brien, defiantly.

Rab grinned and went back to the front. Brien was a diehard and with his crisp toff accent and innate sense of fairness, was a popular officer in the squadron.

They made good time, the prisoners finding an inner strength, knowing they were going to a kinder, fairer place, where they would be treated well and terror didn't stalk the land all day, every day.

Besides the two brothers, who had been arrested on the dhow with Fred, there were two women in their late twenties and four young children under ten. The guys carried the scared tots the last few miles to the pick-up point, the women giving them

177

looks of gratitude from large, heavy-lidded eyes, luminous under the starlight. Rabbie knew he was probably going to get a serious bollocking for bringing them with him.

Policy was you left native prisoners to fend for themselves or in dire straits, you 'disposed' of them. They were the wife and sister of a local sheikh, who had annoyed the 'Crazy Colonel' and was on the run. He knew they would be easily recaptured and subjected to serious abuse prior to a slow death. He may be battle-hardened, but he wasn't a thug and clung to his humanity tenaciously.

They reached the beach and the Zodiacs were waiting for them. Brien Cooper promptly passed out from loss of blood. It turned out he had lost half the back of his right leg after a red-hot piece of exploding truck sheared through his calf.

"How the fuck did he walk on that? Silly bugger should have laid up," said the medic on the submarine heading for Valetta in Malta.

"Not in his nature," explained Rab, "He's an old fighting seadog who gives no quarter."

Rabbie got his severe bollocking off the bossmen and was also awarded the Military Medal for outstanding leadership. Brien Cooper also got a MM for heroism, but he laughed and said it was for just being a stubborn bastard.

Several years later Rabbie watched with satisfaction as the despot Gadaffi was toppled. He had left the marines a year after his award and did a year in the OLG London Office before heading off to New York.

During his time in London, he tracked Brien Cooper down to a dingy bedsit near Charing Cross. Empty whiskey bottles and budget lager cans littered the floor, and Brien lay in a pool of vomit. He had the lower half of his right leg amputated due to infection and sported an artificial one. Having to leave his beloved SBS, he left the forces with an honourable discharge and a war pension, which he seemed determined on spending ensuring the local off-licence didn't go out of business.

He knelt and strapped his comrade's leg on, doused him with a basin of cold water and helped him up and out of the dingy room.

"Where we going?" sputtered Brien.

"New York, mate. Get you dried out and then as near the action as I can."

There were tears of gratitude in the older man's eyes. Battle forged deep comradeship but many succumbed to the insipid horrors of Civvy Street.

"Why you doing this, Rabbie? I'm done for."

Rabbie paused, "Because you're my brother. My brother in arms and a DeJames never leaves a fallen comrade behind, wherever they fall. Now shut the fuck up while I find a taxi."

* * *

As he made his way back to a semi trance and watched Luca, he mused on the strange bond between them now. He guessed she was his comradess now, having gone through gunfire with him. Grinning wickedly, he thought of his rough, tough men of the SBS and the lovely, young, artistic immigrant with the sexy accent he was going to console and help through fear. They would love her and make her an honorary Red Valkyrie.

Adversity under gunfire sometimes made strange bedfellows or…bedladies!

Sod it. He was okay, Luca was safe, and he dropped back into a deep, dark slumber, confident whatever the immediate future threw up he could handle it, and just maybe, this delightful creature may be at his side for some stage of the journey.

Chapter 15
You Might as Well Be 'Hung for a Sheep as a Lamb'
('It's All Too Beautiful'... The Small Faces... 1968)

Late February, 1976, Northern England

As the 'Flying Scotsman' thundered along the edge of the Pennines in the North of England, Jamesey watched Collette gazing out the window enthralled. She had never seen the hills before, let alone two and a half thousand foot mountains shrouded in snowdrifts and cloud. She had seen the Alps and the mighty Himalayas on TV and in books but mountains...? In the middle of England!!! She felt ashamed and small within herself at her lack of such basic facts.

"It's called the 'Backbone of England', Collette," he told the rapt young woman. "Runs for hundreds of miles through Derbyshire, Lancashire, Yorkshire and Co. Durham."

"Crikey, luv. Makes yah feel humble dun it? It's gorgeous."

He looked out with her, passing her over coffee and the cheese with tomato sandwiches he had got them from the buffet. They certainly knew how to put the arm in on British Rail. Captive audience, she guessed.

She blew on her coffee and thanked him. "'Ere, Jamesey, what's them white blobs dotted everywhere?"

That stumped him until he twigged on. "Oh right...err those are sheep, Collette. The farmers bring them down from the hills in winter into the valleys so they can breed."

She looked away embarrassed, "Fuck, you must think I'm a thicko?"

He grinned and squeezed her hand. "Not too many sheep in Watford, honey. Now you know one if it creeps up behind yah and bites you on the arse."

"The only one I want biting me arse is you, love," she paraded suggestively, and smiled, unabashed.

"Is Petrel Hill House Farm in the ...err... Pennines then?" She liked the 'honey' bit.

He explained the farm was in the Cheviots Hills, at the end of them, and how the Pennine Way was the longest footpath in the country and how as a young para his platoon had tried to break the record to travel it on foot.

"Yeah, took us ten days. Bad weather beat us in the last few days. Heavy fog and sleet. We had to make up for lost time on the last day. We set off at four in the morning with fifty pound packs and ran and walked until half eight at night to the end."

"Christ, how far did yah have to go then, Jamesey?"

"Oh, a couple of a hundred miles. Fifty-two miles on the last day; we failed to beat the record by twenty minutes."

She was stunned, "Fifty-two miles! Through those sodding great hills… Bloody hell, mate!"

He drank his coffee thoughtfully, "Yep…longest walk I ever done. Legs were cramping up at the end but it was an achievement, I reckon."

She saw the pride on his face and she subsequently glowed with pride for him. "Reckon so, luv… Bloody amazing feat," then laughed, "Which gave yah sore feet?"

He laughed with her, amused, chewing on his sandwich, "Had blisters for weeks after," and he wondered again what his mother, Beth, was going to make of his pretty, petite, cockney girlfriend, who cursed like a docker. Should be interesting, he surmised.

She eyed him, as if reading his mind. She was so deep in love with him that she was constantly aroused and reassured in his presence and wanted to please him and make him proud of her.

"Don't worry, Jamesey… I'll try and watch my language. Don't wanta let yah down in front of yer mum."

She never ceased to amaze him. "I wouldn't worry, Collette. She may attend Kirk every Sunday but come shearing time, she can cuss with the best."

"I'll go to Kirk with her and mind me P's and Q's…don't want her locking me in the shearing shed, do I?"

He was quite smitten by her, she seemed to get more and more beautiful every day. He wanted her by him like a second skin. She understood him and was a constant source of comfort, solace and amusement. She had seen his violent alter ego that morning when he had beat Slimy Barry to pulp and he thought she might back off a bit after that, but if anything, it had reinforced their relationship. The army taught him that violence was a tool and should be used accordingly. He realised now that the years of training and conflict had partly dehumanised him and that he needed Collette as much as she needed him. She made him see the nicer side of life, and he never knew he could need, or want, someone as much as he did her. She was the best thing that ever happened to him; he let himself decide after judging himself harshly and decided that he could be as decent as the next man.

She bounced from her seat and bounded onto his lap, and he wrapped his big arms around her trim form and they kissed passionately. They had got a six-seated compartment to themselves. He fondled her breasts through her jumper and her breathing quickened. She pulled the blind down on the window. "Lock the door, love… If these hills stretch as far as you say, we've bags of time; anyhow, don't want the sheep watching."

He grinned wickedly and went to do her bidding. When he turned back, she was stepping out of her jeans.

"Told yer, mate," she said, liking the lust in his bearing. "I'm game for bleeding anything once."

* * *

They changed at Doncaster and got the small local line to Hexham in Northumbria a few miles off Hadrian's Wall, an old staging post for the Legions but now a small quaint market town. Famous for its market, ancient church and quaint square, the only legions the locals saw were tourists.

Collette looked smug as she traipsed beside him onto the platform. Imagine that! Doing 'IT' on the famous Flying Scotsman Express. Wait till she told Eadie. She'd wet her drawers.

Jamesey carried his large green army Bergen. He had shown her how to pack it army style. Lining it with plastic bags, then rolling their clothes up so they didn't crease and packing their toiletries in more plastic bags tied at the top. She liked him showing her how to do things and he found her a quick learner.

She had nearly cried with excitement when he told her, on the second Thursday of his leave, that he was going up to visit his mother for a few days and if she wanted to come, he had cleared it with 'The Guvnors' and she was more than welcome.

She furiously counted her tips, £6.38. She'd another thirty quid secreted under her mattress and Ron had slipped her a crafty tenner.

He laughed when she offered to pay for her ticket and showed her his unused army travel warrant, a return for any destination he wanted in the UK, "Besides, you pretend to be sixteen and my sister and you get on for half price."

"Would yah like me to put me old school uniform on then, Jamesey?" she asked with mock innocence. "Not that I get much wear out of it."

He roared out the huge laugh she loved so much, "Don't think mother would approve, Collette, me snatching school girls and abducting them to her farm."

"Okay… I'll wear it for yah when we get back," she replied saucily and pinched his arse. He jumped and gave her that glorious laugh again, and her heart filled and nearly exploded. She loved him so much that at times she thought it was all a dream and she would wake up alone and sad in her little room.

"Jamesey's the type of guy that livens up a room full of people, and he's a go out and getter, not a stuck in the mud, so hold on tight, Collette, be prepared for a fast ride," was Eadie's advice.

"Oh, indeed I do, Eadie… He's a bleeding dynamo, in and out of bed."

That left Eadie speechless and reaching for the port.

When they reached Hexham, a little after five, a green Land Rover met them and a big dark-haired man with a bushy beard and dressed in tweeds greeted them and pumped Jamesey's hand.

"Welcome home, young 'un. You've been missed, so ye have."

Collette loved his accent and his lined, weather-beaten face. "I'm Mac Iass, head shepherd, and this is Bill and Ben, my dogs."

She peered in the back, where two black and white dogs with shaggy coats, tongues lolling, greeted her with gentle barks. "Border collies, specific to the area!" he informed her as he shook her hand with his own gnarled one, "And you're very welcome, lass."

"Cor it's like something from the Bible… Shepherds and sheep."

"Biblical all right," agreed Jamesey. "Mac's been working on the farm before Adam and Eve."

"Specifically biblical!" she laughed as they climbed in, liking the new word she would note down later.

They drove the eight miles to Petral Hill Farm along winding single-truck roads climbing and dipping through the Cheviots. Vast vistas of wild heather and bracken-clad moorland stretched either side.

182

The day was drawing in and a late winter sun hovered over the horizon like a flat yellow plate, and a frosty half-moon had already risen in the east and hung watchfully over them.

Sheep in small flocks were everywhere, often running in a panic in front of the jeep before leaping away into the bracken.

Mac stopped at the Wall. "It's very low at this point, lass. The locals plundered it to build with."

She gazed out at the ancient monument that snaked across the hills and crags either side of them into the distance.

"Eighty-six miles long, forts every mile or so. Some feat of engineering, even by modern-day standards."

She agreed imagining swarthy, armour-clad, homesick Roman soldiers fighting hairy, painted, fur-clad savages. "Should have bleeding stayed in Italy and saved themselves the trouble."

Both men laughed and Mac nudged Jamesey, "She's a bonnie lass... I like her already."

Mac normally reserved his judgement on people until he got to know them. He wasn't standoffish but his job was often a solitary one, tramping the hills with his crook and adoring dogs, herding and caring for the sheep. He could be very reserved with strangers.

A mile past the Wall Petral Hill Farm appeared. It was a large building built of granite, and indeed from blocks pilfered from the Wall, and had stood for hundreds of years on the hill it was named for. It stood sentinel on top of its hill, dominating the wild, vast moorland spread all around, covering the dead bones of Romans and piets.

They drove into the yard at the back. Lights gleamed from the windows to dispel the gloom as they dismounted. The kitchen door burst open and a sandy-haired boy in a shirt and jeans hurtled out.

"It's Jamesey, Ma...he's here!" he yelled. Jamesey grabbed him and twirled him through the air before setting him down and ruffling hair.

"How are yer, Davey boy... You been good? Got you a present."

"I have; I have... What you got me?" the excited lad cried. He caught sight of Collette and looked her up and down. "Who's this then, Jamesey...she your new lassie?"

Beth DeJames came out to greet them. She was a very beautiful woman, Collette thought. Her hair still blonde at forty-six. She was tanned and fit-looking with a fine figure.

She strode over with a confident stride. "Now don't be rude, Davey... Away in and finish your dinner and I've a surprise for dessert."

"'Kay, Mum," and he rushed off full of endless energy, happy his brother, whom he worshipped, was home.

Beth approached Collette and extended her hand, "Hello, dear... You must be Collette... Welcome to Petral Hill Farm."

Collette felt strangely shy. The older woman reeked of self-assuredness and competence. Like mother, like son. She shook hands. They were the same height, and Beth gave her a friendly smile as she scrutinised her through marvellous pale blue eyes, the colour of summer cornflowers.

183

"Very nice to meet you, Mrs DeJames," and she nearly did a half curtsey but caught herself on.

"It's Beth, dear… I hope my big galoot of a son has been looking after you?" and Beth gave Jamesey a big hug before they entered the kitchen, relieved her son was home safe from his war and not letting on, but they both knew it. They were two of a kind. Doers, not worriers. Let's not sit on the fence…let's get off and make our own.

The kitchen was large and well-equipped with a huge Aga cooking range at one end radiating waves of heat. Four men in working clothes sat at a long wooden table wolfing down large portions of stew, hungry after a day's work. Beth fed them every day before they returned to their lodging in the nearby village. They stood respectfully when Collette entered.

"This is Collette, lads, now sit and enjoy your meal."

They did his bidding but not before greeting him individually and welcoming him home.

Collette was strangely moved and felt small and out of place. This was Jamesey's domain…his home, where he had been raised in his formative years, and no matter how far he travelled, or for how long, he would always have this one place where he was wanted and welcome to return to.

She thought of the slum she had been dragged up and abused in and shivered as she wondered at the vagaries of life. She thought she would envy Jamesey his upbringing but instead she was strangely grateful to whatever supposed God there was above that her man had been graced and not blighted like herself.

Beth watched the lost and out-of-place young woman wryly. She was very young but devastatingly pretty. She hefted up Jamesey's Bergen easily. She knew her big son was a good judge of character and this was the first time he had ever brought one of his girlfriends home to meet her. He had broken a few hearts in Berwick upon Tweed and the surrounding villages when he upped sticks and joined the armed forces, so there must be something special about Collette.

"Come on, dear, I'll show you to your room," she said kindly. "You can get a quick wash before your dinner."

Collette wandered after her through comfortable, well-furnished rooms and up a wide staircase and down a long corridor to her allotted room.

Beth shoved the door open. "This is the blue room. There are eight bedrooms, so I run a bed and breakfast in the summer for the walkers doing the Wall…helps make ends meet."

The room was tastefully done in different shades of blue. Collette loved it. Beth showed her the en-suite bathroom. "You get a quick wash… I'll wait for you."

As Collette did her bidding, Beth told her about the farm. Besides thousands of sheep, she ran a small herd of Aberdeen Angus cattle, for meat.

"Finest steak you can get and it's becoming more and more popular worldwide, so it's a nice little earner." She handed Collette a fluffy towel. "Aye, the Japs go mad for it. I wouldn't mind getting hold of one of their Kobi Bulls and cross-breeding with my Angus herd."

Collette mused, "Can't see it, Beth. If the jocks wouldn't accept the Eyeties, can't see them letting the Nips slip over the border," and flounced into the bathroom, much to Beth's amusement.

Collette dried herself and brushed her teeth learning that they also dug peat, which they sold by the sack, and they owned several plantations of coniferous fins. "So if you ever need a Christmas tree, you know where to come."

Collette didn't know what peat was and doubted if she had room for a real tree in her little room. It was all double Dutch to her.

As she brushed her hair and applied some light make-up, she learnt Beth kept some free-range chickens as well, "Just for the eggs and meat. Taste a lot better than those battery hens, poor things. I don't believe in that type of farming. It's barbaric."

She murmured her agreement. She never knew hens run on batteries. She had a lot to ask Jamesey. She'd changed into a light blue pantsuit she had saved up for. Matches the room, she decided. Beth looked at her admiringly as she emerged refreshed, "Oh my, Collette…you do look pretty. I do hope you and me are going to be friends! Nice to have another woman about the place."

Collette sat on the queen-sized bed, "Yah know, Beth… I know sod all about sheep, peat and bleedin' hens wiv batteries but I'm willing to learn. I'm a city girl, ain't I, and this whole trip has me in a real tizzy dun'it? The furthest I've ever been is Southend on bleedin' Sea."

Beth squeezed her hand and laughed with mirth, "I'm so sorry for prattling on dear. I never thought… I'll show you around tomorrow… What you need's a nice big gin and tonic and a good feed."

Collette grinned back, "Now you're talking my language, Beth, and I really appreciate you having me to stay."

"You're very welcome and tomorrow I'll drive you about and explain it all to you."

"'Kay, Beth… Thanks… Eerrr… What size batteries them chickens take then?"

Beth howled with glee, not knowing if Collette was joking or not.

* * *

After a drink they sat at the table and dug into deep bowls of rich, aromatic stew, with dumplings and homemade crusty bread. The labourers were long gone, and young Davey DeJames sat at one end making up the Airfix kit of a Hercules C10 Jamesey had got him and lining up the plastic soldiers in ranks, wishing he was grown up and in the army like his strong big brother.[86]

"This is brill stew, Beth…is this the famous Aberdeen Angus beef then?"

Jamesey grinned and poured her more wine and Davey giggled.

"No dear, it's venison… I shot a stag last week."

Collette gawked, "Ya mean it's a deer… I'm eating bloody Bambi's dad."

They smiled indulgently at her, "Tasty though," she decided, "Must get the recipe off yah, Beth. Didn't know you could put red wine in stew, did I?"

"It's Jamesey's favourite, isn't it, son?"

He nodded in approval as he ate the succulent meal, thoroughly enjoying the homemade food and banter. Good, clean, lean meat.

"No deer in Watford, so I better bring a herd back then if I want ta keep him happy."

---

[86] See Book II – 'The Resurrection of Black Viking Sunray'.

185

"You could keep them in the pub car park along with a few chickens," Beth laughed.

"No battery ones though," Collette shot back, "They can flap around free and lay their eggs down the cellar, and Eadie can pickle them for the punters."

Beth looked at Jamesey's smiling face and decided if he was happy so was she and he caught her eye and winked as Collette went on and told Beth about the Ruby Murrays and Clive the wacky baccie smoking taxi driver.

"Which reminds me, Beth," she prattled on, "Tell me about the time you locked Jamesey up in the shearing shed." Jamesey groaned and hung his head dramatically in his hands, and they chortled merrily at his antics.

Afterwards, Collette insisted on washing up even although Jamesey saw she was drooping with tiredness. Young Davey, much to Jamesey's approval, pulled a chair up next to the huge Belfast sink and dried them for her. Davey liked the pretty woman his brother had brought into their lives. She made his mother laugh and that was good enough for him.

"What yer reckon then, Mum?" Beth tilted her head in thought, then looked him in the eye and saw he was serious and looking her approval.

"I like her, Jamesey... Very pretty and...well...colourful...in language and manner. Brightens the place up."

She saw he was pleased, "Yep, she's some pup... A big, colourful, hilarious, one-woman riot."

* * *

They rose early on Petral Hill Farm. 'Early to bed and early to rise and get as much done in the daylight hours as possible' being the maxim.

Beth had lain awake and smiled as she heard Jamesey creep from his bedroom and past her door to Collette's boudoir. She was no prude, you couldn't be on a working farm with livestock but she sighed, missing her husband Mike, who had passed away five years previously. He had been a fit, lusty man and she missed his touch and presence not only in the matrimonial bed but around the farm and in the house.

A few of the single landowners and men who attended her Kirk had made eager advances for her favours, but she had pleasantly but firmly spurned them. Mike was so irreplaceable in her heart, and she felt she would be betraying him if she lay with another. She knew she was being a fool to herself and that Mike would have wanted her to be happy, but she just did not have it in her to take the first step into a new relationship. She looked up at the shadows on the ceiling, the peat burned red in the grate as the fire slowly died its own death. She watched the flickering shadows on the ceiling in contemplation. Nothing ever really ended. There was always a history and memories. Things had to end to start again but every contact leaves a trace.

Besides, she had young Davey. He was the man of the house now when Jamesey was away. He had been a surprise packet after over eighteen years of marriage, a gift from above. A blessed bonus. She had been married a year, not much older than Collette really, when Jamesey had come along, and despite trying for more kids in the intervening years, and she smiled fondly at the erotic memories, she hadn't fallen with child again until Davey decided to come along. Mike had been gobsmacked and accepted his workers' ribald teasing proudly.

186

Beth Mary Jane DeJames (nee Connally) had been twenty when she first met Michael Robert DeJames at a tea dance in the parochial hall in the nearby town of Roxburgh, where she lived. Her father ran the local chemist shop and her mother kept house. They were reasonably well off, being from good stock, and the local bachelors considered her a good catch. She was young, attractive and intelligent and was enjoying the attention, if the truth be told. But she had ambitions. She could be a stubborn mare.

Her mother had been horrified when she declared her intention to go to Edinburgh University to study Accountancy and Bookkeeping. She had excelled at school in Maths and English and wanted to start her own office, catering to the local farmers and traders. There was a niche in the market, and she believed she could talk the reticent hill farmers into taking their secret stashes of cash from under their beds and putting it into the bank, where she could keep a proper eye on it for them and make it grow through good investments.

"But a woman's place is in the home, darling… It's our duty to look after the menfolk," Beth senior protested.

Beth had scoffed at the old-fashioned view. "Rubbish, Mother. Look at all the women who worked during the war. Without them on the farms and in the factories, we would have lost."

Her mother tried a different tack, "But who's going to pay for it, dear… How will you support yourself?"

"I won a scholarship, so I have and if you won't back me, I'll sleep in a tent on the campus green."

"You'll be seeing men next and Lord knows how that will end."

"Maybe I am already, Mother, and maybe more than one. It is 1947 you know, and I am nearly eighteen," she said, looking away naughtily.

"You'll be seeing no men until you're twenty-one, when it's legal and above board… Over my dead body," Beth senior snapped back.

Hamish watched the antagonists from his rocker chair keenly, a tall man who doted on his youngest daughter and wanted what was best for her. His eldest girl, Deirdre, was already married, had a one-year-old son and was expecting another but he knew Beth was not just a pretty face. He was proud of her education and achievements and feisty nature. She was more than just a pair of breeding hips.

He'd done his national service in the mid-thirties as a subaltern in the Coldstream Guards, the local regiment, and had served in Persia and India. Denied war duty due to a hamstring injury sustained on a dusty polo pitch outside Delhi, he had raised and run a platoon of 'The Home Guard' in the area and was hugely respected in the town and region.

No, another professional in the family would be welcome and young Beth had the mettle to do it. Only a fool failed to see the British Empire was on the decline. Empires came and went, like the Romans, who had built the wall and kept his forbears out of England. They must have seemed invincible to their enemies at one stage but decline they did.

"Now hush yourselves, gals… I think it's a grand idea, and she can help me with the shop and the books on holidays. I'll give her a small weekly allowance to help tide her over."

So that was settled, the man's word in the house being law in that age and era.

So that end of term night in June, 1950, Beth had taken her finals and was expected to pass with honours. Her female peers were in awe of her. Not many women attended university in those days unless they had independent means.

The Summer Ball and Tea Dance run by the Roxburgh Kirk of Scotland was in full swing when Mike DeJames entered with his friends.

Discharged from war service at the end of 1946 after a brief tour in the Far East fighting the Japs, he was a striking-looking dark-haired six-footer. Lithe and muscular... He had rushed home to help his still devastated mother, Janet[87], run the farm. Fighting might have been in the DeJames menfolk's blood but so was farming, and he took to the rugged life like a duck to water and soon had the farm running to full capacity, hiring and firing and tramping his beloved Cheviot Hills in all weathers, impervious to all the elements.

He was a firm employer but scrupulously fair, and the locals said he was a good man to work for, which was high praise indeed.

Mike had seen some atrocious things during the war. He had lost men and been in kill or be killed situations himself. He thought of the night he had murdered SS Sergeant Major Gerhard Muller and shrugged. He wouldn't lose any sleep over it. He wondered what had happened to Justin Webb and if he had checked on young Simon Siminion when he was discharged.

Mike would remain unaware of the strange link the future held for Simon Siminion and the beautiful Luca Valendenski.

No, Mike's only vow was never to leave his beloved borders area. He reckoned he was Scottish/English or English/Scottish and he didn't care. Wars began over borders and he'd seen first-hand man's brutality to his fellow man when constraints of humanity were lifted and the gloves came off.

Lambing season was over and the happy offspring were getting nice and plump on the summer grass and bracken shoots, so when the hands said they were going to go to the dance in distant Roxburgh, ten miles away, he decided to join them after his mother implored him to go. She loved her son but he had thrown himself into working on the farm and needed a break.

"All work and no play makes Jack a dull boy," she barged him. "Away on and have fun. You might meet a nice lass."

He'd laughed. Lasses were the last thing on his mind, and it was near shearing time so he was going to be busy.

They took the Land Rover and roared off into the twilight, a bottle of Islay Whiskey being passed from hand to hand to warm them up, the dance being a teetotal affair.

They parked in the square, and Mike and his five hands toured the pubs, which Roxburgh had no shortage of, having a half of the rich Newcastle Brown ale with a dram of Scotch in each.

When they finally reached the hall, they were flushed and boisterous and the Dean ran a beady disapproving eye over them. Outsiders often meant trouble and the small border town often resembled a scene from a wild west film come closing time on a Saturday night.

---

[87] Janet's husband Major Killian Robert Hamish DeJames was killed at Arnhem in Holland during 'Operation Market Garden' in September, 1944.

They took the place by storm, wolfing down sandwiches and cake from the buffet, whistling at the women and surreptitiously tipping shots of whiskey into their steaming cups of tea.

They found a corner and huddled in it whispering and giggling like a bunch of naughty school boys as they passed the odd comment and ogled the ladies dancing to the waltzes the four-piece string quartet was bashing out from the stage.

Mike felt he was being scrutinised. His senses were still very much on high alert after his time in the Airborne, he slowly turned and gazed down into the most beautiful pair of cornflower blue eyes he had ever seen in his life.

'Don't suppose you've got a spare dram of that whiskey hidden in your coat, for a thirsty lass, by any chance?"

Beth had seen him come in and her interest was piqued at the sight of the handsome stranger in slacks and shirt. She'd been fending off advances all night, and he was the only man to make her heart flutter for some time.

"That's Mike DeJames from Petral Hill Farm over Hexham Way," her pal Mary had told her. "Isn't he just to die for?"

Beth didn't know about that but there was something strong and right about his bearing and manner. The guys with him hung on his every word with respect but they seemed at ease with him. He knew his men and treated them accordingly.

Under the Dean's wife's baleful glare, she broke with strict protocol and crossed the floor to join them, her girlfriends tittering.

Mike's heartbeat rose as well when he turned and first laid eyes on the lovely, curly haired, blonde young lady who wanted to share his liquor. At twenty-eight he had already had a few short-lived affairs with the opposite sex, the most memorable being with the lovely Mrs Willoughby-Lamb Sutton in Singapore[88].

He noted her fine figure and ample bust, "Now it's a new one on me, a lovely lass asking me for hard spirits."

She proffered her tea cup. "Well, this lovely lass is bored witless... I'm Beth...Beth Connally."

He ran her name through his head. He'd noticed the chemist's shop during the pub crawl.

"Your father's the chemist. I wouldn't want you getting into trouble. He might poison me."

She waggled the half full cup at him, "I'll swop you, whiskey for aspirin. You look like you'll need them in the morning to be sure... Besides, it's better to be hung for a sheep than a lamb."

"Depends on your taste, I suppose... I like my meat young and tender," he quipped, amused and secretly flattered this charming creature had singled him out.

Making sure he wasn't seen by the hovering church elders, he poured her a generous measure.

They clicked cups and drank the fiery brew down. The band stuck up some hauntingly beautiful Strauss Waltz as the Dean advanced on them. Mike quickly dragged her onto the dance floor, cups still in hand. She came into his arms so naturally, it was as if she had been there his whole life and he realised he was smitten and wondered if she was some kind of a lovely witch who had cast her spell over him.

---

[88] See Book Three – 'The Birth of Red Viking Alpha'.

Mother would be thrilled, he consoled himself, lost in the depths of her eyes.

She rolled over to his side of the bed and hugged his pillow to her, smiling at the happy memories. It had been a speedy courtship. The Connallys thoroughly approved of Captain Michael Robert DeJames and Janet was pleased for her son. She had never seen him happier.

Beth hugged the pillow to her tighter and remembered. On the last Sunday in August, in that halcyon summer, after Kirk, they packed a picnic and went for a ramble in the hills. It was a glorious day, and they revelled in the heat and blue skies, the purple heather disappearing to the horizons.

On the slope of 'The Dark Cheviot', he spread the blanket and he took her virginity, and she wept tears of joy as the skylarks called to each other and cavorted in the azure blue sky above them. She wanted to know his darkest secret and he told her about killing Muller.

"Should have castrated the sod with a pair of shears first," was her immediate verdict on hearing the tale.

"Ouch," he declared, glad he had unburdened his secret to her, "Nah, would have been too hard to explain away… He went for a gun, so I whipped his balls off before I shot him."

They laughed at that and three months later they married at Roxburgh Kirk, a beaming Dean conducting the service. "I brought them together in a sense," he told the guests at the reception in the Roxburgh Arms.

Jamesey was born on the 12th August, 1950. A big bonny lump of a lad and the marriage progressed happily. Beth took to farm life like a camel to sand and for many years she ran a small accountancy service from a room turned into an office on the farm and made a great success of it.

She was flabbergasted when in early summer, 1968, she fell pregnant again. Mike and all concerned were delighted. Beth was still a relatively young and fit woman.

Davey Robert DeJames was born on 17th March, 1969.

"Isn't it wonderful, Mike," said a joyful Beth, cradling the infant to her in their bedroom where she had given birth. "It's Saint Patrick's Day, patron Saint of Ireland."

Mike had been watching the worsening situation in the North of Ireland on the TV. "I think the Irish need all the saints they can get at the moment… Hope Jamesey doesn't get involved in it," not knowing how true his forecast was to be, Jamesey now approaching eighteen and into his second year in the army. He had joined the junior parachute company at sixteen, based at Malta barracks in Aldershot.

A lump of peat, now near ash, flared brightly as it sank in the fire.

Half dozing, Beth tossed fretfully as she remembered that terrible day in late October five years ago when Mike had quite literally vanished.

Early snow flurries had worried him. Most of the stock was in the lower pasture fields well fenced in, and he had plenty of fodder in for them but a flock of a hundred or so was still up the 'Dark Cheviot'. As the snow fell heavier and the wind whipped up, he whistled for his dogs, and crook in hand he headed out like Jesus to find his lost flock. The Cheviot sheep were relatively short-haired and not as hardy at height as their mountain long-coated cousins in the Highlands and Snowdonia. But their heather-infused meat tasted superb.

The wicked north wind gathered speed and howled around the rooftops of Petral Hill Farm, rattling the slates and bringing more snow. The hours passed and neither Mike nor the dogs returned.

A worried Beth rang John 'Mac' McDouglas in his cottage a mile away and expressed her concerns. "Ach no, I brung that flock down earlier, I could smell the snow coming, so I could."

Beth's blood had run cold, "So Mike's up there looking for non-existent sheep? You know what a stubborn bugger he is."

Mac agreed. Worried, he gathered up the hands and, well clad and carrying torches, they set off in search. They searched and searched, only returning time and again to the farm almost dead from exhaustion, to eat and get warmed up.

Next day the mountain rescue team joined them and a platoon of the Green Howards[89] on exercise at the nearby Otterburn Ranges also joined in.

"There are drifts in the gullies near six foot deep. Just hope he's holed up somewhere," Mac bemoaned to a young platoon commander.

Beth was glad Janet wasn't here to go through the trauma. She had passed away peacefully the year before at a respectable eighty years old.

He was missing until an early thaw the next February, when his remains were found high up the 'Dark Cheviot'. His two dogs lay to each side of him as if to guard and comfort him as he passed from the living realm into the perpetual unknown one. The world had lost another hero.

Beth had the dogs buried with him. The rector had protested but one look from Beth quelled any objection.

Jamesey stood at the graveside with his arm protectively around his mother. He had sat with Mac for a while earlier drinking whiskey in his cosy cottage. "He must have gone round and around the 'Dark Cheviot', looking for non-existent sheep," an upset shepherd intoned.

Jamesey heard the guilt in his voice, "Don't blame yourself, Mac... Dad could be very stubborn when he wanted. He knew the dangers involved."

Mac shook his head sadly, "His dad was a stubborn man as well... All you DeJameses are."

Jamesey smiled at that, "Yeah, runs in the family tree, I guess."

After ten days' compassionate leave, Jamesey left to re-join his battalion. They were being sent across the water to reinforce the much under pressure Royal Ulster Constabulary. Some place called Londonderry, which was on the verge of civil war. Beth had watched him leave, going to Hexham train station with him. Mac had assured him he would look after her. She was a strong lady and would cope.

Beth finally fell asleep and in her dreams she was young and happy and Mike was laughing and chasing her through the heather.

* * *

She awoke clear-headed and refreshed. Jamesey had slipped away in the wee hours. He had been tender and considerate in his lovemaking to her, a side to him that just made her want him more. She felt as if she was in a lovely parallel universe.

---

[89] Green Howards – famous Yorkshire Infantry – now disbanded.

Breakfast was a delicious mix of free-range eggs, bacon, sausage, black and white pudding and thick slices of crusty toast washed down with copious amounts of sweet tea. *A heart surgeon's nightmare on a plate*, Collette grinned as she got stuck in with relish.

Collette was ravenous and cleared her plate, much to Beth's approval. She liked to cook and it was nice to see her efforts appreciated.

Mac and the hands came in and gulped down tea and bannock cakes before heading off to their chores. It was a large farm and high maintenance.

After breakfast Beth showed her the chickens and around the farmyard before heading off in the jeep for an extended tour of the area. "We'll head down the glen to check he cattle. Been a bit of rustling going on recently."

Collette was thrilled. It was a beautiful, still, late winter's day. The sky was blue and the views were magnificent. The air was pure and intoxicating. She never envisaged such beautiful places existed and was rapidly falling in love with it. If she ever had children, she vowed they would spend a lot of their youth in places like this. It was so clean and healthy and just…well…magical and uncorrupted.

She liked that…uncorrupted. Not like frigging Garston, where she had been dragged up. Corruption being the norm there, with a capital C.

Collette, on Jamesey's advice, had taken up reading and every day she tried to learn a few new words.

She looked up words she didn't know in a small Gems pocket dictionary she carried in her bag. She was struggling through a huge Leon Uris novel at the moment about the history of the European Jews, World War Two and the founding of the State of Israel. It was a real eye-opener. Jamesey had lent it to her. "Learn modern history. It will help you know where you stand at the moment in this world," he had instructed her.

He was not only fit and strong but a smart cookie as well, she judged proudly.

"It's a great story and it'll give you a good perspective on modern history," Jamesey told her. He was reading James Clavell's 'Shogun' about the Japanese himself, and they had sat up companionably on Eadie's airbed in his house side by side reading. It made her feel very close to him as they read quietly, shoulders brushing.

"Rustling…cor, sounds like the wild west."

They reached the glen and she helped Beth heave several bales of hay out and spread them around the ground near the gate. The cattle ambled over, snorting and bellowing gently, steam rising off them as the sun warmed their thick, shaggy tan coats.

"Look at the size of their bloody horns!" she exclaimed and hid behind Beth nervously, who laughed and closed the gate. They leant on it and watched the bovines munch lazily on the hay.

Beth pulled out a packet of Embassy Red and they smoked their fags contentedly, Collette even plucking up the nerve to reach over and pet one of the beasts, marvelling at the coarseness of its coat.

They toured the lower reaches of the farm along single-track, bumpy roads, Beth keeping an eagle eye out for breaks in the fencing and open gates.

On a desolate stretch of moorland Beth showed her the peat works. Small bricks of peat stood in conical mounds drying under the weak sun, and two of the hands were digging it out with long bladed shovels.

Beth took them over a thermos of coffee and some scones, which they received gratefully, waving to Collette.

"The ground's thawing nicely," she said on her return. "We only dig enough for our own use and to sell in the local area."

"Never knew yah could burn mud… Do yah drill for petrol too? That why the farm got its name?"

Beth smiled indulgently. Young Collette had a lot to learn. "No dear. It's not Petrol… It's Petrel. They are small, hardy sea-birds who live on the coast in the cliffs. Sometimes, if the weather's extreme, they shelter inland."

Collette smacked her head, "Duh, I put me foot in it again… Petrel, right. It's a nice name. If I have a girl, that's what I'm gonna call her."

Beth looked at her aghast. This young woman, from a world totally alien to herself, that her son seemed to be in love with. "Goodness gracious, Collette… You're err…you're not preggers are you?"

Collette blushed and squirmed. "Yah needn't worry, Beth. Am on the pill, ain't I? We're being careful."

Beth breathed out then laughed. "No offense meant. I'm sure you and Jamesey know what you're doing. Hey… If you ever have a boy, you can call it Pete."

Her turn to laugh, "None taken, mate… Nah, Pete was my sod of a dad's middle name, don't wanta be reminded of him."

Beth was intrigued. She had a lot to worm out of this mysterious girl over the next couple of days.

Beth explained how tens of thousands years ago the area had been covered in semi-tropical forest and swamp land. "Yeah, as the trees died, they sunk and lay atop each other crushing down and then the last ice age came…oh about ten thousand years ago, and killed the forests off and the glaciers crushed them even more before they receded. Peat is just an early form of coal. Hard to light and not as hot but cheap and handy."

Collette was amazed at the older woman's knowledge. She pulled the small notebook out she carried and jotted down some queries, "I'll look that up in Watford Library, won't I? I'm trying to get better educated so I don't keep putting my big foot in and embarrass Jamesey."

Beth eyed her, feeling sad for the poor girl but impressed by her determination, "I'm sure Jamesey's not embarrassed by you, dear… He has skin as thick as a rhino."

Collette smiled, "He's so bloody strong and full of himself but he feels for people, his men and his friends, he's very", she searched for the word, "principled, that's it, principled and decent," she said at last, pleased with herself.

Beth had to agree, that was her son in a nutshell, although she knew Collette was a teensy weensy bit biased, as she probably was herself.

They drove into Hexham for lunch, where they had luscious Cumberland Pie in a small café off the square.

Beth encouraged Collette to talk about herself and told her about Mike and her family, and afterwards, took her to meet her sister Deirdre, who lived in a large house in a pine forest nearby and was married to a man big in the forestry department. "You'll meet my folks tomorrow at Kirk. We're going to theirs for Sunday lunch after."

A firm and fast bond was forming between the two women from different backgrounds and eras, much too both their pleasure. Collette thought she would have been reticent and tongue-tied with Jamesey's mum but she found her easy to talk to and a good companion. Whereas Beth could have felt a mother's jealousy towards any outside female who tried to put roots down on her Jamesey, instead she felt solicitous towards her and was thoroughly enjoying the young girl's companionship and indeed her thirst for knowledge. *Funny old world*, she mused.

The long weekend flew in. Wrapped up warm, Jamesey took her up the Dark Cheviot. She was enthralled when he produced binoculars and scanned the ground before giving them to her and directing her to a copse half a mile away. She watched with baited breath as a huge stag emerged, leading a small herd of does.

"Must tell mother…she can bag one for the pot."

Collette shook her head in wonder. Mrs DeJames was some woman…her husband had taught her to shoot, and she regularly bagged deer, hare, rabbits and pigeons for the pot, he had told her. "She's the Borders version of Annie bleedin' Oakley," she remarked.

On the Saturday night they all headed into Berwick on Tweed. Beth and the hands, Mac and his beloved dogs, Jamesey and Collette.

Before they left Beth lent her a book on the area. "It's history, geology, wild life and fauna. Pop it in your bag, dear, you can return it when you come back to visit."

"I'll never read that in a few days, Beth."

"You can return it to me when you come back next time," Beth told her.

If that's not the seal of approval, then I don't know what is, she thought happily, her heart fit to burst.

"I catch the hallions and they will be picking buckshot out their buttocks for weeks to come," Beth informed her grimly, tapping her Purdey shotgun for emphasis.

They did a few bars, Collette drinking gin and tonics because Beth said it was a ladies' drink, and vodka was for sluts. Collette thought of Suzie and her bunch of roughs and agreed heartily, vodka drinkers all. Then thought of the afternoon in Watford High Street with Jamesey and squirmed hypocritically.

They had a great night. Everybody seemed to know everybody else and they all made her very welcome, her head reeling with new names and faces. *New friends*, she decided. *Decent, honest country folk.*

Their final stop was the Railway Hotel, where a dance was on. She got a few smooches in with Jamesey and Beth taught her a few Scottish reels, and she laughed heartily at the antics of two men, drunk, in kilts and sporrans, who were dancing with each other.

"That's Doug Fitzpete and Pete Fitzdoug," Jamesey remarked. She didn't get it and he refused to explain it to her.

On the Sunday they attended the Kirk at Roxburgh, all dressed sombrely and half hungover.

She met Beth's parents, a spritely couple in their late sixties. She found Mrs Connally a bit standoffish but Beth whispered to ignore her.

"She's a bit of a snob. Still hasn't forgiven me for running off to university."

She listened sombre as the Dean gave a fine, mesmerising sermon in a rich deep baritone, and when he got onto sins of the flesh, she wriggled uncomfortably on the hard bench and glanced at Jamesey.

He seemed half asleep. He was in that mode of mind only soldiers who have been denied a regular routine of sleep can achieve. He was at rest and at ease but his senses were on full alert, and he could come out of his standby state in the blink of an eye. "It's all balderdash," he muttered quietly. "Most of the churchmen I've met would put a warren of randy rabbits to shame."

She stroked his thigh and gave him a saucy wink, a pre-taste of the night ahead she had planned for him.

They left early the next morning, Jamesey's Bergen now carrying an extra ten pound of choice venison cuts for Ron and Eadie and because Collette wanted to make him stew.

He promised his mother he would be careful, and Collette promised her not to be a stranger.

As Mac drove them off, Beth sighed. The place already seemed empty. She liked Collette, felt motherly towards her. She hoped it was a match made in heaven like her and Mike's had been.

On the train they found a seat and Collette began crying. She'd loved meeting Beth and being somewhere so beautiful. It was like a foreign country.

She took his proffered hankie and welcomed his arm around her. "Told yah I can be a right moody bitch," she sniffed.

Chapter 16
"To the Theatre We Will Go"
('Are You Lonesome Tonight...? Will You Miss Me Tonight?' Elvis Presley...1962)

Before all this Luca had lain dazed in an uneasy drug induced stupor in the curtained-off cubicle, listening to the chaotic sounds of the now busy hospital around her and thinking about the man who had come bravely to her rescue. Her very salvation, she decided and crossed herself in the Russian Orthodox manner. She sighed, still in deep shock. Disbelief at the events of the evening, thinking she was in some strange nightmare dream, and she lay motionless, knowing the pain would hit her if she moved, despite the morphine coursing through her veins.

She was extremely anxious about her whole femininity now because she throbbed between her legs, and it was such a vile and personal violation, it caused her great distress and her female psyche had gone into overdrive. Had Rabbie intervened in time to save her chances of future motherhood, which she craved hugely in the course of time? Tears ran down her soft cheeks as she recalled the huge relief she felt as he burst in to save her, the madness of a berserker's blue eyes, ablaze with fury like dark flames under Arctic ice as he waded in fearlessly to beat her cowardly attackers to a pulp. Her Galahad, her Charlemagne, her shining warrior knight.

Luca considered it a miracle and silently prayed her thanks to the unknown gods and deities above who had sent him to be her saviour and knew it was meant to be. The appeasement and feeling of salvation when he had arrived was so intense as she remembered the first sight of him entering and confronting Hanlon. The hairs on the back of her neck stood up and goose pimples rose and a glow in the pit of her stomach reassured her that as far as that part of her womanliness was concerned, she still had feelings of desire. She managed a small ironic personal grin. Drugged or in pain, she still felt feminine and wanted the comfort of Rabbie's arms around her. Love or infatuation? Hero worship or just natural attraction? It was still there. A heady mix simmering in her head.

Then she thought of the humiliation inflicted upon her and the painful throb in her private place and sobbed from the heart, despairing. Who would want her now? Certainly not Rabbie! Not after he had witnessed her near-naked degradation. God, rot Hanlon to hell! She cried so hard, a passing nurse came in to comfort her, checking her drips and monitors at the same time.

Luca mentally chided herself for being such a weakling. She could be lying in the morgue at this minute instead of having these wonderful angels of mercy doing everything possible to mend her sore and battered body. Shame now joined in. Her left forearm ached in its sling, and she could feel the swelling to her left cheekbone.

196

She invoked an old Hunnish curse on Hanlon, angry now as well as upset. After checking all was fine with the catheters and the theatre gown was on right, the kind nurse patted her good hand.

"You'll be going down to theatre soon, honey. They'll fix you up in no time."

The idea of going down to the theatre terrified Luca. She imagined white-tiled walls and masked men in white blood-splattered gowns waiting grimly for her, saws and scalpels flashing under hot arc lights. She shivered. It must be the drugs, she told herself as fresh tears coursed down her face unchecked. She buried her face in the pillow and quietly wept.

"You're a poor excuse for a woman," she berated herself. "Mother and Dmitri would be ashamed of you." And more tears welled, blurring her vision and sparkling opaquely under the fluorescent illuminations.

"Now, what's all this? Those beautiful dove-grey eyes are going to be all puffy in the morning and that would be a serious breach of humanity for us men."

Rabbie was sitting on the bed holding her good hand and wiping her tears away with a handful of tissues. Her heart galloped hard in her breast, and her anxieties vanished like a burst bubble just at the repose of his strong presence. She felt that strange feeling in the pit of her stomach again, which seemed to nullify her bad pain and awoke her femininity. Luca regarded him closely. His left eye was bruised black, slitted and nearly closed, mottled yellow and mauve with bruises, and a large padded bandage covered half the back of his head. Both his hands were wrapped in tight bandages like a boxer's before he put the gloves on, and he was dressed in sweat pants and a long black dressing gown with a dragon design on it. She realised she was gripping his hand and it must be hurting him but he didn't complain.

"I tink your eyes a lot puffier than mine, Rabbie. Is it very sore?"

He grinned. "Not at all. They gave me the funny pills as well. Great stuff, OxyContin."

She sat a bit straighter and stroked his hand gently. "Am so ver' sorry I got you hurt, Rabbie."

He eyed her. This lovely young woman torn and hurting was worrying about him. She was a star. He laughed.

"I had many a shiner and worse when I was in the marines. Bruises fade and cuts heal. Everything's gonna be fine. It's just the way it is. No one's fault."

"You are so gallant, my kind knight. That's a beautiful dressing gown."

"Got it in Malaysia on tour. I have to stay in tonight for observation. Slight concussion."

She was becoming perturbed again. She was the cause of so much chaos and annoyance.

"Just a stupid medical insurance thing. Means I get to take it easy for a day or two, could do with a break, truth be told," he reassured her kindly.

Luca gave him a wry grin. "I bet you could have taut of a few better excuses for getting da break, Rab."

He adored the sexy foreign accent. Undeterred by all she had been through, the dressings, the catheters and unflattering theatre gown, which he could not help but notice was very thin and quite revealing, she still looked undoubtedly attractive. Lost, skittish and nervous but very pretty.

"Anyhow, what will be, will be. You can't put the clock back, you just have to move forward and get better."

197

She smiled. "I tink is a bit of the, 'ow you say? Philosopher in you, Rabbie."

"Not in me, Luca," he protested. "Just positive thinking. Yet stopped clock is right twice a day, but it cannot go backwards even if rewound."

She paused to think about this very complex statement and observed the bruised, good-looking man before her and realised he was just talking to take her mind off things. A huge phosphorescence of gratitude overwhelmed her and she leaned forward and kissed his black eye gently.

"You must tell me about your time in da marines, Rabbie. It will be fascinating to hear about all da different places you have been to."

She sensed his pride at having been in an elite unit and swore he visibly sat up straighter. That pleased him. Not all civilians wanted to hear soldiers telling their adventures. It unnerved them, and they couldn't grasp the concept of deep comradeship forged by arduous, dangerous training and warfare. Luca saw he was delighted and that made her glow even more.

"Ve vill, 'ow you say? 'Pull up a sandbag and swing the lamp one day'."

That stunned him, being a very old army saying.

"Where the hell did you hear that from, Luca?"

Amused, she laughed, "I tell you one day, Rabbie, over a nice bottle of wine. I used to know a soldier in Russia!"

The thought of Luca and him swopping stories over wine intrigued him to no end.

"Now, that's what I call positive thinking, young lady."

The nurse came in with two theatre attendants all scrubbed up. "Time for theatre, honey." She eyed Rabbie up and down, liking what she saw but not showing it. "And you, Mr DeJames, are meant to be up on the ward in bed."

Rabbie gave a half bow, "Certainly, Fräulein, but I insist on seeing Miss Valendenski to the theatre. It's our first date."

The nurse grinned as they wheeled Luca out, Rabbie holding her anxious hand. "Is second date, Rabbie," she reminded him, "da breakfast Friday morning was first date."

The nurse laughed, "Now that sure sounds interesting!" and she ogled Rabbie up and down quite blatantly now as they reached the lifts for the theatres. "You must be some fast operator, man."

"Oh he is, Nurse," quipped Luca. "You should see the mess he made of my bedroom."

Rabbie actually blushed, much to the ladies' delight but was pleased that his embarrassment had taken Luca's mind off things.

* * *

II

Looking down at the young Russian girl still asleep under anaesthetic in the small recovery ward, Dr Buchanon decided they had done everything possible for her and demanded they find a bed for her on a ward. She did not want Luca waking up in ER, which was filling up with crazies and druggies. The dregs and victims of society who thought they could handle a night out in the big city that never slept but by misfortune or pure self-indulgence ended them up in her ER.

"I reckon this young lady has had enough crazies for one night," she remarked to the nurse monitoring Luca.

They had put a tube down her throat and gave her a dose of adrenaline into her left kidney, plastered her left forearm and cleaned and bathed her many cuts and bruises. The bite under her left breast would scar as would possibly the one on her left cheek. The first shot of adrenaline had slowed the bleeding but Mr Shilburn wasn't happy and had performed a quick keyhole surgery from the back and given it a healthy shot from the outside, dosing the small split, and the bleeding had reduced considerably.

"You're right there, Doc. Poor gal will be sore for a time, she don't need to wake up in your mad house upstairs," agreed the nurse in a broad Maine accent. "She'll think she's woken up in the loony bin."

Grace smiled ruefully, "I guess most of them make their own hell, and we have to descend into Hades to treat them."

"Yes, um ma'am. Yer dead right. Them's bad critters that attacked young missy here."

"I don't think they will be hurting any young women for a long time to come once the cops have finished with them."

Grace hadn't been in theatre with Luca. She had too much to do in her own manic domain. Likewise, she had Hanlon and his pair of would-be rapists treated by her junior doctors, not wanting to sully her hands on them. She then had them released into police custody, where they would be taken to the city jail's secure medical floor in the maximum security tower block, glad to see the back of them. She gave a mighty yawn as her pager vibrated against her trim waist.

"Ne'er quits, Doc, do it?"

"Puts the night in though, maybe it's Brad Pitt or Michael Douglas," she laughed as she rushed out to the nurse's derisive snort.

"Ah don't think yah would see the likes of them in our ER, do yah?" she observed to a sleeping Luca.

Grace decided she would call up to the ward when she ended her shift to check Luca. The young Russian girl was quite charming, unlike many of her patients. A refreshing change from some of the thankless thugs she had to treat far too often.

* * *

They wheeled a drowsy Luca up to a mixed ward on the eighth floor and placed her bed in an end bay on the right with five other patients and drew the curtains around her as two of the ward nurses sorted her out, filling in forms and getting her settled down. The nervous, youthful Russian girl now rapidly waking up and glancing around her, skittishly.

"Vot happened to the men who attacked me?" she quizzed a curly brown-haired nurse.

"Now don't you be fretting, child," the older woman in a broad Irish accent replied. "Those skitters are banged up tight in the city jail."

Luca was inspecting the slim plaster cast that covered her left forearm from the wrist to the elbow.

"And there are two huge guys sitting at the entrance guarding you, so there are," she added reassuringly.

"And hastily emptying the vending machine of food and drink," laughed her blonde-haired companion.

"That's Little Danny and Mal," Luca told them. "Rabbie's guys."

"So don't you be worrying, child," responded the older nurse. "Take an Abrams tank to shift those two dudes, so it would."

"Just you relax and try to get a few hours' rest before the doctors come round," advised the nice Irish one.

"Yeah, and your friend, Wendy, will be up first thing and get you changed and all," explained the other. "We'll leave you as you are for the moment."

They left Luca, the curtains closed around her bay, a small night light on low. She surveyed herself again and sighed deeply. She must look a mess and it was very humiliating to have the urine catheter, which led to a bottle attached to the side of the bed. The plaster cast felt strange and alien. Restrictive. She felt her swollen left cheekbone gingerly. The butterfly stitches covered in gauze. The bite under her left breast had been dressed and throbbed horribly. Her ribs were sore and her thighs were badly blackened and scraped. Her left shin was grazed deeply the whole length and dressed with ointment and a gauze dressing. Her lower back was sore and tender.

Again she thought back to the horrific events in her bedroom. She had seen the obscene Hanlon's arousal as he beat her and shuddered as she imagined him raping her. She couldn't seem to get the incidents of the night out of her mind. They seemed to go around and around in her head like a fairground carousel. The traumatic and frightening events flashing before her every time she closed her eyes and tried to rest.

Luca knew sleep would be impossible. She wasn't even sure if she wanted to. She knew for certain that the mythical god Morpheus would be sending his little demons to plague her with nightmares and vivid flashbacks, which would do nothing to help her current state of mental exhaustion.

The Irish nurse peeked her head through the curtain. "Can't sleep? What do you say to a nice cup of sweet tea with toast and marmalade? Might help settle you."

Luca realised she was parched. "That would be lovely. Tank you so much, Nurse."

A few minutes later the curtain parted and Rabbie appeared with a tray. "We will have to stop meeting like this," he said and poured her tea from a small metal pot and buttered the toast for her.

She watched him administer to her needs. She drank two cups of tea in quick succession.

"It's the adrenaline. Makes you dehydrate as it leaves the system. Brings the thirst on yah."

"Why are you not asleep, Rabbie? You need to rest as well," she asked him as she nibbled at the toast, mock annoyed, but secretly delighted at his unexpected arrival.

"Was up seeing the guys. Sent Mal home. He'll have to run the show for the next day or so. Intercepted the nurse. Those girls never stop."

"They are quite wonderful, da," Luca agreed. "I must look da mess," and she yawned heavily behind her good hand.

Rabbie munched on a cream cracker and a piece of cheddar, "Strange how something as simple as a cracker can be so magnificent when you're hungry," he observed just to make small talk.

He sat up on the bed with her, stretched his legs out quite unselfconsciously and put his arm around her. He had to admit she did look pale and wane, strained and hurting. She instantly felt warm and safe so close to him. She put her bad arm across him and rested her head against his strong chest, revelling in his steady heartbeat. Within seconds she was asleep, curled tight to him. Rabbie gazed down at the forlorn woman beside him, marvelling at the length of her eyelashes. Surprised at the surge of protectiveness that nearly overwhelmed him. A curse and shame on Hanlon and on all those of his ilk who gave men a bad name. Fucking crazed predators.

I really should have ripped that bastard Hanlon's head off and been done with it! he chided himself, sensing her pain through his own. More sore than he would admit to. *And shoved my hand down his neck and ripped his foul heart out.*

The older nurse entered the bay, "Mr DeJames! You can't sleep with the patients," she scolded him quietly.

He grinned wickedly, "I don't think Luca is open to advances at this moment, Nurse, and I'm not sleeping…anyway, she's at peace and I'd hate to disturb her."

She digested that, "Well, I guess for an hour or two it won't do any harm."

"What part of Ireland are you from?" he enquired.

"I am from Cork originally."

"Ah, the last port of call for the Titanic."

"Yep, and like the Titanic, I'll be sunk if Matron catches you lying there."

He laughed. "Don't worry. I'll be long gone before morning rounds."

She left them to it, and Rabbie closed his eyes, the warmth of the injured girl next to him making him drowsy now. He drifted off to sleep. Luca opened a heavy eyelid, was astounded at the thickness and length of his eyelashes, before dropping back to sleep, vastly reassured by his male bulk alongside her. Sink or swim, at least they would go down together.

He was awakened by an insistent prodding on the arm and gazing blearily through red eyes; he surveyed a large, portly woman dressed immaculately in white starches scrutinising him closely.

"I am Sister Maureen O'Hara, and I am in charge of the wards on this floor."

"Nice to meet you, Sister," he mumbled. "Am I in trouble?"

"Not if you get up now before Matron does her rounds. Nurse Quigley explained the situation to me." He glanced at the ward clock above the door; three hours had elapsed. "Seems to me I've been meeting lots of Irish people recently."

"So I hear and I hear you beat the bejabbers out of one earlier."

"Should have ripped the bastard's head off!" gently disengaging himself from a comatose Luca. "Would have saved you girls a lot of bother."

Sister O'Hara gave a small grin. "Yes, well, us Irish are actually a very caring race. Now up with you and away to your own bed."

He got up and stretched. "Maureen O'Hara…she was a famous actress, forties, fifties?"

"To be sure, my parents were big fans, thus the name. Now up you get, boyo."

"That's it! She played opposite John Wayne in 'The Quiet Man'."

"Indeed, she did. Now you be a 'Quiet Man' and slip away off to your own quarters."

He looked down at a sleeping Luca, who seemed at peace. Sister O'Hara shooed him gently away. "Now be on with yah. She'll still be there later on."

Rabbie ambled off, tying his dressing gown.

"And don't be hopping into bed with anybody else on your way," she warned him with a mischievous twinkle in her eye.

"Wouldn't dream of it, Sister," he laughed over his shoulder.

Sister O'Hara watched his retreating back, "No, that boyo's only the eyes for the one woman, so he has," she observed to herself and turned back to check the slumbering girl's vital signs. "Quite the romantic that one, so he is, to be sure."

* * *

Luca was in hospital for ten days in total. That first day, true to her word, Wendy was up first thing with a bag of necessities for her and helped the nurses wash and change her into a pretty dark-blue nightdress, shushing an embarrassed Luca and giving her lots of comfort and concern.

"You are da bestest pal in da whole vide world, Vends."

Dr Buchanon came up to see her and told her she would be monitoring her treatment closely. Luca thanked the good doctor effusively.

"Nonsense, it's my pleasure and it's Grace to you."

Wendy had phoned Luca's work and talked to a Mrs Philomena Rourke who was in charge, temporarily, of the office. Simon Siminion was away on a cruise with his dying lifelong partner, Peter Schuster. Philli was aghast when she heard the news.

"Was it that friggin' bastard Hanlon and his pack of thugs, Mrs Havilland?"

"Sure was, but Rabbie beat ten tons of crap outta the dirt bags and please call me Wendy."

"I'll be right over, Wendy," said a distraught head designer, not knowing that she and Wendy were going to become bosom buddies and a new romance was on the horizon for her.

They brought the portable X-ray machine up, and when a tired Mr Shilburn came up, he studied the results on his laptop and seemed happy.

"The bleeding has fairly slowed, Luca. It should heal okay but you'll have to stay in bed until I am satisfied it is healing properly. You're very lucky not to have lost that kidney. Tricky sods they are."

"And I vould have but for you, da? You're ver' kind and clever. Tank you soo so much."

He beamed, his tiredness forgotten as the Luca effect took control.

Rabbie discharged himself at lunchtime, against medical advice, and strolled down to see her. He had rung a contact in the cops and made sure the thugs were securely locked up and unlikely to get bail. He was trying to work out how to justify the expense of two bodyguards for Luca 24/7 and decided if it came to the crunch, he would cover it. He would have a word with his father and work a few shifts himself.

When he got to her bay, she was sitting up in bed, having just eaten a light lunch. He deposited a large plastic cup of the rich Colombian roast coffee he knew she liked on her tray with a handful of brown sugar sachets and studied her. Despite the terrible ordeal she had gone through and her injuries, she was achingly beautiful. Those

202

incredible eyes and clear skin and a figure many women would kill for, and the hair, washed and gleaming, quite tantalised him.

The other five lady patients in the bay for various ailments and operations looked at the handsome guy in a long leather coat and jeans with interest and wondered if they were lovers. They sure made a dynamic, mesmerising duo. Rumour on the ward was the guy had slept with the foreign girl last night... Imagine that!

Luca gave him a shy, tentative smile, "Rabbie, I don't know how da begin to thank you for vot you..."

He quietened her. "Hey, no need. Sure we're both okay...anyhow," and he paused. "Did you not let me sleep in your bed last night?" he added cheekily.

A pretty blush crept across her face and she giggled softly. "Ah, da American humour. Da, I get it. But seriously, Rab, should you not still be in your bed?"

He took the lid off her coffee and began pouring the rich demerara sugar in, "Nah, been discharged. Doc said my head's as thick as King Kong's. Five sugars I believe you took last time we had breakfast."

The other patients were listening with great interest. Breakfast together... Holy cow!

"Da, just da five please. I must watch my waistline, yah?"

"Sure looked okay last night."

She giggled, enjoying the banter and passed him a small plastic beaker they used for water. "Have some wiv me, Rabbie."

He smirked, "I had enough last night. Besides I like it hot, black and strong. How you feeling?"

She shrugged, "I'm not sure. Sore and da confused but ver' happy to see you on your feet. Who dis King Kong guy wiv da thick head?"

Rabbie told her about the giant ape and the movie as she sipped at her coffee contentedly, so relieved he did not seem to have any permanent injuries.

"You look da swashbuckling wiv da black eye, Rab, like da actor in the pirate movie, Johnny Deep."

"Johnny Depp," he corrected her.

"Da, Johnny Deep."

"Yeah, Johnny Deep," he conceded, amused.

They chatted for half an hour before his pager bleeped. He looked at the number and groaned, "Work a beckoning me. No rest for the wicked."

"Are you da wicked, Rabbie?"

"That's for me to know and for you to find out, gorgeous," he retorted candidly.

Luca savoured that with her coffee, "Mm mm...delicious... I think dat would be great fun to find out," and she gave him such a wicked, impudent smile, he nearly doubled up with glee. He hesitated then kissed her on the cheek.

"Must fly," and left, the other patients' heads swivelled to watch the good looker retreat.

The patients were still agog. The ward sure had livened up since Luca had been admitted.

"I vunder where he has to fly to? Probably to rescue more naked women," she remarked to the lady in the bed next to her.

"He can save me naked any day, yah can bet your bottom dollar on that!" the woman replied. A grandmother in her late sixties with kidney stones.

"Vat is this bottom dollar?" Luca queried, looking over, interested. "My name is Luca, da. How do you do?"

* * *

Mid-afternoon and Luca was reading a fashion magazine and eating a chocolate éclair one of the bodyguards had kindly got for her. He was a fresh-faced man in his mid-thirties. Strong looking and friendly. He said to call him 'Buzz' but that the guys called him 'Boomerang'. She asked him if he was from Australia before he returned to his station at the door. He told her no, he was from a small town in Ohio.

She was still trying to work that out, guessing it was another weird American euphemism, when a large, older man with red/gold hair and a plastic right hand arrived with an attractive blonde lady. He introduced himself as Rabbie's father and told her to call him Jamesey and the lady as Simone Parry, who was his head PA as well as being his fiancée.

They pulled up chairs, and Jamesey explained he had been in Boston checking out the new office when Rabbie had rang and informed him of the previous night's dreadful happenings, and they had flown straight to New York in the company jet. After ensuring Rabbie was okay, they had come to visit her.

"Now don't you be worrying about a thing, Luca. I've been onto the Mayor, and he's going to keep me up to speed as to the progress the police are making with those evil bastards, and OLG will have two armed men guarding you twenty-four hours a day for as long as necessary."

He was straight-talking, efficient and very pleasant. She saw where Rabbie got his confidence from. There was an animal attraction that radiated off him, but unlike the brute Hanlon's vile magnetism, Jamesey made her feel comfortable and reassured. Despite his American accent, he still had the traces of the soft burr in his voice like Rabbie's.

"I am soo soo grateful to you all. Rabbie vas so brave last night, da. I tink I vould be dead now but for him."

He laughed softly, "Yeah, he sure is a chip off the old block." Then seeing her confused expression. "He reminds me a bit of me when I was younger," he explained. "I've sent him home; the blighter went to work with a Goddamn head injury!"

Luca was pleased. "Dat's good, Jamesey. He stayed wiv me all da night."

"Can't say I blame him, Luca. At least if you're gonna rescue a woman from a pack of crazed beasts, make sure it's a beautiful one."

She blushed a pretty red, and Simone took her hand gently, "Must say Rabbie has good taste when it comes to damsels in distress."

They chatted kindly to her for a time, and Simone was very pleased when Luca complimented her on her beauty and the elegant light-mauve two-piece suit she was wearing. The young Russian woman was quite enchanting but Simone could still see the trauma in her eyes from her horrid ordeal.

"You know, Luca dear. I went through a similar experience last year. I was terrified. You need lots of rest and counselling."

"Oh my God, Simone. Are you okay now?" asked Luca, shocked.

She patted Luca's hand in reassurance, "Yes, dear, Jamesey came to my rescue in a manner of speaking and sorted the son of a bitch out."

"Yeah, sure did," grinned Jamesey. "The said SOB vacated the building in some style."

Luca bet he did. Like father, like son. "It must be in da DeJames family genes and blood to be da heroes. I am just so glad you are okay, Simone, and tis soo lovely to meet you both, da."

Jamesey laughed, "Dunno about that but we know a good looker when we see one," squeezing Simone's knee fondly. "You must come and visit us in Los Angeles when you're better, dear."

"Sure, we'd love to have yer. The sunshine will do you good," added Jamesey.

Luca liked the sound of that, hoping with all her heart Rabbie would come with her.

The rest of the patients had been eavesdropping candidly. The Luca chick sure got some interesting visitors. They were even more delighted when Simone passed a box of Danish pastries around that she had bought with her for Luca, who had had enough chocolate for the day. They left shortly after, it being the patients' quiet hour, promising to keep in touch.

That evening she had a steady stream of visitors – Philli, Wendy and Bobby. Several of the girls from the office, even Mr and Mrs Chin from the apartments, chattering away to her in broken American-Mandarin. They all brought little nibbles and delicacies for her, which she discreetly shared with her other inmates.

At nine when Wendy left, she lay back on her pillows and closed her eyes, tired. The doctors were pleased with her recovery so far and tomorrow the detectives were coming to talk to her.

"You okay, Luca? What did you think of my father and Simone?"

She opened her eyes, her heart beating a rapid tattoo.

"Rabbie, vot you doing here?"

He was dressed in black jumper and trousers and a long black trench coat as she noticed the other bodyguards wore. She hadn't expected to see him at all.

"I'm doing the night shift with Billy-Jo."

She was flabbergasted. "But, err…your papa said you were not allowed to work wiv sore head."

"Sitting on a chair's not working…besides, I've been sleeping all day."

He sat on the bed with her and they talked quietly. Her eyes were getting heavy. The meds were making her drowsy. He lowered her bed with the remote, pulled up her sheet and dimmed the light. He sat holding her hand until she fell asleep. A couple of the other patients watched, wondering if he was going to jump into bed with her, but they were in for a disappointment. He stroked the magnificent mane of umber hair gently, revelling in the luxurious silkiness.

"Don't worry, Princess," he told the sleeping female. "You're safe tonight. Nobody gets past Rabbie DeJames." He silently left to take up his position by the door, jaw set, one hundred percent alert.

The grandmother in the next bay had been feigning sleep and she wiped a tear from her eye. Goddamn! It was so damned romantic, like a fairy tale. Sure beat Mills & Boon, she reckoned, before dropping off to dream of her carefree days of youth and of the young men who had courted her.

* * *

So the days dragged on as her painful beaten and battered body gradually healed and regained its strength. The two nice lady detectives who had handled her previous complaint against Hanlon had taken her statement, and she was very relieved when they told her he wouldn't be getting bail. They were holding him on suspicion of committing other crimes against women in the borough of Queens, where they found a secret stash of home-made pornographic videos in a concealed safe in his office.

"Very nasty, Luca…depraved, good job that DeJames dude was so switched on," they told her.

Billy Crichton was cooperating with them and had confessed to his part in the affray and had been given bail, but they didn't feel he posed any threat to her. Arturo was keeping his mouth well zipped. He had previous convictions for violence and was denied bail.

Luca thanked them, mightily mollified, and signed a consent form allowing them access to her medical records. She still received a stream of visitors and was the nurses' favourite. Rabbie was a regular visitor. He was back to running the office full-time but did the odd shift guarding her. He never got back into bed with her again, much to the other patients' disappointment and if Luca dared admit it, to hers as well. Although some nights he sat holding her hand or with his arm around her till she drifted off to sleep.

He was a tower of strength and support and still her pulse raced every time he arrived. She was highly aroused and massively attracted to him and wondered if he felt the same or was he just a kind, decent guy. It was something she thought about a lot, pondered on as her bruises faded and her aches and pains eased. Just thinking of him was a soothing balm to the huge mental shock that the attack had given to her female psyche.

After four days they removed the hated urine catheter after Mr Shilburn was satisfied the bleeding from her kidney was minimal, and she was allowed to sit in the armchair by the bed and chat with the other patients and visitors. She was such a congenial and solicitous woman and her devastating exquisiteness and charisma people drew magically to her. They wanted to help and bolster the young beauty that had gone through such a horrible experience. Even the bodyguards slipped in and out with little goodies and luxuries for her. Billy-Jo Sawyer sat with her in the early hours when she couldn't sleep or had woken afraid following a nightmare. She would console Luca and tell her about her escapades in the navy and what it was like to be raised in Tennessee.

An older lady called Judith, a trained rape counsellor, came to see her. She had been held captive by a gang of Hell's Angels for several days before a police SWAT team (Special Weapons and Tactics) had stormed their HQ and rescued her. Judith had been repeatedly gang-raped and now dedicated her life ever since to helping young women who had gone through a similar experience. Luca listened to her in awe, feeling for her, and drew great peacefulness and consolation from the advice Judith gave her, Luca's admiration for her formidable inner strength apparent and gleaming in her eyes.

One day a tall, distinguished silver-haired man came in looking for a Mrs Lustrum. He was dressed in an immaculate three-piece pinstripe suit and had a suntan no artificial lamp could ever achieve.

"She was discharged yesterday," Luca told him.

He eyed the lovely young woman intently. "Oh drat, and I have the theatre booked and all," he answered in a crisp British accent. And who are you, my dear? What happened to your cheek?"

"Why, I am Luca, Luca Valendenski from da Lithuania."

He approached and shook her hand. "James Sturgeon. I'm a plastic surgeon. They call me 'Sturgeon the Surgeon'," and he chuckled at his own joke. "Mind if I have a look? You've beautiful facial bone structure."

She let him take the plaster off her left cheekbone. "Hmm… I can open that and put micro stitches in. Leave no scar at all. Be such a shame for such a lovely face to be marred for life!"

"I can't pay you, "Luca said uneasily. "I am saving da dollars to bring my mama and da brother over."

"Ah, don't worry about that, my dear. I'll do it pro bono. I have a few hours free."

He hastened off to find the ward sister. What Luca didn't know was Jamesey had hired him in secret at a discount. OLG had got him out of a very nasty little blackmail scam that could have ruined his career. After reading her notes, he came back with a nurse and drew the curtains. She wondered what bono, Bono the pop singer, Mr Sturgeon was fixing.

"My poor girl. What a dreadful time you have had. Do you mind if I examine your other injury and see what I can do for you?"

"I don't want to be da pest to you, Mister Studgeon."

He smiled, liking her accent, not bothering to correct her pronunciation.

"It's no bother, my dear. I am only too pleased to help."

He examined the bite under her left breast. She had magnificent tone and structure to them, one of the finest pairs he had ever seen and he had seen thousands. That being what got him into trouble in the first place with an over-amorous patient, who then subsequently blackmailed him and OLG had sorted the matter out for him.

"I'll cut those bite marks away, stretch the skin over and put in more micro stitches. In a few months it will have completely disappeared."

James examined the long scabby wound down her shapely right leg. She truly was a quite wonderful example of the opposite sex.

"I'll trim that right down and plastic skin it. Your own skin will grow back quite naturally underneath and gradually replace it."

For some reason she wasn't afraid. She trusted this man who appreciated and repaired the female form.

"It will need to be dressed and will weep for a while but should heal nicely."

Luca was gratified and told him so and gave him a gleaming smile. Good teeth, he thought, and for some reason the Greek goddess of love, Aphrodite, came to mind. The perfect woman personified. The birth mother emerging from a warm sea, droplets of water running down her beautiful body in the sunlight. He mentally pulled himself back to the present. Randy sods those ancient Greeks!

Four hours later she was back on the ward, still a bit dopey from the drugs. Mr Sturgeon told her that everything had gone swimmingly, and he would see her in a few weeks at his out-patients' clinic.

A worried Rabbie rushed up that evening to see her. He hadn't been told about the procedures but sensed his father's hand in there somewhere and was grateful for the big guy's input. He found her surrounded by visitors, who were listening rapt as she told them about the forests of the Drasnov Valley and how she had found the little missing child. "Oohs", "Wows" and "Wonderfuls" emitted from her audience. She had them in the palm of her hand. She saw him and gave him the smile reserved for the folk on her 'Most favourite people list', and his heart warmed and his pulse quickened. She looked ravishing in a pleated light green nightdress.

"Hey, Luca, I'm guarding you tonight."

"How vonderful, my gallant knight. You are too good to Luca."

The visitors looked from one to the other, realising it was time to go and leave the dynamic duo alone. He sat by her bed all night. Watching over her, mesmerised by her beauty, pondering the future. He knew he could very quickly fall in love with her if he hadn't already. Adversity had brought them together, and he wondered if that little sod cupid was firing his arrows at him, and if he was, maybe he had been hit.

As if sensing his thoughts and presence, she woke in the early hours and held his hand.

"It vill be okay, Rabbie. You see. Ev'ting vill be okay," before promptly falling asleep again.

He puzzled at that. At the road that lay ahead for them, beckoning and enticing.

On Tuesday night, her tenth on the ward, Mr Shilburn and Grace arrived to see her.

"Get a good night's rest and eat your lunch up, and you can go home tomorrow," they told her.

She hugged them both tightly, tears spilling in thankfulness. "I tink I can do dat," she snivelled happily.

Outside the big bad city roiled and boiled in its never-ending cycle as its millions of citizens went through their own routines, many happy, many troubled as a sliver of a sickle moon looked down on the myriad of manmade lights and wondered at the unnaturalness of it all and where the hell it was all heading.

Chapter 17
Around the World Without a Shortcut
(Goodbye Dolly, I Must Leave You, with My Rifle and My Pack on My Back,
Goodbye Dolly, I Must Leave You and I don't Know When I'll Be Back
World War 1 Infantry Marching Song... 'Goodbye, Dolly Gray')

He came awake at 4am, aware of the subtle tick of her alarm clock defining what little time they had left together. He knew there was something wrong. He didn't really need to look at the clock to tell the time, with years of training he knew almost to the minute what time it was. She was cradled in tight to his left side, her head welded hard into his shoulder, holding him tightly in her arms, one leg cocked across his legs. He could feel the heat of her sex on his upper thigh and the wetness of her tears across his chest.

He reached over and flicked on the small shaded lamp, a present from Ron and Eadie, which threw a gentle orange glow across them. She kept her head buried in his neck but he knew she was awake.

"What's wrong, Collette? Why are you so upset, honey?"

She nuzzled her head in deeper and sobbed. He stroked her tousled hair and down her back. He had no idea where this relationship was going. He was a soldier heading off to Belfast in a few days and could not afford to think of the 'love' word. It would be a serious distraction that might prove fatal if he was thinking about Collette and not where the next IRA sniper was going to strike from.

"Right, Private Stark!" he barked, making her startle. "This is your platoon, Sergeant. If you don't respond to my orders, I am going to treat you like a map-reading exercise."

He rolled her away a little and grinned at her, looking deep into her lovely eyes, the colour of fine highland whiskey. Glittering with tears and basking a light opaque yellow beige in the dim light. She gave him a small crooked smile.

"You mean Private Stark naked, doncha? Guess that's how you have me."

"And tis the lucky man, I am to be sure, to be sure," he replied, putting on his best Irish navvy's accent. "You're a gift from the fairies, so you are to be sure, so yah are."

She smiled sadly, the beautiful curve of her full lips rising, "I'll never be able to hear that accent again over the next few months without thinking about you in that awful shit pit of a place."

209

He'd got her talking anyway, that was great. "Oh, I don't know. Most of the people are decent enough and the women are to die for."

She punched him in the shoulder, "Don't use that word and don't let me hear about you and them bloody colleens!"

He laughed uproariously, "Now, now, Collette. Just because one stops and looks in the shop window doesn't mean one is going to go in and sample the goods."

She glanced sharply at him, "If I catch you sampling the bloody goods, you'll have more than the bleedin' IRA to worry about. To be sure, to be sure," she added cheekily, "I'll whoop your nuts off…to be sure."

This was better. He had got the reaction he wanted. Get them laughing and you had half the battle won, the RUC[90] cops had told him in joint riot training when dealing with crowd disturbances.

"Why go out for a hamburger, darling, when you can have a steak at home?" and he pulled her face into his for a smacking kiss, which she responded eagerly to, clinging to him for all her worth.

"And what do you mean you're going to use me as a map-reading bleeding exercise?" inquiring as she broke for air, one eyebrow raised quizzically.

"Well, if I know all the landmarks, and where I'm going, then I'll be coming back without getting lost or going astray, won't I?"

Collette looked bemused, "Well, okay, I guess so. What do I have to do?"

This was good. He had consensual participation, he was nearly there.

"Just lay there and enjoy and tell me when I go the wrong way."

Still bemused she put up no resistance as he pulled the covers off her and laid her out comfortably, eyeing appreciatively the full length of her gorgeous body bathed seductively in the warm orange glow. He ran his fingers through her hair, gently massaging the scalp.

"We'll start in the New Forest, formerly known as 'The Bright Pink Wood' before reverting to nature."

She giggled and he ran his hands down her face and kissed her eyes and licked her tears away. "That last stop wasn't the two Brave tarns, renowned for over-running when upset."

She giggled again, "What's a tarn, Jamesey?"

"It's a small, beautiful glacial lake high up in the mountains."

He kissed down her nose and found her swollen lips again and gave her a lingering kiss. She was getting into it now, especially as his wayward hands were gently stroking her to distraction, the big brute.

"Where are you now, love?" she asked as he broke off.

"I was pot holing. That was the Collette Stark Cave. Famous for its depth and pleasant taste and texture but feared for the pink tongue monster inside that can drive men wild and keep them entranced in its spell forever."

She liked that idea he saw, "So, you're under my spell then, Jamesey?"

"Looks like it, unless I get lost."

"You better get back to the map then, better you?" she ordered eagerly.

He kissed down her chin and into the hollow of her neck, his hands coming up and holding her eager breasts. He stared down at them.

---

[90] Royal Ulster Constabulary

"We've just come over the lovely Chin Ridge and across Milky Hollow and have stopped by the Mountains."

She scoffed, "You mean the South Downs, darling?" Her voice was thickening and he was pleased to hear as he replied. "They ain't the bloody Alps, you know...to be sure," and giggled again.

"The South Downs are very beautiful and a pleasant place to stop for a while."

He kissed down each breast in turn, lingering over each impatient, perk rosy nipple, which he sucked on and nibbled at. He was becoming very aroused himself now, not helped by the little minx stroking his thigh and gently squeezing his balls. He decided he had better continue his journey.

"We regrettably have to leave the magnificent left and right Rose Hip peaks and travel on."

He kissed down over her ribs and licked his way across her creamy warm stomach, which gurgled prettily in appreciation, before licking in and around her flexing naval.

"Where are you now, love?" she moaned.

"I just crossed the bony, arid expanse of Stark's Ridges and explored the fertile, tasty expanse of the Vale of Stark, before stopping at the Oasis of the Belle Belly Button before I go into the dark dangerous jungle in search of The Lost Hole of Love. An ancient legend that describes an area of outstanding natural beauty that puts the Grand Canyon to shame."

She laughed excitedly. "I like the sound of that, although it will never be lost to you, babe," she reassured him.

He gave her a wicked look and grin. "Ah, but there you're wrong, my dear. After every time it's found, alas it's lost again but then comes the pleasure of re-finding it, pure bliss," and with that he stroked her pubic mound and probed through her hairs, ever down, until he was at last insistently stroking her engorged pussy lips. She writhed under him, erotically inflamed. His big meaty digit found her and slithered in up to the hilt in her sticky wetness, searching around deliciously, her clitoris engorged and pressed against him.

"Found it!" he exclaimed, "The Lost Hole of Love that only ever opens to the Sergeant's magic spells. Open Sesame!"

"Truly a magic word," she remarked huskily. "Abracadabra, babe, it's magic all right." She was laughing and crying all at once now, highly aroused and thoroughly enjoying this unusual act of lovemaking.

No man had ever made her feel so wanted or worshipped like this. She felt one hundred percent woman, sensual and stimulated. Very, very aware of her own adult sexuality.

Another finger had slipped in and she felt herself rising in a crescendo of exquisite feelings as she quickened her breath and sweetly orgasmed over his fingers.

"I like it when you bang me off with your magic wands. Christ, I don't know where that came from but I really, really need your big prick up me."

Jamesey eyed Collette wickedly again, her eyes slitted and gleaming with desire, his eyes wide and dancing with mischief. He had moved down the bed, and she could stoke his back and buttocks with her right hand but she couldn't reach his cock as he had turned half away but she could see its turgid tip peeking out cheekily above his thighs, her heightened desire absolutely concentrating on getting that hard rod inside her aching pouch.

"We must finish our travels before we can rest for the night in the jungle," he teased.

He began to kiss and stroke down the inside of her right thigh, "I am now travelling down the shapely White Ridge. One of two long landmarks on the trip."

She reached down and tugged his hair, "No. no, you're going the wrong way. Back to the jungle. Back to The Lost Hole of Love, it's still open."

He laughed again, enchanting in its sexual undertones. She was really into it now, engrossed and relishing every intimate moment. He caught her eye and winked. He had been trained to resist interrogation in the army and stood as firmly as his aching penis. He was gloatingly pleased with his creativeness. *I'll write a book about this one day*, he promised himself.

Jamesey kissed and nibbled down her thigh and over her knee, "Just crossing Mount Knobby Stark."

Collette was lying with her left leg spread and the foot flat, knee bent back. He glanced up and saw her whole womanhood gleaming and inviting. She was watching his every move avidly. She opened her cunt lips with fingers so he could see, hoping to entice him back. Her inner lips glistened like the colour of rich smoked salmon, provocatively trying to lure him back to her throbbing gaping sex. He reached her right foot and kissed her toes and massaged her instep. She groaned in her throat, nerves aflame and alive like electric charges.

"We have now reached the end of Stark Country." He kissed her big toe, "'Stark's Land's End'. A series of Toe Ends and Bays."

Before she knew what she was doing, he rolled her over with his clever hands and began travelling up her legs with his tongue and strong hands. He paused just short of her arse. His voice sounded ragged now.

"After the long journey from the extremities of Toe Ends, we cone to rest at the bottom of the two round peaks that guard Stark's Hidden Gorge."

He began gently massaging and licking her globes. She forced her legs apart a foot or so and managed to reach down and stroke her wet slit with a hungry finger. He parted her arse cheeks and kissed the length of her crack, probing and stroking the round nub of her anus with the flat of his thumb for a while, the sensation nearly driving her crazy and she begged him to fuck her.

"We haven't finished our journey yet, darling." He knelt astride her and started kissing up her spine, not missing one nub.

"Where are we now, love? You lost? I've gotta have some dick. Your big hard dick up my cunt."

He could hear her panting, "I am going up the backbone of Stark Country that reaches back to the New Forest." He reached the nape of her neck and nuzzled her for a minute lovingly.

"Journey's end," he sighed theatrically. "Now where to stop for the night?"

Despite her rampant lust, she laughed delightedly, "That was brill, babe. Now for frig's sake get back to the jungle and hide your snake in there for the evening."

"Okey-dokey." He slithered back down her back. She thought he was going to roll her over again but he spread her legs wide and knelt between them and lifted her arse. She felt a huge shiver of excitement. She had never been entered from behind before, her previous experiences being strictly missionary, with fumbling boys who climaxed in minutes, then thought they were God's gift to the female race. King Knobs. The 'Bulldogs' Bollocks.

She could feel his suffused cock rubbing up and down her spread arse checks and moaned, knowing she was at the hands of a very experienced and sophisticated lover and revelling in every second of it. "Shove it up now, babe. Now!"

"Now we enter the jungle from a different direction in search of The Lost Hole of Love again."

Collette could feel the tip of his cock between her red hot pulsing lips. Her spread flanks shivered and quivered in hungry anticipation.

"You're there, you're there, quick babe. You've found it." She was gasping and writhing impatiently now, at the point of a new total distraction and had already had several more orgasms and her pussy was sopping wet.

"Stick it up, honey, please. Shove it up me. I'm begging yah." She knew he was grinning.

"Are you sure, baby?"

If she wasn't in such a delicate in flagrante position, she would have belted him one. Fuck, he was a teasing god, her sex machine.

"Okay," and he plunged his glorious cock right the way up, and she came in a mammoth mighty splintering climax that nearly blew her to pieces and went on and on as he pumped in and out until a minute later she knew he was about to come as well, all her feminine senses screaming for her to give him the comfort of releasing his hot seed into her. As he burst the full length in a climatic crescendo of hot powerful spurts, she orgasmed again, almost insane with love as she screeched out his name over and over again.

Then the obligatory after love ciggie and his crack about how he didn't know about smoking after sex but she was a fire hazard because she nearly set the bed alight. That pleased her intensely and made her feel sexy. She fell asleep to his endearments of her being his sex kitten, his lurve machine, the lump in his trunks, the queen of the love hole. She loved every crude remark he made. She fell asleep dreaming of The Hole of Love and wondering if he would ever find it again. He frigging better, the big sod.

He watched her sleeping and took a last long swig from the half-empty bottle of vodka, knowing it would be his last drink in months and flicked off the lamp. Collette warm and safe in his protective arms.

Oh dear! Oh dear! he mused. *Oh what a tangled web we weave. Looks like that devious goddess Venus has done her sneaky job and won the game. Job well done, cupid. Hook, line and sinker.*

This was one soldier deeply in love. He lay awake, thinking of their time, planning and scheming their future together. Reckoning this was the end of his footloose, wicked days and not giving a damn. All he ever wanted now was nestled tight into him, a look of such contentment on her lovely face that it almost choked him up and he wasn't a man you could easily choke. He knew to leave her later was going to be a big tug on his heartstrings, but duty beckoned, war duty and he would earn his shilling.

* * *

Much against his better judgement, as he did not want her anymore upset, he decided to let her come with him to the station to wave him off.

After they showered, she dressed in a pretty light-blue cashmere sweater and navy hipsters that gave him the odd tantalising glimpse of her naval. She donned the dark blue coat he had bought her, scarf and jaunty hat and four inch stilettos, which he wondered at. Only women would wear such slick heels on a cold frosty morning. Accidents waiting to happen. He remembered the loud crack when Slimy Barry's wrist had broken and decided he would hang onto her firmly on the way to the station. He would hate to see one of those dainty ankles go the same way.

They took a taxi to the pub, where a sleepy Ron gave him his kit bag and shook his hand and told him he would keep a pint in the barrel for him on his return.

At the station she came on to the platform with him and they had a smoke, waiting for the 7.45 to Euston. She clung to him possessively, taking in his every word, movement, each frosty breath he let out with the fag smoke, so she could remember every detail later. She felt very mature, tender from real sex, she was obsessed with him. She could have never in her wildest dreams imagined she would ever meet a guy like him let alone share his bed and dare she hope have a future with him. He had turned her whole life upside down the last three weeks and she felt like she was living a dream.

Collette told Jamesey that she had saved up for the hipsters so she would look nice for him, and he hugged her and gave her a lingering kiss, totally oblivious of the crowd on the platform.

"You always look nice to me, Collette," as he ended the kiss, reluctantly. "You're definitely more interesting than the army maps. Better features," and gave her a wolfish smile.

Two secretary types on a bench were watching, and she glared at them with venom. She felt terribly possessive of him and resented them looking at her man, and they looked hastily away knowing the slim girl would rumble them. Overhead the clock ticked the minutes away unmercifully. She hoped it would be delayed. Maybe forever.

Collette was wholly aware of everything around her, her senses overacting on her. The cold of the platform seeping up through her soles, the arch of her ankles. The unmistakeable smells of a busy train station, the interactions and sound of porters and restless passengers shifting about. Pigeons cooing and flapping about on the girders above, and she heard an old woman singing some old melody, she couldn't quite place, from behind the frosted window of the canteen kitchen. Her heart thudded as the platform rumbled and shook as the tannoy announced the arrival of the dreaded train.

Jamesey hoisted his kit bag and slung it over his shoulder and pulled her to him.

"Look after yourself, Collette, promise me. I'll be back before you know it."

She told herself she would be strong but still the tears streamed down her lovely cheeks, red from the cold.

"I promise, babe, and you. Don't go taking stupid chances. I wanncha back in me arms."

She heard cries of "Hey, Colour, over here," and looked up to see a couple of fit-looking guys hanging out the windows who opened the door and bounced out and relieved Jamesey of his kit bag. "Got yer a seat, Sarge. Make it nifty, eh. It's chock-a-block."

They got back on and Jamesey gave her a last hug and a teeth-grinding kiss and broke away. "See you soon, hon. We have some more jungle trips to look forward to."

She giggled, "Can't wait. Bye, darling." Tears welling, "I keep me jungle clear of poachers until you return my Tarzan, my King Dong."

He suddenly turned back, "Silly bugger, I am. Here."

He thrust a small, slim packet at her and then boarded onto the train to the impatient cries of his men. War was a beckoning and Jamesey and the guys were going to be the main players.

The train moved off, picking up speed, and Jamesey was waving and she was waving back. She felt like it was some 1930s B movie or some advert for something exotic. All it needed was the clouds of steam and the porter waving a flag. She was very much a young woman, one hundred percent in love and lost already without the light of her life.

Light-headed, she backed over to the bench the secretaries had been on and sat down gingerly, still a little sore from the very heated sex they had engaged in. She wept bitterly, her tears flowing copiously. Whoever sang 'Love Hurts' was right. Her heart felt like an invisible hand was clenching it and squeezing it dry. Her throat was sore from sobbing. The platform was quiet now, just the pigeons arguing and bickering with each other over crumbs and scraps. She watched them, envying them and their companionship.

She picked the paper off the present and carefully folded it and put it in her pocket, as women in love receiving gifts from their new lovers do. Inside was a gold locket on a heavy gold chain. It looked very expensive. She cried heavily. When Collette opened the locket, she saw the picture they had took in the booth of the two of them trying to look serious. The night had sealed THEIR love at THEIR home as she possessively looked upon it.

She put the locket on and vowed never to take it off. She cried for an hour, distraught, bereft, convinced the IRA would kill him and then ashamed at herself for the thought.

A concerned porter told the kindly lady in the canteen, who coaxed her into the kitchen and made her strong tea. She sipped it gratefully, still softly weeping. The lady was extremely nice to her. She knew all about young women and farewells at train stations. She gently pried some details out of Collette and before long Eadie arrived, summoned by the pub phone, thanked the kind woman profusely and got Collette back to the pub and put her to bed in a darkened room for a couple of hours. Poor little pet was totally frazzled out.

When Eadie came down a puzzled Ron asked her what was wrong with Collette. Eadie looked sad, "Poor child's madly in love with Jamesey. Her nerves are fraught."

Ron laughed, "Sure, they're just mates. Jamesey treats her like the sister he never had."

"Well he's committed incest a large number of times then."

Ron grinned, "Ha, he's a dark horse. Good luck to them, I say. Jamesey won't hurt her. He's a true, 'Blue Gent', ain't he?"

"That's not my worry, Ron, a great fella. Not Jamesey. She's babbling about map reading, Collette's country and jungles of all things. She thinks she won't see him again, that the Paddies will nut job him."

215

Ron paused, pensive, "Yeah, that's a soldier's woman's lot. Remember when I did my active service in Cyprus? We'll just have to keep an eagle eye on her, poor little pet."

Eadie smiled, "Do I remember?" she stroked his arm tenderly. "I remember you coming home on leave, you randy sod. I couldn't barely walk for a week," and she moved away off to do her work laughing merrily, her mind flooding with many happy memories.

Ron went for the whiskey. Different bleeding species women in love and way too deep for him. Best avoided when they were snivelling and in cohorts about men. Bloody secret society was the sisterhood when called to battle and men were not allowed entry to their domain until the crisis was over and they were invited.

Eadie was restocking the spirits and dusting away and singing, "I'll be your woman... You be my man... It's the power of love," and giving Ron suggestive looks, making him cringe and reach for the Bello.

Chapter 18
Flashbacks
('Guardian Angel'...Nino de Angelo)

Rabbie was sitting in the office, working out the security schedule for a showbiz bash in 'The Flaming Oasis' nightclub on Wednesday next. It was being hosted by the flamboyant pop singer SassyVanassy. A British artiste in her '40s, who had regularly pumped out hits for the last two decades and was still going strong. A real working-class Britesse blonde bombshell made good from her working-class roots.

Breaking in her fourth husband and considered a bit of a diva, she had sacked her last New York security consultants because she thought them overbearing and restrictive. Mainly working out of the UK, she was No. 6 in both the USA and UK charts with 'Slow Your Love Down, Baby, or I Walk', a catchy dance tune. She kept an apartment on Madison Avenue and visited the city several times a year, and this event was to celebrate her twenty-five years in show business as well as her forty-something birthday party. Celebs Galore, he mused. *Dodgy, set routines and magnets for whackos and deluded psychos with strange, commanding voices in their heads that nobody can hear but themselves but heyho...the celebs didn't mind throwing out the dollars for protection from the shadow people.*

It was a good coup for OLG and Rabbie wanted it to go well. Her new husband, who was also her manager, had rung him.

"She wants good, steady professionals who can react but be as unobtrusive as possible. The last guys cramped her style, know what I mean. She's called the 'People's Pop Princess' for God's sake. She can't be surrounded 24/7 by a shield of giant beefcakes hogging her limelight."

Rabbie assured him they could do the job. He just hoped they could. The price of fame often came high. Look at John Lennon for example. What a tragic waste of talent. Rab had thirty guys on the books, all licenced and ten part-timers. He had another ten guys who worked undercover. He would use a couple of those; maybe put them in as barmen or car valets or something, and the event wasn't publicised or made public, so he was confident enough OLG could handle it without any drama occurring.

He was still musing over his schedule when his secretary told him a Wendy Havilland was on the phone for him. He lifted the phone, still slightly distracted.

"Hey, Wendy. What's up? The Big Man been stealing your equila again?"

"He should dare. I'll lamp the big lump," laughed Wendy. "No, listen. I've been called into work. One of my kiddies took a turn for the worst and the big guy's managed to get a full day's work down at City Hall. Sooo?"

Rabbie twigged. He knew Bobby was finding it hard to get work as an electrician with all the building sites practically closed down because of the recession. Lots of tradesmen in the 'Big Apple' were going down the tubes.

"Got yah. You need Luca picked up. Sure, I'll lift her and drop her home."

"Ah thanks, dude. I dropped her clothes off earlier. She's all excited, bless her little Ruski socks."

"I bet she is. Time's she getting discharged?"

"Dr Grace says if she eats all her lunch up, she can leave at two. I think they would keep her if they could."

He laughed. "Yeah, she sure made an impression."

"And listen, Rabbie. It'll be hard for her going home, so make sure she's settled and tell her I'll be home at eight and do her some supper. She's to stay in bed for a week."

"Yeah, sure, I know. I'm sure between us and that big woman Philomena from the office, we'll look after her fine."

"'Kay, man. Thanks. See yah later," and she rang off.

Rabbie booked the duty driver for half past one. He'd go get her himself and see she got home safely.

* * *

Luca had gone through a busy morning. All the night shift nurses had called up to say goodbye before they went off duty, and Dr Grace and Dr Shilburn had given her a thorough examination on their rounds. They wished her the best for the future, and she had hugged them and thanked them for the wonderful care they had given her.

Judith, the counsellor, had come up for a final chat and given her some pamphlets on support groups and home security.

"Now, I never do this, Luca, but this is my home number. If you need me or just want to chat, ring any time."

Luca was deeply moved and gave the lovely woman who had suffered a similar experience a big hug. Judith had patted her back knowingly. Comrades through adversity.

Ward Sister Mary came and sat for half an hour, telling her she had been a model patient and they would miss her.

"Here's a pack of three pairs of pantyhose. I know you modern girls don't use them now, but you wear them for a week or two, Luca. You don't want to get a chill down there and end up back in here. Now, do you?"

She ate as much of her lunch as she could. She was excited at the thought of getting out and nervous too. Buzz and Big Danny were doing security and they sent her in good, strong Columbian coffee and a box of assorted pastries, which she shared with the other patients, much to their delight. They were going to miss the free handouts and so-exotic visitors.

The ward doctor gave her the discharge papers and a week' supply of the tablets she had to take. Strong antibiotics, aspirin to keep the blood thin and Temazepan to help her sleep.

"You might not need them after a week, but finish the course and see your own physician," he said and shook her hand. Job well done. Another satisfied patient.

She guessed she would have to find a local doctor. She had not been sick once since arriving in the US, and it was ironic that gangsters had been the cause of her first experience with the medical system. She remembered the Director's words about First World countries and there always being bad people wherever you were. He was a prophet. She missed her old mentor's advice. Evil thrived in all cultures once it got its claws in. Look at the Kurds in Syria at the present time and the starving masses around the world.

Luca packed her small holdall, putting the Russian novel Rabbie had given her in fondly. It was a romance about four young men from Moscow who went to the Black Sea on holiday and met four sisters. Country girls who were looking husbands. It was outdated but quite humorous. Rabbie was so thoughtful.

She dressed in the rose-coloured pants suit and yellow jumper Wendy had dropped off. All her bruises were nearly faded away now she saw as she pulled her pantyhose up. The abrasion on her right shin had been stubborn and had become infected but it was clean now and a couple more changes of dressing and antiseptic cream should sort it out over the next few days. She put on the dark check tweed three-quarter length coat she had got in a sale before Christmas and had never worn and sat down to wait for Wendy, juggling her shapely legs up and down impatiently, keen to get out into the world of the 'living' again.

As the hands on the clock reached two, Luca wondered if she should switch her cell phone on and ring Wends, who had said she would be up early to help her pack and dress. The staff didn't like you using your cell on the ward because it interfered with some of the machines and disturbed other patients. She took her coat off again. It was hot in the ward. She was sure Wendy would be here soon. Something must have held her back.

Ruth, a pretty young girl from Ghana, came down to see her. "Luca dear, I've been so busy I forgot to say. Wendy rang and said she has to work but has made other arrangements to get you home."

Disappointment briefly crossed her face. She was so looking forward to getting out into the fresh air and becoming a part of the city scene again. Getting back onboard and caching up on the biz.

"It's okay, Ruthie, I'm sure dat Vendy has it sorted. You people work soo hard and such long hours. You truly are angels."

Ruth smiled fondly at her. It was so nice to be appreciated. Some of the patients moaned and groaned at her. An old boy with dementia had told her to "Get your stinking nigger hands off me" earlier. It was lucky that despite her dark skin she had a thick one.

"I'm sure she has. It's been great you made such a good recovery. Kidneys can be buggers to treat."

Rabbie came in. "Has she been a bugger to treat, nurse? No chocolate for her tonight."

Luca's eyes lit up. He looked great in his dark blue suit and red tie, his dark blue eyes lively and amused. Buzz and Big Danny flanked him. Ruth laughed. "No, she has been a treasure. Now I'll get a porter and a chair."

Ruth left and Rabbie helped her on with her coat.

"Tank you so much. You guys have been so kind to me," she beamed happily.

"Nonsense, it's been our pleasure. Hasn't it fellas?"

219

"Sure has, li'l lady," replied Danny. "It has been a pleasure guarding my adopted 'Yellow Rose of Texas'."

"Yeah! Outstanding. Been a bodacious joy, kiddo," from Buzz, who had a serious crush on her.

A porter arrived with a wheelchair and they got Luca settled in. He put a blanket over her knees. Luca would have been happy to walk to exercise her lovely legs but hospital regulations dictated if you came in on a stretcher, you left in a wheelchair.

"Thanks, dudester. We'll take it from here," said Buzz and proceeded to wheel her proudly down the ward.

The other patients waved and wished her luck. The nurses at their station fussed and hovered over her and thanked her for the big bag of chocolate and candy she had given them. They wished her all the best, impressed.

"Three big hunks to see you home, Luca. Now that's what I call class, girl," giggled the staff nurse. "Send them back up when you're done with them."

"I'll come back for you, any time, sweet honey child," Buzz told her, making her blush, and Rabbie and Danny rolled their eyes. Buzz was about subtle as a turd in a swimming pool when it came to chatting up women.

Luca smiled. Buzz had sat with her a few times when he was on night duty and given her his best chat up lines but he was a sweetie really and married. Out of bounds. They descended in the elevator and through the huge reception area. People watched them, some even stopping and staring at the beautiful young woman surrounded by three big strapping men, wondering if she was someone famous. A visiting famous model or reality TV star, incognito, needing close protection from some wacko on her fan base.

She did indeed feel special and when they got outside, a large top of the range Mercedes Benz was waiting for them. Its black bodywork highly polished and gleaming in the warm mid-March sun, which had chased the earlier showers away and come out to greet her. She raised her face to it, revelling in its natural warmth. The sheer new remembrance of the city air was delightful in her starved nostrils that had absorbed the antiseptic ward aroma for so many days.

Luca sat between Buzz and Danny as they made steady progress through the mid-afternoon traffic towards The Village. Khalid, a pleasant guy from Egypt, driving the big car expertly. She watched Rabbie in the front chatting on the phone to Big Mal in the office about some function this week. His hair was very dark and straight but she noticed it curled a bit where it met his collar. It was very attractive. He looked extremely confident and switched on. He was easygoing and she knew his men liked and respected him.

She gazed out the tinted windows at the masses on the wide pavement going about their business. She speculated about their lives. If they were happy living in this huge cauldron of humanity. She saw homeless people pushing trolleys and very young girls scantily dressed and thick with make-up loitering on street corners, waving cars down and accosting men. Teenage prostitutes. She felt sorry for them, wondering where their parents were. Did they care what their children were doing?

They stopped at lights and a wino, panhandling, came over with his squeegee and bucket to wash their windscreen. Khalid put his window down.

"Don't wet the car, man. Here, get yourself a Big Mac," and gave him five dollars.

220

He shuffled off pleased with his unexpected windfall. The sun reflected off the upper windows of the skyscrapers as they drove down the noisy manmade canyons. A blue and white police car, siren screaming and roof lights flashing, sped past up the service lane. It was surreal after the tranquillity and routine of the hospital. All madness and chaos. So intense in its diversity and vanity the eye didn't know what to latch onto next. It was a hard, vain city, insular and self-centred and any affection, warmth and comfort to those outside the inner circle wasn't given easy to strangers and transients and kept behind closed doors for family, not on the harshness of the uncaring streets.

Rabbie ended his phone call. He turned and winked at her before facing back to the front. Khalid asked him about time off to attend his cousin's wedding and Rabbie said that he would sort it. They passed high red-brick tenements, washing hanging from some of the windows. Two men with shirts off were fighting outside one, watched by a gang of gleeful children. She wondered why they weren't at school.

A yellow cab, steam coming out of its bonnet, had run into the back of a green SUV. The driver, cap on the back of his hand, was standing remonstrating angrily with a well-dressed woman who stood, arms crossed, tapping her foot, ignoring him, chin raised to the rooftop. *A clash of the 'proletariat' and the 'bourgeoisie' classes*, she thought Russianly.

They entered The Village area, and Luca marvelled at the different styles of architecture, the many deviating colours and shapes to the awnings over the small shops and bistros. A lorry was parked and sweating men were rolling large silver kegs of beer into a bar. A hobo who slept on a sheet of cardboard in a derelict shop doorway, people stepping over his feet that stuck out. A yellow school bus went by, and she smiled as the kids waved and pulled faces at them. They pulled up outside The Poplar Trees Apartments.

She was home and suddenly very afraid. The vibrancy she had felt in the air as they had entered The Village expectantly now seemed to fill her with dread, and she shivered in the weak sunlight as she climbed out of the safety of the car and left the comfort and security of her two bodyguards. A cloud covered the sun, putting the street into shadow and she shuddered.

"Come on, let's get you in and you can relax."

Rabbie sent the car on. She took his arm and he carried her bag and they climbed the short flight of wide marble steps to the door.

"Bet you're glad to get home, Luca," Rabbie said. "Get into your own routine again."

She nodded absently, her whole instinct being to flee this terrible place and seek the safety of her mother's arms.

* * *

As the car drove off, Buzz laughed, "Yeah, right. I'll give you a bell in an hour, Khalid, to pick me up. I'll get Luca sorted out."

"What cha mean, Buzz?" asked Khalid. "You've a sick mind, you infidel dawg."

"I mean you won't see the boss in an hour. He'll be sorting her out – in her bed!"

Big Danny gave him an arm-deadening punch to the bicep. "Don't yah be gassin' 'bout Luca like that, hombre. She's one damn fine lady."

"Yeah, man. You just got a sewer for a mind, you dirt bag," Khalid was annoyed. His Muslim upbringing had never quite let him accept the very vile talk many American men seemed obliged to do after they had been in the company of an attractive woman. "In Egypt they would whip the offending dog's flesh off his feet with a bamboo cane."

"Jesus, guys. I was only joshing. Good luck to them, I say. Fuck, Danny, that was sore," he moaned rubbing his arm vigorously.

"Yah all say any more bad talk 'bout Missy Luca and the Boss Hombre and I do yer other arm next, little man."

Khalid laughed. Little man. Buzz true enough was only six foot one to Danny's six foot eight. Buzz sat sulking.

"Friggin' Texan steer shagger!" which got him a dead leg. "Shame his ancestors weren't frikkin' wasted at the Alamo."

* * *

At the tall glass door Rabbie punched in a code on a new key pad.

"What's dis, Rabbie?" she inquired as they entered when the door buzzed and clicked open.

"4057, this month's code. The residents had a meeting about security. Each apartment has an intercom system now so non-residents have to buzz up and identify themselves." He gave her a reassuring look, "24/7, not just at night. Crime doesn't sleep."

Mr and Mrs Chin were cleaning the mailboxes. Mrs Chin rushed over, all five foot of her, and hugged Luca.

"Oh so good to see, Miss Luca. We missed you."

Mr Chin ambled over, sponge dripping. "Great you're back. What cha think of the new security? Got extra bright lighting in the halls too."

"Dat's great, Mr Chin. It was too dark and spooky before."

"Yeah, and a voice and camera inside each door so anybody calls they have to say who they are."

"Wow! Dat's so good."

"Yeah. OLG cut the owners a brilliant deal after Rabbie called a security meeting. How are you now?"

They talked to the concierge and his wife for a few minutes. Mrs Chin got Luca her post and they headed to the elevator.

"That vas ver' good of you, Rabbie. You're ver' clever," *and kind*, she thought.

"Good for business, my dear," he shrugged it off as they stopped at the third floor.

They left the elevator and they walked down to 3B. She clutched his arm very tight and her heart pounded. She knew that her friends had cleaned and fixed the apartment as best they could after the 'incident'. Cleaning away the fingerprint dust, bleaching the blood out of the carpet and mattress. Righting the furniture and fixing the phone lead. They were good people. Salt of the earth.

As they went down the hallway, she began to tremble and when they entered the living room, a cold sweat broke on her forehead and ran down her spine. Rabbie dropped her bag. She flinched and cringed at the sudden thud.

"Right. I reckon a big mug of that Columbian coffee you like is the business. Whatcha reckon?"

She looked at the bedroom door which was ajar and saw her bed. She saw Hanlon's evil face and his big yellow teeth like grave stones, and her body crawled and she felt foreign hands gripping and tearing at her flesh and her shivering turned into a convulsion.

"I'm so sorry, Rabbie," she managed before the darkness caught her and she passed out, her past flashing before her eyes and her post scattering all around like confetti in a gale as her eyes rolled up in her head and the lights went off.

As a concerned Rabbie caught her, he could have kicked himself for being a bloody idiot. He should have seen this coming. He laid her gently on the sofa. He checked her pulse. It was strong, but fast. He mused, "You stupid, stupid prat. Have you not spent the last ten days getting to know her during your hospital visits?" Conclusion: young, kind, compassionate woman thousands of miles away from home. High intellect. Artistic. Huge imagination. What the fuck had he been thinking? She would just walk back into her apartment as if nothing had happened. She was a gentle soul and three bastards had tried to violently rape and kill her. *Call yourself a professional? She was bound to take a nervous reaction, probably a bad flashback. A precursor to post traumatic stress disorder. You're a flipping thoughtless prat*, he scolded himself.

He lifted Luca tenderly. She was extremely pale. Her eyeballs were moving under her lids. He should have seen the signs. Rabbie had witnessed enough of his men succumb to it after violent warfare. Look at his Uncle Davey for Chrissake. He was mentally crippled with it.

Right, he needed to get her out before she woke up and get his doctor out to her. He gazed into her lovely face. How in the name of God above could any man want to hurt such an exquisite creature? He carried her up to his apartment, raging inside his head.

* * *

Luca awoke to a large, airy room in a very big bed indeed. Off to her left, a balcony door was open and a pleasant breeze fanned her face. Rabbie was leaning against the wall facing her, arms crossed. His face lit up when he saw her eyes were open. A grey-haired man with a dapper moustache, somewhere in his mid-fifties she guessed, was sitting by her side, holding her right wrist gently. He had a stethoscope dangling around his neck and a kindly countenance. He reminded her of the old luvvie society actor, David Niven.

"Welcome back, my dear. Please don't be alarmed. I'm Dr Liam McKeever. How do you feel?"

She thought about that. "Okay. I tink, a little light-headed."

"Do you remember what happened?"

"I vas in my apartment with Rabbie and den... I don't know."

"That's good you recall being home. You fainted. Not surprising after the terrible time you've had."

"I remember now. I taught dat Hanlon and them were dere."

"Yes, you had a flashback and your mind decided it was too much so it put you to sleep for a while."

"Oh, dat's so clever. Am I going to be okay, Doctor?"

"Of course, my dear. I'm going to give you a sedative to put you to sleep for a few more hours and leave you some nice herbal pills to keep you calm. Sleep is healing, it's when the angels come down and sit by you and keep watch, my dear, so my dear ol' mum in Tipperary used to tell us as boys, so she used to say to be sure!"

Dr McKeever prepared a syringe and injected her in her good arm.

She yawned again heavily behind a bandaged hand, "I so hope da angels are not da busy tonight because I so, sooo need them."

"Now then. You sleep, we don't want your ending back in Manhattan General, do we?"

Her eyelids grew heavy. "Vould you be my physician, Dr McKeever? I don't have one yet."

"Of course, my dear. I'll call in and see you later."

Rabbie sidled in from the balcony, anxiously, tentative. He looked like a whipped dog looking for his master's reassurance.

Luca was sliding down a long sleepy tunnel now. Her eyelids were as heavy as lead. "So sorry, Rabbie, soooo sorrrreeee."

Dr McKeever rose. "It was lucky I was passing, Rabbie. What a lovely thing she is! A breath of fresh air."

"Yeah, she's great, Doc. She has had a hard time, as you say."

"Yes, well, you know she can't go back to her place. Be very bad for her, so it looks like you've got a houseguest for a while.

"I'll get something sorted, Doc. I'll crash on the sofa."

The doctor looked at him. "You are a decent man. Every cloud has a silver lining, so they say."

Rabbie was amused. "So, what's the one here, Doc?"

"Well, at least after you've been out working all day in this beastly city, you have something beautiful to come home to."

He chortled. "You're an old romantic, Liam. She's too young and good for an old war horse like me.

They strode out and Rabbie opened the front door for him.

"Don't put yourself down, Rab, or undermine the power of love between man and woman. It can be like a runaway train at times."

"I'll behave myself, Doc," he grinned, "That's why the trains have those cow pushers on the front of the locos, so they can toss old bulls like me off the rails."

* * *

In the office, Buzz had been chatting to Elaine Curry, a no-nonsense matronly woman in her mid-fifties who always wore her steel-grey hair in a bun and dressed smartly. Very efficient and good at her job. Rabbie thanked his lucky stars when he had first met her at a veteran's convention in the Manhattan Branch of the American Legion two years previously. His PA had given him a month's notice as she was getting married and moving away. He needed someone who understood ex-servicemen and could handle their often perverse sense of humour and mood swings. She was an expert at handling mental battle scars and putting them back in the box with the lid shut.

He had provided two men free to do the door security for them and had dropped down to see what was going on. Elaine, who was running the convention to raise funds for disabled ex-servicemen, came over to meet him and thank him for the free help. He met an intelligent no-nonsense lady, who had been an army wife married to a Marine Colonel for thirty years and had been around the world several times stationed at various bases and to pass the time had done every qualification going.

Unfortunately, her husband had died after a brief illness, and she was bored and had thrown herself into charity work to put her day away. Her two adult daughters worked as interpreters for the UN and were often abroad for long periods of time.

Rabbie had prised all this out of her over homemade lemonade and meatloaf. He saw a fiercely independent woman struggling on her widow's pension.

"You know, Elaine, I think you just might be what can get me out of a big, big hole at the moment."

She came in for an interview a few days later and never left. She ran the inner office like the bridge of an aircraft carrier, smooth, professional but laid-back.

The guys had a high regard for her. Nothing was too much trouble. They often came to her with their problems or just to chew the cud. She always made time for them. Buzz had got her a cup of the Java roast coffee she liked, and she was spouting on about his latest matrimonial problems.

"Buzz dear, it's simple. Keep your pecker in your trousers until you're home and things will be fine."

"Dat's what I'm saying, Elaine. At home the pecker stays in the trousers. She's no interest. It never gets an outing. It's in recession and there is no end to the drought in sight."

She eyes him, amused. "If you didn't spread it around so much, Buzz, she wouldn't be so afraid of it. The poor girl doesn't know where it's been."

"Whadda I do then?"

"You either re-romance her and stop your wild alley cat ways or cut her loose. You can't leave the poor girl hanging in limbo. It's not fair on her."

Buzz was pondering this as Elaine answered her phone, "Yes, Boss... Yes, of course... Oh, the poor dear... So she's staying with you then? Okay, okay, yes, I must call up to see her, she is quite delightful... I'll tell him. Okay...see you tomorrow."

Buzz, always the ear at the door, sensed gossip. "The boss okay, Elaine? We dropped him off with that Russian duchess he saved earlier."

She smiled knowingly, "Would you tell Mal the boss won't be back in today? He's tied up."

"Witt the Ruski? Lucky dude!"

Elaine knew all about Luca. She had visited her in hospital. She thought her absolutely adorable and believed she could be good for Rabbie, who was going through a drought at the moment in the romance stakes. Such a waste of a fine hunk of masculinity. She sighed, thinking of her late hubby. The epitome of the studly, fit soldier caricature of what a fighting marine should be. "Yes, Buzz...now run along and tell Mal, and don't forget, loose lips sink ships, Buzz."

He ambled grinning into the operative's office. Mal was doing his overtime sheet and Little Danny was chewing on a triple-stacked steak burger.

"See, told ya...the boss won't be back. He's moved the Luca chick into his crib."

225

"Ah shucks, that's so darn nice. She's a fine filly," Dan mumbled through a full chomping mouth, crumbs flying. "Pass the goddam Tabasco sauce, Khalid dude."

Khalid was sitting with a dapper little French man called Charles Brouchard, ex French paras and from Marseille. He shoved the hot sauce over to the devouring hulk.

"If you think about it, Buzz, would you want to go back to live in a place where you've been near raped and killed...? From a sensitive female perspective, that is?" Khalid asked.

Mal laughed, "The only female perspective Buzz likes is when they're horizontal with their legs spread."

Buzz was hurt, "Hey guys, I'm a sensitive guy, I understand the female psyche."

"Yeah, right," Khalid scoffed, "Luca's still ill. The boss is just doing the right thing. He's a true Brit gentleman."

"Yeah and Philli and me are going over tonight to see what we can do to help," Mal informed him. "So wind your neck in."

"You just ze dirty mind, 'mon ami'. You would get up on ze cracked plate," observed Charles. "In la belle francese they would chop your petit monsieur with le petite guillotine."

"Or the crack of dawn," Danny chipped in. "Sleazebag doggone pussy hound."

"Christ guys. Get off the case. I'm trying hard to get things back in order with Katy."

"Yeah, well, make sure you do man, before she gets sick of yah and runs off with someone else," Mal admonished him.

That scared Buzz. "Nah, she wouldn't do that. She knows who brings the bucks in," trying to convince himself.

"As we say in 'La Belle France', 'When ze cats away, ze mouse will play'."

"That's right. She's a fine-looking gal your Katy. I'll go mosey on down if you don't want her no more," said Dan with a wicked glint in his eye, winking at Mal. "I wouldn't mind hitching ma hoss outside her porch."

That was enough for Buzz. "Okay if I head home, Mal? I reckon I'll take Katy out for a nice dinner as a surprise."

"Sure, head on, Buzz. See yah mar man. Don't be doing a boomerang."

Buss sped off, tail between his legs, and they laughed amongst themselves. "Nice one, Little Dan, you scared the crap out of him."

"Yah know what he's like," chortled Dan. "But he's a good partner when the gravy hits the biscuits."

Mal agreed, "Yeah, he's a good worker, just got stray dick syndrome."

They laughed again. "Is 'tres bien' what the boss is doing for Luca, but Buzz could be onto something, spring is in the air 'mes amis' and loves a new blossom."

"Gawd, that's all we damn well need, a romantic French dude in the office," complained Danny.

Mal chuckled and stood. "Let's call it a day, guys. We're gonna be busy next Wednesday with Sassy Vanassy's birthday bash."

"Let's kidnap Elaine and take her to Bronco bills for a drink. She would like the bare-arsed cowboys," suggested Khalid.

Lil' Dan snorted, "Cowboys, pah, thems just imposters. They never rode the range, the horny bum bandits."

"Not the range, 'non', but every spare chick in the place," said Charles.

Khalid chuckled, "And probably not just chicks, know what I mean? They wouldn't know a horse from a possum."

Mal went to see Elaine, "Get your coat on, Elaine, we're closing shop early."

"Oh how thoughtful, Mal."

"Yeah, we're taking you for a drink and to see some bare-arsed cowboys."

"How exciting, Mal dear. You've just made my day."

* * *

He took his work out onto the small balcony; laptop, time-sheets and notes for letters Elaine would get typed up. It was warm for mid-March and the back of the apartments caught the afternoon sun. He left the sliding door open a foot so he could watch her through a gap in the curtains. Just her head was visible, turned from him, the quilt up over her shoulder, rising gently with her soft breathing.

Rabbie rang Wendy at her work and told her what had happened. She was annoyed with herself as well that she hadn't foreseen Luca's extreme reaction.

"I'll be home at eight, Rab. I'll get her sorted out. Big Bobby will bring a bucket of chicken up, and we'll have a confab and decide what to do for the best."

Reassured, he went back to his work. She seemed to be sleeping peacefully. The sun was getting lower. A ray gleamed off her beautiful dark-brown hair and he saw lighter streaks had been brought out in the natural light. He forced himself to concentrate. He was a doorman short for SassyVanassy's function. He didn't want to subcontract. He liked to know the strengths and weaknesses of the men who worked for him and use them accordingly. Buzz, for example, was a superb advanced driver, probably the best he had, but not great with the clients, often being overawed by their status. Whereas Mal seemed to give the clients reassurance when they saw his size and efficient bearing. Always impeccably dressed, he was a good conversationalist and nothing fazed him.

Know your men and use them appropriately, had been drummed into him in the Royal Marines. Encourage initiative but teamwork prevails. The team is only as good as its weakest link. He thought back to the covert missions he had done off various hostile foreign coasts. His small team coming out of the sea like black ninja warriors, completing the operation in the darkness, before disappearing back into the inky sea to be picked up by submarine or boat.

Rabbie grinned. Those were the days. He had never lost a man, a few injured. Lady Luck often shining on him and the boys. Yep, they worked hard, trained hard, fought hard and afterwards, by crickey, they played hard. Happy days. Halcion times.

He mused on that. He wondered why you never knew when you were going through your happiest times until it was over. He loved New York but there was definitely something missing in his life.

He was still smiling, remembering a certain weekend in Valetta on Malta after a particularly dodgy mission in Libya when he sensed he was being watched. He turned. Luca had rolled over and was observing him carefully with those lovely dove-grey eyes of hers.

"Hey, Luca, how you feeling?" He checked the time, it was just after six.

"Hi, Rabbie...vats happen? Why am I in your big bed?"

"Do you not remember? You fainted downstairs. I had to get the doc out to you."

She sat up, groggy. Stretched and yawned. "I tink so… Doc Mac…he 'gave me injection."

He went in and sat on the bed. She had a little colour to her cheeks now. The swelling and bruising on her high left cheekbone, where she had been punched, was nearly away now.

"I'm an idiot, Luca. I should have figured out going back to your place would be hard on you."

She reached over with her good hand and took his. His big hand enveloped hers like an oversized glove. It felt warm and secure.

"Is nobody's fault, Rabbie. You not mind reader. I had attack. I remember now like horror movie in my head."

He glanced down at her hand enclosed in his. He felt immensely protective towards her. "Flashback. You had a bad flashback, but everything's going to be fine. You're safe, Luca."

She shuddered. Remembering seeing the evil Hanlon and his big yellow teeth. She swore she had smelt his foul breath. She looked at the handsome man sitting by her and sensed the safety of him, her female senses awakening. She must look a mess. "I must go the bathroom, Rabbie."

"Sure, it's just over there by the door. How about coffee and something light to eat?"

He stood and she pulled the quilt back and sat on the edge of the emperor-size bed. "Dat vould be nice, Rabbie. Tank you soo so much." She was still wearing her short sleeved yellow jumper and tights.

"The doc took your trousers off, in case you're wondering," he mentioned, embarrassed and averting his eyes from the finest pair of nylon-clad legs God ever created.

She smiled shyly, coy. She had very, very attractive legs, shapely and well-toned. He remembered she had told him she had trained as a ballerina; it showed. He tore his eyes away again but when they crept back, she noticed, "I make things very difficult for you, Rab… Am soo…sooo…sorry," and squeezed his hand. She was secretly thrilled he still seemed to find her attractive.

"Hold on a sec. I'll get your bag for you. Am just glad I can help."

He also got her a long-sleeved light woollen red and blue tartan shirt he used for summer climbing. He closed the balcony door, it was getting cooler.

"Get changed into that, Luca, it'll be more comfortable," and he left to make coffee, whistling. Outside, the city heaved uneasily but they were wrapped up safe in their little cocoon.

He waited outside the closed bedroom door until he heard her enter the bathroom. The doctor had told him on no account must she be left on her own. He made her a selection of cream cheeses with cucumber and tomatoes, crackers and pickles, with a bowl of Peach Melba ice cream.

He knocked and came in with it on the tray with folding legs he used at night when he was watching the late movie and having his supper. She sipped the rich Columbian coffee with relish. She had brushed her teeth and put her hair into a ponytail and looked pretty in the colourful shirt. She ate the crackers and started on the ice cream.

"Is my favourite, Peach Melba. You so clever, Rabbie."

He smiled indulgently and flicked the flat screen TV on the wall to the news, the volume on low.

"Vhat we gonna do, Rabbie? I can't steal your bed for a week."

"Of course, you can. I'll crash in the spare room. Wendy and Bobby are coming up and so's Mal and Philli. I'm sure between us we'll sort something out."

She sighed, "I am such the nuisance to you all, but is wrong me taking your bed. Twenty-six years old and I have to have da baby watchers… Is so da weird and stressing, da?"

He patted her hand, "Nonsense. Look at the kudos you have given me with the guys at work…beautiful, Russian girl lives in the bossman's bed for a week, and we're not baby sitters. We are friends and carers, and you, young lady, are our pal and we do care, so chill, my bed is signed over to you."

She giggled, "Have there been many beautiful ladies in your bed, Rabbie? I bet dair has been." She swore he nearly blushed. He thought of Juliette and scowled mentally.

"No, not too many actually, Luca. The well has run dry as regards that side of things at present."

It was her turn to pat his hand, "Oh, dear…vell, never mind, Rabbie. Maybe it will rain woman soon and fill your well right up again."

"You're an optimist, Luca. I like that. Let's refill that cup for you. You seemed to enjoy it."

"Tank you, Rabbie. Dat Columbian extra rich roast is Number One on my tasty coffee list."

"You and your lists," he laughed. "It's a clever way to do things, I guess."

She grinned at him, "Yep, and it's good you like the Columbian. Now I make the note next to it to say my friend Rabbie likes it so I know vat to give you ven you visit me."

"You're an amazing young lady," he flattered her as he made off with her cup. "You relax and chill out."

She watched his departing back fondly, not knowing he had stocked up with the Columbian coffee just for her when the bodyguards had told him she liked it. Hoping she would come up to visit, of course. Not guessing she was going to end up in his bed for a week. Funny old world. You never knew what lay around the next corner but it sure made things interesting.

* * *

Dr McKeever came at seven, she was still drinking her coffee and had a cup with her, before giving her a thorough examination from head to foot. He had read the discharge letter from the hospital and was pleased with the speed of her recovery but still worried about her mental state. Not all injuries were overtly apparent.

"Physically, you're doing great, Luca, but it's important you rest in bed the next week. That small split in the kidney needs time to heal properly."

"I guess so, Doc. I do feel a little shaky."

"Yep. Now, here is a prescription for a natural sleep aid that I swear by. It's a tablet made from marigold, passion flowers, hops and valerian. I want to get you off the Temazepan. They are highly addictive."

"Yes, Doc. Tank you soo so much," she smiled disarmingly at him. "Passion flowers, how vonderful."

The kind doctor grinned back, "I'm afraid there will be no passionate interludes for you, young lady, for a week or two. Although, I'm sure you're not short of eligible young guys queuing up for your favours who will be happy to wait."

She gave him that one on one smile again that made men feel so special. The smile that drove young men crazy and got them fired up. "Alas, how do you so quaintly put it, Doctor? No one is queuing up for my favours. My well has run dry."

"I find that very hard to believe, young missy. I'll leave you a few tablets to get you through tonight, so no more of this great coffee until the morning."

"'Kay, Doc. I be good girl. Tank you for coming out to see me. Mrs McKeever is ver' lucky lady to have such a kind man to care for."

He chuckled, "I don't know 'bout that, Luca. Now make sure you phone your counsellor friend tomorrow and get a good talk with her. We wanna catch this post-traumatic stress disorder and nip it in the bud."

Dr McKeever left Luca watching a documentary about bottle-nosed dolphins and found Rabbie in the kitchen. They discussed what was best for her over the next week or two.

"I'll see myself out, Rabbie. Ring me if you need me," and he headed towards the door, carrying his battered old black medical bag that had been his father's before him. "By the way, Rab, she says her romantic well has run dry," he threw over his departing shoulder.

Rabbie grinned, he doubted that very much. "Seems to be a dry season, Doc. It will rain sooner or later, I guess."

Rabbie went into see her. She was misty-eyed watching the TV, "Is so bad, Rabbie. The poor dolphins get stuck in the fishing nets and slowly drown and the pod can do nothing to help them.

He sat and viewed the struggling mammal, "What's the pod, Luca?"

"The pod is what you call a family of dolphins. They live together in a close-knit unit just like humans and love and care for each other. Dats the mammy and dats the family you can hear calling for her."

She was near tears now. He didn't want her any more upset, so he put a comforting arm around her, "Yeah, but that one was saved. Sure, the crew cut her loose. I read it in the Sky magazine."

She looked at him then back to the screen, "Oh tank God. She had three little babies to look after."

He switched the TV over to the Comedy Channel and gave her the remote, "Now watch something funny and cheer yourself up."

"Did you know only humans, Bonobo apes and dolphins are the only three mammal species that have recreational sex?"

That stopped him in his tracks, dead. He took in and thought about that, "God, not into apes or dolphins though," making her laugh, merrily.

"Apes…? Naw, can't envisage that happening."

It had never crossed her gentle mind that he might have been lying to her. He watched her fondly as she wiped her eyes with the back of her hands, putting lots of boxes of tissues on his mental shopping list.

Luca stroked the back of his hand softly, part embarrassed. "I guess you tink I am crazy? A silly girl crying over tings I can do nothing about."

He gazed at her again. *A silly girl? All he saw was pure woman. Kind, sensitive and wonderfully quirky.* "No, Luca, I find it refreshing. If everybody cared like you do, the world would be a much better place."

She placed a quick, fleeting kiss on his cheek. "Tank you for caring for me, Rab. You have made tings so much easier for me."

He smiled and got off the bed, "Want to hear the good news?"

Her eyes lit up, "Yes, please. I adore da good news."

"The good doctor reckons a glass or two of red wine at night will help you relax and be good for the heart."

She clapped her hands in delight, "Wow! American doctors are soo, so cool. Will you have one with me, Rabbie, so we can look after your heart too?"

How could he refuse? "Okay... Well, I have Beaujolais, Beaujolais or Beaujolais. Your choice."

She. clapped her hands in delight, thrilled, "Rab, how did you know? My third bestest wine in da whole vide world."

"I had no idea but it's great. I'll go pull the cork."

She watched him leave again. His strong back and confident walk, happy they seemed to share the same tastes in many things. She thought of two beating hearts entwined together – Rabbie's and hers.

* * *

They sat chatting easily together. Luca felt very relaxed. The sleep she had earlier and the lovely wine had lifted her mood. She knew she should be worried staying in Rabbie's apartment, indeed in his bed, for the next week. But she wasn't. Every instinct she possessed told her she was safe and could trust him. She knew she had to take it easy for the next week, even when she went back to work it was to be in a limited capacity so she didn't tire herself out. The doctors had told her she was very lucky not to have lost her kidney.

She had to give it time to heal completely. She laughed at something Rabbie said. Luca was hugely attracted to him. She knew part of it was hero worship for saving her from Hanlon but there was something else there. She had liked him that Friday he had breakfast with her at Jocelyn's. He was world-wise and knowledgeable as well as being handsome and very fit. Okay, he was a few years older than she. So what? She had seen the way the young nurses had eyed him up and down and hung on his every word. She had actually been a bit jealous a few times. There was a charisma around him, an aura of strength and determination that, combined with his looks, was extremely attractive to the opposite sex.

She sipped her wine, it wasn't cheap and nasty. She was surprised he hadn't already been snapped up by some beauty, he must meet a lot of women through his work. Plenty of celeb divas searching for a hunk like Rabbie, he was discerning as well, she deduced. Another plus. Luca shrugged. Their loss and hopefully, fingers crossed, her gain.

Dr Grace had told her to refrain from sexual relations for a few weeks, until she was absolutely sure she was fine 'downstairs', as she so quaintly put it. She was still a tiny bit sore down below. She recalled the flash of Hanlon's shoe as he kicked her and the pain and a shiver went up her spine. Her hand began to shake and she split a few drops on the tray. Anyway, full sexual relations was a family she wasn't a full member of yet.

"You okay, Luca?"

She assured a concerned Rabbie she was fine. They were watching a rerun of the comedy 'Friends'. Luca told him that she used to watch it when she first came to New York because she wanted to try and understand the native New Yorkers' sense of humour, which at times she found very confusing and often still did, truth be told.

Rabbie told her that they used to watch it when he was a marine because the lonely commandos thought Jennifer Aniston, the female lead, was the sexiest woman in the world.

Luca imagined Rabbie and his band of seafaring cutthroats watching television and drooling over her, "Yah, she is very beautiful. I can see why dey tink her ver' sexy."

He agreed, although he wanted to tell Luca she was twice as sexy but common sense prevailed, "Wears a bit thin though, when they show the repeats time and again, year in and year out."

A buzzer sounded and a small screen on the bedside lit up. Luca had thought it was a mini computer. Rabbie showed her a small remote, she could see Wendy and Bobby on the screen.

"Push the green button. Hi, guys, come on in. Down the bedroom."

"'Kay, Rab, thanks," replied Bobby through the small speaker on the remote.

"Press the blue. Opens the front door."

She heard their friends coming through the kitchen, "Dat's so great, Rabbie. So safe, you so da clever."

"Yeah, now watch."

The bedroom door was ajar. As Wendy approached the door of solid teak, it slammed shut and the sound of heavy internal bolts slamming home resounded. "Just press the red button if anyone unsavoury breaks in. Take them an hour with a sledgehammer to get through that door."

Luca was astounded. Wendy knocked, "Hope you guys are behaving yourselves. Handy that, Lucs, if that big galoot sleepwalks."

Luca chuckled, she was enjoying herself now, "You better let Vendy in, Rabbie, she want to get a gossipski, da," and chuckled again, keen to get all the gossipski off Wendy.

Rabbie laughed and pressed the yellow button. Wendy strolled in still in her work uniform, "Well, look at you, Luca. In your pretty plaid shirt, glass of wine and a hunk attending to your every whim. Way to go, gal!"

"Yes, tis great, Wendy. I so happy to be back. Rab so ver' kind."

"I bet he is."

She dumped a suitcase and gave her a hug. "Gotcha enough to keep yah going from your pad. Now, how yah feeling? Do yah wanna get a shower and I wash that lovely hair for yah?"

"Gosh, yes, Wends. Dat would be soo so great."

"Right, Buster Bobby's got a huge bucket of chicken and fries. Go you and talk man speak while I get Luca sorted."

Rabbie left, whistling, glad Wendy was up to take control of the situation, wondering what Luca would look like in the shower covered in soap suds.

Absolutely delightful, he surmised before quickly blocking the image. *Steady as she goes, laddie.*

He was curious as to what was Number One on her wine list.

* * *

The big guy was sitting at the table with a gigantic bucket of junk food before him. "Hey, Rab. Lookee what I got us. Fifteen finger lickin' pieces, fries, beans and 'slaw."

Rabbie grabbed two bottles of Coors out the fridge and got plates. He wasn't averse to the odd trip into the junk world of food. After some of the things he had to eat on Royal Marines survival courses, it was a rare luxury.

Bobby put some on a plate for the girls and put it in the oven to keep warm, "Wends would go ballistic, man, if I didn't save her some Colonel Saunders."

Rabbie grinned, "We wouldn't want that, Bobby. She's a hellcat when she starts. Ask Hanlon."

"She sure showed that muvverfucker," he agreed, demolishing a chicken breast in two big bites before downing half the bottle of beer in one long swallow. "Man, I sure need this. Today's been a total crapper."

"Well, whatever's happened, see it's not ruined your appetite anyhow," observed Rabbie sardonically. Bobby wolfed down another piece of chicken and a handful of skinny fries.

"Thought I had me a day or two's work down the dog pound back at City Hall," he explained through a full mouth, munching furiously as if it was the last supper. "Drove all the way down in the van, in the crazy hour, just for some punk jobs-worth to tell me they were more over the friggin' budget than they knew and they would be in touch." He swallowed and finished his beer before reaching for more Kentucky. "Be in touch, my ass, I'm gonna enjoy this chicken cos tomorrah it could be Cheerios and Pot Noodle, if yah get my drift."

Rabbie knew that as an independent electrician the work had all but dried up with the recession and the building sites were at a standstill. Luca had told him in confidence that they were struggling to survive just on Wendy's nurse's pay and were probably going to have to downgrade to somewhere cheaper to live.

"So the 'Big Bad Wolf's' at the door then, Bobby? Sorry to hear that, man," he commiserated as he got up to get the unhappy man mountain another beer.

"Dunno 'bout the Bad Wolf, man, more like a pack of the frickers; a-howlin' and a-growlin' and prowlin'."

Rab could hear the worry in his voice. As he pulled the cold beer out and de-capped it for him, he remembered the night Luca was attacked and Bobby coming in with a baseball bat. It looked like a child's replica in his giant fist. He had certainly looked formidable and intimidating.

"What you doing Wednesday night, Bobby?"

"Not a lot, bubba. No beer tokens to spare if yer looking to go for a drink."

Rabbie grinned, "Want to do doorman for me at a celeb function? It's shite hours but it pays good."

Bobby liked the sound of that, "Whatcha mean? What do I have to do?"

"Well, it starts at 8pm at The Flaming Oasis off Times Square. Will go on to about 4am. Sometimes they go on longer, you know what the celebs are like when they get blitzed or snort the snow white all night."

He didn't really know what the celebs were like, never having met one. "Yeah, they can be a pain in the butt. You want me to do doorman?"

"Yeah, but you'll have to go back to City Hall and sign on for the 'Private Security Operators' course, so I can put you on my books. It's three times four-hour sessions at Police Plaza over a month, then you do a hundred hours with OLG and you get your licence. OLG are always looking for competent, trustworthy part-timers."

"And you'll use me on jobs? Part-time? Sounds cool."

"Yeah, strictly security only. I'm putting myself on the line here for you, Bobby. If you hurt anyone, I lose my licence, and if you get hurt, you won't be insured until you get yours."

"I won't fool around, Rab. Promise. Just be doing the door, right? Whatcha paying then?"

Rabbie was bending the rule book a bit but he reckoned he could trust Bobby. A friend in need and all that, "Well, it's fifty bucks an hour, then time and a half after eight hours."

The big man's mouth dropped, "Aw, man. You're really pulling me out of Turdsville this month, Rabbie." He clinked bottles with him, "Thanks, guy."

Rabbie drank, enjoying the bite of the cold beer as it slid down his throat. "And you get fifty bucks' allowance for food and travel, so get Wendy to make you a loaf of sarnies up and you can travel with me. Company claims it back off the IRS end of each year."

Bobby was beaming from ear to ear now, "Jesus, man. That's outstanding."

Wendy hollered down from the bedroom, "Run up and get mah hairdryer, wouldcha, Bobby? And you better have saved Luca and me some chicken!"

"Certainly my little angel," and he went off to do Wendy's bidding, bursting with enthusiasm. The sunshine was peeking above the grey, gloomy clouds of his recent working life for a goddam change.

* * *

When he got back down, Big Mal had arrived. Philli was seeing Luca, so he dandered down back up to the kitchen, to chill out and munch on KFC.

"Hear you're working with us Wednesday at SassyVanassy's birthday party," Mal said.

Bobby's mouth gawked again, "SassyVanassy? As in the people's Pop Princess? The sex goddess? Holy schmoly! She's hot to trot, dude."

"The very one. You'll be doing the outside door most of the time but we'll get yah in for a break."

"Awesome! This has to be my lucky day."

Wendy and Philli came down, "She's watching some show about meerkats in Kenya, so Philli and me's gonna have a bit of supper."

Rabbie got the food out of the oven and put some on a plate for them and a separate plate for Luca and poured her a glass of wine. "I'll take this down for her. She has to take her tablets anyway. She loves the meerkats."

234

Wendy and Pilli looked at each other and grinned. The man was well and truly smitten. They snickered. The next week or two were looking to be highly entertaining.

He found her sitting up in bed, hair shiny and brushed and dressed in a black square-necked nightdress with short puff sleeves. She looked good enough to eat, especially when she gave him her dazzling smile.

"Hey, Rab. Do I see da Colonel Saunders secret recipe chicken? Am famished, I tink is the word."

"Your English is certainly better than my Russian, Luca."

He got her settled, and she nibbled at her chicken daintily and sipped her wine as she watched the meerkats, fascinated by their antics. "Dey are so, soo neat."

She took her tablets without fuss, "You know there is petals from the passion flower in the little brown ones?"

"Yeah, what, in the sleeping tablets?"

"Yep, tis strange. You vould tink the passion flower would keep you awake wiv longing, not da make you sleepy," hinting, wondering how he would reply.

He couldn't think of a reply to that, so he went to get her a glass of water for the night.

* * *

In the kitchen the 'Luca Watch', as they were now calling themselves, had worked out a rota between themselves and a few other girls from Luca's work.

"It's all covered, Rabbie, between us and her friends, there will be someone here all day with her and at night when you're working."

"Great, Wendy. She really appreciates all the help."

Wendy was bursting with happiness. Bobby had told her about 'the gig', and she could relax for the rest of the month knowing they had some more money coming in, and all thanks to Luca and Rabbie.

"Hey, Bobby, you should call in and see Brian Cooper tomorrow. He's the Admin Office manager. He needs a spark."

Bobby couldn't believe his ears. This was getting too good, "What's he need done, Mal?"

"He needs switches and sockets put in for three new work stations. He's expanding the Operators Office. I heard him saying earlier when I popped in to see him for a yarn."

"Does he not have a regular guy?"

"Nah, last firm were screw-ups. Blew the main fuse box. He'll take you on, being ex-army an' all."

"Friggin A. I'll call in on my way to City Hall, looks like the long, dry season is about to get hit by a monsoon. Wash all those fricking yappy dogs away."

Wendy was near to tears and she put her arms around his chest from behind, barely able to join her hands, so wide was his girth. Finally, good karma had decided to visit Apartment 3A, The Poplar Tree Apartments, home to Mr and Mrs Robert Eisenhower-Havilland. She would get him downstairs tonight and rock the socks off him, but not for long, as he had to get up in the morning. Oh Sweet Joy! Sweet Joy!

Rabbie had taken Luca's water down. He came back in and making a shush motion with his finger on his mouth, beckoned them to follow him. Luca was fast asleep, her lovely hair spread over the pillow, one slim arm out of the bed. ·

"She looks like a fairy tale princess. Sleeping Beauty," said an enchanted Philli.

The men gazed down at her fondly, "Yeah, well as long as a certain prince doesn't sneak in during the night and gives her a kiss to wake her up. She should sleep through to the morning," whispered Wendy.

Rabbie flicked the television off, blatantly ignoring the last comment.

"Yeah and princesses don't puke bucket loads down yer back," Bobby said, mystifying Rabbie.

He ushered them out. They all took their leave, tired after a long day, Rabbie seeing them out, pleased at the relaxed expressions on Bobby's and Wendy's faces.

He slept in his old army cortex sleeping bag on the couch. He used the spare room as part office and part storage space. He dreamt of giant passion flowers being harvested by meerkats and the petals being made into tablets.

Luca dreamt also of meerkats harvesting passion flowers and of them making a bed out of them for her and Rabbie to lie upon. Hanlon was far from her dreams that night.

* * *

She slept through to six in the morning and awoke fresh and pain-free. The apartment was quiet. She put the radio on low, New York City Beat. She wondered if she should go and make coffee for Rabbie. He would probably tell her off for getting out of bed. Luca opened the drapes. Another nice day promised itself as the sun rose behind the apartments at the back, its warm rays beginning to climb down the poplar tree in the garden below.

She used the bathroom, brushing and flossing her perfect teeth. She put her matching robe on and got back into bed with a writing pad and pen and started to write a letter to her mother. She had not told her mother about the assault on her. It would only make her worry unduly. When she moved her mother over, she would teach her to use a computer and introduce her to the internet. She would love it.

Luca reflected on the standard of living in New York. The technology and instant communications where everyone was in contact with everybody else twenty-four hours a day if they wanted to be. Whereas in the isolated Drasnov Valley where Mama lived, mobile phones were useless because there was no coverage and to use the internet, you had to book a slot to use the computer in the small town library.

She wondered what her mother was doing now. It was nearly lunchtime in Lithuania. Probably still bashing away at her old Singer sewing machine, making a beautiful dress for some hopeful young bride. Her mother had never shown any interest in having a relationship with any other man after Sasha died. She had concentrated on raising her and Dimitri and giving them the best she could with the limited funds available.

Luca's heart swelled with love for her. She had always put them first. She giggled. Perhaps when she finally got Reena here, she would fix her up with some kind, rich New Yorker. After all, she was still a very attractive woman.

Luca stared into space. She would make a list of older, eligible bachelors. Rabbie was bound to know some. She smiled at the thought of Rabbie. She knew he considered her list-making amusing. She liked pleasing him, she understood it would be a few years before she had saved enough to bring Reena and Dimitri over and get them somewhere decent to live and employment. She would ask Rabbie's advice about it nearer the time.

She was writing about the nice man she had met in the apartments and how good he was to her. She knew that would please Reena, who was always asking if she had met a suitable guy yet. Said nice man banged on the door.

"Are you decent? I hope not."

She laughed. She seemed to be laughing a lot recently. "Of course, I am, silly boy."

He came in, "Shame, ah well. Are you ready for breakfast?"

"Sure, it's my bestest meal of the day."

He rubbed his hands together, "Great. Surprise, surprise!"

Mama Jocelyn came bustling in carrying a tray, "Outta the way, big man, before the Special gets cold."

Luca's eyes opened wide in amazement, "What you do now, Rabbie?"

"Now, sit you up straight, gal. Look at yah, you're wasting away."

She complied and Jocelyn put the tray across her lap and uncovered the plate to reveal a full Luca Special. Her mouth watered.

"If you can't come ta Jocelyn's, then Jocelyn ha ta come ta you."

Luca tucked into her breakfast with relish, chatting away to her big roly-poly friend in between every mouthful, enjoying each delicious morsel, whilst Rabbie ate his in the kitchen.

"Ah have to get back, child. Don't expect this every morning. I can't leave that big lump Royston in charge two mornings running, I'll go bankrupt."

Luca hugged and kissed her friend in gratitude, her stomach pleasantly full. Afterwards, Rabbie sat and had coffee with her before he left for work. She took the tablets he gave her with a brave smile.

He fetched the first aid kit and put a new dressing on her right shin, "I don't think that will need changed again, Luca. It has cleared up. It'll fade away in a week or so."

She was pleased, she was proud of her legs, knowing they were one of her best assets, "I never heard Mama Jocelyn buzz the door, Rabbie," a trace of anxiety creeping into her voice.

"I turned it off in case you were asleep. Master switch in the living room. It's a flexible system."

"Oh, that's clever!" *He was soo, so thoughtful. A diamond in a pile of coal.* She liked flexible systems.

He got his work clothes and went to have his shower. She went back to her letter. The strong antibiotics always made her woozy for an hour or so.

He came out in a light-grey suit, pristine white shirt and blue tie set off by highly polished patterned black brogues. With his very black hair and steady dark blue eyes, it was a lethal combination for any young, fertile female, especially for one sitting in her nightwear in his bed. Desire welled and niggled nicely in her lower belly.

"Wendy will be up shortly; I have to shoot on. New client at 10," he told her as he splashed cologne on freshly shaved cheeks.

"Rabbie, come here, vill you? Your tie's crooked. I fix it, da?"

He ambled over, and she turned and pulled him down into her arms and placed her full soft lips onto his and proceeded to kiss him gently but firmly. He hesitated for a brief second, then responded. She stroked the curls on the back of his neck. She was pleasantly aroused, so was Rabbie.

The buzzer sounded and the small screen came on. He left her soft lips – stunned.

"I turned it back on when Jocelyn left," he told her apologetically and reluctantly pulled away to look. "It's Wendy."

He pressed the button to let her in and stood looking down at her. She stared right back at him, her eyes mysterious and full of mischief.

"Dat's just to say a big tanks, Rab. Did you like it?" breaking the silence.

"I think the pleasure was all mine, Luca," he answered her gallantly and headed off to meet Wendy, whistling an old commando battle march. 'That Was One Foxy Lady'. Life had sure got interesting since she burst so flamboyantly into his life.

* * *

Wendy entered a few minutes later after chatting with a very cheerful Rabbie. Luca looked radiant. She beamed at Wendy. Her lovely eyes sparkling silver in the light and full of mischief.

"Rab ses yah slept all night. That's great. Wanna cup of coffee?"

"No tanks, Wends. I tink I go back to sleep for an hour."

"Sure hon, it's the medication. It slows the system down."

Luca was already under the quilt, eyes closed, beatific smile on her serene face, "Soo sorree, Wends, so tired."

Wendy pulled the drapes and left her to it. All her wily female intuition told her something had happened between Rabbie and Luca, and she wondered if the perambulators had changed or was it just a fleeting flash in the pan happenstance. *Sure if no one gets hurt, what the hell! That's karma, babe.*

Chapter 19
A Break at the Oasis

Hexham, Early May, 1976

Collette stood on the platform of Hexham station with Mac and Beth nearly wetting herself with excitement at the thought of seeing her man again. She seemed to be spending a lot of time on trains and platforms recently; she had arrived the day before and been pleased that Beth was happy to see her. She had spent a relaxing evening in the comfortable farm house helping Davey with a complex jigsaw showing Roman soldiers fighting with some tribe of wood-painted warriors. Jamesey had spotted it in a charity shop in Belfast and posted it over to him. He was such a thoughtful man to take time off from his dangerous duties to think of his little brother. *Time he could have spent sleeping*, she thought wryly.

Jamesey…he was constantly in her mind. In the pub, on the street, in his house, where she was living on a semi-permanent basis at his request, looking after it while he was away, and especially in his bed. His huge presence loomed and her mind spun with a kaleidoscope of memories and nuances of thoughts about him. He seemed to be hovering in her head twenty-four hours a day. She often found herself daydreaming about his handsome face and the things they had done, but other times she was sick with worry for his safety in that bastard of a place the army had sent him to, a shiver going down her spine as she imagined a hooded IRA sniper taking aim at her lover's head with a high-powered rifle. Bastard IRA scum, why not just pull the army out and fight the bit out? Then she felt guilty at the thought of the thousands of innocent lives that would be lost and felt a glow of pride for Jamesey, her warrior, for doing his bit.

At times it was just too much and she would break down and cry; Eadie would console her while Ron would shake his head at the fragility of the psyche of a young woman in love. At other times she stood in a happy daze, miles from reality, recalling some special thing they had done and reliving it in glorious technicolour then Eadie would snap at her in frustration to get on with her work, and she would reluctantly drag herself back to the present and silently lament the absence of her man.

Eadie would chat away to her and give her plenty of odd jobs and varied tasks, trying to keep her mind away from these thoughts, because she knew what it was like, she had been through the same thing when Ronnie had been fighting in Cyprus; she knew how hard it was for the women left at home.

When she was alone, all she could think about was Jamesey, Jamesey, Jamesey. She thought at times she would mentally pull herself apart in frustration at his absence. She never believed it when people said mental torture could be worse than physical but she did now and felt like tearing her hair out by the roots.

It was like she was watching a never-ending movie in her head that she was starring in and she didn't want it to get to the final credits and end. She knew it was irrational and unhealthily obsessive but it was her mental bread and butter, and she fed off it and thrived on it. It was what kept her going when he wasn't there.

She felt she had known Jamesey forever but in reality, it was less than three months since the first time they had made love. She had been prepared to accept it as a one-night stand, knowing it would have been something she would have cherished her whole life. She couldn't believe she could hold onto a powerhouse of a man like him. It took time to sink in and it had only dawned on her slowly, the wonderful realisation that Jamesey was also in love with her. She knew he had tried to fight his feelings, not through selfish reasons, but because he cared for her welfare; some battles just can't be won. He had sent her a lovely bouquet of red roses on her twenty-first birthday and a postal order for twenty-five pounds and declared his undying love for her.

Collette marvelled at the miracle of the whole wondrous sequence of events. He wrote her sexy letters on the thin blue free air mail (Par Avion) paper the soldiers were issued with that made her swoon and she kept in a biscuit tin under her bed.

Each soldier on tour in the Province, if they were there for more than six months, was given a short break to go home and recharge his resolve and steady his nerves; nothing like a bit of loving from a wife or sweetheart and a few home-cooked meals to boost morale and it was Jamesey's turn. Oh joy, sweet joy!

Collette could hardly believe it; Jamesey was coming home for six days R&R[91] and he would be here soon. She watched the small four-carriage train come around the bend and her pulse quickened as she sensed him approaching. He had flown in to an RAF airbase near York early that morning and cadged a lift into Doncaster to get his connection. She hopped from foot to foot, chewing her knuckles anxiously.

Beth DeJames watched Collette with part amusement and part concern. There was no doubt in her mind that the anxious, fidgeting lassie was, as her late husband, Mike, would have said, arse over tit in love with her big lad, she just hoped Jamesey felt the same. He could be hard to judge since he joined the army, the harsh discipline and often brutal regime teaching the young soldiers to hide their feelings and display little or no emotion in public.

The train pulled into the station and juddered to a stop, electricity crackling in the air. Collette was holding her breath and chewing her knuckles as the passengers alighted. Watching her, Beth honestly hoped her son felt the same as she knew he had the capacity to break Collette's fragile heart in two. It had happened before with a couple of local girls. Beth knew he hadn't done it maliciously, he had been young and it was part of the growing up process, of his finding his feet as a suitable young man in the love stakes. He was older now and hopefully, wiser in matters of the heart, and she prayed he didn't hurt this young girl, who had obviously fallen hard for him. She didn't think Collette would handle the rejection as well as the other girls in Jamesey's past. From what Beth had heard she had had a fairly traumatic and deprived upbringing and what she needed was someone to show her some love and concern and help her through life's mazes; if Jamesey was destined to be that person, then so be it. She was already fond of Collette, and she knew in her heart that Mike, who was always for the underdog, would have taken to the young girl and thought

---

[91] Rest and recuperation

240

her a 'right tonic' to have about the place; if it was good enough for him, it was good enough for her.

Jamesey alighted from the third carriage down, grip in hand, and paused to get his bearings. He heard his name being called and turned to see Collette waving furiously before racing down the platform to meet him. A huge grin crossed his face and he dropped his holdall, extending his arms in welcome. She flew onto them and he twirled her around, laughing with glee as she clung to him and showered his face with kisses, before he planted her back on the asphalt and they went into a deep, smouldering, lip-crushing kiss.

Mac caught Beth's eye, "Spring is in the air, I reckon. Oh, to be young again."

Beth laughed, watching her son and the girl who was rapidly becoming a new addition to the family get reacquainted, "Come on, Mac, let's go rescue them before they die from lack of oxygen."

They strolled down, and Jamesey released Collette to give his mother a hug and kiss and to shake Mac's hand. Mac took his bag and they headed out to the car park, a lady hanging off each of Jamesey's arms. Beth knew her son well, and as she scrutinised his face, she could see the faint lines of exhaustion and she thought he looked a little drawn. She would feed him up, ply him with good whiskey and make sure he got an early night. He could be stubborn, like his father, but she knew how to handle him; a full belly, whiskey and some TLC and he would be as right as rain in no time.

Collette stuck to Jamesey like a plaster all the way back to the farm, revelling in his physical presence. She could see the tiredness etched in his face as she whispered endearments in his ear. Feeling his warmth next to her, she determined to give him her own type of comfort and support and the bedroom was going to be her main area to achieve that.

While the womenfolk were preparing food, Jamesey escaped to have a shower to get rid of the grime he had picked up while travelling and to think about what had happened when he got off the train.

Collette was not due to be there but when he saw her standing with his mother and Mac, he could feel his expression soften, and he knew he had quite visibly relaxed. She must have conspired with his mother to surprise him.

As she had waved to him madly and then hurtled down the platform to greet him, his heart had filled with joy and had raced like a thoroughbred approaching the finish line. All his instincts told him their short relationship was fast becoming a very important factor in his life and if played out right, would turn into a winning formula. He was more in love with her than he cared to admit even to himself.

His little Collette, his broody mare, who one minute would have him splitting his sides with laughter as she relayed something she remembered, and the next offering her his hanky and plonking her on his knee in a comforting embrace as her mood became melancholy when she thought of the bad times.

Hormones, he guessed, women seemed to have the monopoly on them, an endless, deep well that they dredged up as and when required. He wondered if he was being chauvinistic but decided he wasn't. Collette wore her heart on her sleeve and wasn't afraid to show her emotions in front of him. He reckoned that was an important issue of trust in any relationship and he was secretly flattered that she was so open with him.

She had burst into his heart like an exploding star, a lovely comet aimed from the heavens to land in his grateful arms. He thought about the female softness of her, a softness so surreal, no poet could possibly do it justice; her sweet breath on his face and neck, the wetness of her tears and the salty tang as their lips met; her familiar wanton taste and the texture of her tongue as it urgently sought his; and the satin feel of the nape of her neck as he reached it with his fingers. Brushing through her silken hair, black as a raven's wing, as he pulled her into him and they blended into one, her slim arms encasing him and their combined heat dispelling the cold wall he built round his heart while he was in Belfast. He felt strangely safe, he marvelled at that because he hadn't felt safe for some time and he was only realising that now.

Jamesey went down for lunch feeling surer of his feelings and better than he had in weeks.

II

When you don't have much time and you're enjoying yourself, time seems to go past even quicker, so the next two days passed in a blur for the lovers. Jamesey had not realised just how tensed up he was. He had a heavy burden of responsibility on him, being in charge of a platoon of forty highly specialised fighting men, and that burden became tenfold when on active service. They trained hard but no one could be fully prepared for the horrors of war.

* * *

The war in Ulster was a small, dirty affair, a nasty brutal campaign of attrition fought on the streets, on the hills and in the hedgerows. Outnumbered and out-gunned by the army, the IRA rarely took them on face to face, preferring various forms of elaborate ambush with bullet and bomb. In 1976, West Belfast was the most dangerous place in the world for a British soldier to be serving. Shootings and bombings caused casualties on a weekly and sometimes daily basis and add to that the serious problem of public disorder and riots, often lasting over a period of weeks, which the troops were trying to contain, dressed in full riot gear and looking like futuristic knights. Trying to keep the two factions apart by using only plastic bullets was a thankless and derogatory job, exhausting in the extreme. The IRA's political wing, Sinn Féin (Ourselves Alone), had a clever propaganda campaign going against the hated Brits, heavily supported by various supporters in the media (Loyalists called the BBC, Northern Ireland, Sinn Féin TV) who pumped their slogan out for them, 'An Armalite in one hand and a ballot box in the other'.

The paratroopers were rough and tough, they would speed from one incident to the next, one riot to another, often going two or three days with little or no sleep. Jamesey was proud of his guys and ruled with a firm but fair hand, their welfare always uppermost in his mind. He was aware they had been lucky so far but the odds were not in his favour, and they were likely to have causalities, if not fatalities, at some point, no platoon had served for six months in West Belfast and escaped unscathed.

He found it hard to believe he was still in the United Kingdom when he looked around him in West Belfast. It sprawled along the lower area of the Black Mountain, its peak frowning down on the urban metropolis that was like an unwanted cancer eating into its fragrant slopes. *No*, thought Jamesey. *It's like a foreign country with its tri-colour flags everywhere and its painted wall murals dedicated to dead 'heroes' and the battles they died in. The broken lamp posts and the windows boarded up, where the glass had been broken during riots, the paving stones cracked and broken by rioters and then used as ammunition against the 'other sort' and the army. Even its people, many of them living in crowded, slum conditions, who spat at them when they passed and cursed at them in Gaelic. The myriad of illegal drinking clubs and shebeens run by different fractions and all heavily fortified and sinister.*

Jamesey shivered. It was the complete lack of law and order that got him. The police rarely ventured out of their stations and when they did, they stayed in the town or city centres, where there was less chance of trouble, at least during the day. The Special Patrol Groups, in their grey-armoured Hotspur Land Rovers, were the only ones who ventured into the dangerous areas. Heroes to a man and hated by the IRA and their supporters.

They were a brave bunch of guys, thought Jamesey, *Either brave or crazy or maybe a bit of both.*

The Special Patrols were often made up of ex-forces who had married a local girl and joined the RUC when their time in the army was up. They carried on until were dead, seriously injured or burnt out. Most of them ended up as alcoholics and few of the marriages could survive the long hours the Special Patrols worked, their loved ones waiting nervously at home, wondering if their spouse or parent was going to come home in a wooden box or missing limbs.

Their first few weeks had been an anti-climax as the Provisional IRA were having a ceasefire while their leadership held secret talks with the government. Jamesey reckoned it was just a ploy to enable them to re-group, re-train and re-arm. They weren't stupid by any means; they were a lethal, deadly foe and if you let your guard down at all, they exploited it and moved in for the kill. Routine meant death or injury and it was exhausting trying to keep one step ahead of the 'Bush Whacking Cunts'.

Jamesey smiled to himself, he had been insulted many times during his service but the people in West Belfast had the market when it came to cursing and bitching in your face. He found the daily torrent of expletives thrown at him colourful and often highly entertaining. The women were sometimes more vicious than the men and to have a lovely sixteen-year-old colleen in a mini skirt tell him to "Fuck away home, yah Brit bastard, yer ma's being gang banged by six big niggers" was surreal coming from such a pretty mouth, and to be informed that the IRA was going to "Cut his dick off and shove it up the queen's arse" was definitely enlightening. He shook his head in wonder at the memory.

But maybe he was judging too harshly and being unfair. There were many decent people in Belfast as well, people who wanted law and order to return or didn't want a united Ireland, but they had no voice and to express their opinion in public would result in the loss of their kneecaps or worse. They passed you during the day with their heads low, afraid to acknowledge your presence but at night they would mumble "Good luck, son" or "Thank you and God bless", sometimes they would give a hint as to where there might be trouble and warn you what to watch your back in. Just little things but they made the job seem worthwhile.

The Emergency Provisions Act and the Anti-Terrorism Order gave the police and army carte blanche to stop and search anyone at any time and bring them in for questioning to the dreaded Castlereagh Barracks. Under these laws they could stop vehicles, demand details, seal streets and search buildings. There were a myriad of other obscure rules and regulations designed to thwart the terrorists on both sides of the divide and restore civic order. The ultimate plan was for the police, who were recruiting and training like mad, to regain control in the small, badly battered and forlorn province. *We pay for the sins of our fathers*, Jamesey guessed.

He smiled to himself at a happier memory.

Just after the IRA called off their ceasefire in mid-March and mayhem, death and destruction resumed its daily grind, Jamesey and his team were sent to search a nice four-bedroomed villa on the hillside. 'The Green Slime'[92] had received an anonymous tip that illegal arms were being kept on the premises.

When they arrived, they were welcomed by a pleasant middle-aged couple, who plied them with coffee, cake and homemade scones. They made it quite clear they were republicans and wanted independence from mainland Britain. "We are an island after all and didn't the Anglo Saxons fight to stop the usurper William the Conqueror in Britain back in 1066?" Jamesey had to concede he had a point, as he munched on a feather-light scone. "I live on a border too but I wouldn't kill over it," he told them as he listened to his guys ransacking their house.

"And nor would we," they told him, "Violence begets violence, and we cry every time we hear that a young soldier from across the water has been killed." "We pray for their safety every night," added the woman.

Jamesey was strangely moved and told Smudger to tell the guys to go easy.

The couple had three teenage daughters, pretty little dark-haired things and as he ambled about the house checking on the progress of the search, the eldest tagged along. He made sure any damage was recorded, so that the family could claim compensation from the Northern Ireland Office.

All the time the girl was chatting away about Irish history and civil rights. When they reached her bedroom, she asked him in. When she had closed and locked the door, she removed her T-shirt to reveal the fact that she was braless. Jamesey couldn't help but look at her pert breasts and his erection seemed to have a mind of its own. She sashayed over, revelling in his hot gaze, and stroked him through his combats, "How'd ya like a blow job, I'm up for it and the boys at school say I'm good," she purred.

He looked at her, mesmerised, she was very attractive and he admired both her temerity and her voluptuous young body. Christ, he could dine out on this for weeks, maybe months, at the NAFFI[93] was his not so gentlemanly thought. He pulled his gaze away from her nubile body and handed her back her T-shirt, his thoughts suddenly filled with Collette, "I might regret this later, but no thanks, I'm going steady at home."

She sighed, "Just my luck to meet a true British gentleman. Ah well, suppose I'll just have to make another phone call next week." She carried on to tell him that her and her best mate both shared the secret fantasy of giving a squaddie a blow job and had a bet on as to which of them would do it first. Jamesey had left feeling quite proud of the fact he had turned her down.

---

[92] Army Intelligence

[93] Navy, Army and Airforce Institution. Café and entertainment centre in most bases run by a charity.

The following week X-ray Company was called out to the same place and sure enough, the young officer in charge came back with a smile on his face and a story Jamesey had no problem believing. He dined out on it for weeks and when Jamesey told him what happened to him, he got a few bevvies as well. One of the blokes who did guard on the gates was heard to say, "If she had come down to the barracks any night, she could have had a queue and earned some cash."

* * *

Collette awoke and found him gazing at the early morning mist drifting over the moors. She sat up and began kneading his bare shoulders, the heat from her sleep-warmed body consoling him. "Wotcha muttering abaht, love? 'Ope yah not thinkin' bout those mickey wimmen?"

He smiled sadly, she thought, and wrapped her to him. She pulled him down, "Now let me show ya what a good old Watford girl can do," and his cock rose to meet her hungry mouth.

III

Jamesey was in the hall on the phone. She guessed it was work because when she went to tell him his breakfast was ready, he put his hand over the receiver and looked at her blankly. Collette took the hint and left him to it.

The day before Jamesey had rung a guy at Army Intelligence HQ in Hampshire, who owed him a favour. He was looking for some information and was checking to see if the contact had come up trumps.

"Give me that address again, I missed it... Yeah, I know you can get in trouble, my lips are sealed... Yep, got it. Thanks, my man... Quid pro quo, mate, and remember next time you decide to take on ten drunken Paddies in a bar, the guys and I might not be about to bail you out!"

He hung up and dialled directory enquiries, got the number and asked the operator to put him through. Collette put her head onto the hall, "Yer brekkie's getting cold, love."

He shooed her off with his hand, "Put it in the Aga, my little chicken... Business." She rolled her eyes in mock exasperation and darted back into the kitchen.

Beth had already put the big galoot's meal away in the range to keep it warm, and she joined Collette at the table, where they sat sipping their coffee contentedly and chatted companionably.

They had had a lovely two days at Petral Hill Farm. Jamesey called it his 'oasis' in the stormy desert of life and Collette had to agree with him. The place was sublime, she decided. Liking the new word, she had looked up and added to the lists in her rapidly filling notebook.

When the phone was answered, Jamesey introduced himself and explained what he wanted, that he didn't want to impose or put them out but how he felt it was of benefit to all concerned. After some hesitation and not a little reticence, an arrangement was agreed to and Jamesey hung up, pleased with his powers of persuasion, "You smooth-talking silver-tongued devil you are," he told himself entering the kitchen, "Where's my breakfast then? My belly's stuck to my backbone."

Mac had arrived with his dogs that he doted on as they loved him. Collette stroked them fondly, they were wonderful, intelligent creatures with a gentle, loyal nature and she vowed to have one when she was settled somewhere with a garden. She would see Mac about it in the future.

"I gave it to Bill and Ben, didn't I… If yah can't sit down ta yer meals on time, ya don't get, do ya want some cornflakes?"

He looked at her aghast, his stomach rumbling, "But I'm starving, Coll… I don't even like cornflakes."

He looked at their grinning faces and knew he'd been had. He sat down laughing as Beth deposited a huge plate of a fry up in front of him, "You're a dark and devious woman, so ya are, Coll," he said, amused.

"Enough calories in that to kill a donkey, love," she smirked, "Bill and Ben have more sense."

He broke a succulent Cumberland sausage in two and gave half to each dog. They took them gently and chomped them down daintily. "An army marches on its stomach," and he wolfed his meal down in huge mouthfuls, luxuriating in the fine homemade fare.

"Christ, love," remarked Collette, "The dogs have better table manners. Give it a chance to touch the sides before it goes down."

"As the Proddies say in Ulster 'No Surrender', and I ain't showing no mercy to this fine meal," he gushed through chomping jaws, "God knows, my ma makes the best breakfast under his sky and Lord knows I miss them when I'm away."

Beth looked pleased and Collette vowed she would get her culinary skills up to speed, "Yeah, it's brill and you enjoy it, darling, because you frigging deserve it, 'scuse me French, Beth."

It was Beth and Mac's turn to laugh; they would miss the crack and banter when the lively couple departed. The place wouldn't be the same without them. Beth wondered how Davey was doing at school with his little friends about him; he was a great comfort to her.

Jamesey and Collette had made a huge fuss over him for the last couple of days, spoiling him silly. It was almost as if Jamesey didn't expect to see him again and was saying goodbye. She guessed he was hedging his bets in case something happened to him in that accursed place of evil he would be back in all too soon and she shivered; she would be praying for her son's safety every day, she decided.

"You okay, Mum?" he asked, sensing her unease.

Her big lad missed nothing, she thought. A cold, sinister feeling crept down her spine as a premonition only a mother could have gripped her, and she knew her son was in danger and faced troubled times ahead. She realised everyone was staring at her and had to force herself to refocus and remain calm, "Yes, I'm fine. It was just a 'Will 'o the Wisp'[94] passed across me for a moment there."

Collette squeezed her hand; she sensed a kindred spirit in Beth. "Eat up, son… You've a train to catch."

Beth had decided to give the family car, a very smart Austin Bentley with a walnut dash, a run out and was driving them to Doncaster to get the express to London, Euston, at 11.00am. Jamesey had bet his mother a fiver she wouldn't do it in an hour and a half and she took it on with relish.

---

[94] A phantom light on the moors that when seen foretold bad tidings.

An hour and a half later they were about to board the 'Flying Scotsman' and Jamesey was a fiver poorer.

His mother clung to him for an unusually long time, she normally had good control of her emotions but he saw her eyes were moist, and Collette had noticed and looking at the older woman was getting upset as well. Jamesey brushed his mother's thick blonde hair back with his right hand, not knowing it would be the last time he would ever do that, "We'll stay up here if you want, Mum."

"Yeah, I'll go down after Jamesey goes back," agreed Collette.

Beth got a grip on herself, "No, it's okay, head you down to the sinful big smoke and enjoy yourselves, I'll be all right."

They boarded reluctantly and found seats, "Never seen my mother like that, strange," he intoned, worried.

"She'll be all right, love," Collette consoled him holding his right hand and playing with his fingers, "She's just worried abaht ya, ain't she?"

"Guess so," he agreed, "Fancy a drink, buffet should be open?"

Five hours later they were back in The Robert Peel, sitting upstairs with Ron and Eadie sipping on pints of shandy and munching on ham and mustard sandwiches. Collette looked at her big boyfriend and for a split second such an awful sense of unease gripped her that she wanted to rush out of the room and find a dark corner to hide in.

"You okay, Collette?" he asked.

"Fine, love, just dandy," she answered.

They woke the next morning, groggy from too much free ale well-wishers had foisted upon them, glad the big man was safe. The regulars were keeping track of the blossoming romance with interest. Jamesey dressed and staggered out for his morning run, grunting a short farewell. While he was gone, Collette got his double primus stove out and when he came back, she served him up eggs, bacon, tomatoes and fried bread and strong sweet tea to wash it down.

It was the first time she had cooked a real breakfast for him, and she watched anxiously as he wolfed it down, marvelling at the speed soldiers ate. He mopped up the last of the juice with a slice of bread and drained his second mug of tea, then he belched and rubbed his belly in appreciation.

"Was it okay, love?" she asked tentatively, "It barely saw daylight."

He got up and mussed her hair, "Top of the range, my lamb, fair hit the spot."

He bounded out and crashed up the stairs whistling 'March of the Valkyries' by Wagner. He had told her it was the Parachute Regiment Battle March, "Fairly stirs the blood." She shuddered as she thought of his blood being stirred by a feast of IRA bullets. The imminent return to Belfast of her lover was a constant nag in the back of her mind, like a migraine sufferer knowing the symptoms of an impending headache and waiting for the dreaded pain to explode in their head.

She heard him running the bath and steeled her resolve, even if the confident big bugger didn't know he needed her, she knew. Since his return he had been in a high state of alert, constantly scanning his surroundings, watching doors and windows, his eyes ceaselessly searching for anything out of place. On the train, in the pub, no matter where he was, he never turned his back to the door and any strangers were scrutinised carefully. When a porter on the train had slammed a door, he had flinched at the bang and she thought he was going to jump under the seat. He had grinned sheepishly and she had moved to his lap and given him a damn good snogging, much to the surprise of a travelling vicar and his lady wife.

Ron had noticed what was happening and saw Collette watching Jamesey. He took her to one side to explain, "It's the stress of a war situation, ain't it; he can't wind down 'cause if he does, he daren't see. He knows he's gotta go back, and if he switches off, he's afraid he won't be able to switch on again."

She nodded in understanding, "Guess so, Ron, I'll just be there for him, won't I."

He patted her hand, "You're a good gal, Collette, you're good for each other ain't cha."

Collette had beamed at those words of accolade from a man she had mega respect for, gave him a big smacker on the cheek before going back to stand by her man and join him in his ceaseless vigil.

She dragged herself from the memories just as he turned off the taps, and she heard him climbing into the bath, the water sloshing. Peeling off her pyjamas, she skipped lightly up the stairs, naked, "Room for a small one?" she enquired saucily and climbed in, not waiting for an answer.

He chuckled and lathering up the sponge proceeded to wash her from head to toe, much to the satisfaction of them both.

He told her to dress nicely because they were going to Harpenden, a small town twenty miles north of Watford. They got the Greenline Bus, Collette looked pretty in a blue linen suit and red blouse, definitely her colours. He was dressed smartly himself in slacks, pressed to a razor crease, starched shirt and tie and black leather jacket.

"Who we gonna see then, love?" she asked.

"Just a couple of mates, you'll like 'em," he told her but didn't elaborate.

"Oh, okay…whatever," not pressing the point, content to sit holding his hand and watch the countryside flash past. She'd certainly got about since she'd met him, he'd opened her eyes to the world, and she was thoroughly enjoying the learning curve. Then she thought back to the bath they had earlier and grinned widely. He was teaching her other things too, things she had never thought were possible and never dreamed of, and it wasn't only her eyes he liked to open up.

"What you smiling at then, Coll?" he asked pulling her out of her erotic ramble.

"I'm thinking that cleanliness is next to Godliness, so I think we should have a bath every day."

He smiled broadly, she was outstanding. They got off the bus in the centre of the picturesque little market town, brightly coloured spring flowers in every hue imaginable, lining the wide pavements and grass verges. Ducks quacked and swans honked happily in a large pond as excited little children fed them bread, watched over by protective mums.

Collette watched them enviously as she remembered her own sad childhood. "Lovely, ain't it, darling?"

"Nice place to live, I would guess," he agreed. He popped into a small timber-beamed shop to ask directions and ten minutes later they reached Fosseway Avenue. They found number eleven, a large semi-detached, red brick house with a Dutch barn roof standing proudly in an immaculately tended garden, the cherry trees lining the drive showing their first blossom.

He stopped at the gate, put his hands on her shoulders and looked into her lovely hazel eyes filled with curiosity, "I hope I'm doing the right thing, Coll, I really do...wait here a minute."

He went up the drive and rang the doorbell as she watched, baffled. *What the frig was he up to now?*

A kindly looking lady in her thirties admitted him and then closed the door. Collette crossed her arms and tapped her foot in annoyance, *Bloody charming*, she fumed, *Being left to stand in the street like a discarded coat.*

Several minutes passed and she started to get worried, *What the hell's goin' on? Has he got a bit of strange he prefers to me? Has he got a love child he wants me to meet? Why all the friggin' skulduggery?*

Then the door opened again and he came out with two well-dressed boys in their early teens. As they approached, Jamesey in the middle with a hand on each boy's shoulder, she looked at their dark hair and fine features and her heart skipped a beat. When she looked from face to face and into their curious hazel eyes, she swore her heart was going to stop altogether.

"Say hello to your sister, lads," Jamesey instructed the twins, before rushing over to catch Collette as she passed clean away in a dead faint.

"Knew that bath was too hot," he muttered as he gathered her up and carried her into the house, her anxious brothers scuttling along behind.

* * *

When she came to, with the help of smelling salts and Jamesey fanning her face furiously with last week's copy of 'The Harpenden Gazette', she was prone on a chintz-covered settee. A pleasant woman with curly brown hair had an arm around her shoulders and was administering the foul-smelling salts. A lean man in his late thirties with dark hair and glasses was hovering anxiously behind the sofa.

Recoiling from the noxious fumes, she tried to sit up but was gently eased back, "What the heck's going on, Jamesey? What's happened?"

He perched by her side, "Don't you remember, Collette? I'm a bloody idiot. This is Jim and Sally Mills." They nodded pleasantly as Collette's head rapidly cleared and she sat up again. She put her hands to her face in shock, "Oh sweet suffering Jesus, please tell me I'm not in the middle of some dream... Where's me little bruvvers?"

"Not so little now, Collette," Jamesey grinned, marching out to get the boys who were kicking a ball about in the garden while watching the house, worried about their sister. They came flying in at his shouted summons, shouting her name, they leap on her in a mad hurly burly, hugging and kissing her. Collette squeezed them tightly softly, saying their names over and over in wonder before breaking down in floods of tears. Her heart was fit to explode with love for the siblings she thought she had lost forever.

Sally started crying too and joined the clinging tangle of happiness, Jim leaned over and patted their backs consolingly, his eyes moist and sparkling. Jamesey watched the unusual mixed family scene, raw emotions were exposed and seemed to fill the very air around him. He felt a lump in his throat and realised he was also on the verge of tears. It was a strange and unusual feeling for him and in a way reassuring as it made him feel human again, not the robotic automaton the army wanted him to be, the man who could go into scenes of carnage and deal with it without a flicker of emotion. He felt a huge surge of happiness for Collette and her brothers and glad he had played his part in the reunion.

He pulled the small notebook and pencil he always carried, wrote a note and left it on the sideboard. He was very much the outsider here and surplus to requirements. They needed some privacy.

He left Collette and the twins chattering ten to a dozen, unnoticed but strangely content his devious little subterfuge had worked out so well.

* * *

They talked for ages, catching up. It had been nine long years since they had set eyes on each other and the twins had missed their big sister they adored and who had looked after them and given them love in the face of such adversity. They knew they owed her big style.

Sally and Jim Mills had tried for kids for years but after several miscarriages, the doctors had told them it was too dangerous to continue, so they had applied to adopt and had fallen in love with the twins at first sight.

Jim was a successful businessman in the area, and Sally ran the local Oxfam shop. She kept a good home and the twins settled in well, enjoying the love and attention showered upon them and adjusting well to their new life, but they missed and worried over their big sister and vowed to find her when they got older.

Sally produced tea and Victoria sponge cake, Collette marvelling at her brothers, constantly touching them and hanging on their every word, and gripped with relief that they were safe and happy and so well cared for. She sipped her tea before she realised something was amiss, "'Ere, where's Jamesey? He'll take a cuppa."

Jim retrieved the note he'd seen him write and gave it to Collette. It read 'Harpenden Arms Hotel' room nine – dinner at 7pm – bring the 'bruvvers', xx.

For a brief moment she felt guilty for ignoring her dream lover, then she knew he would understand and turned her attention back to the glorious present.

* * *

On the bus home the next day she cuddled into him, adoration in her eyes. Nobody had ever done such a wonderful thing for her in her whole life. When she had asked him how the hell he had found the twins, he had just tapped his nose with a big finger and said "Jamesey's Ways and Means Act". That he should take the time and effort on his short leave to put her first just totally reinforced her love and trust in him. He was nearly up to God status in her esteem for him. He'd laughed it off when she had thanked him, saying "I enjoyed the challenge and seeing the look on her face. Especially when you fainted, you flashed your knickers to the whole street."

She'd punched his arm playfully but she knew he was pleased. "You know for all yer rufti tufti para philosophy, Jamesey, you're a kind heart, and I will never forget what you've done for me, me whole bleedin' life. Never, ever, mate."

He shushed her with a finger to her lips. "Enough said. When you love someone as much as I love you, Collette Stark, you do what you have to do to make them happy, and you don't need thanks because you're happy too. It's thanks enough."

250

It was a long speech regarding his feelings for her, and she cried tears of happiness that he had stated so honestly his love for her and knew she had never been so happy in her life and that she would follow him to the gates of hell if he commanded. They were meant to be and only death would part them.

The next day he went back to war, and her heart felt hollow at his absence and then filled with a nasty insipid unease and she cried herself to sleep, whispering his name over and over in her head.

Chapter 20
R and R at Rabbie's
Robin Hood... Prince of Thieves
('Everything I Do... I Do It for You'... Brian Adams 1997)

Part 1

'On La Guardia (New York) Office. Security Consultants and Specialists' was emblazoned on a brass plaque by the ground floor. Tinted black bulletproof glass doors that led into the offices off a very busy commercial street, five blocks over from the Poplar Tree Apartments.

Bobby pressed the intercom and stated his business as requested and entered a small, tastefully decorated foyer. There was also nothing tasteless about the big guy in a smart dark suit who gave him an efficient body search and checked his toolkit thoroughly.

"Nothing personal, Mr Havilland. Can't be too careful in this business. I'm Alec, by the way. Alec Green."

They shook hands.

"Hey, call me Bobby. I'm the boss dude's neighbour."

Alec grinned. A large black man in his early fifties with receding hair and very tanned and fit-looking. He had retired after twenty-five years in the Military Police, and OLG had snapped him up for part-time work. This suited him just dandy.

"Yeah, I know. You're working with us at SassyVanassy's party. The boss has pulled me in on overtime. You got a piece?"

Bobby looked blank, "A piece of what?"

Alec laughed. He had merry, friendly brown eyes which had fooled many a drunken GI, who believed they could take him on in a brawl. Highly trained in martial arts, he was absolutely lethal in a one on one. "A piece, a shooter, yah know. A rod."

Bobby twigged, "Oh right, a gun."

"No, that's the big single barrel things the artillery shoot."

He opened his coat and showed Bobby a huge chrome revolver nestled snug in its shoulder holster, "A firearm or a short arm as we call a handgun."

"Errr...no...got a great Black and Decker hammer drill though."

Alec chuckled and gave Bobby a card, "That's my cousin, Vinnie over on 89th. Get yourself tooled up every way, big guy. If yer gonna be working with OLG, you never know what you're going into."

That fazed Bobby, "Okay, thanks, Alec."

"Vinnie do yah a good deal."

A pretty girl stuck her head through a connecting door, "Mr Havilland? Please come this way."

She led him through a large office, where ten secretaries sat clacking away on keyboards and talking on the phones, trying to make extra bucks by selling OLG Security Systems. It all looked very efficient.

He saw Rabbie's name on an open door off to the left and a grey-haired lady writing at a desk inside. He'd seen her visiting Luca in hospital and guessed it was his secretary.

They reached a door with a keypad and she tapped in a code. It said 'Operations Room' on the sign. It buzzed and they entered a room with some desks and easy chairs. On a rack on a wall a number of rifles and shotguns were chained together. The only occupant was a dark-haired woman sitting at the rear facing a bank of CCTV cameras, a radio mike around her neck.

They came to another office door. It had 'B. Cooper' on it. She knocked and on answer, opened the door for him and ushered him in, "Thank you, Melanie."

A short, stocky man with dark hair came around from behind a large desk to meet him, "Come on in and take a seat, Mr Havilland. I'm Brien Cooper. Nice to meet you, old chap."

Melanie came in with a tray of coffee and doughnuts, much to his pleasure. They helped themselves.

"I'm the office manager, Rab keeps me locked up in the back here because he doesn't want me seen by the general public."

"Really? You seem okay to me, Brien."

Brien chuckled, "Only joking, old bean. It's our Brit sense of humour. You New Yorkers sometimes find it hard to understand."

"Sure do. Rabbie winds me up all da time."

"Yes, he's a card. No, it's a security thing but never mind. Have you your Electrician Union card? You don't mind if I check?"

"Sure. There's lots of cowboys about. Putting me out of business."

Brien checked it, satisfied, "Thank God for that. The last clampets I got in cheap botched the whole bloody job. Did a runner, the buggers."

"I stand by my work, Brien. Guarantee it. It not okay, no pay."

"Splendid. Ex-forces, ain't ya? Good man. Us chaps have to help each other out, doncha know?"

Bobby liked the dapper little man with the clipped British accent like you hear in an old World War Two black and white movie, like John Mills in 'Ice Cold in Alec'.

They went out into the outer office, which Brien explained was the Operations Office, "They are all out on jobs at the moment…well, except for the one in hospital. Nasty business."

"Hospital?"

"Yes, lucky to be alive by all accounts. Good thing he was wearing his bulletproof vest. Poor sod, but never mind… This is my wife, Juanita. This is our security desk. It's manned 24/7. Juanita's our Duty Officer."

Juanita was a pretty brown dusky-skinned woman in her thirties, with lovely doe eyes. They seemed an unlikely couple but looked at each other adoringly.

Brien was putting three new computer stations in at the far end of the room. He needed three new double sockets and three cut-off switches above them and a master switch.

"Can't have the staff tripping over extension cables. All health and safety. What do you think, old bean?"

"I'll measure up and give you a quote, Brien," he eyed the gun rack. "That's sure some heavy firepower you guys have."

"Yes, pretty impressive. Fortunately, we only have to use the big guns now and then on operations. The lads normally make do with their handguns."

"Right, handguns," said a worried Bobby, "How often do they use the rifles?"

Brien tapped an M16.556 Armalite semi auto fondly, "Och, four or five times a year on average. Bloody nuisance. Tons of paperwork. Cost of ammo's damn extortionate."

"Ummm, have you ever lost a guy? Sounds dangerous."

Brien gave him a steely look, "I cannot breach that confidence, Robert, but I will tell you every member of OLG is expected to do their duty to the bitter end."

"To the bitter end? Sounds ominous, Brien."

Brien was enjoying himself watching the big giant shaking in his boots, "Yes, indeedy. It's why we only employ ex-service men who can react under effective enemy fire. There are a lot of psychos out there."

"I was only an engineer, Brien, I fixed power lines in Iraq."

Brien eyed him steadily, "You know, I admire modesty in a man. I think you're going to do very well with OLG," and he shook his hand. "And don't worry. We have a great package for the next of kin if the worst happens. Welcome aboard, Robert." He went back into his office and closed the door.

Bobby was sweating. If anything happened to him, Wendy would kill him. He measured up and calculated and made small sketches for half an hour. He could hear Brien on the phone, his conversation muted. He laughed uproariously at something.

Juanita brought him coffee over. She had a kindly face, "You know he's only pulling your leg. No one gets shot. Not in the ten years I've been here, anyway."

Relief flooded him, "Really, Juanita? That's a comfort."

She smiled at the giant. Fear had no respect for size, "Yes, really. But don't tell I said. The odd black eye, broken hand but nothing bad. The guys are too switched on for the average criminal."

He sipped his coffee thoughtfully. He could see Rabbie's hand in this wind-up somewhere. He grinned. It was the sort of trick you played on your comrades in the army. New guys. For some reason it gave him a feeling of comradeship, of belonging already as part of the OLG family.

He gave Brien his quote of $700, parts and labour, "By Jove, that's cheap Robert. Call it $800 and here's $200 down. I'll pay the rest by banker's draft on completion…when can you start?"

"Start after lunch and then I'll work tomorrow and should have it all done by teatime."

"Bloody marvellous. Be good if you finish tomorrow. SassyVanassy's birthday bash's soon. You never know what might happen."

Bobby fixed him with a steady gaze, "Don't you worry, Mr Cooper. Whatever happens, I won't let you down. Nothing scares Bobby Havilland. The hotter and harder the action, the better I like it. Bring it on, I say."

Brien looked at him flabbergasted. The big guy was stark raving bonkers.

II

On the following night, the Tuesday, Rabbie arrived home at seven, expecting to find his new apartment buddy to be in bed watching endangered king penguins in Antarctica on Discovery or something of a similar vein but instead, she was sitting in the front room laughing with Wendy, Bobby and Philli, at a film on his big screen television.

"Hey, Rabbie, trying to teach Lucs American humour. Brought mah 'Blazing Saddles' DVD up. It's outstanding, man." Luca was laughing hysterically as she watched a group of cowboys sitting around a campfire, eating beans and passing wind tunefully. She looked very fetching in a long cream crepe nightgown and robe, and her laugh was unforced and musical. He had to smile, secretly glad she was relaxed and happy.

"Only you Tanks can be amused by a group of smelly farting cowboys," he chided them, "No wonder the Indians kept revolting."

Wendy slapped his leg from the couch, "Hey that's good, dude. The natives revolted against the smelly revolting cowboys."

Luca turned and caught his eye with hers, and he was caught by the smoky beauty of them all over again. "How vas your day, dahling?"

"Okay, thanks, crime never stops," he lifted a large bag. "Got us Chinese. You hungry?"

It was a silly question. She clapped her hands, thrilled. "I am revoltingly ravenous. You are so clever and kind to me, Kemo Sabe."

They laughed at her clever pun and Rabbie marched off to the kitchen area to get the plates. Philli ambled down to help him. "You okay, man? You seem distracted."

He spooned fragrant rice onto plates, "Yeah, I'm fine thanks, Philli... Just a bit overwhelmed having a beautiful Russian flatmate to come home to, and she's really meant to be in bed."

Philli grinned knowingly, "Yep, she's a looker all right, but you need to lighten up, you know. Don't go anal on her. It does her no harm sitting up with her pals, and then Wendy and me will get her settled down for the night."

He spooned beef in black bean sauce over the rice and dished out egg rolls. "Yeah, guess you're right. Only going by what the doc ordered but she's happy, so what the heck... Here, grab the ribs and crackers, chow time."

Philli punched his arm playfully, "That's the spirit, dude." The big Brit was a looker himself and Philli decided in other circumstances she wouldn't mind sharing his bed. She grabbed some plates. "After she's settled in bed, you can kiss her good night."

Rabbie was pulling beer and wine out of the fridge. "You're a sly matching minx," he called after her.

"But you love it, dahling," she threw back over her shoulder, mischievously. Rabbie followed her, grinning. He had to admit, despite the impromptu situation, it was nice to come home to a place full of happy, smiling faces, to people who were rapidly becoming firm friends fast. Truth be told, he had many acquaintances but few close buddies apart from Mal. His father told him when he was going into the forces, "You can't always pick your acquaintances but you can your friends, and be careful who you choose. Keep your friends close and your enemies closer."

He mentally shrugged as he arrived back with the food. Force of circumstances had brought this little group together but he enjoyed their company. They were all individuals in their own right but they gelled well together, and he liked the group interaction and the feeling of belonging it gave them.

Luca smiled her thanks as he placed her food before her. He poured her a glass of Chardonnay. "Ah, my number one favourite wine in da whole world. How you know dis, Rabbie?"

He grinned and plonked down beside her. "I didn't. Just struck lucky, I guess."

They ate companionably, laughing at the antics of the zany cowboys and Indians. "That Mel Brooks was a Goddamn comic genius, I tell yah man, he could make an undertakers' convention roll in the aisles," from Bobby.

"Or a busload of suicidal manic depressives driving over a cliff," put in Wendy competitively.

"Or a trainload of dah deposed Moscow bankers being sent to Stalin's Salt Mines."

Silence fell and everybody looked at her, until Bobby roared with laughter. "Now yer getting it, Luca. Way da go. Yehaa partner."

"Yeah, very good. Must tell the guys at work that," Rabbie chipped in, backing Luca up. She smiled at them. Pleased they were amused and feeling very much part of the group.

The buzzer went and Rabbie let Mal in. "Hey man, to what do I owe the pleasure?"

"Was just passing and thought I'd drop by. Gotta box of beer."

"Hey come grab a pew by me, man. I'll help you dispose of those," said Bobby hopefully. Mal plonked down next to Philli. "You're spoken for, you big galoot… Hi, Philli, you look nice tonight," and he tossed Bobby a Coors.

All eyes were on Philli, who felt herself blush, a rare event in her life. Big Mal had been running a streetwise and basic unarmed combat course twice a week at the firm, at Simon Siminion's instigation, and the female staff were hugely impressed with the prowess and physique of the big Kurd as he put them through their paces. "Why, thank you, Mal, you're looking very dapper yourself. Nice suit."

"Thanks, Hugo Boss. Watcha watching?"

"Blazing Saddles. Mel Brooks."

"Okey-dokey. Farting cowboys. I'm going to the late movies to watch that Jack Reacher movie 'One Shot'. You wanna come?"

The group watched intently as Philli simpered prettily. This was certainly a turn up for the books. "Why, I would love to. I just adore Tom Cruise, thank you, Mal."

Luca and Wendy smiled at each other knowingly. This was interesting. Who would have thought, but seated side by side, they certainly made an interesting-looking couple. They say opposites attract. Was this a match made in heaven?

Luca yawned heavily, "Vell, da cowboys have ridden off into the sunset, and I must hang my spurs up and mosey on down to da bunk house and sleep da fine vitals off."

Big Bobby slapped his massive thighs in delight, "She's got it by all that's made America great. Now she's whistling Dixie."

Wendy and Philli escorted Luca to bed.

"Make sure Luca takes her meds," Rabbie shouted, then looked at Mal as did Bobby. "You're a dark horse, Mal."

Mal grinned wickedly, "The thing about a dark horse is you can't see it coming at night."

Bobby grinned, "That's deep, man, but good luck with it…can I have another beer? My tank's only half full."

Mal tossed him the box. "All yours, big man."

* * *

Rabbie laid his sleeping bag out on the couch, plumped a cushion up and stretched out. After the Luca watch had left, giggling and half sloshed, he had gone and sat with her. She was finishing off a book he had got her in a second-hand bookshop when she was in hospital. He had seen the Russian title and the colourful cover, and not having a clue what it was about, took the plunge and purchased it, hoping it wasn't too raunchy but she had seemed pleased with it.

As he sat by her, she explained it was a romantic comedy about a group of nine to five Moscow businessmen who went on holiday to the Black Sea and met a group of country girls looking for husbands. "It like da Engliski Mills and Boon books. After da trouble and falling outs, they fall in love and live da happily ever after."

"Bit like 'Seven Brides for Seven Brothers', an American musical in the fifties."

"Oh, I vould like to see dat, Rabbie."

He grimaced, "No you wouldn't, Luca. One of the worst films I ever suffered through."

She patted his hand consolingly. "Ah vell, life's never so simple as da movies," and she yawned heavily.

He got up. "I'll make you some cocoa, then it's down to sleep and you can dream about romantic Moscow tycoons."

She yawned heavily again into the back of her hand… "Da Moscow men too busy ripping each other off for romance now. You ever see Doctor Zhivago? Now there's a film and a half." Luca had asked Wendy to get her it online and had watched it with Katarina when he had gone to work. He had told her he had watched it as a young man, and she thought it would be a good conversation piece.

"Yah, Omar Sharif and Julie Christie. She was very beautiful in it."

He smiled, remembering, "Yeah, I think I fell in love with her. A teenage crush."

She gazed at him with those amazing eyes, "Really, dats nice, Rab. You like da older blonde vimmen, then?"

He grinned, knowing she was joshing. "Yeah, well, I bet you had a bit of a thing for Omar?"

She thought about that for a second. "No, not really. Too smooth and da Russian man, Broody, he looks a bit like Mal, don't you think?"

Rabbie agreed, "Yeah. He does now ya mention it, except Mal's about a foot taller."

"Da, Mal big strong man," she replied, "So is Philli. Two powerful, confident people, but lonely. I hope dey find da romance with each other. Be good for them."

Rabbie's turn to consider what she had said. Mal was your typical Turkish ethnic group type of guy. He had a disdain for loose women and in any relationship he believed the man should be the dominant partner. Saying that, he believed in treating

257

his women well and had been through a string of relationships and seemed content to romance them, love them and leave them. He never considered his big mate lonely and from what little he knew of Philomena, she seemed feisty and totally in control of her life. Still, he had to admire Luca's intuition and was rapidly coming around to realising she was a very astute young lady.

"Well, time will tell, Luca. Mal's very old fashioned and from a very ethnic group where a women's place is in the home, but maybe it'll work. Who knows in this crazy city, anything's possible."

Luca yawned, "Or in da bed, but maybe his time in the Big Apple has changed his views," and she gave a jaw-cracking yawn again. "Sorreee."

When he came back a few minutes later with the cocoa, she was fast asleep, book discarded. He marked her place. Pulled the cover up over her bare shoulder, dimmed the bedside lamps to the minimum setting and left her to it, leaving the door open a foot. He felt strangely adrift and lonely for a second, then shrugged it off philosophically as just the consequence of the strangeness of the situation.

He padded back to his makeshift bed, sipping at his cocoa. *Happy dreams, Luca. Hope they're full of romantic heroes and not revolting farting cowboys*, he laughed to himself, glad she was settled and content.

III

Rabbie would have been surprised if he could have gone into Luca's mind and entered her dream. Rabbie was a knight and they were riding through a field of summer flowers on a white charger. She was riding side saddle and his strong arms held her safe as they cantered towards a castle in the distance. Luca wore a garland of spring flowers in her hair and a gossamer gown and the sun was warm on her bare arms. The horse was majestic and snorted gently as they cantered towards the imposing structure. Her hero was taking her to safety, and her soul was singing with the growing love she had for him. Lapwings and peewits soared and flew above them, and she felt carefree and full of the joys of a young woman who had discovered the exuberance of finding a special love every woman should experience at least once in their lifetimes. "Beware Luca, beware!!!" screeched a bluebird from a branch, as dark, ominous clouds rolled across the sky.

They pulled up at the huge wooden gates, and Rabbie eased her down to the spongy turf and galloped off. The gates creaked open and she entered the gloomy courtyard. She crossed it uneasily, a strange force compelling her. She reached a tower and entered and climbed a spiral staircase. It seemed to go on forever. Unease gripped her and menace crackled in the air around her head. Somewhere in the depths of the castle she heard manic, evil laughter, and she shivered and goose bumps rose on her bare arms. She entered a bare, round stone chamber and crossed bare boards to a round bed. A raven sat in an open arched window. It watched her as she lay down, trembling.

"He's back, you silly girl," the raven told her in Russian and took off, dark wings flapping.

She shivered the length of her spine as heavy, slow footsteps ascended the staircase, the tread heavy and ominous. She watched the doorway transfixed. Someone or something pushed it half open.

The footsteps reached the top and a dark shadow filled the door space. A malevolent evil oozed into the room and terror gripped her, and her heart thumped so hard it was like it had a life separate from hers and was begging her to flee the room instantaneously, but she couldn't move, it was like she was bound to the bed. Nailed down. Under some evil spell. Encased in a block of ice.

Her hair rose on the back of her head and her eyes were wide and fixed with fear, and dread gripped her in a firm rigor as the door now swung wide. She gulped and fought for breath as her heart froze solid and told her it was too late to leave. She nearly swooned at the helplessness that seized her. The door crashed against the wall.

Hanlon stood in the doorway, grinning manically. He was dressed as a medieval court jester in a tight-fitting suit of green, orange and yellow squares. He wore a big jester's hat with long floppy horns with bells on. "Ring a ding aling," he snarled at her. "Bubba hubba, sweet Russian thing…time for terror tonic, aring ading dong ding."

He locked eyes with her and abject horror and disgust gripped her even tighter as his manic gaze ripped through her and seared her gentle soul.

Hanlon pulled out a huge filleting knife. "Oh looke here. Time for a song, my dear."

"Who's that knocking on my door? Who's that knocking on my door? Who's that knocking on my door?" said the fair young maiden.

He laughed manically and swished the knife through the air.

"It's only me from over the sea, I've come to get what's due to me. I'm gonna slice you with my knife, then you'll be my wife for life."

"YOU FUCKING DON'T REJECT HANLON, YOU CUNTING BITCH!!!" he shouted and advanced upon her.

An inner strength she never knew she had come to her, and she threw her invisible shackles off and sat up with a mighty heave, praying for her guardian angel to come to her aid. She put her arms out to defend herself and screamed, "GO BACK TO HELL!"

But he didn't and he reached the bed and grabbed for her with his vile, meaty maws, his breath stinking of Guinness and rotten meat as he raised the deadly blade to strike.

Somewhere in her subconscious, she found her voice and she screamed for all her worth, "RABBIE!!! HELP ME!!! RABBIE!!! RABBIE!!! RABBIE!!! RABBIE!!!"

For some reason he dreamt he was riding a horse across a grassy meadow and there was danger ahead. That was strange because he wasn't a great horsey guy. His granny kept horses on Petral Hill Farm and his mother had encouraged him to ride but he hadn't taken to it. He felt alien and exposed on the back of a horse and knew it wasn't meant to be. Horses for courses and he smiled as he thought of the scandal sweeping Europe at the moment where illegal horse meat had been found in beef burgers and other assorted frozen meats. He'd eaten horse meat abroad and couldn't understand the fuss. The horse was a clean, sociable animal, and you could eat worse things, like the dog he had tried in South Korea. Now that was pretty gross. He must have been barking mad, he smiled to the horse. The horse shook its head sadly. "That's pretty sick, Rabbie dude."

He realised, much to his surprise, he was riding fluidly and easily, and there was shouting ahead and he had to get where he was going quick. He drew his sword and looked at it in amazement, then he snapped wide awake, senses on high alert.

He froze and saw by the clock it was past midnight. He had heard shouting. Luca was screaming and calling his name, and he had heard her shout Hanlon. What the frig? Was it a house invasion?

His training kicked in. He grabbed the 8mm Italian Taurus pistol he had placed under the couch, leapt up and vaulted over the back and ran down the aisle, checking the open-plan kitchen to the left and reaching the master bedroom door. He kicked it open and handgun in a tow-fisted grip before him, he scanned the room.

Luca was sitting up, arms outstretched, her attire dishevelled and her hair mused. Her eyes were closed but the sheer look of terror distorting her face froze his blood.

He rushed in, quickly searched the room, checked the patio door was locked, cleared the bathroom and ran to her, all in a matter of seconds.

He knelt in front of her and gripped her shoulders.

"Luca, Luca…it's okay, it's okay."

Her eyes flew open and she stared into his face.

"Hanlon, Hanlon's here. Help me, Rabbie," and she hurled herself into his arms, crying pitifully, her tears soaking his vest.

He dumped the automatic on the bedside cabinet and hugged her to him. He stroked the trembling woman's hair, "It's okay, Luca. No one's here but me. Shush now. You had a bad dream."

She clung even tighter as consciousness and relief flooded her traumatised system. "Are you sure? Are you sure? I saw him. He had a knife. I saw da big horrid teeth. He's gonna kill me."

He eased her back and sat by her. "There's no one here. I've searched the place. He's in prison, Luca. He can't get out," he told her firmly and calmly.

She was taking great sobs of breath and shaking but she slowly calmed as she realised she was safe. She climbed onto his lap and kissed his face wetly with gratitude and clung on for dear life. "Am so, sooo sooree, Rabbie. I swore I saw him. It was horrid. Absolute horrid."

Rabbie had started to get distressed himself seeing her so upset but he got a grip on himself. Luca needed to understand she was safe and nobody could get to her. He sorely regretted not killing the fucker that night and being done with it.

She whimpered and snivelled a bit more as she recalled the horrible sequence of events in her nightmare, but she gradually calmed and took deep breaths, breathing in the comforting masculine musk of this incredible man she was clinging as tight to like a limpet to an encrusted ship's hull. "Sorry, Rabbie. I didn't mean to vake you. You must tink I'm a silly hysterical girl."

He hugged her tight, "Not at all. Glad to be here for you. Certainly livened my night up."

She giggled, then got serious again, "But vot if he gets bail, Rab? Vat is he comes after me?"

"He won't, Luca. He's banged up tight on Rikers Island," he reassured her.

"But vot if he does, Rabbie?" she insisted.

"Well, he won't. He has a snowball's chance in hell of getting out, but if he does, Christ, he'll have to go through Big Mal, Little Dan, Bobby, Charles, Billy-Jo and Wendy. Jesus, no one gets past Wendy," he said with a laugh.

"But vat if he does, Rabbie? Get past them. What then?" she, asked looking for deep foundations of reassurance.

He looked into her damp eyes and wiped a tear away with his thumb, "Well, then he'll have to get past me, and I'll kill him."

She gazed deep into him, searching, "You would kill him for me?"

He gazed back and a deep, unbreakable bond formed between them. "Yes, I would kill him. Should have killed the bastard that night."

She kissed him then and he felt her ease. He eased her off him and got her into bed and tucked her in.

"You want anything?"

She pulled the covers back, "Only you, Rabbie. Don't leave me tonight."

He hesitated, unsure of his ground.

"Is silly you sleeping on da settee when you have such da big comfy bed."

He gave in and climbed aboard. She snuggled into him and rested her head on his chest, and gave a huge sigh of contentment, revelling in the comfort of the solid thud of his heart.

"Howdya know I was sleeping on the couch?"

She smiled sleepily, "I'm a voman. We know these tings."

He was drowsy now. Her heat and closeness was as comforting and old as time itself. It was a natural God-given elemental essence of wellbeing and healing.

"Strange, I dreamt I was riding a horse earlier."

"Da, through a meadows of flowers, and you had da big sword."

He remembered, amazed, "Yeah, that's right. How the deuce did you know that?"

But she was asleep, tight into him, and he didn't want to disturb her. In the morning he wasn't able to recall his dream but he knew something extraordinary had happened between them.

Chapter 21
Cry Havoc and Let Loose the Dogs of War
Part I
"The Art of Warfare Is Deception"
Sun Tzu 5th C (Map and Notes)

18th June, 1976

Colour Sergeant DeJames led his 'Brick'[95] up to the RV (rendezvous point) in the middle of the sprawling Lenadoon Estate, and they went firm to wait for the other C/S (call signs). It was hot for the Lenadoon mid-June afternoon, higher than 20°C, and they were sweating under their heavy para smocks and equipment.

Jamesey had 'hard patrolled' them from their small fortified base at McCrory Park on the Falls Road. The threat of a snipe taking place was always mega high in West Belfast, and he was damned if he was going to lose any of his men due to lack of vigilance. Eyes darting, they steadily progressed.

"Keep alert, lads… All round defence," he reminded.

He mused on his mission as he watched Sgt Smudger Smith and his Brick arrive. A particularly deadly sniper had been operating in the area, and the lads had dubbed him 'One Shot Willy' because he killed with one shot through the head, using an American 'Wood Master' hunter's .30 rifle. He fired from ranges up to six hundred metres but never less than three. He'd taken several Crap Hats[96] out over the past month but no paras and Jamesey intended to keep it that way.

Jamesey scanned the area through his Suit Sight[97] on top of his 7.62 SLR[98], zoning in on likely enemy positions as he covered Smudger and the boys in. The 'Green Slime'[99] believed One Shot Willy was in fact Padraig Micheàl McCarthy, a 40-year-old unemployed bricklayer from County Louth, Southern Ireland. McCarthy had served in the Irish Army for several years and had been their top marksman, fully trained in military sniping and a winner of many international competitions.

He was also a dedicated Irish Republican and hated the British with a blind passion. *A dangerous opponent*, Jamesey reckoned. He had already surmised One

---

[95] Four-man army patrol.
[96] Not paratroopers.
[97] Sight Universal Infantry.
[98] Self Loading Rifle – standard British Army weapon at the time.
[99] Army Intelligence Corp

Shot Willy was militarily trained. He never missed, unlike the rest of the cowboys that manned the ASUs[100] in the area.

Smudger bounded over to him as his own Brick got into cover. He squatted down beside Jamesey, his back to the wall, Jamesey was peering around the corner of it.

"Sod this for a game of soldiers, Jamesey. I'm out of friggin' condition – I am cream crackered."

Jamesey looked at his Sergeant fondly. A tall, lanky six footer with short curly black hair, he hailed from Tavistock in Cornwall, and they had gone through the gruelling para training at Browning Barracks in Aldershot together. They hit an instant rapport because Smudger figured half the Cornish people didn't know if they were English or Celts. Just like the folks who lived in the border area the DeJames originated from. Tough as a bag of nails and with a keen intellect, he ran the administrative and discipline side of the Reconnaissance Platoon and was rarely out on patrol.

"That's because you've been sitting on your fat arse counting cans of bully beef and wanking yourself stupid over Playboy Magazine, you tosser," admonished Jamesey.

Last week one of the platoon's section commanders, a corporal had got badly burnt when his jeep parked at a junction had several gallons of petrol thrown over it from an upstairs window and set alight. The rest of the patrol scrambled out but the corporal, probably exhausted by an average of two hours sleep a night for weeks on end, was too slow. It was still unsure whether or not he would live. Recalling the smell of scorched flesh, the scent likened to roast pork, Jamesey had grimaced in distaste. It never even made the news. Bacon butties were now off his immediate menu. Pork chops a definite no-no.

Another of the Toms[101] had shot himself in the toilets after receiving a 'Dear John' letter from his girlfriend and was now on a life-support machine, looking forward to life as a 'drooling vegetable'.

To boost numbers on the patrol and to raise morale, Jamesey had ordered Smudger out, much to the delight of the lads, who had cat-called and slagged him as he protested and reluctantly put his gear on. Jamesey grinned, he knew it was just an act and Smudger was just playing his role as expected of him.

"Anyhow, better out than having to listen to the Ruperts[102] running about like headless chickens, crying and gurning. Does my fuckin' head in," he moaned. "Tossers."

"Aye, they do some fucking flapping," agreed Jamesey.

"If they just left the lads to it, everything would sail a lot smoother along."

"Hope that wee Martina bird's okay. Pretty thing under that paint. The mind boggles. Fuckers."

"She won't be back in the area, that's for sure," Jamesey said. "She's lucky she never got 'Black and Deckered'[103]."

Smudger shuddered, "Jesus, some of the things they do to their own, you wonder they got the time to go for us at all."

---

[100] Four-man terrorist active service unit.

[101] Private soldiers in The Parachute Regiment.

[102] Junior commissioned officers.

[103] To be drilled through the knee by a power drill.

Halfway through their three klick[104] patrol route, they had come across a hysterical young woman, well no more than a teenager, Jamesey judged, in extreme distress. She had been tied to a lamp post and daubed with red, white and blue paint. Pots of glue had been poured over her and feathers from pillows thrown and stuck to her. She resembled something from a horror movie.

To add insult to injury, they had roughly shorn her hair with a pair of hedge clippers, causing several nasty lacerations to her scalp and hung a cardboard placard around her neck saying 'BRIT LOVER'. She had been, what was locally known as, tarred and feathered. The locals were standing jeering at their open doors and catcalling as they arrived and as they released the petrified girl and called an ambulance. 'Rent a Mob'[105] arrived and a mini riot ensued.

It had taken a full section of SPG[106] and QRF[107] from Battalion HQ at Conway Street Mill a whole hour to quell the disturbance and get the ambulance in and let Jamesey and his lads get on with their mission. He was not a happy camper with the delay.

The youngster had told Smudger her name was Martina, and she had been accused of being a 'sanger banger' because she had gone to an army disco at the barracks with Protestant workmates. He would never forget the deep fear in her eyes.

"Nice body under there, Sarge," commented one of the Toms. "Wonder how she'd like my orange dick up her green twat?"

"You shut your mouth and just remember we're here to prevent things like this, not encourage it," snapped an angry Sergeant back.

"It's just frustration, mate," Jamesey said quietly. "Young guys away from home, cooped up and denying their fear."

"No fuckin' excuse!" barked Smudger, "We're meant to be professionals."

Jamesey glanced at his Oppo, "They will always make time to kill the hated Brit occupiers, Smudger. So never forget that."

Smudger shrugged resignedly, "So, how we gonna play this then, Jamesey?"

"By any way and any means, pal," grinned the bossman. "The aim being to inflict maximum damage on the enemy with no casualties."

He was to live to rue the day.

---

[104] Army slang – 1 kilometre.
[105] In hard Republican areas, the IRA had a rotating crowd on standby to intercept the army patrols and cause mayhem when required.
[106] RUC Special Patrol Group – later DMSUs.
[107] Quick Reaction Force.

Part II

Cry Havoc, and Let Loose the Dogs of War

('We Have Got to Get Out of This Place'... The Animals, 1965.)

18th June, 1976 – 4.05pm – 45, Glenmacadoon Avenue

Padraig McCarthy watched the hated paras go firm at the top of the entry at the far end of Glenmacadoon Avenue, approximately one hundred and twenty metres away. The vertical slats on the louvre blind in the small back room of the bedroom semi No.45 were opened at a narrow oblique angle so he could look out without being seen. He knew the bastards would be scanning the windows with Suit Sights on top of their powerful 7.62 SLR rifles, looking for snipers. The paras were good and it didn't do to underestimate them.

He fondled the stock of the deadly M60 belt-fed .223 American machine gun propped across the back of an upturned chair, its muzzle waiting to discharge a lethal cargo of death at a thousand rounds a minute. He glanced at the other three members of his ASU. Wearing black balaclavas and blue boiler suits, they looked alien and sinister. Two had Armalite Rifles, the famous 'Widow-makers' and the third had a Belgian FN, a rip-off of the SLR, but which could fire on full automatic.

"Not long now, lads. Remember 'Bloody Sunday'[108], boys," he said and they nodded grimly, the air rank with the smell of fear and adrenaline.

It was an elaborate ambush and Padraig was acting out of character. Known as One Shot Willie after the famous WW1 German sniper, by the Brits, he normally killed with a single shot to the head from hundreds of metres away but today it was up close and personal.

"Don't forget your breathing and squeeze the trigger, don't snatch it," he admonished them. An expert firearms instructor after many years in the Irish Army he knew, once the shooting started, his poorly trained troops would forget everything they had been taught, but he hoped that the initial blast of several hundred rounds of high-velocity copper jacketed rounds would take a few of the cunts out and confuse and stun the rest so that they could take a few more out before they made their escape, besides they would be caught in a withering crossfire. He had a nasty little back-up planned.

"As soon as Dekkie's boys open up, give them hell."

His men were starting to fidget; the paras were taking their time. He wondered if their big fair-haired commander sensed a trap. Although the troops didn't wear

---

[108] January 30th, 1972, when the paras shot thirteen protesters dead in the Bogside area of Londonderry.

any insignia of rank when out on patrol, so that the snipers couldn't pick the leaders off, it wasn't hard to work out who was giving the orders when you had observed them for as long as Padraig had, and he had been watching the Recce platoon for weeks now. They were an elite unit within an elite regiment and it would be a major coup to wipe the fuckers out... Good for the morale of the flagging volunteers and a devastating blow to the Brits.

The IRA Intelligence Wing had told him that the six-week course the already highly trained paras endured to get into the Recce was like doing 'P Company'[109] on speed and only the fittest and most aware passed. He watched the big commander conversing with his Sergeant. Kneeling at the start of the alley, even as they talked, they were constantly scanning with their rifles, a worthy opponent for a professional like himself.

The tension in the room was palpable and heavy, sweat coursed down their backs and under their hoods. "Should have stayed across the water. They'll be going back in body bags tonight," he snarled.

The staged mini riot earlier had slowed the multiple Brick patrol down and tied up resources so that Dekkie and him could get in position without hindrance. Sentries or 'Dickers' on every street corner had kept him appraised of the patrol's progress, so they knew where they were at all times. It was a big operation, well planned, and the odds were always on the side of the ambusher. They had fed the information to the army carefully. His wife and kids had been moved out the night before and were ensconced down south in a safe house where he would join them later. He would be ready because after he had been in action, he was always ready for the comfort and embrace of a woman's arms.

"You're looking for me, Colour DeJames, but I'm afraid I'm not at home to your knock, to be sure," and he grinned evilly behind his hood.

His men giggled nervously, arseholes puckering and trigger fingers itchy.

* * *

4.08pm – Glenmacadoon Square

"I don't know, Smudger, I don't like it. It's too bloody quiet. No kids out playing footie, no mums with prams and no one sitting out in the fine weather."

"Probably seen us coming... Bush telegraph, anyhow 12A has the back sealed. Will I send 11A to seal the front?"

Jamesey debated, you sometimes forgot there were people out there who wanted to kill you. The hatred many felt for the British was inbred over countless generations, and it was a strange disturbing sensation every soldier felt and found hard to put into words. He had tried to explain it to his civilian friends but they had looked at him blankly. Ronnie had understood, having seen action, and a few of the pensioners in the bar who had served during WW2 and other nasty little wars like Korea, Malaya and Borneo. He always bought the 'old sweats' a pint, out of respect, knowing many were struggling on a meagre pension.

---

[109] Extreme time during para training where you are just a number which is painted on your helmet and jacket, and you are subjected to extreme mental and physical abuse.

"Strange to think we're tramping around disputed British streets, armed to the hilt, and there are buggers out there looking to kill us."

Smudger scowled, "Keep yer mind on the job, Jamesey. It's no time to get philosophical, I just want to get back to Kim and the kids and you to Collette."

Jamesey pulled himself out of the reveries, "Yeah, you're right, Smudger, thanks mucker." He called Lance Corporal John Bailey, his radio man, over. Each 'Brick Commander' carried a Motorola personal radio but because the dead spots in West Belfast were notorious, they brought a powerful A41 radio when on operations. The thing had a three-foot antenna and along with the spare batteries, it weighed nearly 30lbs and was carried on the back.

Bailey knelt down next to his boss and handed him the rubber-encased mouthpiece and earphones. With the radio, his loaded rifle weighing 10 ½ lbs and 20lb of belt kit, he was sweating profusely. Jamesey slapped the earphones on and spoke into the mouthpiece, static in his ears, "Hello, Zero[110], this is Blackdog B11, is Sunray[111] there, over?"

* * *

4.10pm – Battalion HQ – Springfield Road Barracks

Lt Colonel Johnston Reginald Hedley-Smithers was in his Operations Room at Springfield Road Police Station with his adjutant, Captain Mike Walsh, and his Regimental Sergeant, Major Phillip 'Barnie' Barnaby, a giant of a man who dispensed his discipline through the battalion in a fair but decisive manner. The Colonel took the mike off the Duty Officer, who was manning the bank of radios in front of him, they had only just returned from the riots and were hot and thirsty.

"Send, Colour, Sunray speaking."

"B11 to Sunray, I don't like it, Boss. It's way too quiet, I think it's a 'come on'[112], what's your orders?"

The Colonel, a no-nonsense soldier of many years' experience, had learnt to trust his soldier's instincts and Colour Sergeant DeJamcs was about as good as they got, "Wait out and stay firm, I'll speak to the Slime."

He gulped down a pint of powdered orange and water from a black mug, then walked briskly down to the Military Intelligence Office at the end of the corridor and punched in the security code. It would be a great result for the battalion to nab One Shot Willie and see him go on trial, no doubt sparing a few of his young soldiers' lives, but he wasn't putting his men's lives in danger heedlessly, and he trusted his young Recce platoon commander's judgement implicitly.

He entered and consulted with the intelligence guys, a Captain and a Sergeant in civilian clothes. They ran agents, assessed the threat situation and passed on information. They assured him the information was good, from a reliable source who had proved his worth. The threat was, as usual, high but nothing strange in that, and nothing had come in to indicate that Glenmacadoon was being specifically earmarked by the IRA for an attack on troops.

---

[110] Comms Room.
[111] Commanding Officer (CO).
[112] To be lured into a trap.

He returned to the Operations Room and called Jamesey, "Hello B11, this is Sunray, over."

"Sunray, B11 send, over."

"Roger, spoke to our slimy friends. Carry out your orders as detailed. I'll send the QRF to the area to give you mobile perimeter, good luck."

"B11 Roger, Wilco out."

* * *

4.19pm – Glenmacadoon Square

"He's sending the QRF out to provide a mobile perimeter. We'll give it ten minutes, Smudger. We're close enough to run and grab anyone who comes out. Tell the guys to keep alert."

"Nice one, Jamesey," and Smudger ran off to check the rest of the patrol. There were three, 4-man Bricks in the alley now, Jamesey's B11, Smudger's B12 and B11A Corporal Mike Scott in charge, B12A with L/Corporal Ian Dennison was at the rear of 18 Glenmacadoon Square, where information received said Willie was visiting his wife, they reported no sign of movement in the house.

"Probably up shagging her, the lucky 'Paddy Whacker'," remarked Jim Bailey.

"Have yah seen her, Jim? He must have a guide-dog; she's a fat, ugly cow," said Private Hamish McDonald. "Dunno how we can even find it in the dark."

"He throws talc over her and goes for the damp spots," laughed Private Nigel Sherigan.

"Only bleeding way he can find her twat," laughed Jim. "I like that one, mucker."

"Shut up and watch your arcs," snapped Jamesey. His men flinched and quit the banter. When the colour spoke, they obeyed and when he chastised them, they knew he was jittery. They had learnt to trust his often uncanny sixth sense.

* * *

4.21pm – Springfield Road

Four Land Rovers with a half section of men in each of them screamed out of the gates of the heavily fortified barracks and roared down the Springfield Road on their four-mile route to the sprawling Lenadoon Estate, ignoring all the rules of the Highway Code. Adrenaline-fuelled young soldiers, fingering their rifle triggers anxiously and glaring at the pedestrians and cars suspiciously, who glared back at the oppressors aggressively, noting with satisfaction the twitchy, exhausted state of the overworked soldiers. They were call-signs XB13A, XB13B, XB13C and XB13D and a Sergeant was in charge.

* * *

4.26pm – Glenmacadoon Square

Smudger ran up to Jamesey, "We've been static too long, mate. We need to move position before they set us up."

Jamesey licked his lips; he had a bad feeling about this whole fucking business. His senses were screaming 'come on' in his head. He fingered the trigger and gripped the pistol stock, hard. He stood, turned and shouted down to the Bricks, "Safety on and make ready," as he pulled the cocking lever back with a smart crack and put a round from the magazine into the breach. At least if they came under fire, they could return fire straightaway. He was breaking the rules of engagement, as laid down by the authorities, which said you never 'made ready' unless you were under attack, but he didn't care, it levelled the playing field a little, a second in this game which could mean life or death. The alley echoed to the clatter of cocking handles.

"B11 seal the front, the rest of you cover."

* * *

4.27pm – 18 Glenmacadoon Square

Corporal Mike Scott and his men sprinted across the grass and sealed the front of 18 Glenmacadoon Square. Private Harold Jones fell over a kid's tricycle and cursed, his brother Alan laughed, "You tosser, boyo."

* * *

4.27pm – 17 Glenmacadoon Square

Veteran IRA gunman Declan Murray[113] raised his AK-47 Kalashnikov Rifle and aimed at the soldier to the left of the door of number 18. He was in the back bedroom of No.17, opposite but one house-length down. His partner Kevin 'Cat' Wylie beside him with a powerful seven clip Garand Rifle. Murray stood well back from the window so that he couldn't be seen.

"Ready, Kevin? Here come the soldier, boys."

Murray was in his element, a natural born killer; he was a legend in the ranks of the IRA and was looking to increase his tally of Brit scalps today. He took first pressure on the trigger and slowly released his breath, "Shoot to kill, Cat, shoot to kill."

* * *

4.28pm

"Go Smudger, go," ordered Jamesey, kneeling and covering the square, Bailey to his left. Smudger hammered past like a whippet after a hare, his guys in hot pursuit. His job was to force entry and seal the house. Once inside, Jamesey would join them and the search would commence.

* * *

4.29pm

---

[113] Read Declan Murray's story in 'Mind Over Trigger'.

Smudger and his men were half way across the grass, thirty metres to his front, an icy hand gripped Jamesey's heart and unspeakable things slithered and clawed their way up his spine. Then a calm resolve gripped him as a strange sense of déjà vu hit and for a split second Collette's lovely face flashed across his inner screen and somewhat deep in his mind, in the part no neurologist or psychiatrist had yet explained, he thought he heard her gentle voice, "I love you, babe… I love you," and then the first gunshots blasted through the silence, about forty metres up and to his left. He saw the bullets strike and dig out chunks of the wall of No.18… Corporal Scott dropped in a fountain of blood… Jamesey came up and aimed, clicking his safety off, "Contact, wait out," he said calmly into his radio.

* * *

4.29pm – The Robert Peel – Watford

Collette was sitting in Ron's office crashing away on Ron's Olivetti. She was typing 'THE QUICK BROWN FOX JUMPED OVER THE LAZY DOG' time and time again. She was feeling very nauseous and tired. She wondered what Jamesey was doing, as she did a hundred times a day, when a sensation of such dread and horror came over her that her vision swam before the keys and she felt giddy. She swallowed down bile and hung onto the desk with clenched fingertips.

Eadie came in to see if she wanted a cuppa, "Bloody hell, gal. What's wrong wiv yah? Yah look like yah've seen a ghost." She got Collette a small brandy and made her lie down for an hour. "Yah've been very peaky recently, gal, I'm gonna book yah in ta see a doctor."

Upstairs Collette sank into the pillows, a van backfired outside and she jumped. She fell into an uneasy slumber, nightmares circling and waiting to settle.

* * *

4.30pm – Glenmacadoon Square

"Take cover, cover!" screamed Jamesey and snapped off five quick rounds in the vicinity of the gunfire, an upstairs window, nearly obscured to him by the angle, "Enemy to your left."

He fired off three more rounds, his bullets hitting the area around the windowsill and howling off in ricochets into the distance.

"Return fire, cover your mates," and he fired off three more shots, the heavy recoil in his shoulder going unnoticed, acrid cordite fumes staining the air.

The enemy were still blasting away. Smudger and his men were prone and they started to return fire straight into the ambushers' window. The crackle and rattle of small arms fire filled the summer day with a vicious cacophony of sound. Rounds whizzed and buzzed off concrete and tile viciously. Glass shattered and a chimney pot imploded. Incoming and ongoing returned fire buzzed crazily past each other like angry hornets disturbed in their nest.

Suddenly, the enemy ceased fire. In the five-second gun battle Jamesey had identified two different enemy weapons; different sound, different velocity.

270

Probably an AK and a heavy-calibre rifle. "They're bugging out. Hot pursuit. On me, lads." He led his men towards the back gate of No.17 at a sprint.

Halfway across all hell let loose.

* * *

4.30pm

"Tiocfaith ár lá!" screamed Padraig McCarthy, pronounced 'chucky ar la', the battle cry of the Irish Republican Army and meaning 'our day will come' as he pulled back the trigger on the machine gun he was pointing at the three Bricks of paras in the square, his men opening fire at the same time. In a split second, he saw two paras drop. The noise was deafening. They had stuffed their ears with wet toilet tissue but he thought his eardrums were going to burst. Empty cases, smoking spewed out of the ejection ports and tinkled and tumbled over the floor. Swirls of cordite filled the room, stinging their eyes. Death had come a calling and was unleashed gleefully on Glenmacadoon Square.

In three seconds they fired over a hundred rounds between them. "Kill the bastards, kill, kill!" he roared as he sent a screeching torrent of lead at over three thousand feet a second at the invaders.

Suddenly, the man on his right fell and he realised they were taking fire. They had ripped the blinds apart to see better and saw those same blinds were dancing and swaying as bullets flew through them and became embedded in the back wall of the room, holes appearing in the plaster with meaty thwacks. Another man fell as a round thudded through his shoulder spewing gouts of blood and bone as he dropped his Armalite with a clatter, his blood making the hot empty cases hiss and splutter.

"Feck the paras were quick off the mark, time to go." He gave them another burst of twenty in a random arc. He saw three of the mad bastards were charging them, their muzzles twinkling as they fired from the hips.

Bejesus, they were only forty metres away and they were fit, fast and fucking furious. "Out, out, let's go."

Cry Havoc.... And let loose the Dogs of War 19 11 12

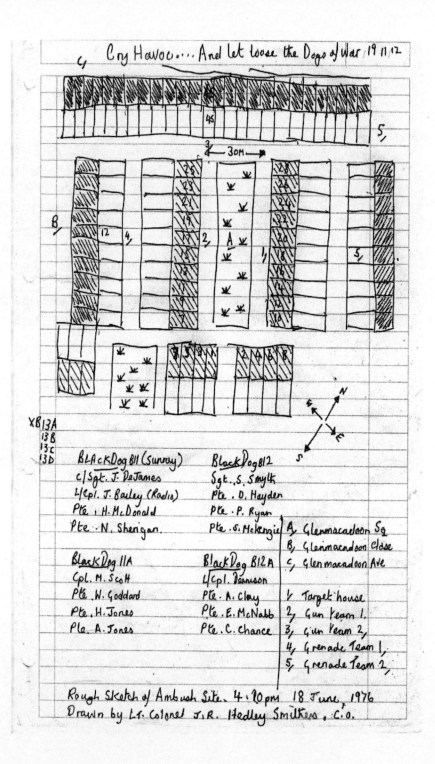

XB13A
13B
13C
13D

BLACKDog B11 (Sunray)
c/Sgt. J. DeJames
L/Cpl. J. Bailey (Radio)
Pte. H. McDonald
Pte. N. Sherigan.

BlackDog B12
Sgt. S. Smyth
Pte. D. Hayden
Pte. P. Ryan
Pte. S. McKenzie

A, Glenmacadoon Sq
B, Glenmacadoon Close
C, Glenmacadoon Ave

BlackDog 11A
Cpl. M. Scott
Pte. W. Goddard
Pte. H. Jones
Pte. A. Jones

BlackDog B12A
L/Cpl. Dennison
Pte. A. Clay
Pte. E. McNabb
Pte. C. Chance

1, Target house
2, Gun Team 1,
3, Gun Team 2,
4, Grenade Team 1,
5, Grenade Team 2,

Rough Sketch of Ambush Site. 4.10pm 18 June, 1976
Drawn by Lt. Colonel J.R. Hedley Smithers, C.O.

272

4.30pm – Battalion HQ – Springfield Road Barracks

"Colonel, we've a contact."

Hedley Smithers was heading off to change his socks. He was getting too old for this game. He had hoped for a half hour to soak his feet in a basin of cold water, smoke a pipe and read a letter from his wife Annalise.

He strode back in, "Who and where?"

"Only got the initial, sounded like 'Blackdog, Sunray'."

"Shit, tell all call signs to keep off the air."

The room started to fill as word spread that gunfire was going on in twinkle town.

When a call sign came under fire, they gave an initial contact report and the airwaves were theirs until they gave another fuller report.

If they were still alive that was!!!

* * *

4.30pm – 17 Glenmacadoon Square

Murray fled down the stairs clutching his assault rifle and Cat's Garand, his comrade was lying upstairs, his brains splattered over the back wall. He had died instantly when a heavy 7.62 round fired by Private Stewart McKenkie of Smudger's Brick had burst through his left eye, tumbled through his brain, scrambling it to mush and burst out of the back of his head, dislodging a large clod of scalp and hair. He was dead before he hit the floor.

Murray had given his comrade a quick salute and closed his good eye, bullets crumping and bouncing throughout the room as he fled pell-mell down the rickety stairs, singing the IRA's Battle March, 'The Soldiers' Song' – Fighting men are we… We will die for Irish Liberty…" and running down the stairs he threw the rifles over to a couple of youths (mules), who ran off like the wind to stash the murder weapons as Murray sprinted off, "Hit them with the grenades, lads, 'Chakagh ar' laigh."

* * *

4.31pm – Glenmacadoon Square

Jamesey and his men flung themselves down as the full weight of four automatic weapons bore down on them in a dancing storm of death. Bullets scythed through the air and tore up the ground all around like a mad invisible harvest, chopping through the grass. He saw Jim Bailey crumble and roll to his right, bullets smashing into the heavy radio, gouging out streaks in the metal. He had gurned earlier about having to carry it and now it might just have saved his life. Thank fuck he was out of the dead spot; this was serious shit.

"Enemy front…fifty metres…upstairs window…open fire," shouted Smudger as if he was on the ranges. Jamesey was impressed as he fumbled for his radio. *Contain, contain and win the firefight.*

273

"'Blackdog… Sunray'…contact, Glenmacadoon Square…am engaging. I have casualties," still the maelstrom of bullets came, trying to engulf them. "Return fire, lads."

The paras opened up a ragged volley, they were pinned down, exposed like beached fish with the gulls hovering above. The spectre of death laughed above, he was having a field day.

Now he had given a fuller contact report the net went ballistic as Zero started giving orders and moving call signs into the area. Jamesey looked briefly round, Private Pete Ryan was lying face down, ten metres away from the door of No.18, not moving and Smudger was kneeling over him blasting away at the enemy position. A bullet tore into the pouch carrying his helmet and twanged off it, and he swore another one parted his hair. The din was horrendous as it reached a mad crescendo. He raised the rifle above his head, emptied the nine remaining rounds and changed the mag in the flash of an eye; training paid.

He came up on the radio again, "'Blackdog… Sunray'…we're pinned down…automatic fire, at least four guns… I'm gonna bayonet charge the varmits."

He caught Smudger's eye, "Fix bayonets, mate. Time to be soldiers."

Smudger laughed and they drew the deadly cold steel and slotted them onto the red hot muzzles of their rifles. It was para playtime. Time to separate the men from the boys.

* * *

4.32pm – Springfield Road Barracks

The room went still, the RSM looked at the Ops Officer, "Did I hear right, sir, did he say he was bayonet charging?"

"If he is it's the first time in this conflict, that's for sure," said the Ops Officer in reply, eager for the festivities to continue.

"Probably the first time since Korea," said the Colonel.

"Certainly the first time on British soil since…probably Culloden, in what, 1754?" from an impressed Captain Walsh, "Bloody seismic."

"He's a madman that DeJames," laughed the Colonel, "Did he really say varmits?"

"Read too many Penny Westerns," explained the RSM, "They all do. Young 'uns think they're in the Wild West."

"They are not too far wrong there," agreed Walsh.

The Lieutenant in charge of the Colonel's bodyguard rushed in, "Jeeps are ready to rock, Boss."

"Well, let's go see, shall we, gentlemen?" and the Colonel marched out, cocking his 9mm Browning.

"God help the IRA if they've killed any of his lads," commented the RSM as he followed, his Sterling submachine gun looking like a toy in his huge hands.

The Ops Officer watched them leave, worried about the guys on the ground but also excited and strangely proud to be part of a little bit of history in the making.

The Colonel mounted his jeep and they passed through the gates as soon as they opened, "Cry havoc…and let loose the dogs of war."

"What's that then, Boss?" asked the RSM, used to the Colonel's little idiosyncrasies.

"Shakespeare, Sarn't Major, Henry the Fifth, on the eve of the Battle of Agincourt, 1415."

"Oh, okay, sir, more a Wilbur Smith man myself."

"Actually, Colonel, in Shakespeare's Henry V, the King said, 'Let SLIP the Dogs of War…' Sir Walter Scott bastardised it in IVANHOE, his novel in 1815," explained the driver, a 20-year-old private from Milton Keynes, who had studied English Literature at Tech.

The Colonel was impressed, his Toms never failed to impress him.

"Well, whatever young Archer is, the dogs are loose, so let's see them back to the kennels."

* * *

4.30pm – The Rear of 18 Glenmacadoon Square

Lance Corporal Ian Dennison had been at the rear of No.18 when the gunfire started. He had been wondering what was keeping the rest of the guys and had tried calling the boss on his Motorola, but to no avail. He was in a black spot, those strange anomalies that could stretch the length of a street or less than ten feet. He shrugged philosophically, he was sure Jamesey had good reason to be behind schedule. A laid-back northerner from Salford, he was content to stand in the back garden enjoying the late afternoon sun on his face.

It had rained for most of March and April so it was nice to be out in the nice weather chatting and helping the 'oh so pleasant' inhabitants of West Belfast.

He had two guys at the end of the enclosed yard, which measured about twenty-five feet by fifteen and was lined by six-feet tall, single-brick walls. The wooden gate had been unlatched. He had one man on the back door and felt reasonably safe as he poked about in the small shed and coal bunker.

Coming out of the shed, he glanced down the garden as a black spherical object came sailing over the wall from the yard opposite and landed at his feet. Suddenly, all hell broke loose as gunfire erupted at the front of the house. The object landed with a clatter at his feet, rolled and parked against his left toecap.

He stared in disbelief as he saw it was a Russian MK6 hand grenade and some bugger had pulled the pin. "Oh, shit on a shovel!"

Grabbing a metal dustbin, he flung the lid off and upended it over the grenade, "Take cover, grenade!" he yelled as he dived to the ground.

The heavy bin was full of ashes from the fire and when the grenade exploded, it blew about six feet in the air and covered the men and the garden in an orangey/grey dust but the bin had contained the blast. If it hadn't been for Ian's quick thinking, they would all have been dead or badly maimed.

They got up, gingerly, wiping the ash that made them look strangely lemur-like, from their eyes. The shooting had intensified, there was a real gun battle going on close by. Ian judged the enemy was at the avenue end of the square.

"On me, lads, we'll flank the buggers," and he rushed out and turned left up the back alley, his men sprinting after him, leaving trails of ash.

4.31pm – Glenmacadoon Square

Jamesey knew it was imperative that they quell the enemy's gunfire and storm their position if he was to avoid more casualties. He rose into the blistering wave of lead-filled air and, rifle butt on right hip and left arm extended on the stock, he charged, screaming, towards the rear of No.45, loosing off a few rounds every third or fourth stride. His bayonet implacably pointed at the enemy, a shaft of sunlight catching its lethal tip and making it twinkle. He picked up speed, Smudger was to his right screaming. "Up the fucking Airborne!" Jamesey had to admire his style.

To his left Nigel Sherigan, a six-year sweat, had decided to join in the fun and was screaming, "Chelsea, Chelsea!" as he charged forward, blasting big holes in the gate. *Have to speak to him about that*, decided Jamesey.

The firing had subsided although bullets still pinged and danced around the window as his guys pepper potted the wall. *Guess the owners are gonna have to read up on their DIY, take a trip to B&Q*, he thought as he crashed through the weakened gate, taking it off its hinges, "Whoops!"

A white sheet appeared from the upstairs window, Jamesey was taking no chances, he crashed through the back door, shattering it, "Sorry 'bout that," Sherigan hot on his heels. He rushed to the foot of the stairs, rifle pointing menacingly up the unknown stairwell.

Smudger, meanwhile, had taken a different route; he bounded off the coalbunker and, screaming like a Comanche Indian, crashed through the kitchen window, rifle at high port to protect his face. He landed flat on his back on the flimsy kitchen table, causing all four legs to collapse, and lay flat on his back and pointed his rifle at the ceiling, dazed. The shooting had stopped, the silence nearly deafening as the echoes crashed into the hills.

He felt something digging into his right buttock and pulled a half crushed packet of Gingernut biscuits. He happily munched away while covering the kitchen ceiling.

4.31pm – 45 Glenmacadoon Avenue

McCarthy and his one remaining standing man were trapped. The dead volunteer had fallen across the door, which opened inwards, and he was wedged between it and the bed. Every time they tried to pull him away, a fusillade of bullets made them duck and cower. The volunteer who had been shot through the shoulder sat in the corner; his eyes slitted and glittering with pain. He had a pillow pressed up to the wound to stem the flow of blood. His name was Finbar Ignaceous Clancy and he was a vicious, diehard fanatic and he wasn't pleased with how things were going, not pleased at all. "Not surrendering, Padraig, I ain't doing the Kesh[114]."

McCarthy gave a wry laugh that was no more than a croak and, crouching low, draped a white sheet out the window. He heard the back door crash open and the

---

[114] Long Kesh, HMP The Maze – Terrorist prison ten miles outside Belfast.

sound of glass breaking below, "We live to fight another day, Finbar, better the H-Block[115] than the coffin." Finbar growled in disapproval but said nothing.

"British Army...come down with your hands up."

* * *

4.32pm

Lance Corporal Dennison came racing around the corner into Glenmacadoon Avenue just as a red Datsun Hiace van screeched away from the front of No.45, burning rubber. He ran into the road to stop it, and his panting men got down to cover him. As it bore down on him he saw it wasn't going to stop, so he shot out its two front tyres. It stopped dead and started to reverse, he put five rounds into the engine. It started to let off steam but it carried on reversing, "Bugger me, those Japs build vans to last," he muttered as he ran after it, followed by his guys.

Suddenly, there was an almighty crash as a big green Land Rover rammed into the back of the van, troops dismounted and swarmed around it. Ian dragged the driver out, pushed him to the ground, spreadeagled, and removed a Colt .45 pistol from the waistband of the quivering man's jeans.

"Naughty, naughty," he chastised the terrorist, "I bet you never got that at Toys-R-Us."

They had the ASU's escape vehicle.

Ian leant down and helped him rise, "Aye up, lad. Don't you know to give way to pedestrians? Wouldn't happen in Salford by gum."

His lads laughed and clapped him on the back. XB13A and XB13B sealed the street and began clearing the houses, just in case of a 'come on', maybe a booby-trap left behind.

It never stopped in Dodge City.

* * *

4.33pm

"What do you mean you can't come down?" Jamesey demanded, his men crowding around him, "You've ten seconds or we're coming up firing."

Smudger barged through the kitchen door, still munching on a biscuit, "Seal the house, lads. This is a crime scene. Yeah, what yah bleeding mean, we are not fucking amused."

"I've a dead man blocking the door."

"Oh for fuck's sake! Wait there and no hanky panky or you'll be spitting lead."

He ushered Jamesey out the back, where Smudger had spotted a ladder. He propped it up against the window, climbed half-way up and peered cautiously over the window sill. He pointed his browning 9mm pistol at them, "Right, Paddy, down the ladder and no funny business. Chop chop."

Sirens were screaming from all directions as McCarthy, and his volunteer, climbed down the ladder and were spreadeagled and cuffed.

---

[115] Secure terrorist prison block.

"Who's left, there were four firing."

"Finbar, but he's shot bad."

"Oh! For fuck's sake," groaned Smudger, "Up and down, up and down. I don't bleeding like heights."

His men laughed, delighted, a para scared of heights. He climbed back up with a first aid kit and disappeared through the window. Jamesey was worried about his own wounded and he felt uneasy again. All his men were highly trained combat medics and were treating the five gunshot victims. He followed Smudger's footsteps, suddenly there was a burst of small arms fire. One – two – three – four – five shots.

Jamesey hurtled up the ladder and leapt into the bedroom, Smudger was lying with his browning extended at Finbar, who now had a third eye, a large Colt Python revolver lay, smoking, in his dead hand. "Fucker had it hid under the pillow. He's away to Independent Heaven," quipped Smudger.

Jamesey found three bullet holes in Smudger's upper left leg. Fuming, he heaved the dead corpse up and away from the door and with superhuman strength heaved it out the window. The guys roared their approval.

He put a tourniquet around the leg and carried Smudger downstairs. "Never knew you cared, darling."

"Oh shut up, Smudger, it's already wearing thin."

"Temper, temper, petal…any chance of some nice morphine?"

He got the morphine ready and slapped it in Smudger's thigh, "Hope that hurt, you Cornish twat."

Smudger rolled his eyes, "Like you, Jamesey, just a little prick."

Jamesey rolled his eyes in mock disbelief, the guy was incredible. "You'll be okay, mate. Trust me."

Smudger went serious, "Thanks, mucker. Don't tell Kim, mate, don't wanta worry her."

"Nay baw, mate, nay baw."

* * *

4.50pm – 17 Glenmacadoon Square

Armoured Saracen ambulances arrived, crewed by members of the Royal Army Medical Corp, who assessed the wounded. Corporal Scott had a gunshot wound to the left side of his head and was in a coma. He was rushed to the Royal Victoria Hospital. Lance Corporal Bailey had been shot through the lower abdomen, his A41 radio had been hit eleven times, and he too was rushed to hospital, where he made a full recovery. Private Pete Ryan was shot through the upper left arm, breaking the humerus and the left shoulder, with serious damage to the deltoid muscle. He was later medically discharged from the army due to complications.

Private Harold McDonald had a graze to the left side of his head from a bullet, he lost consciousness from loss of blood when he refused treatment, preferring to stay on duty. He made a full recovery and was proud of the silver streak in his hair; he got many a free pint in the mess from new recruits when he told them the story of 'The Battle of Glenmacadoon Square'. He later wrote a book about it, which became a Hollywood blockbuster and he moved to a villa in the South of France with a woman from Sweden called Inga, twenty years his junior.

278

Private William Goddard had a lucky escape when a bullet shattered the stock of his rifle, which he was holding across his chest. A piece of plastic pierced his right eye but despite this, he carried on firing. He later lost his eye and the army found him a job in the stores. His party piece was to take his glass eye out and drop it into an unwary drinker's pint. He stopped this practise when it backfired one day and a Captain in the Military Police swallowed it, and he had to wait three days for it to pass through the system. The Captain remarked it was a very trying experience indeed.

But Jamesey wasn't to know these things until much later.

Leaving the QRF to seal No.45, he took the walking wounded and the prisoners to the backyard of No.17, where he sealed the house and set up his Incident Control Point (ICP). Smudger was perched on a stretcher, smoking away, happily watching Jamesey run ragged between the radio and issuing orders.

"The sooner they come for you the better, you heathen," Jamesey pretended to snap at him.

"Ah, all those lovely nurses, top totty," said Smudger, happy in his morphine haze.

The Colonel was up at No.45 making notes, the cops were coming out to re-arrest the surviving gunmen and take them to Castlereagh for interrogation. They were sat out in a line waiting transport, sweating under the hot June sun, being hovered over by tired, angry paras completely spent of adrenaline.

Jamesey had a hundred and one things to do; he had to arrange cordons, reliefs, patrols food and water, ammo resupply, transport, riot control etc. The list was endless.

"You could at least give me a hand while you're lying there, Smudger."

Smudger giggled, "Sorry, mate, ain't got a leg to stand on."

A black spherical object came in a perfect arc over the wall and landed six feet from Jamesey. He knew straightaway what it was and if it went off in this confined space, they were all done for. He bounded over and picked up the grenade in his right hand, bounced and jumped up the wall, reached the top and pulled himself up with his left hand; wind-milling with his right arm, he lobbed the thing towards the alley.

It exploded with an ear-shattering crack and whomp three feet from his hand, blowing him back into the yard. Deafened, he lay on his back paralleled next to Smudger. Smudger was shouting and what looked like fingers were dropping out of the sky.

"What yah saying, Smudger?"

"I said yer gonna need more than one hand now, Jamesey," he shouted.

Jamesey looked at his fingerless hand, shredded and strangely interesting. He thought it looked beautiful as the blood soared in a gushing parabola and the splintered bones gleamed cleanly.

"Oh, suffering sweet fuck…what the frig is Collette gonna say?"

"Best not to tell her!" hollered Smudger.

* * *

279

Corporal Michael William Archibold Scott died at 4.10am, the next morning, in Musgrave Military Hospital, Belfast, his newly-wed bride had just arrived at his bedside.

He never regained consciousness to say goodbye to his sweetheart.

When Colour Sergeant DeJames came round from his operation, minus his right hand, his company commander broke the news to him gently.

It took six orderlies and a large needle full of morphine to put him down.

Chapter 22
Mulligatawny Soup
"Waiter... There Is a Fly in My Soup..."
"Hush Sir, Or Everybody Will Want One..." Peter Sellers

The day of SassyVanassy's function started gloomy. Low grey clouds unleashed a persistent heavy drizzle on the multitudes heading to their day's toil and shrouded the Manhattan skyline like a horror movie graveyard mist, and indeed, the foot commuters trudged along like a cast of zombies from 'The Walking Dead', many of them reluctant to reach work and the tedium of another boring, mundane day.

Luca got up at half past seven with breakfast. Her nose wrinkled with pleasure at the delicious smell of the rich coffee. He had made her a mushroom omelette and grilled Canadian best back bacon and warmed croissants.

"Wow...you're such a good chef, Rabbie...delicious."

She tucked in with gusto. He looked at her slim but shapely figure as she splurged maple syrup on her bacon and put three spoons full of demerara sugar in her coffee.

He shook his head in wonder, he didn't know where she put it and never put a pound on. He showered and dressed casually in jeans and leather jacket. No clients today but an operation they were running at a large electrical retailer in Queens would hopefully come to a conclusion later.

"Listen, Luca. A girl called Katarina is coming to sit with you for a while. You will like her. She's from Russia, St Petersburg, I believe. OLG use her as a translator sometimes. Wendy's on days. She and Philli's going to sit with you tonight. Bringing some films for you to watch."

Luca's heart sank. She knew Rabbie was working today and tonight, and she probably wouldn't see him until tomorrow.

"Wendy's sleeping over. She's off tomorrow and the big guy's working with us at SassyVanassy's do, so you can do girlie things together."

She laughed, "Girlie tings. Vot you tink we are? School girls? We get early night. Wends will be tired."

The door buzzer went and Rabbie went to answer. He returned with a pretty, slim, dark-eyed girl in her early twenties, dressed in a light-green dress. She had lovely, long dark hair, with long natural curls in it. Luca liked her at once.

She introduced herself in Russian as Katarina Tanya Marguerite Bronski from St Petersburg and kissed Luca on both cheeks. Luca introduced herself with her full names as well, as Russians do when strangers meet.

Rabbie ran her names through his head. Luca Sophia Alexandra Sonia Natasha Valendenski. It was the first time he had heard her full title. *It was very pretty*, he decided.

"I see you later, Luca. Have to go make a buck."

Her face dropped. "I not see you till tomorrow. Your be dancing wiv SassyVanassy all night."

"Not at all," he laughed, "She'll be surrounded by her celeb pals. I'll be back at lunchtime. I'm going to make a big pot of Mulligatawny for our dinner. Take a few hours chill-out time before tonight's festivities."

Her face lost its sadness and lit up. She hadn't a clue what Mulligatawny was but it sounded good and what was more important, her gallant knight would be here with her. Pure bliss, then she ruminated, "This ting tonight, dahling. Dair won't be any trouble? You be safe, Rab?"

"Christ, your tablets," he said and got her meds and made her take them with the fresh orange juice he had squeezed earlier. "Yeah, it's no prob, Lucs, main problem will be getting them back out and home without any aggro. Girl bands are the worst...pack of hellcats when slashed... Jaysus this lid's tight... Argh, got it."

She swallowed them, Rabbie hovering over her. She pulled him down, totally unselfconsciously, sub-consciously staking her territory in front of a possible rival, "Kiss for luck," and planted her lips on his, her arms boding no escape.

Her lips, if it was possible, tasted even sweeter with the orange juice. He let her have her way for five long glorious seconds before breaking off and walking out dazed. His previously cold, lonely bedroom, albeit luxuriously furnished and which he hardly gave a second thought to except as somewhere to crash out at night, was now an exotic, lavish, colourful new world and the medically trapped inhabitant was the beautiful focus, indeed of the whole apartment, like a multi-coloured butterfly seeking shelter from life's storms and filling his mind with fantasies and dreams of a very pleasing nature.

"As you Ruskis say, Moscow."

Luca laughed. "American sense of humour. It's so basic. Mosgow. Must go," she said in Russian, glad to have a fellow country woman to chat to, loving Katarina's yuppie St Petersburg accent. "They call this huge guy in the office Little Danny...little? Weird."

"He's very attractive, Luca. Are you sleeping with him?"

Luca pondered on that for a while before "No, doctor's orders, but when I'm better, I think I would very much like to."

"I would. I bet he's a stud in bed. I'll take him on any day."

"You're too young, Katarina," she chided. "Anyway, hands off, he's all mine if I have any say in the matter. Now tell me all about yourself and St Petersburg."

* * *

He took the meat off a shin of beef he had boiled till tender the night before and diced it up very finely. He added it to a large pot of boiling water that was simmering nicely. He threw in a handful of pilau rice. She sat at the end of the long kitchen table watching him. She wore pink cotton pyjamas and a matching robe. With her hair back in a ponytail and no make-up, she looked very young and fresh.

"How'd you like Katarina? She's heard you sing at that club and wanted to meet you."

She watched as he finely chopped an onion and minced some garlic through a garlic crusher, the acidy aroma making her eyes sting. "Dats strong, Rab! Your eyes are watering like a fountain."

He laughed and wiped his eyes with a tea towel before selecting spices from a cupboard. "Spanish onions. Phew."

"I liked her ver' much indeed. She's so, so sweet and so nice to talk the Rodina mother-tongue."

He added hot chilli flakes, very hot chilli powder, cumin, coriander and paprika. A teaspoon of turmeric went in. The aroma of fresh spices in the steamy kitchen air was exotic and heady. Luca's mouth salivated.

He put a can of tomatoes through the blender and added them to finely diced potato, then mixed with some puree and a good sprinkling of black pepper. A diced green and red capsicum was added. A chopped carrot followed and fennel seeds were tossed in.

"Dat smells fantastic, where you learn to cook, Rabbie?"

He added rich beef broth he had got from his favourite deli, popped in some whole curry leaves and a cardamom pod for taste, a taste of chopped fenugreek he grew on the window sill, and put the lid on, content.

"Oh, I dunno. Just picked it up on my travels. I like trying different recipes from foreign lands. This is my dad's recipe. He's a curry fanatic. He had us down the Indian before we were out of diapers."

She smiled at him. Cooking obviously relaxed him and gave him an interest besides work.

"Vell, I tink you are very clever, I'm afraid I am very basis cook. My maman spoil us. I get her to send you some Russian recipes."

He sat by her after putting some crusty bread in the oven to warm through "Yeah, that would be good. Never tried Russian food. Apparently, there's a hundred ways to boil a Russian beetroot."

She slapped his arm playfully. "You joshing wiv me. I take you for Russian meal when you let me out your bedroom." He pondered that, imagining Luca in his bedroom forever with caviar and champagne. Interesting concept.

"And talking of which. Get you back in there and I'll bring this in to you," he ordered, mock sternly.

She clutched his forearm. "Please let's eat it here, together," she pleaded. "Is not good to lay in bed all day."

He considered that. He could think of worse options than to lay in bed all day with Luca. "Okay, I guess so. But after, it's tablet time and rest."

She nodded. "Yes, master. Luca be a good girl after her Mulliefawnandeye Soup."

He laughed and went to serve it up. "Mulligatawny. It's from Mulligaw in India and tawny means brown." He looked at her beautiful tawny hair. It was nearly the same colour as the soup.

They ate from deep porcelain bowls with soup spoons. The soup was rich and delicious. She had two bowls and several slices of the warm bread, dunking it in the bowl with relish. *She was such a natural person*, he thought. *Everything she did was graceful and there was nothing artificial about her at all.*

283

Kind, gentle and of a happy disposition. The simplest of things pleased her but there was also a sophistication and poise about her that hinted at a hidden strength and resilience. He admired her strong intellect and sense of right and wrong. She sometimes came over as a carefree and 'live for the day' type of girl but he guessed she was shrewd enough and could see the wood from the trees. She attracted people to her not just because of her looks but because she had an aura of caring and solicitude about her that drew them to her. Her natural charm and happiness enthused itself onto others like a light being turned on in a dark room. Or maybe he was just biased, he mused. The Luca effect at work. Damn it…She intrigued him on top of the strong attraction he felt for her. She had told him about her upbringing and family. He knew her interests and some of her tastes. Her class quirks, but by God…she just completely fascinated him.

"You okay, Rabbie? You miles away."

He shook his head. "Sorry…yeah, I was lost in space there for a while."

"Vat were you tinking? About tonight and SassyVanassy's legs?" she joked, half serious.

He wanted to tell her that she had the best legs he had ever seen and that he wanted to kiss her mouth deeply and taste her, to see if her mouth was as pleasantly warm and scented as his was after the curry soup.

"I'm sure SassyVanassy's legs are her business. Now, young lady, rest and tablets for you."

She sighed and pouted prettily. She'd loved sitting having lunch with him in the quiet flat. It made her feel close to him. Just like normal couples did every day. He was so clever and organised and kind and considerate, yet no pushover, and he had her wrapped in a large mental comfort blanket of security that was very, very reassuring.

She looked into his fine dark blue eyes. What she really wanted to do now was to kiss him and taste his warm curry breath and enfold him tight in her arms and press her breasts against his strong chest. She wanted to find out what worried him, his secret wants and needs. His very essence. She wanted to be the comforter. His confidante. He was such a confident man, he kept things so well-hidden, relying on his own abilities to sort any problem out on his own. She knew some big time model had hurt him, but he had shrugged it all off when she had asked him as just one of those things. "We parted as pals, Luca. Different cultures. She's away doing good things in the third world. You would have liked her," he had told her nonchalantly, knowing she wouldn't have.

She doubted if she would. The bitch had hurt Rabbie bad. She knew that as only a woman could. She would never leave the man she loved. Never.

Rabbie shrugged and their eyes lost touch as he stood. Looking into her beautiful dove-grey eyes with silver and blue flecks, he sensed she was trying to assess him in some way. He didn't want to make her uneasy with his baggage.

"Tell you what. Into bed and I'll bring the Beaujolais in, and we'll have a glass and watch 'Discovery'."

"Oh goodie. How can any girl refuse such an offer?" clapping her hands in delight.

She lay back under the quilt and took her tablets. She would be glad when they were finished. She sipped the nourishing wine. He sat by her with his legs stretched out. Shoes off, content and complete. Pleased with how his recipe had timed out.

He must get back for lunch more often. It was only five minutes from the office. He liked making her happy, he realised, and liked the thought, the truth of it.

They skipped the Discovery channel and found an old John Wayne movie. 'Fort Apache'. Despite all her social and humane concerns, Luca liked a good action movie.

She pulled his left arm over her shoulder and rested her head against his breast. "I suppose da poor Indians will lose again. John Vayne was such a violent man."

He laughed "'The Duke'? Nah, he was a gentleman. A legend in his time… Anyhow…it's only a film. At least the Indians got paid. 'A man's gotta do, what a man's gotta do' was his motto."

She never answered. He looked down. She was sleeping gently against him, her breath even and relaxed. He took the glass off her and put it on the side.

His turn to sigh. He didn't know where this was going. He was worried about the ten-year barrier between them. Juliette had left him after she had her fun. Okay, for idealistic reasons, but if she had really loved him, she would have found a way around it so they could be together. Not a phone call or post card since.

He looked at the lovely creature nestled so trustingly into him as John Wayne attacked an Apache village with his blue uniformed Seventh Cavalry that in later years became the 101st Screaming Eagles Airborne Division, themselves immortalised in the war film 'Apocalypse Now' with Barry Sheen.

Juliette had been very young and beautiful as well. Educated and intelligent, like Luca. Prone to arrogance at times and argumentative but she had driven him crazy in bed. At times she seemed almost insatiable in her sexual cravings, and Rabbie had often found it hard to meet her demands, but he had always kept his end up, so to speak.

John Wayne was tied to a stake now, and the hostiles were running around whooping and hollering waving tomahawks and spears.

"Yah can do yah Goddamn worst, you critters. No officer in the 7th is scared of you red skinned varmints," he told the chief with thinly veiled contempt. "Yah bunch of bushwhacking crazed coyotes."

Life was all about making a stand, Rabbie believed. *If you were tied to a stake defenceless, about to be killed by your enemies, you might as well go down fighting, even if it was only with words. It was standard Royal Commando philosophy – 'For God. For Queen. For Country' and smile bravely as the knives go in.*

He decided he would take it very slow with Luca. Neither of them needed to be hurt again. He knew he was on the rebound after Juliette and that Luca's feminine ego had been badly hurt after that bastard Hanlon's vicious attack. He seethed inside every time he thought about it.

She snuggled tighter into him. He would have to go and get changed soon into his gear and get his gun out of the safe after the film. He had stood the guys down at lunchtime so they could get a rest and be refreshed for tonight. He had a feeling it was going to be a long one.

The chief relented and decided if John Wayne could defeat his best warrior in a knife fight, he could go free. Rabbie grinned at that. If only life was so simple!

John beat the warrior after a dramatic tussle and held the knife to the defeated man's throat. "Kill me now, White Man, it our custom," ordered the whipped hostile. "Well, it ain't my custom, you critter. That was a darn good, clean, fair fight, git up pardner."

"You're a good man," said the chief, "We smoke pipe of peace."

John Wayne rode off into the sunset, and Rabbie eased Luca off him and went to get changed, warm from her body.

He dressed in a black suit, stab vest, round-neck jumper, shiny black boots and a long black trench coat. Bodyguard gear 'a la mode'.

He packed a Ruger Revolver .357 in a shoulder holster, he preferred revolvers to magazine-fed pistols and stoppages were nearly unheard of, unlike with a pistol which held more rounds. He reckoned if he needed more than the six rounds the revolver's chamber held when bodyguarding, then he would probably be dead anyway. Besides, he had two speed-loaders containing spare rounds and could reload in a matter of seconds.

Wendy and Philli arrived at seven, and Rabbie let Luca sit up in the living room so she could watch the films on the big fifty-six-inch flat screen.

"Got some classics, Luca," said Philli, who was dressed in a pretty blue pants suit, her trademark. "'An Officer and a Gentleman' and 'Sleepless in Seattle'."

"Hope cha got a good supply of tissues in, man, or the floor will be awash," quipped Bobby as Rabbie let him in.

"Oh away and guard Sassy and give us gals peace, right, Lucs?"

"Yes, Wendy. Ve have girlies night. Away and dance wiv SassyVanassy and get her autograph if you can."

Wendy heaved a box of Chardonnay wine out of a bag. "Get the glasses, Philli, while I work this little tap contraption out. It always beats me."

Rabbie took it off her and sat on the couch next to Luca. "There's a knack to it, Wendy. We used to mitch school and all the guys would pool their lunch money together and buy a box and get the girls drunk."

"Oh you're a bad man," cooed Philli returning with the glasses. "But I like that in a guy."

He expertly got the little tap out and poured them a glass. "Right, work calls," he went to stand. Luca stopped him, "Kiss for luck."

They all looked at him. He gave her a peck on the cheek and made a hasty retreat. "Mal's waiting in the car. See you all tomorrow."

"That wasn't much of a kiss, Luca kid," Philli observed.

"No…he embarrassed. I will sink my lips on his later and give him sumting to remember."

They raised their glasses to that one.

* * *

Rabbie stopped outside the elevator door. "Hold on a sec, Bobby," he got his keys out and reopened the door and went back in. The girls were sitting giggling. Philli had her make-up bag out and was about to do Luca's fingernails.

The three good-looking ladies turned their heads as one to look at him, surprised at this sudden, unexpected male intrusion interrupting them so soon into their planned evening. *So much for an early night*, he thought ruefully.

"Vot's wrong, dahling?" Luca asked. "Have you forgot sumting?"

"Yeah, you forgot to take your tablets, Luca."

"Don't worry, Rabbie, I'll sort her out," Wendy assured him.

"Run you on, guy, and don't let Mal eat any rubbish, you'll be late," Philli ordered. "Go, go, go, honey," and made a shooing motion with her hand. "And be careful, my sweetheart."

He left again. They were a formidable trio when together. He subconsciously thought of a 'ménage à trois'. *Awesome concept. Don't even go there, lad.*

He joined Bobby and they started again. He had read somewhere that psychiatrists believed men subconsciously thought about sex every three seconds and women every seven seconds. Interesting theory. He personally thought it was the other way around. The urge to procreate was the basis for the survival of the species and the maternal instinct must be the strongest of all. And what happened when you got older? Surely, your subconscious had other things to contend with? Did babies have the urge to procreate from birth, surely not? He thought of Luca and her mesmerising beauty and imagined her with several little 'Lucas' around her and just knew she would be a natural mother. He imagined the children were his and hers... *Easy boy! Heavy duty or what?*

They left the elevator and headed towards the front door.

At thirty-six he was still a relatively young man. Did he want a family and all the respective responsibilities it entailed? He had never given it much thought since he lost Sammy.

He'd always been fairly easygoing. As a younger man he had just assumed it would come along naturally. He would meet someone suitable, settle down and that would be it... Didn't happen. So what it had never occurred, he was cool with it...or was he? Yeah, he had considered it with Juliette but something held him back. She was too worldly wise for her age, used to being pampered and spoilt. She was probably a surrogate mother to lots of little starving kids in the Sudan by now, but having her own baby would be a hindrance to her. Cramp her style. No, Juliette was a beautiful free spirit. He had met her at the wrong stage in her life.

He climbed into the front of the car, where an impatient Mal was drumming his fingers to a rap beat on the wheel. Bobby nudged him, "Philli says you're to eat no crap, Mal...makes you fart."

Mal grinned, "Men fart but ladies only pass wind – yeah right."

The shocks groaned as Bobby planted himself in the back and slammed the door, the car rocking. Mal found a gap in the traffic and took off.

"Hiho... Hihooo...and it's off to work we go," sang Bobby happily.

The bossman was quiet now, deep in thought. Mal caught Bobby's eye in the interior mirror and they shrugged.

Rabbie was trying to decide if Luca was going to be the significant woman in his life, if she would have him that was. She certainly seemed keen but they had only known each other a few weeks. He would just have to take it slowly, time would tell. It was a great equaliser.

He shook himself out of his reverie. "You okay about tonight, Bobby? Should be pretty straightforward."

"Yeah, I'm keen and ready to rumble, Boss. Prepared for anything."

"Just hope there's no crazies out there with AK47s and a celeb grudge," quipped Mal who had been in on the wind up earlier with Brien and Rabbie.

"The more crazies, the better I say. Bring 'em on. Bobby Havilland is afraid of no man or beast."

287

Mal and Rabbie looked at each other and laughed. Obviously, the big guy had caught onto them.

"Just hope I can get Sassie's autograph, Wendy thinks the sun shines out of her butt crack!"

Rabbie and Mal laughed again. The new man was going to be okay.

They progressed smoothly through the Wednesday night dinner traffic towards Times Square and The Flaming Oasis Niteclub, the current favourite haunt for the 'super celebs'.

Robbie thought again of the lovely Luca watching Richard Gere carrying the maiden off to eternal happiness in 'An Officer and a Gentleman' and probably half way through a box of tissues by now.

Not his kettle of fish. He remembered watching it in a tent in the middle of the desert on a break during 'Desert Storm' two and his fellow commandos laughing and jeering with derision. "Give her one for the boys" and "Away on you, prat" just some of the ribald comments shouted at the antics of the actors on the big screen. Real life wasn't as easy as Hollywood liked to make out, it was all an illusion to tantalise and titillate the masses. There was huge profit in deluding the public, and the entertainment moguls knew it and played on that concept heavily.

He sighed; he knew he was getting cynical. Too many war zones and seeing the seedier side of things had knocked a lot of the sentimental gloss like that out of his system.

In the marines sentiment was frowned upon. It made men act irrationally and slowed their responses down. It wasn't the done thing to show extremes of emotion. Bad for moral old chat, don'cha know? Take it on the chin. Take it like a man.

He grimaced and scowled out at the brightly lit billboards as they traversed Times Square. Young teenage hookers congregated on the corners. Mal frowned at them. "Goddamn sluts, in Turkey they would be stoned."

Bobby remarked, "They probably all stoned anyway. Why they do it."

Mal and Bobby glanced at each other and shrugged again. The boss dude was definitely on a downer. Had to be a woman, they decided telepathically, as only experienced men could, and they could guess who.

Rabbie went deeper into his introspection. He was here now so he might as well see where it led. Okay, he knew he was a decent enough type of guy, he also knew that the extremes of training and fighting for his country in the armed forces had partly dehumanised him in the fact that violence didn't worry or scare him, that it had become a constant in his life for many years. He certainly didn't enjoy it and didn't like to inflict it on anyone, it wasn't in his nature to inflict pain on people and the marines had taught him it was counterproductive anyway. If you hurt someone enough and they got a chance they would get you back, so they would. It was a vicious circle. Violence begat violence.

So what the hell was wrong with him tonight? He liked people. He had a fair sense of humour. He liked to treat his employees with firmness but respect and be considerate to people. Goddammit, he was in the prime of life, fit and reasonably well off. Nice apartment, flash car, good prospects. What was bloody wrong, man?

Then he realised and the cloud lifted. He was already missing Luca was what was wrong.

"Bring 'em on, I say. The more the merrier," intoned Big Bobby from the back.

"Oh shut up, you prat," Rab and Mal said as one and they burst out laughing, ready and raring for Sassy's do.

One of the teenage hookers got into a car with a guy of at least sixty. Mal snarled in disgust. "Only in New York... In Ankara we would cut that dude's nuts off with bolt cutters."

Bobby sniggered, "Blame that chemist guy who invented Viagra... Hiho... Hihooo..."

Chapter 23
The Birth of the Single-Handed Viking
Part 1
('Ride of the Valkeries'... Wagner)
Cassiobury Park

Watford, Late June, 1976

She sat on a wooden bench, stunned and amazed. Uneasy and happy all at the same time. Such a raw combination of emotions that she felt dizzy and nauseous one minute and elated and bursting with happiness the next. "Bloody Norah girl, so much for the little pink pills," she said to herself, "Made me bloated, anyway."

A passing park attendant, with a spiked stick for litter, stopped and asked the lovely young woman who was talking to herself if she was in need of help. "Bit late for that, mate, but ta for asking. Lend me that pointy stick so I can stab meself, mate."

He left, a quizzical look on his face, thinking that the young woman in the thin, mid-thigh, flower-pattern dress had the best pair of legs he had seen in a long time, guessing she was an inmate from the nearby Leavesden Mental Asylum out on day release.

Collette pulled a pack of No.6 out of her bag and lit up gratefully before dumping the almost full pack into the wire litter bin next to the bench, where a few hungry wasps squabbled and hissed around a discarded ice cream cone. "Just a last one, kiddo, hope yer don't mind? Calm me nerves. Don't wancha popping out with a chimney pot for a head, do I...? Jamesey be annoyed, so he would."

A young mother with two sandy haired toddlers in tow stopped, "You okay, ducky? Got a spare fag?"

Collette shooed the angry wasps away, retrieved the discarded pack and gave them to the blonde curly haired woman she judged to be in her mid-twenties. "You can have these. Did yah smoke when you were expecting?"

The woman sat down and her kids stood solemnly by her side, "Had a few but generally, no... I'm Kim by the way and this is Amy and Josh...Kim Smyth. Thanks for the smokes."

Collette struck a match for her, "Bet they keep yer on yer toes. I'm Collette Stark, stark-raving bonkers."

Kim smiled, "Yer right there, love, but I wouldn't be without the little buggers... How far gone are you? You ain't showing yet."

Collette sighed, "The quack reckons baht eight weeks. The big gahoot's gonna kill me. He's goin' places, is Jamesey, and he don't want me as a millstone round his neck," and she began sobbing, causing the other woman to laugh, not unkindly, and put her arm around her. "Not if he loves yer, he won't. Takes two to tango."

Collette sniffed and wiped her tears away. "Yeah, I reckon he loves me all right but he'll be hard to pin down. He's got plans."

Kim giggled, "They all have love and it's normally to get into your knickers.

Grinning ruefully, Collette said, "Naw, it was the other way round. I done all the chasing. He'll go do-lally[116] when I tell him."

"My advice, love, get home, make a nice dinner, candles and all, then shag the brains outa him. Give him the best fuck of his life…then tell him. Be fun as well!"

Collette pondered on this. The kids were fidgeting impatiently now, "Wish I could, Kim, but the big sod's over in Paddy Land at the moment."

Kim eyed her, "Here, wanna come down the play park wiv mw an' the kids? Get 'em an ice cream and we can have a cuppa and a chat."

"Might as well, thanks, Kim." The little girl, Amy, took Collette's hand and skipped along beside her, making her feel maternal. She wondered what sex her child would be.

"Yer guy a soldier boy then, Collette? Where 'bouts is he in Ulster then?"

"Hold on, Kim, I'll get the kid's stuff and us tea, my treat." She crossed to the kiosk as the kids ran off to the sandpit, squealing in delight. When she took their refreshments to the table, Kim thanked her and carried the ice creams over to her children. Collette watched the woman's retreating back, thoughtfully.

Jamesey had given her a bit of a talking to before he had gone back, what he called 'A Security Briefing'. She smiled fondly at the serious expression on his face at the time. "Loose lips sink ships, the walls have ears and all that palaver," he told her. He also told her how the Provos had blown up the paras' Officer's Mess in Aldershot after 'Bloody Sunday' and how they used seemingly innocent, innocuous sleepers to befriend lonely soldiers and their loved ones to extract information and set them up for a hit. "Always expect the unexpected," he said.

"Didn't expect a bleedin' bun in the oven… Can't blame the Paddies for that," she decided ruefully; anyway, she liked the Irish men who came into the pub, they were a lark and a half.

She watched Kim strolling back, a tall willowy, good-looker, Collette had taken an instant liking to her, *but you never knew, did you?*

Kim sat and sipped her tea gratefully before lighting up again. "Yer never answered me question, love. I only ask 'cause me hubby's over there in Belfast wiv the forces. I'm staying wiv me parents till he gets back."

Something clicked in Collette's mind, "Suppose everyone calls him Smudger? Wot's he in then?"

"Yeah! Silly sod's in the paras. A walking friggin' Fig11[117] for the IRA bastards," Kim replied, bitterly, dragging hard on her cigarette.

Collette smiled, "Wot's that word, Kim, for things that are meant to be? You know…that guru guy the Beatles had, he always used it, and those Hari Krishnas…?"

---

[116] Old Army term. Doolally was a posting in India and the heat used to drive the soldiers mad.

[117] Figure 11 target. Man-sized plywood target of an enemy soldier. Used by British Army for target practice.

"Karma, I think. Things predestined…meant to be," Kim answered.

Collette laughed and took Kim's hand, "Your hubby's called Steve Smyth, he's from Tavistock in Cornwall and he's a Sergeant in Recce in 1 Para."

Kim's mouth dropped open wide in surprise. "You'd better close yer trap before a wasp flies in and stings yer tongue," advised Collette.

Kim closed her mouth and eyed the very pretty pregnant girl before her. Steve knew Watford well and often slipped out for a jar or two when up visiting. "How the bleeding hell do yah know my Steve, Collette?" she almost snarled.

"Keep yer wig on, Kim," laughed Collette, her earlier stress forgotten for the moment, "I don't know him from Adam, just by repute."

Kim put her hands to the side of her head, "Oh my Gawd, Jamesey, of course. Jamesey DeJames. They work together, thick as thieves and mad as 'March hares'."

"Both as mad as each other, if what Jamesey ses is right."

"Wow! This is so weird," said a delighted Kim, "So Jamesey's finally been caught. 'Bout bleedin' time. Thought he was married to the job."

It was the turn of Collette's face to fall, "Yeah well, Kim, as I said he's got big plans, and I don't want to be a 'ball and chain' to him. Dunno how he'll take it."

Kim watched her carefully, she quite fancied Colour Sergeant DeJames herself, but she loved Smudger to pieces and he certainly set her fireworks off in bed. The paras were mega fit and with that went sexual prowess. "Get a good look at the floor, darling, 'cause you'll be seeing a lot of the ceiling when I get back," had been his last, crude but exciting words when he left her back in Aldershot.

"Tell yer what, Collette, come back wiv me and have some tea. When the kids are bathed and in bed, let's go for a drink and talk things through."

"I know just the place, Kim." Collette was rapidly warming to her, not yet realising the other woman was on the way to becoming her life-long best friend. "You sure your parents won't mind? Don't wanna impose, do I?"

"Not at all, they love babysitting. Truth be told, I could do with getting out for a break. Change of scene like."

They gathered the kids up and left the play park, the summer heat making the played-out dots drowsy. The summer of 1976 turned out to be the hottest since records began.

"Wait till I see Jamesey," giggled Kim, "He's a dark horse."

"He calls me his thoroughbred mare," Collette divulged.

"You mean thoroughly rid bare, you dirty mare," quipped Kim. "You never heard of the pill?"

"Might as well have took Smarties…least they taste nice."

They got a Number 6 bus to Bushey Arches, just a few miles down the road, and walked up to the High Street where Kim's parents, Mike and Sally, ran a furniture and lighting store. They lived in the spacious apartment above the shop. Both women were still stunned at the strange twist of fate that had brought them together.

Bushey was considered very upmarket by the ordinary Watfordians and Collette was impressed by the smart-looking storefront.

"Yeah, I come up and stay when Smudger's away on tour," Kim told Collette, "Come up and meet Mum and Dad, they've closed up for the day."

They entered by the side door and climbed the stairs, the kids finding a new lease on life and scampering ahead, shouting for their grandparents. Kim blew a wisp of blonde hair away from her face. "Dunno where the little sods get their energy."

Collette was introduced to Mike and Sally Gilbert, a pleasant middle-aged couple. They made her very welcome, seating her and giving her homemade lemonade and scones with raspberry jam.

She glanced round the beautiful room. The apartment seemed very spacious with high ceilings, lovely décor and it was luxuriously furnished.

Kim's mother had embraced and kissed Kim and made a huge fuss of the children, the air crackled with their love, care and concern for each other. Collette thought of her own tragic upbringing and guessed this was how normal families behaved. She felt a fleeting sadness and resting a hand on her belly, vowing that this new life growing inside her would be showered with love and affection. It would have the best of everything; hopefully, with Jamesey's massive presence at her side to help and guide it.

Amy climbed up on her lap, her face smeared with jam. Collette wrapped her arms around the little girl and snuggled into her, and Amy started to nod off. She was feeling very maternal. It was a nice feeling.

Kim watched as she chatted easily with her parents, who were amazed when she told them that Collette was Jamesey's girlfriend and of their strange meeting.

"Well good for you, Collette," said Mike, puffing contentedly on his after work pipe. "About time that big Jamesey met a nice woman to come home to."

"That's right, dear," chipped in Sally, "no man is an island, not even Jamesey."

"He's got an ego bigger than China but us men need a good woman to fall back on and keep us right," reiterated Mike.

"Try telling him that," Collette replied, stroking the hair off Amy's face. "He's such a confident big sod and he's me whole bloody world." She burst into tears and hugged the, now sleeping, tot closer to her. Her hormones were doing Olympian acrobatics. It was just too much for her, what with the news she had received earlier, meeting Kim and her friendly parents and the constant worry of 'her man' off fighting the IRA. It appeared every time the news came on there were more deaths and injuries in the war-torn province. It seemed never-ending and that the sad little country was on the brink of civil war. (Author's Note: During the period 1969-1993, collectively known as 'The Troubles', 1976 proved to be the second-worst year for killing, shootings and bombings.)

Kim's family made a huge fuss over her, Mike got her a small brandy and soda and sat with his arm around her while she drank it. Sally sat holding and patting her hand, "He'll be all right, Collette, it just takes a bit of getting used to when they are away. It's hard on the women."

"Jamesey and Smudger are true professionals. More than a match for them animals," interspersed Mike. "They're lean, mean fighting machines and hard to fool." Kim smiled as she hustled the children off to bed.

"They'll be home in no time, dearie, just you watch," consoled Sally.

"Hope you're right 'cause I'm up the duff, ain't I? And I want me kid to know his 'live' dad, not just his 'dead' memory. "

There was a long pause as they gazed at the pretty, young pregnant woman with the tear-streaked face, before Mike laughed and congratulated her. "Don-t you worry, Collette, Jamesey will stand by you."

Sally gave her a big hug, "Yes, he's a decent honest man and whatever happens, you're always welcome here."

"So don't be a stranger, you hear," instructed Mike kindly. "Or we will be annoyed."

That caused more tears, but happy ones, Collette smiling through them at the kind pair as Kim came back in, concerned, "'Ere, your mascara is running, you soppy mare… Sit still and I'll fix it for yah," making Collette smile, liking the spoiling.

In the five months since Jamesey had come into her life, he had totally turned her life around. She cared for her appearance and tried not to curse. Two nights a week she went to technical college to study English Language and Book-Keeping and she was doing a home typing course, bashing away at Ron's old Olivetti in between shifts at the pub. Jamesey didn't know of these things as her plan was that when he opened OLG, she could help him by doing his paperwork. Make herself indispensable to him, then he might think twice about dumping her, she judged insecurely.

She rubbed her belly, ruefully, hoping the ever-growing bundle would not interfere with her plans. She wanted to surprise him and make him proud of her…he would certainly be surprised now. This would rock him in his size 13 boots. She fingered the gold locket he had given her and imagined the shock on his face when she dropped the bombshell and groaned inwardly. There was no going back on this one.

It must have been that morning he got her in the beer cellar, she thought. The last day of his R&R. Jesus was born in a stable, so what could be wrong with being conceived in a beer cellar? She smiled fondly at the memory, actually turned on, as she recalled how Jamesey had taken her from behind, over the picnic table, and feeling a bit guilty at the thought in front of these decent people. Christ, he was a frigging sex machine and she'd loved every minute of it.

Eadie had sent them down to change the beer kegs as Ronnie was at the bank, and she didn't like spiders.

After a while she shouted down to see if they were okay. Jamesey had shouted up that, there was "a huge big, black hairy one" as he thrust into a moaning Collette, and they laughed long and hard about it afterwards.

She wondered if they still did 'it', they were mid to late forties, or how long it was before the lustre of love faded and the tarnish of discontent and lack of interest blemished such a wonderful, natural gift.

She asked to use the phone and rang The Peel. She was very late and Eadie was worried. Collette reassured her all was well and gushed out about meeting Kim and her parents and how adorable the kids were, how Sally was going to teach her how to make scones and that she was to bring Kim to the bar for a drink and to meet them, not letting Eadie get a word in edgeways. She hadn't told Eadie her suspicions as to her condition, "Here, where did you bugger off to at lunchtime, Collette?" she finally managed to squeeze in. "I was worried about yah."

"Oh I was at the quack. I'm in the bleedin' pudding club. See yah shortly, Eadie," she said and hung up quickly. She could imagine the stunned look on the landlady's face and knew she was in for a serious 'Spanish Inquisition' later on.

After a quick wash at the Gilbert's, Kim helped her with her make-up and brushed her hair, which had lengthened and thickened out. "Ya've got lovely hair, Collette, not a split end in sight."

"Ta, Kim, you're a mate. Jamesey likes it natural, he didn't like it pink."

Kim laughed. "Pink! Jesus, you'll have to tell me all about that in the pub." She liked her new pregnant friend, she was a sketch and a half.

Soon they were on their way, arm in arm, to catch the bus 'up town', chattering away as if they had known each other their whole lives.

II

Jamesey sat morosely surveying the bandaged stump of his right hand or, to be precise, where his right hand used to be. Bloody inconvenient so it was. He was annoyed at being deceived by the IRA but had to admit it was a hell of a well-planned and executed ambush by the bushwhacking scum.

It was heavily bandaged and encased in a protective cage that was strapped to the bed so that he couldn't move it at all. It throbbed, weirdly, and he knew when the morphine wore off, he was in for a lot of pain. He had known other guys who had lost limbs; some of them close mates he had visited in hospital. He had seen the pain and strain etched on their faces and their families', and the dazed looks of the stunned family members as they gazed at the 'whole' man who had left home so confidently and was going to return incomplete, less a man, not 'whole' anymore. He grimaced and felt his head, also encased in bandages, gingerly. When he had pulled himself up the wall and attempted to hurl the grenade away before it exploded, part of his head was exposed and the blast had peppered the right side of it; fortunately, none of it had pierced his skull. He remembered the terrible bang and the thud as he was hurled backwards and landed in the yard. He remembered lying on his back gazing at his fingerless mangled hand, just a lonely thumb sticking up, mocking him, before his training kicked in and he hauled himself to his feet and started shouting orders at his shell-shocked men. "Get after that bastard… Now…and don't trample over my digits," and he used a webbing belt as a tourniquet to strap his wrist and stop the blood pumping out and zipped his mangled hand into his para smock.

"Well, stand there gawping, get that alley sealed tight and light me a fag up."

The young Toms hasted to do his bidding, shaking their heads in wonder. The Colour Sergeant[118] was one hard bastard.

The surgeon, a Lieutenant Colonel in the Royal Army Medical Corp, had come to see him and explained that the hand was too badly mangled to save. He had amputated it at the wrist, cauterised it and put a temporary plastic cap on it.

"We'll get you a nice aluminium hook for when it heals," the Colonel joked, trying to cheer the injured para up, "You'll look like a big pirate." He knew from experience that these guys were tough and resourceful buggers. They had to be. Hard to put down.

Jamesey grinned ruefully, "Better Captain Hook than Long John Silver, though I don't think Tinker Bell will want me anymore." He thought of Collette, she was young and he wouldn't put her through the chore of looking after him so early in her life. "Looks like it's back to the sheep farm for me, Colonel. Thanks for all your help."

---

[118] Rank between Sergeant and Sergeant Major. Wore a red sash in battle and guarded the flag and standards. Not used any more, it is Staff Sergeant now.

He decided there and then that his plans for OLG were now up the Show-waddy-waddy[119]. He'd lost his good hand and who ever heard of a one-handed security operative.

The Colonel left the unhappy squaddie. He knew the man was still in deep shock, it would take time for him to come to terms with his loss and recuperate. Probably worried about his woman. A lot of amputees' relationships didn't survive the daily, tedious grind and routine of intense rehabilitation.

Jamesey looked around his small room. There was a stand with various bags of fluid, attached by clear lines to a catheter, dripping monotonously away into his right arm.

He was in the secure military wing at Musgrave Park Hospital[120] in South Belfast. A two storey, bomb proof, heavily fortified wing guarded twenty-four hours a day by heavily armed guards.

The room was stuffy. He gazed out of the bulletproof window, across the park-like grounds that were dotted with trees, at another block that stood on its own. Also heavily guarded and ringed by security fencing and concertinas of razor wire, this was where injured terrorists were taken and treated.

Jamesey would bet his last pound that would be where the injured IRA volunteers they had captured were. Getting the best of treatment, good food and other comforts, probably better conditions than in the slums they came from, he decided bitterly. He was bitter, very bitter, he had lost a man and six of his men were injured, none of them life-threatening. He had never lost a man to enemy action before, and it was not a pleasant concept for his mind to get round. It was an anathema to him. Fuck's sake, he was meant to look after his young guys, not merrily lead them into ambushes, "You're a fucking disgrace, Jamesey," he admonished himself, as guilt washed over him as deep as a high tide, flooding his mental lowlands with dark, murky, unclear thoughts.

Another thought crossed his mind; he felt under the covers and checked his considerable manhood, relieved when he found it was all intact. "Thank God for small mercies," he grinned sourly at his witticism.

It was one of the greatest fears of a soldier on active service, to have their manhood blown or shot off. When on mobile patrol, the soldiers often took their helmets out of the pouch on their belt and sat on them to protect their genitals if a bomb was to be tossed under their vehicle.

A nurse from the Queen Alexandra's Nursing Corp came in with tea and toast for him. She was a pretty, dark-haired lass, and he thought of Collette again.

"How are you feeling, Colour Sergeant? Matron says you have to try to eat and drink."

"Not as handy as usual," he answered looking at the place his right hand used to be. "How's my men doing? How long do I have to stay in bed? I've things to do."

She marvelled at the man as she buttered his toast. He had been blown up and lost a hand eighteen hours before and he wanted up, he was one tough cookie, strong as a bull. "I'll ask Matron to come down and talk to you, Colour. Jam or marmalade?"

---

[119] Rock band in the seventies. A 'Waddy' (Wadi) is a dry valley in the desert.
[120] Musgrave Park Hospital. South Belfast. The army had a fortified wing there where the injured soldiers were treated by the Army Medical Corp.

He winced visibly, "Saw enough jam yesterday, love. Marmalade, please. How's my Sergeant?"

She checked his vitals and connections, "He's doing very well, considering. He's right next door."

"Smudger!" he bellowed. "Get your skanky arse in here, now."

"Shush, Colour," pleaded an alarmed nurse, "You'll get me in trouble. Matron's a demon for discipline. Besides, he's in plaster."

Jamesey gave her his most brilliant smile, "Go get him for me like a good lass, and I'll eat my toast, drink my tea and be a good little soldier."

She looked undecided, a good little soldier indeed! She was quite in awe of him, if initial reports were correct, he had taken three Provos out and saved his men's lives. "Okay, but just for a few minutes, mind."

She soon returned with Smudger in a wheelchair, a bag of plasma on a line to his arm, and his left leg, in plaster from ankle to hip, sticking out in front of him.

"All right, Limpy. How you doing?"

"Okay, Stumpy. Love the morphine. Cheap piss up, ain't it?"

The young nurse listened to them slag each other off and flatly refused to go out to the off-licence to purchase whiskey for them.

"Ah go on, love," wheedled Smudger, "We'll have a farewell party."

The nurse looked bemused, "A farewell party, farewell to what?"

"Farewell to Stumpy's hand and farewell to my chances for running the next London Marathon. Bring a few pals and some music and we'll have a disco."

Jamesey gave Smudger a steely look. "That's enough of your insubordination, Sergeant Smyth. The next time you address me, it's Colour Sergeant Stumpy to you," and they both laughed uproariously.

The nurse shook her head in disbelief...the paratroopers were all mad in the head. "I'm off before Matron arrives," and she fled.

"Nice little thing, that. I'd give her one," observed Smudger.

"You'd give a dead dog one...now the question is...what are we going to tell Kim and Collette, and when?"

Smudger mused on that, "Dunno, mucker...don't wanna worry them."

III

Ron had heard on the news that one paratrooper had been shot dead and a number had been injured in a protracted gun and bomb attack with the IRA in West Belfast. He nodded with satisfaction when he heard that three of the Provos had been shot dead and more had been arrested. "Good one, lads," he muttered to himself.

Still, he felt uneasy and just knew Jamesey's hand had been in there somewhere, he could feel it in his water, and where the hell was Collette? The sneaky mare had slipped off at lunchtime and not been seen since.

Eadie was upstairs clearing away the tea things; she'd made a beezer of a ham and egg salad, it being too hot to cook. Nearly opening time, so he poured himself a quick shot of Bell's Whiskey before Eadie came down, justifying it as a reward for his healthy eating at teatime.

Half past five…opening time. He opened the doors to find several of his regulars shuffling about impatiently outside. He hoped he would catch some of the office and shop workers going home, thirsty after a sweltering day behind a desk or counter.

The pub began to fill up, the customers quenching their thirst, happy to have ended another day's grind. Eadie was down now, serving in the lounge, putting on her lah-de-dah accent for the more upmarket punters, Ron smiled fondly, his missus was a real George Raft[121].

Eadie looked down and saw him smiling, "Hope you ain't been on the whiskey, Ron! You having a bleeding giraffe[122] at my expense?"

"No, my precious," he chortled, "Just thinking how nice you look," then serious, "And where's that skiving mare Collette?"

The phone in the office rang. "I'll get it," said Eddie, marching down, "Yer obviously having one of yer funny half hours."

Ron heard her murmuring away on the 'ol' dog and bone'. He felt uneasy again, sumtin' bleedin' wrong, he just knew. Jamesey normally rang every other night for a quick word with Collette; he hadn't rung for three nights now. Ron pulled his wallet out and checked that the piece of paper, with the phone number on it that Jamesey had given him, was still in it. He had been told to use it only in case of emergency.

The Irish navvies were in, watching him, "Bejappers, Ron's the pigskin out," said Big Brendan, "The old Queen Victoria, on the note, is dazzled by the light, so she is."

"Are ya gonna buy a round then, Ron?" asked O' Hanlon from Meath, "Or are ya just givin' the moths an outing?" Ron laughed distractedly and, much to their amazement, pulled them a free pint.

Eadie came in, whey-faced. "Pour me a double brandy, love, and get yourself a Bell's."

Ron gaped in surprise, "Bloody Norah…what's wrong, girl?"

"Collette's on her way in wiv a new mate and a bit more from what I can gather."

Ron hurried off to do her bidding, mystified. All would be revealed soon, he guessed. Different Planet, different Species.

* * *

Jamesey and Smudger were certainly not the easiest patients to ever pass through the Military Wing.

They certainly were two rowdies, Matron later wrote in her diary. Both men were meant to be confined to bed until their injuries stabilised. Some hope, no hope and Bob Hope of that.

Jamesey still had concussion, ringing in his ears, trauma and weakness from blood-loss. Of the three bullets that had shattered Smudger's left leg, one had severed the femoral artery in his upper thigh and, but for his comrades' first aid skills, he would have bled out in about eight minutes. "An inch to the right and the old five-fingered widow would have been useless," he told Jamesey, half serious at his lucky escape from a lifetime of no nookie.

---

[121] American actor in the thirties and forties. 'To have a laugh'.
[122] Likewise, to laugh.

Jamesey somehow managed to unstrap his 'cage' and tottered up and down the ward, holding it across his chest looking for his men. Smudger paddled along behind in his wheelchair, nicknamed 'Pegasus' after the flying horse of Greek legends.

When they reached the main ward, the Matron spotted them from her desk and came charging towards them. She was a large woman, six feet tall, with a firm build and ample bosom, a formidable figure who knew her own mind and was used to enforcing it.

"Battleship ahoy!" roared a drugged up Jamesey just before he collapsed. "Lock and load."

"Incoming. Tactical retreat!" cried Smudger as he wheeled about and sped back the way they had come. "Fire depth charges."

It took four male orderlies to get Jamesey back in bed and firmly strapped in, accompanied by the cheers and delighted applause from the bored squaddies on the ward.

* * *

A stern Matron looked down at the fine specimen of a man lying on the bed, "You have your patch[123] out on the street but in here it's my patch, okay. Got that?"

"Only wanted to check on my guys," said a slightly subdued Jamesey.

"Three have been discharged back to barracks already and the rest are doing fine," she told him. "Now you need to rest."

Jamesey sighed, tired now, a depression settled over him like a low cloud over the downs, blotting out his inner sun, "I lost a man, young Derek Webster, he was a good guy."

"You can't blame yourself, Colour, you were ambushed. Not the other way around."

"Yeah, shit happens, Matron. Tell that to his parents." He gazed fixedly out of the window at the clear blue summer sky, his own inner sky grey, frozen and pitiless.

The Matron had had similar conversations with other commanders who had lost men but she knew this man before her was unique, a born leader of men. She had heard his guys talking about him and knew they hero-worshipped him. A special breed of modern day warrior she rarely had the privilege to meet, let alone be in the position to treat.

"As you say, Colour, shit happens. You could all have died, but you didn't. Believe me when I tell you this, we are here to help you, not hinder you." She produced a hypodermic needle and swabbed his upper arm. "Now what say we come to some sort of agreement, you and I?"

She tested the syringe by holding it upright and gently pressing the plunger to make sure there were no air bubbles lurking in the liquid. A tiny drop of the sedative gleamed on the end of the wicked-looking needle like a fresh drop of morning dew on a blade of glass.

"Now let's say you go for a few hours of nice refreshing sleep and then, maybe tonight, I might just turn a blind eye to a bottle of whiskey coming into the ward."

He grinned, "Matron, I think you and I are going to get along very well. I wish you had been out with us yesterday…the IRA would have run a mile."

---

[123] Tactical area of responsibility for an army unit.

She smiled benignly as she plunged the needle in, not knowing exactly how to take that last remark. Jamesey didn't know she had lost her husband, a corporal in the Green Jackets, when his jeep had been blown up in Dungannon[124] two years before.

She knew that when soldiers left for active service, they filled in a 'Next of Kin' form. If they were killed or so seriously injured they could not speak for themselves, the 'NoK' was automatically informed. If the injury was less serious, the soldier had the choice not to have the information passed on until they could do it themselves, meaning relatives did not have to worry needlessly. Both Jamesey and Smudger had opted for the latter.

As Jamesey dropped off to sleep under the influence of the heavy sedative, she wondered if he had a steady woman waiting at home. It would be a terrible waste if he didn't. He looked like an ancient Norse valkyrie warrior and would have led armies in days gone by.

He was sleeping now; she had given him enough to drop a donkey for eight hours. "You'll probably be up causing mayhem in about four hours, Colour Sergeant Jamesey John DeJames," she smiled as she bent and kissed him on the cheek, "You're a very brave man. You were just born a thousand years too late to conquer the world."

Jamesey was impervious to the latest member of his fan club, he was dreaming of Collette and her young, lithe body and her touch, which gave him great comfort in his troubled slumber. She was dressed as a Viking princess, a circlet of gold around her head to denote her lineage, and she lay on a bed of wild animal furs, her breasts bared and her slim arms stretched out to him, "Come, my warrior king, your war is over."

Collette took Kim into the lounge bar and excitedly introduced her to Eadie. It was early evening and the bar was quiet, just a few office workers lingering over their drinks, reluctant to go home for reasons known only to themselves. The men eyed the two good-looking young females, wondering if they were on the pull and what their chances were.

Kim wanted a 'Purple Nasty', a combination of lager, cider and blackcurrant, she was thirsty and Collette took a glass of Chardonnay. Louise, who worked seven to close, had just come in, so she served them.

Eadie sat with them nursing a brandy and port and was eyeing Collette warily as she gushed ten to the dozen about meeting Kim in the park with the kids, Mrs Gilbert's scones and anything else that came to mind. Collette didn't let Eadie get a word in edgeways as she was worried about how the older woman would take her big news. "And the trick with raspberry jam is you dissolve the sugar first, so yah don't overheat the fruit and turn it to mush, so Mrs Gilbert reckons."

Ron mooched in from the public bar, looking worried. Eadie shushed Collette, "Get yourself a whiskey, Ron, and come and meet Kim. Louise," she hollered, "Keep an eye to the public bar for a while please."

Ron joined them with a double Bell's and the soda syphon. He sat down, squirted soda into his drink and shook Kim's hand, "Nice ta meet yer, love, how ya managing then wiv your man away?"

---

[124] Republican town in County Tyrone. Very dangerous and high casualty rate for the security forces.

Kim told him she was staying with her parents and was coping fine but she missed Smudger to pieces. He patted her hand, "Yeah, it's hard for ya, especially when they're on active service…err…have ya heard from him recently?"

Kim looked at him quizzically. "Actually, I haven't. The sod only rings about once a week. Why'd yer ask that?"

Ron shrugged and glanced at Eadie before looking back, "Just wondering is all, how him an' Jamesey's doing an' all that." Eadie knew Ron inside and out, and she knew something was bothering him.

"'Ere, let me get ya annuver drink. It's been a bleedin' scorcher, good for business though. Was bunged earlier," he rattled on as he hastened back to the bar to get them more refreshments. "I'll bring a few snacks back…on the house."

Eadie was definitely worried now, Ron was acting out of character. Free snacks indeed.

She turned to Collette and put her hand up to stop her as she started gushing again, "Right, missy, enough of 'all around the mulberry bush and in and out the houses'…did I hear you right on the dog and bone?"

Collette squirmed and reddened. She played with her glass, afraid to look Eadie in the eye.

"I'm in the Mother's Club, Eadie… I'm havin' Jamesey's sprog, ain't I," she finally declared with not a touch of defiance, "…and wotever ya think, I'm bleedin' well proud ta be carryin' his kid."

Eadie put her hands up to her face in shock before dropping them and taking a big gulp of brandy. "Oh my Gawd…that's wonderful news. Oh Gawd…the big bugger'll have ta marry ya now."

It was Collette's turn to gape in amazement now as Eadie jumped up and enfolded her in a huge embrace. "Cor blimey, I'm gonna be a surrogate granny." Tears flowed down her face, leaving streaks in her foundation.

Collette started crying as well, not expecting this reaction from Eadie at all and mightily relieved by it. "I didn't plan ta trap him, Eadie," she snivelled, "It was an accident, wun it."

Kim clapped her hands in delight. She was having a great time with her new pal. "Yer shouldn't have dropped yer Diana Dors[125] so quick then, Collette," she chirped in, stirring the mud.

"Oh hush, Kim. Yer can't put time back," chided Eadie, releasing Collette from her bosom and collapsing back into her chair. She wiped her face with a dainty lace hankie, streaking her make-up all the more. "Imagine that, me a granny…well, a surrogate one any'ow."

Collette sniffed. "Far as I'm concerned, yer the kid's real granny, Eadie. That bitch of a ma I 'ave ain't gettin' anywhere near it. Ya 've been more of a ma to me than she ever was," they both started crying again and leaned back into another embrace.

Kim's eyes moistened and she joined in, not knowing anything of Collette's upbringing but she had deduced it hadn't been good. Collette had dodged all her earlier questions as to her childhood.

Ron arrived back with their drinks, Louise behind him with a huge platter of cheese, crackers and pickles and an assortment of cold cuts of meat. He looked

---

[125] The 'Blonde Bombshell'. Actress in the sixties. 'To drop your drawers'.

stunned at the three blubbering females all hugging each other, worry again crossed his lined face, and he nearly dropped the tray of drinks, the liquid sloshing about dangerously in the glasses.

"Eadie, Eadie, wot the bloody 'ell is wrong, gal?"

They laughed and sat back, wiping their eyes, amused at his pained look. "Break out the champagne, Ron, you're gonna be a granddad."

He put the tray down quickly before he dropped it, "Tank Gawd for that, I thought summat bad had happened."

They all laughed again and a beaming Louise was sent to get a bottle of bubbly.

For half an hour they drank and chatted, nibbling away at the tasty snacks.

"I dunno where the gherkins went. I thought I had bought a huge jar last week."

"Sorry, Ron, that was me," admitted Collette guiltily, "I get these craving, dun I."

"Better get some more in then, hadn't I," he relied kindly.

"Ah'll pay her back outta ma tips."

"You keep yer tips, love," said Eadie, "Yer gonna need nappies."

The bar was getting busier, music drifted in from the jukebox, the Bay City Rollers were singing 'Bye-bye Baby, Baby Bye-bye'.

"Soon it will be 'Rockabye Baby'," Ron said, smiling. "Come on, missus, back to work."

"Doncha be drinking too much, Collette," Eadie admonished her, "You've a nipper on the way."

"Ya better fix yer make-up," she replied, "yer boat race[126] looks like the Nile Delta. Don't look good in front of the punters, does it, Granny," she added cheekily.

"It's her hormones, Eadie," explained Kim, "Going haywire, ain't they, Collette?"

"Saucy mare," said Eadie, patting her hair back into place, "But she's right, have to keep up me appearances," and she sauntered off, all business now.

"Wonder why Jamesey ain't rung," queried Collette. "He ain't rung for four nights now."

"Nor 'as Smudger. Hope they ain't found a couple of Irish birds."

"Not my Jamesey. They're probably flat out at work," Collette said, not guessing they were flat out, but on their backs in hospital, not at work.

"Yeah, yer probably right, Coll… Still. It's strange though, ain't it?" mused Kim, a trickle of concern crossing her brow.

* * *

The gun and bomb attack on the paras had made the main news on Saturday evening but had soon been replaced by some twaddle about one of the minor royals attending a party in Mayfair that had been raided by the drug squad looking for a major dealer in snow white[127]. Three dead Paddies and a number of injured squaddies in Ulster was old news in a matter of hours. Ron scanned the Sunday papers and found the write-up on page five about the ambush and how several of the paras were

---

[126] Your face.
[127] Cocaine.

still in hospital. It said that two senior NCOs[128] were being considered for gallantry awards.

Ron mused. He went into his small office and got the phonebook out. He knew Gilbert's Furniture Shop on Bushey High Street. He knew it was M. Gilbert and had heard Collette talking about Sally, Kim's mum.

There was a Mr & Mrs M & S Gilbert, 89a High Street, Bushey, Ron was pleased with himself, he hadn't been a rozzer for nothing.

Eadie stuck her head round the door as he was dialling the number, "Wot ya at, Ron? It's getting busy out here."

"One minute, my love. Quick call to make, like."

She gave him a suspicious look and left, slamming the door after her. That big sod was at his work; she would bet her last farthing on it.

The phone rang at the other end and Mike Gilbert picked up. Ron introduced himself and told Mike his suspicions.

"Yes, Ron, I heard it on the news. Obviously, the girls missed it and I never said anything 'cause I didn't want to worry them."

Ron pondered for a second, "And no one from the army has been in touch, Mike, 'cause I would hate to think of the lads lying up in hospital hurt."

"But they would be in touch, Ron, if they were injured."

"Dat's the thing, Mike, only if they are dead or can't think for themselves, mate. It's up to the individual after that."

Mike was starting to get the drift, "So Smudger and Jamesey could be seriously injured and the army can't tell us without their permission?"

"Now ya got it, Mike...and if Smudger's as stubborn a sod as Jamesey, they wouldn't wanta worry the girlies needlessly, would they, know what I mean?"

There was silence on the other end of the line as Mike thought, then, "It's a catch twenty-two really, Ron. What you're saying is, even if they are badly injured and we rang, the army won't tell us anyway."

"Bleedin' stupid, ain't it, mate. It's why I rang ya, for a bit of advice... I have this telephone number see..."

They chatted for a few more minutes before hanging up. Ron sat at his small desk lost in thought, back to his National Service days in the Fusiliers, and his injured comrades lying in hospital far from home, no loved ones to visit and console them.

Eadie opened the door and stuck her nose in, "Who were ya bleedin' talking ta? Ya better not 'ave a bloody bit on the side."

He turned to face her and she knew from the look on his face not to argue with him, "If I friggin' well had, which I don't, I wouldn't ring her from here, now would I, you silly mare?"

She took a tentative step in, "What is, love? Wot's wrong, dear?"

He sighed heavily, "I'll tell ya afta. Hopefully nothing, now I have to make annuver call and I need a diet of peas[129] to do it."

"Okay, love... I'll see ya in a bit."

"Oh and Eadie," he called after her, "Make sure the girls have a good night."

A very anxious Eadie left, and Ron went back to the phone and dialled again, this time a much longer number.

---

[128] Non-commissioned officer.

[129] Peace and quiet.

It seemed to ring forever before a weary voice answered in a broad Glaswegian accent, "This had better be good mon or I'll have yer balls for garters. Ye woke me up yon feckin' eegit."

Ron wondered just what he had let himself in for, "Er...code word God squad."

"Och fer fecks sake...ye that Sassenach Ronnie? Big Jamesey's pal, pal?"

"If you're asking am I Jamesey's English friend then, yes mate, Ronnie Mulligan speaking."

There was a long pause on the line. "Sorry ta keep ye, Ron...and for the language. Only had a few hours' kip the last four days... Where's that bloody single malt gone? Och, there ye are ye beauty. Come to Daddy."

Ron heard the sound of drink being poured, then chugged down a throat. It was a sound he heard hundreds of times a day, and he pulled his own secret half bottle of Dewar's Whiskey out of his drawer and took a long swig. Nectar from God's own golden stream.

"Okay, sorry 'bout that. I needed a good swallow. Reverend Angus McCochrane at your service, I'm the battalion padre, so I am. What can I do for you?"

Ron nearly brought his own drink back up. A whiskey-drinking Scottish vicar, "I'm ringing to see if Jamesey and his Oppo Sergeant Smyth were hurt in that fiasco on Saturday?"

"Ach mon! Ah was afraid yer were gonna ask me that," the reverend answered after another swig of his whiskey, "Let's just say Jamesey's not all the man he was, and Smudger has no a leg to stand on at the moment, and I don't jest when I say that, mon."

Ron's blood chilled. "I need details and to know where they are, mate."

"I could lose my dog collar over this if they find out I blabbed. Back to the Highlands in disgrace the noo."

"Cat's got me tongue, Vicar. Me trap sealed tight. Mum's the word."

They talked for several minutes before Ron hung up, his hands were shaking slightly, "Shit on a shovel, how's Jamesey gonna play pool now?"

Then he rang Mike Gilbert back.

* * *

Jamesey was bored and frustrated. They had taken him down for 'a tidy up' on his stump and to check for infection. The surgeon told him he was pleased with his progress and had cut his pain relief down but kept him on strong antibiotics just in case.

He gazed at his stump with hatred, wondering what the future held for him now. It pulsed maliciously and he swore he could feel his fingers. The Colonel had warned him about that, 'phantom feelings', but assured him that they would eventually disappear, as would the pain. He scowled at it malevolently as if willing the hand to grow magically back. One of his quick-thinking young paras had gathered up several of his severed fingers, snaffled a bag of frozen peas from the raided house and put them inside before giving them to Jamesey as he sat with his back to the wall shouting orders down the radio.

"Here, Colour, maybe the doc can sew them back so they'll grow again."

Jamesey growled at him, "Grr, who do you think I am, laddie? The Jolly Green Giant[130]?" But he put them in his spare ammo pouch anyway, a glean of hope having surfaced at the back of his mind as his men grinned and chuckled. Christ, the colour was one hard bastard, cracking jokes in the face of adversity.

"Get a brew on, young 'un. Maybe I'll grow ten back and keep the ladies twice as happy."

They cracked up at that one, the gallows humour helping to release the tension as they tended to their injured mates, even one of the trussed up IRA men lying face down grinned.

"Don't know why you're smiling, mate," Jamesey remarked catching the prisoner's look, "You won't be dipping your wick for at least the next twenty years. No cause on earth is worth that."

No, Jamesey mused, he was right out of the mix now. Even if the army did keep him on, it would be in a training capacity or, God forbid, the stores, and if he went back to the farm, how could he shear a sheep with one hand for frig's sake. *Try picking your nose and scratching your arse both at once now*, he thought vulgarly.

He rattled the bed in frustration, confined to it for the next twenty-four hours while his stump healed from the op, back in the hated cage. Matron had secured it with a chain and padlock so he couldn't go 'walk about'. Nasty old witch. *I bet she's a big pot of bones boiling down the morgue and she's casting spells*, he thought, then felt ashamed. *Must be the morphine.*

"Bloody evil witch, can't even get to the whiskey in the closet," he moaned and bitched. He was finding it very hard to do everything with his left hand and to cap it all, Smudger was also confined to bed with a high temperature and was on a fluid drip.

He lay and seethed, not used to the quiet and being inactive. Matron strolled in, took his temperature and checked the padlock. "I know you think I'm a bitch, Colour Sergeant, but it's for your own good…you can get up tomorrow. Now there's a pretty young lady outside itching to see you."

That got his attention, "Who's that then?" he asked, curious.

Collette stuck her head round the door, "Only me, mate…'ow's yer doing, love?"

He looked up in amazement… "Collette…here…in Belfast. How the devil?"

She came in, hesitantly. She was wearing the beige midi-suit he had got her and a red blouse. Bare legged and in four-inch heels, she looked good enough to eat.

He gasped in disbelief, wide-mouthed. Matron laughed. "Now there's a sight to behold. Colour Sergeant DeJames speechless. I'm going on my lunch. Aren't you going to greet your fiancée?"

He recovered enough to close his big gob before saying, "Collette…how the dickens… Where the hell did you appear from?"

Collette crossed the room, sat on his bed and took his remaining hand before leaning into him and kissing him passionately on the lips. Matron watched them, amused, and left them to it, kissing was good for morale.

She gave him a good snogging, then drew back and gazed lovingly into his amazing amazed eyes, "Matron ses yer ain't been the best of boys, yer better behave, darling, they're only trying to help ya."

---

[130] Advert in the seventies where a giant grows sweetcorn.

He gazed back into her lovely hazel eyes. She was blooming like a rose and she had even put on a little weight.

"They blew my bloody hand off, Collette. My bloody good hand."

"Well, yer got annuver one, doncha?"

"But what about OLG? What am I gonna do now for a living?"

"Yer'll just have ta try twice as hard, love; besides, yer can get attachments for yer stump, can't yer. Imagine the fun we can have in bed." She lifted the sheet and cheekily reached in and stroked his penis before gently fondling his balls. "Just checking it's only yer hand that's missing," and she chuckled as she withdrew, "All seems shipshape and Bristol fashion down below."

He gazed in wonder at her as she added, "Don't know if they make attachments for down there. Don't think they would have one large enough any'ow," and she laughed gaily at the look of consternation on his face before kissing him again.

An orderly brought his lunch in on a tray and sat it on the swing-table before placing it in front of him. Collette lifted the cover off the main course to reveal mince, onion and carrot, with mashed potato and peas.

"Cor, that looks like a bit of all right, Jamesey."

He grimaced, "Bloody grub's tasteless, I'd rather live off compo packs[131]."

She reached into her bag and foraged for a minute before pulling out a bottle, which she shook vigorously and splashed some over his meat, "Chilli sauce, mate. Got it in the Paki's, didn't I, it's called 'Who Dares Burns'."

That got a small grin out of him as he inexpertly mixed it with his left hand. "Ya'll soon get the hang of it, darling. Like riding a bicycle," and told him about meeting Kim in the park.

He grinned even more when she pulled a pint bottle of Double Diamond out of her bag and opened it with a flourish. "Courtesy of Ron and Eadie. Plenty more where that came from. Got a whole boot-full."

He gulped the golden beer down with relish and let out a long contented belch, "What you mean…a boot-full? I think you've got some explaining to do, lassie."

"Funny old world, Collette. You never know what's around the corner."

"Me and Kim drove up and got the ferry. We're staying in a B&B in Dunmurry…bleedin' weird names they 'ave over here."

"That's some drive," he said between mouthfuls, enjoying the heat in the meat, "Did you rent a car then?"

"Na, mate. Mr Gilbert lent us his Rover. I got it up to a ton on the M1."

He nearly choked on his beer. "Bloody hell, Collette, you can't drive."

"Can now. Kim taught me. Piece of piss when ya get the hang of it; although, I do find going backwards a bit hard."

"Reversing, it's called reversing," he told her, deciding not to mention things like speeding, insurance, driving licences etc.

"Yeah that's it… I'll be able to drive ya about when ya start OLG."

He realised he had forgotten all about his own problems since she had arrived. This slip of a girl had driven hundreds of miles to come to his aid and restore his confidence. "Out frigging standing."

"And I've been doing typing, book-keeping and English at tech, so when we start OLG, I'll be able to help in the office."

---

[131] Army field rations.

He raised a quizzical eyebrow. He was feeling a bit ashamed now of his behaviour over the last few days. As if sensing this, she reassured him, "It's the shock and the drugs. Makes ya feel down and…" she searched for the word, "pess – i – mistic," she said pronouncing it slowly.

He was impressed, very much so, "You reckon we can do it then, Collette? The whole OLG thing."

"Ya told me, mate, when yer get a setback – withdraw – lick yer wounds – assess – advance. Besides, Smudger's gonna need a job, ain't he, to keep Kim in the style she's used to?"

He could only admire her optimism and was caught up in it now. She held his big hand, turning it this way and that, "Besides…even if you had no hands, Jamesey, you'd still be better than ten good men put together."

Hope filled his big heart and soul, "Suppose we can give it a go then."

She jumped up, thrilled and gave him a big hug, "You can be my Single-Handed Viking, love," and she kissed him breathlessly, liking the taste of beer and chilli on him.

He had finished his meal and she took the tray out to the orderly, "The colour's going for a kip for an hour, so don't disturb him," she ordered imperiously.

She went back in, dropped her skirt and pulled the sheet back, "Shift over, my Viking warrior, before that old dragon of a Matron gets back."

She was outstanding, he decided, as she climbed into the bed and snuggled up to him.

"And what was with the fiancée bit? Was that to get in?"

She reached for his cock, "We'll talk about that later, love," smiling enigmatically, as could only a young lady in love, who was mapping out her future with the man she wanted to spend the rest of her life with.

* * *

They had a good old piss up their last night. Collette and Kim sneaked several bottles of whiskey in and a cassette recorder with cracking Reggae, Mud, Slade and a bit of Queen. Several of the nurses off duty came up to boogie on down and supplied more drink. There was even some strange-smelling rolled up fags going around.

It was looking to be a great night as some of the doctors slipped in for a swallow. Jamesey and Smudger got them singing,

"Ten green hand grenades hanging off the wall,
Ten green hand grenades hanging off the wall,
And if one green hand grenade should accidentally fall,
There'll be no green hand grenades
And no fucking wall."

Everyone laughed and nearly burst their breeches when Smudger chipped in with a high falsetto, "And Jamesey's hand flew over the wall and I couldn't hear at all."

The party was swinging, and Collette sat on Jamesey's big knee proudly. The staff were going to miss the two mad paras. They were hard work but, by crikey, the duty flew in because you never knew what they were going to get up to next.

Collette had got Jamesey a big china mug in a joke shop in Belfast. Emblazoned across it in bold red lettering, it read 'WINE ME, DINE ME, SIXTY NINE ME'.

"You can drink yah whiskey outta that, luv, when yer in Germany, so you won't forget me," she whispered in his big lug.

He grinned and gave her pert arse a sneaky fondle, "As if I could ever forget you, my little blossom."

* * *

Matron had finished at tea time but she crept up, suspecting a serious breach of military hospital regulations was going to go down. She listened to the rumpus outside the door, then marched in, wafting her hands at the fragrant smoke.

"So what the devil is going on here, Colour Sergeant DeJames?"

He simpered, "Just expressing our thanks to your magnificent staff, Matron."

"What is that you are drinking, Colour?"

"Finest twelve year old Bushmills malt."

She glared at him, hands on hips, "Well, if you have any manners at all, you would pour a thirsty lady a double measure and find me a seat."

They all clapped and cheered as the music went back on. Smudger chuckled and hugged Kim and began to sing, "Puff the Magic Dragon Lived by the Sea..."

Chapter 24
SassyVanassy's Birthday Bash

"Err...that was a vertical to horizontal neck to crutch, Special Forces incapacitating body slam dunk...so it was."

Bobby Havilland – to the press

Part 1

'Ballroom Blitz'...The Sweet... 1973

SassyVanassy rode in the back of the white stretch limo with her new husband, Enrico (#4) and her personal assistant Vicki, an efficient young lady of twenty-five, with a degree in media and business studies, who let Sassy's often mercurial moods wash over her like water off a duck's back.

She sipped her Manhattan cocktail thoughtfully as she eyed her new husband and latest manager.

A successful man himself in the back corridors of the music industry, he had his own fortune made, and she had known him for years. Romance had blossomed a year earlier when she was on the rebound from #3 and he had rung her up to commiserate. They had gone for a drink, got hilariously drunk and ended up in bed.

She smiled at the memory. Ten years younger and of Puerto Rican descent, he had blown her mind. Okay, he was a whole foot shorter than her but, by crickey, he was well hung and Sassy always believed short guys tried harder. She wasn't complaining, no sir, not at all. He blew her rocks apart.

Besides, he handled her arrangements and business affairs in a smooth competent manner and let her get on with composing and performing her music, which was all she lived for really.

Born in Salford, a working-class suburb of Manchester, in the north of England in 1960, fifty-three years to the day, her mother, a part-time nightclub singer and check-out girl, had raised her on her own after her worthless father, a mediocre bass guitarist, had walked out on them.

Christened Elsie Vanessa Wotton (her mother had been a big fan of Pat Booth, who played Elsie Tanner in the first British televised soap opera Coronation Street), she spent her first few years living in a flat above 'The Pink Pussy Cat' nightclub off Salford's main drag and drifted off to sleep every night to the sound of Blues, Soul and Rock n' Roll. "Hell, music's in my blood, it was in my poor mother's milk," she once said on interview.

She did the circuits of clubs, singing popular songs, a bit of jazzed-up country and western and pushing her own numbers through.

She was a prolific writer of catchy dance songs and at twenty-five she had her own small group 'Elsie's Elsewhere Elsers'. A guy on keyboard, a bass guitarist and a drummer called Keith, who, in a fit of madness, she married in Bradford registry office.

Playing warm-up to U2 one summer night in a mega 'gig in the park' in London, she threw in one of her own numbers 'Don't Cha Get any Ideas Pal… I Ain't Staying'[132].

Elsie was a tall, voluptuous redhead with a fine, wide face, green eyes, long legs and an ample bust, and as she bopped about the stage, the crowd joined in and gave her a standing ovation afterwards.

A middle-ranking executive from Colombian Records watched her with interest, and not a little lust, if he was being honest about it, and approached her at the after gig party. "Hi, I'm Dwayne. Yah know, Elsie, your one talented sassy lady? I want to cut that track and hear the others."

She was on her way. She ditched the elsewheres for 'somewhere else, somewhere better' she wrote in her memoirs.

Colombia liked her stuff. Gave her a complete new image, a new stage name 'SassyVanassy', cut her album 'Sassy's Songs' and sent her on a six-month tour of Middle America with a full professional band.

She was an overnight sensation and 'Don't Cha Get any Ideas Pal… I Ain't Staying' rose, at speed, to number one and stayed there all summer.

After a quickie divorce from Keith (and a not unsubstantial pay off) she married her Dwayne, a Kentuckian twenty years her senior, and gave Columbia a string of hits over a five-year period. When Dwayne dropped dead of a coronary at fifty ("He was very fond of fine bourbons and Cuban cigars but he went happy," she told Music Magazine), she went back to England and opened her own studio and record label 'SassySongs'.

She was mega rich, Dwayne not being short of a few dollars when he popped his clogs, as they say in Salford, and leaving it all to his Sassy.

The big guy in the front passenger seat, swarthy and bald, but comforting in his size and self-assurance, slid the dividing window back, "You folks okay? We'll be at The Oasis in a few minutes."

"Yes thanks, Mal. We're cool," Sassy assured him.

"Great… My pal Boomerang here," and he nodded to Buzz who was driving, "Wants to know if you're gonna sing 'Slow Down Your Love or I Walk'?"

"Sure I am, Mal. Why's he called Boomerang?"

"'Cause his wife can't get rid of him when she throws him out," Mal told her and closed the window, laughing.

"Hold on, Mal, I do have feelings."

"Yeah too many in yer dick."

Sassy finished her drink and gathered her wrap and bag up. She hoped these OLG guys weren't going to be as claustrophobic as the last gang or, like husband number three, a second-rate singer from Pensacola, they would be getting the boot as well.

The limo pulled up smoothly at the kerb by the start of the fifty-foot-long red carpeted, covered walkway to the front door of The Flamin' Oasis Niteclub.

---

[132] For lyrics email the author, copyright D.C. Bond 2013

Buzz and Mal hopped out, did a quick scan and opened the doors for their V.I.P. passengers to alight.

* * *

Rabbie DeJames watched Sassy get out of the car, followed by Enrico, her husband, a pleasant enough little Puerto Rican.

She looked the part at six foot, in a long shiny gold lamé dress, split up the side to mid-thigh, with a plunging neckline to show off her superb cleavage. She wore her hair in a cascade of long gold/red curls down each side from a centre parting.

Rabbie scanned the crowd. Barriers, waist high, had been erected about four feet from the walkway. Rabbie would have liked to have seen them further back but had been overruled.

The crowd was mainly press and news crews. The function had been kept low key at Sassy's wish, she just wanted to celebrate her birthday, quietly, with her friends and associates in the music industry. Although, inevitably, passersby had gathered to see what was going on, you always got the hard-line fans and groupies, who always seemed to know her every move, and a pack of roving paparazzi, who frequented the area, had latched onto the event and were hustling and jostling each other to get into prime snapping position.

All in all, the crowd was lined about ten deep either side and down the length of the barriers. Not too bad…containable.

'The Oasis' had its security inside but they were used to the celebs bringing their own and accommodated them accordingly.

Rabbie had Little Danny and Alec Green just inside the doors. Khalid was with Charles Brouchard, they would walk up through the crowd outside the barriers in pace with Sassy as she paraded up the entrance way to the automatic doors, where she would be greeted by the manager and staff.

The walk from the car to the door was the most dangerous and most likely for the target to be hit, and his team was on high alert.

Danny and Alec would keep an eye on the staff, it had been known for wackos or disgruntled staff to attack celebs inside. Khalid and Charles would probe the crowd for signs of any attack, and he would guard the start of the walkway with Mal.

He'd placed Bobby to the left of the door and told him not to let anyone come over the barriers or impede the client's progress.

He was happy enough. Once Sassy was in, they would keep a two-man presence outside, two men discretely circulating inside and two men resting in the security office cum cloakroom, just to the right of the inside front door.

He'd briefed them before Mal and Buzz had taken off in the hired limo to pick Sassy up at her swanky apartment.

Buzz would be the seventh man after he placed the limo in secure parking.

Flashes popped and cameras whirred, fans clapped and put their hand out, hoping Sassy would 'five' them. The paparazzi were shouting: "Over here, Sassy. Big smile, Princess."

They were about halfway up now. The most dangerous time. Rabbie checked his watch, 9.45p.m. "Keep alert, lads," he muttered into the mike, for the two-way radios, on his left wrist.

311

Bobby heard Rabbie telling them to keep alert as he watched SassyVanassy and her entourage approach. He had to keep telling himself he wasn't dreaming. In the hour or so he'd been standing to the left of the door, a whole clutter of celebs had passed him, chatting away in their Armani suits, the women in the latest designs, Jimmy Cho shoes and glittering with precious jewellery. The musical genius David Bowie past him with his lovely wife. "Peace and Love on Earth and Spiders on Mars," he quipped at him.

Garth Brooks had stopped and shook his hand, "Hi, Big Dude," before going in. John Travolta had nodded pleasantly, and Cheryl Crowe had given him a saucy wink. Smokey Robinson had slipped a big Havana cigar into his pocket and told him to have a good night.

Kris Kristofferson and Bert Reynolds had stubbed their cigars out in the big pot by the door that held a miniature palm and behind which Bobby had hidden a litre bottle of water and a few sandwiches for later. Bobby had gazed, open-mouthed. "You'd better keep that big trap closed, man, or the flies 'a get in," Kris had told him and clapped him on the shoulder.

A couple of members of Oasis staggered up, worse for wear, followed by Bonnie Tyler and Elke Brooks, who winked at him seductively. A girl band and Alisha Cooke looked amazing in matching mini suits.

The up and coming Adele smiled and kissed his cheek, "Hey, thanks for guarding us, big guy."

Wait till he told Wendy, he thought, as a multitude of rich and famous whom he couldn't place passed by to pay tribute to SassyVanassy. He gawked away, in too many celebs passing shock-mode. He sniggered, Wendy would be green with envy.

He felt important standing guarding them and stood erect, hands clasped in front, in full bodyguard mode, as he'd seen Alec and Danny do.

As Sassy was about twenty feet off the door, he noticed some idiot had thrown a lit fag end over the left-hand barrier about fifteen feet to his front. Probably those paparazzi idiots. Without a thought, he strode fast to pick it up. Be a damn shame to burn that fine carpet.

At the same time he reached it and bent down to retrieve it, two guys in jeans and hoodies leapt the barriers, screaming vulgarities at Sassy.

"Death to Sassy – the abortionist," screamed one as he jumped over, clutching a large glass jar.

As he leapt, Bobby straightened up and the man rolled across his back and the momentum threw him in the air, and he landed with a whump on his back in front of Sassy and Enrico, who stopped in shock as the top came off the jar and its contents spilled over the carpet, fizzing.

Simultaneously, the second guy, brandishing a large carving knife, landed to Bobby's left and slashed the knife through the air at Sassy, "Murder-supporting bitch."

Bobby caught his right raised wrist in his left hand, swivelled, kicked him in the crotch with his right foot and then kicked the legs out from under him.

"All-round defence, all-round defence!" screamed Bobby, shouting the first thing that came into his head from his army training days.

Sassy and Enrico watched, horrified. The attacker in front of them jumped up. Bobby grabbed him with his right arm around his neck in a choke-hold and snaked his left arm down and in-between his legs. He lifted him and twisted him horizontal at chest height, knelt down on his right knee and slammed him across his left knee before tossing him aside – he'd seen the move on 'All in Wrestling'.

Alec and Danny rushed out of the doors, guns drawn. An evil vaporous smoke was coming off the carpet, where the liquid had pooled. "All-round defence!" hollered Bobby.

Khalid and Charles vaulted the barriers and the four of them surrounded the clients, arms linked.

Rabbie came running up with Mal, his Ruger drawn, two policemen followed him. "Get the clients in now," he ordered, pointing his revolver in a two-handed stance at the dazed attackers.

The press was shouting and roaring and the fans screaming as the four big bodyguards circled their charges and marched them into the club, where anxious staff waited and closed the door.

"Jesus, Bobby, I can't take you nowhere," Rabbie quipped, covering the assailants as the cops cuffed them and more police arrived, panting.

"Sorry, Rab, was just picking a dog end up."

"You did brilliant, mate. Let's get you in and sorted, your shoes are melting."

Bobby looked down. Right enough his shoes were smoking and so was his right knee, where he'd knelt in the stuff. Goddammit, his best funeral suit. "Hydrochloric acid by the smell," explained Rabbie grimly. "Thank God they never got the client."

Bobby got his big bottle of water and splashed his knee and shoes. One of the attacker's hands was smoking, so Bonny poured it over him, "Not that you deserve it, attacking Sassy, dog breath."

The press snapped away and shouted questions at him. "Don't answer them, Bob," Rabbie ordered as he asked over the radio for more water.

A member of staff came out with a bucket of water and they doused the attackers again.

More cops arrived. "Come on, Bob, let's go in and check on Sassy and Co."

"Ah'll just go get ma sandwiches."

* * *

They got Sassy, Enrico and Vicki into the security office. Their shoes were smoking as well, so Alec and Danny got them off, poured water over their feet and dumped the footwear in a bucket.

"I do not bloody believe it. Some bastard tried to throw acid over me. In my face, for Gawd's sake!"

"And would have if that big guy hadn't moved in. I've never seen a man that size move so fast," remarked Enrico.

"Yeah, he's a true professional," said Alec, winking at Danny.

The manager and staff were hovering anxiously around Sassy, "Go and get us some drinks, and get that big guy outside one and make sure he's okay," she demanded. "He is a bleeding hero."

They rushed off to do her bidding as Rabbie came in, "How are you, ma'am? I've the paramedics coming."

313

"I'm in shock, I think, your big guy stopped me getting a face full of acid."

"And stabbed, dear. Then other guy had a very large knife," added Enrico.

"Bloody hell, I feel sick," she groaned.

Rabbie got her a bucket and patted her back, "Take deep breaths. In and out...that's it."

Meanwhile, outside Bobby had gone to retrieve his sandwiches. Wendy had proudly made him peanut butter and jelly, and he didn't want to be ungrateful and waste them. The full import of what he had done that night hadn't quite hit him.

News crews were arriving by the minute as word spread of what had happened and feelings were running high... SassyVanassy spent a lot of time in New York and they considered her 'one of their own'. An adopted 'Big Apple Gal'.

A senior policeman, a Captain, arrived and asked Bobby what had happened, Rabbie put his head out of the door. "Just talking to the police, Boss. I'll be in, in a minute or two," Bobby told him.

A news crew that had been placed at the top left of the barrier had caught it all on camera and after talking to the cop, Bobby moved over towards them while the paramedics rushed in to attend to Sassy. "Phew, that was a bit hairy," he remarked to the pretty reporter.

The crew had managed to get a live feed through to Fox News as soon as the excitement started, and they had the whole sequence of events on film, talk about being in the right place at the right time. Fox News was screaming for it and talking big bucks. This was going to be a classic and make them a fortune... Pulitzer here we come and U-Tube Yahoo!

"Hey guy, gotta minute?" called the anchor, a pretty, dark haired woman, "What's yah name?"

Ah what the heck! What harm could it do? thought Bobby. "I am Bobby Havilland, ma'am, On La Guardia Security," he told her.

"Cool, you're one of the 'Single-Handed Viking's' men?"

"I guess so, yeah, sure."

"How's it feel to have saved SassyVanassy's life tonight?" she asked.

"Ah shucks, I just did what I'm trained to do."

"Are your ex-military, sir? Don't OLG only employ highly trained ex-forces?"

"Yes, ma'am, I sure am," he answered. "You should have seen the size of our fuse boxes."

"Are you ex-special forces?"

"Well, I done Eye-rack, but no comment. Let's just say I helped light up Bagdad."

"What did you call that move you used to stop the attacker escaping?" she wanted to know.

"Urrghm... That was a 'vertical to horizontal neck and crotch Special Forces incapacitating slam dunk'...so it was."

Rabbie came out, "Have to steal him off you, guys. SassyVanassy wants him."

The anchor turned to Rabbie, "Mr DeJames...you run OLG in New York... Can you comment on what happened tonight?"

"Not at the moment. We're just pleased our clients are okay and that Big Bobby here reacted so fast and effectively, as he's been trained to do."

Rabbie pulled Bobby inside as a further barrage of questions followed them. Bobby's chest puffed out and he was fit to burst with pride.

"Get that out quick," ordered the reporter. "I wonder if that DeJames guy is single," she mused, "I bet he can give a gal a good time."

* * *

The girls were having a great time drinking their wine and watching the movies. Once 'An Officer and a Gentleman' was over, and they had stopped laughing and wiped their eyes, they ordered pizza; well, eventually, when they worked out that the one with the little anchors on it was anchovies, and Luca loved them.

As they ate their slices and chatted about the men, Luca assured a half sloshed Wendy that Bobby had no romantic designs on SassyVanassy.

Philli shushed them just as she was about to play 'Sleepless in Seattle'. "Oh my Gawd! Look at the news flash on television."

They gazed at the small headline banner on the bottom of the local channel that was on the screen.

'ACID AND KNIFE ATTACK ON 'PEOPLE'S PRINCESS OF POP' SASSYVANASSY FOILED IN NEW YORK'

"Quick, flick it onto Fox. Those beggars are always first with the news," ordered Wendy as she guzzled more vino.

"Shit, I hope the guys are all right," said a worried Philli.

Luca held her hand. "Hope so… Who would attack Sassy? She's so talented."

On television a Police Captain was being interviewed, "Investigations are ongoing so I can't say too much but at 9.45p.m. two Hispanic men were arrested after they apparently attempted to stab SassyVanassy with a knife and throw acid over her."

They cut back to the studio, where the newsreader informed them, "There were dramatic events tonight at The Flamin' Oasis Niteclub off Times Square after the popular singer SassyVanassy was attacked by anti-abortionists. Let's see it again as captured by an independent news crew who were on the scene as it occurred."

The girls all raised their hands to their faces as they saw Bobby race down and tackle the villains. "Oh my Gawd, that's his best shoes, they're smoking." They watched gobsmacked as Bobby was interviewed and then, briefly, Rabbie. Luca thought he looked very handsome on television.

The camera returned to the studio and the newsreader continued, "Messages of shock and outrage are coming from all quarters. A spokesman from the Mayor's Office says the Mayor is on his way down there now to see if SassyVanassy is all right and to thank Mr Havilland personally… More on this story as it comes in."

They sat there stunned, the pizza going cold and congealing, unnoticed.

"Who needs to watch Richard Gere and Kevin Costner when our guys are the real thing?" Philli remarked to her stunned pals.

Wendy got up. "I'm going down to get the tequila, ladies, it's gonna be a long night."

Philli got her cell out. "I'll see what they have to say for themselves."

Luca clapped her hands, "Dar is never a dull moment in da Popular Tree Apartments."

* * *

315

When Bobby entered the security office, the paramedics had just finished checking Sassy's feet. A few splashes had put holes in her tights and given her minor burns; they had bathed them and applied a thin layer of plastic skin. Enrico was much the same but Vicki had escaped unscathed as she had been following behind and avoided getting splashed.

Bobby's feet were tingling, as was his left knee, so they sat him down and whipped off his shoes and socks. The soles of the shoes had nearly melted through, and there were splash marks across the tops of both feet, "Ah, damnation, Wendy's gonna flip her lid when she sees mah best footwear's been barbequed."

Sassy eyed the big guy, he was some size, "Bobby, I just want to thank you. You're one brave man."

"Yes, you saved my wife's life, and we'll never forget it," said Enrico, shaking his hand.

Bobby blushed. "Ah shucks, ma'am, I was just in the right place at the right time."

"I'm gonna write a song about you, man," Sassy decided, "It'll be immortalised, what you did, putting your life on the line for us. What size shoes do you take?"

He liked the idea of that, Wendy would be jealous. He tottered to himself. "A size fifteen normally does the job, ma'am."

"And cut out that ma'am crap, its Sassy to you and Mrs SV in public."

Sassy had a string of shoe and clothes shops she owned as an interest as well as a good investment. She was opening a new one on Saks Avenue on Friday, which was partly why she was in New York. "Get onto Ralphie, Vicki, and tell him to get me two pairs of best Italian brogues in brown and black, size fifteen, a couple of pairs of those Italian loafers, same size, and two Armani suits, one black and one blue. What size are you Bobby, honey?"

"Ah am a 52" chest and a 42" inside leg."

"Wow, you really are some specimen! They're working in my new store, 'Cheekie Choos and Clooes' all night, putting the stock out. Oh and get Enrico his usual in a size 6. A dozen pairs of extra-large socks and half a dozen small, new hosiery for me and a pair of those Jimmy Choo 4" heels I like." Vicki got busy on the phone.

"Dammit, where's this guy's drink? What's your tipple, Bobby?"

Bobby looked at Rabbie, the Boss, for approval. "Sure, Bobby, you're in shock," he grinned.

"I'll have me a Jack Daniels and Coke, if that's okay, ma'am," he replied.

"It's Sassy. Get a bottle of that twelve-year-old gold seal in now," she ordered a minion.

A few minutes later Bobby thought he had died and gone to heaven, as he sipped at the luxury bourbon, which he could never have afforded to buy for himself. Detectives came and took brief statements off Sassy, Enrico and Bobby. "That should be enough to hold these guys 'til we get full statements off you and the OLG guys tomorrow," the head detective informed them, "We have it all caught on film anyhow."

The detectives shook their hands, and Sassy signed a few autographs as she drank her Brandy Alexandria, still horrified at the thought of having such a near miss.

"What cha call that Special forces hold you used again?" a Detective Lieutenant asked bobby. "Be one for the recruits at The Academy." Bobby told him and Rabbie grinned behind his hand, as did Alec Green. They had never heard of it and they knew them all.

A small fussy man from the shop arrived and fussed over Sassy. She changed her tights, the men turning their backs but sneaking quick peeks at Sassy's fine long legs.

"Sort that man mountain out, Ralphie dear," she instructed as she slipped into her high heels, "He's a hero."

Ralphie stood in front of Bobby, hands on hips, "My oh my, ain't you a fine looking fellow…! Right, jacket and trousers off…chop, chop." Before he knew it, the assistants had him down to his Homer Simpson boxers. Ralphie unravelled a tape measure, "I'd better check your inside leg, duckie, which side do you hang?"

"No way, pal. It's 42" and I hang to the right," he said sweating.

"He sure does," murmured Sassy to Vicki, and they giggled.

Before he knew it he was decked out in a $2,000 Armani suit and $500 Italian brogues.

"Put the rest of his new clobber in the corner. Just a little thank you from Enrico and me, darling," Sassy explained. "My, don't you look handsome."

"He sure does," agreed Ralphie, fussing over him with a clothes brush. "Are you seeing anyone, sweetie? 'Cause I'm free."

Rabbie and Alex laughed at the big man's shocked expression. "I'll have you know I'm a happily married guy," he retorted, adding, "To a woman. A female one."

"Just my luck," moaned Ralphie, "But if you ever come out of the closet, I'm game."

They all laughed at Bobby's stunned features. "You be careful, buddy," he snarled. "The last guy who told me he was game, I shot."

"You're so manly when you're angry, Bobby," cooed Sassy. "Like a big 'Marvel Action Man'."

"Temper, temper, ducks," cooed Ralphie. "I like a guy with spunk."

The Mayor, a large corpulent man of sixty with a bright red drinker's nose, came in with the chief of police. He rushed over and hugged Sassy in a tight embrace. "Sassy, all of New York is so glad you're safe. What a terrible business."

"It was bleeding terrifying, Al, but for my mate Bobby here and the OLG guys, they saved me from an acid bath."

The Mayor bounded over and shook Bobby's hand. "New York owes you a big debt my boy, a big debt."

"Listen, Al, I want to get his party on the road, but first I want to speak to the Press. Get it out of the way and let my fans know I'm okay."

"I'll get it sorted, ma'am," volunteered Rabbie, "Give me five minutes," and he left, gathering his men up as he went.

Bobby went to follow but Sassy pulled him back. "Not you, mister, you're not leaving my side tonight. Now, what about another quick drinkie-poo?"

* * *

The press had gathered in a feeding frenzy behind a heavy rope placed ten yards down from the door. Rabbie placed his guys in a line in front of them. A couple of mikes on stands had been placed by staff, just outside the doors, ready for use.

Sassy, Enrico, the Mayor and Bobby came out to a storm of questions, and huge applause.

"Let's have one at a time, people!" shouted Rabbie. SassyVanassy has a party to go to," and he pointed to the dark-haired reporter who had caught the action first.

Sassy answered their questions smoothly, she was a real pro. She assured them she was all right and assured her fans it was business as usual.

"I would like to say, I am neither for nor against abortion, but in circumstances where the mother is in danger or there is something wrong with the baby, in rape cases and if the girl is underage, I do believe the choice should be there. Hell, it takes two to tango, people, but it's a sad thing that these crazy, anti-abortionist groups are prepared to take lives to save unborn lives. They are one sad group of hypocrites. What about my right to life, huh? But for Bobby Havilland here, I was a dead person," and she reached up and kissed him on his big, meaty cheek, "He's my hero. My New York Sir Galahad."

"Kiss him again, Princess, for the cameras," they hollered. So she did, several more times.

Bobby beamed with pleasure…sure beat changing fuses.

* * *

Wendy looked on, flabbergasted. "Look, she's kissing my husband, and look…he's wearing a new Armani suit."

"He looks really well, you must be so proud of him," Philli told her.

Wendy took a big slug of tequila straight from the bottle. "Proud of him? She's all over him like a rash. I'll teach her to chat my man up."

Luca patted her hand. "She's only very grateful, Wends, you know Bobby only loves you."

"He darned well better or I'll slice his balls off and whip 'em through the blender to make soup for Mrs Chin's Pekinese."

Luca and Philli laughed, if a little forced, "He only doing his job, Vendy."

"Just as long as he don't do a job on Sassy 'hot stuff' Vanassy."

"She's too old anyhow," consoled Philli, "and she's married."

"Yeah, she's had more husbands than fleas on a dog, and her new one's younger. Bobby watches the porno channel, you know. I caught him."

Philli laughed. "They all do. It's like window shopping. Sure I saw you eyeing up that blonde stud muffin behind the bar in Bronco Bills."

Wendy sighed, deflated, "I guess so." Then she started sobbing. "Ahg, just don't wanna lose the man I love to an ageing Brit pop artiste."

"You von't, dahling, Bobby loves you," Luca reassured her. She was thoroughly enjoying herself, it beat lying in hospital. She wondered if Rabbie watched the porno channel, she didn't even know there was one. Maybe when she was better, they could watch it together…could be interesting.

"And why are they not answering their phones?" howled Wendy. "I'll go to the lethal injection chamber for that poor excuse of a songstress if she touches my man."

318

When OLG went body guarding VIPs and celebs, so they wouldn't get distracted, the guys left their personal cells in the ops room. This meant they couldn't take personal calls in the event of an 'incident', and therefore, they could not be held responsible for the press getting any information of a sensitive nature. It also meant they wouldn't be distracted by incoming personal calls. Instead, they were issued with small secure two-way radios and in this way were in contact with each other and the OLG ops room. In case of emergency, they could call for backup, it was a sound policy which worked well and paid off big time.

Wendy had sent Big Bobby several text messages earlier, asking how it was going and had he met Sassy and was both mystified and a little annoyed that he hadn't replied. She didn't know that the only person carrying a cell was the boss and, after briefing his father in Los Angeles, he had been swamped with calls and had therefore switched it off. There was always the fear that the media would scan the calls and play any recording during the news bulletins, security was paramount.

The girls sat in stunned silence, channel hopping to get any new details of the attack.

"Whatta hell's goin' on?" bemoaned a half-pissed Wendy, "Why won't they answer their Goddamn fricking cells?"

Luca pondered that and poured Wendy a stiff shot of Golden Medallion, "Maybe day don't have dem wiv dem. You know, security."

Wendy gulped tequila. "That's just crazy. I am of a darn mind to get a cab and do a bitta gate-crashing and see what happens."

"No, Luca is right. It makes sense," Philli said, "Say the big guy was texting you instead of watching Sassy, she might be dead now."

"Or maybe Bobby get a mouthful of acid."

"Oh my Gawd!" wailed Wendy, "I want my Bobby. I want to know he's okay."

Luca lifted the house phone and tried the OLG ops room again. "Shitski, is still engaged. I keep trying, Vends." She put her arm around her distressed pal and tried the number again.

Philli knelt beside her and patted her knees, "Listen, babe, Rabbie and the dudes are heavy-weight professionals so don't you be worrying."

Wendy looked up at them with unshed tears in her eyes, "But mah Bobby's only a big softie, he's a Goddamn electrician for frick's sake. He was smoking, his shoes were smoking on the television," and the tears escaped and exploded in a silver cascade like a spring waterfall down her cheeks.

Suddenly, the phone rang causing them all to jump, and Luca snatched it up. She nodded her head at her friends and gave them a thumbs up as she listened for a few seconds before saying, "Okay, Rabbie, everyone's okay. Huh, huh, 'kay, minor burns, 'kay. You have to go, okay. You see us in the morning, huh, huh. Wow, Sassy okay and Big Bobby das hero of da night. Huh, huh da ve are okay now ve know you are all good, tanks. Vould you speak to Vendy just to reassure her, okay?" and she passed the phone to Wendy, who snatched it off her and started talking at once.

"Rabbie, that big gahoot was standing there smoking like a Manhattan toxic waste dump and an hour later he's standing in a new Armani suit and Sassy Vanassy's all over him like fleas over an old hound dog." She listened to what Rabbie was saying and her stance gradually relaxed and she was mollified as whatever he told her sank in. "Well, okay, man, but keep that blood-sucking Brit leech off him or I'll be the next one to have a crack at her…huh, huh, okay thanks, man."

Wendy put the phone down, stunned, "My Bobby's a hero. Who would have guessed? I do declare I need another drink as I'm in a state of shock," and she burst out laughing in sheer relief.

"We are all surrounded by heroes, is like da 'Wild West' but in da modern times," declared a delighted Luca.

"Yea and like the 'Wild West', the little women are left at home to hold the fort and worry," remarked Philli.

"Well, at least we got cable, flushing toilets and goddamn good liquor," laughed a visibly cheered up Wendy.

Philli looked at Luca, "You should be going to bed, honey. Don't want Rabbie coming back and being annoyed, do we?"

"No wayski, hoseaski," she laughed, "I'll hold da fort wiv my friends."

"Thatta gal, Luca. We'll sort the guys out later when they get home and if I find Bobby's been a-messin' with Miss Vanassy I'll shred his balls and put them on that pizza and grill them for sure."

Luca and Philli grimaced at each other, not knowing if their friend was serious or not.

* * *

Back at the Flaming Oasis the party was livening up. The club was decked out with palm trees and tall lamps on stands, which flared up to give the impression of flames. The tables were positioned on islands placed in the centre of a pool full of goldfish and beautiful coloured koi carp and reached by catwalks. He gazed up at the domed ceiling, which depicted a desert night sky complete with stars, revolving planets and, periodically, a comet moving through the darkness. Rabbie was impressed, it was stunning and at the moment definitely the place to be seen but, he guessed, it would lose its appeal to the celebs in time and they would have to rely on the tourist trade.

Very impressive, he thought back to a certain oasis in Libya where he had hidden up a tree with a badly wounded SBS man while the madman Gaddafi's troops searched in the dark for them. He shivered, it seemed like a different lifetime, close shaves like that never left you completely, and he quickly brought his thoughts to more recent events, like the beautiful young Russian he was helping with the trauma she was going through. Now there was a ray of perpetual sunshine if he ever saw one.

He thought back to the night before and smiled fondly at the memory of waking up to her presence that morning. She had shrugged the nightmare off as nothing, and he admired her bravery in the face of adversity, although he knew she was still fragile and hurting.

He was determined to be there for her and not take advantage of the situation, still, he remembered the taste and texture of her lips on his and smiled broadly. Every cloud has a silver lining, and it was a massive ego boost after that bitch, Juliette, to be so highly regarded by such a fine specimen of the fairer sex.

Bringing his mind back to the job, he patrolled the perimeter of the club. Some of the guests were dancing to a five-piece band placed on a stage in the middle of the room, bashing out a string of hits from Sassy's portfolio, along with a few hits from bands like the Beatles, Smokey and the Eagles.

Bobby was sitting at Sassy's side, guzzling down JD and making big holes in the large platters of snacks. Sassy had insisted he stay close by her side, and Rabbie had readily agreed. There was a big police presence outside, at the Mayor's insistence, and his guys had all the doors covered. He shuddered to think about how OLG's reputation would had been tarnished if the attackers had succeeded, and it was the least he could do to let the big guy enjoy the laurels and reap the rewards for his swift action.

Rabbie grinned again, he was the only one who knew Bobby was bending down to retrieve a dog end, but he had reacted well when push came to shove. Rabbie decided it was a case of less said the better.

There were cheers and applause as Sassy got up to sing. She was certainly a refreshing change to many of the celebs he had dealt with, most would have crumpled under the pressure of being attacked and acted the diva. They would have fled the scene, horrified, but Sassy was made of sterner stuff and was smiling as she grabbed the mike and faced her adoring audience.

"Thank you all for coming to my 'Birthday Bash'. Sorry for the late start. A couple of fans earlier delayed me. Thought I needed a facelift I didn't want and some impromptu cosmetic surgery, but my mate Bobby and the OLG guys decided they weren't in my appointment book and got rid of them rather quickly…so quick, their feet left the floor and they left by ambulance."

The crowd roared and stamped their feet in approval. The invited press snapped away and a spotlight found Bobby, who raised his glass to his new best friend, and thunderous applause once again filled the building.

"The things some guys will do to get an invite to a Sassybash," she continued, "But let them enjoy their prison 'lean cuisine'; tonight, my friends, we party. I'm gonna sing and then we're gonna rock the night away… Oh and people," she said as an after-thought, "I don't do drugs, as you know, but if you do, remember 'Acid' is bad for you."

That got another laugh and more applause before she went into her first number, 'Doncha Cramp my Style Babe or I Walk'.

Oh baby, baby, what can I say
Don't cramp my style or I walk
Can't do it all the damn time your damn way,
You think you're cool but you don't talk the talk.
No, don't cramp, don't cramp, don't cramp, don't cramp,
Don't cramp my style or I walk
Yeah, I'll walk, I'll walk, I can do the talk
Don't cramp my style, babe, or I walk.
You think you got it all, ain't nothing special,
You're cramping me serious like stinging nettles,
You're as annoying as a fridge full of hungry bees
Who swarm out from the cheese and the frozen peas.
Don't frickin' cramp my style my boy or I walk.[133]

---

[133] For lyrics email the author, copyright D.C. Bond 2013

Eight verses and choruses later, the room was buzzing and jiving. When the song finished and the cheering stopped, Sassy bowed and announced, "That's my new single, which stands at number four in the Brit charts at the moment." Enrico jumped up, phone to ear, "It's number two now, Sassy."

She laughed with delight, "Shit, I haven't had a number two in ten years. Anyhow, Big Bobby ses his wife's a senior nurse in the Manhattan Hospital for Sick Children, so all the royalties are going to that ward to help make things better for the little kiddies."

The crowd went ballistic. "Hell yeah… I'm just a two-bit singer who got a few breaks and is bloody lucky to still have her face… Goddamn, Bobby's wife is an unsung hero. Let's hear it for the nurses, the fire dudes, the paramedics, the cops…come on, guys, we don't matter, let's hear it for all them Goddamn wonderful 'angels of mercy' out there. The New York unsung heroes."

The cheering and clapping shook the auditorium and nearly blasted the fake sky into space. Sassy had let the news crew who had been the first to catch the incident out front into the party, and they were now on their cells, jubilantly feeding this news to Fox, who broadcast it straightaway.

Sassy was a shrewd business woman; they say all publicity is good and this was great, she knew by tomorrow her song would be number one in Britain and well on the way up the American and download charts.

She truthfully didn't need the cash and money donated to charity could be written off against taxes; besides, she would put out another catchy tune in no time and bring it in by the wheelbarrow load.

* * *

The girls sat enthralled watching Sassy sing her new song on Sky. They had clapped at her opening speech and cheered at Bobby but when she dedicated the royalties to the Children's Hospital, they sat there like shell-shock victims.

"You see, Vends, she da good person."

Wendy was bawling again, "My Bobby got his plates of meat burnt in the line of duty, and then he tells Sassy all about me. I love that man; he's my frigging universe!!!"

"At least his nuts are safe from the kitchen appliances," Philli muttered, relieved.

* * *

Sassy sang for an hour, then they danced and drank the night away. Everybody had the time of their lives. Bobby thought he had died and found paradise as the bourbon flowed and the food kept coming and coming.

"Never had lobster before," he told Rabbie happily, "But by crakey it's goin' number two on my list underneath KFC."

At six in the morning they staggered out of The Oasis and got into the limos. Rabbie sat in with Enrico, who was talking business with him. He wanted Bobby to guard Sassy every time she went out in public for the duration of her week's visit. Rabbie agreed at a rate of $600 a day. He also wanted OLG on their penthouse and place of business and if they went out of an evening. They agreed an acceptable figure and shook hands on it. Rabbie was well chuffed.

At 7.00am a bleary-eyed Wendy heard the door open. Luca and Philli were curled up asleep on the sofa. Wendy was seriously hung over, "Oh Gawd, I've got a mouth like a Turkish tram driver's jockstrap in mid-summer," she mumbled through dry lips as Bobby and Rabbie came into the room.

Bobby grinning and weaving from side to side hollered, "Honey, I'm home!" waking the other two up.

"No, dear, you're not," she reminded him.

"It doesn't matter," he slurred, "Look who I brought home ta meet my precious nursey."

Wendy nearly fell off the seat when Sassy came in, sat down and hugged her to her ample bosom, "Honey, that is one fine man you have there. He's not stopped talking about you all night. It's my privilege to meet one of New York's finest."

She released her and shook her hand. A stunned Wendy introduced Luca and Philli, who stared wide-eyed. "Enrico, where's that darn limo with the grub?" she snapped, then more softly, "I've brought you breakfast. It must have been a worrying night got you."

Waiters came in and served them with eggs benedict, crispy bacon, smoked salmon and all the trimmings. Champagne corks popped and freshly squeezed orange juice flowed, "Mmm, Bucks Fizz," laughed Philli taking a large sip.

It was like something from a dream. A nice dream, Luca decided and looked at a smiling Rabbie, who had fetched her meds from the bedroom. She took them, dutifully, and smiled back at him. She was just glad he was home safe and sound.

Sassy asked her about her singing, "Rabbie has told me a little about you, child. You must come and sing with me one day, he says you're very talented."

Luca blushed, "You must come to da Russian Club, Sassy. We can party when I get better."

Sassy gave them each a bag containing all her albums, signed, and a few other goodies before she left. She also gave Wendy a gift voucher for $2,000 to use in the new store, "Don't see why you shouldn't get new clobber to match your hubby," she told her.

Wendy was over the moon. Bobby was crashed out in a chair like a giant deformed starfish, his snores thundering up to the ceiling.

Wendy walked Sassy out, "He's a fine, fine man, Wendy, but don't worry," Sassy patted her hand, knowingly. Sassy was used to jealous wives, "I like my men like my pet dogs, small, stock and with lots of stamina."

"Oh! Okay. What type of dogs do you have?"

"Yorkshire Terriers, dear. Cocky little things that think they have balls like a bulldog."

Wendy giggled, Sassy was another cool Brit; New York seemed to be coming down with them. "I liken Bobby to a Saint Bernard, big, cuddly and loyal…and they can carry your drink around for you."

Sassy liked that, "I'm gonna write a song about him. I'll see him at twelve for the opening of my new shop. You will come, dear? It'll be fun."

"Try and stop me and my dog will rip you apart," Wendy answered with a smile.

"Oh I don't think so," laughed Sassy, as she headed to the stairs, "He's just a big teddy-bear at heart."

* * *

Rabbie had a quick shower and climbed gratefully into bed. He'd grab a few hours' sleep and then run Bobby down to Sassy's 'Choos and Clooes' before heading into the office to sort out manpower and paperwork for the new contract. He had a busy week ahead.

Luca came into the room with two mugs of cocoa and got in beside him. He sipped thirstily, then, "Don't suppose me asking if you've been to bed is going to have any point to it?"

She smiled dreamily, "I slept on da couch. You sleep, my gallant knight, and I'll read my book and watch over you and chase any bad dreams away." And he did.

He slept like a newborn for four hours and when he woke, she was lying watching him and it was such a lovely sight to behold he said a silent prayer of thanks to a God he, more times than enough, doubted and went to work feeling fulfilled and content, knowing she would be there when he got back.

After he left, Luca lay watching the afternoon shadows play across the ceiling. Spring was coming and the weather was brightening every passing day. She glowed deep inside, her mood as light as a dandelion seen floating on the wind, and she traced Rabbie's name in the air with a finger. Liking the feel of it, the intimacy, she did it again and again and again.

The smile on her lips was fine, fresh and laid-back. She was a woman who knew what she wanted and had just realised that it might very well be possible to turn that want into a wonderful reality.

Part II
'America'... Simon and Garfunkel

Luca had made Rabbie a cheese and tomato toastie and strong coffee, and he came into the kitchen phone to ear, laughing. "Wendy's kicking Big Bob outta bed. We have to get down to Sassy's opening, and I have to get to the office and get contracts sorted. That was some night."

"Can I come with you, Rabbie? I am going da stir crazy."

He sat and sipped his coffee and looked at her. She was fully dressed in a pair of flared jeans and a white cheesecloth blouse. Her hair was gleaming and in her customary ponytail, light from the kitchen window defined the strands of umber, tan and brown, and he swore it had gone thicker over the last week or so. He was entranced. "What about doctor's orders? Bed rest and I bet you haven't taken your meds?"

She came and sat on his lap. He saw her fingernails had grown and were painted a coral pink. It was all very alluring. "Rab, da week bed rest was up yesterday...da meds are all done, and Doc Mac said I could go out for brief periods over the next week or so."

He felt a prat. "Christ, Lucs... I've been ignoring you. Yeah, 'course I'll get you out for a couple of hours."

She pulled his face round and bent hers to his. He saw her lips were shiny and glossy with lipstick, which he tasted immediately because she pressed hers to his and proceeded to give him a breathtaking version of Ruski/Litho liposuction. He responded immediately, marvelling in the freshness of her mouth and their tongues met and entwined and he felt himself stiffen.

The kiss went on for a long time, and he had his hands entwined in her hair and she was holding his head with both hands, gripping his hair.

When they came up for breath, he gazed into her clear, drug-free eyes and marvelled at their mysterious depths, then panted, "You better get your coat; the car will be here shortly."

* * *

In the car on the way to Saks Avenue, Luca was crushed up to a window in the back with Big Bobby, who was seriously suffering after his binge on fine Jack Daniels. Little Dan helped fill the back, Buzz was driving and Rabbie was on the phone as usual, running OLG.

She sighed. He worked so hard and was always thinking ahead. She would love to see him chill out and make some time for himself. He was such a good guy and needed to get self-time.

He ended his call. "Hey, Rab, Doc Mac says dat da swimming would be good da get me back in shape, would you like to go with me?"

Rabbie thought about that. She certainly seemed in good shape already. "Yeah sure, Lucs, I know a good wee club on 47th. Take ya soon."

She smiled "Tank you. I dig my swimsuit out."

The testosterone level in the car rose as their imaginations went into overdrive. *Holy cow.*

She looked out the window. So pleased to be out again. It was another little hurdle over on her road to recovery from the 'House of Hanlon'.

She watched two little girls, no older that four or five, with red bobbie hats and blue puffa jackets sitting on the top of a tenement steps in a shadowed porch playing with a black cat and four similar-coloured kittens, laughing and exclaiming at each other.

A large woman with tendrils of blonde hair watching them carefully. A round, homely face and plump arms crossed on the windowsill.

Is good, Luca thought. *Maman watching her kids with maman cat and kittens.* Life was just a big basic circle, birth, the middle, then away to wherever you go when you leave the mortal coil. Of course some people's circles were bigger that others, and she gazed at the back of Rabbie's head. His classy strong hair. Her life circle might have been considerably reduced but for the intervention of this man's timely intervention.

Fate or lucky chance? Who knew, but she knew for sure his astuteness that dreadful night had prevented her possible death and she was deep in his debt. She reckoned it was meant to be, as Wendy would say, "Karma, babe."

God, it was great to be out. The testosterone level in the car was dense and heavy. She grinned to herself, stirring it up. "Da, I got da nice, black string bikini I never vear yet. I give it a baptism when we go da pool."

Buzz nearly drove into the back of an ice-cream van, and Little Danny eyed her appreciatively, "Ah would like to see that, lil lady. Sure be a sight for sore eyes."

Bobby just groaned, his hangover his prominent feature. He might be the hero of the hour but the effects of too much liquor made no distinction to age, size or gender.

"Chrissake watch the road, Buzz, and you, young lady, behave yourself," he admonished them.

She caught his eyes in the mirror. "I just da say I can't wait da strip off and get da bikini on," she replied innocently.

He caught the mischief in her eyes and laughed as Buzz pulled a hankie and mopped his face. Rabbie grinned. He'd noticed this wicked streak of humour that occasionally rose to the surface and believed it was good healing for her. "Both hands on the wheel, Buzz. We can't wait, Luca. I'll get some photos of you for the office."

Buzz was squirming around on the seat. "Get me one, Boss. Please, please, pretty please."

"Settle, guys. You behave, Luca, or you're walking."

"Yes, master. I be good," she assured him, smiling wickedly, and looked out the window. Two elderly matrons in tweeds, faces rigid with face lifts and Botox, led two tiny silken-haired dogs on leashes, expressions haughty. So New York. She reckoned the rabbits in the Drasnov valley would eat the little dogs for breakfast.

Luca felt her own chin carefully. *I think I just let nature take its course. If I'm old and still graced to be with the one I love, my true love, he won't care. Our bond of loving acceptance of each other will be so strong, it won't matter*, she mused, looking at Rab, wondering. She knew she was in love with him and believed he loved her but it was early days and she didn't want to push, yet!

She smiled dreamily, and he caught her eye in the mirror again and smiled back and gave her a devilish wink.

Buzz swerved to avoid a last minute clash with a refrigerated truck "Frig, Buzz. Whatcha doing? Keep your eyes on the road."

"Sorry, Boss," stammered Buzz, "My heads full of string bikinis."

"Ah lawdy, doncha let Katy know you're thinking of Luca in a bikini, man. She'll make yah do a boomerang again, dude."

"See what you started, kiddo?" chortled Rab.

"Ah think I'm gonna be sick, man," groaned Bobby.

"Pull da over da quick. Bobby sick not da good. He near killed poor Rusty wiv da puke."

Buzz screeched to a halt and Big Bob hurled the door open and heaved copiously over the road.

"Bejesus, now that's what I call a mighty impressive multi-colour fountain, man," Dan said in open admiration. Outstanding duck, that's an organic Picasso."

Luca got him a bottle of water from the mini bar and Bobby chugged it down. "Goddamn, that's better. Twice I've seen my breakfast today."

Rabbie climbed in the back and mixed him a double vodka, tomato juice, lemon juice, Worcestershire sauce, Tabasco and black pepper, wondering who Rusty was.

"'Hair of the dog'. Knock that back. I need you tip top to guard Mrs V."

Bobby chucked it down and belched mightily. "Holy cow, that hit the damn spot all right."

A passing cop on beat patrol stopped. "You folks okay? You're in the service lane."

Luca put her window down. "So sorry, Officer. Da big guy had a bad supper last night. He ver sick."

One look and the cop was hit by the Luca effect.

"You want the paramedics?"

"Nah man, ah am okay now, Officer. Ah had a hair of the dog."

"Sure okay, take your time. Good afternoon to you."

They drove off again, "A bad supper, right," scoffed Buzz, "More like a quart of Jack D."

"And mighty fine it was. I feel great now. Can I have another 'hair of the dog', Boss?"

"Ah reckon he wants the whole goddamn coat!" yakked Dan.

"I think one's enough for now, Bobby. Let it settle."

"Sure, Boss, work a beckons and life is good."

Rabbie turned to Luca. "And who the heck is Rusty?"

"I tell you von night, over a drink or two but not da food."

He went back to work, ringing the office on some matter. She sighed with pleasure. Oh to grow old with such a man! He would be her heart's content. She liked him that first day they met and knew deep down inside she would have made some excuse to 'accidently' bump into him again or turn up at some bar he frequented.

"Oh, fancy seeing you here, Rabbie. Let me buy you a drink," and then later? She shivered deliciously.

"You cold, Lucs?" he asked.

"Niet, am, how you say? Grand," she replied. Thinking that Wendy her world-wise friend would keep her right in that unknown area.

She and Bobby must have sex all the time. All the canoodling they quite openly did and the plain innuendo in their speech all the time, inferring 'the act' was imminent as soon as you left, was transparent.

Or was that just the way married couples got on. Comfortable with each other, like a form of sexual bragging in front of single people. "Hey, we're married and we can do 'IT' when, where and how we want."

She glanced at Big Bobby, who was dozing now. How the damnation did they do that? He was huge and would surely crush little Wendy. She guessed she clambered on him, or did he put her on the table or something? She stopped that train of thought dead.

"You okay young, missy? Glad da be out again in the big bad world?"

She patted Little Danny's huge mitt. "Da, tank you, Danny. So cool da be out with the guys."

"Damn right, little lady. We all just happy and glad you all getting better... Now you all take it easy for a spell."

She gave him a dazzling smile. Bobby and Danny were huge specimens of men, and she thought they were awesome.

"Indeed she will, Dan. Doctor's orders. If she over does it, I'll spank her arse for her," chirped in Rab.

Buzz groaned and the T levels rose again. Somehow the thought of Rabbie giving her a nice gentle spanking on his bed in subdued lighting gave her a nice spear thrust of lust and excitement in her secret place.

"I better overdo it then, master."

Buzz groaned again and Rabbie laughed, "Easy, you minx. You just might get what you don't want."

"Oh, I don't know. I know what I want, I think," she said nonchalantly.

Buzz ground his teeth in frustration. Maybe if he gave Katy a good spanking, she might spread them now and then and stop throwing him out.

"Easy tigress, easy," from Rabbie.

"Yessum, you behave. You been cooped up too long," explained Dan.

Bobby opened his eyes. "Yeah, you gotta take it easy, Luca. Yah don't wanna relapse."

"'Cause we all care 'bout ya, missy."

She patted each of the big guys' hands in turn. You had to keep it fair with men who cared about you. "Luca be good... I don't da know vot I would have done wivout you, Buzz, Mal, Billy-Jo and everyvon. You're fantastic."

Buzz reddened and looked contrite. He'd done his darnest to get a date with the lovely Ruski girl. He knew deep down he hadn't had a snowball's chance in hell of getting anywhere near her. She just wasn't that type. He's heard the boss tell Mal she was 'top totty', which he guessed was Britesse for a 'classy lady'. He pondered on his own marriage. His Katy was a fine-looking filly. She had thrown him out more times than enough for his many sordid transgressions, then forgiven him and let him back home. He smiled ruefully. Yep, the 'boomerang' moniker was well deserved. What the frig was he doing running about with tramps and sluts, buying them drink, then thirty minutes of romping about and ungratifying sex. Hell, he didn't even like most of them. Surely, Katy was worth more than that. Christ, why go out for hamburger when he had prime steak at home? Nope, time for a change of sea. Time to bury the boomerang forever.

"You going straight home tonight, Buzz?" the bossman asked conversationally.

"Sure am, Boss dude. Think I'll take my Katy out to dine and see 'Hangover 4'. She loves those films."

"Talking of hangovers. I think mine is coming back, Rab... I need a hangover cure."

"Nice try, hombre," Dan laughed, "No drinking on watch. We gotta guard Miss Sassy."

Luca smiled at Buzz, "Dat's nice of you, Buzz. I hear dat your Katy lovely lady."

Buzz thought about that. "Yep, she sure is, Luca. She wants to meet yah so you come for supper one night?"

Luca watched the empty steps of a metro station suddenly erupt with people of all shapes, sizes and colours from the hidden depths, "Dar, we would like dat, Buzz, vodn't we, darling?"

Bobby and Dan looked and grinned at each other. *Urrghuh!!! So that's how it was! One for Elaine and the office bush telegraph system.*

"Yeah, be great, Buzz. Thanks man," said Rabbie, liking the darling bit and pleased she'd included him; well, inferring they were a couple. It was a nice feeling.

"Sooo nice to be out. It's a long day in the coop with no rooster about."

Rabbie was on his cell again. Something about a function in Newark. Availability of cars and men.

Imagine growing old with him, she pondered. *All the kids grown and away. The sex not an issue but that being something they would keep going as long as possible. A good love life was important. Passing into old age together. Comfortable with each other and caring for each other's feelings.* She could think of worse things.

Then she beamed widely. They had all this before them, or so she fervently wished.

"What yah smiling at, Miss Luca?" asked Dan.

"Oh, I was just thinking about sex!"

Buzz slammed on the brakes to avoid going into the back of an airport bus. "For frigs sake, Buzz!" roared Rab.

"She's thinking about sex, Boss, Christ's sakes! Is that with or without the bikini, Luca?" he shouted over his shoulder.

Luca looked bemused, "Sex, Buzz. In sex day's time I be outta da hospital two weeks and I go back da work part-time."

Rabbie looked at Buzz with a locked, arched eyebrow. He grinned, Luca was at her work!

"You have a one track mind, Buzz. Now get us to Sassy's in one piece if you can."

* * *

329

The pavements were choc-a-bloc outside Sassy's new shop, Sassy's Choos and Clooes.

It was mainly press, cops, security and fans who had turned out in support.

They were ushered in and Big Bobby greeted his mistress manfully and stood protectively by her, as he would do for the next week.

Wendy had gone early to try on clothes to buy with her gift voucher. Waiters circulated with canapés and nibbles and trays of house red and white. Wendy had already had a couple of glasses, her hair of the dog, and was standing with the Mayor and Enrico in a beautiful black one-piece crocheted dress. Big Bobby thought she looked good enough to eat but instead settled for a plate of canapés, which he wolfed down.

Luca hit the shoes. She loved her footwear. Rabbie watched her try on a pair, admiring her trim feet and shapely ankles.

She finally settled on a pair of Jimmy Choo purple six inchers with an open toe.

She modelled for him, "What do you tink, darling?"

He had to admit they looked good, if not downright dangerous. "Sure look high. Good for the calf muscles."

"Den I get dem. Sassy practically giving dem away." She smiled devilishly, "Maybe I wear dem in bed one day wiv da string bikini."

Rabbie gulped. "You want wine? Red or white?"

"Vhy red, babe. Red wine for a scarlet voman."

She was definitely in a happy, carefree mood, and he admired her sharp wit and repartee.

At six they left. Rabbie got Buzz to drop them at Mama Jocelyn's because Luca wanted to see her big mate and she did Cajun chicken to die for.

Rab had to agree as he shovelled it down. It was delicious. He must tell his dad about this place. Pop was a bit of a gourmet now, and he liked trying food from around the world. He wondered how he was getting on with Simone[134]. Now that was one foxy, sassy lady.

Jocelyn came down and topped their water up.

"Not too hot for yah, handsome?"

"No, it's brilliant. Top marks."

Jocelyn beamed. Happy customers made her day.

"He likes it very hot, don't you, baby?" Luca said innocently, toying with her food with a fork.

"Well, yeah… Err within reason," he stammered.

Jocelyn gave him a huge wink. "The hotter, the better. Gets the sweat flowing, as they say in Louisiana."

He'd no answer to that.

They strolled home after and she held his arm tightly in the hallways, the elevator being 'Out of order' as per.

"That elevator will be the death of us," he moaned.

"Au contraire. I think it saved my life," and she reached up and kissed him, her breath hot and spicy.

She was drooping with fatigue he saw and scooped her up in his arms and straight down to the bedroom. "Right, clothes off and into bed. I'll get your water."

---

[134] Read – 'Mind Over Trigger'.

"You're so gallant, my knight. Tank so, sooo much."

When he came back, she was fast asleep. He climbed in beside her and watched her gentle rise and fall as she breathed easily and content.

He put the lights out. He was smitten by her. Besotted.

What the hell was he going to do about it?

Chapter 25
Curry Night and Confidence Building, Collette Style
(A Lesson in Sexual Etiquette)
('Something's Cooking in the Kitchen... Something's Steaming in the Air'... Dana... 1981)

The wounded men had whisked away as night fell, much to the girls' annoyance, "Talk about a bleeding vanishing act," Collette fumed. "Like bloody ships in the night."

"That's the army for yah, mate," agreed Kim. "Anyhow, they'll be home on sick leave soon," she consoled her.

"Better shift our arses into gear or we will miss the ferry," and she took off with a screech of tyres towards the docks. "'Ere, Coll, you better slow down," Kim advised, "They shoot people for less over here."

Collette lay on her bunk in the cabin, Kim snoring softly above her, rubbing her growing lump, the motion of the ocean making her a tad queasy and thought back to his last night of R & R, when he had taken her home for a cooking lesson.

Now that had been a night to remember, she grinned, whimsically. The big sod still had both hands then, and he certainly put them to good use in every way, she thought as she drifted off.

The next night Jamesey talked Eadie into letting Collette finish at eight, and he took her home in Clive's taxi. He eased himself into the back seat with her, and she immediately wrapped herself around him like a second skin and whispered endearments in his ear, much to the big West Indian's delight and a squirming Jamesey's chagrin.

She was so deeply in love she reckoned her heart was bursting and her insides melted every time he touched her. She had never known feelings like these before and cherished every moment she was with him.

"Yer can wipe that big cheesy grin of yer mush, mate," Collette told Clive as she caught his eye in the interior mirror, "Jamesey's takin' me to show 'ow to make curry. Ain't ya, darlin'?"

Clive laughed, "The hotter the better. You won't be makin' nothin' to eat if ya don't leave him alone."

"Just you stick to yer Waccy-baccy and mind yer own. Ain't that right, Jamesey?" and before either man could reply she was snogging Jamesey again.

When Jamesey finally got up for air, he laughed, "Don't worry, mate, I'll teach her discipline, got me a bag of Scotch Bonnets."

Collette thought back to the spanking Jamesey had given her that first night before and a warm glow of desire spread down below making her squirm against him in anticipation. "What cha on about, Scotch Bonnets? That's those stupid hats the Jocks wear."

Clive laughed loudly, "And also the hottest chilli in da world, babe, grown in ma own West Indies."

"Bloody freezin' in Jockland. Daft name for something so hot if ya ask me."

Once inside, but after an intense kiss and cuddle, which left them both breathless, Jamesey got his portable, two-ring propane gas cooker out and Collette watched with interest as he spread the ingredients on the kitchen bench. He produced two cans of McKeown's Pale Ale and as they guzzled them from the cans, he started preparing the vegetables.

He deftly skinned a large Spanish onion and sliced it paper thin using a potato peeler, making their eyes water, then he crushed eight garlic cloves and added them to the plate with the onions. A red and a green pepper deseeded and thinly sliced soon followed them.

Collette put on the transistor radio and bobbed away to T. Rex's 'Hot Love'. "How's that for a coin cadence, mate? Hot love and hot food, luvva duck."

"Hope you're paying attention, Coll, 'cause I'll be asking questions later."

"'Course I bleedin' am, luv. Where's these chilli hats then?"

He laughed and produced a brown paper bag with near reverence. "Gawd blimey, they do look like little hats," she remarked, fascinated, when he tipped the red triangular shaped chillies o to the counter.

"Took me hours and about ten greengrocers to find these beauties, only the best for my woman."

She liked being called 'his woman', it made her feel safe and loved, neither of which she had felt a lot in her life.

"Some chefs reckon you should de-seed the chilli because the seeds are too hot but really most of the heat is in the fruit itself," he informed her as he diced eight of them up and added them to the plate.

Collette picked up a seed and chewed it, "Nice enough, I like my seeds red hot," she purred as she wrapped her arms around him from behind and rubbed against him.

"Yeah, well one set of seeds at a time," he laughed as he peeled and diced a small potato and a carrot and added them to the pile, "These are optional," he informed her.

After gently unwrapping her arms from around his waist, he placed a pot on the stove, poured in some clarified butter and turned the heat on. "Indians call this 'ghee'," he told her, "It's just butter heated and when the top goes clear, it's skimmed off, but you could use ordinary cooking oil but not olive oil as it's too heavy."

"Oh okay, I'll make a note of that...no olive oil 'cause Popeye won't like it," she joked.

He laughed with her as he watched the ghee melt, and when it started to smoke, he added the chopped ingredients, which immediately started to sizzle and made Collette jump.

"Wow, what a great smell!" and she clapped her hands in delight.

"I have some pals in the Gurkhas and all the little buggers eat is curries," he said as he produced a clear bag full of spices and added three heaped teaspoons to the mix, stirring furiously at the sizzling concoction while adding a small amount of water.

"That's a real witch's brew you're making there," she remarked in awe. She felt so grateful, her bastard of a mother had never even taught her how to fry an egg and here was this handsome man taking the time to show her how to cook properly.

As the delicious aroma filled the kitchen, Collette was intrigued, "Cor, luv-a-duck, what was all that then? Smells great and fair clears the lungs."

He crushed and diced a small bulb of ginger. "Fresh ginger. Absolutely essential. Now the mix was a combination of cumin, coriander, cinnamon, cloves, cardamom pods, red chilli powder and black pepper pods," he listed as he continued to stir the mix. "Secret Gurka measures only known to them."

"Smells fantastic, babe," she breathed in close to the pot, "Looking forward to seein' how it tastes."

He added a can of chopped tomatoes, a teaspoon of sugar and a generous dollop of tomato puree before squeezing half a lemon and adding that to the mix. He gave it a good stir while adding half a pint of water and let it come to the boil before adding a pound and a half of thinly sliced beef, then he turned the gas down low and they watched as the mix spewed up bursting blobs, "Like a volcano just waiting to erupt," Collette observed, smiling.

He smiled with her…pleased she was happy. He added two teaspoons of an orangey powder from another bag, "Garam masala…more mixed spices from my Gurkha pals…sets it off lovely."

"I think I better put a bog roll in the fridge in case we erupt later."

He laughed at that, she was a card. He showed her a pot of fluffy, long-grain rice he had boiled earlier. "It's bleedin' yella, I never seen yella rice before."

"I put some saffron in to colour it and add a little flavour, or you can use turmeric powder, and I'll bung in a handful of peas, carrot and onion when I heat it up in the pan later and stir in a beaten egg."

"You'll be making me as fat as a horse, Jamesey."

"If you become a horse, Collette, you'll be a thoroughbred," he said, eyeing her trim figure and giving his curry a last stir. Satisfied with how it smelt, he put the lid on, "Half an hour should do it."

She eyed him mischievously, grinning. "Yeah, well love, if I'm a thoroughbred I need thoroughly rid…by you," as she wrapped her arms round his neck.

He kissed her deeply before she poked him in the ribs and pushed him in the direction of the sink. "Was your 'ands, darlin', don't want chilli fingers on me tender bits, now do I?"

He did as she bid listening to her as she skipped up the stairs and wearing a smug smile on his face. By the time he reached the bedroom, she was lying on his airbed wearing only a smile and a very skimpy pair of black panties.

"You think your curry is hot, buster, wait 'til ya seed what I've got on the boil fer ya," and she put her hand down her knickers, stroking herself as she spread her lovely legs.

It didn't take Jamesey long to shed his own clothes and join her on the bed.

* * *

334

Half an hour later Jamesey reluctantly dragged himself away to go fry the rice and serve up the curry, pulling on a tracksuit as he went.

He finished off cooking the rice and put it and two good servings of the broth on plates, pleased with the colour and consistency. It had turned out really well, and he was proud of his work. When he returned to the bedroom carrying the two plates of aromatic food, he was surprised to find Collette had been busy in his absence. She had brought a small overnight bag and after a quick wash she had brushed her hair and changed into a sheer black negligee.

He almost dropped the plates when he saw her, she looked gorgeous. How the hell do women transform themselves in such a short space of time? He had left her naked and dishevelled spread wantonly across the bed, and here she was sitting looking beautiful with an angelic smile on her face.

He realised he was standing transfixed with a silly grin on his face.

"For heaven's sake, love, would ya stop gawping, I could eat a donkey between two mattresses. Give us me scoff, it smells great. Me stomach thinks my throats been cut."

He shook himself and deposited a plate gently in her lap and she dug in with gusto, enjoying the delicious curry, blowing and puffing and waving her hand in front of her mouth as the heat hit her.

"Me gums have gone numb," she laughed, taking a large swig of pale ale, "It tastes as good as it smells, I see what ya mean, Jamesey, when ya say it's addictive."

He nodded his agreement as he munched hungrily himself, very satisfied with the outcome. As for addiction, he believed he could become very addicted to the lovely young female sitting beside him. "I promised you a hot one, Coll, and I don't think I've let you down."

"We'll see, luv," she said mysteriously, and gave him an impish grin that melted his big, strong heart.

* * *

They made love again, before starting to fall into contented sleep. Jamesey thought he had died and gone to heaven. Collette was just content at what was rapidly becoming a very serious, life-changing relationship.

Warm and safe in his arms, his massive presence in every way filling her with a contentment she never ever dared think possible, she fell asleep running The Electric Light Orchestra song 'Hold on Tight to Your Dreams' around in her mind... Well, her dream was right bleeding next to her and he wasn't going anywhere tonight.

"Ahh do declare, sah, you all have fair worn me out," she said, mimicking a Southern belle Alabama accent, after the last time.

"Frankly, my dear, I don't give a damn," he had replied in a like accent.

"Wotcha mean, luv?" she asked, confused.

"Famous line from 'Gone with the Wind', Clarke Gable."

"Oh, okay. Never seen it 'ave I? Night, luv."

"Night, my sex kitten."

She purred sleepily at him.

* * *

335

As dawn broke and the first birds were stretching their wings and unruffling their feathers she awoke to his big hand stroking her quim.

She grabbed his hand and brought it up to her breast, "'Ere mate, whatcha doing, what's da rush? You shouldn't treat me like one of your curries."

"Whatcha mean, Coll?"

"Well, prepare me properly, warm me up gently on a slow heat and when I'm nicely tender and bubbling nicely, beat in the meat, luv."

He laughed and kissed her, highly amused. "Or like a big juicy steak. Do both sides until the juices are sealed, then tuck into it, nice and pink inside?"

Now she laughed, then turned serious, "Anyhow, luv, a gentleman always starts up top with a lady and works his way down. It's proper manners. Correct etiquette for the bedroom, mate."

He laughed again, delighted, "I stand corrected, excusez moi," and stuck a big mouth to a cheeky nipple.

She pulled his face up to hers and gazed into his eyes intently, "You do think I'm a lady, Jamesey doncha?"

He saw she was serious, "Absolutely, ladies come in all shapes and forms. You're as good as anybody, Collette, anyhow you're my lady, and I wouldn't change a thing about you."

That mollified her. She pulled her negligee off "That's okay then 'cause whether you're the bleeding Queen or a poxy ten bob whore, the meat all goes in the same package dunit? And it all does the same job so what cha waiting for, luv."

He pounced on her chuckling, needing no second bidding. He liked this adventurous, humorous sex. It was different and took the awkward, embarrassing element out.

Ron had told him if you get the ladies laughing, you have their knickers half off. Jamesey reckoned it was the other way around in their relationship.

After, Jamesey went for a run and Collette had a nice soak in the bath. They finished the curry cold for breakfast. "Always tastes better next day because the flavours are well blended."

"It's brill cold, luv… Well it's never cold is it, it's curry ain't it?"

He had to agree. "The 'Yanks' are working on some microwave thing that reheats food in minutes. It's going to revolutionise the culinary world."

She scoffed, "Never catch on, mate. The poor housewives still be keeping their wayward husband's dinner hot in the oven!"

They wrapped up warm and walked hand in hand into town, Jamesey insisting the exercise would do her good. It was a pleasant, still late winter morning, and she felt proud as punch to be walking so intimately with him in public.

"Do yah love me, Jamesey?" then kicked herself mentally for pushing it.

"Take 'think' out of the equation. I know I love you, Collette, but a soldier's woman's lot is a hard one. Not many relationships last the course."

Reassured, she stopped him and gave him a kiss, having heard what she wanted, "Then we'll just take it one step at a time, luv, and go with the current."

"Sounds like a plan, Private Stark. Come on, I've got my name on a pint of Double D."

* * *

They entered The Peel still hand in hand, rosy-cheeked from their walk and Eadie raised an eyebrow knowingly at the new, radiant couple. Definitely a change in the semantics. They were certainly a good-looking couple. She would give Collette the full Spanish Inquisition over a cup of 'Rosie Lee'.

Collette skipped behind the bar, beaming happily at the regulars to pull Jamesey's pint as he got himself settled. She realised she was deliriously happy and hadn't thought about her tragic past for days and as the tears came and threatened to trip her, she plonked his pint in front of him and rushed out back crying.

Ron came in from the cellar. "What's wrong with Collette then? Thought she be happy now pervy Barry has gone."

Jamesey just shook his head, mystified, "I do not have a bloody baldy, Ron. It's all or nothing with Collette."

Ron grabbed a sneaky nip of whiskey, "Drink that pint down yah and I get yah one on the house… Different species, mate, I told yah, didn't I?"

Jamesey grinned. "True, governor, but bloody fascinating creatures. I love a challenge."

Collette came out later and put Roy Orbison's song on, 'Anything You Want You've Got It' before coming over and giving him a quick squeeze and a peck on the cheek, "And I mean it, mate."

The Irish navvies came in, a boisterous, noisy phalanx of working men cracking away with each other.

"Put him down, lassie, you don't know where he's been," shouted Mike from County Meath, "And get pouring 'The Shamrock' for us thirsty boys."

Jamesey laughed, "First ones on me, lads, now have you heard the one about the Billy goat, the priest and the chicken?"

Chapter 26
Rest and Rivals

She had shared his bed for over ten days now and apart from a few kisses and embraces, he had been an absolute gentleman and she admired him for it. As a female, she felt some guilt for putting him through such carnal torture but she was secretly thrilled by his fortitude.

He often worked strange hours. Coming home sometimes in the afternoons for a few hours before heading out to oversee some function or operation and would make her a nice lunch and then they would lie up and watch a film or Discovery channel and chat quietly. It was quite intimate and she felt more and more drawn to him. He seemed concerned at the age gap between them but she didn't care a fig. Rabbie kept himself fit with regular swimming and workouts at a keep fit club near his work, and she indicated to him she would like to join when she was better. The idea of them breaking sweat together and panting for breath was an intriguing idea.

"Absolutely, Luca. You go down a storm there in a string bikini and the swimming will soon tone you up."

She had punched his arm, "So you tink I need da toned up den, Rab?"

He had scrutinised her slim but shapely form. She was perfection personified, "Well no, but lying about all day makes the muscles get too relaxed and sluggish."

"Oh, okay. I like da swimming... Tell me, Rabbie, are we dating or vot?" she asked bluntly.

He eyed her carefully, "Well, you are sharing my bed and Doc Mac says you have to take it easy for another week, so I guess its kinda dating through force of circumstance, comprendí ciao?"

Her turn to scrutinise him now with those beguiling eyes. "Well, da I know dat, Rab. But if dis crapski wiv dat bastard Hanlon had not happened, would we be da dating?" she asked insistently.

He grinned, "Let's put it this way. I would certainly have been putting myself in a position where I kept bumping into you accidently and asking you out for a meal or a drink."

That seemed to reassure her and she looked pleased, "Ah okay. So we might be dating but now we kinda in a hiatus. Sorta indoor dating."

He laughed, admiring her clever take on things, "Guess so, but it's kinda nice as it is. Main thing is to get you over a very bad experience and get you better," then he followed as he recalled his earlier words. "Frig, I sounded like I would have stalked you if things were different."

She got up on her knees and pulled him into her warm compliant body...upset. "Don't you da dare compare yourself to that brute Hanlon. If you hadn't bumped

338

into me, I vould surely have been sure I bumped into you, da? I would be like dat Sharon Stone in 'Brief Encounters'[135]."

He was reassured and highly flattered. To have this stunner interested in him was a mega ego boost and to be stalked by her he had no problem with at all.

She looked deep in his eyes, searching, "So I guess we are at da stage between dating and becoming da lovers den." It was a statement not a question and it excited him, even more so when she placed her hands both sides of his head and proceeded to mesh her lips with his in a bruising kiss. Her lips tasted incredible, like a wild orchard and pressed flowers, and his tongue found hers and they collided and entwined, hungrily exploring terra incognita and their breathing got deep and ragged. Imaginary sweet singing birds sang and sang around their heads.

He broke off after a while, gasping and smiled into her half-lidded eyes. He had another week of this at least and his heart soared.

The doctor said she could go out for short walks and work part-time from home if she wanted to but nothing too demanding. Rab had brought her drawing board and art materials up and she was working on the ballet scene she had been so violently interrupted in completing. The good doctor had told him quietly it would be better if she didn't go out on her own for a while, not until she had her confidence back and the Luca watch were keeping a discreet eye on her. He had smiled at that. She was Russian/Lithuanian and probably thought nothing of being spied on, albeit in a caring way.

She had enjoyed the opening of SassyVanassy's shop and the fiery chicken gumbo in Mama Jocelyn's but he had seen the uneasy look she gave strangers and she was uneasy in crowds, and he saw the look of gratitude in her eyes when he insisted she stay with him as long as she wished, no strings attached.

He left for work with a spring in his step. He realised now that before Luca his apartment had just been somewhere to rest up and recharge the batteries and he never gave it any particular thought, but now he got a buzz towards the end of the working day knowing he was going home to his exotic flatmate. Or his inside date mate? His bed mate? Friend or potential lover? Both? He would go with the flow. Take it slow. But one thing was certain, she certainly brightened the place up!

A few days into her second week she told him she was going out to lunch with a friend and could she bring him back for a drink?

"'Course you can. I told you. Treat this place as your own," wondering who he was. Uneasy!

He got back at noon. They had a big operation that night in Brooklyn. A rich client who owned several meat-processing plants was being extorted by the Russian mafia, and they were going to tail the suspects and gather intelligence on them before planning a sting operation on them. He was briefing the boys at six and it could be a late one. She came out of the bedroom and joined him at the kitchen table where he was sipping coffee.

He looked at her and everything went slow mo. She looked incredible in a three-piece silk pantsuit the colour of fresh-cut grass. Her hair was up, held by a coral barrette, exposing her fine slim neck and long, dangly silver earrings flashed sexily.

---

[135] Eighties film where Sharon Stone stalks a married Michael Douglas. Famous where she crosses her legs, wearing no underwear.

She was lightly made up and her toenails peeping through strap sandals were painted the same red as those on her fingers.

He pulled a chair out for her and she smiled her thanks. A cloud of perfume assailed his nose. "Wow, that's some fragrance! What is it?"

"Is Issy Miyaki. Is ver' expensive. My friend Constantine got it for me at Christmas."

His mind turned wheels. "Constantine? Do I know him?"

"Niet, he son of owner in da Russian club where I sing," she answered, nibbling daintily on a chocolate chip cookie.

"I don't remember him visiting you in hospital."

"Constantine not do hospitals. Don't like them. He property developer. Ver' busy."

"You won't eat your lunch."

She smiled, "I am ravenous. He taking me da New York Hilton."

"Is he indeed? All right for some."

Her cell beeped. "He's outside. I bring you da doggy bag back."

"I'll walk you down." He knew she still didn't like being alone in the halls.

"Tank you, my gallant knight."

He saw her out and watched as she got into the rear of a stretch limousine. Constantine certainly pulled out all the stops, he guessed ruefully.

He lounged around the flat. Got showered and changed into dark surveillance gear. The flat seemed empty and colourless without her. He hadn't thought about her having a social life après Hanlon. Well, apart from Wendy and Bobby and he knew she sang at the club. He kicked himself for being a fool. She was a beautiful, interesting young woman. Of course she had friends. Look at the masses who had visited her in hospital. He suddenly felt all of his thirty-six years, lonely and foolish. He kinda knew deep down he wouldn't be able to hang onto Juliette for life but Luca? He'd refused to think of a future for them. Too early for that and insecurity gripped him again. Was all the kissing and intimacy she was throwing at him just gratitude for saving her from a fate worse than death? He just didn't know.

They arrived back at about four. Arm in arm. Giggling. Constantine was a lean, sallow-faced guy about Luca's age. He had black curly hair and dark eyes and was dressed in an Armani suit. He bounded over to Rabbie and introduced himself and proffered him a bottle of vodka. Rabbie shook his hand.

"Is very expensive vodka from Siberia, is my thank you for saving my Luca."

Rabbie took it and thanked him. MY Luca, indeed. He would give it to Bobby. He wasn't a great vodka drinker. It was a drink for gangsters and from the state of Constantine, it looked like he'd had a good few with his lunch. He studied his face. The red-rimmed nose and dilated pupils. Cocaine user. Rab knew his drug users.

"Connie had been dying to meet you, Rabbie. He very angry about what da happen to me."

"Yeah, I would have wasted that mother Hanlon."

"Yes well, we have laws in this country, anyhow, less said. Luca wants to put it behind her."

Constantine laughed, "In Moscow he would just disappear, know what I mean, dude?"

Rabbie did. Probably more than this spoilt rich brat did. "Anyway, can I get you a coffee? Drink?"

Luca was watching. Amused, "It's okay, Rabbie. Connie has da go do business."

"Sure have, but you're gonna come down the club tonight, Lucs?"

Rab interrupted, "She has to rest, doctor's orders. That right, Lucs?"

"Da, I mustn't overdo tings. I be back singing in a few weeks, Connie."

"Can't wait, baby. You're missed sorely," and he gave her a tight embrace and a lingering kiss. "I'll see myself out," and left in a wave of alcohol fumes.

Luca regarded him. "You didn't like him, did you?"

Rabbie straightened. "Haven't an opinion either way. A bit overbearing. How was your lunch?"

"Ahgh was fantastique. Beluga Caviar, lobster thermidor. Pavlova," and she laughed, "I am sorry, I make you hungry."

"Not at all. I had canned chilli and rice. Was great. You didn't drink too much? You know what the doc said?"

She sighed and arched her eyebrows heavenwards.

"I know Rabbie. I had three glasses Sancerre."

"Sancerre?"

She came and sat on his lap and played with his hair.

"It's a very dry French white. Nice with a fishy dishy."

"Oh, okay," mollified, adding it to his mental shopping list, "Must try it."

She stopped fiddling. "You know, Rabbie. I can answer for myself. I know I am not one hundred percent fit yet."

He put his arms around her, subdued. "I know you're sensible, Luca. It just me being a little overprotective. Silly of me. I just want you to make a full recovery."

"So you can kick me out and get your space back all to yar-self."

"Absolutely not," he replied stoutly, "My space is your space, it's a done deal."

She sunk her scimitar lips to his and they kissed deep. *Interesting*, thought Luca. *A little chink of insecurity in this amazing man's armour and he definitely had the jealous head on.* She would be careful of Rabbie around Connie. She had seen what Rabbie could do. He was a real man, a Viking warrior, whereas Connie was just a little boy playing at being an adult. Rabbie could rip him apart if he wished. She was quite aroused now. Not at the thought of men fighting over her but at the strength of the man whose knee she was perched on.

She broke off the kiss. "I go and rest now, my gallant knight. Get changed and freshen up."

He released her reluctantly. She giggled and grabbed her clutch bag. "See vot I got my strong man." And she pulled two lobster claws out, wrapped in plastic wrap.

"Now that's what I call a big crab!" he guffawed, touched she had thought of him.

"I make you da sandwich to take to work. Tis better than chilli!"

He knew she didn't like him eating canned chilli. "You're too kind, my dear," he said watching her trim departing ass. Philli and Wendy were coming up to watch films with her. Hangover one and two.

Time to hit the streets. Reassured she would be here on his return.

* * *

When he got back, she was fast asleep.

He gazed down at her dark head, flicked the television off, not wanting to watch Alaskan fishermen getting swept over the side in an Arctic storm.

Luca was unique. You couldn't turn lead into gold but Luca could make anybody or a full room of people think golden thoughts just by her presence. She brought her own unique store of inner sunshine into the room.

She was incredible but he was biased, and he realised now that not only did he feel protective and cared for her but he was also proud of her. Proud of how she had come through such a terrible ordeal but also proud of how she put others before herself.

He stroked her fantastic hair, realising now he was just proud to have her by his side and to be seen out in public with her.

He hadn't liked Constantine. Not liked him at all. Apart from being more Luca's age and having in common the fact that they came from the same vast country and spoke the same language, he detected as shallow weakness in the man and reckoned he would be a 'nobody' if he had not inherited wealth and couldn't get his confidence as a person unless he was snorting copious amounts of cocaine and buying free drinks all night for his hangers on.

Rabbie lingered on that thought. Guys like that were dangerous. Surely, Luca could see that? Sure, did Hanlon not have a similar upbringing? Spoilt stupid by his father and his criminal tendencies overlooked and swept in the corner.

No, he wasn't saying Constantine would go out and harm a woman just for his own perverse gratification but he was sure he got them drunk or high as kites on coke and talked them into bed. Rabbie knew if he had a daughter old enough to go clubbing, he wouldn't want her near the likes of him and would warn her about men like that.

Luca stirred in her sleep, and he pulled the quilt up over her and gave her space.

Surely, Luca could see the type of guy Constantine was? Why was it some women went for the bad guys instead of the ones who would love, cherish and protect them and not treat them as pieces of property or meat to be used and abused as and when they wanted and then discarded when the sell by date was up?

It was the one flaw he saw in Luca's character. She saw the good in everyone and was of such a nature she forgave the bad, thinking people learnt from their mistakes and toed the line after misbehaving.

Big Bobby and Rab had talked about it, and the big man had told him about the severe bollocking he had given her when the detectives had called to see about Hanlon stalking her.

He sighed. A leopard doesn't change its spots or a shark become a vegetarian, and the likes of Hanlon and Constantine go on until they are stopped, but unfortunately, they influence the weak and unwary and drag them down with them until they are put down themselves.

He crawled into bed and fell asleep, a worried old warhorse!

II

The second Friday she had to see Mr Shilburn. He studied her X-rays and declared her kidney to be fine and working well. "Just be careful next month or two about what you drink. Avoid hard spirits. I don't see any future problems. I'll see you in six months, Luca."

342

"I'll just be da little ol' wine drinker me," she sang. "Dean Martin song. Tanx, Doc."

He smiled, "Wine's good. Good luck, Luca."

She left beaming. Billy-Jo Sawyer met her in the hall. Rabbie had flown to Chicago for a meeting and was due back that night and had detailed her to take Luca for her appointment. "What he say, Lucs? All okay?"

"Da, I have da drink lotsa wine. American doctors sooo, so klass."

That night Doctor McKeever called up to see her. He had a glass of Beaujolais with her. He was pleased with how she was doing. She had finished all her meds and hadn't had a nightmare for several nights. She talked to Judith her counsellor when she felt the need. "You're doing great, Luca. Just take it one step at a time. I'm gonna put yah on a multi-vitamin and omega3 fish oil for a few weeks. Good for the insides. How yah sleeping?"

"Vell, I sleep better ven Rabbie here but I rest in the afternoon if I don't sleep well."

"'Kay, I'll keep yah on the herbal sleep aid for a while longer. They are non-addictive."

"Ah yes, the vunderful passion flowers. Tell me, dear Doctor, can I…you know…have da relationship thing now?"

He eyed her. "Well, everything seems normal downstairs. I guess if you've got someone lined up, you could but I'd rather you left it a bit longer. Better safe than sorry."

She pouted prettily, "Ver' well, Doc Mac. I just have da restrain myself."

"Anyhow, I thought your and Rab's wells were dry and barren," he asked mischievously.

She smiled wistfully, "Vell, it would seem dat both our wells are filling up nicely and about to overflow into each other."

He closed his bag and shrugged his coat on, "Well, then you two just go with the flow and God bless the pair of yer. You're a match made through adversity and that gives yah both a little bit of a stronger bond than other couples."

She rose to see him out. "You're da very nice, wise man, Doc Mac. A true philosopher."

"Dunno about that. Just seen and heard it all over the years. Cheerio, Luca dear!"

* * *

Rabbie got back late and crawled into bed. Luca was wearing a white lace nightdress, very low cut. He gazed at the top of her creamy breasts, and she pulled him to her like a mother with a child and he nestled between them content and she stroked his hair and soothed him to sleep. "Soon, my gallant knight, soon."

She dreamed that Rabbie and her were making love in the 'glade' in the Lithuanian forest she and Galen called their own and tears softly flowed down her unblemished cheek because she knew with all clarity that Galen would have thoroughly approved of her gallant knight, and it was time to move on to another stage in the journey of life.

Next morning Rab was up early and was packing a change of clothes in a small carry on. She watched, sipping coffee. He had awoken bleary-eyed pressed into her back, and she had felt his erection and she felt guilty and sorry for him.

Her maman had explained to her that men were different from women in their desires. They felt a sudden urgency that if not satisfied could cause dissent and resentment in a relationship, whereas women tended to build up slowly and simmer. "It's not their fault, poor things, and most men can control their urges but let's face it, if you have a sweet tooth and you live in a sweet shop all day, you're going to give into temptation."

"What are you saying, Maman?" asked a young interested Luca, secretly thrilled her mother was treating her as an equal adult.

"Well at times in a relationship you have to make sure your man's happy even if you have to go without yourself."

"Or what, Maman? What will happen?"

"Well, he might go to a different sweet shop for a different brand of toffee or he might become sullen and withdrawn and a pain in the ass. Men are a different species to us, dear. They live for the pleasure of the moment whereas we tend to live for the long haul and a deeper satisfaction."

Luca remembered those words now. Her period had started the night before. Instead of cursing it, she found it a strangely cleansing experience. Comforting after Hanlon. Her female ID reassuring her that all was well with her womanliness.

"So tell me again, Rab. Why da you going to Boston?"

"Gotta loada new guns for them so I'm gonna drive them up. Check things are running smooth, and then drive back tomorrow. You're staying with Wendy."

She put her hands on her hips indignantly, "No da way da hose. It dair weekend off and I be pussy in the middle."

He had to grin when she mixed her metaphors up.

"And it your weekend off too. Why someone else not take dem?"

"It's boss work. Anyhow you know Wends and the 'Big Guy' love having you to stay, even if you are piggy in the middle," he threw in with a smile.

She hopped out of bed, "You work too da bloody hard. I come wiv you. I help da driving."

"It's only a couple of hundred miles. I'll be grand."

She headed for the bathroom. "You'll be even grander wiv me wiv you. Beside I never have been da Boston. It where da Yankees kicked your Brit asses[136]."

He laughed. "It's full of you mad Ruskis now. I'll be back tomorrow lunchtime."

She turned and looked back through a crack in the door, "It da be our first weekend away. I'm going or I let da air out of your tyres."

He gave up gracefully. When Luca was forceful like this, there was no turning her back. "Fine, I know a nice little hotel by the harbour."

She threw the door open, delighted and gave him a huge hug. "Vunderbar. You da so cool guy. You von't be sorry," and she slammed the door and he heard the shower start.

Their first weekend away. The word dirty crossed his mind, but he doubted that somehow and sighed in frustration. Why the hell could he not have saved a twenty stone Russian shot putter on steroids instead of the most beautiful divine creature on God's earth?

He listened, Luca was singing Dean Martin's 'Little Ol' Wine Drinker Me! Surely not. That lady would never be left sitting alone in a corner like in the song.

---

[136] 1773 'The Boston Tea Party'.

* * *

They drove to the office and Rabbie picked up the firearms for the Boston team. A couple of M16s, two pump actions and some Glock pistols. Hopefully, they wouldn't need them but Boston was the bank robbery capital of North America and better safe than sorry. He knew the importance of superior firepower in a hostile situation from his service days. Battle rules when you come under effective enemy fire:

Locate the enemy! Win the firefight! Attack!

"At least if the Boston crew bump into the robbers, they'll have the tools to fight back."

She agreed, betting her bottom dollar Constantine wouldn't know one end of a rifle from another. She looked at his strong profile as he threaded through the traffic out of the city. "Vell, if someone tries da carjack us, they'll get da big shock ven you open da boot."

He laughed. She looked very pretty in a two-piece navy linen suit, ruffled blouse and knee high boots. When stuck in traffic he'd seen the way other male drivers ogled her and felt proud and jealous at the same time. Then again he couldn't blame them for that. She was a looker all right, and when he was out driving with the guys, didn't they ogle the lady drivers and make comments on them. Christ, Boomerang had a points scoring system. One to ten and they would laugh as he point scored them, often loudly and they would argue and debate the unsuspecting woman's vital statistics.

"Hey, if you don't look, you don't get," was Boomerang's catchphrase, "and you don't get, you fret."

He hit a Starbucks for mega lattes and blueberry muffins. He smiled as he watched her put God knows how many sugars in her coffee, snug in its holder, and dig happily into a muffin.

She caught his grin and wiped a crumb off her lush lips. "Vot? I'm a growing girl. I need da sugar hit," but she was always pleased when she secretly amused him.

They hit the freeway and they cruised along on the speed limit companionably, Bruno Mars serenading them from the radio.

"Couple hundred miles. 'Bout three hours," he told her.

"Two hundred and da eighteen or three hundred and fifteen kilometres, I 'googled' it."

After an hour he pulled over and let her drive and read some paperwork.

She drove confidently and read the road ahead astutely. He was pleased. It was a bonus when you had a beautiful, confident Russian near girlfriend to spell you at the wheel.

When they reached the outskirts of Boston, he took over again. "Hey, I'm impressed. Good, confident, progressive driving, Luca."

"Yah, I used to da drive Mama's old Traskent around da Drasnov, delivering her sewing."

"Bit different over here though. Mega traffic."

"Guess so, Rab. I suppose I should da apply and get da licence then I can drive you all the time."

345

He blanched. He'd assumed she had her test passed and all. "Err, yeah. We'll get that sorted for you." What the heck! The girl was a natural and never ceased to surprise him.

At the Boston office they dropped the firearms off, and Rab ensconced himself in the office with Kung for an hour and Luca went for a walk and browsed the shops. She saw a lovely tan Remo jacket on sale in a boutique that she just knew would look great on him and she counted her dollars and bought it.

Returning, she sat in the office and chatted with Kung's girlfriend, Susie, a petite blonde Bostonian, then when the men concluded business, they went for a late lunch in a small French bistro which did coq au vin to die for.

After, they drove down to the old harbour and booked into a small hotel called 'The Boston Smuggler'. It was old, quaint and comfortable.

They went for a walk along the promenade to help lunch settle, then returned for a rest. The double room was tasteful and boasted a big canopied double bed. She took her boots off, flashing pink hosed legs, pleased to catch him peeking and she stretched out and yawned. "Tis the ozone in da sea air. It da make me sleepy."

He lay down with her and she snuggled into him. "Thanks for bringing me, Rab. Now I can say I had been da Boston."

He was reading a report Kung had given him, "Sure, you can tick it off the list. Glad of the company," and he looked at her but she was asleep, arms across him. He marvelled again at the length of her lashes. She was content, he was content. She had brought him a beige Remo suit jacket. It wasn't a colour he normally would have chosen but when he tried it on, he found it suited him. She had good taste but then again she was an artist and picking and matching colours was a big part of her life.

They dined well, Rabbie wearing his new jacket. He had the rib-eye and baked spud, and Luca a prawn salad because she was watching her figure. He had a grin. She had the metabolism of a Tasmanian devil or one of those wood chipping machines.

After, they had a few drinks in the bar then went to bed early, tired after their long day.

Luca sat up in bed brushing her hair, stunning in a sheer black negligee.

He brushed his teeth, feeling strange to be in a hotel room with Luca. He pulled on a pair of pyjama bottoms and a vest and went to join her.

He climbed in, and she folded herself into him and gave him a long kiss. He flicked the lamps off and they went to sleep.

As she dropped off, comforted by his bulk, she smiled gently, *There more than one way to catch a nightingale in the bush*, she told herself.

* * *

Next morning, she woke early, refreshed. Rabbie was sleeping with his back to her, a heavy masculine heat radiating off him.

She sat up and pulled her negligee off and lay close to him and began kissing his neck and stroking down his back. He groaned throatily. She reached down and found his erection peeking out of his bottoms. It was hard, hot and thrilling. She stroked up and down its shaft, her heart racing.

346

He rolled over and gazed at her through slitted eyes, which opened wide as he spied her naked perfect breasts. She bent down for a hot, sweltering kiss, and his hands reached for and fondled her breasts hungrily.

She increased her pace, and he nuzzled down her neck and throat, then took a breast in his mouth and sucked and chewed on an eager nipple.

He was gasping and writhing under her hand now, and she felt him spasm and she gripped tighter and pumped faster, and he pulled her back into a grinding kiss as he exploded hugely, shouting her name over and over.

When he'd got his breath back, he looked her in the eye. "Not that I'm not grateful but what the hell brought that on?"

She gave him that mysterious woman smile, "Dat to stop you going da different sweet shop."

That stumped him "O…kay. Bit one-sided though. You all right with this?"

She looked up thinking, a twinkle in her gorgeous eyes "Da, was fun. I am gently simmering and can for a long time."

Too deep for Rabbie. "Okey-dokey. Shower then breakfast. You hungry?"

"Always dahling, always."

* * *

They drove back leisurely, a new intimacy between them. He let her drive on the freeway again, not caring if they got stopped or not. It was in the hands of the gods, and he surmised the gods were onboard to keep safe the goddess happily speeding down the road home.

At the end of the second week, the subject of her staying never even came up. He knew she was very reticent about going back to her own crib and was happy enough to stay on. In fact, he relished the prospect. He knew he was in love with her, but he was determined to take it nice and slow. Easy goes it.

He wined and dined her, and they had several more very intimate little episodes. At the end of the third week he took her to get her cast off. She laughed at her pale arm. "Is such da relief. Was so bloody itchy."

"Well, I guess it's another little step towards putting what happened behind you, and you can look forward to happier days ahead."

She hugged him, delirious "But dese are happy days, Rabbie. I am so happy wiv you. It fantastique… Are you da happy, Rab?"

He hugged her back. "Sure am. Life's good."

She got serious then. "You know I go back da work full-time Monday. We not see as much of each other."

'We'll make time. It'll be all the nicer."

"'Kay, we must always make time for each other. Adversity da bought us together, happiness won't tear us apart… Do you like borscht?"

"Borscht? Some type of soup isn't it?"

"Da, Russian soup. I make it for our supper one night."

"Oh, okay. See you then."

He went to work smiling. Culinary skills were not Luca's forte but God bless her for trying.

III

She had returned to work full-time that Monday but Simon had insisted she take no more contracts on for the time being. She agreed, grateful for his concern but then looked inwardly. She felt very restrained in her life at present. Tired of being fussed over. She was Luca...Luca Valendenski... Girl about time, then she felt bad. Her friends and colleagues had been fantastic to her and were only looking out for her best interests.

"He such da lovely man, Rabbie. He too come through da terrible time as a child at da hands of da Nazi pigs and is sooo sad he losing Peter. They da so much lurve for each other."

They were sitting up in bed eating mango cheesecake Mama Jocelyn had sent up, watching some programme about parrots in South America.

"Yeah, it's sad all right but hell, Luca, they made one heck of a success of their lives and hey, Peter's near ninety. Good age and sure Simon's plenty of friends. He'll be okay."

Luca was wearing black silk pyjamas that rustled sexily as she moved about. "Da, I guess so, but I be there for Simon through dis. He my second papa."

He watched her out of the corner of his eye. She was entranced by the colourful macaws chittering and chattering on the screen. "Well, anything I can do, let me know. What about we get them over for dinner?"

Christ, we sound like an old married couple, he thought, grinning. He was happy it suddenly struck him.

She clutched his arm tight and nestled into him. "Dat sooo sweet, Rab. I don't think Peter be able but afta he go to da light, we keep da eye on Simon. Look after him."

He was baffled, "Yeah sure, we can do that... What's the light, Luca?"

She looked into his strong, trusting eyes, not sure how much to say, but she trusted him and didn't want to or see why she should keep anything from him. He was her confidante and soulmate. She knew he would not mock her.

She sat up, pensive look on her lovely face, "When I thought dat all vos lost when thugs were trying da defile me, and my strength vos all but gone and da pain overwhelming me, and I had da no more breath to da curse them for da rabid sick dogs dey were, before my gallant knight came so bravely to my rescue," and she paused and kissed him and kept her slim arms around him before continuing, "I vent into da trance state. Bright light filled my mind. Obviously, my love, I taught I was for da next vorld. The light was bright and warm and it vas comforting. It shone down an avenue lined with blossoming cherry trees and at da end my Galen stood, arms beckoning me, telling me to come da him, dat everything would be okay." She shrugged, "And den you came in like a wild dervish and sorted da bastards out... And it vos", and she kissed him again, "so meant da be. Vasn't my time." '

When they came up again for breath, he didn't know what to say but he knew she was such an honest, natural person he had to believe it. Some of his mates in the marines who had had near death experiences told of strange lights and dead loved ones calling to them with open arms, but he never knew if it was the beer talking or a wind up but he converted now because Luca never lied.

"Anyway, I put dis behind us. We move forward and may our light of love dispel the fetid darkness of unhappiness on the paths we tread ahead."

He looked in awe at her. She was outstanding. That he had come across this heavenly creature in such dire circumstances and had been graced to save her from a pack of violent, hate-filled sexual predators, who were surely going to hell, was reward enough for him, but to still be in her bewitching company weeks after and to be taken into her confidence and be given her deepest thoughts and secrets was mind-blowing. Rabbie wasn't a great believer in the paranormal but he believed every word she had said implicitly and felt blessed to be so trusted. She was near up to goddess status in his mind and eye.

She nuzzled his neck and stroked his hair. "Da small macaws in da Peruvian Amazonian Basin mate for life. When dey leave da nest in da morning to go to da do what da parrots do, dey kiss and cuddle and fly off happy. Small macaws don't survive if caught and put in da cage. Dey don't drink or eat and die of a broken heart so da Indians leave dem be."

He realised he was aroused, and she was stroking him and she slithered down and took his length in her mouth, and he groaned and exploded like a million blossoms taken off a cherry tree in a sudden tempest.

She looked up at him with eyes beguiling and glistening scimitar lips, and he could hear his heart singing and thought it was going to jump out of his chest and dance around the bed.

After she gave him a satisfied, internal feminine look and chuckled, "We just like da macaws in Peru, free to fly with our love forever," and wiped him off her lips and fell into an easy slumber.

As she lay so trustingly into him, her head on his chest, cast-free arm across him, he revelled in her gentle breathing, her sweet breath, the warmth from the contours of her body comforting him. He was replete and content and wanted her by his side like this forever.

* * *

The fast dictates and demands of the concrete swamp they inhabited had little time for a far-reaching mind like Luca's. You conformed. Followed routine, rules and regulations. Fashion, food and diet trends. New model cars. Let on you were one of the gang. "Wow, did you see the latest 'Cruise' movie? So contemporary."

"Yeah, was brilliant," afraid to say it was crap and not be sneered at by the masses… "Hey, dude, try the new sushi diet and soy bean? It's the in thing…"

"Yeah, great," hating that crap but not wanting to be mocked… "Whoa, man. Wise up. Jackets and jeans are out. Get fashion sense, guy." Who really gave a fiddler's fart?

No, Rabbie saw that Luca went with the flow, and she was conscientious at her work and needed 'da dollars' to bring her family over but she really didn't take it too seriously. She was very much a free spirit and mistress of her own mind. Yeah, too trusting and caring and prone to take in every sob story she heard, but it was refreshing and he didn't reckon she would ever be a true New Yorker but with such a rapier-sharp mind, gorgeous looks and an inherent interest in her fellow man, she would fit in anywhere on the globe she ended up on. People just took to her and saw and enjoyed the unique phenomenon she was. She was an extraordinary living work of art and he could study her all day.

Most of urban society lived base, frigid, petty little lives where the bank account balance dictated the dos and don'ts, where the money god ruled supreme and the green dollar was worshipped and shredded and discarded morality like ticker tape in a sandstorm. Gone with the Wind. Another day, another dollar. It was puerile and soul-sapping.

He sighed again and watched the shadows on the ceiling. He saw dark, thundery clouds and evil-shaped creatures lurking in the corners waiting to swoop down and devour them.

Luca rolled over and sat up and pulled him into a consoling embrace "Vot is wrong? My gallant knight. You are da very restless, my love."

He looked into her eyes, luminous and full of mystery in the dark. "Oh, I don't know. I was just thinking about Constantine and what the fuck you see in him?"

She digested that for a while. Sat up straighter. "I feel da sorry for him. I no notion romantically towards him. He drug user and buys friends. He very much under da father's thumb, who, how you say, da Mafia gangster dude." She paused, searching for words, "Da, I been going wiv him da drug rehab scheme. He wanta kick da habit. I just his friend. He wants to change. Be his own man. He is da victim to da drug dealers."

Rabbie felt a complete fucking idiot. Of course Luca knew what Constantine was. She was astute and aware, and he had misjudged her. "Sorry, Luca, I just don't want you getting hurt again. I misjudged you. He's lucky he has you for support."

She kissed him. Liking this jealous streak that had arose in her knight, revelling in the power it held but also knowing it was a dangerous animal that needed kept well and truly locked up in its cage.

"Lie on da front and I give you da massage. You da very tense."

He complied and she straddled him. He could feel her womanly heat through her thin pyjamas as she kneaded his knotted neck and shoulders. "Is da good exercise for my arm after getting plaster off..." she paused, "Did I ever tell you about my Galen? I don't think I did."

His turn to pause, then, "No, Lucs. You haven't, and I didn't want to pry but I gather he was very important to you."

Her fingers probed deeper, separating and sorting his knots out soothingly. "Da, he was my first love. He was ver' special. You vould have da liked he, Rab, and I know he would have da liked you... Vill I tell you 'bout him?"

She was working either side of his spine now. "Yeah, I'd like that," he grunted with pleasure.

So she did, and eventually when she finished, she rolled off him and lay gazing at him, eyes moist. "It his birthday today. I sent Maman money to lay flowers on his grave."

He took her in his arms. "Christ, Lucs. That was rough. That's an absolute crime. What a tragic waste of talent...Do you think... You know... Do you think Galen is happy you're here with me?"

She snuggled in, "Yes, Rab. He be ver' happy I meet such a strong, da decent, honest guy."

"So if a choice between him and me, who would you pick?"

She laughed, not a little unbitterly. "You men always tinking rivals. I don't know and da never will. Dar always little space my heart for Galen. Can a vommen love da two men? Who knows?"

He hugged her tight. "Sorry, Luc… Did I ever tell you about Sammy?"

She flicked the bedside lamp on, intrigued. Luca loved a good secret story. "Dis, your skeleton in da closet, Rab? Please da tell all."

He smiled, ruefully. "In a sense. I never told Mom or Pop she was dead. Mom adored her. I told Mom the relationship had run out of road and it had in a sense," and he hung his head.

Luca got the vodka bottle Constantine had left, and they had a shot each and shared a rare fag.

"Now tell me, my love. It do you good."

So he did. At length. Fighting back tears he felt he had shed over a decade ago.

She listened, aghast, topping his glass up at regular intervals.

When he finished, two solitary tears ran down and hung off his chin. She kissed them off. She was amazed her knight was weeping, she had not thought he would cry in front of her. He was always so self-contained. She felt strangely pleased and honoured.

"And you not know what sex da baby was?"

"Naw, was too wee, but I called it Sammy junior. Unisex name," and two more tears dropped.

She was more upset now. "But vhy did you not tell your parents?" She felt hollow inside for him.

He looked up. "Dunno. Mom had a terribly hard childhood, shite family and she loved Sammy, so I thought it would be easier on her."

Luca thought that was one of the most unselfish things she had ever heard in her young life, and that he could still shed tears and grieve for the one he loved more than a decade and a half ago just made her esteem for him shoot out of the roof. "I'm afraid I was just da bitch. I took my loss out on da everyone."

He took her hands, "I don't think there is any set rules or formulas for grief. For those left behind, you make your own up and get on with it."

"Da, I guess so. Not like you can go da bookshop or ring up and say, 'Scuse me, bastard just blew my fiancée up or a twenty-ton lorry decided to take da shortcut and wipe da future missus out,' vot da protocol for da broken heart?"

He watching her intently, then he burst out laughing, "Fuck, Luca, you should be on television. That's priceless," and he topped their glasses up. "A toast. To my unmet friend Galen. To golden Sammy and little Sammy Junior."

She raised and clinked her glass to his. "Da, wherever dey are, wherever they be, may dey be happy, safe and da carefree."

They downed their drinks, spluttering, half pissed by this stage. They did another toast. Old Scottish one, he told her. "May you live as long as you want, and never want as long as you live."

"They very cleverski," and she hiccupped.

She pulled his vest off, and then took her pyjamas off and stood before him in all her magnificence. He was agog.

"Now I show you how da we can pleasure each other without crossing da border."

The next hour rocked the socks off both of them, and as she slept in his arms, Rabbie wondered just who it was had died and gone to heaven because surely he was there now.

351

Next morning, they went through their routines. Dressed, breakfasted and went to work, both slightly dazed and hungover.

"Hey you okay, Lucs? You look like you've landed on the planet Zog and are lost in space."

Luca sat down behind her desk. "Da, Philli, tank you. I have da nightingale in da bush, trapped, I just have da work out how to get it into da cage now."

Philli laughed, "You da crazski, Ruski, huskie."

* * *

Rabbi entered the office whistling, swinging his briefcase happily. He greeted the guys effusively, shouted to Elaine for strong coffee and went into his office, shutting the door firmly with a back heel and plopped behind his desk, leaned back, hands behind his head, and gave a huge sigh of contentment.

Outside Buzz nudged Mal. "Guess who's got the shagski, alnitski with the Ruski?" he said wickedly.

Big Danny heard and gave him a tremendous dead arm, and he howled with pain.

Elaine passed him frostily with the coffee, "Buzz dear, you have a mind like a dung heap and a mouth like a sewer."

Buzz squirmed, rubbing feeling back into his arm. When she came back out, she was smiling. "But you would be right, Buzz. Rab says to get the paperwork sorted, clean the firearms, then we'll all go to Maloney's for lunch, his treat."

"See, I told yah he's screwing her," laughed Buzz, dodging away from Danny nimbly.

Mal grinned, "Naw, they just sit in bed all night knitting and doing crosswords, you moron."

Even Little Danny looked sceptical at that one.

Chapter 27
The Birth and Rise of On La Guardia

Ten Green Hand Grenades, Sitting on a Wall...
Ten Green Hand Grenades, Sitting on a Wall...
. And If One Green Hand Grenade Should Accidentally Fall...
There Be No Green Hand Grenades and No Bloody Wall.

Part 1

Musgrave Park Military Hospital, Belfast

Late June 1976

Jamesey and Smudger sat in the recreation room feeling sorry for themselves. Apart from being bored witless, the doc had cut their pain relief down and had them on codeine and paracetamol.

"Bleedin' quacks," bemoaned Smudger, "that morphine was friggin' class gear. Now me bloody leg feels like some sadist is poking red hot irons in it."

Jamesey shrugged philosophically, his stump throbbed malevolently, "Guess they didn't want us getting addicted, mucker."

Smudger threw his hands up dramatically, "Oh, the dreams, the dreams. They were class. Now they are making us pop so many pills, I bleedin' rattle when I walk."

Jamesey agreed, "We are a right old pair, mate, and they give me the threepenny bits."

Smudger looked quizzical, "What's them, mate?"

"Just one of Ronnie's from The Peel's cockney slang things. Threepenny bits...the shits. My arse is on fire brother."

Smudger laughed, "Johnny Cash, 'I Got Me a Burning Ring of Fire'."

He had to grin at that, "You got it in one, mate. You could boil a kettle on my butt cheeks."

"I'll pass on that one, mate. Still, never mind, we'll be out of here soon."

An orderly brought them in elevenses; tea and digestive biscuits.

A group of soldiers in dressing gowns and adorned in a variety of bandages, the walking wounded, were playing Gin Rummy at a table across the room. "Oye! One of you go down to my locker. My mother sent a fruit cake over, laced with brandy and there's half a bottle of Scotch. We'll have a swallow with our tea."

One soldier limped off willingly.

"And don't let the Dragon Queen catch you!" Jamesey shouted after him.

Half an hour later the tasty cake demolished and the empty bottle hid under the cushion of Smudger's wheelchair, their mood had lifted when said dragon came in and stood before them. She could smell the whiskey fumes but chose to ignore them.

"So, Colour DeJames, Sergeant Smyth, you're leaving us tomorrow for greener pastures. I'm off tomorrow, so I'll say goodbye now and wish you a full recovery. I must say it's certainly been interesting nursing you."

Jamesey, always the gent, stood and took her hand and kissed the back of it gallantly, "The pleasure, Mein Fräulein, has all been ours. You and your staff are a credit to the Army Medical Corp."

He was then gobsmacked when she pulled him into a huge embrace, crushing him to her immense bosom, "God bless you, my brave boys," and releasing him she fled the room. Jamesey swore he saw a tear in her eye.

"Fuck me, Jamesey," Smudger laughed, "I reckon Matron wants your body, mate."

Jamesey smirked, "I reckon you need a welding set and a pound of TNT to get her drawers off, but she ain't a bad old stick."

Collette and Kim entered, looking pretty in summer frocks. She kissed him, then asked, "Whose drawers yer gonna blow off, love?"

Smudger laughed, disentangling himself from Kim, "You better watch out, Coll, Matron has a serious crush on Jamesey."

The girls had been over for a week now and were going home later because the men were being transferred to Rinteln British Military Hospital in West Germany. They weren't amused at all, "Why they sending yeh to bleedin' Germany for, Jamesey? Why not back to England?" she asked, getting upset.

He plonked her on his knee, wondering how much to tell her. A Captain in the 'Green Slime' had called in to see them earlier and briefed them on developments. A source had told them that after 'The Battle of Glenmacadoon Square', the IRA leadership had placed a massive bounty on their heads. "Basically, chaps, you are open season for every provo in the province and they know you are here, so we have stepped up security, but we think it would be prudent to move you out somewhere safe for a while. Keep a low profile, so it is British Army on the Rhine for you, lads. Pretty Fräuleins and big steins of German beer."

"Sod that, Boss," snarled Smudger, "Give us a couple of gympies[137] and plenty of ammo and drop us up The Falls and we'll soon sort the fuckers out. Right, Jamesey?"

"Fucking A, mate. I hope to be back on duty the week's out."

The Captain looked at them aghast: they were deadly serious. They were madmen. All who wore the Red Beret were, "Gents, you will not be fit for duty for many months to come," he spluttered. "Anyway, it is from the top. You will be smuggled out under cover of darkness tomorrow night to RAF Aldergrove and flown to Germany. End of story!"

Smudger had snorted, "Smuggled out the back door at night like a couple of tarts after an all ranks stag night. Friggin' disgrace."

"Save your breath, Smudger, when the powers to be decide, they are not for shifting," and he pointed his good finger at the Captain. "But mark my words, Captain, Smudger and me haven't finished with the IRA yet."

A flushed Captain left hurriedly, Jamesey scowling after him, not knowing how true his words would be in years to come.

---

[137] General purpose belt-fed machines guns.

So, as he bounced his little Collette on his knee he answered, "Just procedure, my little flower. Rinteln has a good Amputee Unit. They'll fix me up with a plastic hand, probably have a bit of trimming up then we go to the Rehab Unit in Hamlyn, then hopefully home and back on duty."

"When yeh goin' then, luv? I'm gonna miss yeh, babe." She was near to tears he saw, and he hugged her to him in reassurance. "Can we go down to your room, luv? I need to talk to yeh in private."

He gazed into her lovely hazel flecked eyes, "Sure, come on then. Back soon, folks."

As they went, Smudger sniggered, "Away for a bit of nooky, randy sods."

Kim slapped him on the shoulder. "You've a one track mind, luv." She looked thoughtful. "No, Collette's about to drop another bombshell on Jamesey's head, and I just hope he's the man I think he is."

"And what type of man is that, then?" asked a mystified Smudger.

"One that stands by his actions and does the right thing and doesn't run away from his responsibilities."

Smudger shrugged, "Well then, she ain't got nothing to worry about then, has she? Now, tell all, dear wife."

* * *

He sat on the bed and she perched on the edge of the visitor's chair nervously, twisting and pulling at her fingers. Jamesey watched, intrigued, the pain in his stump clean forgotten about now. God! She was a fascinating creature!

"Collette, chill out, kiddo. What's wrong? You haven't met an Irish lad or pranged Mike's Rover, have you?"

She glanced up, "Yeh know I told Matron I was yer fiancée, so I could get in to see yeh? Doncha?"

He smiled, "Yeah, I admired the subterfuge. You're a devious, deceitful little minx, but I commend your style."

A single tear trickled down her cheek, "I ain't deceitful, Jamesey, honest I'm not or devious," she bemoaned.

He was worried now, "Christ! Coll, what's wrong?" then a hesitant smile crossed his face. "You're not asking me to marry you, are you?" It was meant to be the other way around.

She sniffed, "Nah, mate. Nought like that," then in a small voice, "I'm in the Puddin' Club, ain't I?"

He had to strain to make sense of what she had so tentatively revealed, "What club? What you joined the AA or Women's Guild or something?"

Collette stood and took his face between her gentle hands, "No, Jamesey. I'm pregnant. Having our baby, ain't I? It was a mistake and if yeh don't wanna have anymore to do wiv me, it'll break me heart, but I'm gonna have the kid and rear it right and proper."

His mouth dropped and he felt lost for words, which was a rare event for Jamesey. Then a huge smile broke across his face and he spread his arms, "Come here, you soppy mare. So, I'm gonna be a dad. Bloody hell. Bad enough the IRA chucks bombs at me; I think I'm back in shock."

She rushed into his arms and cuddled up to him, tears flowing, "Sorry, luv, I wasn't trying to trap yah."

He stroked her hair, calming her, "Hey, hey, hey. We were a bit careless, I guess. Christ! We were going at it like rabbits before I left."

She sniffed wetly and chuckled, "Are yeh pleased, Jamesey? I ain't gettin' rid of it."

He raised her chin and looked her straight in the eyes, "Right, Private Stark, we'll have no more of that type of talk. I'm absolutely delighted. We're a team, mate, and now we're getting a new member; I'm chuffed to fuck."

The relief she felt was so immense, she felt faint. He sat her on the bed and fanned her with The Belfast Telegraph before bounding into the lavatory and retrieving a bottle of whiskey he had hid in the cistern.

"Come on, let's go tell Smudger and Kim," and he took her by the hand and pulled her out into the corridor before slowing and facing her. "Here, who else knows, Collette?"

She squirmed, "Well, Kim, of course, Ron and Eadie, a few in The Peel…"

He guffawed uproariously, "So, all of Watford, then. Bloody Norah!"

They burst into the room, "Grab your mugs, lads. We're celebrating. There's another little paratrooper on the way."

Kim hugged a relieved Collette.

"You dirty sod," laughed Smudger, "Ah well, at least they never blew your family jewels off."

Matron stood listening inconspicuously in the corridor. Pleased at the big man's news and that the patients were happy, life was so diverse and you never knew what was going to happen next.

* * *

They left at 8pm that night in an unmarked car for the RAF base near Antrim, discreetly shadowed by a heavy armed crew from 14 Int[138].

"Bye, bye, Belfast. Deutschland here we come!"

"And good bloody riddance," said Smudger.

* * *

The following morning Matron was driving a hire car down the Lisburn Road with a male orderly. They were planning to drive up to the relatively safe Antrim Coast to see the famous Giant's Causeway and then have lunch in the picturesque seaside resort of Portrush. She was looking forward to a rare day off from the claustrophobic secure ward and get some decent food and bracing sea air.

As she stopped at traffic lights, a motorbike pulled up and the pillion passenger unleashed thirty rounds from a UZI submachine gun through the window. Hit numerous times across her ample breasts, Matron died instantly. Her colleague died an hour later from a gunshot wound to the head. The IRA later claimed the hit through The Samaritans, alleging they had 'executed' two members of an elite Army Undercover Unit.

---

[138] 14 Intelligence Corp. British Army undercover unit trained by Special Forces.

In West Germany, Jamesey was cautiously pushing Smudger around the grounds of Rinteln, BMH, sussing out the area and where the nearest Bier Keller was.

"Wonder what's happening in Belfast, mate?"

"Probably still killing each other. Same old, same old," guessed Jamesey.

"'Ere, Jamesey, the Matron here's a bit of all right, mate. Better than that cow in Musgrave."

Jamesey pondered that, "Nah, she was okay, was the Dragon Queen. I kinda miss her in a sad, sick, perverted way."

"What we gonna do about OLG now, mate? Is it a no-go?"

"Can't see that, Smudger, I've a kiddo on the way. At least the army pay's steady, if crap."

Smudger grinned, knowingly. He reckoned Collette would have something to say about that!

The ladies arrived home in England without mishap at three, the next afternoon. Collette wore her seatbelt all the way back as instructed by Jamesey, concerned about her being with child. "They should make wearing seatbelts law, Kim."

"Nah, never catch on. Be like living in a police state," she replied. "Now, shake a leg and we can catch Mothercare and look for bargains."

"Sod that, Kim. I need a pint and a jar of gherkins," and they both erupted with laughter.

When Jamesey and Smudger heard about the killings in Belfast, they looked at each other knowingly. The Provisional IRA was now open season… Bastards to a man.

* * *

End of August, 1976. Brecon, South Wales

Jamesey had made a good recovery. They had fitted him with a very realistic plastic hand, which he could slip on and off at will. Smudger had worse problems. The bullets that smashed through his left thigh had done serious damage, shattering his femur and doing colossal nerve damage. They had even talked at one stage of amputation, but an innovated young army surgeon had replaced part of the femur with plastic and titanium screws. He would always have a permanent limp and would certainly never parachute again. His days as an airborne warrior were over, and he was very bitter and detested all things Irish.

Jamesey had tried to console him. "You can't lump all the Paddies in one sack, mate. The majority are decent enough and want nothing to do with The Troubles," and he slapped him on the shoulder soothingly. "Besides, you'll get a nice cushy number in the Stores or somewhere. No more freezing your bollocks off in a trench on top of The Three Fans[139]."

---

[139] Mountains in Brecon, South Wales where the paras train. Pen y Fan, Penny Fawr and Penny Fadder.

Smudger had stared into his pint despondently, "No, Jamesey. If I can't be out with the guys, I'm leaving the colours. I'll take my war pension and sell life insurance or something. I've reached 'My Bridge Too Far'[140], mate."

He was emphatic in his decision and wouldn't be budged, "Besides," he added "You've given up on starting On La Guardia, but at least you can still run and fight."

Jamesey didn't know about that.

On the Battalion's return to barracks in Aldershot after a very successful tour, the Colonel had called him to HQ, "What are we going to do with you, Colour? Can't see you in the Stores or doing Range Officer."

"I just want back to my platoon, sir. I'm one hundred per cent fit."

The Colonel eyed him sympathetically. "You know that's impossible. Queen's Regs forbid it. You'll never see active service again, and you cannot parachute in case your prosthesis comes off."

Jamesey looked glum.

"But tell you what. The Brecon Battle Camp needs a Sergeant Major. Means a nice promotion, more money and with your experience, you'll be doing invaluable work."

Jamesey thought about it. The Battle Camp was a hell hole where recruits had to do so many weeks of extreme training which stretched them to and beyond their limit. A high number of recruits failed the course through exhaustion, injury or terror. The SAS[141] trained there and other Infantry Units on promotion courses. He quite fancied beasting[142] the Crap Hats[143] about and working with the SAS guys. A unit he had been aiming to attempt to join at some stage in his career but that was out the door now. Plus, it was a good five-hour drive from his beloved Collette, who was still in his ear about starting On La Guardia, despite the rapidly growing bump in her belly. No...he had to be practical.

"I'll give it a go, sir. I haven't much choice, have I?"

"You know the offer of the VC for you and Sergeant Smyth is still on the cards? You should take it."

After Glenmacadoon they both had been recommended for the Victoria Cross. The highest bravery award in the army but had turned it down, instead opting for that every man in the platoon be given a 'Mention in Dispatches', a much lesser award.

"No, thank you, sir. I walked my men into an ambush and lost a man. That will always be on my conscience."

The Colonel knew not to argue. They had had this conversation before. DeJames had been found totally blameless at the subsequent inquest, but that was just the type of man he was. He stood and shook the younger man's hand, "Good luck in Brecon, Sergeant Major. I know you'll make us proud."

As he marched out, the Colonel watched the door he had left through intently. DeJames was unique. He hadn't had a better soldier serve under him in thirty years.

---

[140] A bridge on the Rhine in Arnhem, Holland that the paras had to hold for forty-eight hours. After ten days and 8,000 casualties out of 10,000, they gave up when reinforcement failed to reach them.

[141] Special Air Services, the elite of Special Forces.

[142] To give a hard time to.

[143] Any other regiment who doesn't wear the Red Beret.

The Queen's Regulations were outdated. He had no doubt DeJames could fight and perform his duties as well, if not better than, any man under his command. Rumour had it DeJames had some young filly up the duff and was thinking of going solo into private security. He tapped his pen thoughtfully on the table, "Well, if anyone can do it, you can, Jamesey."

He went back to the reams of paperwork that even a leader of eight hundred warriors had to do. *Gets worse every month. Maybe Jamesey will have a job for an old war horse when I hang the wings up?* he contemplated.

* * *

Late September, 1976. Brecon Battle Camp

Warrant Officer Class II DeJames marched briskly across the parade ground, pay stick clasped firmly in his artificial hand and under his arm. Spotting a group of recruits slinking towards the Cookhouse, "On the fucking double or I'll stick my pay stick through your ears and ride you around the Square like a motorbike!"

That cracked a grin across the exhausted men's faces as they sprinted off. The big Sergeant Major was firm but well-respected. No recruit walked at Battle Camp, and he could have put them 'On a Fizzer'[144] if he wanted but he always gave them a first chance.

He stomped into the Cookhouse and the duty cooks quailed behind the array of hot steaming trays of food. He had them terrified. He demanded his men got proper rations and the food was cooked to perfection. He strolled down the hot plates, tasting every selection. It was breakfast time; the most important meal in a soldier's day.

"Scrambled eggs are a bit runny," he growled. Reaching a tray of chipolatas, he hefted one out and bit into it, before promptly spitting it out, "It's raw in the middle, you morons," he roared at the chefs, "It's pork for frig's sake. If you give my men worms or the trots, I'll personally skin your hides!" And he picked up the piping hot tray and tossed it over the counter. It was one advantage of having an artificial hand, you felt no heat.

The recruits cheered and clapped, enjoying the short break in their horrendously strenuous routine. He swung round to face them, "And you can shut it and start stuffing your faces. You've five minutes."

Subdued, they began shovelling food into their mouths as fast as possible. They were heading out into the mountains for a week's exercise and would be on cold compo rations.

* * *

An hour later, Jamesey watched them marching out in full battle gear, wishing he was going with them. With a heavy heart, he sighed, "Sod this for a game of soldiers. Time to move on, old son."

Half an hour thereafter he was before a shocked camp commandant, tendering his resignation from the army on grounds of injuries received on active service. Later

---

[144] To be charged with an offence under Queen's Regulations.

he phoned The Peel from the Sergeant's Mess, "I've resigned, Collette. I'll be home in a week."

"About bleedin' time, luv. I've missed yah and I've found the perfect start-up premises for OLG."

He grinned happily, his heart beaming. She was a true star in a black universe.

II

Watford March 1977

They sat in their office above the bookmaker's office, sipping steaming mugs of coffee and munching on Gingernut biscuits. They could hear Collette bashing away on the Olivetti in the small reception area. It was Collette who had seen the 'To Let' sigh above the bookies on High Street, and Jamesey had snapped it up, paying a year's rent and rates in advance, which had made a sizeable dent in his savings.

"What's she typing anyway?" mumbled Smudger, through a mouthful of crumbs, "Not exactly thriving, are we?"

Jamesey swung his feet off the desk and grinned, "Oh ye of little faith. She's probably doing her homework for Tech."

They had done all the decorating themselves in tasteful beiges and magnolia, the new carpet was a pleasant brown that would wear well and the furniture, although bought in a second-hand emporium in Harrow, was good quality and stylish.

"It'll pick up, mate, it's early days yet. It's Friday…you and Dougie can do the pub run and then we have the Tyre Depot job tonight. So you can get home for an hour or two and we'll meet up again at twenty hundred hours."

Dougie Philpott came in and poured himself a coffee from the flask. He was a lean man in his late forties with grey hair and glasses and was their security system specialist. He had served for twenty-five years in the Royal Signals and was a wizard when it came to all things electrical. Jamesey brought packs of alarm systems from a supplier in Central London, and Dougie made short work of building them and installing them in the premises of their clients.

Dougie had never married, the army had been his wife and family, and when he retired, he had found himself at a loose end, spending more and more time in the boozer filling the hours, there wasn't much work around for someone with his credentials.

He was bemoaning his fate to Ronnie one day when Jamesey arrived. Ronnie did the introductions and, over a pint, the two men chatted about Dougie's qualifications. Jamesey subjected him to a serious third degree before he was satisfied.

"If these qualifications and your references pan out, Dougie, and your crime record comes back kosher, I'll employ you. Thing is it will be minimum wage until OLG takes off, so what do ya think?"

Dougie could have kissed the big, one-handed man's feet; he was bored witless after years of work-filled days and would have worked for nothing, just to feel useful again, but wisely never mentioned that fact to his, soon to be, new boss. His new boss seemed a larger than life guy but there was a touch of the predator about him, always on the hunt and the prowl. An easy gleam of danger in his humorous eyes saying don't push too hard if you can't handle your corner.

Dougie reckoned all ex-paras were mad bastards anyway.

Now he took a good slurp of his coffee and lit a Rothmans Kingsize, "That's Mrs Faraday, in Clancy Gardens, up and going, Jamesey. I put the leaflets through the doors as you asked, and Mr Singh on the corner wants a quote, I told him you'd call at about ten tomorrow morning."

Jamesey rubbed his hands with relish; he insisted on meeting each new customer individually, "Good work, my man, don't know what we would do without you. Would you do the pub run with Smudger and then you can head on home."

"Yeah you're a valuable asset, Doug," added Smudger through a gobful of Gingernuts.

Doug glowed inside from head to foot, he felt needed, part of a team again and to have these two rough, tough ex-paratroopers appreciate his skills was good for his self-esteem. He pulled open a drawer in one of the filing cabinets and produced two small walkie-talkies.

"Here, guvs…stashed these earlier…souvenir from my time in the signals. Three-hundred-feet range, eight-hour battery life and fully charged. My little contribution."

"See, Smudger, he's invaluable. Thanks, Doug."

"Nice one, mate. Good bit of kit."

Doug glowed even more, proud to be in the company of these fierce fighting men and to be accepted by them as an equal.

Collette stuck her head round the door, "'Ere, it's half past two and the pub run's on. Jamesey you have to see that Mr Patterson at 23 Quinto Street, so yer better get yer arse in gear."

"Yes, my little lamb, we're on our way," said Jamesey, standing and shrugging on a smart suit jacket. Collette never ceased to amaze him; she had studied hard at Tech and ran the office, and the men, in a brisk no-nonsense manner. Once she got the yearning for further education, she never looked back, and despite giving birth to Rabbie Hamish three months earlier, she was at the office every day, nicely dressed and putting on a posh accent for the clients, much to his amusement. She was rapidly becoming invaluable to him in the business. He would think of something he needed to do only to find she had pre-empted him and had already nailed it down. It happened so often he started calling her 'Psychic Coll' and she would scowl at him, but he knew she was secretly pleased.

"We're on our way, Miss Stark," Dougie told her as they traipsed out through the outer office.

She looked up from a pile of pamphlets she was examining and smiled, "It's Collette, Dougie, 'ow many bleedin' times 'ave I ta tell yah, we're a friggin' family 'ere, ain't we?"

"Yes, Collette," and he hurried out in awe of the fiery good-looking young woman. Her and Jamesey were well matched; they were both like engines running on full power and it was full speed ahead so get onboard or jump out of the way.

"And don't forget to pick up the baby, Jamesey," she hollered after them, "Or that Eadie one will be adopting him next."

He laughed as he trotted down the stairs, his broad shoulders almost filling the staircase. "Forgot to pick the kid up yesterday," he threw over his shoulder at Smudger, "And she's never gonna let me live it down."

"Told ya, mate, a different species," Smudger laughed, "All from outer bleedin' space."

* * *

The next six months were productive ones for OLG if not for some of the bars in the region.

There was a rise in the number of snatch and grab robberies on pub and restaurant staff. Several had been assaulted and quite seriously injured when they were followed and attacked while they were bringing their hardearned takings to be put into the night-safe at various banks.

In some cases, the gangs had actually got into the premises, usually on a Sunday night or Monday morning, and broke into the safes to steal the neatly counted bundles of cash garnered over the previous weekend. If the landlords lived in the building, they were taken hostage with knives or shotguns and held by one or two of the gang while the rest filled their van with all the drink, cigarettes and anything else they could get their hands on. Ron, a respected member of the Watford branch of the Licenced Vintner's Association, was worried and consulted Jamesey for advice on what they could do and the 'pub run' came about. Every second day, for a small fee, the OLG collected the extra cash from the clients and deposited it in the various banks. By staggering the days and times of the drops, they stayed one step ahead of any would be thieves.

Jamesey had twelve pubs and clubs on his books now, while it didn't bring in a lot of money, it did help pay the bills and it was good for their reputation. He reckoned they were more than a match for any gang of two-bit blaggers if they tried anything. Both him and Smudger carried small, lead-filled coshes and they knew how to use them to maximum effect.

* * *

The company was the proud owner of two Hotspur Land Rovers, Jamesey drove one and Smudger the other. The former battle-grey armoured vehicles with their long wheel base were now painted a glossy black with gold trim and had the company name and phone number embossed on each side in large red lettering. They fairly turned the heads of the locals when they drove past, children wondering at the strange alien vehicles.

They were run by powerful Rolls Royce V8 engines and were still set up with the exterior intercom system the RUC had used to warn riotous crowds to disperse. Using a handset inside the Rover, you could talk to people on the street via a bullhorn mounted on the roof.

Jamesey and Smudger would drive the busy streets extolling the virtues of OLG, whistling at the women and greeting the men. Young folks and kids laughed and cheered in delight but a few angry boyfriends tried to open their doors, when they stopped moving, to remonstrate with them, but hey, the thing was armoured and it would take an explosion to get inside.

They were becoming a familiar sight around town. It was what Jamesey had aimed for; they had actually several new clients, and many more prospective clients had also contacted them, after they had seen the vehicles prowling the streets ominously.

It had been well worth the hassle of the trip to get them. Jamesey and Smudger had flown to Belfast and went to an auction of ex-RUC vehicles at the supply base at Kinnegar a month earlier. They got them for a fraction of their true value as no one in Northern Ireland wanted them in case the IRA mistook them for police and fired a rocket up their exhaust. Not a pleasant experience at the best of times as many a poor RUC man knew to his cost.

The trip back by ferry and the drive down to London proved they were as good a bargain as Smudger had said. He knew about engines, "My old man runs a garage down in Tavistock and I cut me teeth on fan-belts and sprocket sets," he had told Jamesey when they had met all those years ago at the depot and he had remembered. Besides all his other duties he was now OLG's Transport Officer. Know your men's strengths and weaknesses and use them accordingly was the big man's cast-iron philosophy.

* * *

It was almost closing time, and Jamesey was sitting in the bushes watching the southern fence of the tyre depot. It was chain link, a good eight-feet high and topped with barbed wire. The depot building itself was a galvanised steel affair that housed several bays where customers could get their tyres changed and their wheels lined and balanced, there was also a store for the tyres and a small office.

"I don't understand it, Mr DeJames," wailed Mr Kinsallah, the Nigerian owner, "I have good fencing, which I regularly check, arc lighting and a good alarm but still ten to fifteen go every month. At around ten pounds each and seven pounds for re-treads, it's a substantial sum to lose."

Jamesey had commiserated and paced the perimeter, which measured about fifty feet by eighty and was choc-a-block with re-treads and used tyres waiting collection. There was no pattern to the crime; one week Mr Kinsallah would come in and find four tyres missing, a few days later two more, then nothing for a week, then more gone.

"I have sat all night myself, but nothing. The blighters even broke into the office last time and made themselves some tea. It's as if they know my every move."

That's because they do, me old china, thought Jamesey to himself.

The depot was at the bottom of the town, opposite 'The Swan' public house, its front faced the Main Street. Jamesey was watching the fence on the southern side, which was flanked by the River Colne and he had found a spot in the gorse bushes on the bank. Smudger was watching the opposite fence, which faced the sides of several businesses. This was their third random night watching and they planned to stay until four a.m., then pack it in and return to the vehicles, parked out of sight in the patrons' car park.

Jamesey sat immobile, senses alert, totally focused on the job and well screened by the heavy brush. He had an idea what was going on, now all he had to do was catch the villain at work.

Midnight came and he gave Smudger a quiet radio check. Ten minutes later he heard the sploshing of water behind him and quiet rustling as someone crept through the bushes to his right. He clicked the send switch on his radio three times to alert his oppo. Smudger replied and Jamesey watched as a figure clad in black overalls and gloves approached the fence. The figure reached one of the ten uprights, gripped it with both hands and heaved it up. The post came out easily because the heavy lump of concrete which should have been on the end had been removed and hidden in the bushes, Jamesey had found it earlier.

When the gap between the ground and the fence was wide enough, he slithered under it and replaced the post in the hole. He ran nimbly over to the side of the depot, unslung the rope coiled across his body, swung the grappling hook and threw it up fluidly until it gripped the top edge of the building. He hauled himself swiftly up, pulled the rope up after him and produced a screwdriver and soon had the skylight open. He dropped the rope down into the building and disappeared from view closing the skylight after him.

"Sweet very, very sweet," observed Jamesey before calling Smudger. "He's in mucker, come round to my position."

They watched as the intruder re-appeared on the roof and hauled a tyre up on the end of the rope, untied it and let it drop to the ground before going back for another one. Four Pirellis later, at twelve pounds a time, he was done. He screwed the skylight back in place, whooshed down the rope and with an expert flick of his wrist brought down the grappling. Whistling silently, he carried two of the tyres to the fence lifted the fence again and propped them underneath, leaving a nice gap for him to go under when he returned with the other two. He removed his 'props', replaced the post and patted the earth down around it to disguise his entry.

"Good, ain't he…nice little earner," Smudger whispered admiringly.

Jamesey smiled at Smudger, "But we're better, Smudger," he whispered back, "Still, ten out of ten for effort."

The thief wheeled his four trophies into a bush near them, ready to put onto his raft, which was made of wood and some of the tyres he had stolen to help keep it afloat. He would secrete it in a large culvert a hundred yards away ready for pick up later. He stored his hoard in its depths and the buyer picked them up in a van once a month, paying him half the trade value.

He was happy with his night's work as he wheeled two of his purloined charges down to the riverbank, calculating in his mind what his monthly earning would be as tonight was pay night, food and heat in the house for the missus and kids.

Suddenly, a strong flashlight seared his retinas and he hit the ground, hard, face down with two strong hands forcing his arms up his back. "Fucking freeze and don't try anything," a voice snarled, "What's your name?"

"You the cops? It's a fair collar," said the terrified burglar.

"No, we're not the filth and we're asking the questions."

"Then fuck away off and mind your own." The grip on his arms increased and he hollered in pain.

"Get him up, Smudger, but keep a good grip on him and plenty of pressure."

Smudger laughed and pulled him to his feet, "Not the tyre jokes already, Jamesey. I better tread easily, ha, ha."

The tyre thief was thoroughly confused, "Who the fuck are you boys? You'd better get your hands off me."

Jamesey was amused, "Name, rank and number, pal?"

Daniel John Privet was a lean man of forty years, with sparse sandy hair and long narrow features, who had served twenty of them in the Royal Anglian

Regiment. He was an expert in covert and overt surveillance and an expert marksman. He recognised his two jesting captors as ex-army men.

They took him back to the depot, and Jamesey let them in with the keys the owner had given to him. They went into the office and Smudger guarded the door while his boss made tea. Danny watched the big man with the plastic hand carefully, "Ain't ya gonna call the blue bottles then?"

"That depends on you, pal. Let's hear your story."

Danny shrugged, resigned to his fate and told them about his time in 1st Battalion RAR, the famous 'Poachers'. He told them how his wife had got ill with multiple sclerosis and he had five kids ranging from nine to seventeen years old, "Can't live on the pension, can I? The benefits the missus gets is shit and I can't get a day job 'cause I have to help her indoors with the kids, don't I?"

"So you took matters into your own hands then?" enquired Jamesey. "You're on skid row." And Smudger groaned.

"Well, yeah. I'm good at it, besides I miss the job and it's kinda fun, reminds me of being back in Belfast."

Jamesey and Smudger nodded knowingly; it never really left you, the adrenalin surge and sense of purpose of years of service.

Danny went on to explain how a rival tyre firm had asked him to supply them with tyres, as many as he could get. "Bleeding Asian concern. After a few outings, I said I'd had enough but they threatened the wife and kids so I had to go on…been watching the place. Crap security."

Jamesey thought on that. Anybody threatening Collette or his kid would be spitting teeth for a month as indeed any idiot fool enough to threaten any member of his OLG extended family. "You'd better not be bull-shitting me, Danny…now tell me all."

* * *

Two hours later a small flat-bed lorry, with three Asians aboard, pulled up to the side of the bridge. Danny had done well that month and he helped them load eighteen new tyres of various brands onto the back. They paid him ninety-four pounds, which he pocketed hastily. Suddenly, two pairs of headlights illuminated the road as two strange black vehicles careered towards them, engines screaming, before they skidded to a halt, broadside, at each end of the bridge, blocking their exit.

Two bulky figures emerged from the vehicles and moved towards the lorry. The crooks armed themselves with tyre levers but the two paras had their lead filled coshes and they knew how to use them to great effect, cracking heads and bones. When the short, but violent, skirmish was over, the Asians came out as the underdogs and they cowered beneath the assault from the mad paras, crying for mercy.

Danny, never much of a scrapper, had vaulted the parapet and was hiding on his raft at water level. Smudger jogged off to phone the rozzers and returned with the rope and hook, which he tossed into the cab of the lorry.

Jamesey put the time they waited for the law to arrive to good use explaining to the crooks exactly what they would say about the night's adventure and telling them what would happen to them if they didn't follow his instructions. He terrified them, he was like some mythical devil who had appeared from nowhere, and they believed every threat he made.

It wasn't long before two jam sandwiches[145] arrived and they were surrounded by cops. Jamesey gave the three men a look of warning and menace, and they admitted to all the break-ins that had been happening at the tyre depot.

Mr Kinsallah was delighted when not only the eight tyres that had been stolen that night but all that had been stolen that month, and another eighty which were found in his rival's premises, were returned to him. "I can never thank you enough Jamesey, I won't have to place an order for months. Would it be too much if I were to ask you to look at my security for me?"

"Pressure pads and proper fencing, sir. I'll send my anti-burglary expert to see you; he's a new man, very experienced, top of the range," and he strolled off smiling to himself.

* * *

Smudger had been gob-smacked when Jamesey employed Danny 'the Tyreman' Privet. Jamesey tapped his nose with his finger, "It's 'The Ways and Means Act', mate… Anyway and any means to get a result, Smudger…besides, he's ex-army and he was doing it for his family, I admire that."

The Tyreman worked afternoons and a few hours in the evenings and proved to be one hundred per cent loyal. He thanked his lucky stars for the day Big Jamesey had caught him red-handed. Although he was normally a hard man to impress, and cynical by nature, he idolised the two big, easygoing ex-paras. They were from a different mould, he reckoned.

OLG got a nice write-up in the local rag the next week.

* * *

Collette sat with Martha Privet in the living room of her small, shabby home. She'd brought a big box of groceries up, introduced herself and baby Rabbie and now she chatted away with the semi-disabled woman, welcoming her into the OLG family.

Martha felt content in the friendly young woman's company. It had been a long time since she was this relaxed. Her man had a good, honest job with good hours and a good wage but more important, he had a sense of purpose and had gotten his self-confidence back, she saw shades and snippets of the young man she had married.

Collette eyed the tidy but shabby room, "We've got a bit of carpet and paint left from when we done the office up, I'll get the boys down ta sort it."

"We're very, very grateful for all you've done, Miss Stark; it's very kind of you."

"Not at all, it's no bother and my name is Collette. We're one big family at OLG, and families help each other out, don't they?"

Martha beamed. Jamesey might be good at his job and collecting all manner of people to him but Collette was proving just as good at holding them together and keeping them happy. They were a team and it would take an earthquake of seismic proportions to separate them.

* * *

---

[145] Police car with a red horizontal stripe.

Rabbie Hamish DeJames had entered the world at 5.30am on the 18th of January, 1977. He was a healthy, screaming bundle of joy, weighing in at 10lb 4oz.

Collette had opted for a home birth, "Tink we've seen enough of hospitals to last us a while, Jamesey," she told him and he had to agree with her.

Eadie and Kim had been up and down the stairs all night, dancing attendance to the midwife's commands. Jamesey, with Ron and Smudger for support, sat in the living room sipping a blended malt while a ferocious blizzard rattled the windows and tried to batter its way in to join them.

An anxious Jamesey listened to Collette hollering loud enough to be heard over the wind, "Jesus Smudger, I'd rather be tackling a bunch of IRA men with just a knife and fork than sitting here."

Smudger smiled that smile of a seasoned father, "It only gets worse, mucker! Once they have the sprog, they're never the same again."

"Different species, different species, don't say you weren't warned," muttered Ron, darkly.

Jamesey turned to him, "How ya know, Ron? You've been firing jaffas[146] your whole life."

Ron grimaced, "Don't matter, mate, they're all tarred with the one brush and that way since birth."

"Yeah, they get very bossy and clingy. For your own safety, don't let her catch ya looking at a bit of strange," put in Smudger.

"Different planet, different species, I tell ya."

"Oh shut up, Ron," laughed Jamesey. "Here, the storm's stopped…that's a good sign."

"Your storm's only building up, mate."

The door opened and Eadie stuck her head in, excitement showing on her face. "The baby's head is showing. You wanna come up, Jamesey?"

"Do ya not think he's seen enough atrocities in life, Eadie, without seeing one of his own doing?" Smudger sniggered.

Ronnie sunk his head into his hands, "We're doomed, all doomed."

Eadie laughed, "Aw give over, Ron. It's bleedin' brilliant. Making me broody, it is."

Ron shook his head in mock despair. He was thoroughly enjoying himself, it was a new experience for him, the alien female species in total control. "Probably be like something from the 'Exorcist', Jamesey," he said to keep the gallows humour going."

Smudger snickered, "Or the 'Texas Chainsaw Massacre'!"

Jamesey stood and raised his glass to his mates, "'Once more into the breach, dear friends, shot, volley and thunder'[147]," and he downed his Scotch in one swallow. "Tally-ho, a hunting I will go."

He climbed the stairs, none too steady, and entered the room feeling very much the intruder. He was glad to see that the intimate view was obscured by the midwife and Kim.

---

[146] Male infertility.

[147] From Tennyson's war poem, The Charge of the Life Brigade.

Collette scowled at him as he moved towards the bed, "Don't you ever come near me again, ya big sod," she yelled as he, gingerly, took her hand and another spasm hit her.

When another pain rushed through her, he thought she was going to rip off his good hand so he gently prised her fingers off and gave her his artificial one instead, grinning at her, "Everything has its uses."

With a screech that chilled his blood and would have done a vampire victim proud, she gave a final push and Rabbie slithered into the world.

Jamesey was agog, "Bloody Norah, Coll, how the heck did you get something so big outta…that?"

She patted his hand, exhausted, "Don't worry, luv, the next time'll be easier, sorry for shoutin' at ya."

"Oh nay baw, bloody well done, darling."

Then he realised what she had said and that fairly sobered him up… *More? Good grief.*

They all laughed at the look on his face, and as his new son was shoved into his arms, his male ego soared.

Collette watched, tired but content, she knew her big guy would be a good father and provider, "Gawd help him if he ain't," she mumbled to herself as she gently dozed off.

* * *

When Rabbie was a month old, Beth came down for a week to see her much longed for grandson. Jamesey had used the money he got from the army to furnish the house and Collette had enjoyed making it into a home.

The army had wanted Jamesey to remain in badly, he was a unique soldier, but he declined. Soldiers couldn't claim compensation[148] for injuries received while on active duty, it being considered 'not the done thing' when serving your country, but he had received a year's severance pay, his bounty and a war pension.

"Not much for losing yer bleedin' hand, love," Collette had remarked. "Tight-fisted buggers, excuse the pun, luv."

"I'm not complaining. The army's given me a lot of training that helps in my new trade…and besides, I wouldn't 've met you, now would I?"

She looked at him with open admiration. Always the optimist. She was glad he had his confidence back, she would be lost without it. She planted a big smacker on his lips.

* * *

Beth adored her little grandson. He was a bonnie wee boy, healthy and a good feeder. She knew what to look for having reared hundreds of lambs by hand over the years. "He's the pick of the flock, Collette, a born champion. Well done, dear."

That night they left Beth babysitting while they went to the Ramada Restaurant for a meal. Collette was anxious but Beth chased her out, "He'll be fine, bit of quality

---

[148] The rules were relaxed in the late 1980s.

time with Granny while Mummy and Daddy have some quality time together," she told them. "Now go."

The food was lovely but Collette went easy on the drink, as she had abstained during her pregnancy, having only one glass of wine with her meal. She ordered a Cointreau with her coffee while Jamesey had a brandy, and they had just been served when the head waiter delivered twelve red roses to the table.

Jamesey fumbled in his pocket and produced a small jeweller's box while getting down on one knee. "Miss Collette Stark, would you do me the honour of becoming my wife?" he asked and handed her the box. She opened it and kept him hanging in suspense as she looked at the large ruby and diamond engagement ring before laughing, happily. "Took ycr bleeding time asking, didn't ya?"

He smiled back, "Do I take it that's a yes then?"

Collette was thrilled. It was not something she expected of him, he was always so busy and they had never discussed getting married. She remembered the first time she had seen him in The Peel, his first words to her, that first glance and had never dared hope it would come to this. She remembered the insecure, moping, frightened Collette she was then and marvelled that the dream she had then, the dream every single woman has, was coming true. For once in her life she felt truly blessed.

"Ya don't have to ask, love…'course I will, you soppy sod, and get off your knees, yer wearing yer best trousers."

He looked relieved, "Frig, Coll, ya had me heart near stopping there."

She was feeling a bit overwhelmed now and was blushing as the other diners clapped and shouted their good wishes and the manager appeared with Champagne on ice, "Cor, bit like a Mills & Boon novel, ain't it?" Jamesey slipped the glittering jewel onto her finger, and she threw her arms round him and kissed him, much to the delight of everyone there.

Later as they strolled to The Peel and she was still getting used to the strange feel of the ring on her finger, she couldn't help but think how lucky she was to have it there. It would take some serious inner focusing to get her head around this one. It still amazed her that she was truly wanted and loved for herself and for life by this dynamic man who had turned her previous sad, enclosed little world into a whirlwind of new experiences, places, romance, love and hope. She cherished the moment and clung to the happy thoughts that twirled around in her head.

Jamesey interrupted her thoughts to ask, "Do you know what date it is today?"

Without even having to think about it, she answered, "Yep, it's a year to the day since you battered fat Barry senseless and then took me home and screwed me witless."

He grinned. She was a shining star that had filled his dark, violent and emotionless universe, "Sure is, hon…bliss, pure bloody bliss."

"Not for sleazy Barry it weren't, mate," she laughed gaily.

They ambled down the deserted precinct to The Peel hand in hand to meet their friends.

Smudge bounced over and shook his hand and slapped a slobby one on Collette's cheek, "So she said 'yes' then. Cheer up Jamesey, it's a piss up not a wake you miserable sod."

Her brothers stopped forgetting by the door as young men on the brink of adulthood do in the presence of seasoned men of the world and rushed over and gave her big joyful hugs, reunited again in the moment. Big sis had done well and they were proud of her.

"'Ere, how the frig did you arrange all this behind me back, yah big galoot?"

He laughed, "I told you before my blossom. The DeJames ways and means act. Never fails."

She slapped him playfully, "Devious big git." Secretly delighted.

It was too much for her and the tears ran unheeded as he hurried to comfort her. Not their nephew or step-brother but brother. Jamesey just looked on all his friends as family, and she beamed at him through her tears, "Thanks, Jamesey, thanks so much."

He poked her in the ribs making her jump, "Oh stop yer gushing, ya soppy mare, it's your round."

"I'll pay outta me tips, guvnor," she laughed back, ecstatic, in the moment.

Later she took him aside and asked him where the twins were going to sleep. He smiled knowingly, "On Eadie's airbed. You didn't think I would throw that away, now, did you?" and he winked saucily.

* * *

A strange thing occurred in West Belfast the week that Smudger and Jamesey spent in the province purchasing second-hand Hotspur Land Rovers. Four members of the INLA[149] were in a sixth-floor flat of Cullentree Road in the lethal Republican Divis Flats, guzzling Guinness and cleaning two 9mm Berettas ready for a hit the next morning on an off-duty peeler who attended the chapel on the Crumlin Road every Sunday, when two men in dark clothing and balaclavas burst in, practically taking the door off the hinges and riddled them with rounds from two .45mm Colt semi-automatic pistols. They then tossed a toy green cloth dragon onto the chest of the dying leader, who was finished off with a well-aimed head shot.

By the time the police and army gathered in force and ventured cautiously in, the assailants were long gone. Nobody had obviously seen or heard a thing but on door-to-door enquiries an OAP told them in confidence that he was looking out his window and had seen two big men get into a blue saloon car and drive off, "And the funny thing, Officer, was the driver was a big black fella with the dread knot hair like Bob Marley."

The detective had been sceptical. Coloured people were few and far between in the province and as the witness did not want to make a written statement, fearing for his ageing kneecaps, the detective put it down to the onset of senile dementia. They laughed about it in the office afterwards, thinking it highly unlikely the Jamaican Rastafarian Freedom Fighters had linked up with the UVF[150].

The four dead men were well known to the security forces. Killers to a man, who wanted a Marxist Socialist Ireland connected to Moscow. WIS (Weapons Intelligence Section) found the two Berettas had been used in the shooting of a Matron and a corporal in the Royal Army Medical Corps on the Lisburn Road a year previously.

---

[149] Irish National Liberation Army.

[150] Ulster Volunteer Force.

As professional coppers, the detectives didn't condone murder of any kind but they had to admit the four thugs were of no great loss. They puzzled over the mystery of the cloth green dragon as to what exactly its significance was, "Maybe they pissed the Welsh Freedom Fighters off," joked one.

His Inspector shook his head, "You wouldn't bloody know in this place," he said, baffled. "Perhaps they had been sheep rustling."

"Funny about their sheep, the Welsh," his man agreed. "Hey, Boss, what do you call a Welsh man with one sheep?"

The Inspector grinned, being a native of Cardiff, "Faithful and with two he is an adulterer."

They laughed, "Yeah, and one tied to a lamp post is a leisure centre."

The Inspector let them rabbit for a while, good for morale, "Right, back to work. We've murders to solve."

"About as much chance of that happening as sheep surviving a Welsh Rugby team's stag night," muttered the detective constable.

* * *

Later that week Jamesey met Collette in The Peel for lunch. Big Clive came in clutching a small sports bag, looking for Jamesey.

"'Ere, how did yah enjoy your week off, Clive? Where did yah go, mate?" Collette asked him.

"Oh, you know, Collette, just cruised up North for a bit of touring...it was interesting, thanks."

Jamesey took the bag off him and headed out back to see Ronnie. The two Colt .45's were in the bag. Ronnie had won them from an American Serviceman in Cyprus in 1958, and he wanted his souvenirs back.

"What was in the bag then, Clive?" she asked him suspiciously.

"Loads of black and white pudding from up North, Ron likes it. Says it puts hair on your chest."

Collette giggled, "Hate that gear. Heart attack on a plate, any'ow. I don't want hairs on me chest. Jamesey wouldn't approve."

Clive laughed, admiring her shapely bust set off in a tight-fitting red jumper. Jamesey slipped back in and passed him a large wad of notes surreptitiously, but Collette had seen it. She didn't miss much. Clive left grinning and Jamesey sat and got stuck into his beer.

"'Ere, luv, that was a big wedge you threw Clive the Taxi."

"For the black pudding. Great stuff, so it is."

Collette snorted, "You could have fed a village of starving Africans in the Ritz for a week on that."

Jamesey gave her that inscrutable look, which indicated the matter was closed and she knew not to pursue it.

Smudger and Kim came in to join them and over a roast lamb Sunday dinner, the girls quizzed the guys about their trip to Belfast.

"Went off great, didn't it, Smudger?"

"Sure did. Bumped into a few old friends."

"Yeah, they couldn't hang about though," Jamesey continued, cutting happily into his meat.

"No, they had to shoot off!" grinned Smudger and both men erupted into gales of laughter.

Collette raised an eyebrow and looked at Kim, "Oh well, everybody's different," and the men guffawed again.

"Leave them to it, Collette," advised Kim. "Man speak and it's all bleedin' Welsh to me."

* * *

Back in Belfast the Detective Inspector had got the ballistic reports back and was even more bamboozled, "The 45 slugs were from two Colts stolen from the American Embassy, belonging to the marines who were guarding it, and wait for it...in 1958 in Nicosia in Cyprus."

That stunned his constable, "Weirder and weirder, Boss. All four men put down with two rounds to the chest, then finished with head jobs. Very professional."

"Yep, they know what they were doing. Anyhow, you hold the fort for an hour, I'm away to mass up the chapel."

"Sure, Boss. While you're there, ask him upstairs if he knows anything about the green dragon. It's doing my head in."

The Inspector slipped his jacket on, preparing to leave, "You know, Marty, I reckon that dragon is going to remain one of the unsolved mysteries of the universe."

Chapter 28
Borscht
(An OLG Black Op.)
('You'll Never Walk Alone'... Gerry and the Pacemakers... 1962)

New York, First Tuesday in April, 2013

Antonio Salvatori D'Agostino was a big man. Not in height but in girth. At 5'9" he weighed nearly three hundred pounds and, being third-generation Italian, he was dark of complexion, mercurial of mood and hirsute.

Toni ran a very successful delicatessen in the village area. It was a long shop, with glass counters running the length either side displaying his merchandise. Vast arrays of the finest salamis, Parma hams, chorizos, smoked meats, big wheels of cheese, quiches, pizzas and a myriad selection of other delicacies threw their aromas in a heady mix in the air to tantalise the prospective customer. When you entered, the taste buds went into overdrive and saliva swamped the mouth in anticipation. You could nearly pluck the vitamins out of the air with your fingers.

He also had a small selection of canned goods from around the world (only the finest, of course) and a selection of exotic fruit and vegetables.

Despite his build, Toni was fast and articulate and loved to chat with his customers. He liked to see them browse and stare uncertainly at his superb selections, and he would hustle down and advise them on what was what, "Hey, how yah doing... I'm Toni. Try one of my stuffed olives. The First Lady loves them." And the President's wife did. It was true.

Apart from the four staff that ran the front shop, he employed four more, who ran an express delivery and mail order service from a large room out back. He supplied senators and businessmen, pop stars, and celebrities. It was not unusual for a famous film star, rock idol or such like to stroll in and ask his advice. "Hey, Toni. I'm having a party tomorrow for SassyVanassy, any idea what she likes?"

Toni would consult an exclusive clientele list he had started up many years ago. "Yeah, Mr Mayor. She likes the red caviar, not the black, smoked cheese and ham quiche, moussaka, Caesar salad and black pudding."

"Great, send over enough for twenty and a few of your own choices."

Toni would shake their hands, beaming, and rush off to do their bidding. He was a nice man, convivial and larger than life. He loved good food, and he loved people who were of the same mien. Happily married for many years to Maria and the proud, but wary, father of seven dusky, sloe-eyed daughters, he was happy and content.

Business was booming and he was mega pleased with his lot and thanked the blessed virgin every day for gracing him with his good fortune.

But it hadn't always been that way and a small moue of distaste crossed his lips as he thought of the events of a year ago, and then cast the unwanted memories away as he watched the lovely young Russian looking unsurely at the fruit and veg.

He smiled and mentally tried to pull in his big belly but gave up with a cheerful shrug and went down to greet her.

"Hey, beautiful lady, how you today? I'm Toni, how can I help you?"

"Hello Toni, I am Luca, dah, Luca Valendenski. Your shop is so, soo interesting. I love it so much. We so lucky to live close by."

A huge smile crossed his heavy jowls. If anything, Toni was a lover of beauty, after all, he was Italian, and this Luca chick was bellissimo. Quite delightful and heavenly. "Yes, I see you before in with Rabbie. He's a great guy. Are you and him, you know, are you his precious squeeze?"

She gave Toni the full smile, and he was trapped as the Luca effect hit him.

Ravish, protect, plunder, nourish, nurture, shower with cherry blossom, wash and tenderly massage her feet, were some of the thoughts that crossed his mind.

She laughed, the sound like soft Christmas bells or a pleasant breeze rustling through pines, captivating him even more. "Oh Toni, what nice words… Precious squeeze, da. Rabbie is my squeeze and I hope I am as precious to him as he is to me."

He was enthralled. She was no airhead. Brains to match the beauty, "Dear lady, if I could take that smile and turn it into food, people would come from far ends of the world to sample it… Now, how can Toni help?"

Luca looked downcast for a moment. "Toni, I am very, bad cook but I am learning da, and I want ta make my precious squeeze borscht but I see no fresh beetroots?"

It was quiet in the shop, being mid Tuesday afternoon, "Come, bella Luca, to the office for coffee and I sort this tiny problem out for my new friend."

In the office he made her delicious cappuccino coffee, and she went up even more in his esteem when she put several heaps of sugar in. "Ah bravo, Luca. Sugar is good. It gives you energy and is a happy food."

Luca agreed readily. The big guy was highly entertaining. She would find a place for him on her list. He was perceptive too, "I think you have not been well, Luca. You are too slim. What ails you, child?"

"Gosh, Toni, you da pyschicman… I vas in da hospital for a while. How did you know?"

He waved a pudgy hand loftily. "Is no secret. I am a professional food man. We know these things. It's our job to provide nourishment and recognise when it's needed, si?"

She laughed again, "How vunderful, Toni, you so, how you say, astute?"

"Of course," he nodded, pleased, "I have seven daughters, and I learnt when they are sick what food to give them to make them better, comprendí?"

Luca nodded her agreement, "You so clever, Toni, and your girls very lucky to have you as a dad."

He preened, "Yes they are. They are the apple of my eye…now, my caro, Borscht."

374

Lifting the phone, he rang around his suppliers until at last he tracked the elusive beetroot provider down. "Ah Manny, you have a kettle on the boil... I send Giuseppe down for some. Grazie, shalom my friend."

He shouted for Giuseppe to get on his bike and get the elusive vegetables. Luca looked confused, "Why he da kettle on the boil, Toni?"

He patted her hand, "Our problem is solved. No one knows more about beetroots than the Northern European Jew. They are connoisseurs. The kettle is a big tub on legs they boil the beetroot in. Giuseppe bring you bag back, still hot and I peel them for you."

Luca liked the kindness of him and thanked him profusely but he shushed her, "Nonsense, my angel. I am the food provider, and I have my reputation to keep... Now, let's see what else you need so you can give my excellent friend Rabbie a borscht to die for."

She was thrilled. *New York fine food providers were just da coolest.* "Have you known my Rabbi long, Toni?"

He looked at her knowingly. "Are you in a rush, dear lady?"

She told him not, "Then let us partake of more coffee and a slice of Maria's tiramisu and I will tell you a story."

* * *

One Year Prior

It was a pleasant balmy April morning when Toni parked and prepared to open his beloved deli ready for the day's pending business, he was whistling 'The Marriage of Figaro'. He always came in an hour early to check for imperfections and decay in his stock and to ring around his rabbit warren of suppliers. His reputation was second to none, and he intended it stayed that way.

As he opened the back door, two men approached him and one produced a knife and waved it in his face, "Open up, fat boy. We're 'The Mob'."

He was terrified. Toni was a gentle man by nature and abhorred all forms of violence. He pulled his wallet out, "Here, guys, take it. 'Bout six hundred and cards. I want no trouble."

The guy with the blade was about thirty. He was tall and lean and mean, with fair hair in a buzzcut and bad skin. He took the money and thrust it in his trench coat pocket. "Call that a down payment, now get inside, motherfucker."

His partner shoved him into the kitchen, a beefy guy in bomber and jeans with red spikey hair and a round face. His eyes were close-set, green and dead, "Down the office, yah lump ah lard, and we'll talk."

He complied, very aware of the knife. He loved life too much to endanger it for a few bucks, he'd give them the two grand he kept in the safe for provisions.

They sat him down. Menace exuding off them in nasty pulses of nervous energy.

"Take what you want, guys, and go. I want no trouble. I'm a family man."

"We know that shit for brains, now turn that computer on and let's see yah spread sheets."

Toni looked confused. The shorter one gave him a cuff around the head to reinforce his partner's instructions. "Hurry the fuck up, we ain't got all day, for Chrissake."

He complied quickly and they scanned his input and output keenly. The payroll, utility bills and sundry expenses.

"Awesome, never knew yah could make so many green bucks out of 'pooftah food'," from the taller yob.

Toni was affronted, his timidity forgotten for the moment. "My wares are the finest of the fine. Now what do you want?"

"I'm Mr Black and this is Mr White. We're your new business partners."

He looked at the tall Mr Black. *Santa Maria, what were they on about? These were two weird men.* He'd just play along and call the cops when they left.

"You want to buy into the business, guys?"

"You wanna buy into the business, guys?" mimicked Mr White, before slapping him hard around the chops. Toni's teeth rattled and he tasted blood where his molars had cut into his cheek.

"Here's the beef, fatty. You need security because bad stuff happens, and we're yah new task force to keep that stuff from occurring, you dig?"

He nodded at Mr Black. *What the frig...*

"Yeah, man," continued Mr White, "You pay us three thousand dollars a week and we protect you."

"And as much as we can eat, Fatso," added Black.

"But I can't afford that. I've overheads. A family to keep," he answered, flabbergasted.

"Ah yeah, family," and Black reached inside his coat and produced some photographs, which he spread before him. He pointed some out. "Nice one of Maria at the market. There's Carmel going into school. Angelina with her pals... Oh look, there's Gratchia looking out her bedroom window. Sweet sixteen and looking for a good fucking. Do you fuck her, papa?"

"Bet she likes a good go at the old salami," White threw in with a nasty snicker, pleased with his witticism.

Toni was seriously affronted now, "You leave my family outta this, you sons of bitches," he shouted and went for them.

They side-stepped him easily and beat him to the floor. Heavy boots thudded into his ribs and back. He had never felt pain like it.

Afterwards, they told him what 'The Mob' would do to his wife and family. Horror crossed his heavy countenance. Life had certainly taken a turn form the worst. Would he wake up soon from this nightmare wrapped around his Bella Maria's ample folds...? Somehow he didn't think so.

They took him into the shop, produced batons and smashed the glass displays and coolers. Tens of thousands of slivers of glass crunched metallically under their feet as they laughed and horsed about.

Toni looked bereft. Most of his stock was kept in the big walk-in fridge but he shuddered as they played soccer with the big red balls of Edam, stomped on wheels of Brie and flung olives and grapes at each other.

Back in the office they made him sign a contract to 'Black and White Security'.

"Mr Green and his crew will be watching your bitches twenty-four seven. We'll be popping in as and when to check security."

"Yeah, and pay day's Friday. See you then, Fatso," added White.

"Tell the cops two niggers did this and we'll split the insurance money. Them dudes all look alike."

They left in high spirits, two sacks of delicacies between them, leaving cheesy footprints on the gleaming floor.

* * *

His staff found him surveying his smashed empire and clutching his ribs, with tears coursing down his leaden cheeks.

"Ring the cops, Melissa," he told his eldest daughter, "Tell them it was two big black guys and help me up."

Luca listened aghast. Toni being the gent had left the crude parts out but she guessed it must have been a terrifying and vulgar event.

"My poor Toni. So horrible. You were ver' brave to stand up for your lovely family."

He shook his head at the vicious recollections, "Sometimes your faith in your fellow man who coasts along side by side with you in this wonderful world can be a little bit stretched. We are all passengers on life's journey, si, we must get on."

She smiled gently at him and made more coffee. He watched, admiring her lovely form. It was doing him good to talk to this like-minded gentle creature. If only everybody thought like him and Luca. He already had designated a special place in his heart for her amongst his daughters, his wife being his heart.

She sat, "So what happened then, Toni? How did my precious squeeze enter your life?" and she put her soft hand in his, which was a great comfort to him.

"Rabbie restored my faith in my fellow travellers, let me tell you."

She listened rapt as he continued. He was a fluent, descriptive speaker and she imagined his daughters as young children sitting in a semi-circle before him as he recited fairy tales.

Giuseppe dropped a big plastic bag of steaming beetroots into the office and left them to it, the rich, heavy metal aroma filling the corners of the room.

II

Mid April, 2012

Two weeks after Toni's world-shattering visit by Black and White, Rabbie took a much needed day off. He had just been promoted to 'Head of Office', OLG, New York, and had been run off his feet at work. That evening he was having Big Mal and some of the guys over for dinner at his small apartment in Manhattan, and Little Danny was going to show him the finer points of 'Texas Hold 'em'. He needed to stock up to keep the guys happy. Danny and Little Daniel ate like bull elephants.

He smiled as he thought of the big men in his small living room. He would start looking for a bigger place soon, somewhere nearer work, maybe the village area. The fight through the rush hour traffic every morning was horrendous.

His smile faded as he thought of his girlfriend, the supermodel, Juliette Castananda. She hadn't been pleased when he told her he was having a 'boys only' poker night and had slammed the phone down on him.

Then his smile returned. He was going to make a big Greek moussaka, but unlike the Greeks, he was going to put chillies in it to give it heat and serve it up with tossed Greek salad. She would get over it, he grinned. All she seemed to eat was limp lettuce leaves and low calorie cheese and crackers but by crikey, she was a nuclear power plant in bed and he was enjoying being her sexual reactor. He would get her a can of the Black Beluga Caviar she liked.

He entered Toni's deli, his nose quivering in anticipation at the delicious blend of aromas in the air. He had discovered this gourmet treasure house a year ago when he'd hit the famous village area after work one day. After a hilarious hour in Bronco Bills, ogling the topless cowgirls and avoiding the bare-assed cowboys, he had found Toni's on the way to 'Bob Dylan's Bar' and left with a big bag of mouth-watering goodies.

He was an instant convert when he sampled Toni's Mexican chilli and tried to get over weekly. He liked Toni, a larger than life character, full of bonhomie and a walking dictionary on food and who gushed forth on its merits as he helped his keen customers choose.

So Rabbie was disconcerted that morning, as he picked his aubergines, chillies, and sun-kissed tomatoes, to see that Toni looked very pale and worried-looking, and God forbid, even seemed to have lost weight! "Hey, Toni, what you call that ewe's cheese you put in Greek salad? I don't see any."

Toni shuffled down to him. Rabbie noticed he kept glancing at the door nervously and checked his watch again. Rab tried to catch his eye but couldn't, "You expecting Miss New York to arrive or something, Toni? You okay, man?"

Toni grinned wryly. "I should be so graced, Rabbie. I am fine, my friend. What yah looking again?"

Rabbie told him and Toni looked blank for a second. He checked his watch again. "Oh yeah…feta…feta cheese. I forgot to put it out. Melissa," he called.

His eldest daughter of twenty, who was learning the trade, came over, "Si, Papa?"

They talked in Italian for a bit and she went to do his bidding. "It betta she getta the feta for you fella."

Rab laughed, "Getta the feta. Very good, Toni, thank you."

Toni smiled sadly, "Yeah, there a poet in me somewhere. Maybe I'm in the wrong job." He looked at the entrance again, a nervous tick started above his right eye.

"I'm making chilli moussaka. Any tips for the perfect dish, maestro?"

"I dunno know, Rabbie. Just don't burn the muvver, I guess."

He looked at the sweating, nervous man keenly. The last time he had gave Toni an opening to discuss a recipe, he had spoken effusively about how to make perfect spaghetti bolognese. This was not the Toni he knew. He was acting way out of character. Something was seriously eating away at him. Out of kilter.

"What wrong, Toni? You seem out of sorts."

Toni caught his eye very briefly before looking away, but not quick enough before Rabbie saw the combo of dread, fear and hopelessness in his black eyes, the same colour as the lush Italian olives he sold. "You must excuse me, Rabbie. I have some calls to make," and he slouched off, shoulders hunched.

Mellissa came down with his cheese. She was a pretty girl with springy dark hair and eyes like her father. She muttered something quietly as she passed the cheese over. "What you say, Mellissa?"

378

She glanced furtively down at the office, then back to him, and the anxious girl said, "By the grace of Santé Maria, please help him, Mr DeJames," and was gone as quick as she had come.

Rabbie paid at the till and left, his senses on high alert. Something was seriously wrong at Toni's Deli and he was concerned, but also intrigued. A private investigator needed a keen sense of curiosity in all things. It brought results and kept them on the trail, and Rabbie possessed a fine one. He loitered in the narrow street, window shopping and browsing in a small antique shop, watching the customers come and go in Toni's. Well-dressed matrons, young mums and kids, businessmen in smart suits, office girls in trendy gear. He watched them all, assessing the situation, until an hour after he had left, two rough-looking guys in jeans and bombers entered... Rabbie's interest peaked. Definitely what his father called rough trade. Out of place. More burgers and fries type of guys. Fast food junkies.

He dandered back down. He had forgotten to buy Juliette's caviar. Forgotten on purpose.

He entered and Melissa saw him and for a brief instance relief crossed her face. The other staff were helping and serving the steady stream of lunchtime trade as he made his way down to the back.

"I forgot to get my chick some Black Beluga. Can you get me a can, Melissa?"

She looked over her shoulder nervously then back at him, "Sure, come out back. Come and take your pick."

He followed her through and down the hallway, where she stopped by the office. "In there, be careful," she mouthed quickly and fled. He knocked, entered without waiting and closed the door behind him.

The tall mean-looking dude in the pork pie hat was sitting at the computer, flicking through pages with the mouse. The stouter, red-haired one was sitting knee to knee with Toni at the desk, counting out a wad of dollars. Toni was looking forlorn and scared.

All three turned to look at him as he strode in, as if he owned the place.

"What da feck...who you, man?" asked Mr Black.

"Yeah, man. This is a private meeting, dawg. Wait outside. You got no manners or what?" from White.

Toni looked worried as Rabbie pulled an ID card.

"Jim Byrnes. Office of the Department of Public Health. It's inspection day, I did ring."

Black jumped up and snatched it off him, "Lemme see that, this right, Toni? This guy ring?"

Toni looked at Rabbie and nodded, "Si, he rang earlier, I forgot he coming."

"Why doncha come back later, Holmes. We're in a transaction here."

Rabbie looked into White's dead eyes. Crack cocaine user, he guessed. "Sorry guys but I'm on the tax payers' dollar here. You ready to get started, Toni? I've a busy dance list today," and he snatched the ID back off Black. "Satisfied? Who are yah to be checking my authority anyway?"

The ID was one of several he used to assist him in his work. Forged by an expert his father used. "Never you mind, dude. We dun here, Mr White?" White palmed the cash. "Yeah, all's kosher. Let's vamoose, partner."

"We'll grab a few provisions and say goodbye to Mellissa. She's one foxy babe," Black said pointedly to Toni as he left brushing past Rabbie roughly.

Toni sank his head in his hands, "Oh sweet Mama Mia. Whatta I'm gonna do, my friend?"

Rabbie sat and put a big, reassuring hand on his shoulder. "A problem shared is a problem half solved. Tell me about it, my friend."

So Toni did, talking faster and faster as it flowed out of him, pleased to share, his instincts telling him this man sitting with him was tough and resilient, but had an innate fairness within. He put his trust in him and knew it would be reciprocated.

Rabbie listened and made a few notes. "So you see, Rabbie. The bastards came in once or twice a week. They sit in my office and threaten me and my family. They watching my house twenty-four seven. They show me photos of my family, steal my goods and scare the staff. They are having a fine time of it, and 1 am paying for the pleasure. I sign the contract for The Mob to do whatta they want. Whatta I'm gonna do?'"

Rabbie patted his well-padded shoulders reassuringly and stood and flicked the espresso machine on.

"There is no 'Mob', Toni. Gangs of crooks but no Mafia. You're being conned."

Toni groaned and produced a bottle of grappa from a drawer and filled two shot glasses.

"And no Judge is going to enforce a contract signed under duress during the commission of an armed robbery."

"How you know this, Rabbie? You a lawyer?"

He gave Toni his card, "On La Guardia Security, Toni. Now let's see what we can do to get you out of this pickle." He pulled his cell and rang the ops rooms, "Hey, Juanita. It's Rabbie. I've a code red at Toni's Deli. Send the team."

Forty minutes later five huge men, of various shades and origins, and a fit blonde-haired lady, all dressed in long black trench coats strode purposefully through the shop and down the back, the customers chatter ceasing in mid flow as they gaped after them.

"Public Health Inspectors," a strangely relieved Melissa told them, "Just routine."

"Gawd help the rats and roaches," said an ageing rock star looking for tofu and beansprouts.

Two stood guard outside and Toni gawked at the four who entered. One extended his hand and he took it. "Mal Zacharias. Head of Ops. OLG. How can we help, Toni?"

As Toni looked at Mal's competent face and shook hands, hope surged up his veins and filled his heart. He glimpsed better times ahead because he knew these were the good guys and they could just well be his salvation.

* * *

Toni paused for thought. He had produced a nice bottle of Vermicelli, and he watched Luca sip the rich red wine as he popped a cracker and Gorgonzola cheese into his mouth. He saw the enjoyment on her perfect face as her taste buds gave their approval and he was pleased at his new pal's appetite.

He pulled the beetroots over and began peeling them, his fingers staining the colour of wild heather as he worked.

Luca ate some cheese and grapes together as Toni had taught her. The taste was sublime. "They are grown on the lower slopes of Mount Vesuvius by the Bay of Naples, and the Neapolitans say the souls of the Roman citizens of Pompeii, which was destroyed by the volcano, is in the juice."

Luca had eyed the grapes warily before sampling them and smiled, "Then the good citizens must have passed away happily because their souls are delicious."

He clapped his hands in delight, "Bravo, bravo, dear Luca. I make the Eyetie out of you yet."

She had laughed with him. "So, Toni, please carry on your story. Is better than going dah movies. You so, so good talker."

She swore he visibly preened and was pleased her new buddy was pleased. He was a lot more at ease in its unfolding now.

"Okay, sweet child. Let me top up that glass first."

* * *

When Toni got home that night to his large five-bed apartment in a brownstone in a good street on the edge of Brooklyn, he was whistling. Maria met him at the door, where she had been hovering anxiously.

She was a large woman with a sweet face and a kind nature. Like her husband she loved her food and was a superb chef. He pulled her to him as Melissa pushed past to greet her sisters.

Toni kissed her, "Are they here, my caro?"

"Si, they are in the front room with the girls."

"Bueno, Bueno. I must go and greet our guests."

Gratchia, eighteen years, Angelina, fifteen years, Clarisse and Anita the twins, twelve years old were sitting on the sofa watching television while Claudiona and Serita, eleven and nine years old, were sitting on the floor with 'Little Danny', who was showing them how to tie lasso knots with a ball of string. They were engrossed. Billy-Jo Sawyer was standing to the side of one of the large front windows, "Yah know, Dan, I don't reckon there's any varmints in that van. We'll go down later, and check it out."

Danny didn't look up from his knots, "Yeah, ah reckon yah rite, Holmes. Mal dun a drive past earlier. He thinks it's a lil' ol' remote motion job."

"All part of the con," agreed Billy-Jo as she carried out her unobtrusive search.

Toni was happy. He had two armed OLG operatives in his apartment around the clock to guard his family and two more to watch them covertly when they went out. This was stage one and Rabbie and Mai had explained it carefully to him.

He unpacked the extra bags of groceries he had brought home. He hoped it was enough. That Little Danny guy looked like he could pack away enough to fill a pack of hungry coyotes.

Maria began hustling pots and skillets, happy her Toni was home and had taken action to sort out the dire straits they were in, and she liked nothing more than to cook for company.

Three days later Toni sat in his office and rang 'Black and White Security'.

"Mr Black. I don't think I can take much more of this. Whatcha say to a one off payment of say fifty grand and you leave us alone?"

381

Mr Black wasn't amused, "The frig, Fatso. I told yah not to discuss our business over the wires. We'll be in to see you. Stay put."

"Yeah, put your family first, you shit head," White came on the line. "You friggin do as yah told or serious penalties will result. Fucking sonsa bitch."

"Okay, okay. I wait for you."

He hung up and Rabbie patted his back and phoned his ops room. OLG had their own tracing system. It had cost mega bucks but was invaluable. Within minutes he had the address in a small seedy area of the Bronx. He passed it onto Mal for surveillance.

Two hours later the thugs arrived, angry and annoyed. They huddled in the office, making threats and drinking 'Fatso's' grappa.

They agreed on one hundred thousand in used notes. Toni said he would have it by noon the next day. After a further barrage of threats, they left, sniggering viciously.

Rabbie came out of the stationary cupboard and holstered his Ruger revolver. He rang the ops room. They had a clear audio from the pin-size microphones under the desk and a clean picture from the camera in the light fitting.

"Not long to go now, Toni. You'll be able to put all this behind you."

"I hope so, Rabbie; I really, really do."

"We'll get them on camera and take it from there."

"Do yah think they'll be back after I pay them off?"

Rabbie grinned. "But you're not going to pay them off, Toni. Now what about a shot of the grappa Maria doesn't know you hide away."

Toni grinned happily; Rabbie was a man after his own heart. "Whatta the eye can't see can't harm you."

Rabbie didn't know about that. He sipped his grappa thoughtfully. He had seen the blacker side of life since being in New York. The seedy, corrupt, criminal underbelly of the city that never slept. It was a never-ending battle between the strong and the weak, the have and have-nots, the criminally insane and the perverted and just plain greed and envy in many cases, and he liked to think OLG were doing their bit in holding back the criminal floodwaters that so often threatened to overwhelm this fantastic city he had come to know and love so well.

"When you're travelling through snake-infested territory, Toni, always carry a big stick. We're your big stick, buddy, and the snakes are gonna get whacked tomorrow."

* * *

Mr Black and Mr White had severe hangovers and were bitching and cursing when they arrived at the deli half an hour late the next day. They learnt in the extortion game never to arrive on time. You kept the poor saps hanging around in dread. It was part of the dehumanising process they had learnt over the years. Fear and violence were the tools of their trade, and they were experts in using them to exploit weakness in their fellow man so that they could cow them and hold them on a tight leash while they fleeced them down to the last hard-earned dollar, leaving in their wake broken spirits and destitute misery.

It was a lucrative living and they never ceased to wonder at the gullibility of the suckers they preyed on. The rare few who stood up to them they walked away from.

There were plenty more fish in the pond, and a little research and surveillance and they just dipped their net and pulled in another one, terrified and gasping for breath.

They had partied all night in their sleazy tenement apartment at Willoughby Avenue in the Bronx with a couple of teenage hookers they had kicked out, sore and dazed, in the morning. They had got high on crack and popped some diazepam, washed down with vodka.

Mr Black was James Holland. He was thirty years old and had a string of priors for assault and robbery. White was Dean Chambers, twenty-eight. He also had convictions for drugs and violence.

Both were career criminals and had done time in various penal institutions from an early age. Crime was in their souls and it sure beat working for a living. Even in the tough area where they lived, they were feared by the local hoods. They were sadistic and brutal and when high on drugs violently unpredictable.

Possessed of an ornate inner cunning, they knew their rights and having learned some tricks from the cop shows on television, had kept one step ahead of the law for the last six years, since their last stint of incarceration, when they had done three years for blackmailing a happily married businessman who was a harmless cross-dresser at weekends. The authorities had never recovered the eighty thousand bucks they had extorted off him, and if he hadn't broke down and confessed all to his wife, who phoned the cops, God knows how it would have ended.

His wife had stood by him but others had not been so lucky and had lost everything. Lock, stock and barrel. Toni was only one of four businessmen they were scamming at that moment in time and the bucks were rolling in, so when they entered the deli, they weren't expecting any trouble. Toni was a greasy Eyetie slob and ripe for the picking. They would take his generous donation and start on him again a few months later.

They sauntered through the shop as if they owned it, whistled at and made crude remarks to the staff, shocking the customers. They entered the office, keen to get their payment and go back and start the party again.

When they entered the office, a small man in a tweed jacket was sitting at Toni's desk. He had short-cropped grey hair and a pleasant-looking demeanour to him. "Who da fuck are you? Where's that fat bastard Toni?" snarled Holland, his hangover prominent.

The stranger looked up from the paper he was picking through, "Why, I am Charles, Charles Brouchard. I am your worst enemy, oui?"

Chambers crowded in, "What he saying? Whatcha mean, dude?"

"Yeah, get outta here and send friggin' fat wop prick in before you get me annoyed, and yah don't want to see us annoyed, man," Chambers said in backup.

Charles pursed his lips and shook his head sadly, "You two guys... I dunno... Did yer mama never teach you ze manners?"

"Whatcha feck..." but Holland never finished because Charles had rose as fast as a striking cobra and struck him hard across the left ear with the small cosh filled with buckshot he preferred to work with in close spaces. As Holland fell Charles grabbed him by the back of the head with his left hand and smashed his face hard onto the desk, breaking teeth. One down and he wouldn't be getting up.

Chambers was horrified as he reached with his right hand to the knife on his belt, but he didn't reach it because a blow from the cosh broke his wrist, and as he began to howl, a sharp blow to the jaw put his lights out, breaking it in two places.

383

He dropped across his sprawled companion.

Charles put his cosh away and wiped his palms as Rabbie popped his head in, "All done, Charles? That was quick!"

He adjusted his jacket. He was always immaculately dressed. The picture of satirical eloquence. "Oui, Boss. I am losing ze touch. One nearly got his knife out."

Rabbie laughed. Always the perfectionist! After twenty-five years in the elite French Foreign Legion and ten years of those as an unarmed combat instructor, Rabbie didn't think so. Charles was lethal, his diminutive stature and pleasant features a good advantage when dealing with the bad guys.

"They should 'ave listened to their mama. Never talk to strangers. I will take my leave but not before I buy some of Toni's delicious Roquefort cheese and olives," he said in his melodious Southern French accent.

Rabbie clapped him on the back as he left. Big Mal and Little Danny came in as Rabbie finished plasti-cuffing the two thugs.

They heaved them out to the black panel van they used for covert surveillance and with Buzz 'Boomerang' driving, headed off for the Bronx, leaving an anxious, hand-wringing deli owner to get on with business.

As Mal had suspected, the beat up van outside the D'Agostino's for long periods everyday was left unattended. Simple motion cameras trained on the house photographed anybody coming or going or moving at the doors and windows. There was no Mr Green or Yellow. It was strictly a two-man operation.

Reaching Willoughby Avenue, Rabbie tossed Mal the keys, "Recovery time, big guy."

Holland and Chambers watched from the floor of the van. Gagged now as well as trussed up. Fear was deep in their eyes and pain etched across their faces. They had come round to a world of pain to see two huge guys with hard eyes watching them. "Any ol' trouble from you greenhorns, and I'll be happy tah break yah pinkies one by one, hombre," Little Danny informed them pleasantly.

Inside the apartment they found over $150,000 in various denominations secreted in a cash box under a floorboard in the bedroom.

Rabbie counted it deftly and whistled. Like most crooks they didn't trust banks and liked to keep their stash close to hand.

They also found a notebook with the names and addresses of four other businesses inside. Rabbie later visited all four and found the same scam had been going on there. A tailor, a chemist, a man who ran a string of hotdog vans and a garage owner. They were so grateful and relieved to be free to trade without hindrance again that they each agreed to pay a quarter of OLG's cost, which was a great help to Toni.

Also in the stinking apartment was about $10,000 of crack cocaine and a lot of extorted prescription drugs from the scammed chemist.

They drove for a late lunch. Leaving the crooks firmly secured as they tucked into huge steaks at the local Hanlon's Steak House.

"Hey, all yah can eat for ten bucks at night," said a happy Lil' Danny. "I'll come back here."

Rabbie wasn't so sure. He didn't like the look of the horsey-faced owner nor the way he berated his staff.

Afterwards, they drove back to the office. They sipped coffee and chewed the cud, and Rabbie caught up with any outstanding business with Elaine Curry.

He rang Billy-Jo at the D'Agostino's, "Okay, you and Alec can leave now. The threat has been neutralised. Get Big Alec to hot wire the van and bring it back to the office."

They would sell the camera surveillance gear at auction to defray costs and the van would go to OLG ranges to be used for target practice.

All in all, the day was going well. After the office closed, they drove back to the Bronx. The two perps were lying semi-conscious in the back, wondering when their hell was going to end.

When it got dark they pulled up outside the apartment and hauled them inside. Rabbie had not wanted to drag them in during daylight hours. It was a dark street. Most of the street lamps either didn't work due to lack of maintenance or were vandalised.

Once inside they sat them on the sofa. Danny ungagged them. Their throats were raw and constricted. Holland spat two teeth out.

"You go near people again we'll kill yah," he told them pleasantly.

"Slowly," added Mal, who then shot them both in the right knee with a throw down. He emptied the chamber in the sixty-inch flat screen and tossed the gun down.

The villains screamed in agony, then pleaded for mercy as he produced another throw down, a .38special; they picked them up on ops, always handy to have.

Rabbie made the call to the cops on the cheap pay as you go he had purchased earlier and would discard.

Mal tossed the other throw down into the kitchen. Something for the cops. Felons were not allowed to carry firearms.

"Just in case you think we're fucking about, lads, we've got your last visit to Toni's on film, so you'd best forget you met us today."

They drove off and watched as several blue and whites zoomed past, sirens and lights blazing.

"They certainly go in mob handed down the Bronx," observed Rab "Home, Buzz, and don't forget to change the plates on the van."

They left mightily satisfied with a good day's work done.

"So you see, Luca. I get my life back; I get all my money back. I have enough over to pay OLG for a great job done, si, and all because my friend Rabbie go to bat for me. He and the guys were fantastic."

Luca was agog. "Wow, dat sooo so amazing. Vot happen to the bad men? You no more trouble, Toni?"

He laughed happily, "Oh it was a clever job OLG done. The bad men they get done for possession narcotics with intent to supply, possession unlicensed guns and other stuff. They doing big time, lady. I tell you."

Luca was delighted and proud of her lover Rabbie. Well, not quite her lover but did she not share the same bed as him? She had to admire his self-control because she had accidently, well maybe not so accidently, brushed up against his erection in the mornings and it had thrilled her to pieces.

That night she served him pickled Rollmop Herrings on a mixed leaf salad, before she served up delicious borscht made from the elusive beetroots, fresh chicken stock, white wine and herbs. Rabbie had tucked in with gusto and complimented her effusively, much to her satisfaction.

Later she lay in bed, watching him sleep. "Sweet dreams, my gallant knight," she breathed before she spooned into him and closed her lovely eyes, safe and secure.

Luca grinned knowingly as he left whistling the next morning. He had complimented her effusively on her culinary feat.

What he didn't know was that Toni had took her home to meet Maria, and the girls and the older woman had helped her make the tasty soup for her to take home.

She shrugged philosophically. *Oh well!* she decided, *All's well in the hood, everybody is happy, the baddies are in the clinky and new day is a blessing to be enjoyed and lived to the full.*

Chapter 29
Felix... A Hero and His Wheelbarrow
(Zoom...and the Whole Wide World Went Boom... 'Zoom' by Fat Larry... 1981)

The Robert Peel Pub, Watford 5ᵗʰ November 1980

The bar was quiet in the early evening as medically retired Sergeant Major Sebastian Justin Pugh sat in his wheelchair and contemplated his bleak future through the bottom of his glass. He was a strong-looking man with dark hair brushed back, dark intense eyes and despite having no legs, he radiated confidence and self-determination, but it wasn't how he felt tonight.

If the army would pull its finger out and get him fitted with new artificial legs at their centre in Leatherhead, Surrey, he might be able to look to his future and get some type of job to supplement his pension. Soldiers on active service were not allowed to claim compensation for criminal injuries inflicted on them.

At the moment he was living in a ground floor adapted flat in the local Leonard Cheshire[151] home on the outskirts of town, but he missed the craic and going out for a pint with the guys. So he had took the bull by the horns and ventured out on his own, tipping the big West Indian taxi driver for helping him out of the car and into the hated chair.

"You'll be okay in The Peel, mon, big crew of ex-army dudes drink there."

Reassured, especially after Clive told him he would pick him up again at eleven and see him back to the home, Sebastian was enjoying his pints of best bitter and drams of fine Bowmore Whiskey. Louise, the pleasant blonde girl who did nights in the saloon bar, shouted over, "You okay, mate? Give us a shout when you need another."

He toasted her in thanks, listening to the craic from the public bar next door, men playing pool and darts and telling jokes. He wished that he could join them but his confidence just wasn't up to it yet.

A big, fleshy guy with grey hair, a whiskey nose and a limp came over and introduced himself as Ron the landlord, "Yeah, Ronnie Mulligan, mate. You ex-forces?"

"Yeah, I done my bit. God help me."

Ronnie eyed him keenly, "Well, you're in the right pub, mucker. Why don't yeh come on through to the public and meet some of the boys?"

Sebastian thought about that, then, "Maybe later, I've got a bit of thinking to do."

---

[151] Group Captain in the Royal Air Force who founded homes for disabled servicemen.

Ronnie could see a man in distress and turmoil, he was an astute and kind man under his tough landlord exterior, "What's that you're tippling?"

"Bowmore's? Good choice. Louise," he hollered, "give this guy a double Bowie on the house." Louise hastened to his bidding and he offered Ron his hand.

"Sebastian Pugh. Thanks very much, Ron."

Ron shook. He knew an ex-squaddie in strife when he saw one, "My pleasure, mate. Have da go back and run the public. Eadie's up roasting half a pig for dinner, Gawd lumme. See ya later!"

Sebastian watched his departing back. Nice guy but his insecurity, through his disability, had made him deeply uneasy in public. Sure, hadn't his wife upped and left him and took their kids back to the native Northampton? He cursed the fucking IRA, devious bastards. They had only not wrecked his life, they had destroyed a career and decimated a good family future.

Louise brought his drink over, and he downed it in one with no water; the Scotch coating his throat and bursting like a big ball of molten wax in his belly. Louise looked concerned, "Hey, you're safe here, mate. You wind down and relax."

The drink had indeed chilled him out. He produced a blue fiver, "You're a darling, get one for yourself and big Ronnie. I'm fine. Thanks for the hospitality." Louise left with a smile. She knew a gentleman when she met one. Legs or no legs.

And that was the problem, Sebastian thought, Cathy still rang to see he was all right and suggested he come up for the weekend, but she was finicky and he knew his sex life was over. The kids missed him like blazes but he wasn't ready. He was still waking at four in the morning with the nightmares. The vivid blue flash[152] and muscle paralysis that left him drenched in sweat, disorientated and wanting to fight back, to throw himself out of bed and seize the bastards by the neck and throttle the life out of them.

He gulped some beer down and took a good slug of whiskey. What the fuck was he going to do? The IRA had taken his legs from the knee down but they hadn't taken his manhood. He could still look at a pretty woman and get aroused, but there was nothing he could do about it except for the five-fingered widow, which left him feeling degraded and perverted. Sebastian guessed he would never feel a woman's soft flesh and heat in bed again, and it made him feel desolate for the lonely destiny that lay ahead of him.

* * *

A group of punks came into the bar, six in number, with their strange spiky hair dyed in all shades of fluorescent colours, pierced noses and lips, outrageous clothing – wearing heavy boots and spiked dog collars and chains.

Louise served them hesitantly pints of Purple Nasty[153]; they took their drinks and sat in an open horseshoe-shaped booth and mumbled unintelligently amongst themselves.

Sebastian snorted and decked more whiskey. They certainly were a good marker for bringing back National Service. One of the punks with hair like a Mohican, dyed

---

[152] Certain commercial and military plastic explosives give off a vivid electric-blue flash when detonated, Semtex in particular, as the author can verify.

[153] Beer, Cider and Blackcurrant.

388

pink and purple, looked over, "You gotta prob, Granddad? Why don't you hop off home?" and he laughed uproariously and his mates joined in. They keep glancing at him and sniggering and he heard 'Spastic' and 'Cripple' mentioned several times.

"Granddad, indeed," grunted Sebastian loudly to the ceiling, "I'm only bloody thirty-two!"

Mohican looked at him and sneered, "Listen, Crip...fuck away back to your home for spastics and hide your sick body away from us. Spastics should be seen and not heard and not allowed in public with decent folk."

Sebastian grinned, "You're cruising for a bruising, mate, as they say in America."

Mohican snickered, "Well, get out of your fucking chair and go for it, you crippled wanker. His friends chortled and giggled into their Nasties.

Louise couldn't hear the conversation fully but she sensed it wasn't good. She came out from behind the bar, hands on hips and confronted them, "Right, five minutes to down your girlie drinks, then out... Comprendí, dickheads?"

They jeered again at her like a pack of rabid dogs, "Listen, slut, we'll go in our own time and have another after. So, go get your poxy, smelly twat behind the bar and pour us another if you know what's right for yah."

Sebastian observed with intent interest. Louise was a cracking looking young woman, well-dressed, well-coiffed and, as the guys in the NAAFI[154] would have said, a wee cracker. He could see she had pride in her appearance and hygiene.

"Well, sod, you wankers, time's up. Get out now before I call the landlord."

Mohican grabbed her wrists and pulled her onto his lap, "What about a little kiss, and we'll talk about the first thing that comes up."

His mates whooped, "Yeah, let's take her out and give her one each for Watford."

Louise slapped him hard across the foul fiend's chops and the pack rose in unison to attack her. Sebastian decided enough was enough. He may be physically disabled but these vicious thugs were seriously mentally disabled. He wheeled over to the horseshoe, pulled Louise away from the prat onto his lap, then grabbed the thirty-six-inch-long baton the army used for riot control from the adapted sheath on the left of his wheelchair. He smacked Mohican full force with a horizontal blow across the bridge of his nose, breaking cartilage and blackening both his eyes. Louise clung on tight and all hell erupted. The pack rose as one and attacked 'the crip' who had assaulted their alpha wolf.

* * *

Jamesey, Smudger and 'Hedge' Privet had slipped off early and were throwing Double Diamond down their necks and sipping on the Hennessey Brandy. Kim and Collette were down with Myrtle in Colne Avenue. They had taken her and the kids out shopping and the plan was that about eight, the guys would arrive down with a takeaway from the 'Mandarin Garden'. They would chill out then set the fireworks off for the kids, "Yah can set my firework off later in privacy, luv," Collette had told Jamesey, much to his delight.

---

[154] Navy, Army, Air Force Institutes cafés and recreation centres for troops.

Jamesey knew the girls would be guzzling wine, playing good 'reggae' and spoiling the kids. Then they would all head their own happy ways after an hour or so and tomorrow was a new day. He loved going to bed with Collette, whether anything happened or not. It was a loving, warm, secure thing, and he just adored folding himself to her hot, deft, compliant body.

Ronnie had told him about the guy in the wheelchair next door, ex-army fella, but shy about coming into the public.

'Let the hare sit, Ron. We'll assess him later."

Smudger was about to pot the black and win a much needed score off Jamesey when all hell broke loose in the saloon bar.

"Call it a tie, brother," Jamesey laughed and vaulted the bar as Ronnie reached for his trusty slugger; Smudger hot on his heels. They bounced through the divide and crashed over the bar into the saloon. Stopped and looked gobsmacked... What the fuck was going on here?

* * *

A twenty-year-old prat with a multi-coloured Mohican was curled up in a ball holding his nose, blood seeping through his fingers. Another punk was clutching his family jewels, coiled up in the foetal position. A wheelchair was on its side and a big guy had his teeth in one guy's ear, chewing like a Rottweiler, and had another cretin in a chokehold with his left arm. Louise was fuming and ranting and slapping another around the head, every slap raising the hemline of her lime green skirt up to knicker level, flashing her fine legs.

"Feck me pink, Jamesey," remarked Smudger, "that guy's bouncing on his stumps like a yo-yo."

Jamesey gauged the situation in the blink of an eye, "Well, he seems to be handling his own."

The remaining gang member pulled a switch blade and made his aggressive way towards Sebastian.

"Mine, mates!" shouted Hedge and bounded over and gave the cunt the 'Smoker's Punch', twisted his arm up his back and relieved him of the wicked blade, "Up the Mighty Poachers!" he roared and delivered a 'Liverpool Kiss', which put the guy's lights out.

"Not bad for a crap head," observed Smudger.

They strolled over, slapped the assailants about and threw them out.

"Never judge a book by its cover," Jamesey snarled. "You come back, you'll know what crippled means."

"Fucking wankers," injected Smudger. "We know your faces. WATCH YOUR FUCKIN' BACKS!"

Back in the saloon, Ronnie had got Sebastian back into his wheelchair, had calmed Louise down with a brandy, and Eadie had rushed in from upstairs and dusted her down. Jamesey grinned at a shell-shocked Sebastian, "Suffering Jesus, brother. Where the fuck did that come from?"

Sebastian looked cowed, "Dunno, but don't like young women being subjected to physical abuse and foul language," and emptied his whiskey, which had miraculously surfaced.

390

"Indeed, he does not," reiterated Louise, who was smoothing her skirt over her fine body. "A girl can certainly feel safe and secure when Sebastian is on the scene."

The hero of the moment blushed ,and Smudger took place behind his chair and pushed him forward, "Dunno why you're drinking in the Yuppies part anyway, Sebastian. It's for pussies…come and meet the guys." Jamesey smiled. Always on the make, he sensed an opportunity here.

They played pool and filled Sebastian with whiskey. They wheeled him around the pool table and Eadie supplied them with roast pork sandwiches, crackling and apple pie with custard. Sebastian was blocked but knew he was in good company and safe. Even more, he liked the smouldering looks Louise gave him, smiling occasionally from the partition of the bars as she flitted in and out. Sebastian watched, mesmerised, but putting himself down. He had no hope there with a looker like that.

* * *

Jamesey and Smudger plied Sebastian with even more drink and prised his story out of him. When he needed a piss, they pushed him down to the Gents, whipped him out of the chair, whisked his kecks down and plonked him on the bowl until he was done.

"For fuck's sake, I can handle myself!" he yelled.

"Yeah? Well, fuck up, you craphead. Time is money!" bellowed Smudger.

"Plus a waste of drinking time and it's your bloody round."

* * *

What Jamesey and Smudger deduced was their new buddy, Sebbie babe, was one hard, mean fucking dude. He had told them he had joined the Royal Army Ordnance Corp in 1962 and had gone through the system and by 1968 was a fully qualified Armourer Warehouse Supply Officer and Quartermaster Sergeant.

"Yeah, practically ran the Ordnance depot in Pirbright until I made a fatal error."

"What was that then?" Jamesey asked, interested.

"I applied to join the bomb disposal mob. Did the course up at Sutton Coldfield and became a 'Felix'[155] and before I knew it, I was up to me neck in IEDs[156] in Ulster."·

"Lummy, Seb. Were you mad in the head or did you just take a funny turn?"

"No, Smudger, I wanted to see a bit of action, and I was sick of seeing the young 'uns coming back in body bags after triggering booby traps."

Jamesey clapped him on the shoulder and sent Hedge for more drink, "Bravest of the brave, those ATOs[157]. Nerves like stainless steel bear traps."

"Yeah, well, I always liked tinkering with things – mechanics and electrics. Did three tours but the fourth proved to be my Waterloo."

"What happened then, Seb?"

---

[155] Mythical cat with nine lives.

[156] Improvised explosive devices.

[157] Ammunition Technical Officers.

Guy Fawkes Night, Belfast. November the 5th 1979. Exactly one year prior.

Warrant Officer Pugh was based in the Old Grand Central Hotel on Belfast Royal Avenue in the city centre. The army had taken over the hotel, lock, stock and barrel, and it was a bustling hive of activity as patrols, both mobile and foot, came and went. Squaddies hustled about doing a thousand and one tasks and Ruperts and NCOs stood about looking important and barking orders. Radios squawked and hissed with static and the crew in the comms room controlled operations and monitored the ever-changing situation.

Around a square mile of the city centre was ringed by a cordon of steel gates and fencing; all pedestrians were searched entering. Vehicle access was restricted to buses, delivery vans and, of course, security force vehicles. They were trying to keep out the bombers but they managed to slip the odd car bomb in, which caused mayhem for a couple of days before they cleared up and reopened the shops. But you couldn't fence off the whole city, and there were plenty of other targets in and around the periphery of the street barriers and devices still exploded on a frequent basis. The brave Felixes risked life and limb daily to defuse the bombs, big or small, and frustrate the IRA godfathers, who retaliated by making even more sophisticated explosions laced with booby traps to catch the wary defusers out. Glaziers and carpenters were never out of business in Belfast.

Sebastian was tired. He sat in the standby room fully dressed, waiting for the next call out. His crew and bodyguards sat playing cards or dozing, rifles to hand. The atmosphere was tense. The night previously, the IRA had blitzed four provincial towns, causing millions of pounds of damage and killing a squaddie in Dungannon. A secondary device was placed behind a concrete pillar he had taken cover behind the cordon.

The terrorists were good at leaving little surprises behind or staging elaborate come ons such as road traffic accidents or robberies. The cops and army rushed out to attend only to find themselves being pulled into a trap of bombs and bullets. Yep, the Felix teams province-wide were stretched to the limit, and they were number one on the IRA hit list.

Sebastian had already been out three times that day, defusing small tape cassette fire bombs that the IRA got their women to smuggle into the city centre and hide in the stores under piles of discount wallpaper, designed to detonate at night and cause maximum damage.

From 'Information Received', they had searched Littlewoods off the High Street and found three in the ladies clothing department. They were easily deactivated, and he had placed them in a bag of sand and handed them over to CID. A grateful manager had given them a free steak and chips before letting the staff and customers back in. If the bombs had gone off, thousands of pounds of damage would have been the result. Seb and his men had enjoyed the break in routine. He found the vast majority of Northern Irish people pleasant and easy to get on with and felt sorry for their troubles. It always seemed that violent patriots inflicted more suffering to their own than the intended regime they appeared to want to overthrow.

Seb shook his head. The mind boggled and was way too deep to think about in his exhausted condition, plus it was his birthday and he was heading home for a week's leave in the morning. He missed Cathy, his wife, and his lovely eight-year-old twins, Ben and Kirsty, and looked forward to spending some quality time with them.

Suddenly, the call-out buzzer went off with a screech like a pig being slaughtered, and the boys threw their gear on and headed out to the vehicles as Seb and bodyguards rushed down to the Operations Room for orders. The Colonel of the Green Jackets, Colonel Sharp, was there peering at the map and the Ops Officer was directing call signs to the target area.

"What's the score, Boss?"

The Colonel swivelled round, "Got a Brahma for you, Sergeant Major. Ten-thousand-gallon oil tanker hijacked in Andytown. Dumped in Flack Street off the Crumlin Road. Couple of yellow Calor Gas cooking cylinders sitting on top, wired up. Driver's door lying open and a cardboard box, also with wires, coming out on the seat."

Sebastian felt a sense of déjà vu. This was the big one. This is what all the training, the commitment and dedication to duty had brought to fruition – the climax.

'Did they give the authorised code word[158]?"

The harassed Ops Officer spun round in his chair, "Yeah, the bastards did. Two-hour warning PIRA job."

Seb studied the map. It was a densely populated area on the peace line between the staunchly Republican Ardoyne estate and the outer fringes of the Protestant Shankill. If that tanker blew, it would decimate the area for several hundred yards and spray an umbrella of burning oil for at least half a mile.

"Area sealed? We are going to need a massive evacuation on this one."

"'A-company' have sealed the scene and are clearing three streets either side but they are being hassled by rioters from the Doyne."

Seb scrutinised the map. Time was of the essence but he needed as much knowledge as possible to ensure the safety of the civilians and sanitise the area as quickly as possible.

"I need the area cleared at least ten streets, Colonel. No line of sight. I need the inner cordon at least two hundred metres in a 360° and in hard cover. Inner cordon with me at an ICP at the city side of Flack Street and the Crumlin Road. I want fire brigades and ambulances on standby at the junction Oldpark Road and Crumlin Road."

"You got it, Sergeant Major. I have crashed 'Gordon Highlanders'[159] from Palace Barracks. They should be en-route now."

Sebastian went through a mental check list, "Might be an idea to get a few leisure centres and church halls opened for the residents. I've a feeling this will be an all-nighter."

"Welfare and press officers will sort that."

"Right. Thanks, Colonel. Am en-route."

They watched him rush out, "Rather him than me, Boss."

The Colonel sighed, "Brave guys those Felixes. Saved my guys several times last few months. I'll say a prayer for him and his men." The Colonel was well-known for his religious beliefs.

---

[158] The terrorists gave code words weekly to verify their claims.

[159] Infantry regiment – now disbanded.

"Don't know about prayer, Boss. Good body armour and a steady hand is what is required here."

The Colonel shrugged, "There but for the grace of God go I. I'll pray anyhow. Maybe someone up there will listen."

The Ops Officer turned back to his bank of radios. He somehow doubted that in this godforsaken place.

* * *

They screamed out in convoy – two jeep-loads of gun-toting bodyguards. A Saracen armoured car with all the gear any bomb disposal man could need, and Seb in a jeep crammed with radios and frequency-blocking gear[160] and his personal equipment. A driver and his assistant, a Corporal called Stewart Blythe, who helped him with all the small tasks an ATO had to do.

The journey was only ten minutes; they roared through the Royal Avenue gates, traffic scattering before them. Turning left up North Street onto the Shankill Road, attracting a few bricks from kids loitering at the entrance to the Republican Unity Flats, they squealed up the road at full throttle. Then turned right down Tennent Street past the heavily fortified RUC station, left onto the Crumlin Road. This had been sealed by troops on the ground and screeched to a halt at the junction with Flack Street, putting the vehicles in a lager, like Wild West settlers; bonnets facing out, leaving a relatively safe area to work in in the enclosed centre space.

Sebastian gave his arrival time over the air as his bodyguard debussed, got into cover and secured the area around the vehicles. He knew not to get out until the bodyguard commander told him. ATOs were big on the hit list for PIRA command; any IRA sniper who whacked him would get a nice big cash bonus. The 'Come On'… Beware the 'Come On' had been drilled into them time after time during training. He got the all clear and climbed out and looked up Flack Street.

There it was – the dreaded tanker sitting bathed in headlamp light from two RUC Hotspur Land Rovers attached to the SPG[161] in Musgrave Street. It looked sad and abandoned, like a beached whale or some pet prehistoric dinosaur disregarded by its callous owner. More call signs arrived. The QRF[162] company from Palace, "Get the area cleared at least ten streets deep. If that bugger goes off, it will be catastrophic!" he ordered the Major in charge. There was no rank issue here. When a Felix was on the scene, he was the man in charge.

It was now eight twenty-five pm. He had an hour and a half left but you couldn't trust the IRA time warnings; they were very rarely accurate or true. Over the next half hour, they sent the wheelbarrow up to take photos and X-rays. Wheelbarrow was a four-foot-long vehicle on tank tracks with cameras, an extending robotic arm and high powered lights.

They monitored its progress from the television screens in the back of the Saracen, Stewart working the remote control box like you would fly a remote control plane. He surveyed the pictures. The two gas cylinders right on top of the tanker had,

---

[160] Radio jamming equipment to prevent remote controlled explosions.

[161] Police uniformed anti-terrorist and riot squad. Highly trained and suffered high casualties during The Troubles.

[162] Army squad on immediate standby to head out as backup at incidents.

what looked like, small explosive charges attached with electrical wires; one on top of each cylinder. But he also noticed a concealed wire painted white leading down under the lorry. Okay, where the frig did that lead to? Or what?

They brought the barrow back and studied the results. The barrow had a sniffer device, which could detect various explosives up to thirty metres in radius. Sebastian pulled the litmus strip out and analysed the progress of the machine. It couldn't climb and the lorry was obviously too high but it had extended its robotic arm and circled the entire vehicle. What he saw he did not like.

"Right, Blythy. We have no trace of explosives off the gas cylinders. But look here! See the deep purple, that is under the lorry. That indicates plastic, probably C4, and see the pink from the box in the cab, HME[163], possibly Annie[164]."

Sebastian had one hour left. He was helped on with his apron of body armour that weighed thirty pounds, blast-proof gloves and a heavy Kevlar helmet with reinforced visor and radio mike connection. The only way he was going to sort this bugger out was by taking a close look.

He began the long, dreaded walk; the eighty metres to the tanker. The walk many had started and some had never come back from. Sweat broke and soaked him, his body repelling the unexpected weight and heat. Two of his dedicated bodyguards followed him down, loyalty blazing in their eyes, rifle butts on shoulders.

Halfway down, he waved them back. If the bugger exploded, their flack jackets wouldn't save them. They would be blown into fragments, vaporised, only leaving a red mist. Sebastian did not want that, this was his job and his alone. He was a professional to the core and took his responsibilities seriously.

* * *

For the next hour he clambered carefully over the lorry. He ascertained the charges on the gas cylinders were just plasticine but the strange wire led under one of them. Underneath the tanker he discovered an Adidas sports bag that it led into. He opened it by cutting a square out with a Stanley knife. Blocks of white C4 explosives were exposed by his torch. He gingerly followed the wire and carefully pulled out the Canadian detonator they were attached to. Safe.

Sneaky bastards but so far so good. He scrambled back onto the tank and peered under the cylinder, the wire disappeared under. The bombers hadn't done a good job, they had left a space of an inch or so, he was able to look under with a torch. His blood ran cold. It was a mercury tilt switch that the INLA had killed the MP Airey Neave with in the underground car park at Westminster. As he drove off up the exit ramp, the mercury had tilted down and made the connection complete and detonated the bomb. If Sebastian moved the gas cylinder at an angle, it would have activated the pound of explosive below the base, blasting them all to kingdom come.

Perspiration blinding him, he cut the wire with his snippers and prayed to God for deliverance. Time was up but he was not one to leave a job half done. His Oppos and the cordon party were observing anxiously, shitting bricks. Sebastian climbed into the cab, straddled the box and investigated it. His torch showed and he smelled

---

[163] Homemade explosives.

[164] HME made from industrial fertiliser, diesel fuel and icing sugar.

the distinctive smell of almonds that accompanied HME. The IRA only had so much commercial explosives and used them sparingly.

He was uneasy about this sod of a box. He carefully eased up a flap and shone his flash light in. The explosives gleamed wickedly, ground into a fine light brown sand. The detonator stuck out and wires led down below the box. He couldn't see any timer. He struggled down, flat, not an easy task with all his armour on and shone his torch under the driver's seat. Wires ran down through a hole in the floor.

Sebastian was twenty minutes over the detonation time now but he reckoned he had a handle on things. He climbed out, laid flat under the lorry and flicked his Maglite on. Dirty devious cunts. The wires led to a large sausage-shaped tube of explosives wrapped in cling film. He looked at its tiny black switch attached to the evil detonator. Again his blood ran cold.

His hands were shaking now and the sweat flowed like a newborn desert spring after the rain had fallen in the desert. If he had moved the box in the cab, the 'trembler' would have set the whole fucking thing off. The tanker and its lethal load of diesel would have gone up in a devastating fireball, destroying and razing the area to the ground and claiming many lives.

Sebastian was very scared now. His wife and children were there like a photograph in his mind. For some reason he thought of when he was a young boy and his dad would take him to a reservoir near Huntingdon, fishing for carp. He would tell him the swans were the reincarnations of all the kings and queens of England and to hunt them would bring bad luck to the land.

He could have walked away then. He was happy the lorry wasn't going to explode. He could get another Felix team to help him, then he thought of all the displaced people wondering if the terrorists were going to leave them a place to live in, of the massive disruption this incident was causing. He even thought of the families with empty oil tanks who would not have heat tonight. Sebastian's hands steadied, "Fuck you, fuck the sons of the sons of the sons. We don't give into violence, so go screw yourselves!", and he clipped the wires each side of the trembler, pulled out the detonator and went back to the cab, defused the box of explosives and ambled back to the ICP[165].

Radio procedure had been maintained. Blythy helped him out of his gear, "Bloody hell, Boss. Class call."

"One-hour swamp time[166] but I reckon it's safe now. Send the barrow in to retrieve the goodies for forensics."

"How many devices, Boss?"

"Four defused but let's not get complacent. What about a cuppa and a fag?"

"Got some good tuna and onion sarnies, Boss."

"Nah. Some reason I've no appetite."

* * *

The barrow pulled the cylinders down, the box out of the cab and blasted them with controlled explosions, which was basically a shot of water fired at Mach speed with the power of two shotgun cartridges.

---

[165] Incident control point.
[166] To wait for safety.

Sebastian left another half hour swamp time, then with the RUC, scores of crime officers retrieved and bagged them for evidence. He then bagged the explosives under the chassis and engine block. He felt good now, "I guess we can declare the area safe and leave the rest to the cops."

"Reckon so. Great job, Felix par excellence," grinned Blythy, lighting him up another Rothmans.

Sebastian came up on the radio, he liked this bit, it meant the mission was over and things could get back to normal, "Hello Zero and all call signs. This is Foxtrot 74, device secured. Open the roads and let the residents back into their homes. Am handing control over to Rucksack[167]. Out."

* * *

Sunray came up on the Net, "All call signs, hold firm until Felix is extracted. Excellent work, lads."

Blythe was helping Sebastian off with his heavy armour and wiping the sweat with an army towel. He placed the body armour at the back of a lamp post by the pig, "I'll get you another jacket, Boss, that one's soaked through."

And Sebastian was drenched both mentally and physically drained. That was a tricky one, plus a close call. Blythy was unzipping his smock, fresh one to hand, when the two pounds of C4 in the metal face of the post detonated. The body armour behind it channelled the blast forward.

Blocks of iron ripped Blythy apart and Sebastian, who was half out of his smock, felt a powerful kick to his lower legs and somersaulted ten metres through the air, his lower legs spiralling in front of him like Wellington boots thrown by a giant's hand, "Oh shit! Happy birthday to me," he grimaced before losing consciousness.

* * *

The guys listened aghast, "Fucking hell, Seb, that was some experience. You saved a lot of lives, mate."

Jamesey was impressed, "Yeah, I think I remember that on the news. Fucking outstanding."

Sebastian shrugged, "One does what he has to do."

Hedge said, "One Hero with his Wheelbarrow…" then hollered, "More drink, landlord!"

* * *

The night flew in, Sebastian was having a ball but refused Jamesey's offer to come home for supper, fireworks and meet the kids, "I've had enough fireworks to last me a lifetime," he said ruefully. "Besides, that big Jamaican taxi driver is going to pick me up at eleven."

Jamesey left it at that, not wanting to push things.

* * *

---

[167] Royal Ulster Constabulary.

Sebastian woke up next morning with a thumping head and a whiskey mouth. Something very soft, warm and tender was draped over him like a skin rash. Louise peeked from below the covers, "You okay, lover?"

He gazed at her, stunned, thinking he had or was in a weird dream, "Hangover. Am parched like a desert with a drought."

"I'll get you a glass of water and I've Anadin in my bag," and she hopped out of bed, naked but for a pair of scarlet knickers.

He gaped amazed at her pert arse and small pert breasts. She was perfection personified. Sebastian gulped the water down, took his Anadin dutifully as she absent-mindedly played with his chest, "Uhmm…what the hell happened last night, Louise?"

"Well, you were a little bit inebriated, so Clive and me saw you home. I thought I'd stay to make sure you were fine and slept well."

He looked at her, amazed, "Argh, did anything happen, you know?"

She laughed salaciously, "Not really, you randy git…you got my gear off, then fell asleep.

"Okay. Sorry about that," subdued. "No offence."

"What yah mean? I'm a girl on heat," and she jumped up, peeled her knickers off, tossed them carelessly away and proceeded to shag his brains out.

After she lay in happy delirious aftershock, "Bloody suffering fuck, Sebastian. You don't need legs, mate! That is one great middle leg you've got," and slapped him playfully on the chest. "What the feck more does a girl need…? Now, let's up and dress, Skandia for breakfast, and this afternoon we can dally a while in bed, play a bit of reggae and go exploring…whatcha think?"

Sebastian was very much up for that. Very much indeed.

* * *

Three days later they were in The Peel, wolfing down scampi, chips and mushy peas when Jamesey rolled in, wheeled Sebbie babe out to the pavement, lit two Embassy up and shoved one in his mouth. "Sebbie, you're a cunt. I made a few phone calls about you to my contacts."

Seb looked at him warily. He did not like people getting into his business, "And what the fuck does that mean?"

"It means you never told me or the guys you got awarded the bloody Victoria Cross[168] for actions above and beyond the call of duty."

Sebbie babe shrugged, "Didn't feel it was relevant."

"Listen, how you feel about going to work in Hexham in Northumbria for OLG? I'm going to open a training camp for operatives. Lots of live firing and explosives. I need a chief armourer and guy who knows explosives. You'll have a staff of five."

He was shocked, "Jamesey, I've no fucking legs. I can barely shit on my own."

Jamesey guffawed, "Just trivial problems, mucker. Three times your army pay, free housing and board. What yah think of that?"

He hesitated, "Legs, mate, I have not got any."

---

[168] Highest military award for gallantry.

398

Jamesey grinned, "Doncha worry, mucker. OLG will get you a new pair. On the house. We are a family, we look after our own."

Sebastian was near crying now, "Whatever you think, you put your trust in me, I won't let you down."

"I know, mate," Jamesey proffered his right hand, and Seb shook it vigorously and was amazed when it came off in his hand. Jamesey laughed uproariously, "Mind over matter, mate. Mind over matter...now get back in there... Louise is missing yah."

He wheeled himself back in, stunned, eyes brimming with tears. The big ex-para had given him his life back and seriously restored his self-confidence.

He wouldn't let the big man, or himself, down.

In the public bar Jamesey called for order, "New addition to the OLG family. Seb's gonna run the Hexham operation for us." That got a cheer and a round of applause.

"You better get the drinks in, Seb. OLG tradition for new recruits," Smudger ordered.

Seb smiled, "My absolute pleasure... Landlord!"

Later Louise came through and plonked herself down on his lap and gave him a smouldering kiss before coming up for air, "I hear it's beautiful up at Hexham. Near that bleeding Hadrian's Wall. When we going then?"

He gazed into her gorgeous eyes, mesmerised. If ever a man's cup was full to overflowing, it was retired Sergeant Major Sebastian Justin Pugh's.

Jamesey regarded the engrossed couple from across the room. Looks like he had killed two birds with one stone on this one. Louise could be in charge of catering for the trainees. She was a good lass. Flexible and adaptable.

He said his goodbyes and left for home, whistling a para marching song, wanting to spend some time with 'er indoors', his little broody mare, who quite fascinated him. To him, it had just been another day at the office.

Chapter 30
"He Spermed Me in the Heart"
('Are We Human'... The Killers... 2013)

29th April, 2013

Wendy Havilland watched her friend sitting on their couch sipping the strong Columbian coffee she liked so much. She thought Luca appeared unhappy, which was unusual for her even with the hard time she had gone through the last month or two. Plus, the pressure on a stunning young woman living alone in this huge, sprawling, impersonal city that could make or break a person very quickly. Her companion was normally of such a vibrant, happy disposition that usually just being in her presence was an utter pleasure.

Wendy was an attractive woman herself. Curly blonde hair, brown-eyes, with a very pretty round face. She had a fine full figure that, despite her and Bobby's liking to party now and then, and a predilection for binges on junk food, she kept well-toned. She knew Bobby had no problem with her curves because he was always trying to get his hands on them! This was okay with Wendy, as she had an exceptionally high sex drive. She was a thoroughly modern city girl whose maxim was, 'If you have sexual inhibitions, then lose them, baby, and go thrive on the sex drive'.

After a long shift on the children's ward, there was nothing she liked better than to get home and get down and dirty with the Big Guy to get rid of the stress. Just to start all over again in the vicious circle that working with sick kids brought. Even though she was very dedicated to her little patients, Wendy was a strong-minded, resourceful woman who very much wore the pants in the marriage. At times she let Bobby think he did, knowing that the male ego was often temperamental and needed flattering and bolstering up every now and then.

In spite of this, Wendy and the Big Guy could be so laid-back that their small circle of friends often said that they were so chilled out they were near comatose. Quite content to go with the ebb and flow of the often hectic schedule of life that living in the heaving metropolis relentlessly threw up.

They had been trying for a baby the entire ten years of marriage but so far the stork had denied them its presence. They had not bothered to get tested for fertility or look at other options as some of their friends did. Wendy's view was if it happened, hey, it happened. If not? Well they could always adopt in later life. Bobby's opinion was that he could bounce his foxy lady's sexy bones anytime he wanted without the nuisance of contraception.

"Hell, Wends, this whole goddamn wonderful city is our baby at the moment, kiddo," he once said when he had been on the Jack Daniels and she had to agree.

The place did tend to suck you up into its vast atmosphere, and she never wanted to leave the city or live anywhere else, despite being born and bred in the huge human rabbit warren that was Brooklyn.

She watched her friend again. Luca was outstandingly stunning. Her features were striking and achingly beautiful and Wendy had observed the men ogle her when they were out. She never had to open a shop door because the nearest passing male rushed to do so. Yellow cabs screeched to a halt beside her whether she summoned one or not. Children and animals adored her, sensing her kind, compassionate nature. Old ladies on the metro made room for her to sit by them and chatted away to her as if they had known her their whole lives.

During the ten days she had spent in Manhattan General, the doctors and nurses had hustled and fussed over her and she had an endless stream of visitors. Hell, even the two humongous hulking bodyguards Rabbie had kept lurking near the ward entrance were half in love with her. Bringing her little pastries and running down to the shop to get her magazines, and, goddammit the girl could eat like a horse and never put an ounce on!

Wendy grinned, not being a vindictive or jealous woman by nature, except for the odd occasions she had caught a sneaky Bobby watching the porn channel. He got cold shouldered for a while and his huge bulk confined to his lonely side of the bed until she was ready to lift the invisible line and let the drooling yob in between her hot thighs again.

No, Luca was totally unaware of her charisma. She just presumed that is how people normally acted to each other because that's how she treated everybody herself. No wonder she was a stalking magnet, thought Wendy. Her naïveté and her oversized ability to regularly see the good side of things in life and the decency in people was endearing. Get a few drinks down her and an animated Luca was great company. When they went out as a foursome, Luca and Rabbie, Bobby and her, it was always fun and often turned into a hilarious riot. Luca dancing the feet off Bobby and Rabbie, forever considerate and well turned out, ensuring they all had a good time and went to the best places. If Wendy and Bobby were a few dollars short of the tab, shoot, Rabbie sorted it and never a word said.

Shit! If it hadn't been for Rabbie, they wouldn't be sitting here now, him taking on Bobby nearly full time with OLG and giving them a bit of financial security. Hey, if Rabbie had not met Luca, who knows where she and Bobby would be now, there being very little work for electricians during this awful depression. She would be content living in a rabbit hutch of a tenement if Bobby was with her, but it was certainly a lot more comfortable where they were, and well, whatever will be, will be.

Wendy was a great believer in karma. You could fight and struggle against life, try and change things to suit yourself but if it was preordained, then you might as well go to Brooklyn Bridge and try and count every rivet blindfolded. You weren't going to change what was set out on the road ahead, and she really had no doubt Rabbie and Luca were destined for a life with each other.

She understood Luca had been making most of the running, and Rabbie was hesitant because of the ten-year age gap and insecure from being dumped by some stuck-up model. Hell, he was tearing the arse out of things now, and if he didn't pull his best worsted socks up, he could lose this exquisite creature very quickly for good.

Luca had already informed her she was thinking of moving back into her own apartment. Wendy thought this would be bad for her. Bad karma. She knew that, in the face of a few lustful clinches, they had not made love yet. Although, Luca had certainly made it obvious to Rabbie she was keen and willing to move the relationship up a notch. In fact, desired it intensely and if Rabbie didn't give her one damn good seeing to soon, Luca was going to give into the rejection and leave.

Goddammit, had she not shared his bed for the last six weeks? Was he some type of monk who had taken a vow of celibacy? Luca was gorgeous, for heaven's sake. Wendy grinned wickedly, shoot, if she'd been sharing a bed with Luca for weeks, she might be tempted herself. If anything, Wendy was game to try most things, much to Bobby's delight. She was a thoroughly modern New York lady.

Wendy could see Luca was getting very annoyed now. Luca stood and paced over to the window, arms crossed, chin raised, teeth clenched angrily. She had never seen her furious before. Scared, yes. Upset over things on television, saddened at other people's misfortune, but angry…nyetski. Not Luca, the Russian 'Mother Theresa', for heaven's sake.

"You're so lovely when you're cross, Luca…your flashing eyes, pouting lips…rigid poise."

Luca actually scowled. Wendy was amazed. "Bah…what is beauty ven the man you idolise… Yes, Vendy, damn well idolise… Who I would gladly die for… Sperms you day in and day out," and she burst into a deluge of bitter tears.

Wendy rushed over to her and led her back to the sofa and comforted her. Part of her wanted to roll around the floor laughing her head off, the other part wanted to cry with her. Goddamn, men were so insecure. Christ, Luca was such a sketch! She reached over and topped Luca's cup with the strong coffee from the carafe.

Luca had been staring out the window at the apartment across the street, wondering if the other couples were enjoying their Sunday morning lie in and making love to each other. She loved Rabbie so much but the last week she had physically ached for his touch, and he had seemed to draw back even more.

He had come in late last night after supervising some do at a yuppie club, crawled into bed, given her a perfunctory kiss on the cheek and fallen fast asleep. That was fine. She could understand that. He worked hard and was very diligent towards his job as indeed he was very diligent towards her in every way. Well, every way but the one she ached for most with him. Rabbie spoiled her and treated her like a queen and was great fun and immensely interesting and attractive in every way.

Well, diligent in every way but that one. She wanted him to make love to her so badly it was hurting and she had given him plenty of opportunity, and he hadn't taken them. It was making her very uneasy and she felt unwanted as a woman. She realised she was depressed, which was a strange scary animal threatening her normal confident, cheerful persona and that in itself made her feel even more down. She had never done it with Galen before he was killed and regretted it terribly and now when she had finally found a man she loved deeply, he was rejecting her.

She sighed very deeply and with utter dejection as her bestest friend filled her cup. Wendy sensed a flicker of worried alarm.

"Goddammit, Luca. You better tell me what's wrong, or I'm going to stick my head in the oven and turn the gas on."

Luca's lips twitched despite herself. Wendy was so funny at times. "Don't be silly, Vends. Sure, we have electric ovens. Sure, it vill take too long and frizzle your hair plus your fair skin burns too easy, dahling."

Wendy winked at her, "So it'll take a bit longer. Now come on, honey. Get that lovely trap flapping and tell me what's up. It has to be Rabbie in there somewhere, am I right?"

Luca chuckled in spite of herself. "Yes, it's Rabbie. He come home. Into bed. Asleep. Datsfine. I tink to myself. I get him when he wakes up, like you advise me, Vendy. Men are what you say, 'Horny buggers' first ting in the morning."

Wendy laughed now. She loved it when Luca's Russian accent got deeper and she dropped her vowels. Normally when she was excited or pissed.

"Yep, they sure are. 'Go to work on a shag' is what Bobby says."

"Yes, so I'm tinking. I put on dis nice, black negligee and nuttin underneath, you know. Verry sexy. When he wakes, I'm draped over him, you know. Verry close, giving off all the vibes blowing in his ear, playing footsie, you know."

Wendy's agog now, "Wow, what happened?"

Luca sighed, "He spermed me, he spermed me good."

"Well, yahoo. Good for you girl. About time too," and Wendy clapped in delight and yahooed, "Way da go, gal."

Luca scrutinised her pal crestfallen and hung her head, looking disgusted.

"But you did it, Luca. The Biz, the dirty deed. He played hide the sausage with yah…yeah? You tamed the python? The one-eyed spitting dummy."

She looked confused. "I told you…he spermed me…badly spermed."

Now Wendy was confused. "Yeah…he spermed yah. Never heard it described like that, but wow!"

"He just rolled over, said 'You look nice, Luca' and went for a shower."

"But you said that he spermed you good and then badly. Did he hurt you? Is that what you mean?"

"Yes, Vendy. He hurt me. He spermed me badly. He spermed me right in the heart," answered an exasperated Luca, the first tears rolling down her fantastic cheeks. ·

Wendy left her chair and went and sat by her friend and put her arm around her, totally perplexed.

"Right, 'kay, Luca. Take your time, dear. What happened when he came out of the shower?"

Luca sniffed. "'Kay. I went and made him coffee just in my negligee, and when I heard him come out, I brought it in and made sure dat he got a good eyeful of what was on Luca's menu."

Wendy laughed in spite of her friend's expression. "Sorry, Luca. You're so funny at times. So did he throw you on the bed and give you as damn good sperming?"

"What are you on about, Vends? No, he got dressed and said that he had paperwork to do at the office and left," and she burst into floods of tears.

Wendy hugged her to her. She wondered if there was a 'Spermed Russian Woman's Helpline' in the phonebook. She was lost in outer space on this one.

"Right, we're going to sort this out, Luca. Slowly and steadily or I'm going to have to get the tequila out," she paused, inspired, "Actually, that's not a bad thought, hold that one, Luca,", and she galloped off into the kitchen and returned with the fiery drink in two glasses and lemon slices. "Right. Get that down you. Davstravia!"

They clinked glasses and knocked the drink back and gasped and spluttered.

"Right," said Wendy, "Let's start over. You dressed up for him. Tried to seduce him. Showed him the goods on the menu and offered it to him on a plate and he didn't…you know, sperm you?"

Luca raised her hands in frustration. "No, Vendy. I told you this. He spermed me…he spermed every advance I made on him."

Like the lights being turned on at Times Square after a power cut, Wendy finally twigged on. She raised her hands in the air in supplication.

"Oh, thank you, lawdy. Thank you." She turned back to a weeping Russian girl. "He spurned your advances, Luca… SPURNED. Rejected you. You didn't make love and get his seed his white hot stuff, his sperm. SPERM."

Luca stared at Wendy as if she was a simpleton. "Yes. Dat's what I have been telling you, Wend. He spermed me."

Wendy bowed to the inevitable and got them two more slugs of tequila. Luca's mobile rang and she answered. "Yes, Rabbie…? Oh, are you… I don't know if I really want to go… Yes, it's a nice day… I'm singing at the club at six… I suppose if you want to come… What am I doing? I'm drinking tequila with Wendy… Yes, I know it's half past ten on a Sunday morning… Yes, I'm okay… I'm Russian… I am going now to get a shower and dressed…I leave Wendy to go back to bed, you know how her and Bobby like to lay in bed on Sundays and spurn each other…Yes, spurn… Never mind, Rabbie, it's complicated… I see you at twelve… You love me?" she made a humphing sound and she hung up.

Wendy clapped and squirmed in delight. "Bet that's one confused dude, Lucs."

She grinned. "He's taking me to the zoo for chilli dogs, then to the deli to get goodies for supper, then to the club to hear me sing. He's even finishing work early just for me."

"Sounds like he's got it all planned out, kiddo. They are only little boys, really. Men!" She nudged her friend and winked. "Seems like you're gonna get a good sperming tonight."

"I won't hold my breath," snorted Luca. "As little Kylie Minogue sings 'I should be so lucky, lucky, lucky, lucky… I should be so lucky in love'. I see you later, dahling," and she left her friend doubled up, howling with laughter, tittering away to herself.

Bobby came mooching down from the bedroom in his dressing gown all tousled looking. "What the heck you gals scheming over a bottle of tequila at this time of a Sunday?"

Wendy gave him a hundred-watt beamer. "I'm scheming on taking this bottle to bed and having a little fun, whatcha tink, Big Guy?"

Bobby's eyes lit up. She could wrap him around her little finger. "I think I'll go and brush mah teeth, little lady," he paused. "What's wrong with Luca these days?"

Wendy simpered. "She's been badly spermed and don't even ask."

II

He sat behind his desk munching on a blueberry muffin Elaine had brought in, staring into space wondering what in damnation he was doing there, when he could be comfortably ensconced at home with Luca. His lovely, charming, endearing, gorgeous flatmate who was making it perfectly clear she wanted to take their hesitant, fledgling romance across new borders. Borders he was reluctant to cross, being mentally stuck at a passport control of his own stupid making. He was waiting to see if his entry visa was going to be stamped or not and if he was going to allow himself entry into new pastures.

It wasn't like it was terra incognito. He'd been down that passage before with Juliette but the two women were as different as chalk and cheese; although both undeniably very beautiful. He couldn't decide if Luca was still looking upon him as a huge security wall and risk control after her near-death experience with Hanlon or did she want him for himself? That she was genuinely attracted to him and saw the worth in him as a serious contention as a long-term partner or was she also blanking out what had happened to her and deluding herself?

Rabbie sighed and dumped his muffin in the waste basket, picked up his pen and, brow furrowed, tried to concentrate on his work. He just didn't know, and he didn't want to be cast aside like a piece of flotsam on the tide after a few months, like Juliette had done to him, seriously denting his male ego.

He threw his pen down and gazed into space again. No, Luca wasn't like that but what if after a few months she regretted getting involved? He knew she would feel trapped but would be too decent to tell him and then where would they be?

Elaine Curry came in with more coffee and seeing his stricken, distracted look, sat down.

"You know you didn't have to come in, Rabbie. I told you I would sort this for tomorrow," and she sat down, her body language demanding attention.

She adored the boss dude, in a motherly way of course, and wanted to help put him right with this silly Luca business. They were a match made in heaven but he just couldn't see it. Typical man. They had such fragile egos when it came to women. They couldn't see the trees for the woods at times. She knew the Juliette escapade was only going to be a flash in the pan affair, Juliette was a hard, self-serving bitch that controlled Rabbie with the devouring demon between her legs. Luca was different, she had class and poise but most of all, Elaine believed, she truly loved Rabbie.

He looked disconsolately at his PA. "I know, Elaine; I should have stayed at home with Luca. I guess I'm in the doghouse now. I have a very strong gut feeling I've hurt her feelings."

Elaine put some sweeteners in her coffee and stirred briskly. "You in the crapper, then? Oh, dearie! Wanna talk about it? A problem shared and all that palaver."

Rabbie exhaled heavily. He felt like a teenager under Elaine's unscrupulous gaze and wondered what his mother would have made of the whole thing. He took the bull by the horns and told Elaine what had transpired earlier and how he felt about Luca. She was the closest thing he had to a mother in New York, and he trusted her implicitly.

Elaine listened poker faced as he poured his heart to her. The boss dude had it bad, that was for certain. When he stopped for breath, she raised her hand, the bracelet her daughters had given her for Christmas jangling.

"Now, Rabbie. Sit back and look at this sensibly; it's simple. Do you love her or not?"

He squirmed like a naughty schoolboy asked a difficult question about the homework he had learnt.

"Well, yeah, I guess… I mean I love her company but…"

She shushed him. "Don't prevaricate, Boss. You're thirty-six not seven. So there's an age gap, so what! You're a young man. Luca's incredible. She's making all the moves and you're blanking her out. For Chrissake she puts that stuck-up cow in the shade. Juliette screwed your head up, man. Don't lose out on a chance of happiness because you're insecure. If you love her, go for it! If you don't, cut her loose, but I reckon that would be a huge mistake for you both and you both would be unhappy."

Rabbie looked at her in wonder as she paused for breath. "But I thought you liked Juliette? Everybody did."

Elaine snorted, "No, Rabbie. I passed myself with her for your sake but the general consensus in the office was she was a self-centred, two-faced bitch and it would all end in grief. Which it did."

"But why did no one say anything?" he asked, flummoxed. "The guys seemed to like her."

She gave him a sympathetic look and patted his hand. "Because your head was so far up your arse, you couldn't see the light. The guys didn't like her; they lusted after her, dear. Sure, the operatives were running a book to see how long it lasted."

He leaned back and blew air out, "Christ, I've been a friggin' idiot. I had no idea!"

"Don't worry yourself over it, Rab. Women like Juliette pick up decent guys like you all the time, chew them up and spit them out like bubble gum and move on. She is a predator and you deserve better, dear."

He grinned, "Yeah, she was a man eater all right. So advice number one. What am I gonna do about Luca?"

"My advice, go for it. She's good for you. Put your fragile male ego away in the safe, otherwise you'll regret it your whole life."

He puffed his cheeks out, lost in thought, "Right, I've invoices to email, then I'm heading down the Legion for a nice liquid lunch."

"Yeah thanks, Elaine. I'll lock up…thanks again."

She paused at the door, "Seriously, Rabbie. Don't lose Luca now. You don't get many chances in this crazy world for genuine happiness," and she left, pleased with herself.

"That is one sage old bird," he said to himself. "I had no idea. Wonder who won the draw?"

Love is warfare, he decided. He would treat it as a battle. A battle to win Luca's trust and affection back. He was at the crux of the fight that every soldier knew. That critical point where you press forward on the enemy and possibly take more casualties or retreat and take cover and lose the advantage.

Rabbie opened his top drawer and pulled a postcard out. It was from Paris and showed the Arc de Triumph at the top of the Champ-Elysees. The message on the back was written in Juliette's childish scrawl.

'Have missed you, baby. Will be in New York 30th April. Staying Excelsior. Meet me at 8pm in the bar. I'll make it up to you, Juliette xxooxx' ☺

It was dated a week previously. He smiled sadly. What the fuck was he to do? His heart had skipped a beat when he had received it. He had briefly wondered if they could start again. He still did but Luca was always in his mind and, as Elaine said, Juliette was poison. He knew before he did anything he had to lay Juliette to rest and hopefully Luca was the antidote.

He left happily, jaunty, humming a Stevie Wonder song, 'For once in my life I have someone who needs me', Elaine grinning at his departing back like a Cheshire cat who has got the cream.

III

Juliette Naomi Castananda was born in the Ethiopian capital, Addis Ababa, on the 21st of June 1986. Her father was a rich Malaysian silk merchant and her mother a local beauty, descended from nobility and whose family were owners of vast tracts of land in and around the dusty capital.

Her mother told a young Juliette that she must always remember her roots and that she had royal blood flowing through her veins. That indeed she was related to the famous Emperor Haile Selassie, who headed the disposed Ethiopian royal family. They were driven out by the Italian dictator Mussolini in the Second World War and the icon for the modern day Rastafarian movement and immortalised by Bob Marley and the reggae music of the seventies and eighties.

Juliette remembered that her entire life, recalling what her mother had told her as she bounced her up and down on her knee. From a young age she acted with poise and regal grace and played the part of a princess to perfection, or a 'prima donna', depending on her mood.

They lived in a luxurious villa in a walled compound guarded by armed sentries. Ethiopia was a troubled country, prone to drought and famine and often at war with its neighbours. She was a beautiful child with big almond eyes that slanted slightly upwards, high cheekbones, creamy coffee-coloured skin and lustrous black hair. As black as pitch.

As she grew, so did her beauty, and she soon realised the power she had over men and used it accordingly to get what she wanted. She had the best of education and travelled extensively with her father, who was happy to indulge his beautiful daughter on trips he made to the fashion capitals of the world to sell his fine Chinese silks – Milan, Paris, London, New York were common destinations.

Juliette grew tall and willowy and everywhere she went she was complimented on her looks. Taking an interest in the world of fashion she demanded, and got, the latest clothes and trendy accessories. She could throw impressive tantrums if she didn't get her own way.

Aware of the starving masses in her own country, as a young teenager she would fill the car with food and get one of the armed guards to drive her to the shanties downtown. She would distribute it to the starving children, the ones with the extended bellies and the eyes that showed no hope in them, flies swarming about them. It assuaged her guilt at all the things she had, and it gave her a kick to be seen as the angel of goodness. Her parents turned a blind eye, secretly delighting in their daughter's kindness and increasing her allowance to cover it.

At fourteen she lost her virginity in the potting shed to a gardener and took to sex like a shark to a shoal of distressed fish. Working her way through several of the servants before her father put an end to it and sent her to finishing school in Switzerland.

By sixteen she had grown tall and even lovelier. Her flashing Oriental eyes and impossibly long legs making men drool and crowd around her like a flock of starlings fighting over breadcrumbs, when she entered a room. She exalted in this power she had over men and picked them up and discarded them as often as she changed her fashionable clothes. She returned home in disgrace after a torrid affair with a married minor celebrity visiting the ski slopes but secretly revelled in the sordid headlines in the tabloids, and her lust for media coverage began.

At eighteen she stood five feet eleven inches tall and was incredibly attractive with high, firm breasts, long hair in dreadlocks and those fabulous long legs that would make her a household name on the catwalk. She enrolled at New York State University to study humanities and took to campus life immediately. No party was a party unless Juliette was there. She discovered cocaine and cannabis and happily got stoned most nights and screwed her way through the rich and good-looking under grads, breaking hearts carelessly. She was a free spirit and lived life to the full, never giving a second thought to the shattered guys she left in her wake like garbage thrown over the stern of a ship.

Despite her self-centredness, she was shrewd and stuck to her studies and helped two nights a week at a soup kitchen the Students Union ran in downtown New York. She knew she was spoilt and pampered and accepted it as her God-given right, but something about the seedy down and outs fascinated her.

At twenty she stood at six feet and was modelling part-time for a fashion house off Saks Avenue. She had been spotted at a student charity function doing a gig for Aids relief in Africa by an agent, and he signed her up, dollar signs in his eyes.

When she turned twenty-one, she got an acceptable second in humanities but she was modelling nearly full-time now. Her legs were plastered across billboards and in catalogues across the whole eastern seaboard. An up and coming fashion house 'IsMe' signed her on full-time; she had it made and quickly became a household feature, making regular appearances on television and in the papers.

The paparazzi loved her and followed her about like adoring puppies, tongues lolling and tails wagging. The money rolled in and as the fame hit, she gathered up a coterie of hangers on and became famous for her wild parties in the huge swanky apartment she had in upmarket Soho.

Rabbie pulled a bottle of Glenfiddich out and took a slug. He rarely drank during the day but he felt the need as he recalled the crazy parties Juliette used to throw. He used to kid himself they were fun, and he got caught up in them but now he realised they were meaningless, self-serving and puerile. He grimaced as he remembered the mornings he had crawled into work hung-over.

He cast his mind back to that fateful day he had first cast a lusty eye over the stunning woman. She had took his breath away, but he knew she was out of his league. 'IsMe' were doing a fashion shoot down the zoo and had hired OLG to provide a discreet presence to keep nuisances at bay. It was mid-June and the weather was fine and hot and Rabbie decided to go down himself and get out of the office.

He arrived at two with four operatives and after recceing the area around the primate house, where the shoot was to take place, his guys spread discreetly out and the models and photographers arrived in several SUVs. Soon there was activity as they set up. A mobile home the girls used as a changing room arrived and a swarm of glamorous models got out, chittering away like a flock of exotic birds in all shades and colours.

Juliette stood out from the kaleidoscopic swarm. Dressed in a turquoise bikini with a multi-coloured sarong around her slim waist, arms and neck adorned in jewellery. Her hair in beaded dreadlocks, she looked like the Queen of Sheba. She stood elegant and immutable as she gazed about her regally. Totally in control of herself and her surroundings.

Rabbie tried not to stare but it was hard. He part understood then what it took to have the essence to be a supermodel. They were one in a million, and he knew why they earned big bucks, and Juliette had what it took to make it in bucket loads. She was mesmerising.

She briefly caught his eye as she strolled over to take her position in front of the monkey cages. Assistants fluttering around her like pilot fish and looking away haughtily, almost with contempt. Cameras started snapping and the models posed and pouted, strutting and doing what they did best to promote the latest modes in swimwear, kaftans and accessories for the supercool poser.

Unknown to Rabbie, there was trouble brewing in the baboon house. Saxa, a large ten-year-old male, had been causing commotion in the tribe. Jealous of a younger male rival, he had been ranting and raving all morning and the keepers, fearing he might injure the rest, had isolated him from them in a small compound at the rear.

He could hear the hustle and bustle of activity at the front of the monkey cages, and his curiosity had piqued at the change in routine. He sniffed the air through his large nostrils and detected the music and perfumes of the models and his senses were inflamed. He growled lustily and gnashed his large canines together. Who were these strange female interlopers invading his territory so blatantly? He mused, his anger rising, his alpha nerves going crazy with their foreign scent. If only he could get out, he would drive them off his patch, and then the tribe would welcome him back as their undisputed leader again. Numero Uno!

Then Lady Fate cast her fickle hand and raised the ante. A young foreign exchange student called Jorgen from Denmark felt sorry for Saxa. Against all regulations, he entered the connecting corridor at the rear with a bowl of mixed fruit for him. He unlatched and swung open the outer gate, crossed the six foot gravelled sterile area and gazed at the big baboon through the mesh.

Saxa looked at him sadly and ambled over to the inner gate, chattering softly. Jorgen reached his finger through and Saxa bowed his head, letting him scratch it. "See, you're not so bad, my friend," and fed him a pineapple slice. "Stand back, Saxa. I leave you the bowl. I want to go and watch the lovely ladies."

He moved back a few feet and again, breaking all health and safety laws, unbarred and opened the gate to slide the dish in. As fast as a cracking whip, Saxa sprung forward and pulled the gate wide and bowled Jorgen over. The fruit salad became a tossed salad and before the fruit hit the ground, Saxa was through the outer gate and bounding up the corridor to freedom.

A dazed Jorgen sat up, "Oh God, I think I am deep in the pit of shit!"

Juliette was laying on a sunbed in a Gucci bikini of various colours of the rainbow. A two-year-old chimp called Stardust, provided by Mr Warren, the head primate keeper, was perched on her shoulder, watching her adoringly, munching on a banana. Two photographers were filming her from all angles, trying to catch that famous pout that was her trademark and captivated her fans worldwide.

And pouting she was. She was bored and hung-over and the cocaine buzz she had earlier was going fast. She wished they would hurry up and get done so she could get a quick snort and a good stiff screwdriver to sort herself out. Juliette eyed her fellow models standing around in small groups in skimpy outfits, watching intently. Some with feigned looks of indifference and others looked with open jealousy.

She knew she wasn't particularly well liked, that she was considered a bit of a diva, but she didn't care a fig. It didn't stop them coming to her parties, guzzling her booze and snorting her snow white.

"Tomas," she called to the Shoot Director, "Can we lose the fucking chimp? It's making me itch."

"Just a few more, sweetie pie. Near done."

"Well, hurry the fuck up! God knows what I might catch."

Mr Warren peered at her with disdain. He was more worried what Stardust might catch! Such language in public. He sometimes wondered, after dealing with the public for many years, why he had to lock his monkeys up at all. They had more manners, common sense and family loyalty than a lot of folk who visited the zoo. They stood before the cages pulling inane faces and acting the fool, scaring his gentle captives. No, the wrong breed of primate was banged up, he decided, then quickly changed his mind as an angry Saxa came hurtling around the corner. Baboons were the gangbangers and trouble-makers in Mr Warren's kingdom, and Saxa was hell-bent on causing mischief.

The area in front of the monkey cages had been cordoned off to stop the visitors interfering with the photo shoot. His four guys were up by the ropes keeping the public at bay, and he was amused at the ribald comments and jokes that were coming through the small earpiece as they remarked on the models. It was a good job nobody else could hear.

"'Kay, fellas…stay alert. Enough of the monkey business," he told them, "Or you'll be in the doghouse." To groans and titters from his crew.

"Watch out, Boss! There's a mega-sized baboon coming up fast behind you," Buzz shouted over the net.

"Yeah right, Boomerang," he laughed prior to glancing over his shoulder to see a three-hundred-pound male baboon coming at them on all fours, at twenty miles an hour, teeth barred. The laugh died on his lips, "Oh suffering fuck! It's a man-eater."

Pushing the chimp off, Juliette stood and put her hands on her hips and gave her famous pout. She had had enough, cameras whirred and whizzed as the happy snappers finally got what they wanted. She gazed regally around her and wondered why her cohorts were screaming before she looked to her front and locked eyes with the blazing red ones of a very irate Saxa, who was coming straight for her. Terror seized her valuable limbs.

"Oh my God," she whispered to herself, hangover forgotten, "It's King frigging Kong's son!"

Rabbie did a double take ahead of bounding into action, still not believing his eyes. His first thought was to pull his Ruger revolver and shoot the brute but there were fleeing bodies everywhere and it was too dangerous. He smashed his heel down on a wooden bench someone had dedicated to the zoo, breaking several of the timber spars, ripped one off with a satisfying crack and holding the broken slat in both hands, sprinted over the intervening space to confront the beastie as it advanced menacingly on Juliette and Stardust.

Saxa saw red when the strange tribe began screaming and running around like headless chickens. He lunged towards a tall one standing facing him with a small chimp sitting petrified on the sunbed by her. Was this the matriarchal leader of this strange group? So grotesque with their bare hairless limbs. Saxa would soon show her who was kingpin. He'd rip her throat out, he decided as he skidded to a halt a few feet in front of her. He rose on his haunches and beating his strong chest and filling his lungs, gave a tremendous screeching howl. Lips pulled back, exposing his vicious teeth, three-inch outer pointed molars flashing in the sun.

Juliette's blood froze as the creature stood before her pounding on its chest and screaking horribly. There were baboons in the jungles of her native Ethiopia, and they had a fearsome reputation. Despite not being particularly religious, she vowed never to touch men or cocaine again, crossed herself and wondered if there were catwalks in heaven, or was she already in hell?

DeJames got up speed and crossed the space in a matter of seconds and rammed his right shoulder into the roaring animal's upper left arm. Saxa was knocked over and rolled to his right, enraged. He tumbled over and bounced agilely back up on all fours and confronted his new enemy. A new kid on the block looking to thwart his claim to supremacy. Hell show the false contender.

Giving a hideous scream designed to cowl and put fear into the stoutest of hearts, he charged straight at Rabbie, murder foremost in his mind. As the howling beast reached him, he side-stepped Saxa, and spar of wood gripped firmly in his two hands like a baseball player, he lifted it and whacked him full force across his large red buttocks as he passed.

It landed with a resounding crack and Saxa hollered in shock and spun around and came right back at Rabbie, although with considerable less momentum. He stepped in front of a cringing Juliette and bat raised skywards in a strong two-fisted grip, faced his adversary.

Saxa stopped and rose to his full height and did the chest pounding and roaring thing again. Rabbie debated whether to shoot again and be done with it, but predetermined another ploy.

"Right, let's be having you, you hairy beastie," and he lowered his head and ran full tilt at Saxa, connecting with his chest, bowling him backwards.

Saxa rolled several times, head over heels, stunned, who was the demonic antagonist sent by the great ape God to make a fool of him? Rabbie thumped him hard again across the arse and Saxa screamed and retreated a few feet, back to him and looked fearfully over his shoulder. Another echoing wallop and he fled a few more feet, his arse on fire.

"Right, back to your cage, Big Boy," ordered Rabbie with another swipe.

Saxa withdrew further. That bowl of mixed fruit looked more and more appealing. He turned and faced Rabbie and sat down in capitulation and stared him in the eye. *Hasta la vista, amigo... I'll be back!* he chittered softly to himself. After my fruit salad and my butt stops throbbing.

He eyed the big ape carefully as his guys arrived, weapons drawn. They encircled Saxa, four unwavering barrels pointed at his head.

"Will I waste the chimp, Boss?" asked Buzz eagerly. "It's one scary looking monkey."

"It's a baboon, you nuthead," he replied, throwing the plank down, making Saxa flinch. "Probably more afraid of you, I reckon."

Mr Warren came running up, "Don't shoot. Don't shoot. He's given up," and took the dazed creature by the hand. "Come, Saxa. Back to your nice safe enclosure," and he led him away.

"Guess you're king of the tribe now, Rab," joked Mal.

"Yessum, you'll get free bananas and lady monkeys on demand," from Little Dan.

Rabbie smirked, "Put your weapons away, guys. That was one weird experience," and he headed over to check on Juliette and the girls, as the guys began singing the theme from 'Jungle Book'.

She was even more exquisite close up. She observed from eyes the colour of rich liquid tobacco, slightly mellowed from the sun by impossibly long dark lashes. Her small firm breasts prominent above a firm creamy abdomen that tapered then flared atop those magnificent legs that seemed endless.

"So, are you 'King of the Jungle' then? A jungle VIP?"

He stopped before her and gave her a self-depreciating smile, "Dunno about that. Never had to fight a giant ape before... Rabbie Hamish DeJames at your service."

"Juliette Estelle Clarissa Castananda, if you're going to be formal... Come, I need a drink and I think you do," and she took his arm and led him off to her trailer, his men watching agog.

"You'll be hearing from my goddamn lawyer, Tomas. Putting me in fucking danger with wild animals," she bellowed angrily before slamming the door.

In his compound, Saxa flinched at the shouting. "Don't worry, Saxa," Mr Warren consoled him, slicing up bananas. "That one's bad news. You mark my words."

Saxa rubbed his tender posterior in agreement, glad he was back safely in his cage, wondering just which two of the species were most uncivilised, the brutes.

IV

He shifted more comfortably in his chair as he recalled their stormy relationship and sighed wistfully. God, she was some handful, in every way. That afternoon she had locked the trailer door, made them two huge Screwdrivers from the minibar she insisted on having at every shoot and disappeared into the small bathroom. To snort coke, he now knew, but didn't know then.

She came back stark naked and stood in front of a seated DeJames in all her glory, and he gaped in awe at her magnificence.

"I like to screw after I get near killed by horny baboons. What about you?"

He needed no second bidding and gulped his drink down. The sex was fast, furious and inventive. DeJames was fit and strong and knew his way around women and how to treat them right but Juliette was something else. She seemed insatiable and unshockable. He couldn't get enough of her firm, lithe young body and thought he was in heaven.

The incident with Saxa made great press and various humorous starts on it were portrayed in the big tabloids. The gossip columnists picked up on the romantic sideline and had a field day. It was all good publicity for OLG, which pleased his dad, and Juliette was even more in demand.

As the relationship grew, they became the couple to be seen around town with. They went to all the top clubs and restaurants, often on free invitations, and mixed and mingled with New York's in set. The mighty and the wealthy. Juliette knew her way around town and could backstab with the best of them. He watched amazed as a person or a couple who were flavour of the month became persons non gratis the next, as the pack tore them apart behind their backs.

"Like a pack of hyenas ripping apart a disabled antelope," he growled one night as he scrutinised them bickering in the current drinking hole the celebs congregated in. She laughed, on a cocaine high.

"But such fun. Enjoy it, my king. It could be us next week."

Rabbie discovered more about her drug habit. She didn't do much to make a secret of it, assuring him she had it under control. He chose to turn a blind eye. Infatuation does that to people. You choose to sweep the bad sides, the faults under the carpet. Hide them away in a dark cupboard, and Juliette had DeJames chained to her from the start. She could be as sweet as pie, kind and attentive, endearing, even feigning innocence, but when she blew, she blew hard.

She became famous in the press for her tantrums in public over supposed slights or bad service. When Rabbie tried to calm her, she would direct her anger on him and storm out, saying it was over between them. He would stand hands raised in exasperation before slinking off home, confused and infuriated.

Juliette spent a lot of time on location doing fashion shoots, often in far flung places and despite the luxurious lifestyle she led, it was a hard, demanding life. She was a very wealthy young woman and knew her career as a supermodel was of limited duration. She had invested wisely and had more than enough money to last her several lifetimes. She was seriously considering a career change. She had seen the suffering around the world, in her own country; hell, even in the good old US of A, there were starving people.

Rabbie used to stay at her top of the range apartment she had in Soho. She wouldn't stay at his cramped place in Manhattan. She considered it beneath her and besides, his guys used to call around and drink cheap beer and ogle her. Oh, she played the part and had them eating out of her hand, but they were rough and common and talked about things like football and watched crap movies... No, if Rabbie and she had any future at all she had to get him away from their unsavoury influence.

After a gruelling shoot in Morocco and Tunisia in August, she had made her mind up. She had a degree in humanities and friends in UNICEF. She wasn't an airhead. A couple of years working with deprived kids, then into African politics. Power, prestige and prominence, and she wanted Rabbie by her side. She knew she was more than a little in love with him. He seemed to understand her more than any man before, and she felt safe and protected in his presence. She knew also she had him, metaphorically speaking, chained in the bedroom stakes and had never had a lover with such stamina. Those ex-commandos were incredible.

Juliette rang him from a shoot on Gibraltar, "Rabbie, I miss you. I know I'm a spoilt bitch. I'm taking September off and I want to spend it with you."

Rabbie got the message on his machine and was ecstatic. Could this be a new start for them? Was Juliette finally coming around to seeing life with a mature eye? He hoped so because he missed her and was half in love with her.

They had a great time in September. Rabbie was owed time off and they flew to Acapulco for two weeks. Juliette got even blacker with the sun, and as they made love every night, he gloried in the luminescence of her eyes, contrasted to her dark skin, and exalted in his own masculinity as she came again and again under his stiff probing rod.

Back in New York they avoided the masses. They had candlelit dinners, walked hand in hand in Central Park, went to art galleries and Broadway shows. They even visited the zoo and Juliette gave Mr Warren a cheque towards the upkeep of the primates. They visited Saxa, who ran off in a panic when he saw Rabbie, guarding his rear end fearfully. Juliette coaxed him forward with ripe figs, his favourite, and he took them gently, which Rabbie regarded as a good sign.

"Not too many couples can say a mad baboon brought them together," he remarked, gazing deeply into the world's most highly insured eyes.

In the last week of September on the Sunday evening, they came in from dinner. She poured them a drink and sat by him. She looked into his strong face and told him her plans for the future. He listened with interest, then mounting unease.

"I leave on Tuesday, Rabbie, for Khartoum. UNICEF have a base there for operations in the Sudan. I want you to come with me. They need men with your experience."

He was too shocked to speak for a minute, then, "Juliette, I love you, you know that," and he clasped her hand tightly. "But I can't just up sticks like that...leave OLG. Let my dad down."

She laughed, "Of course you can. I've enough money for both of us. If you love me, you would."

Rabbie knew emotional blackmail when he heard it and could be as stubborn as the next man. "I need time to think, Juliette. It's all so sudden."

She got up and ambled over to the bedroom door and facing him dropped her Christian Dior white satin sheath dress. She was wearing nothing underneath.

"Let's discuss it in bed, my warrior king."

He had his pride and stood and walked to the front door, "I'll ring you tomorrow, Juliette."

"If you leave now, Rabbie, it's over. For good," she replied icily and lifted a porcelain bust of the Emperor Selassie off its pedestal.

He left without a word and as he closed the door, the bust shattered behind him.

No, he thought, it would never have gone the distance, and he pondered on the lovely Luca. Different horses for different courses, he remembered his Uncle Davey advising him about women when he was a teenager on his granny's farm.

He shrugged on his jacket and pocketed his keys. No, he would go and make it up to Luca because she was surely the finest filly he had in his life's stable, not that he had enough fillies at the moment to stage a two horse race.

Chapter 31
On La Guardia Goes Global
('Rocking All over the World'... Status Quo)

Part I

They said Jesus Christ and his disciples were fishers of men, and if they were, then Jamesey Robert DeJames was a modern-day version and they would have been proud of him. He cast his nets far and wide; he fostered loyalty, demanded commitment, gave praise when it was due and could give a serious bollocking when warranted, but he prided himself on being a fair and considerate employer.

As his OLG Security firm grew, if he needed men, he didn't need to advertise. He trawled the pubs and clubs, the markets and precincts, parks and other places where people congregated. He wasn't looking for saints or scholars, he just wanted mortals who could do the job professionally and would not let him down. After all, OLG was his baby, his creation, and the good name of the firm was paramount. Sacrosanct.

Jamesey demanded dependability and he got it big style from his employees. He was big and likeable, firm but fair, and people wanted to please the big ex-para who oozed confidence and was so bloody keen to make a success of life that they got caught up in his exuberance and clung onto his coat-tails so they weren't left behind.

Collette remarked of him one day, "He's a bleedin' steam engine goin' at full speed and I'm enjoyin' the ride!"

Kim laughed, "In more ways than one."

Collette blushed prettily, "Saucy cow!"

Jamesey was a convivial man by nature, and his close brush with death during the ambush in Glenmacadoon Square just made him even more so. He loved Collette. He loved the challenge of OLG, and he lived each day to the full.

After a year, OLG Watford had secured several lucrative contracts for guarding local car parks, shopping arcades and public buildings. At night his men did doormen and security at clubs, functions or other events. The pub run was now fully established and expanded to banks, shops, businesses and anybody else who wanted their valuables moved around safely.

Jamesey even fought tooth and nail against other firms to secure a government contract to move used notes for incineration from money establishments to the Bank of England's secure facility at a secret location in England. He commented to his staff, "It's a class act. The government's paying us good money to help destroy money." He liked the irony of it.

OLG even guaranteed their customers their money back if it was stolen. It caused him to break a bit of sweat in the early days when the cash flow was slow. But as the business expanded, the cash began to roll in and he slept easier at night. A few opportunist thieves tried to snatch the odd satchel of cash or hold a van up but they were no match for OLG's battle-hardened veterans, and the firm's reputation grew and word spread that it was a good, solid operation, scrupulously honest and could take on any task at a drop of a hat.

After eighteen months Jamesey moved the whole shebang to a new office block at the top of the town. He had forty people working full time for him now and a retinue of part-timers he used when and where he wanted. He rented an entire floor, and the owners gave him a discount when he provided two doormen and installed an alarm system.

Collette had left the old office above the bookies reluctantly. It held happy memories for them, and she thought fondly of the first day she had met Jamesey, and he had backed 'Collette's Dream' at 20/1 in that very shop. Sometimes she still had to kick herself to make sure it wasn't a dream. She didn't recognise herself at times the smartly dressed, confident and efficient executive PA to the guvnor. She was very much an integral part of the firm. Despite running the home, she oversaw the other office staff, which seemed to multiply monthly, kept Jamesey's appointment book and nagged at him if he was late. She also helped with the hiring and firing, took a personal interest in the employees' welfare, kept an eye on the payroll, kept up to date with all new aspects in the security business and a thousand and one other details needed to run an expanding company.

She was Jamesey's rock, and she knew it and revelled in it. She never knew one person could love another so much and it amazed her how deep her love for him was, and the wonderful thing was she knew with one hundred per cent certainty that Jamesey felt the same.

"Couldn't have done it without you, Coll," he liked to tell her, and she would look up from whatever home correspondence courses she was doing, spread across her desk, and grin happily at him.

Regardless of having young Rabbie, Collette had maintained her trim figure, and both their sex drives were more than satisfactory. Her thirst for education and reading hadn't abated and her language had improved, although she could still curse with the best of them when the need arose. Dougie still lived in awe of her as did most of the staff, but she was massively popular, and it was to her that the younger members came to her with their problems. If Jamesey was the searcher and finder, then Collette was the welder and binder, who held them all together in a tight bond.

II

OLG HQ, Watford 9th April 1983

It was mid-morning and Jamesey and Smudger sat in his office munching on chocolate digestives and sipping a rich Java roast Collette had installed in the office. Insisting on freshly ground coffee impressed the clients, and both men got quickly hooked on it. Smudger took a good wallop and smacked his lips in appreciation, "Sure beats the army ration, mucker. This gear's top notch."

Jamesey agreed and pulled a bottle of Black Bush whiskey out of his drawer and added a healthy slug to their mugs, "Whilst the cat's away and all that...remember the Nescafe sachets in the compo packs? When you got it open, it was as hard as a brick."

Smudger concurred, "Yeah, and you freezin' your nuts off and knackered and needing a hot beverage. Stuff was probably pre-war. No sell-by dates, you see. How is the Queen Bee and the nipper then?"

Jamesey ruminated for a bit, Collette was heavily pregnant. Her first six weeks she had bad morning sickness and a month later a small showing, which had ended up as a week of rest and care in the hospital to prevent a miscarriage. It had spooked him and he had fussed over her and made sure she followed orders and had lots of reading materials.

"Yeah, they're okay, thanks. Enjoying the visit to me mum's, and Beth loves to have them stay, still, truth be told, I miss them in the house."

Smudger stretched, Kim and the kids were away to Cornwall to visit his parents. "Yeah, they kinda grow on yah," and he laughed. "Kim's only gone visiting 'cause Collette's gone walkabout."

"Yeah, bleedin' joined at the hip, them two," agreed Jamesey. "Here, see there's a sell-by date on this pack of biscuits. Bloody things are getting everywhere!"

Smudger squinted at it, "Best before March 1987... Bleedin' hell, so what do they do with all the stuff when it's outta date?"

Jamesey shrugged, "Probably dump it or build mountains with it."

"Food mountains," he chuckled. "Never catch on. If the government's any wit, they would send it the starving masses in Africa or somewhere... Christ, we ate some dodgy meals in the paras. Never done us any harm."

Jamesey was of the same mind, "But tell you what, Smudger. It's all a plot by the supermarkets. Means the stock is always turning over. It's gonna put the small High Street shops out of business, you mark my words. And as for government, you have to be kiddin'. Pathetic."

He was well on his soapbox and liked an audience.

"What yah mean then, Jamesey?" he asked, interested.

Jamesey topped their mugs up.

"The coffee's rapidly turning yellow and smelling of heather," complained Smudger.

Jamesey gave him a wink, "Put hairs on yer chest...now listen and learn. Say the government has a series of meetings and decides to send two plane-loads of say, out-of-date corned beef and spam to, let's say, the hungry in Ethiopia. First, they'll be moaning and gurning 'bout the cost. They'll be worried the Ethiopians will be insulted or consider our planes in their airspace as an act of war. So they'll have to send a delegation to speak to the chiefs and warlords to clear the way. More time consumed. With me, so far?"

"Yeah, and more dead kiddies. Go on."

"'Kay, say it gets that far. Then they'll have to consult the European Commission in Brussels because they are rapidly calling the shots now, and Maggie Thatcher can't pass wind without their say so."

"Okay. More time wasted."

"Exactly. So the commission eventually get around to it." Jamesey put on a mincing France/Galle accent and pantomimed with his hands. "Oh no, you cannot send ze corned beef to Ethiopia. It too hard to open with ze little keys and they might

417

cut themselves…and sue ze trouseaurs off us. Oh no, you cannot send ze spam. It is pork and the Muslims will be insulted and call a Jihad down on our 'eads."

Smudger laughed, "Ham in spam? I don't think anybody knows what goes into it and having ate too much of it in the army, I don't want to."

It was Jamesey's turn to laugh, "It's a national secret, mate, but you don't see too many stray dogs or cats near a spam production plant," and he carried on his pantomime, "Any'ow. Ze can is marked in pounds and ounces, not ze kilo or gram. You must re-weigh and re-label it."

"As if the starving give a flying fuck. Grub is grub when your bellybutton's sticking to your backbone," growled Smudger.

"True, mate. So let's just say it does get the go ahead. The wankers on the commission pocket a nice fat overtime bonus for burning the midnight oil and clap themselves on the back for averting a famine which has been going on for years. The RAF spends tens of thousands flying it over just for it to be grabbed by the warlords, who sell it on the black market or to Saddam Hussein in Iraq for his army, and the hungry, well, they stay hungry!"

Smudger agreed grimly, "Never change, will it, Jamesey? Poor buggers, I reckon we are going to have trouble with that Saddam cunt in years to come."

"Yeah, God helps those who help themselves and the masses will starve. They don't give a flying fuck."

June Semple, a lady in her forties, whom Collette had befriended down the Legion after her husband had been killed on the 'Sir Galahad' during the previous year's Falklands War, put her head around the door, "You two finished putting the world to rights? You've visitors."

Jamesey looked at her. Another of Collette's strays but truly a valuable find, she was a top-notch secretary, and the missus had given her on-the-job training and she filled in when Collette needed time off. Jamesey had big plans for her, "Yes, my treasure…who's calling? I've no appointments."

She grinned. She was attractive, with long dark hair and blue eyes and kept her figure well. Talk in the office was Dougie Alarms was chasing after her. *Be a good match*, Jamesey reckoned. *Two ships on a lonely ocean.*

"Three guys from the government. Home Office. Probably going to arrest you for treason," and she smirked wickedly.

Good sense of humour too. Collette could pick them, "Give them a coffee, June, and send them in after fifteen minutes."

She left closing the door, The boss was a true character.

"Nice one, Jamesey. We done our bit. Now they can wait for us. The tables have turned full circle."

"Yep, the prerogative of power. It's brill…wonder what the bastards want. Very, very interesting."

"Maybe they want us to guard the food mountains from the starving masses."

"I smell something deep, dangerous and dirty, me old china, but I also smell government money and lots of it."

Smudger snorted derisively, "Yeah, they won't spend money to alleviate the suffering but they will on making it worse. This smells mega dodgy."

"You're getting cynical, mate. Could be all neat and above board."

"Fuck off, Jamesey!" he replied. "Them bastards don't known above board, just down and dirty."

418

Jamesey swallowed his coffee-flavoured whiskey and savoured the burn, "Ain't life so interesting, mate?"

* * *

"I want to just remind you, gentlemen, you're still under the dictates of the Official Secrets Act. Anything repeated outside this room could result in you being arrested and held in prison incommunicado."

Jamesey and Smudger eyed the three men who had entered the office with interest. They were well suited and booted, with light overcoats to protect their expensive attire from the heavy April showers the day had started with. The speaker was a short, thin aristocratic-looking guy with silver hair combed back, in his early fifties. His two companions were taller and stockier, about ten years younger and stared at them unwaveringly. They reeked of spooks, he decided. "No introductions. No chit-chat. No handshakes," he paused, assessing. "So, tell me, what does MI5 want with us today?"

The speaker laughed softly, "No fooling you," and offered his hand. "Colonel Swain[169] retired. Secret Service and my staff, Johnny and Phil."

They shook quickly and pulled up chairs, all business. "Long words for this time of the morning," sneered Smudger. "Bullshit baffles brains, eh?"

"What he's saying, Colonel, is that we may have only been NCOs but we're not stupid."

"Yeah, you can't teach your granny to suck eggs."

"What he means is you can't teach an old dog new tricks," interrupted Jamesey, "We know the score."

The Colonel laughed, "Lovely metaphors. As long as we understand each other, what I have to say is highly classified, doncha know?"

"Before you go on, do I want to hear this? I'm a happily married man and a civilian. I've done my share of active service."

Smudger had the thick head on, Jamesey saw. He'd never been a great fan of the established officer class system. Smudger believed it was outdated and fostered an 'us against them' mentality. He thought a man should only become an officer on merit and experience and not because of money and that daddy came from Belgravia and could afford to send their spoilt brat to Sandhurst. He used to drive young subalterns to distraction by acting the thick Cornish yokel, making them explain their orders numerous times, and then with a look of disdain plodded off to carry them out.

"Why don't you cut to the chase, Colonel?" suggested Jamesey. "We may have been low on the food chain but we are patriots."

"Glad to hear it. Basically we need help, Mr DeJames. Since the PM's stance against the IRA during the hunger strike in 1981, the PIRA received a massive influx of recruits to the cause and money and arms from abroad. Phil?"

Phil was a tough-looking man with close-cropped dark hair and battle-weary eyes. He'd seen a bit of action, Jamesey decided. "Yes, Maggie claimed the victory over the hunger strikers as a great moral victory but it strengthened the IRA cause for victory through violence. The Armalite in one hand and the ballot box in the

---

[169] A main character in the author's book 'Tour of Terrorism 1'.

other. The IRA active service units have never been stronger or better-armed, and they are over here and dedicated on causing as much mayhem as possible, and she wants them stopped by all means…"

Jamesey raised a hand to stop him, "By over here, you don't mean in dear old Watford, do you?"

"Yep, and the MI5 is swamped keeping tabs on them and the armed forces are still recovering after the Falklands, so we are subcontracting so to speak."

Jamesey looked at him knowingly, "Argh, I see. So you've come to the professionals for help?"

"That's about right," interjected the Colonel. "Technically, you and Mr Smith are still on the reserve but we don't want to enlist you. Part of MI5's remit is to keep an eye on private security firms in the UK, and On La Guardia is making a good name for itself and we are impressed."

"So you want to employ us to watch the IRA in Watford?"

"Yes, Mr DeJames, and a few other places. What do you think?"

"It's gonna cost you, Colonel. Jamesey and me have already shed blood for our country. They call him the 'One Armed Bandit' down the pub," Smudger informed him.

The Colonel grinned knowledgeably. "They are still singing songs in the shebeens in West Belfast about the martyrs of Glenmacadoon Square. I can assure you money is no object."

"Then let's talk business," he pressed his intercom, "Coffee please, Miss Moneypenny."

"Real coffee," said Smudger smugly. "None of your powdered crap at OLG."

"Glad to hear it. I hated that shit we got in the rations," said Phil. "Always went hard."

June brought a tray in and left them to it, curiosity across her beak. The Colonel drank with approval then, "Okay, gents, down to business. Take notes, Johnny. This is the first briefing for what we are going to call 'Operation Hornet'[170]. Present are…"

9th April 1983; 10.15pm

Major Victor Ivanhoe Berkeley II, thirty-three years and formally of the Royal Green Jackets and 22 Special Air Service Regiment, regarded the group of eight men who stood menacingly in a half circle before him, his back pressed into the hard wood bar of The Three Bells pub on Watford's main street. Victor was an attractive man with clean-cut features, long dark hair and 'come to bed' blue eyes that many a willing female had fallen for and subsequently had their hearts broke. Wide in the shoulder and lean in the hip at five foot nine, he had the build of an Olympian swimmer.

He knew he should have taken his drink in the lounge bar, where you got a better class of clientele, but he had got used to slumming it with his guys in the SAS in various dives around the world and liked the commonality of it. He regretted it now as the thugs pressed upon him. Strangers in strange public bars were often regarded with suspicion by the regulars, but Victor could be quite charming when he wanted

---

[170] Named after Watford Football Club 'The Hornets'.

and had inveigled himself into their company. He had his sights set on a pretty little redhead, who had been covertly giving him the eye as he stood at the bar drinking gin and tonic with a slice.

Sighing, he mentally chided himself for taking the bait. He was a sucker for a pretty face, and this penchant for the female species had got him into more scrapes and fights than he cared to remember. Victor collected woman like a football fanatic collected programmes and often played away from home in hostile territory, like tonight. He enjoyed the chase but once he had snared his prey and drunk at the Golden Well, he moved on at the first hint of commitment and wandered off to track down another.

He was like some type of lusty nomad who plundered the oasis then disappeared into the vastness of the desert before moving on to the next watering hole to seek the forbidden fruit again. Time he settled in one spot, he decided, and put some roots down. But first, he would have to extricate himself from this delicate scenario as hastily as possible. The critters arrayed before him were not happy bunnies at all. Fists raised and cheeks red with anger, they were tough working men form the Basildon Bond paper mill outside of town and considered themselves hard cases.

"I think there's been some misunderstanding here, old Beans," he said, hands outspread. "What say I buy us a round and no hard feelings?"

"What say I ram yer teeth down yer throat, old Bean?" said the ringleader, a strapping man, who had unfortunately turned out to be the provocative harlot's husband, "So far yer have to put a toothbrush up yer arse to clean them."

Victor tut tutted, "Such language from one so young. I really didn't mean to cause offense. Anyway, I took a vow of celibacy many years ago."

"Celibacy…wot you a pooftah, then?" asked another.

"I'm sure my sexual orientation is of no interest or really any of your deuced business."

"We don't like pooftahs in our pub. Do we, lads?" from the leader.

They muttered their agreement, "But we like a bit of queer-bashin'," said another, "And Paki-bashin'."

Victor bristled and adjusted his dark turban. His parents were from Delhi gentry, and his skin was as brown as a hazelnut. "That really is very insulting. The Pakistan people are proud but maybe not as proud as us Anglophile Indians."

"What the fuck is he wafflin' about? Do the Paki cunt," said one, hate eschewed on his racist face.

"I apologise if I insulted your wife but she did come onto me, and my hand accidentally slipped onto her rather fat thigh. You should keep her indoors, young fellah. She's a danger in public."

"Enuf of your crap, you Paki pooftah. Yer leaving through the fuckin' window," snapped the enraged leader.

He gave it one last not very diplomatic stab, "Listen, gents. Let me leave the premises with my head high and with dignity, and I won't have to wipe the floor with your racist faces."

They gawked in amazement, "Enough of this shite," and the leader swung a haymaker at Victor's head with his right fist as the others moved in eagerly.

He may as well have put a signpost on it because Victor caught it easily in his right hand, spun under the upright arm, twisted the arm up the back and with his left hand slammed it into the back of the neck. His attacker's forehead cracked onto the edge of the hard bar, and he crashed down to the floor screaming. One down, seven to go. He really didn't want to hurt them but his dander was up by jingo, and he spun to confront the rest, who rushed forward, livid.

In a flurry of blows and swipes with the sides of the hand, almost too fast for the eye to see, he felled the first three in a blurred kaleidoscope of movement, connecting hard. *Careful*, Victor he reminded himself, *you don't want to kill anybody like that poor, mislead docker in Mombasa.* He swung to the remaining stunned thugs and adopted the 'Horse Karate' stance. Fists up and clenched, elbows bent and arms tight into his sides, legs splayed and bent.

"I must warn you I am a high don in the martial arts."

"Now he fuckin' tells us," mumbled one mesmerised by what had occurred in front of his eyes.

Then, unfortunately, Lady Luck intervened. The barman saw his chance and swung a golf club with devastating force into the back of his head, "Fore!" he shouted as he connected, delighted with this shot, before quickly stashing the club behind the bar in case the cops came a visiting.

Victor saw stars and little birdies were singing in his head. He'd been sucker punched. He reeled, then a kick to the stomach and he doubled over with a whoomph.

"Stomp the black bastard," and a battery of blows sent him to the floor. Time to do a hedgehog, and he curled up into a defensive ball, trying to regain his breath. Bloody uncouth heathens.

The redhead watched greedily, turned on. She'd seen the guys stomp a Paki before, and it fired her engines. She hated the little bastards, with their smelly curry breath and pokey shops selling weird goods and thinking they could come over here and live amongst white people as if they were equals. The men would smear his face all over the bar, and she egged them on, wanting blood and shivering in anticipation.

As they lashed viciously with their Doc Martins into the human ball, the doors burst open and two big guys in black burst in like fired rockets and ran into them with hard shoulders and bowled them over like skittles. Gathering themselves, they charged back to the intruders standing over the prey, only to be felled by solid thwacks and whacks by expertly used coshes. They cringed away, cowering in a group, eyes blackening, jaws swelling and several spat teeth from bloodied lips.

"Watch them, Smudger," said Jamesey and helped Victor up. "You're losing your touch, Major."

Victor took his turban off and fingered the dent in the inlaid metal lining, "By George, Colour Sergeant DeJames, as I live. I had it under control, doncha know. Blighter would have broken my skull but for this," and he showed him the dent. "How in damnation did you know I was in town?"

"We have eyes everywhere, mate," laughed Smudger. "Don't we, Jamesey?"

"Come on, Major. Let's beat a hasty retreat to a real pub. The natives are restless."

"Yes a change of venue, I do believe. Much obliged for your timely intervention."

"Not the first time the paras had to pull you guys out of trouble," grinned Jamesey as they headed out.

"Bye, Victor. Nice to meet cha," waved the redhead.

"If you were mine, dear, you'd be going home to a damn good spanking."

She sighed as they left, "I'd probably like that," she said softly as she went to attend to her battered hubby.

In a quiet corner in The Peel, Jamesey and Smudger quizzed the Major.

"Heard you were on the loose, Boss. What you doing for a living now?"

"Please chaps, call me Victor. I resigned my commission after the Falklands. Thought I'd give civvie street a go, doncha know?"

The paras and the SAS often worked hand in hand on operations in war zones. The SAS gathering info on the enemy and planning ops and the paras acting as backup and going in hard when summoned to battle.

Victor's reputation preceded him. He was probably one of the world's top operatives in counter terrorism, close quarter undercover surveillance and unarmed combat. Legend had it he spent five days in a compost heap, breathing through a straw, watching a nest of IRA men on a farm near the staunch republican town land of Cappagh in Tyrone. Finally calling in the paras to scoop them when they received a shipment of arms.

Other stories abounded, and Jamesey wanted him especially now they were doing sneaky beaky work for the government. "Listen, Vic. Smudger and me run a pretty tight ship. On La Guardia security. We are going to branch out into undercover work and we need someone to head the operative's division. Train them up and supervise and plan ops. Whatcha think?"

Victor eyeballed them keenly. He'd lost a lot of good mates in the Falklands, especially when a chopper full went down in the South Atlantic. Men who didn't care about class, colour or creed. All they asked was you covered each other's backs and when the chips were down, you stood your ground.

"Well, I must admit I'm bored. Best offer I've had is selling double glazing. Damn degrading. Tell me more."

"How does Major's pay twice over sound and expenses?" beamed Jamesey back.

"Golly gosh! Must admit the family finances have took a tumble recently," he paused, "Count me in," and they shook hands on it.

"Just a couple of things, Victor," interspersed Smudger. "No loitering with the female staff. OLG's one big happy family."

"Yeah, we're happily married, and we look after our girls, so no hanky panky."

Victor looked hurt, "As if I would, perish the thought," then he looked over his shoulder at Eadie behind the bar and back at them with a twinkle in his eye. "But the landlady's a cracker. Bit old but I don't mind a bit of motherly experience, by jingo."

"She's out of it too, Vic. Sorry. This pub's what we call our second home."

"Yeah, Ron and Eadie's family like. We use the place as a safe house. It's well run and one hundred per cent secure."

"Enough said. I know not to do the dirt on home turf."

"Eadie, bring a bottle of 'Bush' over, and you and Ron come and meet Victor."

A few moments later they joined them, and Victor stood gallantly and pulled Eadie's chair out for her. "Must say the ladies in Watford are top totty. I think this calls for champers, landlord. I've just joined the family."

Ron got up to get it, seeing a nice profit, and Eadie simpered and fawned over Victor.

"Just remember, Vic. What goes on in the family stays in the family," the dynamic duo told him.

III

He sat sipping a pint of Double Diamond in the corner of the lounge bar in The Peel. Ron and the locals knew when Jamesey sat there, he wanted his own council and was thrashing some mental problem out or coming up with new ideas and strategies for OLG.

Ron watched him proudly. Many of the OLG 'family' used his bar as a second home and often took clients there for lunch or after hours for business meetings. Jamesey's trade was booming and he had been there from the start, well him and Eadie, and Ron liked to see a man make a success of things. Jamesey was a bleeding phoenix rising out of the despair of losing his hand. Devouring and sucking up all opposition before him, the man seemed unstoppable, and the bigger the challenge, the happier Jamesey was.

Ron regaled new customers with the story of how Jamesey had wiped the public-bar floor with Slimy Barry's beak, and Eadie told their better halves the fairy tale romance of the beautiful desolate barmaid and the handsome para.

Because of the upturn in business, Ron had hired a full-time chef called Antoine. He was a fiery little man from Brussels, but he made beef and Guinness pie and his coq au vin was to die for. He got along great with Eadie, who ran the food department, so he was happy enough. Eadie had gone up-market with the foreign crap on the menu, though Ron was a pie and mash man.

Chef arrived with a big platter of eggs, sausage, bacon and chips, "Ronnie, I tell this so many times, I am ze chef not ze waitress. My huge talent is in the kitchen. Is demeaning, I am ze artist."

Ron took the plate off him, "Yeah well, the girl's off tonight. You take your over paid talent back to yer stove and I'll sort this for yeh."

Antoine threw his hands up, "Pah...if you pay peanuts, you get ze monkeys. I am ze best, Monsieur Ron," and he looped off, hand on hip.

Ron was laughing as he put the food down in front of the hungry security tycoon. "That Antoine. I swear he's queer, bent as a nine bob note."

Jamesey pulled himself back to the present, "Oh right, well, it takes all different acts to make a circus."

Ronnie recharged his pint glass, "There yah go, mate, real food and real ale. What more does a man want? Not into all that poxy foreign grub goin' baht the pubs at the moment."

"You're a diamond geezer," said Jamesey, lavishing salt and pepper on his grub, "Now, bugger off, I'm thinking."

Ronnie grinned, "You'll harden your arteries, son. What yer thinking baht then?"

"I'm trying to sort out the Irish problem, so sod off."

"Well, if anyone can do it you can, mate," he said in leaving, half meaning it.

Jamesey munched on his scoff, the vinegar biting his throat nicely, and replayed the meeting with MI5 over again in his head. Once they had thrashed the protocols and criteria out for 'Operation Hornet', Colonel Swain had given them a very large cheque by way of a deposit. "Lots more where that came from, chaps. H.M.'s coffers are very deep," he said by way of departure.

Jamesey looked at the plastic hand on his stump. The war in Northern Ireland showed no signs of abatement. Previous IRA campaigns against the British since partition in 1922 had normally fizzled out due to losses, lack of popular interest or decrepitude. But the flame of Irish independence, although low at times, could never be fully extinguished by the authorities. It only took one fanatical finger on the trigger to start it all up again, and this time it looked like the IRA and their splinter groups were going to take it the whole way or die in the process.

Jamesey chomped and munched his way through his meal. Collette had been trying to get him to eat healthier and would have nagged him for eating crap but she was visiting with Kim and he reckoned a good binge was allowed now and then; after all, an army marches on its stomach and OLG was like an army and they were thrusting forward... Well, that was his excuse and he was sticking to it.

The Irish problem, 'The Troubles' as they had become known, was more complex than people thought. As a young soldier he had been sent to the Province when it was on the point of civil war. They had spent a few weeks frantically polishing their skills in urban warfare, learning the rules of engagement and pouring over maps of the high-risk areas, the Catholic areas in green, the Protestant in orange. Jamesey knew very little about Ireland or its history but it became very clear that the troubles were in the working-class areas. Although there were cries for equality, better housing, equal pay and seats in government, the overriding demand was for the six counties of Ulster, Armagh Antrim, Down, Fermanagh, Londonderry and Tyrone to be freed of British rule. They wanted the border to go and North and South to join as Eire, under one government based in Dublin.

He splurged sauce on a sausage and ate it in three mighty bites. Antoine skipped down to him, "Is ze food okay, Monsieur James? You should try ze good French cooking. Is 'ealthier."

He eyed the little man, amused. There was no doubt he was bent as a bottle of crisps. "Only good thing to come out of France is the Dover ferry. Hey, do you have frog's legs?"

Antoine jumped up and down enthusiastically, "Mais oui, I can get them, monsieur."

Jamesey grinned, "Then go get some and hop off, I'm thinking."

The little chef laughed delightedly, "Monsieur...hop off...very funny. I leave you to your swill," and he turned to leave.

Jamesey called him back and gave him a tenner, "Here Frenchie, get yourself a bottle of that plonk Ron calls wine, merci beaucoup."

Antoine minced off happily, despite being Belgian, he was used to the cockneys mistaking him for French. He had tried to explain but they were a breed and culture of their own and couldn't care less. No wonder the Germans couldn't beat them down in WW2.

He mopped up the juices with a slice of bread and belched in appreciation. When he came back from the first bloody tour, he had decided to read up on Irish history and it was an eye-opener.

Pre-Christianity Ireland was dominated by large groupings of fierce tribes, who lived in hill-forts and spent most of their time raiding each other, stealing cattle and women. Despite this, they were civilised and cultured, God help any would be invaders because the tribes would unite and drive them back into the sea. It was an effective strategy. The Romans came, took one look and decided to leave the mad Irish alone. They called Ireland 'Dementia' then, which he thought very apt!

Then came Christianity and that, Jamesey decided, was when their trouble began. Saint Patrick started it, a former Roman slave, he converted the tribal leaders and 'the Word' travelled the country and became law. Monasteries flourished and towns grew around them. By the fifth century, Dublin was considered the foremost learning centre in the known world and was fully endorsed by the Pope in Rome. Catholicism gripped Ireland in a fierce grip like a fever.

In the eighth and ninth centuries, the heathen Vikings invaded but the tribes massed again and kept them out of the interior and they settled in the coastal areas. Dublin became a thriving Viking port but the yoke of Christianity soon got a grip on them as they interbred and their mighty war god, Odin, was replaced by the pacifist Jesus Christ.

The eleventh century saw the arrival of the mighty Norman war machine. After thrashing the Saxons at Hastings in 1066, they tamed the English, bombarded through Wales and Scotland, making them satellite states, before crossing the Irish Sea. They built mighty castles and ruled with an iron fist but could never quite quell the stubborn tribes, who attacked their armoured columns as and when they could. The soil around Dublin was light in colour for several miles, to go beyond that the Normans had to go mob handed, thus the saying 'Don't go beyond the pale'.

He finished his pint and signalled Ronnie for another, solving history problems was thirsty work.

"You the world sorted to rights then?"

Jamesey sighed, "The world's simple compared to the bloody Irish, their stubborn love for their island makes them dangerous."

Ronnie left, shaking his head, and Jamesey went back to his musing. Like the Vikings, the Normans interbred, married off the fair French maidens to the tribe leaders. They made the tribe leaders Earls and things settled down for a time. That's when Rome and the Catholic Church really got into things. They preached doom and gloom, hell and salvation, heresy and damnation. They literally lived off the backs of the terrified common populace…pay up or go to hell.

But even through all that, the native tribes were never quite beaten. The Protestant Queen Elizabeth I ran a war of raging battles with them, but they had perfected the art of guerrilla warfare even then and they became masters of the game.

Then came the 'New Model Army'. After James I, the last true Catholic king, Charles I came to the throne.

The Puritan Oliver Cromwell raised an army against Charles, defeated him and executed him for treason by removing his head in 1649. England was now truly Protestant.

The Irish had to practice their religion in secret as the Proddies arrived and stole their land, Cromwell prohibited the Catholic faith and when the tribes again rebelled, Cromwell put them down, committing many atrocities, for which he is still hated by the Irish. *A sad legacy to be remembered by*, Jamesey mused.

The Irish have terribly long memories, decided Jamesey, a fierce but cultured people. Not stupid by any means, able to survive several invasions but still keep hold of their unique Irish identity. They also bred like rabbits; at the extortion of the local priests, the bigger the family, the more money for the church and more fresh blood to fight the excommunicated Prods. In 1983 the Catholic Church in the North of Ireland still banned any form of contraception, and even Protestants living in the South had to smuggle in condoms and the pill and use them in secret.

Cromwell's heinous activities had fostered in the Irish a deep-rooted hatred of the English that still prevailed but the Battle of the Boyne, in 1690, between the Catholic King of Scotland, James II, who laid claim to the English throne, and William II, who was on the throne, was the icing on the cake. Protestant William beat James resoundingly, and the Prods sang about it ever since, rubbing their Catholic neighbours' faces in it and never letting them forget. They ruled the roost and Protestant settlers came and were given the land that had once been owned by Catholics, after they had been driven off. History referred to this as the 'Plantation Period' and was another nail in the proverbial Catholic coffin.

Many Irish left for the colonies, America, Australia, Canada and the West Indies; they became a transient race. Having been encouraged to have large families by the priests, it came down to leave or starve, as the sons and daughters had no prospects, so they left.

Still the flame of Irish freedom could not be quelled and, through the eighteenth and into the early nineteenth centuries, although the English were the landowners and the Irish little better than slaves, there were numerous small rebellions, which were quickly put down.

Then came 1845 and the Potato Famine. *That, as they say, really put 'the cat amongst the pigeons'*, thought Jamesey. When the potato crop failed due to blight, the masses were starving, and although the government in England could have alleviated the problem by buying Irish corn, they sat back and watched the situation in Ireland get worse and bought Dutch corn instead. The uncaring rich called the starving, 'Greenmouths', because in desperation they ate grass.

Tens of thousands left Ireland for the 'New World', and the pioneering Irish became famous worldwide for their toughness, ingenuity and sense of humour in the face of adversity. They worked hard and sent money home to sustain their loved ones. They waxed lyrical and sang sentimental songs about their 'Homeland', the sacred 'Emerald Isle', taking their music all over the world; they also cursed the hated English to hell and back.

"Can't say I blame them," Jamesey said into his pint, "It was all downhill from there, especially when the Republicans stormed the Dublin Post Office at Easter in 1916." He gulped down more ale, "Way too soon for an armed insurrection," And he shook his head sadly.

The 'Irish Republican Brotherhood', forerunner to the IRA, was raised and their 'flying armed columns' took on the mighty British Army. Still reeling after WW1, the flower of British manhood lost to incompetent decisions made by uncaring Generals, the British sued for peace.

"And that's when they made their biggest mistake," he told his diminishing pint, "They should have gave them the whole shebang. The place, after all, is an island."

The Provence of Ulster was the heart of Unionist Ireland and the centre of industry – ship building, linen and textile mills, steel and banking and commerce – all owned and run by the Protestants, and the British wanted to keep control of it. Incredibly, the IRA General Michael Collins agreed they could keep six of the nine counties of Ulster and signed on the dotted line… Partition had arrived.

"You silly, silly man," said Jamesey, "A child could see the trouble ahead."

"Who ya talking to then, Jamesey?" asked Smudger, who had arrived with Victor.

"I was talking to the spirit of a dead man who was killed by his own for being an idiot."

"That's okay then," replied Victor Berkeley, "I talk to my ancestors all the time," and grinned.

"What ya got for me? Is 'Hornet' a viable gogo?" asked the boss, giving Victor an odd look.

"Sure is," said Smudger, "We are ready to rock and roll."

"Great. Whatever the rights or wrongs of the Irish problem, we can't have them coming over here bombing and shooting innocents, can we?"

"Absolutely not," they agreed. "Wot ya eating?"

"Proper squaddie stuff but don't tell Collette, mate."

IV

Two weeks later the three of them were sitting in a small council flat, watching a line of garages stretched out below them. Jamesey had given the tenant, an old grizzled WW2 veteran, a hundred quid and put him up in a hotel near the motorway, "We can claim it back as expenses off H.M.G.," he told Smudger.

'Operation Hornet' was coming to fruition. Victor had nobbled together a team of six undercover operatives, ex-special forces, and he had a string of informants in the Watford pubs. They had joined the Irish drinking community to watch and listen. Their brief was two-fold, identify new arrivals from the 'Emerald Isle' and identify groups and individuals who openly supported the IRA's campaign of violence.

What they had discovered was that the majority were decent, hard-working people who didn't give a hoot one way or the other about The Troubles but there was a small, relatively silent minority who were prepared to get involved, if the godfathers of violence called upon them, to wage war on the mainland. When these people were identified, the operatives tailed them, found out where they lived and worked and reported back any suspicious happening to OLG HQ.

They were now watching four guys who had recently arrived and shared a council flat in Carpenters Park, a large estate between Watford and Harrow. They drank most nights in The Green Man and seemed to have plenty of money, despite having no visible means of income. They had recently hired a Ford Transit van from Hertz and a lock-up garage where, the operatives said, they spent a lot of time with the door closed.

Jamesey had ordered a covert entry the night before, and they had found nearly a ton of home-made explosives in fertiliser bags, timing units, detonation cords, fuses and all the other trappings for an improvised bomb factory, four fully working Armalite rifles were the icing on the cake.

Colonel Swain had been told and plans had been made; now they were waiting for the four suspects to return, "The Provisional IRA are the most professional terror group in the world at present. The Irish, far from being the stupid race portrayed by various comedians and the media, are highly innovative and creative. Never underestimate your enemy."

Smudger snorted, "Innovative and creative or not, here they come, Jamesey. Bloody amateurs, if ya ask me."

They watched the van arrive and back up to the door. The terrorist got out and started loading it.

"Talk about caught in the act," chortled Victor. Jamesey picked up the phone and spoke into the receiver, "The hungry chicks have returned to the nest."

He put the receiver down, "Let's watch the fireworks, lads, Beats Hill Street Blues[171]."

"Wonder how the New Yorkers would feel if some terror group started bombing them?" asked Smudger.

"I think their day will come, my friend," Victor answered.

Two blue Sherpa vans pulled up with a squeal of tyres, one blocking each end of the entrance-way to the line of lock-up garages. Eight black-clad figures armed with sub-machine and shotguns burst from the side doors; stocks in shoulders and muzzles trained on the bombers; they raced towards them screaming at them to put their hands on their heads and get down on the ground

The bombers froze. They knew they were being raided by Scotland Yard's elite Blue Beret Tactical Firearms Unit. Several unmarked police cars pulled up and detectives raced out, brandishing heavy calibre revolvers. They took cover behind their vehicles and watched their uniformed comrades move in.

Three of the bombers decided they didn't want to die for Ireland at that moment in time and threw themselves down, terrified, trying to burrow into the concrete. The fourth was made of sterner stuff, he leapt into the van and came out brandishing one of the Armalites, shouting the Proves war cry 'Tiofaidh ár lá' (Chucky ar la), and faced his enemy.

He managed to get off a half-second burst of six rounds before he was cut down in a withering fusillade of fire, his body jerked in a mad caricature of some wild savage dance as the heavy rounds punched through him, gouging fist-sized chunks of flesh off before a bullet blew his head apart and he dropped like a brick.

Jamesey grimaced, "Another one bites the dust... Good track that... Freddie Mercury and Queen."

"Yes, indeed," agreed Victor, "Oh the folly of the sons, of the sons, of the sons."

"Good enough for the murdering bastards," snarled Smudger, who still resented nearly losing his left leg and the permanent limp it had left him with.

They watched as the Blue Berets put brown paper bags[172] over the prisoner's hands, to preserve any traces of explosives, and cuffed them before the jubilant Anti-Terrorist Squad Detectives arrested them, faces flushed, victorious.

The ATO (Ammunitions Technical Officer) arrived in his armoured truck and secured the scene and deployed uniformed local officers to clear the flats. Colonel Swain, who had been listening from the local operations room, rang, "Bravo, DeJames. Score a big one for the good guys. I suggest you bug out, we'll talk soon. Well done, chaps."

Jamesey hung up, grinning, "Time to go home, boys. Mission accomplished."

He stood and gathered his belongings as the phone rang again. He picked it up.

"Where the hell are you, love? You've been gone ages."

"Collette? How the hell did you get this number?"

"It was in the safe. You coming home? Me waters have broke and I'm contracting."

---

[171] Popular American cop show in the early 1980s.
[172] To preserve explosive traces.

He paled, she wasn't due for another week but obviously Mother Nature had other ideas. "I'll be there in fifteen, love, hang on and keep your legs crossed."

Collette laughed, "Yer better hurry. This one's like you. He ain't gonna hang about…'ere, I hope you haven't been eating any crap while yer've been doing all that secret squirrel stuff?"

He looked sheepishly at the Wimpy cartons, half-eaten kebabs and Mars Bar wrappers, "Not really. Lots of salads and high-fibre cereal bars."

"You lying bastard. Kim saw yah coming outta the Wimpy with a huge sack of burgers and fries."

It was his turn to laugh, she was a sketch, his little Collette, and love swelled his heart for her. "You're in the wrong job, my love, you should be doing the covert stuff. Now get off the phone and practice your breathing. I'll be there tout suite."

"Oh bugger off and get your arse into gear, you randy sod," and she hung up.

They trudged down the stairs, "No point in lying to them, Jamesey," remarked Smudger. "They got a full-blown bullshit antenna built in when it comes to us men."

"Yes, they are a different species," from Victor, "You can't fool the sisterhood."

"Okay wrap it up, guys. Let's shift it," and Jamesey broke into a jog. "Collette's about to drop a sprog, and if I'm not there when it pops, she'll kill me."

Victor nudged Smudger as they trotted after him, "See how the mighty warrior is cowed by a slip of a girl, is why I never married."

Smudger agreed, "You ain't seen Collette when she kicks off. She's a one-woman army."

Victor grimaced, "Thank Shiva she wasn't born Irish and in the IRA. We would be up the Ganges without a paddle."

* * *

Colonel Swain called into OLG HQ next day beaming like a Cheshire cat and shaking hands all round. The press had a field day, MI5 had leaked that the bombers were going to ram the gates of Buckingham Palace, set off the bomb and shoot all round them. Jamesey had his doubts, thinking it was all hyperbole, but the public was outraged and the fact that an unstable bomb had been made in a densely populated area added fuel to the fire.

After he had paid OLG a substantial figure for services rendered, Colonel Swain suggested they open a sub-office in Central London and gave Jamesey a list of service personnel leaving the armed forces that year and who might be interested in joining the company. Jamesey and Smudger agreed it was a good idea. "Maybe an office in Belfast and Liverpool."

Jamesey was keeping a cautious eye on the phone, Collette's labour pains had eased and she had been sent home, "Don't know about that, Colonel, lots of expense and man-power involved."

"Oh, fiddlesticks, Jamesey," he answered, "H.M.G. will find you premises and help with overheads until you get established. As for men, there are hundreds of young, fit ex-servicemen out there looking for work."

"Especially after the last round of defence cuts and redundancies. Soon we won't have an army," said Smudger darkly. "What if the Krauts kick off again? Cromwell must be turning in his grave."

"Exactly," beamed the Colonel, "That's why we need you chaps, fighting terror is an open, free enterprise now."

Jamesey had to agree it was feasible, he could see his empire expanding quicker than he had planned, but it was all good.

"Then it would be nice to get into North America, see where the buggers are getting their arms and money from, and cut it off at the source."

Jamesey was stunned, "America. I think you're rushing ahead without headlamps here, Colonel."

"Not at all. New York, Boston, Chicago. Cities with big Irish links. We can smooth the path, clear the diplomatic channels, so to speak."

Smudger liked it, "I'll have some of that. We could get an office in those twin towers they're putting up."

"No way, Smudger," objected Jamesey, "I had enough of heights when I was in the paras. We'll stay on the ground so we can see our enemy coming face to face and stop them in their tracks."

After discussing plans and tactics for another hour, they were interrupted by the phone ringing. Jamesey answered it at once, "No, Coll. I had a prawn salad and sesame whole grain baguette, I'm on my way."

He jumped up, "Have to leave you gents to it, Collette's about to calve and I better be there," as he rushed out the door.

Smudger pointed to the empty curry and fried rice carton in the waste bin, "She'll find out, Colonel, and they'll have a barney."

The Colonel smiled and agreed, "Yes, the ladies are psychic at times. Built-in radar when the chaps are spinning lies."

"Yep, different species, Colonel."

V

Jamie Killian DeJames weighed in at a healthy 10lb 2oz at 10.10pm that night in the Maternity Wing of Shroddell's Hospital. The couple gazed at their own creation, happily. Jamesey counted the baby's fingers and toes, "He's perfect, Collette. Bloody well done, lass."

She gave him the impish grin he loved, "Couldn't 've done it without yah, love. Now bugger off home and get some kip, I'm exhausted."

He kissed her lovingly and started to leave but she stopped him at the door, "I smelt curry on your breath earlier, love, but I'll let you off just this once, in the circumstances."

'Sorry, Coll, but they're addictive."

"Yeah, well bring me one up the marra and we'll share it. A good bum-burning vindaloo."

He readily agreed, "And all the trimmings for my baby-making queen."

Collette was feeling a bit maudlin, and her eyes moistened as she remembered that first curry he had taken her for. She had needed him then in ways she had never thought she would need a man, and now they were a team. She loved the interaction with him and she loved looking after him. She had so much to be grateful for and she thought she was going to explode; she expected to wake up in pieces and find it had all been a dream. The tears spilled down her cheeks unchecked.

Jamesey rushed over and wrapped her in a huge, comforting bear hug, which was just what she needed, and whispered sweet nothings in her ear while he stroked her hair. She ran her fingers through his tawny mane, "You know I only nag because I care about ya, Jamesey? I don't really mind ya havin' the odd binge."

"I know, Collette. We care for each other and that's all that matters to me. You and the kids."

She was calm now and, gathering herself, gently pushed him away, "Away on wiv ya now, love. Get some rest. There's a chicken salad in the fridge. See ya the marra."

He kissed her again and left, if he hurried he would just catch 'The Peking Garden' on Vicarage Road.

Collette opened her Leon Uris novel 'Trinity' about the history of Ireland.

By the end of 1984, OLG had offices in New York, London, Liverpool, Manchester, Newcastle, Dublin and Belfast. MI5 had kept their promise to help smooth the way and help with expenses and personnel. They also supplied OLG with what seemed a never-ending list of jobs they needed done 'off the books' and paid through the nose for the privilege.

The IRA campaign to bomb the mainland in the mid-eighties was minimal and largely unsuccessful. They managed to set a few devices off but the majority of the volunteers were either caught in the act with the goods, or they fled back home, tails between their legs. The IRA godfathers in Dublin and Belfast suspended many operations and swept through the rank and file of the volunteers with their torturers looking for non-existent touts, snitches and informants. They nearly got Maggie Thatcher, the PM, at her hotel in Brighton when a bomb went off, during the party conference, but a near miss was as good as a mile in Jamesey's book.

Colonel Swain and his team sat behind their desks in Whitehall feet up, twiddling their thumbs and letting the OLG do their work for them.

OLG Watford remained the UK HQ and Jamesey and his ever-loyal sidekick Smudger became a bit like the transient Irish, travelling from office to office, overseeing operations, troubleshooting and boosting morale. At every chance they took the wives and kids with them. Collette loved to travel after her cramped childhood.

On 4th August 1987 Petral Elizabeth was born in Liverpool General Infirmary. Jamesey was in town overseeing an operation to stop the IRA bringing explosives in on car ferries. The Provos were looking revenge after the SAS shot dead nine of their members at Loughgall in May of that year.

They were delighted at having a daughter and new addition to the family. She had Collette's eyes, hair and heart-shaped face; Jamesey was smitten, he felt fulfilled. They said no man was a man until he had a daughter.

The Single-Handed Viking and his warriors were on a roll and he intended to keep it that way.

VI

November, 1988. OLG HQ Watford.

The Colonel had called a meeting. Victor had rushed down from Petral Hill Farm, where he used its large isolated wastes to train up new operatives. The twelve-week course was long, punishing and arduous. The majority failed and went back to the armoured trucks or to installing alarms but the ones who passed went on to become members of the elite Undercover Operatives Division. They were the best of the best. The farm was churning out more than wool, meat and peat, it was producing some of the greatest undercover men since WW2 and the Colonel was impressed.

When they arrived, he introduced them to a large taciturn man in his early sixties, who had world-weary eyes, eyes that had seen it all, and didn't seem to be a person easily impressed.

"Colonel Archie Harrison Lang. My counterpart in MI6."

They nodded at him carefully…he looked dangerous.

He began, without any preamble, "The IRA campaign is nearing an end, they are still attacking but are finding it hard to get volunteers to engage us. The ones they have are young and inexperienced; they often botch jobs and make mistakes, sometimes on purpose, not wanting to engage the security forces and get themselves killed," he paused and sipped his brew, "Mmm, good coffee… No after Loughgall, the Enniskillen Poppy Day Massacre and other atrocities, they have lost a lot of popularity both with their own people and overseas support. Arms and money has practically dried up from America and Libya. The experts believe that in a few years' time they will call a ceasefire; of course, they will call it a victory and we will call it a surrender but it should signify an end to this present spate of hostilities."

"That's all very interesting, Colonel, but where does that leave us? We've got a terrible lot of resources tied up in watching the IRA for you," asked Jamesey.

Swain took over, "There's always going to be an Irish problem whilst the border remains. You'll always have the doves and the hawks. At the moment the doves are strongest. Gerry Adams, Martin McGuiness, Mitchell, Morrison, McLaughlin and a host of others…these people are going to be in government, you mark my words, but you're always going to have a small group of dissidents, splinter groups who will keep on with the campaign of violence."

Smudger snorted derisively, "What, murderers, bombers and torturers in charge of education, transport and industry? Can't see it. Jailbirds in power. No way."

Jamesey jumped in, "Yeah, it's coming, Smudger – especially if Labour get in. Their shadow spokesman, Kevin McNamara, is a rabid republican, as is his side kick Mo Mowlem. The Tories are so busy back-stabbing Maggie, they are going to fold."

Smudger had to agree, "Well, yeah, with friends like Heseltine and Archer, who needs enemies. They make Brutus look like a lamb and look what he did to Caesar."

"Yeah, you can hear the knives going in," and he switched his attention back to the Colonels, "But what has it to do with us, and why are MI6 getting involved? You're foreign affairs."

Colonel Harrison Lang took the reins up, "Well, Colonel Swain has agreed you keep your brief to keep an eye on IRA suspects home and abroad but MI6 is worried about the Arab countries. We are particularly worried about that blighter Saddam Hussein in Iraq and the Ayatollah in Iran. They are mad men and we see war coming. As for the rest of the Arab countries, Algeria, Tunisia, Libya, Egypt and Syria to name the main ones, they are ripe for revolt – and mark this carefully – when one goes up, they all will."

Jamesey let out a long, slow breath, "I guess so, it's feasible, but what can OLG do about it?"

433

The Colonel smiled, showing pristine white teeth that must have cost an arm and a leg, "Well, we don't think it will kick off for ten or twenty years but it would be nice if OLG had offices in say Riyadh, Cairo, Tunis, Constantinople, Ankara and Jerusalem."

Jamesey and Smudger looked at each other in amazement when the Colonel produced a cheque for almost ten million pounds, "This is just to get you started. We want the best and H.M.G.'s prepared to pay."

The partners were gobsmacked, "Bloody hell, I guess I better get my Arab phrase book out!"

Jamesey laughed, "Guess so, mucker, OLG UK has just gone global."

VII

June 2013, Los Angeles, California

And then all hell was let loose, and Collette died and things were never the same again.

In 1989 OLG UK had 500 employees on its books and by 2013 it had 10,000 – all from the idea of a single handed ex-soldier who backed a horse called Collette's Dream at 20/1 and rented an office above that same bookmakers.

When The Single-Handed Viking was interviewed by Johnny Carson on American TV and asked the secret of his success, he stated, "There would be no OLG Empire if my little Collette had not dragged me up from the wall of self-pity, kicked my sorry arse into gear and not took no for an answer. They say behind every good man is a good woman; well, I had the best. God must have broken the mould when he made her because he was afraid of the competition. She was small in stature but huge in life. They say no one is irreplaceable, I disagree, she was."

For the first time in living memory, OLG employees saw a tear sparkle in their chief's eye and trickle down his cheek. Their admiration and respect rose another notch at this open show of love and devotion for his dead soulmate.

Smudger watched from his couch in his comfortable LA apartment, Kim cradled in his arms, weeping for her lost friend.

"Different species, Jamesey," he said softly to his mate's image on the screen, "Different bloody species – and so are you, my friend," and he thought back to that terrible winter in 2011, in Hollywood, and he began to choke up himself, and as always happened when he got stressed out, the ache in his left thigh came back and niggled at him from when he had been shot so many years ago in Glenmacadoon.

Chapter 32
Chilli Dogs, Zoos and Russians
('Apeman'... The Kinks... 1968)

Part I

He knew in his own heart he had really been a complete and utter twat that morning and that he had probably hurt Luca's feelings deeply. What the hell was he playing at? He didn't want to lose her but he was certainly going the right way about it. Why the hell had he not just stayed in bed and let Mother Nature take her course? She was a stunning, highly desirable young woman and for her to pick him out from the stable of suitors who were clamouring to get their evil way with her was a huge ego boost.

As the OLG duty driver weaved through the busy Sunday lunchtime traffic, mainly consisting of the innocuous yellow cabs, tour buses, mini buses and cop cars, he wondered if he had left things too late. He hoped not.

"I should get Big Mal to kick my stupid butt," he decided.

He realised Luca was upset. She was drinking tequila at ten thirty on a Sunday morning for Gawd's sake! Not like her at all, especially before singing at the club, and the phone call he had with her was difficult. She had, it seemed, not been too happy to hear from him. He knew that slime ball Constantine had been making heavy moves on her. She sometimes mentioned him after singing at the club.

"Constantine said this. Constantine did that. Blah, blah, blah."

He slapped the dashboard in frustration.

"You kay, Boss?" asked Buzz, the duty driver and Gulf War veteran.

"Women, Buzz. They are a different species."

Buzz grinned, "True, man. You can't live with them, and you can't live without them!"

Rabbie snorted and went back to his reverie. Buzz left him to it. He'd guarded the lovely Russian girl the boss was dating and had indeed run her around in the duty car a few times. She seemed a great gal, and he wondered what the problem was. If she was his, she would be getting a good look at the bedroom ceiling several times a day. He leered, glad the bossman couldn't read his thoughts and questioned if Rabbie was having penile dysfunctional problems. A woman like that would take an awful lot of lurvvving!!!

"Don't even go where you're thinking, Buzz, or I'll have you on night shift for a week."

Buzz nearly ran into the back of a busload of Swiss tourists. Jeepers, creepers, the guys said that the boss dude was psychic and that just proved it. Rabbie smiled to himself, Buzz wasn't hard to read. From a small town in Ohio, his poor, long-suffering wife had thrown him out more times than enough when he found the fleshy delights of New York City too hard to resist. She always took him back though and the guys called him 'Boomerang Buzz'. Plus, the fact that after six years serving with a hairy bunch of Royal Marine Commandos, it wasn't hard to work out what was uppermost in young men's minds. Sex, drink, sex, food, sex, football, sex and more sex! Normally in that order.

The car pulled up outside the apartments and Rabbie jumped out.

"Thanks, Boomerang. Straight home to that nice wife of yours and no detours to a certain little club off Times Square."

He entered the building, leaving a flabbergasted Buzz openmouthed behind the wheel. He took the stairs, still musing. He knew after he rescued her from Hanlon and her stay in hospital, she had developed a crush on him. It was understandable that she had seen in him a big masculine safety net she could fall into and bounce around in. The fact of the matter was he was hugely attracted to her and loved having her around; in fact, he loved everything about her. Her quirky little ways, her grace and poise and her high intellect and she was great fun, so why in damnation did he keep rejecting her advances?

Sharing his bed, it had been hard to keep his hands off her lush, fantastic body the times she had woken up with her arms around him and her head on his chest, looking so beautiful and safe. Her long lashes adorning her soft cheeks and her gorgeous umber hair spread over her slim shoulders and nestled between her breasts, had almost broke his resolve. The week Luca had to spend confined to bed after hospital had brought out a caring side for the opposite sex he didn't know he fostered as deeply as he did. It pleased him and made him feel good about his masculinity.

Rabbie enjoyed catering to her needs and spoiling her. He felt she was worth it and deserved it. He had to pinch himself at times to make sure it was real when he saw this outstanding female specimen sitting up in his bed, flicking through the Sky channels, looking for documentaries on endangered species and crying over orphaned baby baboons. This necessitated him having to put a comforting arm around her and drying her tears with a Kleenex and switching to something safer.

He shook his head ruefully. There were not too many Lucas in the world, in what was rapidly becoming a global village. She was an endangered species herself and if she left him, he sensed she would take a part of his humanity away with her. Luca wore the world on her sleeve. He sighed as he trudged slowly up the stairs. He thought her infatuation for him would pass with time but if anything, it had intensified. Rabbie half hoped it wouldn't, not wanting to get involved again after Juliette and hoping that they could remain friends, go out together the on the odd occasion and have fun. He realised that was not an option, it was all or nothing with Luca.

He got to the last flight that led to his door, pondering what he would find behind it. What kind of reception he would get from this enigmatic young Russian sex bomb? He guessed he had slipped way down Luca's 'Bestest Man in New York' list and it saddened him. She looked absolutely ravishing in that black negligee this morning. The sunlight from the window making it transparent and outlining every hidden treasure and soft curve. Her nipples standing proud like precious rubies waiting to be found and mounted on a hot demanding crown. Christ! He was such a complete and utter pathetic wimp, a poor excuse for a man.

He searched for his key as he reached the landing. He had surmised and gleaned from conversations he had with her that she had been through some man crisis in

Lithuania when she was younger, but she had never talked about it and when he broached the subject, she had patted his hand.

"It's 'kay, Rabbie dahling. Is over. First love is the hardest, da?"

He reasoned that was why she had come to New York. He had asked Wendy if she knew, and she had blanked him with that woman's look only another woman understood and that men shied away from. Rabbie inserted the key and the act flared an image of Luca and him engaged in a loving full-on sexual performance. He fucking well knew he loved her with all his heart and regretted his stupid reticence over age, work, culture and social constraints.

"You're a wanker, Rabbie," he chided himself as he entered his apartment. "A total prat."

She was standing waiting for him, expression neutral.

"I saw the car drop you off, Rabbie. Is the elevator out of order again?"

Luca was dressed in a fluffy mohair short-sleeved jumper in various shades of blue and green and dark blue figure-hugging hipsters with short black boots. Her pink bra strap curled over her shoulder sexily and her beautiful hair, gleaming, was in a ponytail hanging across her shoulder and furled around her left breast. She looked a million dollars.

"Ready to rock and roll? They are bringing the baby pandas out at two."

She donned a half-length black leather coat and slung her bag, with her work clothes, over her shoulder. "Wow, they are so cute," and joined him as they reached the elevator and she took his arm. "Tank you for taking time off work, Rabbie. I've been a bitch to you dis morning."

That stumped him. They went down in the elevator. As they passed the third floor, she said. "This is where we first met, my gallant knight. It was sooo, so to be."

He gave her a huge hug and a quick kiss on her eager lips and their mood lightened. Maybe not too late at all?

Rabbie walked her out into the early May sunshine and watched as she raised her lovely face to the healing warmth. His heart melted as he felt her relax into the curve of his side. He absolutely adored her. Love was too small a word; cherished came to mind. He cherished her whole being, presence and essence when she was with him. Yep, deeply cherished! He just cherished her completeness as the epitome of anything he wanted female in his life. Rabbie whistled and waved for a cab but one had already stopped, the eager male driver waving them in. The Luca Factor at work.

* * *

The zoo was heaving with families and tourists who had come to see the first showing of the panda twins, Mitzi and Majou. Born ten weeks earlier and, by all accounts, doing well and already munching their way through several pounds of young bamboo shoots daily. Luca had followed the story avidly in the media and enthused happily over the little furry black and white bundles shown on television.

"They are so cool, Rabbie, and safe in the zoo, where no son of a bitch poachers can shoot them."

Luca believed all endangered species should be placed in well-kept zoos and looked after by humans and bred until they were no longer in danger of extinction. Rabbie hadn't the heart to tell her it was totally impractical, due to cost, space and

437

manpower. But he loved her for her empathy and it reiterated her status as an idealist. Which was refreshing in what his work showed him was often a grubby, grasping world, where the stronger dog gobbled the weaker dog up.

They weaved through the milling crowds of photo-snapping tourists and excited families. The kids waving cotton candy around, faces smeared with chocolate and ice cream, goggle-eyed with wonder. It was a pleasant, warm spring afternoon, and Rabbie was enjoying being out in the open after being cooped up in the office all morning putting the final touches to the 'Big Conference' gig they had starting Monday.

The sky was sapphire blue and cloud free and hundreds of sparrows and pigeons flocked around and got under their feet, pecking at and squabbling over crumbs. Luca smiled at them indulgently, her lovely eyes, dove grey in the bright light, crinkled in amusement at their antics. An elephant trumpeted through its trunk happily from its enclosure.

They visited the Monkey House first. Luca had a season ticket to the zoo and often came on her lunch hour. All the staff seemed to know her. Mr Warren, the chief keeper of primates, spotted her and they discussed how poor Pauli's foot was and indeed Mr Warren led her to a small ward at the back. It turned out poor Pauli was a one-year-old chimpanzee who had fallen and broke his left foot and was in a cast. Pauli seemed delighted to see Luca and jumped up and down and into her arms chattering insanely. He began picking through her hair as she fed him a Twinkie.

"Not too many people Pauli takes to but he loves your young lady to visit."

Rabbie liked the 'your young lady' bit. It seemed Pauli had been intercepted at the docks, stuffed into a cramped crate, starving and near death from dehydration.

"Probably for a private collector or an illegal vivisectionist doing trials. Bastards! Oh sorry, Luca," explained Mr Warren.

"Tis 'kay, Mr Warren," said Luca, cuddling Pauli, who was now totally under her spell. "Bastards they are. I put them in crates and nail them down good!"

It transpired Luca had adopted Pauli under the zoo's 'Adopt an animal for life' scheme and paid a few dollars every month to ensure he got good food and vet care.

"We do depend a lot on donations in these hard times. But for people like Luca, they would not get as good care as they do."

They left and went and watched the antics of the tribes of various primates in their compounds, Luca happily observing as they swung from branch to branch or sat picking nits off each other, gibbering happily in the sun.

"You never told me you had adopted a chimp, Luca."

She grinned wickedly. "Did I not, dahling? I probably didn't want you to get the jealous head."

He laughed. She was outstanding. He'd scored a few points with her when he gave Mr Warren $100 donation towards Pauli.

"I liked Pauli. I'll help you with the costs. We'll make great parents."

She looked him in the eye. "I'll tink about it. I tink you make good papa, Rabbie," and she skipped away towards the Reptile House, Rabbie running to catch up, mentally digesting her last statement. She didn't like the snakes or spiders but knew Rabbie did, so followed him around trying not to look too closely. She thought the boa constrictors were evil, repulsive things and shuddered at the cold, hungry look in their eyes and thought of Hanlon and then surveyed Rabbie surreptitiously. Two different species of men.

Rabbie sensed her unease and ushered her out into the sunlight, which dappled pleasantly through the new foliage on the large plane trees. He had a surprise lined up for her. OLG did some part time security work for the zoo management and he'd pulled in a favour.

The outside of the panda pens was thronged with an eager crowd waiting to see the panda cubs for the first time. Rabbie guided Luca down to the front, where an area had been roped off for the press. He flashed his OLG ID to the attendants, and she was thrilled when they were shown to the front, where Benni the male panda sat chewing bamboo shoots contentedly in the horseshoe shaped rock-lined pit.

An expectant hush descended as a hatch was raised at the rear and a two-hundred-pound mummy panda called Matilda came wobbling out, her ducts still heavy with milk. Close to her side, scampering in and out and under her legs, were two bundles of black and white fur, weighing about ten pounds each. The crowd oohed and aahed and whistled and clapped. The big mama stopped and acknowledged the applause, then sat by her mate and began munching herself at the bamboo fronds. The press snapped and filmed away. Luca watched dreamily.

"It's why they are so endangered. They are so kind and gentle and loving. They don't know how to defend themselves."

Rabbie looked lovingly at her and saw the pandas reflected in her eyes. He thought they looked like old fashioned bank robbers from a dated black and white movie with the rings around their eyes like masks. Luca was overjoyed when they were led with the press into a small, sunny enclosure at the back and the keepers brought Mitzi and Majou out for a solo photo shoot, the little fur balls utterly unfazed. They let Luca hold them and the press went mad snapping the stunning young Lithuanian woman petting and making a fuss over them. She made page five of 'The New York Times' the next day, holding Majou to her face.

"Miss Luca Valendenski, 26 years old, Interior Designer, welcomes Majou to 'The Big Apple'."

She was ecstatic and gave Rabbie a kiss by the gates as they left. "You are always full of surprises, Rabbie. Tank you."

His heart glowed as they searched for a cab to take them to the club.

* * *

The Village was absolutely heaving with tourists and locals looking for an early dinner when the taxi dropped them off late afternoon. A tour group of Japanese were doing the 'Bob Dylan' walking tour as they climbed out, and a band of old hippy buskers with peace signs and long greasy hair were singing Janis Joplin songs.

They made their way to the small side street where their favourite deli was, but not before being stopped by a group of Buddhist monks in bright saffron robes and sandals. They made a great fuss over Luca and she sang 'Hare Krishna' with them and twirled around with her arms in the air as they clashed their small finger cymbals and rang bells.

"She has beautiful aura about her. A true Earth Mother. She has been hurt but is strong. You are there for a reason with her," an old wizened monk told him in a San Francisco accent.

Rabbie dropped a ten dollar note in their tray, extracted a laughing, giddy Luca from the swirling colourful melee. She hugged his arm as he got her into Toni's Deli, still dizzy. Her eyes were radiant and full of silver light. Her cheeks were flushed and her sweet lips were curved in a happy smile, and he was happy because she was. The monk never spoke truer words. She had an incredible presence about her and the great thing was she was altogether unaware of it.

They needed provisions and quickly filled a small cart with the basics and their favourites, each knowing the other's tastes. At the checkout the girl packed three large, thick brown bags for them. Cans, juice and drink in one bag, veg, fruit and bread in another and meats, cheeses, ham and fridge stuff in the last one. Rabbie grabbed the first two heavier bags and Luca the other and thanking the girl, they headed off the short distance to the club.

"We'll eat well tonight, Luca. I'll make us a great supper."

She smiled knowingly. He liked to cook; it relaxed him and helped him wind down.

"Yes, well, but none of dat 'Red Mex Hot Chilli'. It upsets you late at night, Rabbie. Gives you da vindys."

"Yes, mistress. Christ! We sound like an old married couple."

She glanced sideways at him, "Yes, veil, I just don't like to see you end one of your verrry rare days off ill. You deserve better, dahling."

He looked contrite. She had him down to pat. She curbed his tendency to eat heavy, spicy food late at night, which bloated his stomach and led to poor sleep. It was an old Commando habit that you ate as much as you could, whenever you could, because you never know when the next meal might come along.

"It'll be cold cuts, prawns, fine cheeses and Rabbie's famous tossed salad," he promised her.

She approved, "Oh, yum, can't wait. I am always starving after I sing my spot."

He glanced at her fondly, Luca had quaffed two huge 'chilli dogs' at the stand in the zoo and a mega Cola. She had the metabolism of a Tasmanian devil, or, and he smiled at the idea, 'Road Runner' in the cartoons. The little desert creature that zoomed from A to B at high speed but was always full of fun and mischief and continually one step ahead of the bad 'Wily Coyote'. That was Luca to a tee, then he thought of the old monk's words and Hanlon and his thugs and thanked his lucky stars again he had got there just in the nick of time.

Walking alongside her lovely, strong man, because that's how she thought of him, her highly perceptive mind sensed a slight shift in his mood and she said, pointing to the French breadstick poking out of his bag and the huge onions peeking through. "You look like a Frenchman with the bread and onions. All you need is a beret and a bicycle."

"Blimey, Luca, never call an Englishman French. It's an insult across the pond. We were at war with them for hundreds of years."

She absorbed this, "Nonsense, my love, sure your family doesn't know if they are English or, how you say, Skittish?"

"Scottish."

"Yes, Skittish. Sure did the French not send an army in the 1700s to help 'Little Bonnie Prince Charlie' to throw the English out of Skitland?"

They arrived at the club and sat on the bench outside so Luca could have a rare cigarette; it calmed her and helped her focus on her singing. He was amazed at how well-read she was.

"Well, yes, the English won and the French beat a hasty retreat."

She lit her cigarette with a lighter the same colour as her dark blue hipsters, "And little Charlie escaped and lived his days out in France," she paused. "You know, they say the Frenchmen in Paris are the most romantic in the world."

"They stink of garlic and eat big, slimy snails and frog's legs."

"I would like to go to Paris one day. I tink I could make a living singing in the clubs," she paused again and looked him in the eye before glancing away, puffing on her Gitane. "Would you like that, Rabbie?" she probed nonchalantly, but not really teasing.

He stared at her profile: her straight nose and well-shaped chin, her smooth forehead and high cheekbones – she was dazzling! He sensed the warning in her words and perhaps sense of insecurity. He chose his words carefully, "I think you'd be a great success, Luca, but I wouldn't like it! I would not like it one bit at all!"

She turned her face to him, and he moved his closer, leaning into her. Their heat met and cushioned them together. "Would you be jealous of the Frenchmen in Paris, Rabbie?" she asked, insistent.

Their lips were inches apart. Hers were slightly moist and invitingly apart and beckoning for him to seize and possess them with his own. His heart pumped fast.

An old wino of indeterminate age tapped her on the shoulder and spoke to her in Russian. He knew her name. She shrugged and sat up normal and replied in kind to him, gently. She broke off a chunk of crusty bread, delved into the bag and came out with Camembert cheese, Italian salami, an apple and a packet of chocolate chip cookies. The wino shoved them in his coat pockets, and she gave him the remaining cigarettes and lighter.

"Lend me ten dollars, Rabbie."

"He'll only buy alcohol, Luca."

"I know, but it's too late for him now. He was in Stalin's Gulags – he lost his family."

Rabbie extracted a fifty dollar note and gave it to him, "Here, old timer. If you're gonna go out, do it in style."

Luca beamed at him, "You just jumped back up to 'Number 1' on 'My Kindest Man in New York' list, dahling."

The old man bowed to them in turn and mumbled a few lines in Russian.

"What's he saying?"

"It's an old Russian prayer for luck[173]. He used to be a University Professor of Literature and a famed poet."

Rabbie watched the old man trudge off. *There but for the Grace of God go I*, he thought.

"Come on, my love, I tell you later. I am late."

They headed in, he stopped her in the foyer, "So, who have I replaced as 'Number 1' then? Not that slime ball, Constantine?"

She laughed merrily, "You are crazy, man, I don't do drug dealers. No, you have taken over from Mr Warren, who retired last week and is working in the Monkey House for nothing."

Luca placed a kiss on his cheek and rushed off to change, shouting over her shoulder that she would see him upstairs after. He shook his head ruefully, she never ceased to astound him.

---

[173] What the Russian poet told Luca.

The Russian Club attracted a section of the large Russian émigré community that had swelled in New York since the fall of Communism and were now allowed to travel freely. What better place to head to if you wanted to make something of yourself than America – the land of the free and opportunity galore!

A huge stuffed bear wearing a stars and stripes bowler hat greeted you in the foyer, where you passed through double doors into a vast two-tiered room as big and high as a grandiose church. An executive bar was off to the right, a stage at the far end, with a large dance floor in front of tables and chairs dotted about the periphery. Booths and long tables lined the left-hand side, and Rabbie spotted the innocuous Constantine and his gang of about eight quaffing down their free champagne and, no doubt, working out where the next line of coke was going to come from.

The decor was all reds and whites and jumbo photo motifs of Russia, past and present, adorned the walls. The dance floor was a huge jigsaw of The Kremlin; the idea being the dancers could trample all over the seats of government that oppressed them for so long, *And probably still does, to a large extent*, mused Rabbie. He figured their leader, Putin, was looking to expand the new Russia and there was trouble ahead.

The bar boasted over two hundred different types of vodka, wines from across the federation and brandy from Georgia. An enormous hammer and sickle, lit by red bulbs and on a white background, hung above the bar dramatically. The barmen were dressed as Cossacks and the pretty waitresses wore various forms of national dress. One showed him up to the balcony on the second floor, which ran three sides of the room and where people could eat and drink away from the throng downstairs, the club often getting very busy, and watch the show. Their waitress was dressed in the peasant costume of the Ukraine, with a multi-coloured flared skirt and red bodice. *The Ukraine was Putin's next move*, Rab judged.

He ordered a bottle of heady Georgian red wine and a selection of cheeses and crackers. He was nervous for some reason and always got peckish when so. Rabbie joined Big Mal and Philomena, who were seated half way down and had a good view of the stage. The lighting was low and canned music of various Russian-themed songs emitted from hidden speakers.

He shook Mal's hand, who was looking very dapper in a two-tone mohair suit, and kissed Philomena on the cheek. She was quite chic in a red jumpsuit and beret, having dressed for the venue. He thought her and Mal were a good match. Bobby and Wendy came rushing over.

"Wassup, man? Thought we'd be late by the time Wendy got her make-up through the cement mixer."

Wendy, in a black button up crocheted dress with knee-high boots and bare legs, kicked him, "At least I made the effort, yah big galoot."

Bobby was in a leather jacket and jeans, as indeed was Rabbie, "Chill, honey, chill, so did I," and he donned sunglasses. "Rabbie and I are OLG secret police dudes."

They sat and chatted and drank for a few minutes before the lights went down and the stage was lit by a single spotlight and the MC introduced Luca Valendenski, 'The Russian Nightingale', in Russian and English, much to the delight of the hundred or so clubbers who clapped and cheered their approval. Rabbie was anticipating a look of surprise when she saw her friends had come to hear her perform. She was so easily made happy at times.

She came on to catcalls and whistling, face glowing. She loved to sing and she looked spectacular. Her hair was pinned up, which emphasised her slender neck. Luca wore a thin-strapped halter-neck top, which showed off her shoulders and bust, ending just below her ribs, exposing a flat midriff. A short, black mini skirt, pink hold-up stockings and black ankle-high boots completed the ensemble.

Every eye in the house was on her as she went into her trademark first song – Alicia Key's 'New York (Empire State of Mind)'. She waved up to them as she sang the first few verses, delight on her face.

"It's in Russian, Wendy," remarked Bobby.

She then switched to English, much to their pleasure.

"Concrete jungles where dreams are made

There's nothing you can't do

Here in New York, New York, New York."

Luca had a wonderful voice, pure but with a huskiness underlying. With her accent and ability to hold a note, they were enthralled. She went into Sinead O'Connor's 'Nothing Compares 2 U', then Bonnie Tyler's 'Total Eclipse of the Heart'.

Rabbie remembered that was what she had been listening to the first day they had met. Their eyes engaged as she swayed and gyrated around the stage. Couples danced and others moved up closer to listen, drinks in hand, mesmerised; she was wowing them. Mal and Philomena held hands, and Bobby sat Wendy on his knee and kept helping himself to Rabbie's cheeses and biscuits behind her back. She had him on one of her surprise diets, much to his annoyance.

Luca livened up the beat with an Abba medley: 'Mamma Mia', 'Waterloo' and 'Super Trooper'. More took to the floor and the place was buzzing. She went up the years and sang some songs by Snow Patrol and Razorlight and a fantastic version of Imelda May's 'Mayhem'. She sang for an hour without stopping, accompanied by a three-piece combo the club provided; guys on guitar, drums and a keyboard.

"Okay, tank you all ver' much. I go now for short break. Davstravia."

She got thunderous applause and when she passed Constantine's table, they mobbed her. He hugged and kissed her on both cheeks, his hand very near her lovely arse, Rabbie noted wryly. A waitress, wearing the national costume of Bela Russe, appeared with a magnum of champagne and dispensed glasses.

"Compliments of the Management for Miss Valendenski."

Bobby ogled her and Wendy pulled his hair, he scowled. Goddamn diet. The only diet he liked was a 'see food diet'. He saw food – he ate it. Soon a perspiring, panting Luca emerged, and they stood and clapped her in. She shooed the praise and made them sit.

"It's vot I like to do, and my friends are happy…den I am happy."

She downed a glass of bubbly in one and Rabbie poured her another. She giggled as the bubbles tickled her nose. He wiped her perspiring face with the cold cloth that was wrapped around the champagne.

"Mmmm…dat's so good," she purred, and slapped Bobby's hand away as he made a foray towards the cheese and crackers. "I tell Vendy. You on diet, big guy."

Wendy turned from watching the dancers, "What's that?"

"I say, I tell you how nice you look, Vendy dahling."

443

She beamed and turned back. Luca slipped a cracker to a sulking Bobby, "Here, just one, you big behemoth."

He wolfed it down covertly, and they grinned at each other, friends again. Rabbie was impressed, he had never heard anyone called a behemoth before. He figured it to be some type of barbarian; he would google it later.

Luca did another hour; mainly obscure Russian love songs they had never heard of.

"What's Luca singing about now?" Bobby asked a waitress dressed as Miss Georgia.

"She is singing about making love in a raspberry bush full of nightingales."

"Wowww... Sounds good, Wendy."

Luca glanced up at them, "I sing now for my special man, Rabbie. It the Enrique Iglesias cover of 'Hero'," she paused. "For my hero, Rabbie DeJames, my Sir Galahad."

"I can be your hero, baby,
I can kiss away the pain,
I will stand by you forever
You just take my breath away."

She sang the rest up to him. A lot of studly young Russian males looked disappointed and Constantine was scowling. She ended her set with Paper Lace's 1974 hit, 'Billy, don't be a Hero', but changed it to Bobby and waved to the big fella, much to his and Wendy's delight. Her finale was Dr Feelgood's 'Milk and Alcohol', which finished to rapturous applause and cries of "Encore", so she did a quick LeAnn Rimes number and ran off the stage.

After, they sat for another hour drinking, Luca winding down and accepting the accolade of her friends and passing guests.

"Hey, let's all go to 'Bucking Billy's'. I wanna get me some 'Country and Western'," suggested Bobby.

"Yeah, come on, Luca. They got them cowboys just wearing leather chaps and their asses all bare," cajoled Wendy.

"And them topless cowgals on the mechanical broncos," chipped in Mal and Philomena punched him playfully.

Luca laughed, "Sounds sooo, so kinky, but dis little Russian girl is going home for nice supper and long, hot shower... Aren't we, Rabbie?" and she held his hand, insistent.

"Aw, shucks, Luca," bemoaned Bobby, "I wanna get yah up and line dance with yah, girl."

Wendy got off his knee, "Oh, give over, you big Yazoo. You up for it, Mal...? Phil?"

The others were game and they gathered themselves up and said their goodbyes. Wendy kissed Luca and winked, "Good luck, kiddo," she whispered.

* * *

Getting their shopping from the checkout booth, they strolled the short distance home.

"We better put da shopping away first, Rabbie, before it spoils," she said, "I hope the ice cream has not melted."

Staring into her lovely eyes, he knew his heart had.

II

('When I Said I Needed You'... Elvis Presley)

They rode up to the elevator, "That was a good day. I am looking forward to my supper ver' much."

Rabbie looked at her fondly over his laden bags, "Same here. You deserve it after keeping us entertained singing."

Rabbie went to put his bags down. "Is okay, Rab, I get key for you." She reached into his right-hand jeans pocket with her left hand and burrowed deep. She found the key nesting amongst his loose change, then burrowed around a bit more towards the middle, a mischievous glint in her eye.

"Is ver' deep pocket...ah, I tink I have it." She moved her hands towards the middle and could feel the side of his penis with the back of her hand. She ran her knuckles up it. It was thick, hot and dangerous-feeling. She shivered deliciously. He was half turned into her, his hips cocked to facilitate her searching hand.

"Got it," she pulled the key out and opened the door for them, a wicked gleam in her eyes.

They moved through the living room and turned right into the large kitchen/dining area and dumped the groceries on the long table.

"Phew...tis great to be home," beamed Luca. "Bucking Billy's hah...tis so tacky, dahling."

She opened the fridge at the end of the kitchen, the light illuminating her face and the cold air cooling her skin. She dived into her bag and began unpacking.

Rabbie opened the larder cupboards above the work bench on his left, "Are you saying Bob and Wends are tacky?" He began to unpack his hoard of beloved, chilli, curries and stews.

"No, silly, they enjoy themselves wherever they go," she replied, looking over her shoulder at him. His back was to her, she turned and grabbed a can from his bag and slipped it into her own. "It too much for me, although the bare bum cowboys are interesting."

He chuckled, "The bare arsed cowboys are, quite frankly, downright scary. Not my scene either."

She put the half-melted Peach Melba ice cream away; her favourite, "I tink it be okay, it still quite hard." She reached back into her bag, "Ooops...silly girl has put can in with the perishables."

His back was to her as he reached up and placed dried spaghetti and pasta shells on the top shelf, distracted. She moved in behind him.

"Red hot chilli, your favourite," and reached and stretched up behind him to put it in the cupboard. She never made it. He swung around fast, knocking into her.

"What's that, Lucs?" and she staggered back nearly falling, arms flailing madly.

His quick reactions kicked in and he caught her in his strong arms, and they half turned with the momentum so they ended up with her back to the table. Her left hand around his trim waist and her right arm, handing still holding the can, went over his left shoulder and behind his neck.

"Whoops-a-daisy," he said.

She didn't know what that meant and didn't care. Their eyes met and he pulled her in and their lips crashed into each other's, starting a long, hot, hungry kiss; their tongues meeting, entwining, exploring and tasting each other. She hugged tighter into him, her left arm moving up and down his back. She dropped the can uncaringly on the table with a thud and put her hand on the back of his neck and kissed back harder, her heart pounding as he pressed his groin into her and she felt her own liquid heat melt with his hard hotness. The kiss went on for an extremely long time. She could feel the need and urgency in him, it matched her own, yet still the hesitancy in him. She had taken him by surprise, she wanted him and she wanted it now. She had to move things on.

Luca had taken her coat off when she began unpacking. They broke and breathed air, eyes locked. He broke that contact and started kissing and nuzzling down her fine neck, pausing at her pulse thrumming frantically like a butterfly caught in a web. Rabble's hands were caressing up and down her back inside her jumper. She reached around and eased his coat down and off his broad frame and tossed it on the table. It missed and hit the floor. She pushed him away, criss-crossed her arms low and removed her jumper in one fluid movement and flung it carelessly aside. Luca then sat on the table and pulled him into her spread legs and back into another passionate clinch and deep kiss. She hadn't bothered changing out of her skirt.

He revelled in the softness of her full lips and her darting, probing tongue; the incredibly smoothness of her skin. For some reason he wondered where her front door key was. She always carried her own religiously after Hanlon. It was security for her. She liked to spend as little time alone in the apartment hallway as possible. It spooked her. Sometimes at night, Rabbie went down and met her at the door after she phoned him ahead. He cast the notion aside as he kissed across the top of her bust, licking at and tasting her creamy mounds. He was very aroused and she was breathing heavily in his ear, her breath hot and fragrant.

She sat up and faced him, pulled his dark blue Ben Sherman shirt out from his jeans and began unbuttoning it from the top. Luca thought dark blue suited his colouring. He had a nice dark blue suit and she decided he looked very distinguished when he wore it. She kissed flesh as it was revealed, nipping and licking him. He stroked her shoulders. She eased his shirt off and ran her hands all over his chest – his chest hair was very dark. She kissed and sucked each nipple in turn and he moaned. She had to keep it moving. She could see his prominent arousal through his jeans. She felt light-headed with desire and revelled in her own wetness seeping out of her. *Move it on, Luca.*

She had assumed control of the pace, and he sensed it and was happy to go with the flow. He rubbed and caressed her shoulders and back, nuzzled and kissed her earlobes, neck and cheeks. She reached around her back and unhooked her bra. He helped ease the straps down her arms and it dropped to the floor, light as a feather. Excitement tore across his chest, his heart beating an erratic tattoo.

She leant back on one arm and wrapped the other around his neck. He reached for her and squeezed and rolled her breasts in his hands, they felt bigger and heavier than he expected. Over two good handfuls each, he judged. They jutted firm and well-shaped, the aureoles were large and pink and sloped into round nubs that he sucked on greedily; the nipples rising like studs to his inquisitive mouth, "Oh, Rabbie, Rabbie, my dahling."

He stroked her stomach with his left hand, then from her right knee up her pink nylon sheathed leg until he reached the hot firm skin of her upper thigh, her skirt rose up at his touch, and he could feel the heat from her hungry sex, "Oh God, Rabbie."

He kissed and chewed on her breasts, still fondling her silky thigh. She opened her left leg wider, cocked and placed her booted foot on her back of a chair, the unspoken invite plain and as old as time itself. He found her with his strong fingers and stroked up and down outside her very damp panties. She gasped and mumbled some endearment in Russian as he caressed her swollen lips through her fine mesh pink knickers. He eased the crotch aside and petted her silky, hairy pubis before guiding her pussy lips apart with his eager digits and inserting his middle one into her hot wetness, skimming her clitoris and probing deep as she arched up to meet him, "Oh God, yes, Rabbie, oh yes, sooo, so good."

She held the back of his head, left hand twisting and pulling at his hair, as he nuzzled her breasts and fingered her tightness vigorously, making sure her clitoris got plenty of action. Old feelings she hadn't felt since Galen infused her. She grinded and moaned at him as he eased her back more and another finger joined the first. As the climax burst out of her in a hot searing torrent, she arched her back. He had her utterly and completely trapped and immobile on his two relentless fingers.

Luca wanted to feel and stroke his cock. She wanted to feel flesh on flesh. The comfort of his weight on her as he covered her, she needed him to take her, right this Goddamn minute or surely she would die of sexual depravation!!!

"Rabbie, Rabbie," she tugged at his hair. He was totally lost in the moment. "Rabbie, bed…take me to…da bed, please, my dahling."

He straightened, breathing heavily, "God, yes, God, you're beautiful, Luca." He picked her up easily in his arms and walked down the corridor and into his bedroom, Luca stroking his hair, kissing up and down his face. "I like the way you always carry me around Rabbie," she purred, "It's so da cool and sexy."

He placed her on the edge of the bed. She sat up and positioned her legs either side of him again and began unbuckling his jeans, kissing his stomach in fast, impatient lines of kisses. She slipped them and his boxer shorts off and he kicked out of them.

His cock was long, hard and beautiful, it was eager for her touch. She fondled up and down its length, and he groaned deeply and stroked her lush hair with both hands. She peeled him back and gazed at the shiny rosy head, a drop of fluid glistening at the tip. She took him deep in her mouth, glorying in the male taste and texture of him, the power reversed now, and sucked and stroked him simultaneously. He gasped and his breathing bellowed as he writhed his hips with the rhythm, his hands gripping her shoulders now.

Rabbie could feel his testes tighten and deep embers of pleasure igniting on the banked fire that had smouldered so sullenly within since Juliette had left him. He felt alive and powerful, sexually for the first time in ages, as he watched this incredible head bobbing up and down his starved shaft. He pulled out, and she looked up at him with those incredible grey eyes, glassy now with wanton lust and sexual promise.

He pulled her up and they kissed again. He sat before her and eased her pink mesh pants down, his gaze fixed on her gorgeous quim. She whimpered now as he

447

ran his hand up her leg and entered her again with his fingers; she was exceedingly wet. It excited him even more if that was possible. He squeezed and pinched at her firm right buttock with the other hand. Her breathing came in fits and spurts as she muttered in Russian again, and she held onto his upper arms tightly. He thought his cock was going to explode, he was so turned on. The joint expectation between them of the now inevitable coupling to come was dynamic. An earthquake coming of huge power on the seismic sexual scale ahead. Luca had a small orgasm as his searching digits teased at her. She nearly fainted at the pleasure of it.

She pulled away and clambered past him, she crawled up the bed. The two wall lights above the headboard were on low. She reached the middle, her head near the top. He watched her eyelids hooded. Intense. Mesmerised. Carnal. She glanced over her shoulder at him, her fantastic arse dazzling his eyes, her womanhood shadowed and mysterious.

"Are you not joining me, my kind sir?"

He stood rampant and faced her, a near bestial stance. She rolled over onto her back, legs wide and stroked her pubis with long ringed fingers, ogling his erect member through slits for eyes, the whites gleaming. "I tink I vant you now, Rabbie. I tink I vant you and your big dick ver' much."

He didn't think she would be so wanton. Sexy, yes! Sweet and innocent? Maybe, but this! She was just a sex magnet to him, which was a major bonus. Luca never ever ceased to surprise him. He growled at her and likewise crawled up the bed and in between her gaping legs and watched her stroking herself. He moved her hand and began gently licking her engorged lips, she urged him on in Russian. He licked faster, making her writhe. He licked up and down her gash, driving her delirious and chewed and ran his tongue across her clitoris, which drove her wild. His hands slid up and found her breast, and he pulled and fondled them mercilessly. She panted and wriggled as he revelled in the taste and texture of her. She cried out his name incessantly as she climaxed hugely, her cunt gushing and quivering. She pulled him up with frantic hands, "Please Rabbie…you driving me crazy woman…now, Rabbie. Now," as she gazed into his eyes.

He covered her fantastic body, transfixed by her. She arched up to meet him, and he shoved his cock in her, she was very tight. He thrust harder until he was fully home, and she let out a low howl very deep in her throat, pulling him into a meshing tongue-twirling kiss.

"Oh, Rab, do me, dahling. Do me ver' good," she gasped in his ear.

He was calling her name out as he began to pump in and out, faster and harder. He marvelled as her fanny gripped and clasped him; he knew he wasn't going to last long. She groaned and gyrated under him, trying to match him stroke for stroke but losing it sometimes in her inflamed state. Rabbie would pause before thrusting forcibly in again to get the stroke back, ramming into her as his passion soared. She dug her nails into his back and flailed her arms and wrapped her long legs around him, squeezing her thigh muscles. She was nearly incoherent now, and he knew he couldn't hold back any longer.

Rabbie plunged harder and deeper at a furious pace and came in a white-hot blaze that seemed to seize and strangle every nerve and sinew in his body. Luca screamed out his name, "Rabbbiiieeeee… Rabbbiiieeeee!" He didn't feel her clawing his back as he blasted what felt like an impossible torrent of cum into her delectable velvet void.

She had come in a gigantic explosion of unconstrained nerve endings as she felt his hot release flood her entirely. She had never experienced anything close to such emotions in her life and to do so with the man she loved made her ecstatic with happiness. They were both clinging to each other now, dazed, sexually traumatised. They lay there for long minutes, just holding each other and getting their breaths back, their bodies settling with just the odd twitch and jerk, which eventually subsided.

He gazed down at her in complete adoration – he utterly idolised her. He'd been a fool and had nearly lost her; he knew deep down he loved her but this really sealed the deal for him. He had noticed she still had her ankle boots on and was amused. He suspected she hadn't realised. She stared up at him, rapt and full of love, fit to burst. He went to pull out so he could lie by her side, she held him firm.

"Leave him in me, Rabbie. He'll go ven he's ready."

He chuckled, "He never may go."

Luca went, "Mmmm…he can always come back to visit," and eased him out tenderly.

He liked that and kissed her, reassured she was genuine. She punched his arm playfully.

"Wow, Rabbie…you really spurned me good, dahling."

He looked back at her lovingly. He had heard her and Wendy on about spurning and sperming in the club and got the drift, "Was my pleasure, my love. I will spurn you to distraction from now on but I will never sperm you again."

She hugged him tightly, "Tank you, baby, you so good to me."

He was enjoying himself now, "They are an endangered species, you know. The Japanese have them near harpooned to extinction."

Luca arched an inquisitive, sexy eyebrow, "What, baby? You me near harpooned to death, you brute."

"The Great Spurn Whales, getting very scarce."

"Okay…dat's not good."

Rabbie noticed then she was crying, concerned, he stroked her hair, "Hey, come on. They will be okay. Greenpeace have it under control."

She gave him a small wry smile, "Dat's good. You can get off me now, I vant to take my boots off."

He eased himself up and saw the smear of blood on her thighs. He hesitated before lying by her, he knew now why she was crying and his love surged for her, "Why didn't you tell me, Luca?" and pulled some tissues from the box she kept on the side for when she was watching the Discovery channel.

She dried her eyes and kissed him, "I didn't tink I had to, love."

He beamed from ear to ear, "Hugely flattering, Luca, thank you. I've never ravished a maiden before."

She was happy he was happy as she had been anxious about how he would react. As for Luca, she was ecstatic she had lost her virginity to this great guy she loved from the bottom of her heart.

"Yes, vell, Russian tradition dictates after losing, how you say, your cherry, the couple must have long, hot shower together and then supper in bed."

He liked that but doubted the veracity of it, "I reckon you made that up, but I'm game for it."

She laughed saucily, "You'll never know, vill you, Rabbie, unless you go to Russia and find another maiden to deflower?"

It was his turn to laugh, "No, I think one beautiful Russian maiden will do for me this lifetime."

She liked that and "Awed" her thanks at him.

He padded off to the bathroom to get the shower going and popped his head around the door, "I miss you already."

She shooed him away, "Me too, dahling."

She pulled her mobile out of her drawer and checked her messages. One from Wendy to say they were home safe. Luca texted a quick reply, glowing inside and out.

* * *

Wendy and Bobby were canoodling in front of the television, half sloshed, and Wendy was playing hard to get after teasing him about ogling the topless cowgirls, although she had every intention of giving in eventually. Her cell phone beeped an incoming message, she slapped his wandering hands off.

"Oh, my Gawd… Rabbie gave Luca a damn good spurning. About time too."

Bobby was none the wiser. Women a different breed and not to be taken lightly.

III

The Émigré Hobo's Poem to Luca

'May you always roam and live free,
And never feel the cold weight of chains!
May every door in life open for you
Without need of a key.
May you always be strong and free of pains.
May you bear beautiful children, a girl and a boy.
May they be healthy and bring you great joy.
I wish you and your lovers well,
And may Stalin burn for eternity in Hell.

Chapter 33
Yeehaa... Hollywood, Here We Come.

March, 2013, Los Angeles, California

They got back late from the studios in Culver City, where the link for the Carson show had been done. After, they have driven up to a restaurant they liked at the top of Topanga Canyon. They sat on the terrace watching the vast sprawl of LA below them, enjoying the cool mountain air after the smog of the vast city below. A coyote yipped in the dense mesquite brush and its partner answered a few hundred yards away. Jamesey cocked his head, trying to track them. They were out hunting to survive, he thought. Finding food and teaching their pups the ropes to ensure the survival of the species. Unlike four-legged creatures, Jamesey had been a hunter of men for many decades. Seeking out criminals, terrorists and the drags of society who preyed 'on' its citizens, after perpetrating violent, senseless deeds on them! Most wild animals avoided modern man like the bubonic plague, and he couldn't say he blamed them.

He sipped on a vintage Pinot Grigio and picked through his oven-baked cassoulet. The Italian-based mixed meat casserole was rich and herby and the restaurant served it as a speciality, slowly cooking it all day until the meat literally melted òn the tongue. The meal was costing him a small ransom but he considered it worth it. You paid for what you got and he never stinted when he was in the company of a beautiful woman, and Simone did indeed look lovely in the wavering candlelight, the subdued lighting softening and mellowing her striking features and making her look mysterious and feminine. She gave him a look of promise that only a certain beautiful woman can achieve, capturing all the basic elements of a confident, content lady in love, happy to be in the company of her lover and knowing conversation was unnecessary.

She knew he was in a pensive mood and he was probably thinking of his late wife but she could handle that and knew he looked upon her as his companion in her own right and didn't draw comparisons. Walking in the footsteps of a dead person who was idolised could be a tricky, uphill path with emotional ambushes waiting at every bend but, to the pleasant surprise of them both, the transitional period between them had been relatively easy. The relationship was open and honest, and Jamesey was an easy man to love. He was as tough as old leather but unfailingly civil and solicitous towards her.

She forked through her seafood risotto, enjoying the luxurious surroundings and unexpectedness of the evening. Jamesey had decided on a whim to take the drive up the dark, winding canyon road, phoning ahead for a table. The staff knew him and knew he was a big tipper and a connoisseur of fine dining and had made room for them on the terrace. She suspected a few Ben Franklins had changed hands but she was delighted at the impromptu break. Her lover was a beast of decisiveness. When a whim took his fancy, he looked at the practicalities, made a plan and went for it. Life had speeded up and opened up and had been a dizzy cascade of exciting discoveries and pleasure the past six months.

She gazed out at the lights of traffic on 101. Los Angeles never ceased moving. At night from a distance it was a fascinating, never-ending laser light show.

A senior PA of OLG Global, she wasn't complacent but she was confident in her own abilities and had made herself invaluable to him both at work and home. It was a heady mix to be loved and appreciated in both arenas of life by a man she adored. Jamesey was a powerhouse, a one-man nuclear reactor, fit to burst, and when he set his sights on something, he went out and got it, bulldozing any obstruction away until he had it. It was an exciting, arousing trip to be on with him.

She chewed thoughtfully on her squid and prawns. She'd never believed she would love again. Not since Steve 'the beater' had died so unexpectedly, well not unexpectedly to her, as she had murdered him and got away with it but she didn't like to dwell on that.

She knew Jamesey had run a full background check on her, it was something a man in his position had to do and he was astute and very perspective. He had only asked her about him once, and she had quite candidly told him about the years of abuse and his fall from the seventh floor balcony of the Hammaret Blue Azir Hotel in Tunisia. He had just grunted and said, "Surprised you didn't give him a shove, he was no loss to no one." Then he had taken her out for a drink and dancing on Sunset-Boulevard, and they had never talked about the matter again.

The wine was smooth, expensive and plush on the palate, the flavour simmered on the tongue before sliding silkily down her throat. She knew Jamesey was as much at home in a rough pub, swigging pints of ale, or in the finest French restaurant, picking and choosing the wine for each course. He was adaptable and flexible and could pass himself in any company. He could talk the talk and walk the walk when he had to. People were drawn to him, and he made firm friends fast and had the knack of keeping them on side.

His show of emotion for Collette on the interview that night had brought a lump to her throat but it showed the canny inner man and she loved him even more for it.

She chewed on a chunk of swordfish. The garlic in the sauce was ripe and tangy. "You won't be wanting to kiss me tonight, Jamesey, after this," she said merrily, pulling him out of himself.

"What, the garlic?" he smiled, "I'll get some fresh parsley off Marco. We'll chew it. Old fashioned breath purifier and good for the digestion."

She never knew that. He was a bottomless mine of golden nuggets. "Cool, you can tickle my tonsils afterwards to your heart's content."

He laughed, "Tonsil tennis, Christ, we sound like teenagers. Had mine out years ago in the army. They didn't want ya getting a sore throat when sneaking up on the enemy, in-case you coughed."

She gazed into his fine eyes. Still clear and focused despite his age. She knew he had killed men in the army, indeed was a venerated war hero, and had turned down some high award out of some misguided sense of honour because he believed he had walked his guys into an ambush. He had also turned down a knighthood from the British Queen because he considered himself a simple working man and medals and awards were a load of twaddle, but she had talked him into accepting it if offered again, saying it would be good for business. He had reluctantly agreed. "You just want a new hat and outfit and a freebie to Buckingham Palace but I guess it'll look good on the headstone when they plant me six foot under."

"Which won't be for many years yet, dear," she consoled him, "You've the constitution of an ox and the hide of a giant turtle."

He liked that, "Yep, there's life in the old dog yet. Still, a lump of tin on a man's chest doesn't make him any better than the rest," he paused, "Anyway, the giant turtles are near extinction, not a great example of the survival of the fittest species."

She smiled at him. He was a unique breed himself. A rare, hard surviving breed.

The Chef, Marco, a portly man with black curly hair and a walrus moustache waxed to points at the end like an old time opera singer, came out to ask Jamesey what he had thought of the cassoulet, "I putta da sun-dried tomatoes in instead of da fresh. What you think, my good friend?"

Simone was amused. Everyone he met genuinely sought his approval in things.

"It's magnifico, Marco. They give it a bounce and hold the flavours together before letting go and allowing the taste to starburst across the palate, like sitting on a hot Italian beach on the 'Bay of Naples', taste buds overwhelmed, revelling on how exquisite life can be."

Marco was delighted. He called a minion over and made him write it down. "I putta dat under description on menu. Grazie, Grazie. Is fantastico, such a descriptive turna da speech."

"You know, Marco, you're a true artist. It's very hard to put into words such exquisite food. Truly you have a God-given gift and this, Padrone, is 'manna from heaven'. Exquisite does not justify it."

Another convert, grinned Simone. He had him eating out of his hand. A beaming Chef bounced joyfully back to his hot domain. Signor DeJames knew his food, and it was a pleasure to cook for such an appreciative gourmet, not like a lot of these crass Americanos who wanted hot dogs and burgers and chips with everything. He shuddered theatrically at their gastronomic vulgarity.

Afterwards, they drove home at their leisure, chewing on the fragrant parsley Marco had supplied.

"You know, Simone. I didn't think I would take to LA at the start. Too big and noisy, and I thought the people would be insular and living in a hyperbole all of their own making."

"So what changed your mind, Jamesey? You seem content, dear."

"Yeah well, I guess I was judging it from the movies and books I read. You know, Clint and Arnie, then Connelly's Harry Bosch and then all the hype about it being the 'Centre of the Universe' for serial killers, but I was wrong."

"Well, it's certainly had its share of bad publicity, especially after the riots in South LA after Rodney King, but I like it. People are basically all the same but there seems to be an added ingredient to the Angelinos, an extra gene or endless battery life to them. They're certainly go out and getters."

He agreed with her, "Yep, guess the spirit of the pioneer hasn't quite diluted in their blood yet."

"Yeah, Davey Crockett and the Alamo, Butch and Sundance and the strong women they attracted," she injected.

"Then you've all the transients coming in from all around the world, many from war zones or abject poverty, determined to make a future for themselves. It's such a complex mix and match of cultures. It's fascinating."

She had to agree. "Yes, it's colourful all right, and the climate's so great when you can avoid the smog. It's a class act. We'll keep the Malibu beach home when we move to Chicago and commute."

"Yeah, LA is bloody addictive. It is a powerhouse of a trip."

Simone was quiet, thinking. "You know I think you like LA because it is like you. It has a vast personality, it never slows down, gives up or quits and anything's possible, just like you, my love."

She squeezed his strong hand, "You pioneered OLG from scratch, then went global and the Yanks respect you for it."

"Okay, okay," he laughed, "I'll give you a bigger dress allowance. My head's big enough."

She turned sideways on the seat and stroked his upper thigh, her profile dark in the car and enticing. "I don't want a bigger allowance, I just want you, Jamesey."

He waggled his eyebrows like Groucho Marx, "Well, I'm all yours tonight, you wicked woman."

When they got in, he checked his answering service at OLG. She saw him frown, "Trouble in New York, have to ring Rabbie."

While he made the call, Simone made coffee. The call was a long one. "Some bastards tried to kill some Russian girl, and Rabbie baled in and stopped it. Shots fired and everything; he's okay but for a sore head and a shiner."

Simone poured him a coffee, "Like father, like son, we going up before Boston?"

"Well…we'll hit the new Boston office first, and then fly in to see them. He seems to have everything in control. He's no panicker, is my Rabbie," pride in his voice.

"You just never know what's around the corner, do you?" she sighed. "It's a never-ending battle of good over evil. I'm going up, Jamesey… You won't be long?"

"No rest for the wicked, I hope?" he answered.

They made love, clinging passionately to each other, finding comfort and solace in each other's wants and desires, ensuring they were both fulfilled.

The next morning at first light they flew off to Boston. Jamesey settled into his seat and opened his briefcase. He rubbed his hands enthusiastically. "Hey, Boston is two hours ahead, gives me two hours catch up time, and time, my dear, is money. Ready to take notes? We sleep later."

She shook her head in wonder, "Yep. Ready when you are, Boss." The man saw the positive in everything. No wonder he had an empire and he was undisputed kingpin. "Sleep's for wimps."

II

They got into Boston at lunchtime and sped off to the new office. It was still winter in Boston and Simone shivered, forgetting how cold the extreme northeast of the empire could be as she climbed gratefully into the limo.

Twenty minutes later they reached the business area, rushing past quaint Georgian buildings, immaculately restored, many with coatings of a late snowfall hanging precariously off their eaves. "Don't be fooled by Boston. People think it's

454

safe and a time warp because it's one of the oldest in the country. It has the same crime problems as any major city."

"Oh sure, like throwing bales of tea in the harbour and refusing to pay you Brits taxes.[174]"

"Exactly," he grinned, "They started early and kicked our Brit arses, and now it has the highest bank robbery rate in the USA and with the Ruskis and Albanians moving in, OLG needs a foothold."

"Don't forget the triads in Chinatown," she warned, "Read about those guys in a book. Very scary."

He leant back. "Essentially, when a system loses its integrity, the whole system is corrupted and the system lost."

She sensed a speech coming, "You want me to write this down?" she chided gently.

"No need. OLG prides itself on its integrity. Our operatives have proved in their years in the forces their commitment and honesty and ability to serve within legal perambulators. The young men and women in our offices are highly vetted. They are trustworthy, quick off the mark and loyal," he paused, marshalling his thought process, "I open my offices where they are needed. Boston needs one. It's no reflection on Boston. Indeed, it's a small office, but you mark my words, it will have a major effect on the hoods and malcontents, and Boston will be a better place for its good people."

Simone mulled on this for a while, fascinated.

Finally, she said, "Are you linking OLG to a private police force or some secret type of anti-crime army?"

"In a sense. There's no integrity in crime, no written laws in their structure for them to follow, okay. You get misguided loyalty in gangs and family limits crime but a thief will steal off another thief. A killer will kill another killer. They are professional criminals but their infrastructures are weak and not regulated by society. OLG exploits those weaknesses and strikes hard when tasked."

"So do you think the cops, the FBI are losing the battle then?"

"Certainly in some towns and states. They are proud and able but under-staffed and underpaid. A crime wave doesn't stop because half the town's cops are off with the flu or the budget has run out. That's why OLG is so successful. We're a profit-making corporation. We have our own politics, and we only take on what we want to do – no corrupt congressman or self-serving politician can tell us what to do. We look at a job, if we don't like it, we tell them to bugger off."

"But that's just giving business to other competitions in our trade."

"Not at all," he replied smugly, "The OLG empire's too big and wide, with friends in the highest places. We came, we saw, we conquered. OLG's the biggest shark in the private security ocean."

She was impressed and not a little excited by the magnetic speech and the power that radiated off him and filled the car.

He thought back to all those years ago when he had taken a nervous Collette to see Jaws at the cinema in Watford and smiled at the memory. "But never drop your guard, Simone. Watch your enemy so you can see him coming."

---

[174] The Boston Tea Party of 1773 when the colonists refused to pay tax on imported tea and threw it into Boston Harbour, thus starting the 'American Revolution'.

"True, Jamesey, even paranoid 'schizos' have enemies. And you, Jamesey, are definitely top 'Great White'."

He reflected on that for a while, "Yep, but even the Great White shark is afraid of the mighty 'Killer Whales' who attack in pods, military fashion, so we must never let our guard down or get complacent."

"We are an experienced tactical company and that's the way we will stay."

III

He went through the Boston office like a whirlwind. The plane was on standby at Logan to fly them to New York at a moment's notice. Simone knew that Jamesey wanted to check for himself if Rabbie was all right. He didn't like inconsistencies and liked to be hands on wherever possible, but she also knew he was a fine and caring Pop. Firm but fair. He was certainly a massive inspiration to her and had changed her life around but then he was unique and it was just part of his nature.

The new office was small by OLG standards. The head of the office was Kim Sao Fanchung. A former Major in the South Korean Defence Forces, he spoke fluent Mandarin, Japanese and passable Russian, besides English. At forty he had come to America looking for excitement and better wages. Jamesey had snapped the man up. After years keeping communist North Korea out of the South and running agents, he was a seasoned security operator. After training in LA and three years in Chicago, he had proved his mettle and been promoted, just like every head of office before him. His friends called him 'Kung', which he tolerated with a wry smile.

The office was on the first floor above a small exclusive bank that OLG traded with. Kim had his own PA, four clerical staff and six operatives. They were a tight, hand-picked team, highly motivated.

"Is great, Mr DeJames. When we're not chasing robbers or triads, we're selling alarm systems," he said in his deep sing-song voice that did indeed remind Simone of the late Bruce Lee at the small, informal reception they had arranged for the big boss.

"Yeah, well, take no rash chances, Kim," Jamesey told him. "No amount of money recovered is worth the loss of an OLG operative."

He gathered the staff around him and gave them one of his famous pep-talks, leaving them feeling very much a team and bubbling over with enthusiasm. By half two they were back in New York and speeding towards a hurt son, whom Jamesey firmly, but kindly, sent home, boding no argument.

Despite not having slept for over forty hours, they rushed off to meet the girl Luca, who had so quite unexpectedly come into their lives. There was no time for fatigue. Rushing from place to place in private jets and limousines and meeting new and exotic employees who could kill you with one swipe of the side of the hand was rest enough. Simone thrived on the adrenaline buzz.

After the visit they headed back to La Guardia Airport, important clients were meeting them at the Beverly Hilton that night. "Should make it if these bloody yellow cabs would stop hogging the road," he snarled. "Still, we'll have three hours in LA, so we can sleep on the flight and have time to sort the paperwork before the meet, works out well."

So damn positive, he amazed her at times. She thought of their visit to Luca. Jamesey was on the car phone to the Miami office about a ship full of drugs they were watching for the DEA (Drug Enforcement Agency) and hoped to hit soon. "And when you hit it, hit the sods hard," he ordered. He didn't like drug smugglers, thinking of Collette's past.

Simone had been quite bewitched by the lovely hurt creature Luca, who despite her horrendous ordeal and injuries, had given them a dazzling smile. Quite mesmerising, with her charming accent. She had an aura about her that was very hard to put into words. Intelligence sparked off her. She had kind eyes and a compassionate nature, and she seemed thrilled to meet them and within a few minutes, Simone felt she had known her for years as she prattled on about things and gushed over her hero Rabbie.

She brought the compassionate side in her out, what she called her older woman's syndrome, and she wanted to help and nurture the younger female. Simone classified herself a fairly hard-nosed no-nonsense workaholic and after Steven the beater and the miscarriage he had brought about, it was refreshing to still know she had that side to her nature and it pleased her immensely.

No, it was truly nice to have met Luca and satisfying to be in a situation to comfort and help her. You didn't meet many Lucas, and the ones who did cross your path, you made it your business to keep in touch with in case you never knew another like her again.

God knows what Rabbie was truly feeling. To have such a divine creature fancy the socks off you was heady stuff enough but to have come to the rescue of such an angel and to be hero-worshipped was the stuff straight from the covers of a romantic work of art and mind-blowing to all concerned.

She smiled fondly as she recalled how Jamesey dealt with the serial sex bigot Jim Hooper and how Hooper had vacated the Chicago head office in such a bizarre manner. It was amazing how from such a horrid event romance had flowered between her and Jamesey.[175]

No, Luca definitely had a mega crush on Rab, and she could play him like a hooked fish. Simone wondered if he would bite and fall hook, line and sinker for her or would he swim hastily away, afraid to take on more that he could chew.

The limo sped through the gates to the private runway and they quickly boarded. "How does that song go, Jamesey? 1970s hit. 'From New York to LA... From LA to New York'."

Jamesey hummed it. "Yeah, bet you never thought you'd do it in one day."

Ten minutes later they were cruising at 35,000 feet southwest, heading towards the prairies. "Wouldn't fancy going all that way in a covered wagon. Get some sleep, honey," he advised, and he reclined his chair back and was asleep in seconds as only old soldiers can do.

Soon Simone was dozing too, holding his hand lightly and relishing his touch.

* * *

Hollywood, California, May, 1999

Jamesey smiled. Collette was at the window. It was their first day in Hollywood. "'Ere Jamesey, get yah arse up here, luv. It's only got one them Jacuzzi thingies."

---

[175] See book two in the trilogy – 'The Resurrection of Black Viking Sunray'.

IV

Bel Air, California, July 2000

Jamesey watched amused as Collette excitedly fiddled with the knobs and began filling the Jacuzzi. It wasn't as if she'd never been in one before, many of their friends in New York had one and held 'Jacuzzi Parties' and the gym they attended boasted several. He knew Collette wanted one of her own, and the apartment they had off Madison Square, although large and comfortable, just wasn't suitable. It was an older, turn of the century building, so he was pleased he could finally get a Jacuzzi and make his little mare happy.

He gazed out from the deck at the thick mosquito scrub that lined the hills, highly satisfied as Collette squealed in delight as she found the bubble maker, and when he turned she was half naked, hopping on one foot as she wrestled her jeans off, "'Ere, get yah kit off, mate, and we'll go for a plunge."

He smiled indulgently. Collette reverted back to her cockney accent when excited but normally her speech was clear and erudite. He loved it when she did, especially in bed, where, regardless of three pregnancies, she still never failed to arouse him. Jamesey eyed her appreciatively; her body was still firm and supple, despite a few stretch marks that she called 'Battle Wounds'; she was a fine-looking filly.

"What if the kids come out? Be a shock to see the old fogies in the altogether."

"Then they'll have to bleedin' get used to it! Any'ow, I ain't ashamed of what Mother Nature gave me."

He shrugged, resigned, and began taking his togs off. You don't argue with Collette when she was being what she called 'emphatic'. She would come to him with a request or a problem and finish with, "And I'm being emphatic about this, Jamesey." He shed his boxers and climbed in to join her. An hour's soak would do him no harm. He had business to attend to later, but it would wait until after lunch.

She splashed over to him and got him between her legs and began kneading his shoulders, "I'll give yeh a massage, mate, cos I bleedin' love yah, don't I? Wiv all me heart. If I had to, I still wouldn't have enough room for the entire love I have for yah, and that's 'emphatic', ain't it?"

"And I love you too, babe. We wouldn't be here now if you hadn't supported me. You deserve only the best," he told her with the utmost sincerity.

"Bollocks!" she cackled. "We're a team, mate, and always will be."

"Fifty cents for swearing, Collette."

"Bollocks! Bollocks and ten times bollocks! I'll pay yeh later in bed."

Jamesey knew she was pleased at his praise but tried not to show it. He was indeed proud of her, she was well-read, had a great vocabulary and was brilliant with the finances. He had made quite a few good investments with her astute appraisal of the financial markets. Must run in the family, he guessed, look at her brothers, Frankie and Mike. Fiscal wizards who looked after the OLG finances cleverly and wisely. One hundred per cent dependable, not like their whore of a mother, who he surmised had been a business woman in a sense. Always ready to open her legs for a profit and constantly on the lookout for the next mug to scam.

458

He recalled Christmas Day, 1984. He had purchased a four-bedroom detached house in South Oxley, a mile or so out of town and rented the house out in Croxley Green to a nice Asian family. He was going up in the world and was determined his loved ones and extended family got full benefit from their hard work.

Smudger, Kim and the kids were down, as were Frankie and Mike, who had grown into fine young men who had passed with honours from the London School of Economics. Jamesey was going to put them out for a year or two with his accountants and bankers to show them the ropes.

Kim and Collette were sweating away in the kitchen, preparing a magnificent feast, when the telephone in the hall rang. He answered it and listened before thanking the caller and hanging up. He put his head around the kitchen door, "What time's dinner, then? Smells great."

Collette blew hair out of her face, "Bleedin' Norah, Jamesey, you sure that's a turkey and not an ostrich? Enuf there to feed Bangladesh. Who was on the dog and bone?"

"Oh, just work checking in," he answered ingeniously. "Have I time to take the twins for a pint?"

She scowled, "Work? I smell skulduggery. Back in an hour or your dinner's in the dog!"

"Yes, my precious," grinning, undeterred by the phone call.

They didn't have a dog, although Collette was waiting for Mac the shepherd to get her a Border Collie pup. He grabbed the guys, who needed no second bidding, and they strolled the hundred yards to 'The Happy Hour' pub and settled in with pints of bitter and measures of Scotch.

The twins observed him shrewdly, "So, what's up, Uncle Jamesey?" asked Frankie.

"Yeah, not that we aren't grateful for the gesture, but it's unusual for you to take us to the pub."

And it was true. He seldom encouraged them to drink. He had high expectations of them. He eyed them keenly, "No easy way to say this, lads. Your mother's dead. Cirrhosis of the liver. Contact of mine in Hendon rang."

They both looked at each other blankly, unsure what to say.

They both looked at each other blankly again, unsure what was expected of them.

"Thing is, guys. You have to decide what you want done, arrangements, etc. I'll do anything I can to help. I don't think we should bother Collette with this just yet. You're the men of the family."

They went into a huddle, then Mike said, "Well, our first reaction was to put her in a sack, weigh it down with bricks and throw her in the Thames, but…"

"I guess even a dead dog should be buried," Frankie put in. "Our dad was a bastard and I'm not making excuses, but Mum might have turned out different if he supported her. We best do right by her."

"Yeah, let Collette enjoy her Christmas. Um…we'll sort it tomorrow."

Jamesey was mega impressed with their mature approach. He had seen them grow from gangly teenagers into mature, sensible men, "Okay. We'll get the ball rolling tomorrow. I'll get her kept on ice."

The twins grimaced, "Ice ran through her veins, Uncle. Her heart was frozen solid," remarked Mike.

"Yeah, well, you've us now, and Sally and Jim, and you just move on and make Collette proud."

"Oh, we will, Uncle, we will," they chorused.

* * *

Christmas dinner, 1984, was a great success. The turkey was cooked to perfection and Collette's homemade chestnut stuffing was superb. Jamesey leant back in his chair stuffed to the gills, "Abso...bloody...lutely fantastic, girls. I will be spitting feathers for a week. Outstanding!"

Collette swelled in his praise, "You'll be getting turkey for the next week."

They all groaned and then laughed. Collette watched, glowing, bouncing a sleepy Jamie on her knee. She adored Christmas...well, now she did. It was a real family time, although the twins seemed a trifle distracted.

Sally and Jim arrived down from Harpenden for egg noggin and a, yep, turkey salad supper. They all got half pissed, played charades, and Jamesey chased her around with the mistletoe, making her scream in gleeful hysterics.

Later in bed, a drowsy Collette nuzzled into him, "That was a brill day, honey. You never did tell me who was on the phone."

He considered telling her, then decided it was the twins' job. Sometimes men had to stand up and be counted and it was their time, "Go to sleep, my precious. Tomorrow's a new day."

She dozed off, fingering the locket he had given her on a railway platform eight years ago. She knew something was up but it would all come out in the wash if she needed to know...if not...then she knew her lover had it sorted and would always do what was best for her.

* * *

Next morning the twins took Collette into the parlour and broke the news to her. Jamesey donned his sweats and went for a run. When he got back, she was standing with her back to the kitchen sink, pose rigid, sipping a balloon of brandy.

"Why the fuck did you not tell me yesterday, Jamesey?"

He eyeballed her warily, "Well, one, it wasn't my job, and two, I think that bitch done enough to ruin your life without spoiling your Christmas."

She flew at him, fists raised, and he grabbed her arms tight and clasped her to him. An elbow found a jar of Haywards Pickled Onions and they smashed dramatically over the tiled floor, "You, feckin' git! I had a right to know," and she broke free and slapped him hard across the face. "Always think you bleedin' know best."

He went to hug her but she pushed him away, "Leave me alone!"

The twins tentatively edged in, "I'm going to the office. Look after your sister, she needs you," he said.

* * *

He sat with Smudger and they demolished a bottle of Hennessey, then cracked open another, "She'll come round, Jamesey. It's just the shock, you done right, mucker. Anyhow, probably the time of the month."

Jamesey gave him the big eye, "Don't trivialise it, mucker. That bitch traumatised her. I'll book into a hotel for a couple of nights until she takes the pot off the boil and calms down."

Smudger sunk more brandy, "'Kay, mate. I told yah, different species. Kim's wiv her, she'll settle. Come on," and he put his coat on, The Peel beckons and I gotta get that tenner back you took off me at darts."

* * *

Come teatime, Jamesey and Smudger were well steamed. Ronnie had been partaking of the whiskey and Eadie the Queen's Counsel Sherry.

"Can I stay at yours tonight, Ron?" slurred Jamesey. "Collette's a right hump on."

Ron giggled, "Yah can have the 'Presidential Suite', last slept in by JFK and Marilyn."

Collette walked in and looked at her large inebriated mountain of a man' and she felt like a piece of shit. "'Ere, Jamesey, you okay, love?" she asked gingerly. "You comin' home? Cos I made yah a real hot turkey curry."

He gazed at her through bleary eyes. His little Collette, his broody mare, the love of his life and his heart filled and overflowed, and he grabbed her, wrapping her in a crushing embrace.

Ron and Smudger winked at each other and Eadie "Ohhed" and "Ahhed", "Nothing like a good row to clear the air."

"Take him home, Collette," ordered Ronnie, "he can't even pick out the colours of the balls on the pool."

* * *

And she did and next morning when he woke, she was leaning over him, contrite, "Sorry, babe. I was all confused and in a tizzy. I was a right bitch to you."

He stared at her, "Au contraire, my sweet. It was a one-off tricky thing that life throws up now and then," and he proceeded to shag her brains out for the next hour. Sure beats going for a run. The Sun newspaper had carried out a survey that said that twenty minutes of rigorous intercourse was the equivalent of a three mile run.

"We'll go another six later, love," she promised getting out of bed, panting. "Gonna make yah the full English fry, keep your strength up," and she whisked off, still feeling extremely guilty.

Jamesey smiled. It was water of a duck's back to him. After some of the matrimonial fights he had witnessed in the married quarters in Aldershot, it was just a storm in a teacup. At least she hadn't stabbed him or took a meat cleaver to his head as he'd had to deal with, at times, when Duty Sergeant.

Six days later, Janet Elaine Stark was cremated at Tooting Crematorium. Present were Collette, the twins and the proprietor of The Queen Boadicea pub in Garston, a big fleshy slab of a man called Jeffers. The service was brief and they gave Collette the urn.

461

"Yah know, she had a hard upbringing herself, young 'un, and yer Dad, if yah mind me P's and Q's, was a right mean sod. Me missus, God rest her, used to send up food and do what she could for yah, but it was a no-win situation."

Collette reflected on that and in a deep memory vaguely dredged up Mrs Jeffers, "Yeah, I think I remember your missus. Ah well, what goes around comes around. Thanks for coming."

She went back to the car where Jamesey was waiting and got in and kissed him, "Thanks, mate. I still feel a right fuckin' bitch to yah."

He stroked her hair, "Rubbish. They say you hurt the ones you love, I don't know. Let's put this behind. Tactical withdrawal, lick the wounds, assess the situation and advance."

Collette was flummoxed, "Why? What's going on?"

"I'm taking you away for a week. You need a break."

"Oh, okay…where we going then?"

"New York. Always wanted to see 'The Big Apple'."

She gawked at him, speechless – an uncommon event for her.

"Close your mouth, love, before the flies get in," he admonished her, "And go pack your things. We haven't got all day."

She hastened to his bidding. Things were just getting better and better. It was the last and only serious argument they ever had.

* * *

Jamesey luxuriated in the warm, hiving water, fondly remembering. Collette grabbed his manhood enticingly, "What about a quick bonk, love?"

"What about the kids?"

"They are watching 'Shrek 90' or something. I've always wanted to do it in a Jacuzzi."

He laughed and obliged her, "See, told yah I'm game for anything," and she gasped and climaxed.

Collette thought her veins were going to burst, so deep was the love for him that coursed through them, "You are a bloody limited-edition, Jamesey. I love you with all me soul, heart and body. I friggin' owe yah big style."

He gazed into her fine hazel eyes, the colour of a Scottish moorland stream with the sun shining on it, "You owe me bugger all. You're my life, now how about lunch in The Skandia because if I get any more bleedin' turkey, I'll be turning into Bernard Matthews[176] products."

She chuckled, "Let's do the Indian in Abbot's Langley, love. And there was no Captain Curry, you made that up. Curry means gravy in India."

He chortled, "See, education's a great thing. Now you can hold your own in a debate and outshine me." He kissed her again, "Maybe, but I will always treasure Captain Curry." They drove off, Jamesey happy he was going to be allowed to feed his curry addiction in the open, "Here, Coll. What you gonna do with the ashes then?"

* * *

---

[176] Huge turkey breeder in Norfolk, famous for his television adverts.

They stopped by the pond in Cassio Park. It was a cold, freezing day, and Collette shivered as she scattered the ashes on the frigid water, "Hope she don't poison the ducks," she muttered, then pulled two carnations out of her coat pocket that she had nabbed off the wreath. One was red; one was white.

She tossed the red one in. "Here, Mum. Red for blood, it's thicker than water. More than you deserve." Next she threw the white flower in, "White for peace and purity, Mother. I hope where you're going you find both." She was crying and Jamesey took her in his arms, moved in spite of himself.

"I'm impressed, love. You can move forward now."

Collette snivelled a bit and he led her back to the warmth of the car. She watched as he confidently drove away, sucking on an Embassy Red, a rare treat but consoling.

Yep, forward and onward and with this Herculean man by her side the world was her bloody oyster. No retreating. No fucking surrender.

* * *

A few days afterwards, his mother arrived down. Collette greeted her joyfully, "Oh my Gawd! What a bleedin' lovely surprise."

Jamesey joined them, "Mum's down for a week to watch the kids."

V

As the jet cruised across Arizona at 38,000 feet, Simone cracked a weary eyelid and scrutinised her lover.

He was perfectly at ease, stretched out, ankles crossed, shoes off, his big hands laced across his still flat stomach, which she marvelled at, because he ate like a starved grizzly bear after hibernation and drank like a fish.

He was smiling in his sleep and even gave a subconscious chuckle now and then.

She wondered what he had been like as a young man and only one word came to mind. 'Powerhouse'. Even now at sixty-three he was a dynamo, and his positivity and generous nature had certainly rubbed off on her.

She thanked the day he had come to her rescue at OLG HQ in Chicago and they had become lovers.

He didn't talk much about his late wife, Collette; his little broody mare, as he called her, whatever that meant?

Simone closed her eyes again. Best get another hour before landing. Jamesey could be a hard taskmaster when in full flow, so one grabbed whatever sleep one could, when possible.

She guessed it was an army thing… Carpe Diem! Seize the day and get as much done as possible before collapsing from exhaustion.

She smiled as the Goddess Morpheus put her under, her beautiful eyes closing.

Collette must have been some woman, it was a shame she never met her to compare notes, she decided, as Johnny Nod took her down.

Now that would have been an enlightening, powerful conversation.

* * *

463

And Jamesey was indeed laughing in his sleep. He was remembering the hot summer day his PA in the office had tentatively put her head around the door and said, "Uhmmn, Mr D, I've the LAPD on the main line."

He looked up from his paperwork, "What do they want? Is it business?"

Cindy, his very efficient and attractive PA with dreadlocks to die for, squirmed and visibly grimaced, "No, Boss, they want you down at Hollywood Police Station to bail Mrs DeJames out."

That stumped him and he threw his pen down, "Whatcha mean? Bail her out? What the damnation is my Collette doing in the Cop Shop?"

Cindy cringed. "I best put them through, Boss dude." Which she did.

He picked the telephone up, scowling. "DeJames... OLG... LA... What the frig have you arrested my wife for?"

He listened carefully, jaw dropping, Cindy peering fearfully around the door, wondering, as the bossman's colour rose, if he needed a heart attack pill.

"What the fuck do you mean...? Possession of an unlicensed firearm...? She doesn't have a bloody firearm."

He listened some more then roared, "Discharging a firearm in a public place... Criminal damage to a plate glass window... Public affray and assault... Yes, I am calm, can I speak to her?"

He groaned, "She won't speak to anyone and in her agitated state you are best just to let her calm down, is that right?"

He groaned, "Okay, Officer... I'll be down straight away... Yeah, let her cool down, she is a one-woman bleeding army when she starts. See you soon."

Cindy, who had heard every word, put her head around the door, "I'll get Pete the duty driver to run you down, Boss."

She fled back to her desk. Wait until the girls heard about this... OLG LA had certainly livened up since the DeJameses had hit town. It was like something from a forties John Wayne western.

Jesus, she couldn't wait to meet Collette. Talk about Annie bloody Oakley!

She put her head around the door, "Pete will be outside in two, Boss."

Jamesey had put his shoulder holster on, holding his chrome-steeled .45 Colt Python with the six-inch barrel, and was throwing his jacket over it.

"Scuse, Boss," she hedged tentatively, "You might want to drop the gun... LA Cops, especially after Rodney King, can be a bit twitchy around them."

He stormed past her, "Yes well, mine is fully licensed, not apparently like my wife's."

Cindy watched the strong departing back and hit the telephone to her best friend in accounts and sales... "Myrtle, babe... You will never guess what's happened..."

* * *

Big Pete, a Kansan in his thirties and ex-Navy Seal (Sea, Air and Land) Special Forces drove the new boss competently through the mid-afternoon traffic.

Jamesey sat there musing. Stumped. What the frig was going on? They had been here a month. Collette loved the big, spacious six-bed apartment, especially the Jacuzzi, which she was never out of.

The kids, Jamie and Petral, they loved their new school and the climate and they were all getting on nicely with the California tan.

464

Collette was getting along great with the neighbours, had joined their wine club and had enrolled at the Adult Campus for a course in Spanish and American History.

And now she was in the police station on a firearms offence in South East LA. The mind boggled!

He had got her a nanny, a nice Mexican girl, very competent, to watch the kids so she could go out when she wanted, a housekeeper who came in four mornings a week and a BMW...SUV that she could run about in and take the kids out when she wanted.

He had given her carte blanche on furnishing and decorating the flat and got her a platinum visa so she was never short of dollars.

No, life was good. His mother was coming over tomorrow to stay for a few weeks, and Collette and the kids could not wait to see her.

Yeah, LA was a vast, sprawling jungle, but he had given her a map and a good security briefing about where and where not to go. She was sensible normally. She knew about the myriad of gangs and the high crime areas and that there were still areas of the city not rebuilt after the Rodney King riots.

For Christ sake, she was a Watford girl. She was streetwise and knew how to look after herself.

They pulled into the precinct grounds. Pete said in his Kansas drawl, "Listen, sir, bit of advice if you will take it?"

Jamesey looked him in the eye, "Drop the sir crap, that's for officers... What is it, Pete?"

Pete put his hands up in a placatory manner, "'Kay, Boss, one, don't go in there like a young bull in a rodeo, they will only keep yah hanging...two... I've rung Tobias Mathias, he's the OLG attorney at law, and he says don't do nothing until he gets here to keep you and Mrs D right...and three, lose the gun, they will mess you about for an hour checking the licence before you even get to see the little lady," he grinned. "Believe me, I've been there in my après Seal days, before I joined the OLG family."

Jamesey eyed him keenly, pulled his Python and handed it over. "Loaded but safe."

Pete grinned, "What Clint Eastwood used in 'Dirty Harry'."

Jamesey managed a smile, "Yeah, well, make my day and go and find some decent coffee. See you inside," and he climbed out and marched towards the enquiry office.

Pete watched him admiringly. Things had certainly got a whole lot more active since the day the big man had moved down.

Brothers in arms really. Both ex-special forces.

He unloaded the Python and pocketed the rounds. Big gun for a big guy.

God knows what the next few hours would bring, and he best keep it away from Mrs DeJames, who sounded like a one-woman rampaging tornado.

* * *

Earlier That Day

Collette had always wanted a Tiffany Lamp. She had seen them in a shop window, the beautiful stained glass shape dazzling and reflecting the suffused

465

colours and design and then saw the price and wondered as the young, confused adolescent if she would ever have one.

Then, many years ago, she truly believed it was probably just a pie in the sky fantasy, but now it was a real deal and her mother-in-law and friend Beth was arriving tomorrow, and she could imagine a beautiful Tiffany Lamp glowing in welcome in the living room with its beautiful colours.

But Collette was practical and wasn't going to pay the exorbitant prices the dealers were asking and trawled the internet and found one exactly as she wanted in 'Sucker Saul's', pawn shop in South East Los Angeles, going at a third of the price.

She rang, "Yeah, don't sell it, I'll be down in an hour."

So keys in hand, she set out to the garage to get her BMW and head off.

A little voice niggled at the back of her head. Jamesey had told her in his 'security briefing' not to go to South LA alone or unarmed. It was full of violent gangs and had a huge crime rate.

She shrugged as she drove off. It would be a quick in and out, and who would hurt a mother of three on a shopping mission?

She had found the Los Angeles people friendly and considerate, and she could see the lamp shining in the corner as they had pre-dinner cocktails, both Beth and Jamesey enthusing over it and admiring her good taste.

* * *

She found 'Sucker Saul's' pawn brokers and cash checking shop okay by use of the GPS.

It had been an hour's drive, and she marvelled at the huge sprawl that Los Angeles was.

South LA was a vast expanse of low-rise single-storey clapboard housing and rows of colourful shops and cafés of all kinds and stretched for miles.

Gangs of coloured and Hispanic youths hung around every corner, wearing their gang colours and stared at her curiously when she had to slow down. There certainly were not a lot of white faces around.

But she wasn't worried. They were only kids and young guys. They had mothers who loved them, and if they wanted to strut about in the street, that was their business. More power to them.

She chuckled, "All I want is a Tiffany Lamp," a childhood ambition and today she would fulfil her dream.

Parking outside the shop, a single-storied shop front in the middle of a row of commercial premises, she climbed out and entered, glad to stretch her legs.

Saul was a slim Asian man in his late thirties whose head was adorned with a bright saffron-coloured turban.

He looked surprised to see a diminutive well-dressed white woman enter his domain.

"Welcome, memsab," and he bowed graciously. "How can Sucker Saul help you this beautiful day or are you lost, looking for directions?"

She grinned, liking the man instantly, "Naw, mate, we spoke earlier, Mrs DeJames, about the Tiffany Lamp."

Realisation crossed his features and he gave a beaming smile, his pearly-white teeth contrasting with his silky dark complexion.

"Welcome indeed, lovely lady. Yes, we agreed a price subject to an overview of the goods. I don't think it will disappoint," and with a flourish he produced a spectacular lamp, its glasses in all the colours of the rainbow; he plugged it in and threw the switch.

Collette gasped in joy and gazed in amazement at the lighted tapestry of colours before her.

"Cor luv a duck, it's like being in a bleeding church on a sunny day. Let's haggle, Saul my friend."

They soon agreed a price much lower than anticipated and both pleased. Saul bubble wrapped and boxed it for her.

"There…safe and sound. It would take a full hit from a Taliban RPG 7 and still be fine."

They chatted for a few minutes and Collette, well pleased with her haggling abilities, prepared to leave.

Saul stopped her, "Memsab…if you don't mind me being impertinent but South East LA very dodgy for young memsabs. Would you be interested in an insurance policy?"

She eyed him. "Like what, Saul?"

He produced a small box and took out a small gun with a flourish, that nestled in the palm of his hand.

"Cobra .38. Two shot over and under. Packs a punch at close range, easily concealed. I call it, my dear, 'The Muggers Equaliser'."

She looked at it, and he demonstrated its actions and showed her how to load it.

"I do you a good deal. You fill in the form and when it clears, it's yours. Great thing for a young lovely lady to give her the 'get out clause' in any unfortunate situation that hopefully will never arise."

Collette mused, a manicured fingertip to her lip. "Yeah, I reckon that might be handy to have. Certainly pay out quicker than any insurance myself and the old man have," and laughed merrily.

At that point in time the door burst open and four tall black men in T-shirts, jeans and sporting red bandanas burst in and encircled Collette.

The tallest, a mean-looking brute in his mid-twenties, mean-looking scars on his face and arms, no doubt from many gang fights over the decades during his troubled upbringing, got face to face with Collette, who had turned in surprise.

Well, not really face to face, as she had to look up at the thug who was over a foot taller than she was, "'Ere, what's bleeding going on?" she asked him quite pleasantly.

He snarled back at her, lips curled up in a nasty sneer, "You're in our territory…and we don't want no white honky trash in our crib."

Collette was quite afraid, especially as they were all sporting big, wicked-looking knives but she wasn't going to be talked down to, "Yeah well, I'm here on business, but I'm leaving now, so shift your arse and let me through."

Sucker Saul glared at them, "Put those knives away, such behaviour in front of a lady. You should be ashamed of yourselves."

"Shut your Goddamn mouth, you Paki shit. If she doesn't give us the damn keys pronto, she's coming with us and she will be on the serious end of a lotta Black Snake… And empty that frigging cash register while yah are at it, dude," the leader snarled viciously and grabbed Collette by the arm with his free hand, waving the long steel blade around nastily. "And what's in the box, it looks expensive?"

Collette tried to pull away but he wasn't having it, "Yer can have the bloody BMW but yah ain't taking my Tiffany Lamp. The mom-in-law is coming and its special, ain't it, now get yah bleeding paws off me."

"You pay for this, you heathens," roared Saul indignantly. "I pay my protection money every week right on time to the Cribs. When I tell Mr Henry the Slasher, he will bliddy deal with you most severely… And I am from Bombay in India, not bliddy Pakistan," he ended, seriously insulted.

The leader threw his head back and snorted derisively, "You're outta luck, pal. We're from the Bloods, we taken over this street…" and he issued more orders, "'Key, missey, and grab that box and the register, and we'll go and party on down."

Collette was fuming. She produced the Cobra Derringer she had palmed and promptly aimed and shot the knife out of the bandit's hand, the gunshot deafening and causing the rest to flinch in shock and bow down looking for cover. The .38 copper jacketed slug hit the knife blade at eight hundred feet a second and it flew out of the Blood gang leader's hand, breaking his wrist, and he howled in pain and clutched it across his chest in agony.

She stepped back to a safe distance and pointed the small gun right between his eyes, "Now I told you that you were NOT taking my lamp, so I suggest you gather your little crew up and vamoose before I give you a third eye and the back of your nut explodes over the floor and makes a mess on this nice man's floor…what's it to be, hombre?"

The other three gang bangers eyed her warily. She only had one shot left, they could take her, even though they would lose their leader, before she could reload.

There was no honour amongst thieves, and they edged menacingly forward, blades brandished.

Then Saul came up from behind the counter with a double-barrelled pump action shot gun and emptied a thunderous blast into the ceiling and the failed crime spree ended when the gang fled the scene hastily. But not before one grabbed the box with the lamp in it on his way out.

Collette waved smoke away from her face, "The little sod got my bloody lamp!" she roared in rage and promptly reloaded the small revolver from the box of ammo on the counter, "And I ain't bloody having it," she muttered darkly as she headed after them.

Saul was on the telephone to the cops, "I told you the bliddy Derringer was a good piece of kit, memsab!" he grinned after her.

Collette raced out and saw the gang was a hundred yards up the road by now, so she jumped in her SUV and roared off after them, rapidly gaining on them, passersby and onlookers gaping in amazement at the action going on.

She caught up rapidly and slewed the car off the road and broadside across the pavement and skidded to a stop and hopped out and pointed the pistol meanly at them. "Put that box down right away and be on your bleeding way. I'm right frigging annoyed now, so I am."

The gang screeched to a stop and gazed in disbelief. They were not used to being confronted on their turf by gun-toting small-statured good-looking English women.

Street cred was at serious threat here and they advanced warily.

Collette fired a warning shot between the legs of the nearest goon, the round whanging off the pavement and howling across the roofs into the distance. "I mean it. PUT THE BLOODY BOX DOWN…or the next punk gets plugged," and she jangled her coat pocket, "I've got plenty more rounds left," and she eased back and jumped back into the car and deftly reloaded then aimed through the open window. "I mean it," and fired another round into the grass verge, causing them to jump in shock. "Leave the box and head home to your mamas and pappas before I really get annoyed."

Suddenly, the street was filled with a cacophony of lights and sirens and was swamped with blue-shirted gun-waving cops. "Freeze, Motherfuckers… Get on the ground and put your hands on your heads."

The gang complied hastily and were soon cuffed and their rights read to them.

Collette watched amused, then deeming it safe, got out to retrieve her lamp. *Wait until Jamesey heard about this, then she grimaced, maybe not, least said, soonest mended.*

"She's got a gun. She's a frigging mad motherfucker. She tried to shoot us," shouted a gangster from a cop car.

Two officers approached her warily, hands on gun butts. "This true, ma'am? Do you have a licensed fire arm and have you been discharging it in public?"

Collette shrugged, "Well, it ain't exactly licensed but I can explain," and produced the Derringer to show them.

Before she knew it, she was flat on the ground and the cuffs were being slapped on, "You have the right to remain silent… You have the right to an attorney…"

* * *

Jamesey approached the desk Sergeant warily.

The outside area of the enquiry office was a hive of activity as citizens clamoured for action over various matters or stood angrily waiting to make complaints against the boys in blue.

When it was his turn, he snapped, "DeJames, I believe you have my wife, Collette, in your custody?"

The Sergeant grinned and shouted over his shoulder, "Mr DeJames is here for Mrs DeJames, Lieutenant."

An attractive blonde woman in an immaculately pressed uniform came through and escorted him through into the inner sanctum of the bustling hive of law and order, "I am Lieutenant Anne Pedlow, I've to take you up to see the Captain."

He groaned, "The Captain. Must be serious. I hope she hasn't caused you too much trouble."

Anne looked surprised, "Trouble? No, sir. She's been terrific. Great shooting and fortunately nobody hurt."

That bamboozled him. He'd given her a few lessons on the range but she had not really taken to the complexities of firearms training, saying the guns were too heavy, noisy and hurt her wrists.

"So what happened and where? I thought she was at a tenants meeting."

They left the elevator and headed for the Captain's spacious office. "She'll tell you herself. It was in South East District, Palm Tree Boulevard."

Jamesey growled but stayed silent. He had told her never to go to South East LA without being accompanied by a person from the office and it would be better if she avoided it all together.

When he entered, Collette was chatting animatedly with a group of senior officers, sipping coffee, a plate of pastries balanced on her knee.

"What the hell, Collette, were you doing in South East alone? And say nothing until the lawyer gets here."

"'Ere keep yer hair on, love. I was getting us a Tiffany Lamp and some gang bangers tried to tea leaf it off me."

A heavy, florid-faced man hustled around from behind his desk. The word 'lawyer' was not one senior officers liked to hear, "Now, Mr DeJames… I'm Captain Ed Bain," and shook his hand, "Mrs DeJames prevented a serious robbery, which led to the arrest of four very serious criminals. We are very grateful to her and indeed proud."

"Yep, the boss is gonna recommend her for a 'Citizens Commendation'."

Jamesey was flummoxed, "But she doesn't have a gun."

Collette beamed, "I do now, love," and mimicking a Wild West Cowboy accent, "Ah got me a dandy little Derringer and the Goddamn constitution ses ah have the right to bear arms."

They all laughed, except Jamesey, who listened as the Captain explained the details, and he shook his head in stunned disbelief. His little broody mare could have been killed and where would the OLG family be then?

But he lightened up when the Captain produced Jim Beam.

"So we had to arrest her as a precaution," the Captain was explaining as the OLG lawyer arrived and Jamesey explained it was all a big mistake.

"No problems, Mr DeJames. All's well and all that crapo… I'll only bill OLG for the hour and the trip down… Nice seeing yah all," and he hastened off, back to the golf course.

The Captain gave a pained look, "All the damned same, those shysters. They make the shark Jaws look like a pet goldfish!"

Jamesey grinned at Collette, who smiled back as she remembered the film they had seen together in the Watford Odeon so many years ago.

"Well, no harm done. Don't suppose you have one of those electronic ankle things to spare, Ed?"

They all laughed and on the way home Collette sat proudly in the rear of the car with the Tiffany Lamp protectively on her knee and regaled them with her antics.

Jamesey could not ever stay annoyed with her, "Yeah well, next time, my sweet, heed advice and follow rules and no one will get hurt."

"Yes, my Lord and Master," she told the back of the head of a man who would break every rule in the book if he could get away with it.

Pete just smiled knowingly. *Talk about the 'Dynamic Duo'.*

* * *

And Collette did get a 'Good Citizens Reward', presented by the Mayor, which still hangs on the wall in his office.

The plane landed smoothly at LAX International, and Jamesey was instantly awake and out of his seat before the craft had finished taxiing to a stop.

He shook Simone awake, all thought of the past forgotten as he concentrated on the hours ahead, energy and determination exuding off him in waves as he grabbed his briefcase.

"Let's go, sleepy head... No workee, no payee. We're on a tight schedule."

Simone stumbled out after him to the steps. God, he was a brute of a hard taskmaster, but she revelled in every blessed minute of it.

Chapter 34
The Power of a Darn Good Spurning
('Goodness Gracious... Great Balls Of Fire'... Jerry Lee Lewis)

She woke wrapped around him like a second skin, revelling in the feeling of contentment and fulfilment that cloaked her whole being. She had never in her wildest dreams believed she could have felt this way. As a woman she was touched by such wholeness that she couldn't even begin to unravel it in her head. A strange sense of achievement and vindication gripped her; vindication that the love she had searched for was a true one. A wholesome, natural and ancient phenomenon.

Gazing lovingly at Rabbie, who was in a deep, comatose sleep, a relaxed half smile on his face, she gently ran a fingertip across his cheek and through his hair. Life was all about overcoming obstacles and climbing to the top in the various endeavours you chose to do or were thrust in your path. She reckoned she had just surpassed every expectation in her love lottery.

She was on a high pinnacle now; a pinnacle of love so high, it took her breath away. All the treasures of life she would travel through with Rabbie were spread tantalisingly in the valleys below, waiting to be found and explored. She knew in the depths of her full, beating heart that Rabbie was her man, her lover, her soulmate, and that they would swoop down into the valley together and explore its many enticing trails. They would go from destination to destination as a single unit, helping and supporting each other over any obstacles in their way. Yes, there would be trials and tribulations on their route, hairpin bends and rock-falls to traverse, but their love would carry them through. She knew in her heart that their love would grow stronger and deeper and that nothing could come between them.

This love was so strong, it amazed her. She was stunned by the intensity and purity of the feelings she was experiencing. They were sublime in their majesty; a royal and pure thing in its timeless lineage.

She had never believed she could feel so comfortable and safe with anyone. After they made love, they had showered together and she thought she would be inhibited and shy in his presence but as she stood naked before him, it seemed so natural and right that she enjoyed the closeness it brought them.

They made love again, and she was so relaxed and easy with him that all her inhibitions disappeared and she thrilled to the touch of his hands and mouth on her body. She moaned as he speared his strong masculinity into her tender core and squirmed in time to his incessant probing as he brought her to a peak of feeling she had never before reached, watching his face as he reared back and exploded inside her, causing her to reach her own crescendo as once again they became one entity of pure sensation.

The bond she felt with him was magical. It was overwhelming and she felt encased in its mystical net.

He was so caring and considerate with her after they had made love, she felt like she was in heaven. They had a nice supper and he catered to her every whim. She adored him for it and when she saw the way he looked at her with his strong, dark blue eyes, she knew she was very special to him as well. After all that had happened with Hanlon, it was such a great feeling of comfort and security that she now knew she could bury the events of that terrible night away in a corner of her mind she need never visit again.

In the early hours of the morning, she took the initiative when she felt his male hardness pressing against her and, straddling him, she gasped as the full length of his manhood slid inside her. She was mesmerised at the depth of feeling the joining of their bodies gave her, but it was more than that, it was a joining of mind and soul, so special and new to her but it was as old as time itself.

That morning he had to go to work. The operation at the electrical retailers in Queens, which had been dragging on for weeks, looked like it was going to come to fruition that day.

"Sorry, Luca, I have to be there for the climax. Show the boys the boss appreciates them."

She grinned wickedly, "I tink you were there for several climaxes last night, dahling."

He laughed, she loved his laugh and was pleased to hear it, happy that she amused him. "Sure was, you're incredible, babe."

She glowed in his praise, "Yes, veil, no climaxing wiv any strange vimmen you might have to rescue today."

"After you? No way, honey. Your name's on my heart. Anyone else would be an anti-climax."

"You say da most lovely tings to me, Rabbie," simpering prettily, her breasts half exposed.

He gave her a lingering kiss. "That's because you are," and left, a jaunty spring to his step.

* * *

She lay in bed hugging his pillow, not wanting to leave the place where she had discovered her true womanhood. She replayed every moment over in her head, every move, kiss and caress of the night before. "Luca, you are a wanton woman and loving every minute of it, you spoilt bitch," she chided herself in Russian before hopping out of bed and pirouetting round the room naked, only to flop back, splayed out, delight shining on her face as she enjoyed the uniqueness of the situation. She thanked her lucky stars and prayed to God for making life so glorious for her and her lover.

Quelling her exuberance, she had a luxurious bath. Relaxed and dressed, she made coffee and decided to write to her mother and extol the virtues of the wonderful man she full intended to spend the rest of her life with, through thick and thin.

* * *

473

Luca spent the next few hours between reading and dozing, hearing nothing from Rabbie until he phoned her at 3.00pm, sounding very pleased and satisfied with himself. "Hey, Luca, get your coat on. I'm sending the duty driver for you, we're celebrating downtown at Maloney's. We got a great result."

She hastened to do his bidding, glad he was safe. Khalid, the duty driver and teetotaller, explained on the way that the OLG operatives always had a bit of a 'hoedown' after a successful op and often brought the wives and girlfriends along. "I just dropped that reprobate Boomerang's girl, Katie, off. He's keeping an eye on her because Little Dan's got his sights set on her."

Luca smiled as they pulled up at Maloney's, "Hopefully, her and Boomerang make da nuver go of it. He's a big sweetie at heart. Tis great to be in love, da? It not happen often in life."

Khalid watched her trip gaily into the building. "Now there's a girl in love, I do believe. Good fortune, Luca," he wished her and thought about the blonde body builder he had met down at the gym. "Takes all sorts, though."

* * *

Maloney's was a large, old fashioned Irish bar on Third Avenue. All polished woods, shiny mirrors and even shinier brasses, and you could imagine you'd stepped back a hundred years by walking through the door. With its tall ceilings, patterned tiled floors and original plaster cornicing, it made the customer think he was drinking in a real Irish bar, which he was.

It was run by a lady called Bronagh Maloney, who took over when her father passed away. Attractive, with long straight brown hair and the pale skin and flashing blue eyes of a true Irish Colleen. She was a no-nonsense businesswoman but convivial company, and she could put on the best Irish accent heard outside the Emerald Isle, for the tourists, despite being born and bred in New Jersey.

"Sure, we pull the best pint of Guinness outside Dublin, so we do, and our champ and sausage was sent from the Good Man Above for us to eat, so it was," she told them.

OLG used the bar regularly. She valued their trade and was discrete, which they liked. The bar had a fine restaurant, which served the best of Irish stews, salmon steaks and of course the famous champ, all served with just the right amount of craic and banter. About twenty of the OLG guys and their women were now celebrating and cavorting at a big table in the eating area.

Bronagh watched the pretty Russian girl come in and smiled ruefully, she was beautiful. Her and Rabbie had had a bit of a thing going for a few months when he had first arrived but it had fizzled out when they decided they were better as friends than as a couple. They had remained good pals and spent quite a few hours 'putting the world to rights' over a drink or two.

Rabbie had expanded at length about his dazzling flatmate during one of those evenings, and Bronagh had seen he had it bad even before he knew himself. She felt a tinge of jealousy because deep down she still carried a torch for him and had hoped to rekindle the flame one day.

Coming out from behind the busy bar, she smiled wistfully, "Hey, you must be Luca. The guys are up the back, I'll show you."

474

Luca was gazing around her, "Vow, vot a fantastic place, is gorgeous! I so like the Irish, dey are kind and clever and so, so good company." She offered her hand, "I am Luca Sophia Natasha Sonia Alexandra Valendenski, so pleased to meet you."

Bronagh hesitated for a fraction of a second, then shook, "Hey, I'm Bronagh, the proprietor. How do you do...? Céad Mile Fáilte... Irish for a hundred thousand welcomes."

Luca had noticed the slight hesitation; she was very perceptive. "I am very vell, tank you so much. You must be so proud to own such a cool place. Such a nice saying. We say in Lithuania, 'May your roof be strong and the wind always behind you'."

"Class keeps me busy and bread on the table but yeah! Love it. I meet different people every day. When the bar is busy, time whizzes by and when it's quiet, it seems to stand still, giving me time to read, think and just count my blessings."

They moved through the bar, "Dat is so neat, Bronagh. Is good to be happy at work. Tell me, dis Guinness stuff, why is it black?"

"Well, a couple of hundred years ago some dude fell asleep in Dublin and the barley he was roasting burnt. As they couldn't afford to throw it away and start again, they brewed it anyway and, voila, Guinness came into the world. As black as night and as dark as sin, my old Pops used to describe it, lovingly."

"I would love to try it. It is so typically Irish...discovered through a laid-back guy and turned into a success through his failure."

Bronagh liked that, "Never looked at it that way before. They sure made their burnt crop into a fortune."

"I'll get you a Guinness, Luca. First is on the house."

"Tank you, Bronagh," she answered as they reached the back of the room. Rabbie bounced up to greet her and giving her a kiss, led her off to join the others. The party stood and greeted her fondly and, as always, she felt immediately at ease in their company.

Bronagh watched, *Hot damn, you couldn't dislike that girl if you tried*, she thought to herself. *Ah well, if she's good for Rabbie, so be it, and hey, I've just made a new buddy.*

* * *

Luca listened as the guys enthused over the successful op while guzzling down schooners of beer from large jugs that the staff kept topped up. Everyone was in good humour and it was a case of 'live for the day and sod tomorrow, it'll take care of itself'.

"So yah see, Luca, it was a goddam three pronged op. The night cleaning staff were slipping the camcorders and Walkmans into false compartments in their wheelie-bins..." said Mal.

"Yessum, little lady, they hid them in a skip outside, then before the garbage contractors came on Monday, crooked security staff put the spoils in a big sack and the bin men smuggled it out..." continued Dan, proudly.

"I don't know 'ow you heathens drink zat swill," said Charles Brouchard, sipping on a fine Pinot Grigio, "Le vin de rouge a la belle France is better for you," completely changing the subject.

"Oh be quiet, you rascal," admonished Billy-Jo, "Anyway, Luca, when the garbage crew arrived, we were waiting. We'd arrested the cleaners earlier with the goods on them… That's when Buzz fell into the skip."

"Yup, and ah had to pull the little guy out by his withers afore he drowned in all the gunge."

"Holy Moly, I was chasing a garbage operator and slipped but you've got my undying gratitude."

"You sure have, Danny," agreed his wife Katie, a very pretty girl with long fair hair and big dark eyes, who hugged the big man and kissed him a big smacker on the cheek, "You're my hero, man."

Lil Danny beamed, "Should've left him to sink, missy, then ah could have come a-courting."

Buzz squirmed, embarrassed, and everyone laughed, "Goddam it, Dan, can yah not go to the circus and find an Amazon or something and leave my gal alone?"

That got more laughs. Luca was enjoying the banter; when Rabbie had introduced her to the others, they had made her feel at home and part of the group.

She asked Katie why her husband was called Buzz as well as Boomerang. Katie smiled, "Well, everyone knows why he's called Boomerang but after the Gulf War his hair fell out, so he got it all cut off in what we call over here a 'buzz-cut'."

Luca digested this. "So he got da crew-cut because he had da alopecia da?"

"Yeah, he won a Bronze Star when he took out an Iraqi machine-gun post. They reckon he saved a lot of lives. So you see he is a hero, my hero."

Luca reached over and squeezed her hand, "Da, he's a dahling. I hope his boomerang days are over because you are da nice couple. It takes two hearts to beat a tune, da?"

Katie grinned, "It's just his nerves, Luca. He's got a lot better since he went to work for OLG. Rabbie's very good to him, and he knows I'm always at home for him when needed."

"I tink dats vunderful, Katie. It so great when we can help and care for each other."

She smiled, half envious of Luca, a young woman obviously in love, deeply content, and recalling the heady moments at the start of her romance with her Buzz, her silly, but loving Boomerang.

Rabbie stood and asked the guys to join him in a toast to OLG and their successful operation. The team all stood and raised their glasses.

While he had their attention, he gave them a short pep talk, "So another satisfied client, six arrests and thousands of dollars in stolen goods recovered but most importantly…" he paused and eyed his staff, "no one was hurt, except for Boomerang's pride. I salute you all," bringing a smile to their faces and a chuckle around the table.

They raised their glasses again and drank deeply. Luca was so pleased for him. She could see the respect and affection they had for him. She realised she was proud of her man and hugged that thought to herself.

"Yep, the only casualty was Buzz's dignity. You should have seen his little legs flapping in the air," put in Billy-Jo with a laugh.

"And his clothes," added Katie, "they were covered in gunge."

"Like his mind," laughed Dan, "dark and gungy."

The craic went on all through the meal…big plates of thick sausages and lamb-chops served with large bowls of champ swimming in butter, the pieces of spring onion sticking out of the mash and adding a pleasant crunch to the potatoes.

"Dammit, why do calories and cholesterol taste so good?" groaned Billy-Jo.

Luca sipped at her Guinness, when she tried it at first, she had found it quite tart and heavy, so Bronagh added some blackcurrant juice, "What we call a 'Black Velvet', honey. Smooths it down," she told her.

"Tank you, Bronagh, it's lovely," Luca said after trying the mixture.

She noticed Rabbie watching Bronagh's departing back, "She's ver' nice, Rabbie. I like her ver' much."

Rabbie looked at her. Women could be very intuitive about possible rivals, and he sensed Luca had guessed about his short, pleasing fling with Bronagh. He tested the water, "Yeah, she's great, we had a bit of a thing going a few years back but we're just buddies now."

He expected her to be surprised but she just shrugged and stroked his hand, "Okay, I hope she meet nice man to make her as happy as me. She deserves it," and went back to her meal.

Rabbie was pleased. Luca could be quirky and wore her emotions in plain view when it came to injustices, whether it be human or animal issues, but most of the time she had her feet well planted on the ground. She had a good, steady, realistic outlook on life, and he respected her for it. He watched her chatting away easily with the gang and his love surged, the girl was a natural.

When she finished eating, she rose and kissed him, "I'll be back in an hour or so. I have to go out, it's a woman ting."

He helped her on with her coat, flummoxed, "I'll go with you…everything okay?"

She pushed him gently down into his seat, "I go get da injection…ya know…da morning after ting. You stay wiv da guys and rest on your laurels," and she was gone, a whiff of discreet perfume loitering after her, male eyes discreetly watching the beauty's departing hips.

* * *

It was 6.30pm and Juliette was sitting in the Excelsior Bar drinking her fourth Screwdriver and buzzing on coke. Several men had tried to pick her up, but she had given them her haughty withering look and they soon got the message to get lost. She was playing the ice-maiden but when Rabbie arrived, she would go onto best behaviour mode, shower him with affection, and once she got him up to her suite, she would show him what he had been missing for the last six months. She would soon have him enslaved again.

She watched the entrance to the luxurious bar from her perch on a stool at the end. Yeah, Rabbie had grown on her, he was a steadying influence and good for her, she saw that now. She'd had a brief affair with an Italian aid-worker in the Sudan, but he was almost as big a prima donna as she was and it just didn't work. Dealing with the desperate, starving masses had sapped her will, and she realised it wasn't for her. The sheer negativity and hopelessness of the situation, the corruption and unchallenged violence against the helpless refugees had decided her belief that it would never change. While the Western governments held back, afraid to get involved, it could never get any better. She might as well try to hold the tide back on the Hudson for all the good she could do.

Juliette believed it was time she settled down, and she wanted to do that with Rabbie DeJames. All she had to do was convince him, and she didn't think she would have much trouble doing that.

A striking woman entered the bar and looked around her until her gaze lit on Juliette, and she strode purposefully over. "You are Juliette Castananda, da? I recognise you from the posters, I am Luca, I have a message for you."

Juliette looked at her warily. Years of drug abuse had made her paranoid and suspicious, she sensed bad news coming. "Luca. What type of name is that? Good name for a cat. What's your message and hurry up? I'm waiting for someone, and I don't do autographs."

Luca snorted, "You're ver' arrogant. Vy vould I vant the autograph of you? It not as if you the 'Brain of America' or you do anyting vorthvile."

Juliette bristled, "Who the fuck do you think you're bloody talking to? Give me the message and then piss off, Luca, meeowww," and sniggered cattily.

Luca leant into her, "The message is, Ju-li-ette, Rabbie DeJames won't be coming. He is otherwise engaged. Got it?"

"Whatcha mean…not coming? Where is he and what the fuck has it to do with you?" Juliette's voice rose with every word, her cheeks infusing with colour in anger.

As Luca watched the arrogant supermodel in front of her go very red in the face, undeniably gorgeous, she wondered what Rabbie had ever seen in her. This woman could never love anyone but herself, let alone a decent guy like Rabbie. She reeked poison like some nocturnal tropical plant leaking a deadly fragrance to attract its unwary prey before closing its strong petals over them and slowly digesting them with its acid.

"He is otherwise engaged. Wiv me…ve are in love, and I ask you to leave us alone. Ve are ver' happy, and I don't vont him troubled by da likes of you."

Juliette leapt off her stool and glowered at Luca, almost shouting now, "Whatcha mean, the likes of me? Rabbie and I have something special…so butt your skanky arse out. Now where is he?"

Luca stood her ground, "He is with his friends, people who appreciate him and don't abuse his trust. After he vill come home with me to bed…our home and our bed. Do you understand, Ju-li-ette? He doesn't love you, he loves me with all his heart."

Juliette snarled and put her face right into Luca's, the bartender watching anxiously, "Listen, you ignorant, immigrant ignoramus, and listen carefully. I am Juliette Castananda of the Royal House of Ethiopia, and you don't tell me what to do." She contradicted herself, forgetting her roots and that she was a guest in the USA herself.

Luca pushed her away with both hands, lifted the full glass of Screwdriver off the bar and dumped it over her dreadlocks. "Then you should act like the princess, now leave us alone in future or dis immigrant will, as Arnie ses, be back."

Luca turned her back on her killer stilettoes, and strode purposely towards the door. She heard Juliette come storming up behind her, side-stepped, turning at the last second, and put her foot out and Juliette tripped over the dainty ankle and crashed full length across a table of shocked onlookers from Oslo, spread-eagled across the table, drenched in spilt alcohol, legs flailing.

478

Luca laughed, "Dat suits you, princess, you spread dem too easily in public."

The drinkers tittered behind their drinks, and the bartender smiled as Luca walked out, not a care in the world.

When she got back to Maloney's, Rabbie looked at her quizzically, "Okay, Luca? You took your time," he looked at his watch.

"Yeah, der vas a queue, must have been a whole lotta spurning done at da weekend."

"Sure was," he said, smiling fondly at her, he glanced at the watch again, a nice Oyster Rolex.

"You gotta be somevere, lover?"

His face cleared, "No, nothing important. Whatcha wanna drink?"

"I stick to da Black Velvets. Is a drink fit for a queen, I tink."

* * *

The next morning over breakfast Luca was gazing dreamily into space. She could sure get used to regular spurning. To think that something so deliciously wonderful was absolutely free. She tried to pull her thought back to the present but when she looked at Rabbie over her coffee cup, its rim halfway to her lips, the coffee was forgotten as she lost herself in thoughts of the previous night's lovemaking.

He was frowning at the paper, "Vots da matter, my Gallant Knight? Vot disturbs you?"

Sighing, he put the paper down, "Just some super-rich model wrecked the Excelsior bar after a confrontation with an unknown female." He looked at her intently – could it be? No not his gentle, caring Luca, "Then the cops came and found coke in her room and arrested her."

Luca shrugged, "Life's a lottery, dahling. You vould tink someone like dat vould be out doing good in da vorld, not acting da spoilt brat and wrecking it."

He looked at her, doubt creasing his brow, she stood and her wrap fell open, revealing her curves, and all thoughts of the news story disappeared.

She put her hand out, enticing him, "Come, my Knight, you can spurn me again before we go to work."

The next fortnight passed in a blur for the two lovers. Rabbie wined and dined her and they made love whenever they could. although at times they were content to just relax in each other's arms and talk quietly about whatever came to mind. Enjoying the nearness and warmth while they got to know each other.

Luca became very relaxed and kept herself busy at work. Philomena came in every morning for coffee and would extol Big Mal's prowess, and Luca would smile, knowingly. What Rabbie and her had was special and not for the office gossip circuit.

Peter Schuster passed away on May Day after a long illness, and Philli was made a full partner. Luca had Simon over for dinner once a week and visited him regularly. He had been with Peter for a long time and missed him very much. She could see the gratitude in the distraught man's eyes, happy that he hadn't been forgotten. "I lost my Papa very young, and it is da pleasure to me if you would be my new Papa, da."

Rabbie was relaxed too and so chilled at work, Elaine noticed the vast difference in his mood. Juliette rang several times demanding his attention but Elaine fielded the calls, telling her Rabbie was unavailable for the foreseeable future. Rabbie never answered his cell to her. One day she arrived at the office demanding an audience, but Elaine sent her away with a flea in her ear. Elaine grinned to herself. The boss was getting a good boffing... Luca was getting a good boffing. Everybody was happy and it was full steam ahead in the OLG household.

"Whatcha tell her, Elaine?" Rabbie wanted to know.

"Just the truth, Boss, that you were happy without her and to go find a high catwalk and jump off it or I would clock her one."

Rabbie returned to his office shaking his head and laughing, "You put the whole meaning of the term 'Protective Executive PA' off the scale. Thanks, Mum," and closed his door.

Elaine leant back in her chair, satisfied, if the boss was happy, she was happy and the SS OLG New York was full steam ahead, without any outside distractions. "See, Boss," she told his closed door, "Ah told ya Luca was good for ya."

At that moment said Luca came traipsing in carrying bags and looking very fetching in a mid-thigh, flared summer dress in a pretty shade of green, which set her figure off to perfection. "Hey, Elaine, I found da great little café off Eleventh vich does da most fantastic pate, rolls and cheesecakes...come and join Rabbie and me for lunch."

Elaine followed her to the door and watched Luca laying the goodies out while the boss gazed at her adoringly, "I don't want to intrude, guys."

"You're not, Elaine, you're family," Rabbie told her.

"Yes, we love your company, da," agreed Luca. "Now sit vile I fetch da coffee."

Elaine sat glowing inside. She was so happy she wanted to hug herself in delight and shout to the sky with joy. Luca brought in three mugs with the coffee pot and administered to the older woman's needs before settling down to eat her lunch.

"You know, I tink I see dat supermodel in da street. You know da one always in da press with da long skinny legs? She not look ver' happy."

Elaine blew on her coffee, "Oh, don't worry about her, dear. She's a has been...has been here and now she's gone. Queen for a day, then gone forever."

Luca smiled knowingly, "Da the higher you climb, the harder you fall. C'est la vie."

II

A few days later, Wendy summoned her bestest buddy down for coffee, eager to hear all the juicy business. She sat her down and placed a big steaming mug before her, "Made yah a Russian coffee, babe, four sugars. Right, I want an inch by inch account of your night with Rabbie."

Luca sighed dreamily. *She looked radiant and content*, Wendy thought. *A rose in bloom.*

"Oh, Vendy, I soo, so in love. He so da kind and thoughtful and, vell, he Mister Vunderful," and took a slurp of her coffee and near choked. "Fruckski, Vends...vot da heck?"

Wendy patted her back, "I put a double Smirnoff in. Calm you down after your hard night of lurve."

Luca giggled, "It vasn't a hard night, it vas vunderful. Although I must da admit, my knight vas hard for me on demand. I am so da lucky and da spoilt bitch."

Wendy laughed and patted her hand, "Well, enjoy it while it lasts, Lucs. The guys tend to fade with time and it gets a bit rusty."

Luca stared at her friend, "Rusty…like in da corroded? I don't tink dat happen wiv me and Rab," semi-indignant.

"No, dear, I just mean the element of surprise dies off, and it becomes routine, but it's still great."

Luca sipped on her strong coffee thoughtfully, "Da, I guess so. I mean you and da big guy at it all the time, da?"

Wendy clapped her hands in delight, "I wish, Lucs. Between working long hours, being pissed and generally knackered, we just get down and dirty when we can. But I tell you, kiddo, he still rocks my boat, if yah get my drift."

Luca pondered on that, "So all da talk and innuendo is just da bragging?"

"Absolutely, kiddo," smiled Wendy. "Wind them up and keep them guessing. It's class and it's free and it's legal."

It was Luca's turn to clap her hands, "Dats sooo cool, and now I do same situation. I vant da crew da tink Rab and me doing it all the time," and she paused, thoughtful, then, "Veil, which we are at da moment. It's so brilliant."

"And long may it continue, Luca. He's a great guy and you're well matched. So happy for you."

Luca glowed, "Da, we sure are and I vill keep it going. I soo so in lurve…tell me, Vends, how da you and Bobs do it?"

Wendy looked at her with an astonished open mouth you could have drove a tank through, "Whatcha mean, Lucs? Whatcha wanna know?"

"Dis Ruski coffee so cool, babe. It's just, yah know, Bobs so huge and you're so sweet and petite…we just curious."

Wendy reflected, "Well, obviously he does not do a big belly flop on me. I would be hamburger mince. No, I very much dictate, and we manage and he seems content enough so there yah go. Thought you down to give me the gory details of you and 'Superstud'."

"No, it just too da intimate and sooo incredibly personal, I don't want to share it wiv nobody but the angels of love, who have given this wondrous blessing to me," and she slurped more vodka-rich blend and took Wendy's hand, "We vundered, you know…do you and da big guy do it on da kitchen table? Do you recommend it as a good position?"

Wendy went into hysterics, tears tripping her, "Yeah, it's class. He gets right in like Errol Flynn…frig's sake, Lucs, just buy a copy of the Kama Sutra and work your way through it. You're happy. I'm happy."

Luca was pleased and hugged her, "Tanks, Vendy, I never forget all dat you do for me, and I always be your bestest buddyess."

Wendy was chuffed, mollified, and made Luca another Russian coffee. They sat and chatted away like two sparrows in a gutter after a prolonged bout of rain and the sun had just come out.

"Hey, Lucs, what me and the Big Guy got yah. Had them made specially in the T-shirt shop in Bloomingdales. You can wear them tonight when we go to 'Texas Tom's'. It's our treat," and thrust a bag into her hand, grinning wickedly.

Luca thanked her, drank her doctored coffee down and hugged her, "I go now, Vends. Maybe I catch him coming outta shower and give him a Luca Special."

"You are so special, babe," Wendy said, "Am so frigging happy for the pair of yah."

Luca left, eyes moist and horny for her lover.

He was indeed showering when she arrived back, so she made two Ruski coffees and took them down to the bedroom. She had missed him and wondered at that. He was wearing just a towel round his waist, drying his hair. She gave him a lingering kiss and took over. She pulled out his T-shirt, a nice navy blue and put it on over his head.

"Vends got us these, says it da cement our love. We vear dem tonight in public."

Rabbie looked at the front and laughed. A big 'HERS' with an arrow to the right, in big white letters dominated it. Luca opened her coat and showed him hers, which said 'HIS' with an arrow.

"Well, I guess the thought was genuine and as we are only going to Texas Tom's Chilli House, I'll just go wiv da flow," he agreed.

"Da, you can scoff da red hot chilli to your heart's content," she promised, combing his hair, liking the domesticity of the situation, "And his BBQ ribs da die for. Then ven we get home, you can give me da spare rib all right."

"Spare rib, Luca?" puzzled.

Her eyes lit wickedly, "Da," and she fondled his manhood. "The one I love and that shoots da BBQ sauce when chewed."

He had to laugh, this was a new Luca. Happy, carefree and wanton. Whilst he loved every faucet of her personality, he liked this devilish lady in lust aspect to her. He pulled his jeans on, "You are one horny, outrageous vixen but I'll certainly give it my best shot."

"Oh, don't you da worry, my knight, you vill. Now come, we are running da late and I'm ravenous."

He chuckled again, "You're always hungry," and drank his coffee down. "Wow, new blend. Now that's what I call strong."

"Da, it da extra strong Columbian wiv da Ruski surprise. Now, come, we go, my love."

He happily followed her out, none the wiser.

'Texas Tom's' was full of high-spirited, beer-guzzling, rib-munching beefeaters, cavorting and chewing the cud merrily. They located a table and shed their jackets and watched the antics of the line dancers, laughing at their mistakes, cheering when they got it right. It was great fun and congenial, and Luca loved every minute of it. It was good to see people happy and enjoying great food and company.   '

Mal, Lil' Danny, Philli, Billy-Jo, Buzz and Katey joined them and soon they were quaffing down pitchers of Bud and chomping on foot-long ribs and steaming bowls of red hot Tex chilli.

A pretty waitress dressed as Dolly Parton leant over Rab's shoulder, "Your T-shirt's awesome. Such a bold public statement."

"Yeah, par'ner. Ah didn't think yah'll would be so open, man. Guess yah want ta whole goddamn world to know," Danny remarked.

"Took yah time, Boss dude," Buzz put in, "but hey, what a thing to brag about!"

Rabbie was munching contently on the fiery repast, "What are you guys wittering about?" he wanted to know, bemused.

"It's not the sort of thing we brag about in Turkey, Rab, only after the couple are wed. Guys have been stoned to death for taking maidens' flowerhoods," Mal told him darkly.

Billy-Jo chuckled, "In the depths of Tennessee, y'all be heading for a shotgun wedding."

Katey put her oar in, "Buzz wouldn't last down there, Billy-Jo...stop ogling the waitress, Buzz."

"Just wondered if they were real, Katey. Always wondered if Dolly's were kosher if you get my drift."

Katey punched him, "Real or not, you're with me tonight, so just appreciate whatcha have."

Buzz put his arm around her consolingly, "Doncha worry, honey. My eyes are stuck on you and every guy in the room is jealous because I'm with the prettiest gal in New York."

They all smiled at them and Lil' Dan gave Buzz a pat on the back, "Good on yah, par'ner. Ah guess ah better rein mah horse up and hang up mah spurs where yah Katey's concerned."

Everyone laughed at that, and Rabbie excused himself and went to the bathroom. He was confused because muffled laughter and tittering behind hands followed his departing back. Washing his hands in the rest room, a large guy said to him, "Now that's what I call a sexual contemporary fashion statement, man. Hope she was worth it."

Rab quickly finished up, "Don't know whatcha on about, guy, but if you're trying to pick me up, you need to keep it simpler," and he hustled out hastily.

More laughs followed his back as he returned to his table, and when he looked at the back of Luca's T-shirt, realisation dawned, and he nearly dropped with embarrassment and wished the floor would open up and swallow him.

On the back of her T-shirt it read, I lost my 'cherry' in the 'Big Apple'.

Everybody looked at him. Amused.

He pulled his T-shirt off, and twirled it around and read it. I took her 'cherry' in the 'Big Apple'. He began to chortle and guffaw and then he was howling with laughter as was the whole table.

He dressed and sat down next to her, gasping.

"Oh Chrissakes, Lucs, that's brilliant. Talk about being had... Apparently, we have made a new sexual fashion statement," and he looked at a victorious Wendy, the tears tripping her. "And you, Staff Nurse Havilland, watch your rear for a while... I'll get yah back."

Luca hugged him. "I just vant da world dah know we are in da love and you very special."

He went happily back to his chilli, delighted.

Buzz nudged Little Danny. "Lucky dude. Wish I'd been there," and promptly got a dead arm.

* * *

Later at home, Luca looked unsure, "Vas da T-shirt thing a bit too much, my love?"

He pulled her into a clinch. "Outstanding, my angel. Unusual, but definitely a huge ego boost."

She went tight into him. "It just I so in lurve and proud, I want the whole world to know."

483

He pulled away and looked into her outstanding eyes. "And I'm proud and love you completely and entirely. Okay?"

Reassured, she let him go. "Da is ver' good now, let's go hide da spare rib between the meat sandwich and make some cement."

He followed her down to the bedroom, chuckling. Now that one would certainly need some working out.

She was outstanding.

III

A few nights later Rabbie woke in the early hours to an empty bed, Luca's side of the bed was cold. Unease gripped him as he pulled on trackies and checked the apartment but all was quiet, except for the humming of the big Frigidaire. He took the small 8mm Taurus he kept for personal protection at home, checked the load and chambered a round. The front door was ajar an inch and the alarm system had been turned off.

Dread seized him, you didn't run a successful security firm in a huge high crime metropolis without being aware you would make enemies, and Rabbie was an aware kind of guy. Something was seriously out off kilter here. He knew Luca didn't like going out alone at night and the dimly lit, silent halls and stairwells spooked her.

With his pistol before him in a two-fisted combat stance, he searched for her, each corner and door, methodically making his way downwards. When he reached her old apartment, he noticed the door was slightly open, and he was gripped by déjà vu as he recalled the night he had disturbed the pervert Hanlon and his thugs.

He nudged the door open with the barrel of his gun. Light filtered down from the living room and soft music came down the hall to meet him. He sidled forward, weapon raised, and pushed the door open.

The living room was lit by candles, casting flickering shadows on the walls. Tchaikovsky's 'Nutcracker Suite' played softly from the stereo, and she had pushed all the furniture back to give her space to dance.

He gazed mesmerised as she pirouetted, leaped and twirled on tiptoe in full ballerina mode. She looked magnificent in her full ensemble of pink nylon, chiffon and lace.

He lowered his weapon and edged through the door and eased himself onto the closest armrest, as the beautiful creature danced unerringly to the lovely music. It was magical and mesmerising, and he had never seen anything quite like it in his life and was totally caught up in the moment. Time seemed to stand still and, when the music reached its crescendo and gradually petered out, she swooped down to the floor, legs out straight arms up and head bowed. Proud, inspiring and the mistress of her own femininity, the eternal flame to the mystery that is woman.

She slowly relaxed, regained her breath and looked him in the eye, "So sorry, Rabbie, tis something I had to get out my system."

He grinned sheepishly, "I was worried. I thought you had run off and left me for the milkman."

She came over on her knees and wrapped her arms lightly around, with her head buried into his chest, "I vould never leave you unless you told me to go."

He stroked her hair, "Can't see me doing that. Wanna tell me what it's all about?"

484

She looked up at him, the candlelight illuminating her face and making her eyes shine. Tears had gathered and welled at the corners, and he gently wiped them away with his thumbs.

"I had to cleanse my flat for the next people, chase the bad spirits out. I had to face my demons and cast them out of my life."

"And have you cleansed, chased and cast you demons away?"

She ran her hand across his strong chest, "Yes, I believe so. It was scary, but it had to be done."

"I think that's one of the bravest things I've ever seen," he told her truthfully. "You know, Luca, you're under no obligation to me for what I done that night, no debt of gratitude, you're a free spirit. I don't want to hold you back through a debt that was never offered or planned."

She gave him a hesitant smile, "Vill you make love to me now, my Gallant Knight, to complete the ritual? I don't want to be a free spirit because my spirit is entwined with yours for life. It is karma, my darling, and so meant to be… The past is the past and all I see is the long summer of our future together.

He helped her off with her outfit and they made love on the floor, slowly and gently, then reaching the crescendo like the music that had gone before them, both making timeless moves and rhythms of the ageless dance of procreation. It was all the reassurance she needed, and their everlasting love and fate together was sealed forever that night on her Kaftan rug.

Afterwards, they lay together, and Luca smoked a rare cigarette, feeling pure and replete. She felt at ease with her love. "Tis strange dis love ting, Rab," she mused, "Who is giving and who is taking?"

He shrugged, "I guess it's a bit of both. It's what makes for a good relationship and makes it stick the distance."

She blew a perfect smoke ring, "Ven you take me, I am giving but when you come, you know, I am taking part of you and you are giving. It's da quid pro quo."

He laughed, "That's way too deep for me, Luca. I'm just a simple security man."

She gave him a mischievous look, "Vell yes, you were well deep…deep inside me, and ven ve both come the same time, ve both taking off each other at once."

He pulled her to her feet, "Come on, Socrates. Let's get you home. I'll take the morning off, and we'll have brunch at Mama Jocelyn's."

She was thrilled. He was so understanding, and he gave her so much without even realising he was doing it. "You know, Rab… I think God broke the mould when he made you because he didn't want any more competition."

He closed the door to her apartment after them with a satisfying finality.

IV

Santa Monica, Los Angeles, Mid June, 2013

Rabbie threaded his way across the busy boardwalk to the steps that led to the beach, keeping a wary eye out for skateboarders and rollerbladers.

He liked the Angelinos but they always seemed in a mad hurry to get from A to B as fast as possible.

Carefully weaving through the throng of bikini-clad beach-babes and bronzed muscle-bound posers out enjoying the mid-day heat, he skirted the family groups playing and cavorting on the beach or just lying catching the rays. It was a hive of good-natured activity.

He ducked as a Frisbee whizzed past his head and then hopped to one side to avoid a small dog scampering around and digging up the sand. "Hey sorry, dude," said a stunning, well-toned lady in a micro bikini, "One of those ices for me?"

He grinned, "Sorry, ma'am, already names on them."

"Shame, handsome. I guess lil' old lonesome me will have to get one for myself."

Laughing, he plodded on, "Guess so, ma'am." Christ, the Californians were so forward, friendly to a fault but there were no back doors in them, and they said what they thought. They gave a whole other layer to the term laid-back.

Luca was lying under a beach umbrella, chatting with his Uncle Davey. She looked magnificent in a black bikini, which set off her perfect figure. No liposuction or implants there and he reckoned she put the rest to shame, but then he was a teensy weensy bit biased. He counted his lucky stars every day that this incredible female was sharing his life, and amazingly, their love seemed to grow stronger all the time. Even on the short trek to the ice cream shack, he couldn't wait to get back to her.

He knew he was over protective but Luca said it would pass in time, especially when the trial was over in August, and they would grow relaxed and comfortable with each other like a pair of well-loved slippers. Worn in and happy together but one would not be the same without the other.

He liked that metaphor. The girl was amazing and kept him amused with some of the gems that came out of that luscious mouth, a mouth he constantly wanted to devour. He wanted to captivate and keep conquering that perfect Cupid's bow at every opportunity. Was he a guy in love or was he a guy in love? Life was good...no...it was fan-fucking-tastic and the best thing about it...he knew his Luca felt the same.

He placed the tray of ices down and mock scowled at his uncle, "How come it's always me has to go get the ice cream?"

"Because you're the big tough marine and we're the guys who served in the real army."

Laughing, he plonked himself down on the towel beside Luca, "Tank you so much, dahling," she said as she kissed him. That made it all worthwhile, he would have walked to the North Pole to get her ice if she asked him.

"Anyway, Uncle Dee, without the Royal Marines to pull you guys out of the crapper, where would you be now?"

Davey grunted non-committedly, eyes inscrutable behind his Ray-Bans as he gazed out to sea, "Guess someone had to do it. Come on, Sharon, let's go swimming."

Sharon, an attractive blonde in her thirties and twenty years his junior, pouted. "You know I don't like the water when it gets deep. Freaks me out, man."

Davey pulled her up, muscles rippling. At six foot three he was fit, tanned and no pushover. A number of scars adorned his body, hallmarks of the years he had spent on active service.

His friend and comrade in arms jumped up, "Oh leave her be, ya big galoot, I'll go with ya. Don't want you scaring the sharks."

Philip 'Scoobie' Martin was a giant of a man. Close-cropped dark hair and the build and girth of a human bulldozer, he had a wide-open face with a large nose, which had been broken on numerous occasions, splayed across it.

Scoobie had served with Davy all through their army days and now both worked for OLG Los Angeles. In what capacity Rabbie wasn't sure, but he knew they often went abroad and when he asked, his dad just said, "Troubleshooting," and didn't elaborate.

"Don't you be messing with the sharks, love," his wife, a no-nonsense English lady called Marlene, warned, "The Great White's endangered and so are you," she laughed.

"I'll bring one back for the pool," and, grabbing an ice, he ran off after Davey.

Rabbie grabbed an ice too, "Sod it, better go keep an eye on them," and he bounded off down the beach.

Luca watched his departing back, fondly. He was so kind, thoughtful, caring, considerate, handsome, strong, and sexy, well just near perfect, except for his penchant for hot canned chilli but she could live with that. The fact was he was her life and she was so in love. She couldn't imagine life without him, and they had known each other less than four months.

Luca gave a huge sigh of contentment. Marlene watched the beautiful young Russian, happy for both of them, "Boys, oh Luca. They are so easily pleased. God help the sharks."

Luca came back to reality with a start, "Sharks, oh St Mary of Moscow! I tink dey were only kidding, da."

"It's okay, Luca, there are no sharks this close inshore," she consoled the worried girl, "Anyhow, only a suicidal shark would go near those mad men."

Sharon sighed, she felt very much the outsider. Marlene had been at her work and done a bit of matchmaking, but she knew Big Davey picked women up and discarded them like used coats, and there were no vibes of interest off him at all. He had no romance in his soul, hated shopping and trivial conversation. He would drift off into his own world for hours and didn't seem to realise he did it.

Marlene had told her he had been badly hurt a few years ago and just needed the right woman to help him get over it; somehow she doubted it was her, besides he was too much hard work.

"This ain't working, Marlene. Think I'll go browse the boutiques," and grabbing her sarong, trudged off dejectedly, shoulders slumped.

They watched her go and Marlene shrugged, "Oh well, easy come easy go. How are you enjoying your trip, honey?"

Luca gave her the satisfied smile of a woman who was getting copious amounts of loving and special attention. Watching the lovely girl, Marlene felt happy for her and Rabbie. She remembered fondly Scoobie's rough but tentative approach to romance and how she had to take the bull by the horns and steer him in the right direction to win her affections. She thought whimsically of how he had chased her till she caught him, and laughed to herself, those were the days, and she wouldn't swop her life now for a second.

"You look like the cat who got the cream."

Luca pondered that, "Vot a lovely saying, yes I am indeed a happy, fulfilled pussy."

Marlene looked at her in disbelief, then cracked up. "I don't believe you said that," she chortled merrily.

Luca answered, perplexed, "Vot I say so funny, Marlene?"

Marlene explained and Luca laughed, "Ah I see, da pussy...ver' good. What a nice name for it. Yes, that part of me is also ver' happy. It gets a good stroking and loads of cream."

That got Marlene going again, the Ruski was hilarious, "And long may it continue, Luca. The more the better, I say."

Luca looked at her straight-faced, "If I get much more, Marlene, I be able to open da dairy."

Marlene looked her in the eye and saw the mischievous twinkle and burst into stitches, rolling and holding her sides, eyes watering.

Luca grinned, happy, "I tell Scoobie you need some cream, and he should fill you up tonight. You can put it in your coffee in da morning."

Marlene gathered herself and looked at her, gasping, "No more, please don't Luca, I'm an old married woman."

"It's nice when in da espresso, whip it in da mocha, beef up da Nescafe, ole."

Marlene's lips started twitching again and then she was off. Rolling around, legs waving and howling in delight, to the amusement of the other sun worshippers.

"Espresso, oh my Gawd!" she roared.

Luca smirked and went back to her magazine. She was finally getting the hang of this strange Americano/Brit humour. It was very simple really, and she had been putting too many slants on it. Marlene looked at her panting. "Please, Luca, no more."

Luca turned a page nonchalantly. "You can whip it, Marlene then put it on da trifle with da cherry on top."

Marlene thought she was dying as she screeched with glee, breathless and lost in the sheer absurdity of the thing. "That's freaking brilliant, Luca... You should be on the stage."

Luca thought, finger to mouth, "Da, I am on da stage on Sundays at the club, den I go home to the dairy express to get cream for da pussy. Rabbie da 'Milky Bar Kidski'."

Marlene was curled up in a ball now, helpless with mirth as the men came trotting back, and they stood round Marlene, amazed. "Oh maaah Gawd!!! 'The Milky Bar Kid', that's brill."

'Is she okay?" asked Scoobie, helping his overwrought wife up, brushing sand off her fine tanned legs.

Luca looked up from her magazine. "Da, she fine, Scoob. We were just talking dairy products and she took da turn. You have to produce da cream tonight, big guy, for Marlene's espresso machine."

They had to carry Marlene away and put her under a cold shower, Scoobie looking perplexed.

Rabbie plonked himself down next to Luca. "Good to see you girls have bonded. I don't even want to know... Where's Sharon?"

Luca rolled over and pulled him down into a smouldering kiss. When they came up for breath, she whispered in his ear. "Sharon has gone. She not getting any cream. Tis so sad."

Rabbie kissed her again. Happy she was happy. He reached for the sun cream, and Luca smiled sweetly and rolled onto her front. Sure was good fun on Malibu beach.

V

They ate a scrumptious dinner that evening at Jamesey's Malibu Beach mansion. He had sold the Hollywood apartment after Collette's passing, and Simone had moved in with him at the beautiful Mexican style hacienda but their plans were to move on a more permanent basis to Chicago, where OLG had their flagship office and command centre. The 'Windy City', where they had met and fell in love. A love they neither thought they would ever experience, capture or have again.

The men had dressed for dinner and the ladies in all their finery, and Luca was enjoying the fine seafoods and meat courses served at the long mahogany table in the airy dining room…she had never seen such opulence as she drank from fine crystal and ate off bone china with solid antique silver utensils. Waiters in crisp whites catered to their every need, and Luca was savouring every minute. It was her last night in LA, and she had thoroughly enjoyed her week. She sipped on a crisp Chablis and pierced huge prawns out of her avocado pear as she gazed around the table and mused. The Angelinos called the king prawns shrimps. It was so typically North American. Everything was bigger and totally unreal at times in this vast country of 550 million people. It made a poor immigrant like herself often feel overwhelmed despite being here several years, but also anything was possible and it was an exciting and challenging prospect to know she was part of the huge American highway that zoomed along at high speed relentlessly and didn't stop for those stuck on the hard shoulder. No, you had to get in there and go with the flow or you got left behind.

Rabbie's younger brother Jamie had flown in as had his sister, Petral. Jamie was a muscular, stocky man with eyes full of mischief and luxurious dark brown hair, which he wore longer. He had flirted outrageously with her. He too was an ex-army man and ran his own security firm in the West Midlands of England. 'Stand to Security'. She liked him immensely. There was a huge charisma to him and like Rabbie, an inordinate trust and honesty in his demeanour. Very appealing to the female sex. She noticed Rabbie watching and gave him a reassuring special 'our look' and a wink.

Petral was beautiful with long dark tresses, flashing hazel eyes, a heart-shaped face and a figure to die for. She had a degree in Criminology and was in charge of some anti-terrorist unit in Northern Ireland. She knew Rabbie was worried about her serving in the troubled province and that big Jamesey wanted her to leave the force and join OLG but she was very much her own woman, and Luca was impressed. Petral was cool, calm and collected, with a huge presence of self-assuredness about her, and God help anybody who got in her way in life. She had quizzed Luca about Lithuania and Russian politics and then told her a dirty joke about three Cossacks, and Luca had liked her razor-sharp mind that could switch from topic to topic so astutely.

There was quite a gathering of OLG Global there tonight that Jamesey had flown in, and the conversation was loud and often raucous as the men caught up on things and the ladies got all the biz as to who was going with who and who had done what.

She bet she had been a topic for them. The Ruski who had snared Rabbie and would it last? She gazed over at her Rabbie, who was deep in conversation with Jamesey's partner Smudger, who ran OLG UK, and a dapper dark-skinned man in a turban called Victor, who was head of OLG operatives training worldwide.

Other, younger members of the firm, up and coming top guns were hanging on the veterans' every word and vying for position to throw in comments and suggestions.

Jamesey, very much the patriarchal figure, gazed down from the high-backed wooden carved chair at the head of the table and watched fondly, if not a little regally, and threw in the odd remark that the young bloods seized on and expounded upon, which he would benignly digest, along with his food, before answering his interested acolytes. Luca saw very much where he had got his Viking moniker from. Despite being sixty-three, he still had a full head of dark blonde hair and a thick moustache, which tapered down to the edge of his chin and she could imagine him at the prow of a long-ship in the dark ages, battle axe in hand, looking for lands to conquer.

Rabbie had told her Jamesey had gathered them together because he had important announcements to make. There was an expectancy that underlaid the vibrant atmosphere. It was a gathering of strong, powerful people, many who had been to war and had killed their fellow men, albeit in a kill or be killed capacity, and Luca didn't want to dwell on that too much, being very much a pacifist at heart, but there was also an underlying strong sense of fairness and honesty aboard, and she guessed Jamesey picked his leaders carefully and commanded their loyalty and respect by leading by example.

Her thoughts were reinforced a few minutes later at the end of the meal when Jamesey stood and took a swathe of white envelopes off a silver platter a waiter offered.

An expectant hush fell across the gathering as he eyed them keenly, before he began, "As of this time next year I am standing down as chairman of OLG."

Looks of dismay and disbelief crossed the faces of his audience. "I will be staying on the board and will be open for consultation and any advice an old warhorse like me can give." He eyed them one by one. "It's been a long, heady journey. Hugely satisfying and I know I leave the company in the finest hands and the best minds possible," he took a draught of the fine Laphroaig whiskey he had recently took a liking to. "In the envelopes I will be handing out are the new promotions and transfers you have been waiting for and richly deserve," he paused for effect, then raised his glass. "Open them tomorrow. Let's enjoy tonight... To OLG Global. From strength to strength."

They rose as one and drank deep. He sat, satisfied, and took their thunderous applause as his due.

The King is dead, long live the King.

* * *

Collette would have loved this, he mused as the whiskey did its magic and dulled the memories.

On the flight back Luca watched him intently. "Vhy don't you open the envelope, dahling?"

He sighed and pulled it out of his inside pocket, ripped it open with a thumbnail and read it quickly. He gazed out the window at the clouds, pensive.

"Well, vot it says?"

"He wants me to head Los Angeles and oversee Houston and Miami. It's a huge promotion."

She hugged him, "Dat's vunderful! Congratulations dahling. Can we live on da Malibu Beach?"

He looked at her in wonder. "But what about New York? Your job?"

She shrugged. "Then we enjoy our last year in the Big Apple. I can work from home. Life is a never-ending journey till the road stops."

He kissed her, relieved and amazed. She was incredible and his mate for life, 'by hell or high water', as they say in the Royal Marine Commandos.

* * *

Back home safe that night they relaxed, enjoying the privacy. "The light doesn't shine on you…it's in you," he whispered in her ear.

Luca stroked his face tenderly, "Dat's so sweet, Rab. Dere is a poet in your Viking heart, I tink."

He grinned, "Naw, my dad's the Viking. I'm just good ol' Rabbie, Security Consultant par excellence."

She moved closer to him, "Oh no, my dahling, I don't know what you did in those dark years. You won't talk about in da special boat thingy but you fought da fight on da foreign shores like the Vikings and returned triumphant," and she caressed his face again and gazed at him adoringly, "and came back alive, albeit with a few scars; physical and mental, so you could meet and rescue your Luca… Is karma, dahling. You'll always be my Viking…" and she chuckled deep from the throat… "Especially in da bed, you heathen. You have certainly conquered my fertile plains and valleys."

Rabbie mused on that, she was so bloody intuitive and smart, and he had no answer to it. He decided to do some more ravaging on her beautiful body and made love to her again, much to her intense pleasure.

After they lay panting, Rabbie bounced out of bed and produced a bottle of good Beaujolais and a selection of cheese, fruit, olives, pickles and assorted crackers. They sipped and chewed happily, listening to Loretta Lynn on an oldies radio station.

"She was a great artiste and poetess," she informed Rab, munching on a ripe Bric and Ritz cracker, "her talent as a singer took her from a hovel in Kentucky to luxury in Hollywood." She popped a grape into her mouth and popped one into his mouth too, "But unfortunately, she lost 'Bobby Magee' on the way… Such is the price of stardom."

Rabbie had never heard of Loretta Lynn or Bobby Magee and decided not to go there, "Yeah, she sounds good, but you're better. You could make a mint yourself if you went commercial," then he paused, "and be famous and make a 'Bobby Magee' out of me."

She handed him a Jacob's cream cracker with Danish Blue, "No, my love. I don't think Bobby Magee was very good to her. Anyhow, if I didn't have to sing to raise da extra dosh to bring Mama and Dimitri over, why I would sing for free? I am an idealistic woman, not da materialistic."

He nodded, "You sure are, and it's very refreshing in this sad, money-orientated world."

She agreed, "Pass me a slice of that Jarlsberg, dahling, please... Thank you... Vhen I sing if one unhappy person in the crowd cheers up and goes away happy, den my job is done. I have obtained my goal for the night and my art form has been a success...otherwise, why sing in public at all if it has no impact on others beside yourself?"

Rabbie didn't know if it was the wine talking through her, so decided to play devil's advocate, "Hey, I've heard you singing in the bath to yourself, so how does that impact or influence anybody else?"

She chomped on Edam and a pickled onion, "Veil, it had an impact on you, Rabbie, because yesterday I was singing Sinead O'Connor in the bath and before I knew it, you were in the bath with me."

Rabbie laughed, "Yeah, it's like a mental health food for me. I guess you have to practise."

Luca went for the Stilton and Melon, "Veil, yes, but hey, it had da impact on you, so I prove my point."

He smiled, "It certainly did, I have to say that Camembert is superb. Our Toni always comes up trumps."

Luca chewed on a knob of Jarlsberg and added a few blueberries, "Norwegian cheese is good...extremely pure. I bet da Vikings ate it for strength."

He went for the Gruyere and grabbed a few remaining grapes. "Hard to beat mature Batiste Cheddar melted on toast... Now that I would sing for."

"We love what we know, my dahling. I sing on my own to practise so I am good so I can sing better so people can feel better after they hear me and leave happy in their minds."

She repeatedly astonished him – with her unselfish, astute mind, "And you do. Now supper done, you must be tired? Let's get a few hours' kip, Johnny Nodd is swinging off my eyelids."

She stroked his thigh enticingly and moved her hand higher, "Is time, am tired but cheese makes Luca horny. Will you spurn me once more before Johnny Nodd comes, please?"

Tiredness forgotten, he rolled her over, brushing crumbs off her fine breasts and as he covered her, he put lots more selections of world cheeses from Antonio's tomorrow. Know your enemy but know your lover better to keep her happy. As Mary Poppins said and his life was now, 'Practically perfect in every way'.

Chapter 35
Marriage... A Triumph of Hope over Adversity

Early October, 1984, Garston, North London

She crumbled the paper up and hurtled it across the grotty room. "How the frig had her wet dish rag daughter landed a cushy number like that? And found an up and coming businessman to sponge off as well," she wondered. Christ, life was so unfair. She kicked out at the cat, which ran off hissing.

At forty-five, despite years of self-abuse through alcohol and soft drugs, Janet Stark still retained relative good looks. After her husband was murdered six years ago, she had given up her job in the Queen Boadicea pub and operated from home, much to the annoyance of the neighbours, but the area was rapidly deteriorating and the housing people used it as a sink hole for the homeless, down and outs and newly arrived immigrants, and the crime rate was soaring and the 'Old Bill' had enough to contend with and left her alone, unless they got a specific complaint. To prove a house was being used as a brothel took many nights of observation, gathering evidence of men coming and going, car numbers, unusual behaviour late at night and then they had to raid the place on warrant, catch the punter in flagrante delecto (in the act) and prove money changed hands, and they didn't have the resources. It was easier to catch the street walkers and curb crawlers around Casio Park and the top of town and haul them before the magistrate. It kept the traders happy and looked good in the paper.

Anyway, Janet was careful. She only took enough punters to provide her enough for drink, wacky baccy and to pay the rent and gas, and if she was short one week, she would pop down the local and do a bit of business out back.

She had run a couple of girls for a while, scrawny little mares from up north, but they were always squabbling and leaving their mess lying about and tried lying to her about how many tricks they turned a night and nobody short-changed Janet Stark.

Besides, the steady stream of randy drunks attracted 'Lily Law', who swooped several times to stop fights and other disturbances, and she threw them out on the street. No, Janet was a lone operator and that's the way she liked it; after all, the council had been kind enough to take her kids away and raise them so she could be alone and her sod of a hubby had been decent enough to dip his wick in another woman's snatch, where it wasn't wanted, so she could utilise her time to her own ends and she should show her appreciation for the free space it gave her.

She stared around the room. Wallpaper was peeling from a damp spot in the corner, the carpet was threadbare and the TV was on its last legs. She lit up a Regal Kingsize and put her feet up on the scarred coffee table, deep in thought. She was alone in the world now. She felt no regret at her children going into care. Better off for the little sods. She wasn't born to motherhood, she knew that and it was for the best, but she was getting older and the barren years stretched ahead of her. Oh she'd had a fine old time, she thought, as she took a slug of vodka from the bottle. She had taken to sex like a duck to water from an early age. An only daughter too, her father had been at her from an early age as had several of her five brothers. There was no violence. They gave her sweets and pop to make her keep their dirty little secret, and she realised the powerful hold sex held over men. Pathetic sods, addicted wankers.

She grinned ruefully. God, over the years she had accommodated more dicks than a regiment of guardsmen and never paid a penny in tax. She should get a reward for services to the male libido but somehow she didn't think the snotty old Queen would be asking her to a garden party. Probably be afraid she would shag the staff, then she laughed as she glugged more vodka, or that stuck up toff of a hubby of hers, who was always slagging off the foreigners. Now that would be one for the papers, imagine that splashed across the Sun or the Mirror. 'Duke of Edinburgh Abdicates for Garston Sex Bomb'.

She tottered over to the crumpled paper and took it back to the sofa and read the article again.

'Local Security Firm Goes from Strength to Strength' blazoned the Watford Echo.

'Security firm, 'On La Guardia Security', in offices at 149, High Street, announced today it has brought another four armoured trucks after landing a lucrative contract to collect and deliver all monies to the Ladbrokes chain of bookmakers in Herts and North London.

'"We have already made a great success of our own alarm systems, having our own factory in Harrow," explained Managing Director, Mr DeJames. But with another four trucks, we can employ another sixteen guards, which is a good boost to the local economy."

'OLG already employs sixty staff full-time and provides a full service in all aspects of security work.

'"We pride ourselves on our professional service and discretion when needed. All work guaranteed and no job too small," said Mr Smyth, Joint Managing Director. 'Full force! Full Discretion', company motto.'"

Janet read on "Blah, blah, blah," she scoffed as the journalist detailed the successes the firm had achieved and services provided but what caught her eye was another quote from the DeJames bloke.

'"The office is run by my fiancée, Collette, and she runs a tight ship, I can assure you, so I have to be on my best behaviour at all times."

'"Without Miss Stark the office would be turmoil but she is a one-woman army and keeps us all up to speed, and all the staff wish her and Mr DeJames many years of happiness for their impending wedding," said Mr Waton, OLG Head of Security Systems.

'In their open-plan office OLG exudes an air of calm, competent efficiency. Clients are met in pleasant interview rooms and the staff are well turned out and pleasant. It seems to be a winning combination. Miss Stark, an attractive brunette with a no-nonsense manner explains, "We treat all employees as an extended family and strive to give them the best work conditions and on-the-job training possible. We respect their views and are open to ideas. The boss' doors are always open to them."'

What really got Janet was the group photo of some of the employees and the top brass. DeJames was a looker all right and there was his Collette. Looking smart in a top of the range suit, hair immaculate and looking wet, happy. Like the bleeding cat who had finally got the canary. She thought back to the skinny little snot-nosed brat she used to slap about and used to whine to be fed and cried when she locked her in her room at night so she could go and make a few bob so she could put a crust on the table.

She finished the dregs in the bottom of the vodka bottle and hurled it at the cat that was peeking around the door warily. Fucking ungrateful bitch! Here was her mother on skid row, and her ponce of a waste of a daughter was getting married to a hunk and living the high life. I don't think so, daughter, unless...? Pound signs flashed across her eyes, and when Janet Stark sniffled out a nice little earner, she was a force to be reckoned with.

She pulled the phone over, an essential tool in her line of business, and dialled. "Hello, is that On La Guardia Security? Can I speak to Miss Collette Stark, please...? Who's speaking...? Tell her it's her mother..."

The cat watched her from the hall, wondering if he was going to get fed today or was it time to move on.

* * *

Acapulco, Mexico, October 2013.

Luca lay on the sun lounger on the beach of the six-star hotel and watched her husband emerge from the crystal-clear sea and trot across the hot white sand towards her. He was a phenomenal swimmer and loved the sea and back in New York they swam several times a week at the club they went to. "One of the only exercises that utilises all the muscles in the body," he told her.

She had to agree as she was well-toned and supple again after her difficult spring, and as she was eating for two, she found it great exercise for a pregnant woman.

He was tanning nicely but she would slap more cream on him, she didn't want him burning and ruining their last few days. It calmed her to see him relaxed and happy, and her love for him surged as she watched his well-muscled, co-ordinated form approach. He was coming back to her, his Luca, and she knew it with all certainty this man would always come back to her, and the thrill of it was incredible and she had to pinch herself at times and bring herself back to reality, because since they had become lovers life had taken on a whole new meaning for them and she cherished every moment. If ever fairy tales came true, hers had and she relished the realisation of her dreams.

Till death us do part, she mused. It was strange. A near-death experience had brought them together. It was so, so meant to be. She rarely thought of Hanlon now. He was locked up for the next fifteen years before eligible for parole and the way Luca thought about it was that fate had dealt a double-edged sword. What she had suffered at that deviant's hand had brought Rabbie into her life and an unbreakable bond had formed between them, and Hanlon was sealed up safe, away from inflicting suffering on more unwary woman.

Rab plonked down beside her and gave her the dazzling smile that always melted something inside her, water beading down his face and body. She made him sit up and dried him off with a fluffy towel and lathered cream over him. He let her have her way, knowing she liked to administer to his needs and truly cared for him, and she was a soothing balm in his often hectic life and just being in her presence was calming and when she let him into her inner space, it was like a bolt of electricity, the intimacy was so intense.

He watched her surreptitiously as she dried his legs. She took the sun well and was turning a nice mahogany. Her bare breasts jiggled as she dried his hair. She had been a bit reticent about going topless but after making friends with some of the other lady guests, she had decided to go with the flow.

Discarding her top one morning on the beach, she showed the world her vital assets, and twirling her bikini top above her head, she said, "There I am now da hippy lady and burn da bra."

The guests laughed and the male members looked at her in approval, if with not a little lascivity, much to Rabbie's wry amusement. He saw the look of lust, if not indeed envy, in some of the men's eyes and marvelled that a pair of breasts could be such an issue, but they were a magnificent duo and he was proud she was all his. Empires had fallen for less. Caesar and Cleopatra. Helen of Troy. Romeo and Juliet.

He grimaced when he thought of Juliette and realised but for Luca he had effected a lucky escape and would have gone back to the nubile, high-breasted model and probably to a life of meaningless grief.

No, Luca was a one-woman show and despite her high sensual nature and high sex drive, which had grown since he took 'her cherry' and seemed to have expanded even more in the first few months of her pregnancy, he had no worries about her straying. He trusted her implicitly and cherished her deep sense of loyalty and after Juliette, it was clean and refreshing, and he never had flares of jealousy when she talked to other men as he had with his ex.

No, he was cool and content and if they had a high sex drive, so what? Enjoy it when it was there because it was a mega bonus and it certainly cemented the relationship and would give them many happy memories in old age.

Wendy said they were like two hands in the same glove, and he couldn't agree more. Entwined.

She finished with him and rubbed cream on her stomach, "Can't have da bambino burning. It come out wearing a sombrero," she quipped.

"It will be like the cartoon mouse 'Speedy Gonzales' if it takes after his mum," he quipped.

"You were like 'Speedy Gonzales' at the conception, dahling. You spurned me senseless."

He smiled, "After all the chillies and fajitas we've had, bambino's probably going to be born clutching a fire extinguisher," and he bounded up to get them a drink, ignoring that last blatant remark.

She watched him leave again. He was tireless, like a cat on hot bricks, and she saw several of the women blatantly watch his strong, departing back. She placed a hand across her abdomen protectively. Fourteen weeks pregnant and she was just rounding nicely. All was going to schedule and the 'gyni' was pleased with her. It was so kind of Mrs Obama to refer her to 'her man in New York', as she called him. She had sent a postcard to her and her lovely husband of the hotel and wrote that they must try it and come down for a break. It was a little bit of paradise on earth.

Luca gave a deep sigh of contentment. Life was sublime. The poor President worked so hard. Being the top man in charge of the free world was a hard watch, and she reckoned her and Rab were happy as they were. Politics was a dog eats dog business, and she would leave it to other hands, living in this fantastic-free democratic nation.

Rab came back with a waiter bearing a tray of juice, tortillas and fruit. The waiter fussed over her and soon she was munching happily on the spicy dish.

A svelte blond was still ogling Rabbie. She had seen her flirting with him in the bar the night before. She wasn't worried. Rabbie oozed a primal toughness and stamina, which was appealing to the opposite sex, coupled with an inordinate sense of security and sincerity and his obvious good breeding and gentlemanly conduct, it was a heady mix. Fertile women knew good genes when they found them and Luca knew they would welcome him into their pool with open arms, and she snickered, or legs, but she knew he had only eyes for her and that was enough.

"You 'kay? Chilli not too hot?" he asked.

"Nietski, it's brilliant. Tanx so much, honey."

He was pleased she was pleased. "You're happy, I'm happy. What are you thinking about?" He had caught her soft chuckle and thoughtful smile. She never stopped intriguing him, and he liked delving into her mind at times and seeing what was going on inside. It was a treasure trove of gems for him to mull over and ponder on.

"Oh, I vas just tinking, you know. How as a little girl I would pray I would meet a gallant knight one day and then as I got older, I saw da knights were a ting of the past but den I met you and I realised da knights have never gone away."

See, he told himself. *Everyone's a gem.* "Said knight has found his Queen. What you say back to the Royal Chamber? It's scorching and too hot for my lady."

"Da siesta time is good. The Mexicans are so sensible to split da day up!"

They gathered up all the paraphernalia a morning on the beach demands and headed gratefully into the shade.

As her eyes adjusted to the gloom, she smiled fondly as she thought back to her wedding day.

* * *

October, 1983, OLG HQ, Watford

Collette put the phone down with a shaking hand and looked furtively around the office. She felt sick to the stomach and light-headed after what she'd just heard. It was lunchtime and most of the staff were out fuelling up with calories for the long afternoon and enjoying the unseasonal sunshine. They were having a bit of an 'Indian summer', and she hoped it lasted for a week or so more because she was getting married in less than a week's time to the man she loved and she was determined nothing was going to get in the way of that, especially her bitch of a mum, whom she never expected to hear from again, but who like the proverbial bad penny was at this very moment in time about to turn up again.

Jamesey was out meeting a couple of potential recruits down The Peel, and Smudger was interviewing a new client. What to do? What to do about that bastard of a mother of hers? One thing was sure, wherever Janet Stark turned up, trouble was not far behind her, and if she wanted to bring discord and grief into someone's life, she would. She was an expert at it and could win Olympic Gold for stirring the shit.

Collette's guts had run cold when she heard her mother's voice after all these years, demanding to meet her, and a nasty taste had entered her mouth. Images of her deprived childhood had flashed across her mind, bad thoughts she believed were buried forever, and she had visibly paled and realised just how strong a hold those terrible years still held her. She couldn't believe the audacity of the bitch. She was a reformed character and had seen the light? She wanted to make amends and be part of their lives and was coming straight down to meet her perspective son-in-law, before hanging up.

Collette lit a Consulate menthol with a shaky hand. She rarely smoked these days, thinking it was bad for the children, but she kept a pack in her drawer for emergencies and liked the odd one after a meal or sometimes after Jamesey had made exquisite love to her.

She pondered on what to do, dragging deeply on her cigarette, her mind a conflict of emotions. Then she thought of her Jamesey and all they had achieved over the last six years and a steely resolve came over her. He had taught her that only the weak allow themselves to be intimidated, and when a problem cropped up, you took it by the horns and dealt with it before it had a chance to get a grip and cause more mischief.

She stubbed her fag out and called one of the office juniors over. "Hold the fort, Melanie, and take Jamesey's calls. Anything important, take a message. I'll be back in an hour."

"Yes, Miss Stark. No problem."

"It's Collette, love. Back soon." And she shuck her smart double-breasted suit jacket on and left.

Outside it was indeed a lovely day. She sat on a bench in the busy pedestrian precinct and raised her face to the healing rays and let the healing warmth calm her as she waited for her mother.

She had looked up 'Indian summer' in the encyclopaedia. Apparently, when the Indians used to attack the wagon trains on the Great Plains during the Wild West days, they would stop when the first snows came and hole up for the winter, but when the weather stayed fine like today, the attacks would continue and more pioneers would die.

Her mother was like an Indian summer. She just never knew when to retire and leave her alone. She spotted her mother tottering towards her on six-inch stilettos, midi dress that buttoned down the front and a long thin cardigan. She looked lean and wane, and her hair was long and thin and needed attention.

Collette called her over, and she waved madly as if they were lost friends. She staggered over and plopped herself down. "Collette, oh my Gawd. Look at yer in yer lovely suit, all grown up and all."

Collette looked at her non-committally, taking in the shifty eyes, the small vicious mouth and the prematurely lined face. Her mother had aged something shocking, and she could smell the drink dying on her breath. "I thought we'd go to the Skandia for lunch, Mum. You look like you could do with feeding up."

"Ohkay. Guess I could manage a toastie, duckie. Am watching my figure."

The Skandia restaurant was a hundred yards down the precinct opposite the Odeon. Collette looked over her shoulder at it as she entered and recalled with nostalgia that very first day she had met Jamesey and the hilarious time they had watching the film Jaws. She believed she had fallen in love with the tough paratrooper the first time she met him and reminded herself of the timid shell of a girl she was then and how by falling in love and giving herself completely to him she had transformed into the confident young woman she was now. How her zest for life was so strong and the many interests she had, but most of all, she was a mother now and Jamesey and her kids were her life. She would let no bastard interfere or wreck what they had, especially this bitch of a sad excuse who called herself her mother. In Collette's book mothers should be there for their offspring, to guide, nourish and nurture them as they grew on unsteady legs and wary minds into life but most important was trust, and if you couldn't trust your mother, then you were beat, and Collette shuddered inside as the waiter seated them at a table for two and asked if they wanted an aperitif.

"I'll have a Bloody Mary, please. What about you, Mother?"

"Just a coke, ducks. I am off the booze."

Collette laughed, "Get her a double Smirnoff, twist of lemon and coke."

The waiter departed, and Janet went to speak but her daughter stopped her, "I can smell it off you, Mother. Don't worry. My treat."

Janet prevaricated. "Yes, well, I fall off the wagon now and then but I'm most times sober. Times have been hard for me."

Collette looked sceptical, "Oh fucking dear. Get the violins out and play a sad song." She paused as the waiters deposited drinks and left. "Just what the fuck do you want, you evil bitch?" she snarled.

Janet feigned shock, "I just want to build bridges, not erect fences, love. I'm so sorry for the past but I want back into your lives now. I was wrong and I apologise. I am older and wiser now. Let us let bygones be bygones."

Collette leant back in amazement. "Let bygones be bygones. You fucking used and abused us. We were into care like friggin' yoyos. You put the twins into care because they cramped your style... I don't know what you're after...JANET... But you're not going to get it."

A tear ran down Janet's cheek, and she covered Collette's hand with her own, making her flinch and feeling repulsed. "I just want to make amends, love. I was very, very wrong. I know now. I was stuck in a trap."

Collette pulled her hand away and winced. "You're frigging unbelievable... You know the Elvis song... 'Stuck in a Trap, I Can't Go Back'? Jesus wept, Mum, for what you done to us. You've burnt your bridges with me and the twins. I think it be better if we just left and went our separate paths."

A steely resolve crossed her alcoholic eyes, "I need money, dear... I am on me uppers. I'm sure you wouldn't want that nice big bloke to know you used to be a prostitute. A willing one at that."

The waiter came down to take their order. "I'll have another drink, love. This is my daughter; we're just catching up."

The waiter knew the OLG crowd. They were regular clientele. "Yes, I know Miss Stark and Mr DeJames. Valued customers. Please take your time, ladies."

"Just call a spade a spade and not a shovel and cut to the guise. What is it exactly you want, Mother?"

"Well, I won't make your past public knowledge or make any trouble, as you know I can, I'll be a torture if I want to be, you know that... Five grand and I'll never darken your door step again… How is the little lad? He's at school now. Maybe I'll call down and see him."

Collette rose, knocking her chair over. "You go near him, I'll swing for you." And she threw a tenner down. "That'll cover the drinks and get you pissed," and turned to leave, then thought better, "Did you ever love us, Mum, even a little bit?"

Janet laughed scornfully. "Five thousand smackaroos, in cash, in forty-eight hours or I swear by the demons that drive me, I will be a millstone around your neck and destroy the happy little scene you have going now."

Collette stormed out in deep shock and went straight to the primary school and took her son home and double-locked the front door.

The waiter had seen her departure and had heard a lot of the conversation and felt sorry for the lovely Miss Stark.

He went to the staff room and picked the telephone up and dialled.

* * *

Jamesey put the phone down. A thoughtful frown across his strong features… *Hmm, so the reptile has crawled out from under the fetid stone.* He was expecting it. He wouldn't have his wife upset by a low life like that. He would sort it, and he would sort it DeJames style.

* * *

Acapulco, 2013

She lay looking at her husband sleeping. Husband, her husband, what a magic word! She perused the ring on her third finger on her left hand. *Till death us do part.*

When they come up to the room she had peeled off her black string bikini and walked naked across the room and hit the shower. She knew he was watching her. It pleased her that he did. At first she had been a little shy at undressing in front of him but now it seemed the most natural thing in the world to walk around naked in front of him.

It wasn't too long before he joined her in the shower and they washed each other down then kissed deeply, and he led her to bed and made love to her before dropping off to sleep.

She thought back over the past few months. After the rather humiliating public announcement of her pregnancy at the trial, Rabbie had been all care and concern. She had been worried about his reaction to the news but realised she had nothing to worry about. He was thrilled and fussed over her like crazy.

A week later he took her to a little Italian restaurant called Giovanni's on Staten Island that their friend Toni from the deli had put them onto and they had come to love. The cannelloni was to die for and the ravioli rich and tangy. As they sipped after dinner coffee, Luca told Rabbie she was going shopping next day to get ingredients to make stew. She wanted to improve her culinary skills. She knew she was a lousy cook. It amused Rabbie, she knew, but she was determined to get better. She'd a kid on the way and soon she would be feeding a family of her own.

"Yah, Wends give me her mother's great recipe. I got lean beef in da fridge, so tomorrow I go Toni's and get da onions, potatoes, carrots and da stock you like."

"So you'll be coming down with carrots then?"

"Why so, there no carrots in da kitchen, is there? We ran out. You eat them like da Bugs Bunny."

He grinned hugely, "I got carats, honey, but not ones you get in a greengrocer." And he knelt and opened a small jeweller's box before her. "Luca Sofia Natasha Sonia Alexander Valendenski, will you do me the great honour of becoming my wife?"

She gazed at the ring. A big square-cut diamond surrounded by smaller ones. She was speechless. "Diamonds for my future Queen. Watcha say?"

She took the ring out and he helped her put it on. "Is beautiful, my knight. Tank you sooo so much."

"I take it that's a yes then?"

She threw her arms around him, "Da, da, da, da, da, da," and lathered him with kisses.

A few weeks later he told her he had to go to Europe for a week to a security conference and would she go with him? She got time off work and flew to London and transferred to the OLG (UK) jet and took off.

"Vere we going now, Rab?"

"Russia. Company business."

They landed four hours later and Luca deplaned amazed. It was late afternoon. "Vhy, we are in Vilnius, vat we going here, Rab?"

"Oh just me being downright sneaky."

When they reached the terminus, there to meet her was her mother, brother and the old Director. They had a tearful reunion and Rab was pleased. He was good at skulduggery and liked to practice it now and then. 'Like father, like son'.

On the way to the Hilton, Luca asked what was going on. "Well, Dad and Simone, Wendy and Bobby and Mal and Philli are already here. Got in earlier."

"But why are they here, Rab? They tell me dey going to Atlantic City to play da casinos."

"They were telling 'porky pies', Lucs."

"Well, my granny, and brother and sister get in later. Jamie's my best man."

"Best man? Vot's going on?"

"We're getting married tomorrow. Big Bobby's giving you away. Okay?"

She was deliriously happy at seeing her family again but this was the icing on the cake. "You are one amazing guy, Rabbie DeJames… Oh God, what about da dress?"

He laughed. "Everything's arranged. Your mum's one made for you. I've been in touch with her for weeks through Katarina Bronski to interpret. It's been fun."

She punched his arm playfully, nearly swooning with joy. "You are da one dark horse but I love you so ver' much."

* * *

They married the next day in the small Russian Orthodox church Luca had attended as a girl. The whole village turned out to see the local girl made good.

She looked stunning in the beautiful full lace dress Reena had so painstakingly made.

She took her vows solemnly, meaning every word, her heart filled with love for her gallant knight.

Who would have thought that after coming through such a horrendous event things would come to this? Life certainly was diverse, and you never knew what direction life's wind would blow.

She said to Rabbie afterwards, "Marriage truly is a triumph over adversity, my husband."

"Or adversity waiting to happen," quipped Wendy gaily, "Welcome to the club, dear."

* * *

She had dozed off herself and when she awoke she saw the sun was well down, a hot shaft of light streaming through a chink in the drapes. Rabbie was still out cold. Good, he deserved it and besides, and she grinned with anticipation, he would need all his energy for the coming night. Being pregnant seemed to make her hornier than usual.

She went and sat on the balcony. It was so tranquil and lovely in the late afternoon. After the wedding service, she had asked to be taken to the graveyard on the hill.

'I need a few minutes alone, Rabbie. To say goodbye to someone."

She went to Galen's grave. Laid some wild flowers and knelt. "Please keep the ring, Galen. There will always be a corner in my heart for you. Wherever you are, I pray to God you are as happy as I am."

She had wiped a tear and gone to join her husband. "So what you got planned for me now?"

"Oh a few days with Maman and then it's off to Acapulco. Sun, sea and sex and lots of it.

"I think I can handle that, my dahling," she cried happily.

* * *

Watford, October 1984

Twelve hours before Janet Starks' vicious deadline was up, she was sitting in her house with two pissed up punters who were arguing about who was going to have the first turn at her. She was pleasantly drunk, the punters having provided a bottle of White Horse Whisky and a lump of hash, and they had enjoyed a couple of humongous joints.

She really didn't give a flying fuck who screwed her first. She wanted to get the deed done, get shot of them and finish their whiskey.

Besides, she had to get up in the morning and meet her prat of a daughter for lunch, and a very profitable lunch it was going to be as well. She'd seen the look on her girls face when she threatened her with her children, soppy mare. She would get her dosh, get nicer digs and in a year or so, go back for more. It was a nice little earner.

"God bless yah, Collette," she toasted to her in the harsh whiskey, then to the squabbling men, "Err...if yah can't make yah bleedin' minds up, I'll take yah both at once, no extra."

Suddenly, the front door crashed open and two uniformed police officers burst in, batons drawn. "Freeze. Nobody move or yah get a mouthful of truncheon."

The drunken trio looked at them in stunned amazement. What the frig was going on?

A tall dark-haired man in a trench coat entered. Hands in pockets. "Chief Inspector Douglas. Drug Squad. I have a warrant signed by a magistrate to search these premises for illegal substances."

Janet jumped up, spitting venom, "Get yer filthy arses out of my gaff, rozzer. Yer not find anything here."

"So what's that lump of brown and paraphernalia on the table?"

She snatched the warrant out of his hand and read it, then ripped it into shreds and threw it in his face. "Only a bit of brown pig. It won't even see court."

He cuffed her around the head and pushed her none too gently back onto the sofa. "It's more than brown I'm looking for, now sit there and less of the clap trap... Search the house, men."

He spun to the two punters, "I bet your prints are all over those rizlas. I've no beef with you two. Beskaddle and keep it shut or I'll come seeking you out for special attention."

They needed no second bidding and grabbing their jackets, fled like hares out the trap.

"Yah cowardly bustards. Call yourselves men?"

"Shut yer septic tank, whore!" snarled the Inspector. "God help your poor neighbours living next to a trollop like you."

A uniform stuck his head around the door, "Kitchen, Inspector. Enough snow to coat Hyde Park."

He grabbed her roughly by the arm and dragged her protesting into the squalid kitchen.

"Found this in the larder behind the cornflakes."

A large packet of white powder wrapped in clear plastic and cellotape sat on a counter.

The Inspector weighed it in his gloved hand, "Jesus, must be two kilos in that."

Janet sneered. "Never seen it in me life before, you planted that, you rotten nark!"

The Inspector grabbed her hand, forced her fingers viciously apart and slammed them down on the parcel.

"Then why's your fingerprints all over it you poxey, slut?"

"Did you bleeding see that?" she implored the boys in blue. "He's stitching me up."

"Never saw a thing," they chorused.

"You're under arrest, whore, and the Judge is going to throw away the key."

He dragged her out to the patrol car. "Get in the back with her, Kevin."

"No way, Boss, I don't want to catch crabs. The missus will kill me."

"More like lobsters," laughed his mate, "and I'm driving."

"Cuff her and toss her in the boot then, we'll hose it out later."

Thoroughly degraded and scared now, they put her in the boot, handcuffed, and drove off.

Two hours later she was still sitting in an interview room, still cuffed and wondering just what the frig was going on, the drink drying in her.

A tall blond-haired man came in with a smaller man in a pinstripe suit. She thought she recognised him.

"Mrs Stark, I'm DeJames, your future son-in-law. We need to talk."

She gaped at him. "What the bleeding hells going on?"

"I heard you had been arrested and decided to intervene. I have quite a bit of influence with the local constabulary."

Relief crossed her face. "So you gonna get it all squared then?" a crafty look crossed her face. "I mean we're near family now and I can be very, very good to yah," and she uncrossed then re-crossed her legs to reveal she was wearing no knickers.

He looked disgusted, "I wouldn't touch you with a ten-foot electric cattle prod. How the hell you gave birth to a cracker like Collette beats me."

"Then what the fuck do you want?"

He gazed at the raddled wreck of a woman, amazed Collette had come from her loins, "Oh and the twins say hi. Remember them? Probably not. They are at university… Doing very well. Then they'll be coming to work for me."

"Noisy little buggers. Whatcha want then?"

He sat down before her and gingerly took her restraints off. She winced as the blood rushed back into her hands. "Possession of two kilograms of cocaine carries what? Four years, Jeffrey? Oh sorry, Jeffrey Waite, my brief."

"About that, if you get the Judge on a good day."

"Plus, that cocaine belongs to some very nasty East End gangsters, who like burying people alive in concrete and want to know who stole it off them."

She looked very worried now.

"Now, to make this all disappear, I just need you to sign a couple of pieces of paper. Move to Tower Hamlets, where I have arranged a nice council flat for you. Never come back to Watford again and most importantly," and as fast as a snake, he gripped her face hard in a strong hand, "If you ever come near Collette or my kids again or I even get a whisper, I'll fucking bury you alive myself. DO YOU FUCKING UNDERSTAND ME?"

Looking deep into his arctic blue eyes, she saw the berserk inside and nearly wet herself. She nodded with difficulty in his tight grip.

He grinned evilly. "Good. You've wasted enough of my time…Jeffrey."

Jeffrey gave her two documents to sign. The first one she waived all her rights as a maternal grandmother to the DeJames children, and the second she agreed not to approach or contact Collette ever again.

She signed with a flourish and a sneer. Jeffrey gave her the address and keys to her new abode and an envelope with a £500 pound in it.

"Moving expenses or put it away for a rainy day. You can only open your legs for business for so long, and I reckon you'll soon have to put the shutters down…INSPECTOR… Get this trollop out of my space. She's polluting the air."

He rose and Jeffrey snapped his briefcase shut and followed. "Bye-bye, Mum… Rot in hell."

504

Smudger arrived back half an hour later and found Jamesey and Dougie Alarms in his office sipping Remy Martin. "Took the stripes off the escort, and Harry will return the uniforms in the morning."

"And I'll put the Persil back in the box. Shame to waste good washing powder," sniggered Dougie.

"That is one confused, mixed up girl," observed Smudger. "Gis a brandy, mucker."

"Yeah, well, what goes around comes around. Should have raised her kids right. They're our future."

"Would you have buried her, Jamesey?" asked Smudger.

"Waste of a good shovel but I doubt she'll darken our lives again."

* * *

He crawled into bed. Collette stirred and rolled over to peer at him, "Where yah bleeding been, love? Yah stink of brandy."

"On an Op. Didn't mean to wake you."

"More like on the end of an optic in the bar."

"Life is but a stage and we are all actors in the same play."

"You only quote Shakespeare when yah pissed, now go a kip," and she buried her head under the pillow.

He went to sleep grinning. A job well done.

* * *

Next day he grabbed Collette at lunchtime. "Fancy going to the Skandia for lunch?"

She scowled. "You've to see that Gillespie guy about the Sainsbury contract at one."

He grabbed her coat off the hook, "Smudger's doing it, and I've barely seen you recently, what with the wedding arrangements."

She looked tired and stressed as she followed him reluctantly out.

Once seated, she looked about her nervously. Jamesey covered her hands with his, "She's not coming and you won't be seeing her again."

She looked at him, mouth agape, "You better close that before a bee stings your tongue."

"How'd yah know? What ya do, love?"

"We promised no secrets, Collette, she's gone; I used utmost force and utmost discretion."

A tear trickled down her cheek, "I'm sorry, Jamesey, and I didn't know wot tah do. I was gonna tell yah."

He released her and perused the menu, "You're forgiven, now what about soup of the day, then hotpot. You need to keep your energy levels up, honey. Big day soon."

She smiled, a heavy cloak of dread lifted off her shoulders. "Sounds good and tell yah what, we'll get Mr Singh's extra-hot vindaloo for supper, then have an early night."

He grinned, "And Jamie's going to let us get an early night, him teething and all.'

Collette's turn to grin. "Eadie's got him tonight. She dotes on him."

"Then I'm your man and all yours."

She took his hand. "Thanks, Jamesey. Dunno what I'd do without yah."

As they slurped their soup, a thought came to her and she gasped and put a hand over her mouth, "Ear', Jamesey... You didn't kill the bitch, did yah?"

"No, waste of good cement. I made her my leading lady for a while; now eat your soup up before it goes cold."

She knew not to press him and did his bidding.

* * *

Three days later they got married in the afternoon at Saint Martin on the Green Church off Watford High Street.

Ronnie proudly gave a ravishingly beautiful all in white Collette away, Kim was matron of honour and the twins were ushers.

Smudger was best man. "You sure about this, Jamesey?" he whispered as they stood before the altar, waiting for Collette. "They're a bleeding nightmare once they are hitched and got the ring on."

Jamesey licked his lips nervously. "Well, I'd rather charge an IRA machine gun nest with a knife and fork but too late now, said the rabbit to the lamp."

Afterwards, they had a jolly old knees up down The Old Peel, and the newlyweds left to honeymoon in Paris.

Collette clutched his arm in the plane and looked adoringly into his eyes. "You're so romantic, Jamesey. Every bride's dream to honeymoon in the city of love."

"Nothing but the best for my lady," he replied stoutly, failing to tell her Colonel Swain wanted him to open an office there, and he was going to scout it out.

Anyway, why not mix business with pleasure, he justified to himself. He could claim it back on his tax return.

As they flew over London, Janet Stark looked out of her tower block apartment and saw the lights of a plane in the sky and winched at the nagging pain in her side and poured herself another Smirnoff to deaden it, not knowing that the cirrhosis in her liver would kill her within three months.

A slow, lingering and very lonely way to go.

The Trial (Rubber Bullets. 10cc) – Mid August, 2013

The trial of Harold Henry Hanlon and Arturo Calvos got properly underway on the third Monday in Courtroom Number 6. The Central Criminal Court Building in Manhattan, an imposing classical neo Greek monstrosity that impressed the visitor and awed the violator with its magnificent fluted columns, wide stone stairways and decorated triumphal arches.

"Tis something you would see in ancient Greece," a nervous Luca remarked to Rabbie as they ascended the broad outer steps. "It da intimidating. It musta cost da fortune."

Rabbie pulled her to a stop and pointed to the statue of a robed Greek goddess on top. "See her, Luca? I forget her name… Minerva or something but see her hand? That's the scales of justice and that's what you're going to get when they send Hanlon and Calvos down the line for a very long time. Justice."

She tugged him forward, "I hope so, dahling. Dey can break rocks for a new building to house the many homeless in New York in da luxury…dis just crazy waste of money. Where da justice for them?"

He laughed as he followed her graceful light tread up the dazzling marble facade. Always the idealist, but he was uneasy. The District Attorney, Elaine Williamson, had warned them that Hanlon had concocted a fairly reasonable, if perverted, defence. Although highly implausible to trained ears, it might sound possible to people more gullible.

"We have to be on our guard, guys. He only has to put reasonable doubt in two members of the jury's mind, and the bastard walks free to offend again. And mark my words, he's a serial criminal and will be a danger his whole life," she told them at a pre-trial meeting. "We have to put him away, period."

Rabbie had squeezed Luca in reassurance but he had caught the nervous look in his lover's eyes. What the DA and Luca didn't know was at a bar on Swinging Third Street a few nights previous he had met with Big Mal, Little Danny, Billy-Jo, Buzz 'Boomerang' and Charles Brouchard. He had listened intently to their plan if Hanlon and Calvos walked free. It involved a stolen van, a fishing boat, incapacitating drugs, firearms and fishing nets weighted with lengths of chain.

"Give the muvvers some of their own medicine," growled Buzz. "Only thing fuckers like that understand."

"Yeah, before they join the ranks of the disappeared," put in Mal with an evil grin that a number of Saddam Hussein's soldiers had glimpsed before their demise.

"City ain't safe for us gals if them douche bags get loose," from Billy-Jo. "Them critters are mega diseased; I say feed them to the hogs."

"Oui, c'est la vie," Brouchard agreed. "Le scum must be dispatched to meet their maker, tout suite."

"Prefer a darn good lynching, hombre, but y'all are right. Gotta be done, dude," said Danny, picking meat out of his teeth with a pick after demolishing a twenty-ounce rib eye steak with fries.

Rabbie eyed them keenly, "You know technically we are all guilty of conspiracy to murder?"

"Wouldn't be the first time, would it?" replied Mal mysteriously. "We know the risks."

"Yessum, it's for Miss Luca an' all them others them sick jackals have preyed on, man," Danny agreed chewing on his toothpick.

Rabbie looked at Danny, "'Kay, I'm touched, guys. I'm in. Hopefully, it won't come to such extremes, but thanks from both of us."

Buzz snickered, "Won't come to it? Ask Billy Crichton," and he laughed softly.

Little Danny gave him a mighty punch to the arm, "Sweet Jesus, you just dunno when yer goddamn trap should flap or not, Boomerang!"

Rabbie glanced at his crew avidly as Buzz rubbed his arm vigorously, "Hot shit, Dan, I think you broke mah goddamn humorous and it ain't funny."

Mal caught Rab's quizzical look. He knew he had done a few Black Ops in the Commandos, "Least said, guys. Here's to Luca," and raised his bottle of Coors, and they clinked necks and drank deep.

"And here's to OLG. Murder Incorporated," guffawed Buzz, and receiving another dead bicep from Dan. "Chrissake, Dan. Frig off back to the Lone Star State and punch some steers!"

"You sound like a page from a James Patterson novel, but this is real life, so here's to sealed lips and deaf ears and no mercy to our enemies," toasted Rabbie, which they all drank to.

* * *

They entered through the huge polished mahogany doors and succumbed to being searched by eagle-eyed security staff and through the metal detectors into a huge cavernous hall. This was alive with activity as numerous lawyers, cops, barristers, detectives and members of the public were wheeling and dealing in small groups or sat on the marble benches, looking lost or feigning indifference.

The clamour rose up to the vaulted ceiling. They passed stone busts of famous deities, thinkers and judges, who gazed down from sightless eyes from their lofty niches onto the scheming, lying and disparate throng of humanity below, the machinations of man as old as time itself.

"Oh what tangled webs we weave when we contrive to lie and deceive," he said as he led Luca through the crowd to the elevators.

"Vat are you saying, dahling?"

"Just something from a play. 'Schoolboy Shakespeare'."

"Da, life is but a stage," she agreed, "And we are all actors to some degree. Was Sir Walter Raleigh actually clear, in his memoirs?"

He smiled at her. She was so smart and aware, besides being beautiful. He knew if he had to, he would kill Hanlon without a qualm for her. Like swotting an annoying fly or crushing a stinging insect underfoot.

"Come, we take the stairs. Is only one level."

She had dressed that morning in a navy blue trouser suit with high heels and with her gleaming hair in a ponytail, she looked demure but business-like. He had detected the odd look of worry cross her lovely face as he watched her dress and apply her make-up in front of the mirror. He knew she was anxious about confronting Hanlon and being in the same room as him in public and knew he had to give her as much moral support as possible.

Rabbie observed her as she climbed the stairs firmly with a feminine understated poise, and the grace of a natural dancer, oblivious to the innate rhythms inherent to her. The long umber hair casually furled across the side of her beautiful face, the dove-grey eyes reflecting the light from the atrium above. He had learnt from Luca that life was a precious gift and that many things were different now they had bonded as a tight couple. Also that things that were once individually his own were now hers too and vice versa. He revelled in the sharing between them. Whilst they both had their own pasts, pasts Luca said you must not deny, there were no secrets separating them, and the future loomed ahead invitingly and tantalising, and Rabbie rejoiced at the idea of the fascinating, glorious road that was in front of them. He realised now his life had been cruising along in a self-imposed vacuum and then Luca had entered and filled that void, demanding commitment. Although at the beginning he had shied away from giving it for various reasons that seemed puerile now, he was immensely happy, content with his lot and lived every day to the full in the company of this marvellous woman.

Luca watched him out of the corner of her eye and stopped on the landing and faced him. She sensed his deep protective mood and was secure and grateful, but she was worried what his reaction would be when he saw Hanlon.

Rabbie was usually cool, calm and collected. Well-organised and knew his own mind. True, she had to prod him somewhat at the start of the relationship. He had held back for reasons he considered honourable, not wanting to hurt her or get her on the rebound. She loved him for it; in fact, if she admitted the truth to herself, she loved him from the first time they met but now their love had finally bloomed. What she now felt for him was so deep it was bottomless in its intensity, in her desire for him, just to be close to him. Luca luxuriated in being his mate and confidante, and she knew from the bottom of her heart, as a young woman, she would never find a love like it again and considered herself so lucky, she counted her blessings each glorious morning she woke up.

"I love you, Rabbie," she told him, stroking his strong arm gently. "Don't be getting annoyed in court at what that bastard say, da? Ve get dis over wiv, den put it behind us forever."

He kissed her, "Don't worry, Luca. That son of a bitch is going to prison and by the time he gets out, the desert will have turned to ice and the camels will be skating with the penguins."

She giggled, "Ah… Royal Marine sense of humour, da? So it vill be," and they entered Courtroom Number 6 arm in arm, tittering like two school kids sharing a juicy secret.

They had arrived early at the DA's request, so she could go over any last minute details with them. They sat on the front bench reserved for witnesses behind the prosecutor's table. The court started to fill. Bobby and Wendy joined them and whispered their "Hellos" even though the court hadn't begun. It was that type of atmosphere.

The DA emerged from the Judge's chambers with a small dumpy man in a smart suit that did nothing for him. He had a sallow complexion and a balding pate, and his eyes darted around the room like a hungry ferret looking for rabbits in distress. Elaine spoke briefly with her team, then approached them.

"Bad news, guys. The Judge has decided to allow Crichton's written statement in evidence. It won't make a lot of difference but it does kinda back up Hanlon's defence."

The man in the suit, who had hung back, came forward. "Miss Valendenski? Mr DeJames? Sal Moreno, defence counsel. I was wondering if you might like to avail of an interpreter because I am going to have some very difficult questions for you, young lady."

Luca stiffened as he ran his eyes rather blatantly over her body, "I don't tink so. I was an English student of language at Vilnius University in da Lithuania, and I am quite au fait wiv da American vernacular."

That stumped him, "Oh, okay, just don't wancha misunderstanding and saying something you regret."

"Just slink away over to your own table and stop scaring my complainant," Elaine ordered.

He left with a lewd grin. Moreno was a seasoned defence veteran of many years and took on the cases many defence attorneys wouldn't touch with a barge pole. He put forward incredible, outlandish defences and made them feasible in the eyes of the jury. He lost as many as he won, but he had no ambition to sit on the Supreme Court bench as a Judge plus the money was good, and money was God.

He was quietly confident. His client, Hanlon, was a psychopath, and they were good liars with no morals and his sick defence just might pass muster, and Calvos was backing him up to the hilt as was the late William Crichton's statement. Crichton had posted bail but it hadn't done him any good. His body, weighted down with chains, had been found on the shores of the Hudson two weeks ago, when the water level dropped with the heatwave they had endured.

He sat at his table and briefed his three assistants. The trial had actually started the previous Thursday, when a jury of twelve had been sworn in. Six men and six women. Sal had gone for young guys in their thirties, sexually active and not easily shocked by the spectre of kinky sex. Elaine had gone for older ladies; upright members of the community, decent and straitlaced, who would empathise with Luca's ordeal. It was an even mix, and Sal only had to put reasonable doubt in their minds.

He likened his cases to battles and always carried a quote from Shakespeare's Henry V on the eve of the Battle of Agincourt in 1415 with him.

"Listen in, guys," he told his troops. "'Once more into the breach, dear friends, once more, or close the wall up with our English dead...and you good Yeoman, whose limbs were made in England, show us hero, the mettle of your pasture... Let us swear, that you are worth your breeding'."

He paused, eyes gleaming, "It's a dirty job at times but someone has to do it... Let battle commence," and he stood and high-fived his team.

"Oh Gawd's sake, he's doing his Henry the goddamn Fifth routine," groaned the DA. "He thinks he's a frigging General."

"Now that was Shakespeare, dahling," Luca informed Rab, "Part I."

Rabbie laughed, "Yeah, Agincourt. The French knights used to cut the captured English archers' first and second fingers off to stop them shooting their bows. Thus the two-fingered salute, sign of defiance."

"Really?" said Elaine interested. The Brit guy was a mine of useless information. "Well, we can't give him the fingers now, just not done, but after we win, guys, he'll be wiping egg off his face."

Luca stared at them, bemused, then smiled, "Oh, okay. Ve throw eggs at him. Dat be fun." They laughed amiably at her and she beamed, pleased she had amused them.

"Got a good Judge too. Old school. Scrupulously fair and takes no bullshit. Great on women's issues," she reassured them.

The court had filled now. The stenographers and clerk fussing about under the raised bench where the Judge would sit to conduct the proceedings. Philli rushed down, out of breath, Mal behind her.

"Sorry I'm late," and hugged Luca. "It's a bitch to get parked here."

A tall, strong-looking Afro-American in the uniform of the Court Bailiff stood by the bench and hollered, "Silence in court! All stand for his honour Judge Cyrus Hyran Wallganger Front de Boeuf the Third!"

A sprightly grey-haired septuagenarian in his black robes strode up to the bench, sat down, surveyed his domain and gave a brisk rap with his gavel.

"Court in session…take the weight off, folks."

Luca shivered as Hanlon and Calvos, in orange jumpsuits, were brought out and stood in the dock.

"Supreme Court of New York Case Number 9047-versus-Harold Henry Hanlon and Arturo Calvos."

"Luca, Luca, I forgive you. I love you, baby!" shouted Hanlon, staring straight at her. "Come back to me, baby."

Her blood ran cold and something very evil with many legs ran up the centre of her back as she heard the voice of her would be rapist/murderer. She trembled.

Rabbie jumped up, enraged, "You shut your mouth, Hanlon, or by God I'll swing for you!"

The jury, who had filed in a few minutes beforehand, getting settled in their seats aware of the important job ahead, gasped at the two antagonists. They had not expected fireworks so early.

Cyrus rapped his gavel furiously, then pointed it at Hanlon. "One more goddamn outburst, Mr Hanlon, and I'll have you removed for the duration," and he swung it towards Rabbie.

"And you, sir. Thought you were ex-military. Restrain yourself, man… Bailiff, read the charges."

The cops had done a good job charge wise against Hanlon and Calvos. They had charged Harry with attempted murder of Luca. Attempted sexual assault. Assault in the first degree. Unlawful discharging a firearm. Unlawful possession of a firearm. Possession of obscene material, namely extreme pornographic DVDs. Breach of a court personal protection order, and they had thrown in burglary with intent at Luca's apartment for good measure.

He had pleaded not guilty to them all, except the obscene DVDs and the breach of the order. In his statement he claimed the gun was Luca's, which she kept for personal protection and he had pocketed it for safekeeping. He claimed that she had restarted the relationship despite the order, for financial purposes, that she liked very rough sex and had consented to make a home movie for a large sum of money involving, him, Calvos and Crichton. He claimed Rabbie was a possessive rival, who had broken Luca's door down in a fit of jealous rage, had in fact assaulted them and not the other way around. That it was Rabbie who fired the shots, and forensic confirmed there was firearm residue on Rabbie's hands and clothes. He also claimed it was an unlawful arrest that he had been beaten by a large man with a baseball bat and that Luca was a lying, devious bitch.

Arturo backed him up every step of the way and was also charged with the same crimes or as an accessory to the same. The very dead William Crichton's statement was a lot sketchier, although he did say Luca was a very willing participant and that Rabbie had fired the shots.

"It's all ludicrous, of course," stated Elaine. "But we have to go through the whole nightmare to send the sad S.O.Bs down."

The cache of violent homemade movies found in Hanlon's office looked very promising at first to the detectives. They had watched, teeth clenched and grim faced, particularly the snuff movie of a young Albanian woman being beaten and then strangled. Despite vigorous enquiries, they were unable to locate most of the women starring in the sick productions or the locale of the filming. They did trace several prostitutes involved, who readily admitted their consensual inclusion for financial reward. To complicate matters further, a number of copies turned up at various bars and dives across the borough, and Hanlon happily admitted buying them off persons unknown in those places.

The first three days the jury heard the police and medical evidence. The testimony of forensics and CSI experts.

On the Thursday, Luca, nervous as hell, entered the box to testify. Hanlon gave her a saucy wink, which the Judge caught and warned him off. Elaine led her through her testimony step by step, and there were gasps of shock and horror as the public heard the horrendous ordeal the lovely young immigrant had endured. When she described being kicked downstairs and being bitten, one lady juror fainted and two openly wept. If looks could kill, then Hanlon was six feet under and worm fodder. Elaine was pleased. Luca was erudite and sincere.

When it was Sal's turn, he took her through it all again but put Hanlon's slant on things.

"He said it was your gun?"

"Not true."

"He claims you agreed to make the movie?"

"Any woman who consent to da ting like that need head examined," annoyed, eyes flashing.

"How long did you go out with Mr Hanlon?"

"Never, it all in his sick head."

"So you never ate with him at his steakhouse?"

"Veil yes, but…"

"No buts, young lady. Are you still in love with him? Is this your idea of revenge for some slight?"

She glowered, "Some slight? Bah…if being near da raped and killed is da slight then yes, I want justice."

And so it went on until he released her. He saw the Judge was becoming impatient. He had her measure now and would crucify her on cross-examination. He was well pleased the way things were going.

It was Rabbie's turn next. As part of his Royal Marine training, the ones remaining towards the end of the rigorous course went through a particularly painful and humiliating week, where they were treated as prisoners of war by an enemy that didn't recognise the Geneva Convention. After the DA had finished with him, he put himself in anti-interrogation mode and refusing to look at Moreno, gave as short and succinct answers as possible.

"'Kay, Mr or should I say Captain DeJames? You served eight years in the British Royal Marines?"

"I did."

"And you are the recipient of the British Military Cross for actions undisclosed? And you were trained in unarmed combat and how to kill with your bare hands?"

"I refuse to answer that under the premise of the Official Secrets Act."

Moreno sniggered, "I think you've just answered that…now, your last two years were in charge of a detachment of the Special Boat Service? That, your honour, is our equivalent of the Navy Seal."

The Judge growled, "I do read and watch Discovery Channel. Move it on and it's Squadron not Service, Counsellor."

"I refuse to answer that for the same reason."

Elaine jumped up. "Relevance, your honour."

"Mr Moreno?"

"Your honour, I want to prove DeJames is a violent man and can plan complex, deceiving operations as he did when on active service with the SBS and how he could have easily distorted the facts of the night in question. He's an intelligent man, used to thinking on his feet."

The Judge sighed, "Totally ludicrous, Mr Moreno. Denied, now move it on."

"No further questions, your honour. You may stand down, DeJames."

"It's Captain DeJames!" snapped Rabbie. "As you brought it up!"

Moreno sneered. He'd made his point and they all knew it.

Wendy was next, saying how she had heard the shots and rushed in and described the poor girl's injuries. "She was in deep shock and if that was play acting, then I'm Angelina Jolie and Moreno's a Harlem Globetrotter." Which got a laugh from the court and a mock stern finger wagging off the Judge.

Bobby got more laughs when he denied hitting Hanlon with a baseball bat, "Hell, Judge, I'm a professional, I helped light up Baghdad. I wouldn't waste a good slugger on that dirt bird. That's a no-brainer. I'd've just threw him out the window and saved you folks a lot of time 'stead of having to listen to him bleat like a spoilt rich kid."

"Very colourful, Mr Havilland," said the Judge. "Now please resume your seat."

Calvos took up his right not to give oral evidence without prejudice to his defence, and Billy Crichton's statement was read out in court, and the jurors looked thoughtful after said account.

Elaine patted Luca's hand, "Hang in there, kiddo. We've still got an ace or two to play yet."

But she was worried, it could go anyway at the moment, her fine mind thought. Then it was Hanlon's turn. He gave his evidence firmly and clearly. He was an accomplished liar and enjoyed his time in the limelight.

Moreno stressed time and time again about the fairy tale relationship he had with Luca, until at one stage she nearly believed it herself, before shaking herself and forcing herself to look at the brute who was leering down at her. He stared back with soulless eyes that led to hell.

"You see, Mr Moreno, I only went along with the kinky stuff to please her because you see," and he spoke with all sincerity, "I loved her and indeed, despite what she's doing to me… I still do," and he hung his head dramatically.

Luca was aghast. Hell would freeze over before she would love a demon like Hanlon. Rabbie gave a slow hand clap and Bobby, Mal and the rest joined in, "Oh bravo, bravo Hanlon. Oscar-rated performance."

The Judge gavelled them quiet. *Hot dog, this was turning out to be one damn fine trial. Life really was a stage.* "Court adjourned until Monday morning, when we'll start cross-examination."

"Make or break, kids," said Elaine. "Make or break."

Moreno caught them on the way out and looked Luca full in the eyes, "Oh what tangled webs we weave when we decide to lie and deceive. Shakespeare, my dear."

Luca flinched and Rabbie put his face into the shithead little attorney's, "She's not your dear, and it was Sir Walter Raleigh's in his memoirs before Elizabeth the first cut his head off, which I would surely love to do to you."

Sal tut-tutted and ambled off glad, he had rattled them.

Luca watched him waddle off, "Knowledge is power, my love, but used properly it is a good thing."

* * *

The Cross-Examination

The court went quiet, an expectant hush as Luca walked from the prosecution table and into the witness box. She looked very pretty in a two-piece primrose yellow shot silk suit that ended demurely mid-thigh, showing off her shapely pins. Her beautiful hair, in its customary over-the-shoulder ponytail, gleamed under the court's lights, bringing colour to the proceedings and emphasising Luca as the centre of attention. Long drop gold earrings with red garnets and matching gold necklace completed the ensemble.

The Clerk of the Court reminded her she was still sworn in, and the Judge bade her sit.

"Now you still understand the oath okay, Miss Valendenski? You must tell the truth at all times or you could get into trouble. Your English is very good, but if there is anything you don't understand, please do not hesitate to tell me and I'll get the interpreter."

She turned her liquid, limpid grey eyes on him, "Tank you so ver' much, your honour. You're ver' kind and please do call me Luca."

The Judge, all seventy-two years of him, wished he could call her Luca, over a champagne and lobster dinner at his club. He had a feeling today was going to be good sport.

"'Kay, Mr Moreno. Let's get this show on the road."

Sal strode into the arena, glanced over at the jury and faced the young woman. If he could break her and convince just two members of the jury she was complicit in the events that night and that things had just got out of hand, he might get his clients off. He began gently, going over her background again, her qualifications and job.

"So, am I to believe then, Miss Valendenski, that your aim is to bring your mother, Reena and your brother over to live with you here in New York?"

Luca glanced at him surprised, and Elaine stood, "Relevance, your honour. What's this to do with my complainant nearly being killed?"

"Mr Moreno?"

"It's very relevant, your honour. It proves Miss Valendenski needs more money than she is earning at present to bring her family over and settle them from an extremely poor country."

The Judge let him continue his line of questioning, eyebrows raised enquiringly.

"Answer the question, Miss Valendenski."

"Vell, yes your honour. I intend to bring them over. I have been saving every month from my salary. Lithuania a very poor place."

"But another source of income would certainly come in handy?" Sal asked.

"Vell, yes, I make a bit on the side by doing the markets and getting collectables and curios for my clients and sell them on for a small profit."

Sal stood facing her, arms crossed, thoughtful. "A bit on the side, you see my client maintains you were his bit on the side for a number of Sunday nights for nearly three months."

Luca snorted, "I get him some nice French mirrors and candlestick holders but I never saw him on Sundays."

Sal paced up and down before the jury. He reeled off ten dates he had memorised. It was time to strike.

"Those are Sundays and my client claims, in his full and very frank statement to the police, that on those dates, normally between 9pm and the early hours, you and him engaged in full sexual intercourse on numerous occasions and that he paid you for the act in full."

You could have heard a pin drop in the court, or as Bobby said later, a mouse fart, as all eyes stared at Luca. Rabbie sat there seething, Big Bobby gripping his arm tight as Rabbie turned his furious gaze on Hanlon, who was sneering provocatively.

Luca stood up and crossed her arms and half turned away, her head tilted proudly, cold fury radiating off her.

"Bah!" she spat out. She looked fantastic in her anger, cheeks flushed, her spine ramrod straight.

"You insult me, Mr Moreno. Do you seriously tink I vould have any romantic interest in an ogre like Hanlon? Why, he could lay all your gold from Fort Knox at my door, begging for my favours, and I would spit in his perverted eye."

The audience clapped and cheered, and the Judge banged his gavel furiously. "Order...order. Order in court!"

The din eventually subsided. The crowd was really caught up in her now.

"Please sit down again, Miss Valendenski."

"Ver' vell, your honour."

She shrugged and sat, her eyes sparkling with anger still.

"Miss Valendenski...let's move on. May I call you Luca?"

She eyeballed him in disbelief, "Bah... I don't tink so. I don't tink I let strange little men who intimidate I am a common prostitute call me by my Christian name."

"I think you mean insinuate, Miss Valendenski, or do I intimidate you because I'm getting near the truth?"

The Judge rapped his gavel, "Move it on, Mr Moreno."

"'Kay, your honour. So you deny my client came up to your apartment on these dates for sex with you."

Two red spots of rage suffused her cheeks, "I deny any man come my apartment for how you so crudely put it...sex. I do not do sex. Sex is for hookers!"

She stood again and glared at Moreno, "I, Luca Sonia Alexandra Sophia Natasha Valendenski, make love, and I only make love to the man I love!"

The crowd was transfixed. They watched her in open admiration. She was mesmerising like a modern day Cleopatra, mysterious and beautiful.

"You're a bum, Moreno!" someone shouted.

The Judge gavelled again, "Order, I say!" He was transfixed himself. He liked witnesses who stood up for themselves, especially glamorous ones with sexy accents.

"Mr Moreno, let's go."

"Yes, your honour… Miss V…and please think carefully before you answer this… I remind you that you're under oath."

She stood again, eyes blazing, "It's Miss Valendenski to you, mister. You keep reminding me I'm under oath. The kind Judge explain dis; I am not a simpleton like your client. I speak da whole truth for da Judge."

"Please sit, Miss Valendenski," ordered the Judge, eyes twinkling. "Unfortunately, Mr Moreno has to ask these very distasteful questions and you must answer."

She turned to the nice old boy, eyes downcast, demure, and tugging at his heartstrings.

"I am ver' sorry, your honour, for bein' a pain in the butt. I know to speak dah truth in dis court of free law in this fantastic city that has taken me into its bosom and made me one of its own. Has fed, clothed and nurtured a poor immigrant… I would not insult your constitution by lying… I don't tink I could. It would demean freedom of speech."

They hung on her every word. Two ladies in the jury had tears coursing their cheeks and mutters of "Shame on Moreno" and "Bullying motherfucker" from several men.

Rabbie had never been as proud of her. Her high intellect was shining out and that combined with her good looks was a staggering combination. Moreno looked down at his feet, perplexed. She was good, very good. He wished she would let him call her Luca. The Judge was the epitome of sympathy.

"No one's saying you're not telling the truth, my dear. That's for the jury to decide, or that you're being a pain in the…umm, a nuisance. We just decide on the facts put before us."

A solitary tear ran gently down her cheek and she gave the nice Judge a hesitant smile with her beautiful lips, "Am sorry, your honour… I understand… Tis just hard being called a hooker in front of these nice people."

Every male in the place stared hard at Moreno and Hanlon, wanting to punch their lights out. Elaine got up and strode over, giving Moreno daggers before putting her arm around Luca.

"I will speak to my witness, your honour. She is upset and I think a recess is in order?"

"Yes, of course. We'll break for an early lunch. Reconvene at one folks."

The crowd filed out. The Judge got to his chambers and said to his clerk.

"Make sure your audio typist got that down. Verbatim. I have never heard a prettier witness speech in forty years on the bench."

"You gonna stick it in your memoirs, Judge?"

"You bet your dunkin' donuts I am. I think that gal's gonna give me a whole chapter before the day is out."

* * *

They went to a small park nearby and found a bench to eat the chilli dogs they had bought from the kiosk at the entrance. The sun was hot and young mums and couples with prams and toddlers were out in force to take full advantage of the fine day. Rabbie observed Luca watching the antics of the children, a whimsical look on her face. She broke part of her roll up and fed the crumbs to the sparrows gathered at their feet, waiting. She fed the more trusting ones by hand. She put her chilli dog back in its Styrofoam box.

"I'm sorry, Rab. I don't tink I want tis. I disgrace on all the hungry little kiddies in the world."

"You can't take the whole weight of the world on your shoulders, honey."

She sighed, "Why are people so bad to each other, dahling? We all feel the same and have the same needs."

The idealist was coming out in her, he saw, "It's just greed and power, love. But there are plenty of good people like yourself, who make things a bit better."

"And you, Rabbie," and kissed his cheek, then laughed. "I put chilli sauce on your face."

He wiped her lips with a napkin and then his face, "You're doing great in there, Luca. You just have to keep the outbursts down a bit or you might get done for contempt of court."

"Yes, I know. Elaine explain. They can put me in prison until I apologise," she scowled. "Apologise for being called a common hooker in front of my friends and strangers. Not while a bear shits in the woods will I say sorry. No way, Jose."

He smiled, admiring her spunk, "No one believes it, Lucs. They know it's all crap."

"Yes, and when the crap hits the fan and flies about, it tends to stick to the one it hits."

"You're full of all these wonderful metaphors today, hon. No wonder the Judge likes you."

"Yes, veil, like me or not he can still put me in the Gulag."

Rabbie held her hands, "We'll get it sorted, honey. Don't worry."

She broke free, "I feel queasy, excuse me," and she walked off to the nearby toilets, rubbing her belly.

He was worried about her but when she came back a few minutes later, she appeared happier.

"Were you sick, Luca? I'll see Elaine and try getting the trial delayed for a day or two."

"Just a little, 'kay now. No, I get it over with, I vant get back to the witness room and get changed."

They left arm in arm, "Why do you want to change, Luca? You look great."

"I look like a high-class hooker! You never told me you got a medal for bravery, Rab."

He looked pensive, "It's only a piece of metal, Lucs, main thing we all got back safe." .

She looked at him in open admiration. He was some piece of work.

Luca re-entered the box at 1pm sharp. She had changed into a light linen two piece the colour of her eyes. She wore a small pearl choker around her neck and single stud pearl earrings. She looked very feminine and sedate. The men of the court enjoyed the fashion show and the jury approved. The court was called to order and the now hated Moreno continued his line of questioning.

"Miss V," he knew she hated that. "I want to ask you about the intimate sexual relations you had with my clients."

"You may ask but as it's all a figment of his mind, I don't know what I can tell you."

The DA got up, "Objection, your honour. What does Mr Moreno mean by clients in the plural?"

"Mr Moreno, explain yourself!"

"Your honour, I'm just trying to prove that Miss Valendenski had consensual sex with my client on numerous times and on the date of the alleged offences. She was engaged with Mr Hanlon's two friends as well, at her request."

"This is ridiculous, your honour. There is no evidence to say the complainant agreed to this except the defendants' own statements and the word of a dead man."

"I agree. Mr Moreno, keep your questions strictly about the relationship between her and Hanlon."

"Yes, your honour." Moreno was pleased. He'd made his point and hoped he had cast a bit of doubt in the jury's mind.

"Now, Miss Valendenski. Did you or did you not have a sexual relationship with Mr Hanlon?"

The onlookers were hanging on every word.

"Not while there are dogs in the street, no. You insult me again."

The court tittered. The Judge smiled behind his hand. She was classy. "Okay, folks, enough for one day. Reconvene tomorrow nine thirty sharp."

The next day Moreno grilled her relentlessly.

"You have a very small birthmark in the shape of a butterfly just about an inch or two down from the top of your left buttock?"

"How do you know dis, Mr Moreno?"

"Mr Hanlon told me. Yes, or no?"

"Veil, yes, but he…"

"Miss Valendenski, I am asking the questions, not you. You also have a small black beauty spot hidden under the crease of your right breast. Yes, or no?"

"Did Hanlon tell you dis? He must have seen it ven he was…"

After pressing her more about her sexual activities with Hanlon, which she denied vehemently, and seeing the Judge was getting impatient and he was losing ground with the jury, the beady-eyed little lawyer decided it was time to pull his rabbit out of the hat.

"Abracadabra," he muttered under his breath, then out loud. "So, please tell the court, Miss V, who is Galen Levi?" Moreno asked innocently.

The annoyed witness visibly blanched, then stammered, "Galen…vot he to do with dis? How you know about my Galen?" and a single tear ran down her cheek, stark in its loneliness.

Sal sighed theatrically, "Judge, please tell the witness to stop answering a question with a question and to answer my question."

The Judge harrumphed, annoyed, "This better be goddamn pertinent to the defence or I'll be very annoyed, Counsellor."

"It is, your honour, and I will prove it."

The Judge glowered and turned to Luca. "Best answer, my dear. Get it over with."

She stood again, "Galen Levi was my first true love. He was very brave man," her eyes were sore with misery.

"And it is true he was killed serving his country in Chechnya in 2007," he pushed on, hard.

She gave Sal such a look of pure hatred, he took an involuntary step back, "I don't know vhere dis is going, mister, but if you sully my Galen's name in dis court, I vill heap a thousand curses on your foul head," and Luca gave him circled fingers, the Russian evil eye.

The Judge rapped sharply on the gavel, "Best just answer the question, Miss Valendenski."

An amused Moreno shook his head, "Never been cursed before in court. Do you practice witchcraft full time, Miss V? Or is it just a hobby? Did you put a spell on Mr Hanlon?"

Another rap on the gavel, "Just get on with it, Counsellor. Going up and down your blind alleys is getting tiresome."

Luca glared down, "Da, Galen died defending a country of gangsters and thugs, who threw him to da wolves. Why do you vant to know dis, Counsellor?"

"Questions, questions," Sal tutted, and grinned knowingly at his team. "How did Mr Hanlon know about Galen, Miss V? Through a crystal ball?"

"I tell you again, it's Miss Valendenski, if you have to address me at all, and I don't know how da pervert knows about Galen!"

Sal pounced, "Because my client will say you used to shout his name out when you climaxed when making love with him, and you told him about Galen by way of apology."

Luca's cheeks flushed. An enforced silence gripped the court – strained and ugly. The Judge looked disgusted, "Is there really any need for this, Counsellor? What is it proving?"

"It's proving my client had sexual relations with the witness. How else would he know about Galen Levi? Her intimate body markings? Her family, who need money?"

Rabbie had had enough, he had seen the look of loathing cross his lover's distraught face. He jumped up, "You lousy piece of shit! I'll not have my fiancée put through this filth." He bounded over the waist-high divide, a number of spectators rising with him, shaking fists, faces red with infused rage. Bobby and Mal managed to grab an arm and drag the infuriated Rabbie back as the Judge gavelled furiously.

"Order! Order! Order in my court!"

Hanlon smirked in delight at the mayhem he had caused. The several thousand dollars he had spent on an internet detective unravelling Luca's background had sure paid dividends.

"But I forgave her. Cos she knows I love her. It was only pillow talk," he hollered in glee, which just added fuel to the fire. Luca began weeping uncontrollably.

Court Bailiffs and cops hustled around defusing the situation as the Judge got a sore wrist banging away with his hammer. Luca scowled at Hanlon with contempt as gradually the situation eased and people took their seats again, muttering obscenities.

The Judge stared at them wearily from a weary eye, "My last warning, folks. I will CLEAR THIS COURT if there are any more shenanigans. You, Mr DeJames, take a hike for half an hour and calm down. Both you and Miss Valendenski are pushing me into a corner. So, quit and quit now! Go and get defrazzled, sir!"

Rabbie was led out, white-faced. The Judge beckoned Sal over, "Get on with it, man, and less of the vile speeches or you will be joining your client in the cells."

He sauntered back to mid court, his confidence increased. Cause mayhem and confusion and witnesses often said things they regretted and once said in court, they could not be retracted.

"So, Miss Va…len…denski," he emphasised snidely, "Do you still really expect the jury to believe you never had free consenting sexual intercourse with Mr Hanlon?"

The DA jumped up now, "Objection, your honour. He's coercing my witness, trying to put words into her mouth. Gossip and innuendo bruited around, confusing everyone."

The Judge gave a sharp tap, "Sustained. I am sick of warning you about confusing the witness. Rephrase your question, Mr Moreno."

Luca had sat but rose again, "Tis okay, your Highness, I answer, den vould it be all right if I take da short break to have a very rare cigarette and da compose myself?"

The Judge agreed readily. By Jiminy Cricket, this was an outstanding venue! Wait till he told his cronies in the club about the beautiful, defiant Russian Princess and the obnoxious, deviant little toad of a Counsellor.

"Well, what's it to be, Miss V? Aye or nay?" Lou asked, dripping with sarcasm.

Luca stared at him loftily, a steely glint in her eye, "Da…" and she let it drag out before, "I had da near sex with him. Now go get cigarette because da air in this court is fouler than any Winston can put in my body!" And she stepped daintily down and walked out, head high, every eye watching her departure.

Moreno raised both hands in dismay, "What the hell she mean by that? What the goddamn is 'near sex'?"

"Don't answer a question with a question, Counsellor," and he rapped his gavel. "Fifteen-minute recess," and clutching his robes about him, he headed off to his chambers, chortling, pleased with his own wit.

When the court reconvened, Sal took her up on that very subject. Rabbie had been informed of the goings on and sat grim-faced, wishing he could stick his highly polished brogues very hard up a dark part of Moreno's anatomy. Luca 'tanked' him for sticking up for her but assured him she had everything under control, before they went back in. He certainly hoped so. He didn't like the way the questioning was going and who the hell was going to suffer if Hanlon got off. He glowered at the loathsome creature in the defendant's box, who gave him a cheery thumbs up.

No, it wouldn't be Luca, Rab determined. Hanlon would be disappearing if that occurred, because OLG would be putting Plan B into operation, and the revolting brute would be food for the fish in the bay.

"So, please explain for the jury what 'near sex' with my client means?"

Luca ignored him and faced the sweet old Judge, "Your Worshipfulness, I am a bit overwhelmed, may I say something for da record? I von't waste too much of da court's time."

Cyrus sensed more gems were about to come out of that lovely mouth and pulled a pad and pen so he could make his own notes, "Of course, my dear. The defence has wasted more than enough of our time as it is, so feel free."

The court tittered, and Sal lifted then dropped his hands in exasperation.

"I understand I must tell da truth, da whole truth and nothing but da truth. Da truth is sacrosanct and that is branded upon my heart. To be able to do so in a free court, in a free country, before dese decent citizens." Every face was riveted upon her, "People I feel small to call my peers, and in another situation, it would be to my honour to appear before them. For surely, in da country where I come from da truth was rarely heard, and there were no free courts. Just kangaroo courts where da beasts of state had already decided da outcome of da case before it was even aired. There vas no 'For God, For Freedom, For Justice'. No, it was just there to reinforce da harsh, cruel girders that held up a totally inhuman, uncaring totalitarian regime which stifled free speech. In fact, trampled on it and recognised it for da danger to its vile existence it posed. Afraid da mere act of free speech would rot its foundations and bring da whole stinking structure tumbling down."

The Judge raised a hand furiously, "Hold on, Luca, just got to trampled on… Okay, carry on."

Sal watched her, gobsmacked. She was outstanding and the Judge was calling her Luca now, for frig's sake. Maybe she was indeed a witch.

"Da, I am so proud to be a member of dis society of free men and women, da foundations of which make da U.S. of A so great that to lie in court is not an option for me. For surely it vould break my poor heart, already branded a liar by dis sad excuse of a man, and I vould die like a grape on the vine denied vater and sunlight, and quite rightly so.

"I apologise for my behaviours. I vas a pure woman, chaste and unblemished, until Hanlon decided I was to be his unwilling play chattel and put his hands upon me. Tarnished, vile mitts surely blessed by satan, so if I had been a little da over emotional, then I beg the court's understanding and vill try to keep my many emotional heads in check for da rest of da duration of dis trial," and she sat down demurely.

They had watched and listened to her with open mouths, stunned by her eloquence and oratory skills. Not a sound or movement was seen or heard for a very long pause. It was like time had stood still, until Luca broke it, knowing she had them trapped in the palm of her hand. Like a beloved canary who had escaped its cage and was heading to a dangerous open window.

"So, da answer da question on 'near sex'. I had 'near sex' with dat brute Hanlon because he neared raped me, but my gallant knight came to my rescue. I can still hold my head up high and look you all in the eye, knowing my name not besmirched, tanks to Mr Rabbie DeJames. Tank you all ver' much for da patience."

Someone began to clap, it caught on, and they were soon all clapping and cheering. Cyrus surveyed his court. Women were crying; goddammit, even some of the men were crying. Moreno approached the bench.

"Judge, I want to appeal for a mistrial. That vixen has them all on her side. My clients ain't getting a fair trial."

Cyrus guffawed, "No friggin' way, Jose. I am thoroughly enjoying myself, besides you started all the melodrama. You just have to take your medicine and lump it. Away back to your table," and he rapped the court to order.

521

When quiet eventually descended over the courtroom, which was standing room only now, Sal tried again. He stood and paced over to Luca, who watched him impassively.

"Very fancy speech, Miss V. Now, no more smokescreens. Did you, or did you not, have sex with my client?"

She stood and pointed her index finger straight at Hanlon, "I DID NOT HAVE SEX WITH DAT MAN."

The court laughed and clapped. Sal shook his head in annoyance, "I seem to recall a certain leader of the free world saying that a few years ago, and he was proved a liar. Can I have a few minutes, Judge, to consult with my troops?"

"Ten-minute adjournment, folks," beamed a happy Judge.

Moreno eyeballed the young beauty chatting with her oh so spiffy fiancé, jealously. He wasn't finished with her yet; not by a long chalk. Like Henry V at Agincourt, he still had a quiver full of arrows to let loose.

* * *

When they reconvened, Sal got right back at her.

"Miss V… I am going to ask you some questions about marks on your body again…"

She interrupted him, "Why you want ask about my body? I tink a bit of Hanlon's perversion rubbing off on you."

The crowd teeheed, and Cyrus gave a little rap with his gavel.

Sal shook his head slowly from side to side. "Question, questions. There is no such thing as unflawed beauty, Miss V…although if you don't mind me saying, you are very close to it. Now, if I may continue…"

She butted in again "Vell, yes, I do mind, but vhy you vant to talk about my body in da public arena beats me. Are you perhaps frustrated, Mr Moreno?"

The audience loved it and giggled and smirked away, animated, shuffling in their seats.

"Your honour, please instruct the witness not to answer a question with a question," interrupted Moreno.

"You must answer the questions as fully as you can, my dear, and only ask a question if you don't understand."

She was blushing furiously, and Rabbie was tense and grim, "Yes, I do have such a mark."

"And you still deny having sex with my client?"

"Are you mad? Of course I do, idiot."

"Miss Valendenski," warned the Judge.

"Okay… Let's chill here," Moreno advised. "Are you sure I can't call you Luca?"

"Not while the selfsame dogs are in the street still."

"Pity. Okay. What do you think of Mr Hanlon? You know, as a client, as a friend…as a lover, perhaps?"

The DA objected but the Judge overruled. He wanted to hear this. She was confused.

"Vot you mean? As like, vot do I tink of him as a person?"

522

"Sure. You told the cops you got to know him quite well in a client-employee relationship. You had steak dinners a few times at his restaurant. Did you pay for those dinners?"

"Okay, I see… I keep lists of people, Mr Moreno. People I like. Kind people. Nicest man. Best service…"

"You keep lists, Miss Valendenski? People lists? That seems a bit bizarre." He turned to the jury, arms out, palms up, as if to say, Is she crazy? "Client lists, I'm sure."

"Of course I do, I'm from Russia. Now you interrupt me, you're a ver' rude man," she answered prettily.

He spun back to her, sarcastic, "Then put me on your Rude Guys list…can we get back to my client?" he snapped.

She retorted, "I told you, I have good people list and bad people list too, but your client is top of the pile on my shit list!"

The court absolutely exploded with laughter. It was packed, Rabbie noticed. Word had got around about the sexy, feisty young Russian girl in Court Number 6, and they arrived in their droves to see her. Court artists were sketching her and the press, which seemed to have trebled in number, were scribbling away furiously, sensing a big byline.

"Order! Order! Order or by jingo, I'll clear this court."

They gradually settled. Not guessing the best was yet to come. Elaine nodded to Luca, who nodded knowingly back.

"Come on, Mr Moreno, and make it snappy. This demeaning line of questioning is getting very tedious."

Silence ensued.

"Very well, Miss V, you know the Sunday dates in question between nine and let's say, for ease, midnight?"

"I always go home after singing at the Russian Club and work on my plans for a few hours, ready for Monday."

"And you deny you entertained Mr Hanlon on those dates and times at your apartment?"

"Yes, I deny it, of course."

"Even though his driver, Mr Arturo Calvos, states he dropped Mr Hanlon off on those dates at your apartment and picked him up later?"

"Oh yes, Mr Calvos, the brute who ripped my pyjama top off and punched my breasts. Yes, I deny it." Scathingly, "Or was I meant to enjoy their perverted act?"

"Please stick to the facts, Miss V. Mr Calvos also states he drove you out on other times for, I quote, 'Romantic candlelight dinners at various late-night eateries around the borough' from his evidence earlier."

"Bah! He should be writing fairy tales. Do you seriously believe," and she pointed her outstretched finger at Hanlon, "that I vould allow myself to be seen in public with that perverted, ugly beast? I vould die of shame."

The court laughed and hurrahed. Cyrus gavelled. "Easy, Miss Valendenski."

"Please call me Luca, Judge."

"Carry on, Mr Moreno. Speed it up, man."

"Look, we have the dates and times. We have evidence of personal marks on your body Mr Hanlon could only have known about. He describes," he consulted notes with his team and hurried back to stand before her, "He even describes in detail

523

the first time he had sex with you in depth. The Sunday before Christmas last year. Why not just come clean? Stop wasting the jury's time."

Luca was enraged again. She stood up slowly and glared down at Moreno.

"Bah. Come clean? How can I come clean about anyting that pervert did...and as for him describing the, how you say it? The Act...bah! It must have been a very quick, small, lonely and short act in his own bed, because it certainly vas novhere near mine."

Again there were claps and whistles the Judge gavelled out. Moreno wasn't giving up.

"I'm calling you a liar, Miss Valendenski. I put to you that you and Mr Hanlon had a full sexual relationship. Mr Hanlon paying you well for your time and company and that you engaged in numerous acts of sex with him on many occasions."

The DA looked at Luca and nodded. Big Bobby and Mal were physically restraining Rabbie in his seat, and Hanlon was staring at her lustily. She rose to her full height, tall and proud. Cold palpable anger soared off her. She turned and gave Hanlon a look of such contempt, it could have shattered glass, before turning back to Moreno. She raised her beautiful chin in defiance and her eyes flashed.

"Bah. Bah. Bah," she said. Complete silence followed as the court watched the outstanding woman, hypnotised. They knew when she went "Bah" something good was coming.

"How could I have da sex vith your client when I was a virgin up until the evening of Sunday, 29th April, this year, when I lost, how you say, my cherry, to my one and only lover, Mr Rabbie DeJames and who I am in child with."

There was a huge and (excuse the pun) pregnant pause before she added, "And I tell you, he gave me a damn good spurning that night, something I would guess would be outside Hanlon's sick remit!"

A stunned silence dropped across the court. The DA winked at Luca. The gal was a trooper. The Judge gawked at her, Moreno gawked at her and the jury gawked at her. In fact, the whole court gawked at her, except the prosecution team and Bobby and Wendy, who were gawking at Rabbie, who was sitting in shock, before pure turmoil ensued as the court erupted into pandemonium.

Luca sat down, watching Rabbie intently. She was six weeks pregnant and was going to tell him soon. Preferably over a candlelit meal, but oh well. He caught her eye and gazed in wonder at her. He gave her a thumbs up, and her lovely face relaxed. She gave him one back and blew him a kiss.

The shocked Judge let them have their noisy fun. Quite amazing. This was surely a whole chapter of his memoirs. He beckoned the Clerk of the Court over.

"What the goddamn Ace of Spades does she mean by 'a damn good spurning'?"

His Clerk ruminated, "I would hazard a guess it's a Russian euphemism for the full sexual intercourse act, your honour."

They studied Luca. "Lucky, lucky, lucky man," Cyrus decided before, "Get me Moreno!"

The clerk agreed as he found the dejected lawyer and brought him over, "Go speak to your client, Sal. He's proved a liar; it would be in his own best interest to cop a plea."

Moreno hesitated, "Could be a clever strategy, Judge. I would like forensic tests to prove she was a virgin and DeJames in the box so I can grill him."

The Judge glowered, "Do you not think Luca has gone through enough public humiliation and indignation? It's degrading. Go speak to your client." He banged his gavel, "Fifteen-minute recess," and called the DA over to get her assessment.

Rabbie sat up in the box with Luca. She was embarrassed and looked shyly down at her feet, "I didn't vant to tell you like dis, Rab."

He hugged her, thoroughly delighted, "Well, I guess that's one way to break the news."

"Am sorry, Rabbie, was going to tell you. Was that night after we had dinner at Giuseppe's? I forget to get the injection. Was bank holiday, remember?"

What was it with women and special dates? It was almost like a female physic thing. How could he forget? What a night that was with Galliano and bananas involved. He kissed her to reassure and comfort her.

"I'm so proud of you, my darling. Little Pauli's going to be jealous," he ribbed her.

"He's only a monkey, silly. He vill understand."

The court reconvened and they took their places, Luca still resplendent in the box.

"Mr Moreno, what's your client's instructions?"

Moreno spoke quietly, huddled up to the Judge, who looked more and more irritated. He summoned the DA over, who looked disgusted and gave him more daggers.

Luca got her make-up compact out and fixed her lipstick and mascara. Every able bodied male drooled. She was totally unconscious of the effect she was having. The conference at the bench broke up, and they returned to their respective tables.

"Your submission please, Mr Moreno?" his eyebrows bristling and face livid, "and make it snappy. You have wasted enough of my time today."

Moreno stood. He really did wish he had become a civil engineer as his father had been.

"Your honour. On my client's instruction, we would like a four-week adjournment."

The Judge leaned back. Tapping his pen on the bench in a rapid tattoo, his face a mask of scepticism. "And why would you like a mere four-week adjournment? Do please tell."

"We would like a statement off Rabbie DeJames to confirm he did indeed…ummm…take Miss Valendenski's…umm…her virginity."

There were angry mutterings from the court.

Moreno knew there was no escape from this. The Judge whispered to the Court Bailiff. "You get your guys to reinforce the court and ring the precinct. I smell a riot coming."

"Your honour, two more small things. One…a forensic test to determine Miss Valendenski was a virgin on 29th April last, and…two…a medical DNA test on the embryo to determine if the unborn child is Mr DeJames. If it's not, it will prove she is a liar, a loose woman and sleeps around."

Another absolute stunned silence descended, but this time it was a dangerous, strained one. Faces darkened and suffced with rage and gasps of disbelief rose in the air. Hands angrily clenched backs of the seats. Feet tapped angrily. People hissed, the mood dangerous and ugly, nasty mutterings and annoyance filling the air in the room.

Luca shot to her feet. "How dare you impinge upon my chastity on the 29th of April and not losing, how you say…my cherry? To Rabbie DeJames, the man I love and as to the parentage of my beloved embryo, you insult and disgust me." She looked strong and powerful and utterly tenacious in her stance. "Bah. Forensics, medicals. YOU CAN STICK YOUR TESTS UP YOUR ASS, COUNSELLOR!" she shouted and raised her fist in a victory salute. "PROTECT THE EMBRYO, LADIES PROTECT THE UNBORN CHILD!"

"Contempt, your honour, she's in contempt!" shrieked Moreno as the whole court rose as one shouting and applauding and stamping their feet before surging forward in unity, coming over the dividing rail to chants of, "Get Moreno. Get Moreno." A human tidal wave of angst roared at him.

Chairs and bottles of water started to fly as a group of angry students ripped the seating off the fixed tiers and used them as weapons. The Bailiffs ushered the Judge and his staff back to his chambers, where they barricaded the door. The prison deputies got Hanlon and Calvos out the back door but not before Hanlon got hit on the head by a tome of New York penal amendments, giving him concussion.

Moreno darted left and right, back and forth. He was trapped. Cops rushed in to grapple with and shoo people out into the corridor. Rabbie grabbed Moreno by the scruff of the neck and dragged him over to the witness box. He shoved him in past a still-standing Luca, where he cowered down in the corner, terrified and whimpering. Rabbie stood in the little doorway guarding her but he didn't need to. Different groups had banded together and were jumping up and down, arms across each other's shoulders, rapturous. They chanted, "Luca, Luca, Luca Valendenski", "Luca, Luca, Luca Valendenski."

"Luca, Luca, Luca Valendenski. Protect the embryo." A group of first-year female law students were gathered below, shouting questions up at her.

"Vimmin. You must alvays speech freely and the truth. The rights of the unborn embryo are sacrosanct. Believe me, I have come from a dark land where that is impossible."

They scribbled her answers down and later formed the 'Luca Valendenski Women's Free Speech Society', where she was a guest speaker for many years to come.

Bobby and Big Mal stood around, looking menacing and giving out OLG business cards to cops, always on the lookout for part-timers. Wendy sat up in the Judge's seat, swivelling around, laughing uproariously and shouting, "You all needa damn good spurning. Spurn for America… Yeah you dudes."

Luca watched it all, bemused. She really hadn't wanted to cause the lovely old Judge any trouble. She guessed he was going to send her to prison. She placed a hand across her stomach protectively. "Is okay, bambino. Is no Gulags in New York."

Her mother had said to save herself for the one she loved and by the great Russian Bear were her words prophetic. She gazed adoringly at her Rabbie, who was talking to a police Captain, calming things down. Always the peacemaker. It took an hour before they considered it safe enough for the Judge to come back in.

He took his seat and surveyed his wrecked court. The prosecution and defence teams sat at their reset tables, nervously watching him.

"Mr Moreno, what have you to say for yourself?" he roared.

He stood abject. The young woman he had so verbally abused and who he thought he could break had turned the tables and broken him. In fact, she and Rabbie DeJames had saved his skin, despite everything.

Had stood guard over him and even got him a cup of coffee from somewhere afterwards. They had certainly given him a new perspective on life through eyes that had been jaded for years.

"After consultation with the DA, your honour, and talking to my clients, we are going to drop my previous application requests. They are going to plead guilty to attempted murder in the second degree and all other charges."

The Judge relaxed a bit, "Well, now we're talking dandy Dixie doodle. You happy enough with that, Mrs Williamson?"

"Sure am, your honour."

"'Kay, arraign them."

Hanlon and Calvos were brought in to boos and hisses and the amended attempted murder and other charges re-read to them. They pleaded guilty; Hanlon, a white gauze bandage pinned around his head.

"Take them down and prepare pre-sentencing reports."

"Goddamn crazy woman," muttered Hanlon. "Dunno what I saw in her."

"Okay, Luca. I think I can call you that now. What are we going to do with you?"

Moreno jumped up, "Your honour, I think I was extremely coarse and vulgar with Miss Valendenski, which attributed to her outburst. Plus, as she's with child. Hormonal and stuff, I feel I must share in my part in her contempt."

"Yes, I feel you must. The minds of pregnant women are prone to outburst and over-protectiveness. I must apologise, Luca, for letting Moreno even suggest those tests. I certainly know I would not have let my daughter go through them."

"Tank you ver' much, your honour. I have been a little high strung but now Mr DeJames is aware of my state, I am much happy," and she gave him a demure smile, head tilted down shyly ,which tugged at his old still strong heart and nearly threatened to pull it asunder. It was a very personal gesture.

He looked fondly at her, "You're an inspiring young lady," he turned to Rabbie. "You look after her, you hear me, young man," and he banged his gavel. "Court dismissed."

The press rushed out, jostling each other. Luca breathed a sigh of relief and took Rab by the hand. "Let's go home, lover, all this drama has given me an appetite. After all, I am eating for two now."

* * *

They were mobbed outside the court and had to take a circular route home to avoid reporters, a police car escorting them. He ushered her into the bedroom and took her high heels off and propped her up with pillows and gave her the television remote.

"Your choice, you'll probably catch yourself on the news at six."

"Bah… I have seen enough of the court to last me two lifetimes. I watch the meerkats on Discovery."

He fussed about her, "I think you deserve a nice glass of the young Beaujolais you like, cheese crackers and grapes."

527

Rabbie strode off and stopped at the bedroom door, laughing, "Up the ass, Counsellor." He turned and saw she had stood and taken her suit top off. He gulped. She had gone to court braless.

"We'll see. It would need some experimentation."

He watched mesmerised as she dropped her skirt to reveal sheer black stockings and garter belt. The white of her thighs contrasting to the black was very erotic and made him stiffen up with excitement. She pulled down and stepped out of a pair of very sheer, scanty black knickers.

"Don't be long, dahling. I am totally addicted to your spurning. At least I don't have to get da morning after jab for a while."

* * *

Ten days later they attended the court again to watch Hanlon and Calvos get sentenced.

Luca had said to Rabbie prior, "I vant da see da barbarian go down, then I feel secure and I can close the book on this sad chapter in my life and throw it away for good."

Quite a crowd gathered to see the thug get his comeuppance and the Russian girl's revenge, and they were mobbed by reporters and supporters, shouting questions and wishing her well.

When Hanlon and Calvos were arraigned, the packed court hissed and booed, and Judge Cyrus gavelled them quiet, winking at Luca, who looked very fetching in a pale blue twinset and her six-inch killer heels from 'Choos and Clooes'.

The Judge listened to the presentencing reports and faced the two cringing defendants. "Mr Calvos, you're a sad little man, easily led and with no morality at all. I don't think you would have the intellect or organisational skills to plan or commission a crime such as you stand before me today of committing; hell, my big ginger tom cat treats his lady cats better than you will ever treat a woman, but then again, you're a deviant and a social pariah, so I am a gonna help you and send you to prison for thirty years, with a first parole hearing after ten years. Take him down."

The crowd huh-hurghed their approval. Hanlon looked at Luca, who winked at him. He knew this was going to be bad. "Harold Henry Herbert Hanlon. You have absolutely no pity, scruples or morality in your soul at all. You're a danger to our lady folk, and I suspect you always will be. I also suspect that the entirely unprovoked attack on a sweet innocent guest to our shores is but the tip of your dirty iceberg, your catalogue of weird perversions you seem to feel you can go about and commit with impunity, not caring one single iota about the effect you have on the victims, indeed damaging them for life. No one woman is safe when you're stalking the streets. You're a glib, seasoned liar whose only interest in life is your own sad sexual gratification. You quite happily accused Luca Valendenski of being a whore, a prostitute and a woman of low morale character, which all proved to be a figment of your imagination and a clever, if perverse, false defence. Miss Valendenski stood up to you bravely in court, and I commend her for her courage... No, I can't have a serious threat to society like you, an organised, very dangerous serial pervert able to mingle freely with decent people and plan more criminal perversions." He paused and raised his gavel, "Life imprisonment and a minimum parole hearing in fifteen years," and he banged his gavel crisply in its knocker, "Take the SOB down. His presence disgusts me."

The crowd cheered and clapped, and Cyrus beamed at them, thinking how his little speech would look in his memoirs.

"Rot in jail, Hanlon, and a curse of ill health on you," she muttered in Russian as the ogre was led away.

"Judge would like to see you and Miss Valendenski in chambers," the Court Bailiff whispered in Rabbie's ear.

* * *

In his chambers the Judge offered them sherry and Luca had an Amontillado. "Tis my bestest sherry on my list, Judge," she told him.

He smiled indulgently. "Please sit, now 'The Luca Valendenski Free Speech Society'?"

Luca looked at him prettily, "Vot about it? I want da tackle vimmen issues."

The Judge pulled a wad of papers out of his drawer. "Lotta lotta interest in it, people been sending money in. Cheques, money orders, even cash." He pulled a letter, "From Julie in Nebraska. Ten-dollar bill. She says you inspired her to leave her violent boyfriend and get counselling. Reckons you're the Joan of Arc of America."

She blushed, "Da gosh. I just standing up for myself; anyvay, Joan da Arc burnt at da stake."

The men laughed. "Don't do that to heroines these days," Rabbie reassured her.

"What do you want me to do with these, Luca?"

She thought, "Vot about I put some proposals down on paper, you hang on da them and open da bank account, and we meet up for dinner in da few weeks?"

Cyrus beamed, "My club does a great lobster thermidor."

She clapped her arms in delight, "Ahrgh, I just lurve the shell fishy dishy."

Wait until the other members saw this cracker on his arm in the club. "Then we'll swap numbers and stay in touch."

They made their farewells and left.

* * *

"You sure about this, Lucs?" asked a thoughtful Rab. "Could be a lot of work involved."

Her turn to think, then, "Da, it good chance to right some wrongs. From being a victim of a serious, degrading crime I met the most vonderful man. A good ting came out of it. Now annuver good thing emerges. Who do know what vill come of it? Hanlon in the pokey and unable to commit evil, and I arise from his shadow into da sun."

He kissed her. She was phenomenal. A one-off, an endangered species, and he would be at her side to keep danger away from her.

They broke off and she took his arm, "Come, ve go do Mama Jocelyn's. She da crap cake special on. My treat."

He grinned. Always hungry, but obviously her fast mind burnt the calories off because she was as slim as a winter deer.

529

Two days later he drove home around six. He was taking Luca to the club for a swim, then they were meeting up with Wendy and Bobby for dinner in Mama J's, and then probably find some music somewhere.

He was right about her string bikini. She looked magnifico in it and turned many a male head in the club, indeed even some female ones – truth be told and it being New York.

He noticed there were groups of people outside the apartment talking excitedly, and Mr and Mrs Chin were hovering at the top of the steps, shooing people away and generally barring entry.

He parked up and dodged through the throng.

"Whassup, Mr C? Why all the gawkers?"

"Luca had visitors, man, and they won't go home."

He guessed it was something to do with Luca. It always was. Luca the magnetic force. "Who was it, Mr Chin? No trouble?" he asked worried.

"Naw, all good in the hood. Ask her yourself. You'll be surprised."

When he entered, Luca was arranging a huge bunch of flowers in several vases. Roses, carnations, lilies, tulips and a myriad of others. A good few hundred bucks worth. "Hey, have I got competition or what? Where is he? In the wardrobe?"

She laughed gaily "Niet, silly boy. My friend Michelle called for da coffee wiv her children."

He sat and she jumped on his knee. "We going da swimming, then eat? Am hungry and so's da baby."

He eyed her, curious. "Well, you are eating for two… So who's Michelle?"

She ruffled his hair. "You do know, Michelle Obama. Da first lady. She very pretty."

He must have been staring open-mouthed because she put her face to his and their tongues met.

He pulled away, "Whoa whoa… You're saying the President's wife just popped in for coffee, then left?"

She pondered that, "Vell, more like dropped in, because they landed da helicopter on da roof…"

"What the heck she call here for?"

Luca put her finger on her lovely chin. "Vell, she in da New York da see her jinny colonist, and she followed da trial and she came to see me because she wants to be the patron of vimmen's free speech society."

Lost for words, he just gaped at her. "Yah, she lovely voman and da kids so vell-behaved. I gave dem cookies and milk. Can we go da swimming now?"

He recovered himself. "Life just gets more and more interesting."

"Da, we going da supper soon in Washington in dar big white-painted house."

He just shook his head. Absolutely incredible. "Come on. I need a swim… Errr, what's a jinny colonist?"

She blushed. "You do know. Da ladies doctor. Michelle da insists I use hers for da birth."

They left, Rabbie thinking he was in some parallel universe type of dreamy place, where life was always good and the woman were beautiful, but no pushovers, which he decided was a good thing, for everybody concerned.

Chapter 36
'When Will I See You Again'

When will I see you again?
When will our hearts beat together?
Are we still lovers? Or just good friends?
When will I see you again? When will I see you again?
When will we share precious moments?
Is this the beginning?
Or is it the end?
When will I see you again?
When will I see you again?

The Three Degrees, 1972

January, 2011 – Belaire, Hollywood, California

Collette liked the small supermarket a few blocks down from their apartment in Bellaire, it was clean and well-stocked and had a deli counter to die for, plus the staff were friendly and helpful and would engage in a good natter with their regulars when it was quiet.

She pushed the trolley towards the checkout, then stopped and pulled her clutch bag and delved into it and pulled out a packet of Tylenol and dry swallowed three. She glanced at her watch. Ten after two. "Christ, Collette," she mumbled to herself, "You only took three a couple of hours ago," but the headaches were getting worse, and she had that strange tingling in her fingers again. "It's the quack for you tomorrow. No more farting about."

She nearly dropped the bag before catching it and placing it carefully on top of her goods, she seemed to be getting clumsier too and seemed tired all day. What in damnation was wrong with her? Had she not the best of lives? Good pals and to top it all, she was still in love with the love of her life, Jamesey.

Reaching the checkout, she dumped the groceries onto the belt and got her purse out.

Mona, the cashier, began pricing the goods and bagging them for her. "You okay, Mrs DeJames? You're very pale looking. You wanna sit down a while and I get you a glass of water?"

Collette liked Mona. They would call her in North London 'The salt of the earth'. Collette wondered why she looked so blurry.

"It's Collette, dear, how many times?" she replied with a rueful grin, "Naw, I'm okay, got guests for dinner and have to get back, could do without the hassle, if the truth be told."

"I could get these delivered for you pronto. You need to take it easy, hon, or you'll be getting a takeaway!"

Collette really did feel quite ill now. Apart from the pounding headaches she had been getting on and off for months, she kept getting hot flushes and felt nauseous. "You know, Mona, I might just take you up on that," and she lowered her voice, "I think I'm going through the change of life, if you know what I mean?"

Mona did. She'd been through it herself. "Sure do, a woman's lot and all that, but you hardly look old enough, Collette."

And Mona was right. Approaching fifty-six, Collette was still slim and pretty and could have passed for twenty years younger in the right light. Collette laughed in spite of her sore head. "You sure know how to boost a gal's confidence, Mona. Put it on my account. I'll go sit in the car and guzzle coke for a spell."

"I'll get Donny to drop it off, Collette, you put them up. Holler if you need me, honey."

Collette grabbed a can from the cart and headed out to the car park. Perhaps a healthy dose of caffeine would help, but the bright sunlight seemed to sear right through her eyes into her poor head and dark spots raced across her vision. Her legs felt weak, and she felt like she was going to vomit.

For frig's sake, get a grip. Kim and Smudger were coming for dinner. Petral was flying in, and they were going to celebrate her promotion to Sergeant in the Northern Ireland Police Force, and Jamesey was bringing the head of Miami and his wife up to dine. *I don't reckon spare ribs, slaw and chips from Fernandos would please them*, she thought.

She made it to the Subaru SUV and leant against the driver's door. She ripped the coke can open and took a huge gulp. She always seemed thirsty these days. God that was good. What was it again? Oh yeah…Coca Cola…stupid mare.

Annoyed at her body letting her down, she ran through the menu again, trying to put mind over matter. *Scottish smoked salmon with asparagus, baby corn and hollandaise sauce. Check! Cumberland pie with cheese gratin, petit pois and mixed veg... Check! Mango, orange and lime cheesecake with butterscotch ice cream. Cheese and biscuits, and Jamesey was sorting out the wines and spirits. Check! Sorted. Easy-peasy, chicken cheesy. Go girl, go, you're not gonna let Jamesey down.*

Well, at least the mind's not going, she mused and took another big chug of coke. The fizzy drink hit her stomach like a weighted brick and she felt bloated. The mere thought of going home and cooking seemed an impossible task and that was a strange animal in the yard because Collette loved cooking and liked seeing her friends and family enjoying her culinary creations, and she didn't give up or fade from doing her duty. A job was a job. Bob-a-job, knobby. Christ, she felt weird.

The spots swimming before her eyes were big black planets now, and she jack-knifed forward and vomited in ferocious gout over the asphalt. *Now that's what I call a technicolour yawn!* she shakily thought. *Talk about the magic bleeding rainbow!*

She leant back down again on the car, perspiration streaming down her face. "Looks like takeaway after all, Jamesey," she said as her legs gave way, and she passed out in a merciful faint, onto the hot roadway.

Mona had been watching her through the window, concerned. "Donny, dial 911 and get the paramedics. Mrs DeJames just fainted in the car park," and she grabbed a bottle of water and ran out. *Jeepers, glad my change of life wasn't that severe!* she thought thankfully.

* * *

Jamesey was on the telephone to Chicago when Cindy, his PA, put her head around the door, looking perplexed.

"Jamesey, some woman on your private number says she's Mona from the store and it's urgent."

Jamesey frowned, made his excuses to the Windy City, and connected Mona from the store.

"Jamesey DeJames, On La Guardia. Can I help you, err Mona?"

"Yah, Mona from the store on Upper Wilshire. I'm on your wife's cell and got your number."

He sat up straight. "What you doing with my wife's cell? Is she there?"

"Well, that's the thing, Mr DeJames," said a flustered Mona, "Your wife passed out in our lot, so I got an ambulance and went with her to Mount Sinai Hospital."

Jamesey cut in, "She passed out? Is she okay?"

"She's in with the doctor guys, so I grabbed her bag for safe keeping, and I hope you don't mind but I went though it for her cell and called yah. Took me a while to work it out, it being a fancy phone and all."

"Of course, I don't mind," he reassured her. "Can you wait until I get there? Was she conscious when they took her in?"

There was an ominous pause, then, "Well, no, she was outta it but she was breathing and all."

"Well, guess that's good. I'll be there in fifteen."

"Okay, and Mr DeJames, they're very good here, my Ma was in for a bypass in the fall and they were outstanding."

Jamesey was shrugging his blazer on, "Thanks, Mona, and call me Jamesey. See you soon."

He rushed into the outer office. "Cindy, get someone to lift John Carter from Miami at five. I'm going to Mount Sinai. Collette's not well."

Cindy, an efficient Afro-Caribbean in her late forties, who used to work in the Pentagon for many years calming flapping Generals down, shooed him out. "I'll hold the fort; now off you go and ring me when you can."

He grabbed the duty driver, a rangy Missourian called Pete Slater, and they sped off. He had suspected the missus hadn't been herself for a while now but whenever he broached the subject of seeing a physician, she just said she was okay and it was just the early onset of the change of life. She could be a stubborn mare at times, which was part of the attraction he felt for her, and then he inwardly grimaced as he realised she said the same about him.

God, let his little Collette be fine. Let it be just a wee glitch in the pan. He wasn't a great man for scripture, believing a man made his own way through life. *Made his own mistakes and successes, without any help from some guy sitting on a golden throne somewhere high above, somewhere unreachable to mortals like himself, a cynical look on his face as we stumble about cheating, stealing and living off each other's backs as we slowly kill this magnificent planet. Where the frigging hell did that come from?* Jamesey wondered. Stress, strain and worry did the strangest things and threw up weird notions, no matter who the recipient was.

As the car sped through traffic, Pete expertly weaving from lane to lane, Jamesey felt worried and not a little humble because if Collette had not kicked his big, fat sorry ass after he got his hand blown off in Belfast in 1976, he very much doubted he would be Chairman of a mega global security company. No, he would probably be selling life insurance policies door to door in faraway Watford and living in a rabbit hutch.

She had stood by his side through thick and thin, borne his children and made a home for them wherever they ended up, and when after a few whiskeys he would say he couldn't have done it without her, she would laugh and shrug it off, but he knew she was secretly pleased and it pleased him to please her. He worshipped the ground she walked on. People like Collette were few and far between, a special and rare breed.

He had no right hand but he didn't need one. She was his bloody right hand, and the Barry White song came to him. 'You're My First, You're My Last, My Everything', and that was what Collette was to him, and he changed his mind and said a silent prayer to God to look over and bring his broody little mare through what was surely a simple hiccup in her health, and then he put a little caveat on the end… *Because if you don't, I'll get up there somehow, pull you off your golden seat by your beard and cast you down into the hordes of desperate humanity down here on earth, and you won't like that at all when they rip you apart. Not one little bit. It's dog eat dog down here.*

Pete crashed through an amber at a busy intersection, swerved around a camper van full of boy surfers and sunk the pedal to the metal. His driving was fluid and progressive, and despite Jamesey's anxiety, he couldn't fail to notice his professional skill.

"You okay, Mr DeJames? Shouldn't be long now," asked Pete, watching him carefully from the corner of an eye the colour of strong tobacco leaves.

"When we get there, Pete, arrange two operatives to guard my wife 24/7. I don't know how long this is going to take, I am just praying it's something simple and easily treated."

"You got it, Boss… They're great at Mount Sinai, best teaching hospital in the good ole U.S. of A."

"They fucking well better be," growled Jamesey, and then said another silent little prayer, asking for forgiveness for his first prayer, feeling a total hypocrite.

Pete glanced out of the corner of his eye at the old warrior dog of a man who was his boss. He not only respected the guy but he enjoyed his company. The man was a millionaire, but he treated his staff on a one to one and had the gift of making every employee matter, regardless of how young or menial their job was. He grimaced to himself…for all his dollars…no health, no wealth.

* * *

Petral Collette Beth DeJames had landed at LAX at 2pm and got the shuttle bus to the hire car lot to pick up the nifty little Lamborghini convertible her Dad had insisted on hiring for her. Although fiercely independent, it had its perks having a pop who was chairman of a global conglomerate in the security field, so she let him throw her the odd titbit now and then. She had mega respect for the old man, who had made such a success of OLG, but she wasn't in awe of him, as many were. Petral was in awe of no man or woman, it was the way she was, but she held him in the highest esteem and had learnt a lot from him, at his knee so to speak. Life was a learning curve and the old man had gone full circle.

At twenty-four she was a very beautiful young woman in her prime. Long black hair with a natural sexy curl, flashing hazel eyes with green and gold flecks and a heart-shaped face and snub nose. She stood at five feet six inches, was full breasted, a trim waist and legs made in heaven, and when she walked into a room full of men, the conversation settled and the testosterone level rose, and she knew it. In fact, the power of the thing turned her on. But she was no easy pull, and the several short-lived affairs she had achieved so far had been with men of her picking and careful choosing, and although highly satisfying, the sparks had soon fizzled out and she had moved on to greener, fresher pastures. She guessed Mr Right and romance would come along in years to come, but she was in no rush and the whole world was her playground at the moment and that's just the way she intended to keep it, not get tied down at an early age like many of her contemporaries, with a hefty mortgage and a squad of squealing brats hanging off her apron strings demanding attention. No way, Jose.

Petral was a shaker and a mover. She was her father's daughter on that score but there was a lot of her mum in there too. She knew her mum had suffered a terrible upbringing and the subject was taboo in family circles, but she had raised Petral and her siblings with love and devotion and apart from that, she was interesting and could discuss so many topics, and Petral was amazed at her wealth of knowledge. Her mother had told her when she was leaving home that there were two types of love. That you could love a man for his attributes, but when you met the real one meant for you, you knew and it was for life. She held her mother in the highest regard and reckoned at times she was very much the power behind the throne, albeit in the most discreet, encouraging and supportive way. She was really looking forward to seeing her mum. It had been nearly a year, and Petral scolded herself for ignoring the old folk. Still, she was here now and she bet Mum had pulled out all the stops for a nice dinner.

Petral smiled. She was currently lodging with her Uncle John and Aunt Mary[177], in the rural village of Maralin, twenty miles outside Belfast. She had studied Criminal Psychology at Edinburgh University and passed with honours, and the new police service had snapped her up and for a year she had learnt the ropes at Brooklyn, the Police Headquarters in East Belfast, but six months ago she was promoted to Sergeant and sent to lead a unit of uniform anti-terrorist cops in Peat Island in Mid Ulster. It was dangerous, exhausting work, and the guys had shown their dismay the first day she arrived at getting a petite little woman to lead them against the Real IRA but she soon showed them she was as tough as old boots and whipped them into shape and if she now said follow, they said lead on, without question or debate. She was where the action was, right in the thick of it, and happy as a pig in shite; after all, she was a DeJames and leading seasoned men and fighting tyranny in the little country she loved so well ran in her blood and coursed through her veins.

---

[177] See sequel: The Rebirth of a Warrior – Lost Relatives

535

After all, hadn't her dad given his right hand to the often God-forsaken place? She laughed. Some guy on the plane had chatted her up all the way over. Said he loved her accent and was big in studio film marketing and offered to get her an audition for the movies. She had played him along and agreed to meet him at the Beverly Hills Hilton that night, but she had no intention of going. She had noticed the white band on his ring finger, standing out from his tanned hand, and he never answered his cell; in fact, turning it off. Divorced with kids and making a fresh start in LA. Yeah right, mister married man... If Petral was anything, it was observant, and she hadn't come down from the sky in a bubble...

No, she had moved in with Uncle John and Mary because it was handy for work but also a relatively safe area. She had considered buying a place of her own, but the previous labour government and the bankers had certainly screwed the property market up. She knew her dad would buy her a palace at the drop of a hat, but she was determined to make it on her own. She was a free spirit and intended to stay that way. DeJameses liked to make their own way, whatever their gender, and didn't take hand outs easily.

Whizzing down the freeway, her cell rang, and hoping no cops were watching, she answered, hands on.

"Petral, it's dad... Your mum's in Mount Sinai hospital, can you come?"

"Christ, what's wrong, Pop?"

"She's in a coma. I need you, Petral. I don't know what to do."

For her dad to plead for help was such a rare event in Petral's life, she thought she was imagining what she heard, then the trained, practical head came on and she punched the directions up on the GPS. "Hold on, Pop. I'll be there in twenty. Everything will be fine. Love you."

* * *

Jamesey hung up and marched back into the hospital and down to the cubicle in Accident and Emergency, hoping against all hope that Collette would be up and sitting, laughing with the nurses and swopping recipes, or knowing her, dirty lady jokes that men never heard and thank God would never understand if they did.

Pete stopped him with a big rancher's hand and thrust a cup of coffee at him. "Doc says they want more X-rays and to wait here. Deeko and Christa will be here shortly, fully tooled. John Carter's flight was delayed, and Cindy caught him before he left and cancelled. Mr Martin is heading into the office and is going to run the business for as long as needed and..." he consulted his iPod, "his wife Marlene is going over to your crib to get Mrs DeJames a case of basics, and Mr and Mrs Smyth will be here within the hour from Malibu. Cindy wants to know do you want anybody else rung?"

Jamesey looked at him transfixed, and then shook his head, his red and gold locks just starting to show the faintest of snow, gleaming under the fluorescents.

"I'll just have to go with the flow, Pete. I'm afraid this has all rather caught me unprepared."

Pete squeezed his shoulder hard. "Might be nothing, Boss. Some allergy or aversion to something? What's Mrs DeJames always saying? We're all one big goddamn family in OLG? You hang in there, Boss dude, and think positive and me and the guys get yah through this."

Jamesey looked at Pete. He didn't know him that well, having transferred him down from the Kansas office six months prior. Six foot two inches of lean, tanned, whipcord muscle and a chiselled craggy face. Hair a neat short, back and sides. Jamesey could imagine him riding the range, roll up fag between his lips, lassoing steers. He knew he had been a Navy Seal and had served in Afghanistan and Iraq. He was clean-cut, efficient and reassuring, and Jamesey was glad he was here. He had a strange feeling he was going to need a port in a storm soon, because he had an inkling he was going to have to drop anchor and ride the rough weather out.

* * *

They sat in the relatives' room nervously waiting. Collette had gone through a huge bank of tests, and they were waiting the results with bated breath. To say the atmosphere was tense was an understatement. The matriarchal figure was ill, and it was a strange and scary monster that prowled the corridors of their minds.

Petral sat holding her Auntie Kim's hand. Although not related by blood, Kim had been there right through her childhood and she and Collette were like sisters. "I bleeding told her to go to the doctor's weeks ago. Sore heads she was getting but you know how stubborn she is, silly mare," tears making her eyes shine and her voice quiver.

"And whatever's wrong that streak of stubbornness will get her through it," Petral reassured her. "Just you watch. Mum will be up effing and blinding soon, just you watch, Auntie."

Smudger put his arm around his distressed wife. "She'll be okay, luv. Bleeding indestructible that one. Take a squadron of tanks to put Collette out of action."

Petral excused herself and went out into the corridor and rang her brother Rabbie in New York, chewing her lip nervously. She was more upset than she cared to admit. This was a twilight zone for her.

"Hey, sis, what's up? Still hounding the Real IRA?" Rabbie asked, delighted to hear from his hard to get, wayward sister.

"I'm in LA, bruv… You better get down. Mum's not well."

There was a stunned silence, "Whatcha mean? Mum's never ill. Where is she?"

"She's in Mount Sinai. In a coma. We're hoping she just took a bad reaction to something."

"Bloody Norah! How's the old man taking it?"

She paused, "He's lost in space on this one, Rabbie. I dread to think what will happen if worst comes to the worst. You know how much he loves her," she gulped saliva, "as we all do."

Rabbie scoffed, "Nothing's gonna happen to Mum. She's as tough as he is. Probably bad shellfish or something. You know how she loves her prawns and cockles."

"Yeah, you're probably right, now stop gabbing and get your arse into gear. Let's get some family support going here for Mum and Pop."

He laughed, "That's my girl. See you soon. Everything will be hunkey dorey!"

But Petral was worried. They had been here three hours now, and she guessed if it had been a simple allergy, they would have known by now. They had called her father down an hour ago to speak to the doctors, and he wasn't back yet. His absence spoke volumes.

She wandered back into the room. Marlene Martin had arrived with Collette's case; Marlene's husband Scoobie was second in command in LA. A ferociously strong man who had served for many years with her Uncle Davey in the elite Special Air Service. They often travelled abroad together troubleshooting for OLG. "Any word, dear? Scoobie's at the office now. He has rung your uncle and he's on his way."

"No, Dad's with the doctors. You want me to get you coffee?"

"Something cold would be nice dear, thank you."

Petral strolled down to the Coke machine and using her loose change, got Marlene a can. Debating, she pulled her cell out again and rang her brother Jamie in Cairnchester in the West Midlands of England, where he ran his own security firm, 'Stand to Security'. She got his voicemail, probably out on a job or more likely doing the business with one of the local beauties, she guessed. "Jamie, it's Petral. Don't get too alarmed but Mum's in hospital in a coma, could be anything but I'll ring you when I know more."

She hung up and took Marlene her Coke. Her Uncle Davey had arrived and stood to greet her. He was an extremely strong, fit, attractive man and the mystery uncle of the family. She knew he had lost his fiancée, the love of his life, in Afghanistan at the battle of 'The Fort of the Dark Raven's Wing', a few years ago, and was still grieving, and her father had warned the family not to bring it up as it brought his post-traumatic stress disorder on and turned him funny. Uncle Davey could be very, very dangerous when he so wished, and she knew her Dad had got him out of trouble a few times over the last year. But she had always felt safe and reassured in his strong presence and knew he loved the family.

"You okay, Petral? Christ, I hope Collette will be okay," and he surprised her by giving her a hug and a kiss on the cheek.

"Fingers crossed, Uncle. I didn't know if you were in the country or not."

"Just back, Scoobie rang me. Christ, I hate these bloody places; I'm going out for a smoke."

"Those things will kill yah, mucker," Smudger told him. "Not that the Taliban could," and he grinned.

"Oh well, at least I'm in the right place then," he threw over his shoulder without a trace of irony.

"Two VCs, a MM and a DSM and God knows what else, I guess it would take some brave dose of nicotine to harm Major DeJames," Petral observed, proud of her uncle, and left the room.

"It's only an addiction, I reckon the nicotine calms the system."

Petral snorted. "Cancer doesn't respect war heroes; still, if it keeps him happy and calm, what's the harm?"

"Very true, because believe me, you don't want to see him when he goes off his trolley," Smudger said darkly. "When Major DeJames kicks off, the whole bleedin' world wobbles."

"Yeah well, let's just keep positive and pray for Mum and be there for Dad. That's all we can do until we know more." Smudger looked at her in open admiration. Petral was a DeJames all right. A right chip off the old block.

"Yeah, and tell yah bleeding what," chipped in Marlene, "there is no better man to have in your corner than the Major when the shit hits the fan!"

Smudger raised his coffee in a toast, "Amen to that, Marlene."

Jamesey sat on a bench in the rear parking lot. Trying to get his head around what he had just been told by the specialists. He would give his right hand for a cigarette but he had given up many years ago, just smoking the odd Cuban cigar on special occasions. Births, weddings and funerals. Hatch, match and dispatch. He didn't even have a right hand. He'd given that for his country and the lives of his young soldiers. No, his right hand, metaphorically speaking, was lying out cold in intensive care, and what the specialists had told him had chilled his blood and scared the crap out of him. What the fuck was going on? The Los Angelinos were watching for the next mega earthquake, but he sincerely hoped his had not arrived.

The head of physicians and the duty neurologist had sat him down and gently spoken to him. The X-rays had shown up a large grey shadow on the left side of Collette's brain, so they had sent her for a MRI and a CAT scan. Resonating imaging and computer assisted technology or something. The terms were irrelevant to him. All he cared was they gave a three-dimensional image inside his loved one's head and what it showed was inside her beautiful mind, and it wasn't very encouraging at all.

"It's a tumour, a melanoma, Mr DeJames. The size and shape of a duck egg. It's inverted and angled at forty-five degrees," said the neurologist grimly.

"I'm surprised your wife has survived this long. You say she was walking about okay? This thing is pressing down on her cortex nerves and by rights, should be affecting her functioning properly in a considerable manner."

"Well yeah, she's had sore heads and hot flushes, and she seemed a little unsteady and confused but she thought it was the change of life," he explained.

"I see, and you say the headaches have been going on for six to eight weeks?" asked the head doctor.

The neurologist tut-tutted, "That's very fast. Not good at all, I'm afraid."

"What you mean? Not good? What are you going to do about it? Just zap the bastard. Expense no bother. I'll pay for the stars and skint myself for my wife."

"The thing is, Mr DeJames, brain tumours can form over many months, sometimes years, and if caught early, can be treated with some success but for one this size to have grown so fast, it shows it's a particularly virulent strain. I'm surprised she didn't have more pain with it. Unfortunately, there are many strains of melanoma of the brain, and this one is particularly virulent."

Jamesey fidgeted. He wanted action and he wanted it right now. "Well, she's a tough little filly. So what you going to do? Cut it out or what? For all the size of her, she is as strong as an ox."

The head doc took it up. "Not as simple. We can operate and laser it. Burn as much out as we can but the chances of getting it all are minimal, and it'll just grow back all the faster. The speed it has grown so far, Mr DeJames, is very discouraging from an operational viewpoint."

"Yes," put in the neurologist, "and she may never come out of the coma or walk again. I doubt very much she will see the week out. We can only keep her comfortable and pain-free. Palliative care is the only option. I am so sorry. I know it's hard to accept."

He was horrified. He stood spluttering, "But, hey come on, you gotta save her. She's only fifty-six. You have to do something. She has to come home. She is going to lay and give up in hospital. I forbid it. Her family… I need her…" and he sobbed.

The neurologist put his hand on his shoulder kindly, "Let's run by this again slowly. If we operate, there's a fifty/fifty chance she'll die on the table. If she survives the op, there's only the same chance she'll regain consciousness or walk again. Of course, it's your choice but she'll be dead in a month at the most."

He was aghast. "That's impossible. You have to be joking. I can't believe this."

"I'm sorry, Mr DeJames," from the head, "You can get a second opinion of course, your prerogative, but that's the way we see it."

The neurologist patted his back in sympathy. "We'll keep her comfortable and pain-free. Why don't you go for a little walk and think about it then get back to us?"

And that's what he did and was sitting on the bench, horror stricken when his younger brother Davey came around the corner and found him. He gave him a big hug, which was a rare thing and tried to look at him assuredly.

"There you are, Jamesey," and he sat down, looking into his brother's stricken face, "I presume the bone saws gave you bad news? What they say? Let's take it one step at a time."

"Gis a fag, Davey. I need one bad. It's not good, bruvver."

He lit Jamesey one of his trademark Du Maurier from the orange box with the full lid that lifted up that he ordered from Pall Mall in London. Jamesey sadly told him the devastating prognosis. "Looks like I'm not even going to get a chance to say goodbye to her. It's a total fuck up," he ended, eyes brimming with unshed tears. "The beautiful light of my life. My heart, my world," and incredibly, tears ran down his hardened cheeks.

Davey put his arm around him, thinking furiously. He'd never had a chance to say a proper goodbye to his Sonja either, the light taken out of her dancing, lovely green sea blue eyes by a cowardly Taliban bullet. His brother had been there for him then, and he was a man who knew the importance of goodbyes. "Bollocks to that, Jamesey." And he pulled his cell and rang Rabbie in New York, "You coming down, lad? 'Kay, grab the company jet and a relief crew and put it on standby to fly anywhere in the world at a moment's notice. I'll explain later. No chill, just fucking do it. We need you, nephew."

He got a number off Google and dialled. "This is Major DeJames. On La Guardia LA. Can you modify a Gulfstream to take a comatose patient on possibly a cross Atlantic flight as soon as possible?" He listened. "Money's no object; I want all the gear, crash, medical. Can you recommend a top-notch emergency nursing agency?" he punched a number in "'Kay, I'll be back to you with landing details and funds in a few hours. Don't let me down. Bankers draft from Bank of California or Visa Gold, whatever… Okay, sweet."

He called another number and arranged for two experienced extensive care nurses and an ER doctor to go to LAX in five hours' time and await instructions. "Make them comfortable, no expense spared, but no alcohol, they are looking after my sister-in-law," and snapped the telephone off.

Jamesey sat with his head down; strangely grateful his brother had taken this terrible burden off his shoulders.

"Right, let's get back to the quacks."

"What are we doing, Davey? I'm afraid, bruv."

Family stood together through thick and thin.

Davey gripped his shoulder. "We're going to get the best expert in the world, email him the tests and fly her over ASAP. At best, you get lots more time with her; at worst, you get to say your goodbyes. You okay with this?"

Jamesey nodded his head. "'Kay, least we're doing our best by her." He gripped his upper arm, "Thanks Davey, I mean that."

They hunted the experts down and met up in their office. "Who is the top-most expert in this field of brain tumour intrusion in the world?" Davey demanded.

They looked at each other in silent agreement. "It would be Doctor Jürgen Bergenhaffer, but he's in Basle in Switzerland."

"Can Mrs DeJames fly okay with this thing in her head?"

"Well sure, but you will need a MedAire jet, equipment and a full medical team."

"That's being arranged. Could you get me Bergenhaffer's number and email the scans and notes to him?"

"Well, sure," said the head doctor, relieved the problem was being taken out of his hands, "But I warn you, he doesn't come cheap."

"Money's no object when it comes to Collette," snapped Davey. "A million bucks a minute I'd pay to save her."

"He is absolutely brilliant," enthused the neurologist. "If anyone can get her out of the coma, it's him."

"But we still stand by our diagnosis," said the head, with a sympathetic shake of his head.

"One step at a time, gentlemen. You have the papers and Collette ready to move in six hours. Thank you for your great care and efforts. Come on, Jamesey."

"It's in the hands of Gods but with proper professional medical care," and he paused, "you have nothing to lose. I am so sorry, Mr DeJames."

Davey hustled the stunned man out. and they headed to the relatives' room, bearers of bad news and slim hope. "Come on, Jamesey, I've more calls to make, and I'm going to personally see Collette gets sorted and on the plane and gets to 'Cuckoo land' asap."

Jamesey was weeping now. "Thank suffering Jesus you're here, brother. I have no grid reference or direction on this one."

Davey enfolded him in a huge bear hug, "Family, brother, we pull each other out of the snake pit, no questions asked. Right… Compose yourself. Let's not upset the ladies."·

A passing nurse had seen the grim expressions on the men's faces and put the 'Do Not Disturb' sign on the door.

Jamesey was sipping coffee when Davey slipped out and telephoned Cindy. "Tell that Kansan Pete Slater he's going to Switzerland and my brother needs a PA."

* * *

True to their word the medical team was waiting at the Executive hanger at LAX, and they immediately took charge of a comatose Collette and supervised her transfer onto the modified Gulfstream.

Davey DeJames watched grimly as they hooked her up to various monitors and life-support machines but was quietly reassured by their confidence and caring attitude. He'd seen it all before when he had accompanied wounded men from the

541

hell holes of Iraq and Afghanistan on long haul flights to bases in Germany and the UK, the injured being tended to by the Brit forces medical team, whom he considered the best of the best, but this was different, this was his sister-in-law, the much loved little Collette, and it was family, which it made it a different ball game and he had pulled out all the stops on this one.

He looked over at his older brother, who was standing on the asphalt, looking lost and confused. He went and put a tentative arm around his big shoulders. Jamesey like this was an unknown animal to him. "Chin up, bruv. You never know what this Professor Bergenhaffer can do. Europe is always ten years ahead."

Jamesey sighed so long and deep, Davey thought he might pass out as he saw the anguish in his brother's eyes, "If she makes it over, Dave, she's gonna die, mate. I just know it."

Davey steeled himself, "No, she fucking wont, she's a big fighter in a wee body and you know it. Anymore talk like that and I'll kick your arse up and down the runway, now get a fucking grip, for both our sakes. For Collette's sake, get switched on."

It was the way the soldiers talked to each other, and Jamesey grimaced and shook himself, "You're fucking right, mucker. I've been a waste of space. Gotta be there for her. For myself and everyone."

"Now you're bloody talking, mate. I've pulled in every marker I have on this one. You'll be in Switzerland in no time, and Collette will be getting the proper treatment before you know it."

And he had. The Gulfstream would hop over to an America Air Force base at Tampa, Florida on the East coast, where it would get priority refuelling before the long haul to a Royal Air Force base at Truro in South West England, where it would top up, and ninety minutes later it would land in Geneva, where it would be met by a Swiss Army ambulance and Collette would be taken to the clinic thirty miles away in the forested foothills of the mighty Alps.

The bond between Special Force operatives worldwide was very tight, and Davey had managed to cut nearly two hours off the overall flight plan by cutting landing, take off, clearance and fuel times, meaning the jet could go at maximum speed.

Davey wasn't going with them. He would stay in LA and help Scoobie run the office and do any troubleshooting. He had done as much as he could.

Pete Slater arrived carrying a grip and casually dressed in a rawhide jacket and jeans. "My pal Jean Pierre in the Swiss Special Forces Mountain Troop is going to meet us at Geneva and has arranged transport and accommodation around the clock."

Davey was impressed, "How the fuck did you sort that?"

Pete grinned, "Easy, Boss, me and the Seals pulled him out of a shit pit of gunfire in Helmand a couple of years ago but as soon as I mentioned your name and the bosses heard, they couldn't do enough. You must be some legends."

Davey looked pensive, "Yeah, legends. Legends fade into history, it's the way it is."

Jamesey stood and stretched, "Hope you brought plenty of fags, young Slater. My nicotine addiction has just kicked in again!"

"Got two hundred Camel in the bag, Boss."

Major Davey DeJames groaned, "Fuck me, lad. If you've seen as many camels in life as we have, you never want to see another one again."

Pete laughed, "Cheer up, Bossman. You can light these ones and they smell a hell of a lot better than camel shit!"

* * *

Go to Switzerland.

* * *

Davey DeJames saw them off and headed back to the office to confer with Scoobie. They would keep the OLG ship afloat until Jamesey got back with hopefully a recovering Collette.

As he marched back to his car, he had a strange feeling of foreboding. Experienced soldiers of many years' service, who had put their lives on the line, developed a strong sense and Davey's had kicked in strongly, and he sensed doom and gloom ahead. The 'Gremlin' factor kicking in.

He wasn't a praying man and believed if there was a God, he must have one hell of a sadistic streak, judging by some of the horrendous, atrocious things he had seen over his career, but he prayed anyway.

He judged his brother and wife were going to need all the luck the gods could muster.

* * *

In the end the flight went smooth and uneventful.

The Gulf G5 was a long range executive jet that normally took up to sixteen passengers and baggage.

It had been decided Pete Slater would accompany them as driver and fixer, Petral for moral support and her unflappable demeanour, Rabbie to keep an eye on Jamesey and to liaise with OLG, and Kim Smyth because she refused to be left behind. "She's my best friend, no, more than that, she's my bloody sister and where she goes, I go."

That, plus a very competent team of a doctor and two nurses, who hovered over a comatose Collette on a special medical air bed, hooked up to a bank of monitors and oxygen plus baggage, which had been hastily scrambled to the airport, made for a heavy payload, and they had to refuel at RAF Truro, in Cornwall, after Davey had pulled a favour in.

Dawn was breaking as the sun beat its way up the Alps and a Swiss Army ambulance and a seven-seater SUV were waiting for them on the apron, another favour pulled in my Major DeJames.

They arrived an hour later at Le Clinique Salanger, high above the city on the pine-forested slopes.

Collette, with no change at all in her condition, was immediately rushed off for tests with a group of rushing nurses issuing instructions in a mix of French and German.

"Is the Professor's orders, ja," a portly Matron told them, leading them into the palatial red-tiled, three-storied villa.

When they were settled in, Jamesey was fetched to the Professor's office, itching to get things going to help Collette.

He was still numb with shock and having serious trouble getting his head around things but Petral and Rabbie had talked long and comfortingly on the flight as he sat holding Collette's hand forlornly and knew the matter was out of his hands, and he would just have to go with the flow and do what he could or thought best for her.

Professor Jürgen Bergenhaffer was not what Jamesey expected. Certainly not the stereo type of a fumbling grey-haired genius wearing glasses and a tweed suit.

Bergenhaffer was a tall, athletic-looking man in his late forties, wearing his long brown hair in a ponytail, dressed in a Ben Sherman shirt and Levi's and sporting a flamboyant pair of cowboy boots with shiny silver design.

He greeted Jamesey and bade him sit. He had all the test results and images from the scans on his laptop.

"It's a very bad melanoma and must have grown very quick for your wife to still have functioning so recently," he told him in flawless English.

"So what can we do about it?" asked Jamesey, wringing his hands unconsciously.

The Professor eyed him sadly. He hated this part, "Well, by rights she should be dead. Those bastards can grow at a tremendous rate, and the tests confirm it's a very virulent strain."

Jamesey hung his head, "So I can't even get to say goodbye to her, then?"

Bergenhaffer injected some hope into his voice, "What we need to do is burn out as much as we can as soon as possible. I have got a state of the art micro laser the Germans have perfected. I can probably get most of it, but," and he paused, "we don't have the ability yet to get one hundred percent clearance rates... Sadly, it will grow back and probably quicker."

Jamesey seized on that, "I don't care, do it, Professor... And the coma?"

"Yes, we have been making groundbreaking work there using strong drugs and chemicals. I believe I can bring her round at the right time, and you will get a limited time together."

"How long, Professor?"

He leant back in his chair, fingers steepled, deep in thought, "Maybe a month, six weeks, it depends on the patient's general health."

Jamesey was stunned to the core. "A month, a bloody month?"

"Yes, maybe longer. Of course, she will be bed-ridden but she will be compos mentis and aware of her surroundings, albeit she will be on strong medication for the pain."

"And the alternative?"

"Leave her as she is and let her slip away peacefully."

* * *

Jamesey talked it over numbly with the rest.

"Bring her round, Dad. She won't want to go without saying goodbye," from Petral.

"I don't know, Dad," from Rabbie, "But a son could not have asked for a better Mother. I don't think she would want to just leave us like this."

"I just want to see her again and give her a hug goodbye," cried Kim.

He even went out and sat in the grounds and had a smoke with Pete Slater, just to get an outsider's perspective.

Pete mused and blew out a plume of smoke into the pristine Alpine, resin scented air.

"Guess it's what separates us from animals," he mused, "We know for certain we are going to die at some time. I knew a lot of guys who got slotted in Afghanistan, mostly young guys, who never got a chance to say cheerio to anybody. I reckon if they had the choice, they would have liked to go with kith and kin around them. I sure would."

Jamesey thought back to a young paratrooper mercilessly gunned down in Belfast many years ago.

He patted Pete on the legs. "Thanks, Pete," and he went for a long walk in the beautiful grounds before heading back to find the Professor.

* * *

They spent a week at the clinic. The laser surgery went smoothly and on the third day, the Professor brought her back to consciousness.

Collette looked around her confusedly "'Ere where am I, Jamesey? What's going on, mate?"

He was holding her hand tightly, "You're in Switzerland, honey. You're not too well."

"Cor, Switzerland. Always wanted one of them cuckoo clocks."

He smiled sadly, "I'll see if they have any in the pawn shops."

She laughed at that, "No, seriously, Jamesey. What's bleedin' wrong with me?"

So he told her, and they both shed a few tears till she squeezed his hand, "That must have been a bloody hard choice to make. Thank you, my love, from my heart."

"You are my heart, my darling," he told her before breaking down again.

She consoled him now, "Come on, mate. We all have to go sometime. It's been a great ride, but I'm getting off at one station and you're just getting off at a station further up the line. We'll meet up again."

He looked into her eyes, the drugs making her pupils the size of pinheads.

In the face of probably the most devastating situation a mortal could find themselves in, she had something positive to say.

His wonderful, loyal, clever, feisty little mare. She was outstanding. Unique.

* * *

They flew home three days later, Collette marvelling over the plane and cracking away all the way back.

* * *

Six weeks later they buried her in a quiet cemetery in the Hollywood Hills, birds singing and chirping happily in the trees in the warm sunshine.

"I'll take you home to Petral Hill in a few years, once I get my head sorted," he told her through his broken heart.

Chapter 37
Let's Get Together Again

Week Before Christmas, 2013

She was asleep on the couch, curled up on her right, dressed in a thin buttery coloured short nightdress and matching negligée. He gazed fondly at her, she looked so sweet and content, her head resting on her hands and her left leg cocked over her right, the gown open and showing the length of her perfect legs. She was a masterpiece waiting to be painted.

He hung his coat up and knelt before her, she opened her eyes and smiled as she came out of her sleep and saw her dream lover looking intently at her. She decided after the birth was out of the way, she would paint a portrait of him in oils, so when he was away working he would always be with her in spirit and she could feel his absent presence.

She stretched and yawned luxuriously, and her breasts strained against the thin fabric and her toes curled like a cat's before she relaxed and pulled him into a warm kiss, her cheeks flushed from sleep. Nuzzling into him, she purred in contentment.

When they broke off, she traced his face with gentle fingertips, so happy he was home safe and sound, his reassuring presence so vital and comforting to her life. A dream life she never thought she would have so soon.

"I think I am going to put you top of my list of 'Most Beautiful Girls When Asleep in New York'," he declared, stroking her beautiful hair. "If not the world."

She smiled, "I tink I put you number one on my list of 'Sexiest Man To Wake Up To in the World'."

He lifted her gently in his arms and carried her easily down to the bedroom. He pulled the covers back and put her on her side of the bed. She got comfortable, and they embraced again before kissing deeply and tenderly.

"I 'ave done us some supper, Rab. Nice seafood salad, vill I get it for us?"

He was hungry but not for food. He stroked her bare leg and nuzzled her ear and neck, enjoying her warmth and smoothness. Ever the gentleman, he said, "If you want it now, Luca, I'll get it for us." And he stroked her rounding belly, "After all, you're twenty weeks preggers now and eating for two!"

She hugged him to her, "I know, it's great, but vill you still vant me ven I am as fat as Big Mama?"

They had watched the Eddie Murphy film on Classic Films where the famous comic had dressed up as an overweight old mama so he could get a job as a housekeeper. "Of course, I will. Sure it's only padding, like Eddie's. It'll soon drop off you. I find it quite sexy actually."

Reassured, she ran her fingers through his hair, "Tell you vat, ve 'ave supper then ve 'ave long, hot bath and I wash your hair and give you a massage."

He liked that idea very much. They had made love in the bath before but he wouldn't try it on tonight with her so far into her second trimester.

Reading his intimate thoughts, she said, "Den afta you can give me a gentle massage in bed."

He liked the sound of that, "Now that certainly sounds like a viable game plan," and he bounced off to get their supper, full of beans and love for her. Maybe he should invest in a hot tub…more room to manoeuvre.

She watched him go, so full of renewed energy and zest, she thought he was incredible but she was just a teeny weeny bit biased. Her asking him to give her a massage in bed had become their secret code for when she wanted to make love since she had fallen with child.

His lovemaking to her had been gentle, tender and incredibly fulfilling. Her whole body seemed ultra-sensitive, especially down there, although her breasts often felt tender and sore. She wished, sometimes, he wasn't so careful. She missed the times when they would roll around the bed and tear their clothes off and ravish each other before he took her hard and frantic, making her scream out in ecstasy, clutching his hair tight and running her nails down his back.

He put her salad down before her, and she smiled her thanks. She could eat for America at the present moment in time.

Those days would come back, she would make sure they did, she vowed as she squeezed lemon juice and dribbled vinaigrette over her seafood. She popped a king prawn into her mouth and nearly swooned with pleasure. She had purchased them in Toni's Deli and the convivial Italian had popped a few extra in, "For the bambino and his rose of a mom, King Neptune's harvest, my caro."

The first few weeks of her pregnancy she had quite bad morning sickness, Jocelyn had guessed early on, and Luca had sworn her delighted second mum to secrecy, explaining that was why she was off her food. Rabbie had thought she was worried about the upcoming trial. Jocelyn had mixed her up a tea using cloudberries, an old Indian cure, and the sickness had cleared up overnight.

She certainly was not off her food now, and Rabbie certainly seemed to be enjoying his as he wolfed it down. Ex commandos did not hang about when it came to demolishing plates of scoff.

She had taken a terrible craving for peppermint ice cream with hot butterscotch sauce. Rabbie thought it was just a fad she was going through and it was a strange concoction Lithuanians liked. *He hadn't a clue*, she thought fondly as she watched him eat and scroll down through the messages on his cell.

"You arranged to meet da mistress ven your fat lady falls asleep?"

"Absolutely not, my lover," he declared stoutly, "You're more than enough of a handful for me," he glanced at her large, firm breasts, "Well, two or four handfuls actually," and he grinned suggestively and waggled his eyebrows, making her giggle.

"You doing your 'Groucho Marx', I lurve it ven you do that, my dahling!"

She loved his easygoing manner and sense of humour, her mother would love him, she knew. She must sort her mother out with an English language course; she would need it if she was to meet a kind American widower when she came over in a few years. Her maman was thrilled over the news and demanded regular updates.

Luca sighed and wished her mother was here to help her through the pregnancy. Deep down she was scared. What if something went wrong? What if she needed a caesarean? It would be such a comfort to have Maman by her side. Being pregnant felt so natural but it could be thought-provoking when she was alone and sometimes scary, but her female buddies were such a great support and had been great but sweet mother of baby Jesus she so wished for her darling Maman, who was so far away. She wanted her by her side as a mother and daughter bonding mechanism. The succour of having the one who shed blood to birth her to be with her and be proud of her achievement in getting to this status in life.

Rabbie sensed her pensiveness, "You okay, honey? This salad's great."

"Yah, am 'kay…bit of a nervous wreck at da moment. Must be da hormones."

He patted her hand. "It's your body changing. Getting all geared up for motherhood! It's understandable," he reassured her, "They live on the seabed and shake you know," he added mysteriously.

"Vot do, dahling?" she asked to please him. God, she was so easily fooled.

"Nervous wrecks."

She looked at him sceptically, "Is no such thing. Is dis American humour?"

"No, Royal Marines. I'm only codding," and he chuckled.

"Vat is dis 'codding' mean?"

"Codding, you know…the fish."

She was bemused, miles away in her own thoughts.

"Never mind, I'll go run the bath and put lots of that apricot and mango smelly stuff in. You can relax to your heart's content."

"My heart is only content ven it's wiv you, lover."

It suddenly hit her hard how lucky she was to be in love with and be loved by this fabulous guy. She was nearly weeping now. All that he had done for her, she had refused to face how lonely she had actually been in this huge metropolis. Yeah she had Wendy and Bobby, but she had sometimes envied their intimacy and felt the odd one out when they were canoodling, as Bobby called it, quite openly with each other. She felt embarrassed at times and left them to their devices and hastened back to her lonely apartment.

But Christ on a crutch was she glad she had waited and Rabbie had come along. She didn't think Christ had ever used a crutch, but she had heard Rabbie use the expression when he was frustrated, which was rarely. Probably a silly saying he had picked up in the marines. He came out with some crackers at times that made her howl with glee.

Luca had no great religion in her soul but she half believed there was a God looking down on them but when she saw the starving little children on the Crisis channel, she sometimes wondered what his game plan was? Why were some people blessed and some cursed? Was it just luck of the draw or some cruel masterplan from an unfeeling God?

She also didn't believe in organised religion, telling anyone who would listen that a person should be free to believe in and worship the deity of their choice; they were all one and the same, surely. She smiled, remembering Bobby reminiscing when she said it, "Ah used to worship the Baywatch Babes, especially Pamela Anderson. She can give me the kiss of life any day," and Wendy punched him and gave him a dead leg and sulked for an hour.

548

Rabbie watched her out of the corner of his eye. He had thought she was going to cry a minute ago. God, she was such a fascinating creature! He could watch her all day and never be bored, just intrigued.

Once he had got used to the idea of being a dad, he had found the whole pregnancy scenario fascinating, which stumped him. He had thought he would back off a bit but every week there was something new and different happening, and he relished watching his Luca transform. He found her incredibly sexy. She just oozed femininity way and above her normal quota, if that was possible. She was positively blooming and radiated good health. He even had a book on pregnancy, which he read, behind his closed office door, totally engrossed. Elaine had caught him at it and praised him for being a real 'modern' man, although he had forbidden her to tell Mal and the guys, but secretly, it was a really good male ego boost that made him feel king in his own wee realm.

"I go for annuver scan nex' week. Dey vill be able to tell me baby's sex."

* * *

That stopped him in his tracks as he headed off to run the bath. He turned, "Really? Do we want to know? I like surprises."

"I guess not," she answered, "What vill be vill be…karma, as Vends says."

He turned back but she stopped him again, "Can ve call the baby Brooke if it's a girl?"

"Err. Yeah…sure…it's nice but why Brooke?"

"Da first bridge I crossed in New York, Brooklyn Bridge. They say in Russia when you cross water to get to a new place, you say a prayer for luck."

"That's class, Luca, I love it, and a brook is a small stream in England, so there's another water connection."

She loved him talking and taking an interest in their child, "Da, and you were a Commando who fought on the water and returned safely from da war. It's just meant to be, babe."

"Cool, and you could call her Reena as a second name after your mum."

"And Sasha after my papa and Collette after your mum."

"It's all sorted then. Brilliant…err…Sasha?"

"Yes, is unisex name in Russia, like Toni over here."

He trotted off, "That's if it's a girl, hon."

She stroked her tidy little bump. It was so neat looking and she knew, with her maternal instincts, it was a girl. He would be thrilled and dote on his daughter.

The baby stirred and kicked. She grunted, those weren't the little flutterings of fifteen weeks, this was a physical, healthy punch from inside.

She stroked her tummy, "Calm yourself, my little babushka, we will meet when it is time…Da."

When they had finished their bath, dried each other off, and he had massaged her with baby oil, one thing led to another and he made wonderful love to her.

By now he knew every inch of her beautiful body and just exactly where to touch to give her the most pleasure, and they both reached a dizzy plateau of intense sensual pleasure and release. Afterwards, they just lay gazing lovingly at each other before falling asleep in each other's arms.

A few hours later Rabbie was suddenly awake. Not sure what it was, he snuggled closer to Luca and listened to check if it had been a noise, then he felt it, a small flutter just where her small bump touched him. Brooke was letting him know 'she' was there. Christ, he was so lucky to have his beautiful Luca next to him, he felt truly blessed. He knew he was a very, very lucky man to have her in his life and to be her significant other, and by hell or high water, he would lay his life down to keep her safe.

On Friday morning they went to Jocelyn's for their breakfast, Luca looking cool in green denim dungarees, a long brown leather coat and matching knee-high boots. *The girl would look sexy in a plastic bin liner*, Rabbie thought as he walked alongside her, proudly carrying her drawing case.

It was snowing lightly, and he made her hold his arm tightly. It was still dark and slippery out. "You know the baby's due in mid-April, and my granny's birthday is on the twelfth."

"Wouldn't it be neat if Brooke arrives the same day, Rab?"

"Yeah, be nice, spring arriving and all, won't be long going in. It'll be lambing time back in Scotland."

She looked at him fondly. He was living and breathing her pregnancy, and he couldn't wait for the baby to arrive.

"Yah, it good time of year for babies. You be able to take Brooke to the park with da other dads, and me and Vends go and get pissed."

He looked at her aghast. She had totally given up alcohol, and even her rare cigarette, since she found out she was expecting.

She smiled and patted his arm reassuringly, "Tis joke. Maybe ven she a few months old, ve go away for a dirty veekend."

"Mmm…sounds interesting, I'm up for that," he answered with a saucy smile.

"You be ready for it, love. No sex for six weeks afterwards, and I probably not in da mood last few weeks when I get big as a whale."

His mouth dropped. "Shit on a shovel, that's like…ten, twelve weeks."

She laughed, "You can always go see dem topless cowgirls in 'Bronco Bills'."

"I'd rather abstain, what a man's gotta do, a man's gotta do," he stated manfully.

She pinched his arse, making him jump, "Don't you worry, Luca keep you happy. Dar more than one way to peel a banana."

He didn't know exactly what she meant by that, but he did get the gist.

He guided her into the warmth of the diner, and Jocelyn welcomed them in her usual effusive manner. When they were seated, Jocelyn brought Luca the concoction of herbs and vitamins that her mother had sworn by, and Luca took it, just to please her, and washed it down with orange juice. "Yum da yum time for the tum… Get the 'Specials' on, Mama dear… Luca is wasting away, da?"

Rabbie watched the scene contentedly. All their friends and work colleagues were fussing over her; the Luca effect was in full flow.

After they had eaten, he walked her to work and reminded her to be home by one. "Don't forget the people are coming to take your old furniture to the shelter. See you back at home then."

"Okay Rabbie, I'll be sad to see it go but at least it all going to a good home. Bye dahling, see you then," and she kissed him and headed off to her office.

Derek, the office junior, watched her and then regarded Rabbie with nothing short of awe. The concept of being with a woman like Luca and her having his child was mind-boggling to a seventeen-year-old boy.

The lease on Luca's flat was up at the end of the year and as she was living with Rabbie, she no longer needed most of her furniture, so she had decided to give it to a shelter for the homeless, and Rabbie had made all the arrangements for her. The building's owner was keen to bring in new tenants and with Christmas so close, she wanted to get the flat cleared quickly. Clear the cobwebs away from her old life and head forward refreshed and keen to move on.

Rabbie grinned. Who would have thought that day in March, when she passed out in her flat on her return from hospital and he had carried her up to his big bed, that she would still be there nine months later. He had to pinch himself at times to make sure he wasn't dreaming.

He popped in to see Simon, who was bearing up well after his long-term partner, Peter Schuster, had recently passed away. Simon was pleased to see him, he had become a regular dinner guest at the apartment, and Luca fussed over him and treated him like the father she had lost at such a young age.

The two of them sat sipping coffee and reviewing the security on the building.

Rabbie checked his watch. "Must fly, Simon, got an airport run. Incoming VIPs, and you know how mad JFK can get for parking."

Simon walked him out, he liked the big ex-marine. He had certainly made a big impact on all their lives in the past nine months or so.

"Safe journey. Go get your VIPs and give them my regards."

* * *

Luca spent the morning drawing plans for a small Georgian town house conversion down in the South Village. At eleven she had coffee with Philli, who had taken to being a full partner like a duck to water. They chatted about babies and then their men. Philli and Big Mal were going from strength to strength since they had moved in together. Both were strong willed, and they were a good match for each other. Maybe not one made in heaven, they both had a chequered past, but it was a good strong match, and Luca hoped it lasted the pace.

Philli's usual quip was, "Just a darn shame I didn't meet him years ago, could have saved a fortune in alimony."

Mal said, "She is like a tigress, she would have made a great guerrilla fighter!"

Luca was happy for her big pal, she and Mal were going to be godparents to Brooke, and Simon would be her grandfather. Life was nearly perfect.

When she got back to the apartments at five minutes to one, she was glad to see Rabbie's Beamer parked outside. Mr Chin was dry mopping the hall, and he beamed at her when she entered the building. When she got to the elevator, the 'Out of Order' sign glared at her.

"Hey, Mister Chin, you trying to tell me I'm fat and need exercise? It was okay dis morning."

"You lovely, fat pregnant lady," he chortled, "I tell owners."

She laughed and started up the stairs, one hand on her stomach, protectively. "Mummy doing her exercises, Baby. Means we can eat more at dinner."

When she got to the third floor and reached her old apartment, she saw the door was open. She felt an overwhelming sense of déjà vu. A tingling up her spine and a pleasant light-headedness, as she felt angels gather around her and cherubs stroke her hair.

She stood in the hall for a minute and then Rabbie appeared. "Oh there you are… I thought I heard you…come and see what I have found."

She followed him in, holding his hand tightly for some reason she didn't quite understand.

He led her into the living room and there sitting on her old couch was her mother, the old Director and Dmitri were standing looking out the window.

"The new tenants," Rabbie said softly to a stunned Luca.

Nearly perfect had just shot off the perfect scale.

As Luca rushed to embrace them, Rabbie grinned a self-satisfied smirk. *You are one serious, sneaky, devious sod*, he laughed to himself.

But he had been taught by the best teachers in life, the old school, and surely, he had the best of training.

God only knew what the future held ahead for him and his new extended family but he was sure it was going to be very interesting and satisfying.

Epilogue

'The Light Can Only Shine If Surrounded by the Darkness'

Luca gave birth to Brooke Collette Reena Elizabeth DeJames on the twelfth of April, 2014. The child weighed in at seven pounds fourteen ounces; had all her fingers and toes, and both parents were thrilled.

Reena got work as a supervisor in a top-class sewing house and like her daughter before her, marvelled at the wealth and avarice of the huge city. She soon picked up the use of the internet. Dimitri went to community college to study English and dated the lovely Katarina Bronski, OLG's translator. Mikhail, the old Director, after a brief visit went back to his beloved Lithuania and died peacefully at home, two years later. Content in the knowledge he had given Luca a chance in life, that she had fulfilled her potential and that she would carry his legacy on. They all attended his funeral and many tears were shed, he was a legend in his own right, a giant who had suffered the horrors of war and bigotry but who had stood firm and had brought love, hope and wisdom everywhere he went and to everyone who crossed his wise even path.

Jamesey retired, married Simone, and he moved back to the UK and settled at Petral Hill with his mother. He had travelled full circle and what a journey it had been! He regularly returned to war zones to do aid relief for refugees and to broker under the table peace deals for various governments. He accepted his knighthood off the Queen he had served so well, in 2015.

Ron and Eadie Mulligan ran The Peel for many more years and remained an important part of the OLG extended family. As did the twins, Mike and Frankie, who rose high in the financial side of the huge security empire.

Big Mal and Philomena Rourke married and lived happily together, and he ran OLG New York for many years to come. Little Danny went back to 'The Lone Star State' and operated the new OLG office in Dallas. Buzz 'Boomerang' Michaels stopped philandering and wooed Katy back.

As for Rabbie and Luca, they settled in well in Los Angeles, living a fine lifestyle and still deeply in love. They travelled extensively and Luca, a minor celebrity after the trial, chaired meetings of 'The Luca Valendenski Free Women's Speech Society' across the nation. The patron was the First Lady and it became a tradition over the years at each change of office, the First Ladies and Luca tackling women's issues worldwide and making it a better place for them to live.

Her friends, Bobby and Wendy Havilland, were regular guests to LA. Wendy continued her vital nursing job with sick children, and the big guy became head of maintenance for all OLG offices, North America. The Police Academy taught his 'Vertical to horizontal crutch to neck incapacitating slam dunk' to their new recruits. SassyVanassy, who visited frequently when in town, wrote a song about him called

'The Streets Are Safe When Big Bobby's on the Case'. It was a big hit, and all proceeds went to the children's hospital.

'Handsome Harry Hanlon' was found dead in mysterious circumstances in his cell. Someone had broken his neck during the night. Someone of great strength, although nobody was ever made amenable for the crime. Several OLG staff from the New York office had visited the prison earlier to interview a Russian Mafia Godfather, serving time for extortion, about matters unknown.

Smudger ran OLG UK for many years, Kim became Welfare Officer. They kept an apartment in LA, so they could vacation there regularly with their friends.

Mama Jocelyn opened several more bistros in New York, financed by Jamesey, who knew fine food when he ate it and a good business opportunity when he saw it. She was one of many godmothers to Brooke, who was baptised in the Russian Orthodox fashion.

Beth DeJames stayed on Petral Hill Farm and kept an eagle eye on the running of it for years to come. She doted on her grandchildren and great granddaughter. Mac the shepherd eventually retired and bred Border Collies for the rest of his years. He still blamed himself for Mike's death.

And so the DeJames clan grew and prospered. On La Guardia Security went from strength to strength, employing ex-forces and police, helping law enforcement and over-stretched governments globally to fight terrorism, crime and bring peace to troubled territories.

Rabbie DeJames, Managing Director, America, said in Time Magazine, "We liken ourselves to a stop gap between bad and good. When the tide of evil surges and rushes in, a wave towards the shore, they have to get past our defences. I liken OLG to a giant seawall, and the current of evil won't swamp us. It just crashes against us now and then, looking in, before we knock it back out to sea again."

In 2015 Jamesey Johnny DeJames had the remains of his beloved Collette exhumed and re-interred on hallowed ground at her cherished Petral Hill Farm. The entire DeJames family attended the small open-air service at the foot of The Dark Cheviot mountain, conducted by the Dean of the Presbyterian Church of Roxburgh.

Jamesey said to his dead wife's spirit. "Light can only shine bright if surrounded by darkness, and you were such a light and you have left behind a legacy of such light in the family you loved so much. No retreat, darling, no retreat."

Many a tear was shed over the fragrant sweet blooming heather that day.

When they later dispersed to their various locations around the globe to carry on and to push the fight into the face of evil, Jamesey grinned, "She's probably up there now cussing like a trooper and calling me a fool for disturbing her peace," he said to an ageing landlord.

"Different bleedin' species, Jamesey," replied Ron. "Different planet."

Jamesey laughed and clapped his old friend on the back, and they headed down to the farm for whiskey and Beth's famous Cumberland pie. But the adventures weren't over for the DeJames family; for some they were only beginning, because huge adventures and dangerous trials were going to face them on the next stage of the big 'circle of life'.

* * *

28ᵗʰ April, 2018, 1.15pm

Jamesey marched down Watford High Street. It was lunch time, the weather was fine and the pedestrians and workers were heading out for lunch.

He was looking forward to his in The Peel with Simone Parry, his fiancée. At sixty-six he still had a good appetite and could drink with the best of them.

A black Volkswagen Golf pulled up, windows went down, and high-velocity gunfire ripped through the air, the gunshots ricocheting between the buildings.

Jamesey fell to the sound of screaming passersby. He hit the pavement hard and a huge puddle of blood formed under him stickily.

The Volkswagen Golf screamed off, "Inshalloh Allah!" shouted the gunmen behind their hoods.

Jamesey's mobile trilled 'March of the Valkyries'. He fumbled it out, his eyes glazing over, and answered.

It was his brother, Davey Robert DeJames, "Just thought I'd ring and give you a sitrep on the Peshawar caper, Jamesey."

"Fek that, I've just been plugged, bruv... And it's not bloody good!" and he passed out, blood dripping off his fingers onto the hot pavement.

* * *

And so the story goes on;
Read Part II of the DeJames trilogy: 'The Resurrection of Black Viking Sunray' (The Rebirth of a Fallen Warrior).

Meet and go on adventures with more great characters around the world.

* * *

Inspiring books for inspiring people.